STORY I

*The Library of Wales
Short Story Anthology*

Edited by Dai Smith

PARTHIAN
LIBRARY OF WALES

Parthian
The Old Surgery
Napier Street
Cardigan
SA43 1ED

www.parthianbooks.com

The Library of Wales is a Welsh Government
initiative which highlights and celebrates Wales' literary
heritage in the English language.

Published with the financial support of
the Welsh Books Council.

www.thelibraryofwales.com

Series Editor: Dai Smith

Story I first published in 2014
© The authors and/or their estates
Introduction © Dai Smith 2014
All Rights Reserved

ISBN 978-1-90-894641-6

Cover Image: *Penrhys* Ernest Zobole, ©1951. Oil, 810 x 595
Cover Design by Marc Jennings

Printed and bound by Gwasg Gomer, Llandysul, Wales
Typeset by Elaine Sharples

British Library Cataloguing in Publication Data

A cataloguing record for this book is available from the British
Library.

In Ireland for Lily

INTRODUCTION

If the novel offers the reader entrance to its expansive world through the hospitality of an open door, the short story presents us with the more guarded perspective of a window into life. The short story must select and edit its revelation, glimpsed not dwelt upon, if it is to be a telling one, and worth a second glance. What it wishes to show is, to an extent, foretold by all that frames it, yet which remains unseen. This is why the chosen field of sight is crucial to the meaning of the vision vouchsafed for an understanding. The portal of the window defines not only what we will see but how we will view. The short story window, then, will come in many shapes and sizes, and some will have stained glass for panes and some will have bars across them, whilst, depending on which aspect of human behaviour they have decided to unveil, some will be open to the sky and others will cast their light into the cellar depths of existence. Once upon a time, it is true, in a world in which, literally, there was no glass in the holes or slits of the buildings, whether hovels or castles, through which the outside world was eyeballed, so there was no imaginative conduit into the lives of significant others which, first, the novel and then the short story proffered for those readers with the available leisure to look. By the mid nineteenth century increasingly glassed-off sectors of human anomie yearned for the connective compensation of an inner-eye's resolution of life's strange bewilderment and alien otherness, which a completed narrative alone could bring. The novel's finite dream world made up for the infinite messiness of actual living in the new urban and industrial world. Yet, notwithstanding the structured ordering which such fiction could bring, the chance, ephemeral, disturbing, enticing diorama of street encounters and haphazard incident, the unaccountable and the unknowable, needed the explication of epiphany. The flash bulb. The thunderclap. The whisper. The rumour. Often, amidst the unstoppable flow of modernity, there was no time for anything else. Or, as John Updike put it, the importance of the short story now derived from the way it had of 'bringing Americans news of how they lived and why', and not only Americans. Everywhere, if you blinked you might miss something. If you stopped to do anything more than gulp it down, you might choke. Such speed of motion and instant memory would, soon, find its blurred articulation captured via the shutter of the stills camera or the sprocket whirr of the movies. From the late nineteenth century the short story especially was the literary cross-over form which pictured new vistas, distant horizons and close-up faces, in an array of montage and edited cuts.

None of this came about because of some species of reified aesthetics, though a subsequent aesthetic crafting of subtleties of form and language was to be key to making the short story such an effective witness to the psychological and emotional upheavals engendered in individual lives by the weight of unbidden social developments, and through the devastation wrought by unheralded historical circumstances. In all this, Wales, except in the spurts and starts of particular places and industries, was a latecomer until with a landslide shudder as the twentieth century began there was no country of comparable size so overwhelmingly marked out by all that industrialisation entailed. Some Machine. Some Garden. Even rural Wales, its agricultural and artisan and mercantile economy there included, had become an offshoot, de-populated and migratory, of the new Wales of tinplate and iron and slate and copper and steel and, feeding all the roaring fires of Industry and Empire, of coal – anthracite, bituminous and steam, the fossil fuel of modernity itself. Two out of three workers in a Wales approaching three million in population by 1914 were in the coal industry. Wales was urban to its molten core, if only urbane in the marmoreal, statuary of its prosperous Edwardian heyday, and tricked out for the first time in our history with a panoply of national institutions.

Yet, Wales had no cities or deep civic traditions, no wide gradation of rank and hierarchy beyond the bourgeois and proletarian, to compare with Scotland or Ireland, let alone England. Its university colleges were as young as its national sporting endeavours and its literary glories were embedded in Welsh, its most distinctive and, down to 1914, thriving characteristic. Whatever the decline in numbers, both absolute and in percentage terms, which would within a few decades first assail and then fatally threaten the language, there was, before the 1920s, only a sporadically expressed sense of any national cultural crisis around linguistic usage, whilst, emphatically, there was no dilemma, political or otherwise, about the being of Welshness and the embrace of a British identity.

Before the First World War, James Joyce had written the short stories he used to skewer the evasions and illusions, their dreams as well as their acts, of his fellow countrymen. The struggle he had to publish *Dubliners* in 1914 was, in part, a reflection of the power of his devastating, unacceptable, ultimately undeniable stories of love and indictment. Crises and civics were the twin breeders of his consciousness, and of Ireland's conflicted nation. It would take, in different circumstances of crisis and civic outcomes around class, at least another generation before Wales would find comparable voices. For a while after 1914, Wales was buoyed up, as nation and society, by the centrality of coal in both peace and in war, and its force-fed ambitions took it to the forefront of the Celtic queue in power and aspiration. The triumphant foie-gras outcome was the production of the cocky, confidently self-promoting, Welsh-speaking politico, David Lloyd George, as Prime Minister of Britain and wartime leader of its Imperial Dominions. It would take a mighty shake of the social and economic kaleidoscope after the Great War to see the mosaic of Welsh life thrown into shards in a disarray which would now overturn all previous set patterns of expectation and order. It was all this, no more and no less, which saw the Welsh short story emerge as central to our understanding of knowing how and why the people of Wales have lived as they have over the past century.

The very first batch of stories in this volume are uneasy outriders of all that will be. Not quite tinged with the late Victorian romance of Celtic exoticism and otherness, yet suffused with strangeness, playful with morbidity, helpless in the face of encroaching death. They are enchanted tales because they are in thrall to magic and all its spells in a Wales gasping through religion and respectability to breathe anew under the suffocating toxicity of a noxious capitalist system. This Wales was a-buzz with contradictions. Curtains fretfully twitched across these particular windows of intellect until, the spell abruptly broken, winds began to howl through all the shattered glass of post-1914 Wales. It was Caradoc Evans – of whom his friend and admirer, Gwyn Jones, in 1957 said that he had 'flung a bucket of dung through the Welsh parlour window and ... had flung the bucket in after, with a long-reverberating clangour' – who put a capstone on any fantasy Wales which lingered on. That his collection, *My People* (1915), appeared in the midst of a World War which shape-shifted Welsh history entirely is no more a happenstance than Lloyd George's own contemporary elevation. If England, as Keynes informed us, had Shakespeare when she could afford him, the great economist who would shortly dilate on the *Economic Consequences of the Peace* (1919) delivered by Lloyd George at Versailles, might have added that Wales only joined the discordant chorus of twentieth century literature when its economy slid into bankruptcy.

The stories which follow on into the disenchantment of the world, through the inter-war years and in the Second World War itself down to the 1950s, are utterly distinctive in tone even when, occasionally, they tell this wider Big Story in oblique or sidling ways. They are time-bound and socially observant as a measure of historical experience. It is this focus which makes them so Welsh. Contrariwise, the critic, Tony Brown, has pointed out that most women writers in English of this entire period, formally educated and necessarily middle-class, had 'connections with the actual social life of Wales (which was only) socially and/or geographically tenuous (and that their) stories tell us very little about the actualities of Wales itself between 1850 and 1950 ...nothing ...of industrialisation, nothing about the huge shift from the boom years at the end of the nineteenth century to the disasters of the 1930s, nothing of the struggle of working-class families to survive'. The perception of such activities was one which contemporaries, as writer practitioners and reader participants, did not hesitate to emphasise in their work: What was socially marginal, for whatever valid socio-historical reasons, was not the work which brought the news of how and why the Welsh had lived and endured in a dramatic if enforced commonality of being.

At the end of this first period, from the late 1920s to the late 1950s, one of its first generation of writers – those born before 1914 – came to edit the third major collection of stories to be published. That was George Ewart Evans (b.1909), whose **Welsh Short Stories** came out for the English publisher, Faber & Faber, in 1959. He was clear, as he wrote in his Introduction, dated May 1958, that over 'thirty years or so, the short story in Wales has emerged and reached its present maturity', and he was just as firm in his answer to his own posed question:

> What caused the Welsh short story to appear when it did? This is a question that cannot be answered if we try

to restrict the inquiry to purely literary terms. For the Welsh short story, like the Irish story just before it... flowered during or immediately after a period of acute social stress... The Irish experienced their upheaval in the first quarter of the century; the renascence of Irish letters roughly coincided with it. The Welsh were entering the 'Hungry Thirties' when the tempo of events in Ireland was slowing down. It seems no accident that the writers who have had the greatest influence on the direction of the Welsh short story grew up during the twenties and thirties in industrial South Wales, chiefly in those valleys and coastal towns that were so devastated by social and economic crises.

In that Wales of the late 1950s, so much was clear to that generation which had indeed seeded the 'first flowering' of 'Anglo-Welsh' literature. It was a drumbeat to which the prominent Welsh writers in English marched in step as much as did the whole culture and society, formed and perhaps already static, of their known world. Gwyn Jones (b.1907), his shadow as critic and contributor looming authoritatively over the literary landscape, had anticipated George Ewart Evans' thoughtful remarks in his own typically more flamboyant editorial note to his influential collection *Welsh Short Stories* (1956) for Oxford:

> An editor who is part of what he edits cannot show free from prejudice. My book has been built around those authors who seem to me at once creators and most distinguished practitioners of the Welsh short story in English... if we except the patriarchal Caradoc, these writers belong to one generation, and all of them except Caradoc and Goodwin belong to industrial South Wales. Remove the Swansea-bred Dylan Thomas, and the others belong to the mining valleys, where they grew up in the hungry twenties.

For better and worse the contemporary Welsh story is the product of a passionate, rebellious, and humorous generation, with a huge delight in life and no small relish for death.

He who edits, as Gwyn Jones assertively admits, also selects. And in the 1950s, as in the 1930s, the selectivity was indeed all one way in its regional skew. Twenty years had separated the first collection from Faber, *Welsh Short Stories* assembled by a collective anonymous panel of advisory editors, in 1937 from the offerings of the 1950s, with only Gwyn Jones' slim *Welsh Short Stories* from 1940 for Penguin in between. The dates are significant for, in the 1930s the fate of the Welsh industrial valleys had first impinged on a wider consciousness, whilst by the 1950s the emergence of 'Welfare' Britain after the Second World War was unimaginable, in shape and in aspiration, without the wider contribution of South Wales. It was, in a sense, a pinnacle from which these editors, and their acolytic readers, could accommodate all of Wales.

In the Faber volume of 1959, out of 25 selected stories by single authors, three were in translation from Welsh, including one of the stories by three of the women there included. The 1956 OUP volume had been almost a mirror image, with 26 stories, though by 18 authors, with four stories translated. Gwyn Jones perfectly reflected the contemporary sensibilities of the 1950s in his fulsome declaration that 'all 26 stories are by Welshmen... and about Welshmen, and... he who dips his head into this book will hear music and taste mead'. Sufficient mead, perhaps, to ignore the fact that two of the stories he selected were in translation by that honorary 'Welshman' Kate Roberts. At a time, perhaps, of a different tempo of crisis for Welsh-language writing, his further remark that 'There is not one Wales, but many; and no one voice and one language can serve them all' might sound as truthful as it is contentious. It is a double condition, even so, to which our selected stories over these two current volumes will return again and again.

A way of avoiding it was to take the more fanciful road chosen by Aled Vaughan in *Celtic Story*, from 1946, where 24 stories were assembled from 'Ireland, Wales, Scotland and the West country'. The editor, no doubt whistling against the wind of post-war British triumphalism, contended that 'The central theme of this collection is "Celticism", that indefinable quality that makes the work of the true Celtic writer stand out on its own in any collection'. But, by then, the concept of Celtic sensibility outside a rooted and structured society was a feeble throwback to the idylls and/or grotesqueries which the writers championed by Jones and Evans had long swept away. Gwyn Jones, for one, was clear about what the first generation of Welsh short-story writers had sought to do, and the examples from elsewhere by which he, and they, sought to be measured. He introduced his own selected short stories in 1974 and, again, his collected stories of 1998 with the confident modesty of one who knew where his texts would find their context. It is where, too, I hope that *Story* may be located and assessed:

> ...literature has never lacked far-questers and exotics, but for the most part, what men are, what they know, what they feel, grows from a place or region. This can be provincial (in the literal not pejorative sense), metropolitan, or in respect of some Nations national. For me, it seems unnecessary to add, this means Wales, and therein South Wales, and still more narrowly the mining valleys of Gwent and Glamorgan on the one hand, and the thirty-mile central arc of Cardigan Bay and its hinterland on the other.
>
> Regionalism of this high and honourable definition has a status as estimable as any other form of writing, and has been a main feature of the European and American literary tradition. For this region – it can be as small as Eire, Calabria, or Berlin, or huge as the Deep South of America – the regional writer will feel an

inescapable though not necessarily an exclusive attachment. He will understand its people, as no intruder will ever understand them, and be driven to act out that understanding in words: their character, personality and traditions, patterns of behaviour and impulses to action; what they believe in, their hopes and fears, bonds and severances; their relationship to each other, to the landscape around them, and the creatures they share it with... If his gifts are modest but genuine, his following will be small but appreciative; if he is a Hardy, Joyce, or Faulkner by virtue of what his region has given him he will be heard with reverence throughout the world.

Every editor should end with a confession: implicit or explicit. Implicitly this selection over two volumes will speak for itself as to its specificities and its inter-relationships. Explicitly, I constructed a few principles, or rather made up some rules, some of which I broke. There happens to be 42 stories in each volume. That was, as it turned out, a coincidence. What was not accidental, however, was the decision to have more than one story by certain writers, and even to give a few authorial stars more than two stories by which to represent themselves. The familiar or the classic, then, rub together with the unexpected and with what is raw but powerful. By so doing, I hope, the representational intent of *Story* will become clear. And that is, to touch upon the lives of Wales in the past one hundred years or so without any literal attempt to suggest any kind of overall objective survey or even a foray into history. My chosen windows onto Wales do precisely what windows do: whether the weather outside changes, stones are thrown, night blots out day, rain streaks or sun shines, with figures at play or bodies at rest. These are moments. It is why they are, therefore, momentous. None more so than the two World Wars which have marked out destinies, individual and social, more than most histories of Wales until very recently have wished to consider. Those stories are most definitely flagged up here. As are the ways and means, humorous and defiant and forlorn, with which Wales suffered its equivalent of the Famine in Ireland – the locust decades between those wars.

I think it is plain, too, that the Wales which strove to put its house in order after 1945 did so in a way which proved to be an uneasy marriage between a cold-headed refusal to endorse its immediate past by anything other than fierce rejection and a warm-hearted embrace of the things and people so loved and succoured that they soon crystallised into nostalgia or into a sentiment almost too large to withstand. Here, the 1940s will end with withering backward glances but also with the cracked grace note of Rhys Davies' masterful 'Boy with a Trumpet', a tale set outside Wales completely yet redolent of a yearning for expressive horizons and a settlement that cannot, in all its paucity, be resisted.

The story will, too, end Rhys Davies' involvement in *Story*, though not, as will be apparent, his paramount place amongst the first generation of our short-story writers from Wales in English. His influence, more and more appreciated, has been as deep as it has been understated until recently. In the second volume of *Story* the 21 men and only 5 women of this volume will be replaced, numerically anyway, by 19 men and 13 women. Tone and the intended effect will change as well, and all that comes from the alteration of our story over time. No anthology, however, even two of them arriving together, can, even if it is perforce, omit so many good stories and ask to be regarded as definitive. But what I can hope is that *Story* (Volumes I and II) may serve, overall, as a definition, one amongst many to be sure, in a language and style fashioned here in Wales of what it has been to live with Welsh breath in our lungs and with Welsh stories to tell the world. This was our news. Read it, and think that you and we may yet know the how and the why of it.

Dai Smith

THE STORIES

AFTER FOREVER

ENCHANTMENT

THE GIFT OF TONGUES

Arthur Machen

More than a hundred years ago a simple German maid-of-all-work caused a great sensation. She became subject to seizures of a very singular character, of so singular a character that the family inconvenienced by these attacks were interested and, perhaps a little proud of a servant whose fits were so far removed from the ordinary convulsion. The case was thus. Anna, or Gretchen, or whatever her name might be, would suddenly become oblivious of soup, sausage, and the material world generally.

But she neither screamed, nor foamed, nor fell to earth after the common fashion of such seizures. She stood up, and from her mouth rolled sentence after sentence of splendid sound, in a sonorous tongue, filling her hearers with awe and wonder. Not one of her listeners understood a word of Anna's majestic utterances, and it was useless to question her in her uninspired moments, for the girl knew nothing of what had happened.

At length, as it fell out, some scholarly personage was present during one of these extraordinary fits; and he at once declared that the girl was speaking Hebrew, with a pure accent and perfect intonation. And, in a sense, the wonder was now greater than ever. How could the simple Anna speak Hebrew? She had certainly never learnt it. She could barely read and write her native German. Everyone was amazed, and the occult mind of the day began to formulate theories and to speak of possession and familiar spirits. Unfortunately (as I think, for I am a lover of all insoluble mysteries), the problem of the girl's Hebrew speech was solved; solved, that is, to a certain extent.

The tale got abroad, and so it became known that some years before Anna had been servant to an old scholar. The personage was in the habit of declaiming Hebrew as he walked up and down his study and the passages of his house, and the maid had unconsciously stored the chanted words in some cavern of her soul; in that receptacle, I suppose, which we are content to call the subconsciousness. I must confess that the explanation does not strike me as satisfactory in all respects. In the first place, there is the extraordinary tenacity of memory; but I suppose that other instances of this, though rare enough, might be cited. Then, there is the association of this particular storage of the subconsciousness with a species of seizure; I do not know whether any similar instance can be cited.

Still, minor puzzles apart, the great mystery was mysterious no more: Anna spoke Hebrew because she had heard Hebrew and, in her odd fashion, had remembered it.

To the best of my belief, cases that offer some points of similarity are occasionally noted at the present day. Persons ignorant of Chinese deliver messages in that tongue; the speech of Abyssinia is heard from lips incapable, in ordinary moments, of anything but the pleasing idiom of the United States of America, and untaught Cockneys suddenly become fluent in Basque.

But all this, so far as I am concerned, is little more than rumour; I do not know how far these tales have been subjected to strict and systematic examination. But in any case, they do not interest me so much as a very odd business that happened on the Welsh border more than sixty years ago. I was not very old at the time, but I remember my father and mother talking about the affair, just as I remember them talking about the Franco-Prussian War in the August of 1870, and coming to the conclusion that the French seemed to be getting the worst of it. And later, when I was growing up and the mysteries were beginning to exercise their fascination upon me, I was able to confirm my vague recollections and to add to them a good deal of exact information. The odd business to which I am referring was the so-called 'Speaking with Tongues' at Bryn Sion Chapel, Treowen, Monmouthshire, on a Christmas Day of the early Seventies.

Treowen is one of a chain of horrible mining villages that wind in and out of the Monmouthshire and Glamorganshire valleys. Above are the great domed heights, quivering with leaves (like the dear Zacynthus of Ulysses), on their lower slopes, and then mounting by far stretches of deep bracken, glittering in the sunlight, to a golden land of gorse, and at last to wild territory, bare and desolate, that seems to surge upward for ever. But beneath, in the valley, are the black pits and the blacker mounds, and heaps of refuse, vomiting chimneys, mean rows and ranks of grey houses faced with red brick; all as dismal and detestable as the eye can see.

Such a place is Treowen; uglier and blacker now than it was sixty years ago; and all the worse for the contrast of its vileness with those glorious and shining heights above it. Down in the town there are three great chapels of the Methodists and Baptists and Congregationalists; architectural monstrosities all three of them, and a red brick church does not do much to beautify the place. But above all this, on the hillside, there are scattered whitewashed farms, and a little hamlet of white, thatched cottages, remnants all of a pre-industrial age, and here is situated the old meeting house called Bryn Sion, which means, I believe, the Brow of Zion. It must have been built about 1790–1800, and, being a simple, square building, devoid of crazy ornament, is quite inoffensive.

Here came the mountain farmers and cottagers, trudging, some of them, long distances on the wild tracks and paths of the hillside; and here ministered, from 1860 to 1880, the Reverend Thomas Beynon, a bachelor, who lived in the little cottage next to the chapel, where a grove of beech trees was blown into a thin straggle of tossing boughs by the great winds of the mountain.

Now, Christmas Day falling on a Sunday in this year of long ago, the usual service was held at Bryn Sion Chapel, and, the weather being fine, the congregation was a large one – that is, something between forty and fifty people. People met and shook hands and wished each other 'Merry Christmas', and exchanged the news of the week and prices at Newport market, till the elderly, white-bearded minister, in his shining black, went into the chapel. The deacons followed him and took their places in the big pew by the open fireplace, and the little meeting-house was almost full. The minister had a windsor chair, a red hassock, and a pitch pine table in a sort of raised pen at the end of the chapel, and from this place he gave out the opening hymn. Then followed a long portion of Scripture, a second hymn, and the congregation settled themselves to attend to the prayer.

It was at this moment that the service began to vary from the accustomed order. The minister did not kneel down in the usual way; he stood staring at the people, very strangely, as some of them thought. For perhaps a couple of minutes he faced them in dead silence, and here and there people shuffled uneasily in their pews. Then he came down a few paces and stood in front of the table with bowed head, his back to the people. Those nearest to the ministerial pen or rostrum heard a low murmur coming from his lips. They could not make out the words.

Bewilderment fell upon them all, and, as it would seem, a confusion of mind, so that it was difficult afterwards to gather any clear account of what actually happened that Christmas morning at Bryn Sion Chapel. For some while the mass of the congregation heard nothing at all; only the deacons in the Big Seat could make out the swift mutter that issued from their pastor's lips; now a little higher in tone, now sunken so as to be almost inaudible. They strained their ears to discover what he was saying in that low, continued utterance; and they could hear words plainly, but they could not understand. It was not Welsh.

It was neither Welsh – the language of the chapel – nor was it English. They looked at one another, those deacons, old men like their minister most of them; looked at one another with something of strangeness and fear in their eyes. One of them, Evan Tudor, Torymynydd, ventured to rise in his place and to ask the preacher, in a low voice, if he were ill. The Reverend Thomas Beynon took no notice; it was evident that he did not hear the question: swiftly the unknown words passed his lips.

'He is wrestling with the Lord in prayer,' one deacon whispered to another, and the man nodded – and looked frightened.

And it was not only this murmured utterance that bewildered those who heard it; they, and all who were present, were amazed at the pastor's strange movements. He would stand before the middle of the table and bow his head, and go now to the left of the table, now to the right of it, and then back again to the middle. He would bow down his head, and raise it, and look up, as a man said afterwards, as if he saw the heavens opened. Once or twice he turned round and faced the people, with his arms stretched wide open, and a swift word on his lips, and his eyes staring and seeing nothing, nothing that anyone else could see. And then he would turn again. And all the while the people were dumb and stricken with amazement; they hardly dared to look at each other; they hardly dared to ask themselves what could be happening before them. And then, suddenly, the minister began to sing.

It must be said that the Reverend Thomas Beynon was celebrated all through the valley and beyond it for his 'singing religious eloquence', for that singular chant which the Welsh call the hwyl. But his congregation had never heard so noble, so awful a chant as this before. It rang out and soared on high, and fell, to rise again with wonderful modulations; pleading to them and calling them and summoning them; with the old voice of the hwyl, and yet with a new voice that they had never heard before: and all in those sonorous words that they could not understand. They stood up in their wonder, their hearts shaken by the chant; and then the voice died away. It was as still as death in the chapel. One of the deacons could see that the minister's lips still moved; but he could hear no sound at all. Then the minister raised up his hands as if he held something between them; and knelt down, and rising, again lifted his hands. And there came the faint tinkle of a bell from the sheep grazing high up on the mountainside.

The Reverend Thomas Beynon seemed to come to himself out of a dream, as they said. He looked about him nervously, perplexed, noted that his people were gazing at him strangely, and then, with a stammering voice, gave out a hymn and afterwards ended the service. He discussed the whole matter with the deacons and heard what they had to tell him. He knew nothing of it himself and had no explanation to offer. He knew no languages, he declared, save Welsh and English. He said that he did not believe there was evil in what had happened, for he felt that he had been in Heaven before the Throne. There was a great talk about it all, and that queer Christmas service became known as the Speaking with Tongues of Bryn Sion.

Years afterwards, I met a fellow countryman, Edward Williams, in London, and we fell talking, in the manner of exiles, of the land and its stories. Williams was many years older than myself, and he told me of an odd thing that had once happened to him.

'It was years ago,' he said, 'and I had some business – I was a mining engineer in those days – at Treowen, up in the hills. I had to stay over Christmas, which was on a Sunday that year, and talking to some people there about the hwyl, they told me that I ought to go up to Bryn Sion if I wanted to hear it done really well. Well, I went, and it was the queerest service I ever heard of. I don't know much about the Methodists' way of doing things, but before long it struck me that the minister was saying some sort of Mass. I could hear a word or two of the Latin service now and again, and then he sang the Christmas Preface right through: "*Quia per incarnati Verbi mysterium*" – you know.'

Very well; but there is always a loophole by which the reasonable, or comparatively reasonable, may escape. Who is to say that the old preacher had not strayed long before into some Roman Catholic Church at Newport or Cardiff on a Christmas Day, and there heard Mass with exterior horror and interior love?

THE COFFIN

Caradoc Evans

Captain Shacob owned *Rhondda*, the rowing boat from which he fished and in which he took folk on the sea at Ferryside. A plump widow named Ann who had sailed in his boat for pleasure said to him: 'My son, Little Ben, is a prentice to the carpenter; be you a father to him. My husband, Big Ben, is in the graveyard; be you my second husband.' She also told him that she rented a house and ten acres of fertile land on the bank of Avon Towy.

Shacob sold his boat and married Ann, whose fields he trimmed at what time he was not repairing the ditches on the public roads. Now Ann fattened wondrously; her flesh almost choking her, she was wont in hot weather to throw up her hands and scream that she was dying. On arising on a July day, she went into a fit and fell back upon her bed. At midday she would not sup of the gingered and sugared bread and water which her husband offered her, nor again in the evening.

'Eat, woman fach,' said Shacob.

'Let me perish on an empty belly,' answered Ann.

Having milked his cow, tended his two pigs, and shooed his fowls to roost, Shacob walked to the workshop of Lloyd the carpenter. He stood at the threshold of the workshop, his hands, like the claws of a very old crow, grasping the top of the half door, his eyes wearing the solemn aspect of the man who is soon to revel in the mournful joy that Death brings to us Welsh people; his long underlip curling over his purple-stained chin like the petal of a rose, Shacob stood at the door as if he were the reporter of sacred messages in the chapel.

This is what he saw inside the workshop: the crutched figure of the carpenter, whose mouth, from the corners of which dribbled tiny streams of tobacco juice, was like the ungainly cut in a turnip lantern; the hairy face of the cobbler, much of whose wooden leg was thrust into the earth through the shavings and sawdust with which the ground was strewn; the bright countenance of the broken-out preacher, whose skin was of the freshness of that of a sucking pig; the head of Little Ben, whose nose had been twisted at birth, bending over a birdcage.

The preacher was declaring that Jonah was not swallowed by a fish, even though the fish was a whale whereat the cobbler, driving his leg farther into the earth, cried: 'Atheist!'

'Hoit!' said Shacob.

None of the company heard him, so low was his voice.

Presently Little Ben looked up, and after his gaze had rested for a while upon his stepfather's hands he set to improve the perch-rod of his cage.

'Hoity-ho!' Shacob sounded.

'Why do you stand there like a thirsty ox at the gate?' asked the carpenter. 'You have seen millions of whales at Ferryside. Sure, indeed, they can take in a man at a gulp.'

'Hist-hist,' said Shacob. 'Ann is going for the sail.'

'For two shillings – for one shilling and a morsel of butter,' said the preacher, 'I'll make a memorial song to the dead.'

'Don't let him,' cried the cobbler. 'Be you warned by me.' He struggled to free his leg. 'Little Ben, pull her out.'

'I am here about the coffin,' Shacob announced.

'How can I make the coffin,' Lloyd replied, 'when I am haymaking all the week? Why didn't you come a month back? And Ann is so stout that it will be a longish job.'

'Where else can I go?' Shacob wailed.

'That's it!' the carpenter growled. 'Take your custom from me. Don't bring your breaks here any more if you talk like that. Go away with your wheelbarrow and spade and pickaxe and shovel.'

'The perished – the stout and the thin – must be housed,' the preacher proclaimed.

'Hay must be gathered and stacked and thatched before the corn harvest,' Lloyd answered. 'How are the animals to live in the winter? Tell me that.'

'All the dead – tenors and basses, praying men and men who cry "Amen", old and young, big and little – must be housed.' So sang the preacher in his pulpit manner.

The cobbler moved before he was freed and fell upon the floor, his wooden leg breaking in two.

'The Big Man's punishment for discussing the Beybile with you,' he reproached the preacher. 'The breath in your body is the smoke of hellfire.'

'I have not the timber to make Ann a coffin,' said Lloyd. 'No; not for stout Ann.'

'There are many trees,' said Shacob.

'Great will be the cost of the coffin.'

'I'll sell the cow,' Shacob began.

'Hearken! If I make the coffin, you must pay the day after the funeral. You shall not make a debt of it.'

The preacher blessed Lloyd. 'You are behaving in a most religious spirit. Houses of stonemasons crumble, but the houses of carpenters will be placed in the lofts of the White Palace.'

Husband, stepson and carpenter then passed through the village and the deeply-rutted, cart-wide lane to Shacob's house, which is in the midst of marshland.

As the three unlatched their clogs at the foot of the stairway, Shacob shouted: 'Ann, here is Lloyd Carpenter. Are you perished?'

Ann made an answer, whereupon they went up to her. Lloyd drew back the bedclothes and bade the woman straighten her limbs; then he measured her length, her breadth, and her depth. 'Write you down two inches extra every way for the swellings,' he commanded Little Ben.

'We ought to write four,' said the youth.

'Clap your head. Have I ever made a coffin too small?'

'If it only fits,' said Ben, 'how can the angel flap his wings when he comes to call Mammo up? Mammo, you need the angel?'

'Why, iss, Son bach,' Ann replied. 'Are you not ashamed, carpenter, to deprive me of the angel?'

'It is the large cost that is in my think,' murmured Lloyd.

'Drat your think! I will not go into a coffin that will smother the angel. Have I not suffered enough?'

'It will be many shillings more. Maybe ten. Maybe fifteen. O iss, a pound.'

'Be good,' said Shacob. 'It is well to obey the perished.'

For three days Ben and Lloyd laboured, and as the coffin was carried on the shoulders of four men, the haymakers who came to the hedges were amazed at its vastness.

By the side of the bed it was put. 'For,' said Lloyd, 'she will be a heavy corpse and easier to roll down than lift.'

At the end of the year the carpenter said to Ann's husband:

'Give me now the coffin money.'

'On the day after the funeral,' said Shacob.

'I will have the petty sessions on you, I will, drop dead and blind. I'll poison your well. And your cow. And your pigs. Is it my blame that Ann is alive?'

'It shall be as you pledged. Broken-out preacher heard you.'

'Tut-tut. He is a bad man. He disputes the Beybile. That is why he was broken out from the capel.'

But Shacob was soon puzzle-headed. Ann fancied to see herself in the coffin, and holding a mirror she tried to enter it, but the breadth of it was too narrow. She made such a great dole that Shacob hurried to discover Lloyd's iniquity. 'Little Ben,' he shouted at the door of the workshop, 'come forth from the workshop of the sinner. Bring your birdcage and coat and tools. Have a care you bring nothing that is his.'

The youth obeyed and remained like a sentry by his stepfather.

'There's glad I am I did not pay you,' cried Shacob. 'If I had, the law would find a thief.'

'Be quiet, robber,' Lloyd returned.

'Who made Ann's coffin too small? Come out, neighbours bach, and listen. Who made Ann's coffin too small? Who tried to cheat the perished dead?'

Many people came to hear Shacob reviling Lloyd and were very sorry that the carpenter answered in this fashion: 'Reit. 'Oreit. Little Ben, go you in and find the paper with the figures.'

'And keep it tightly,' Shacob counselled his stepson. 'Nothing new must be put in it. Don't you be tempted by Lloyd because he was your master. We are honest.'

After Lloyd had measured Ann, and while he was measuring the coffin, Little Ben went under his mother's bed and wrote anew on another paper and in accordance with the fresh measurements.

'Carpenter,' he said shyly, 'you are wrong. Study the figures. I cannot work for a scampist master.'

'Why do I want a useless coffin?' Ann shrieked. 'A mess I would be in if I perished now. And what would be said if I reached the Palace in a patched coffin? Ach-y-fi!'

That night Little Ben, who was unable to sleep for his mother's plight, stole into Lloyd's workshop and brought away screws and nails and a few planks of timber, and with these he enlarged the coffin.

In the ten years that followed, the trouble between Lloyd and Shacob brewed into bitter hatred; it attracted one to the other, when they fought as fiercely as poachers fight for the possession of a ferret. Shacob died, and there was peace for a little while, but in the after-season Lloyd did not subdue his rage. 'Shacob is gone,' he whined. 'Cobbler Wooden Leg is gone and Broken-out Preacher. The next will be Ann. Oh, there will be a champion riot if I don't get my money.' His spoken and unspoken prayer was that the Big Man would allow him to live longer than Ann. Every summer evening he watched the weather signs, and if they foretold heat, he said joyfully to himself: 'Like a poof she'll go off tomorrow.'

As Ann fattened so Ben enlarged the coffin with iron staples and leathern hinges. This he did many times. The fame of his skill became a byword, and folk brought to him clocks, sewing-machines, and whatsoever that wanted much cunning to be set in proper order.

He had married, and his four children were a delight to Ann, who often tumbled into her coffin and closing her eyes said to them: 'Like this Grand-mammo will go to the Palace.' The children pranced about with glee, and by and by they played hide and seek in it.

On a day when Ben said: 'If I stretch the box any more your perished corpse will fall through the bottom, Mammo; even now it will have to be well roped before you are lifted,' before sunset a horrible thing happened: three children hid in the coffin and the fourth swooped down upon them, and the sides of it fell apart.

Ben viewed what had been done. 'It won't repair,' he told his tearful mother. 'I'll make you another, Mammo fach.'

He laughed as he separated the pieces, for those that belonged to Lloyd he was returning to Lloyd.

THE DARK WORLD

Rhys Davies

'Where can we go tonight?' Jim asked. Once again it was raining. The rows of houses in the valley bed were huddled in cold grey mist. Beyond them the mountains prowled unseen. The iron street lamps spurted feeble jets of light. There were three weeks to go before Christmas. They stood in a chapel doorway and idly talked, their feet splashed by the rain.

Thomas said: 'There's someone dead up in Calfaria Terrace.'

'Shall we go to see him?' Jim suggested immediately.

They had not seen any corpses for some weeks. One evening they had seen five, and so for a while the visits had lost their interest. When on these expeditions they would search through the endless rows of houses for windows covered with white sheets, the sign that death was within, and when a house was found thus, they would knock at the door and respectfully ask if they might see the dead. Only once they were denied, and this had been at a villa, not a common house. Everywhere else they had been taken to the parlour or bedroom where the corpse lay, sometimes in a coffin, and allowed a few seconds' stare. Sometimes the woman of the house, or maybe a daughter, would whisper: 'You knew him, did you?' Or, if the deceased was a child: 'You were in the same school?' They would nod gravely. Often they had walked three or four miles through the valley searching out these dramatic houses. It was Jim who always knocked at the door and said, his cap in his hand: 'We've come to pay our respects, mum.'

At the house in Calfaria Terrace they were two in a crowd. The dead had been dead only a day and neighbours were also paying their respects, as was the custom: there was quite a procession to the upstairs room. The corpse was only a very old man, and his family seemed quite cheerful about it. Thomas heard the woman of the house whisper busily on the landing to a neighbour in a shawl: 'That black blouse you had on the line, Jinny, it'll be a help. The 'surance won't cover the fun'ral, and you know Emlyn lost four days in the pit last week. Still, gone he is now, and there'll be room for a lodger.' And, entreatingly: 'You'll breadcrumb the ham for me, Jinny…? I 'ont forget you when you're in trouble of your own.' The dead old man lay under a patchwork quilt. His face was set in an expression of mild surprise. Thomas noticed dried soapsuds in his ear. Four more people came into the bedroom and the two boys were almost hustled out. No one had taken any particular notice of them. Downstairs they asked a skinny, cruel-looking young woman for a glass of water and to their pleased astonishment she gave them each a glass of small beer.

'It didn't seem as though he was dead at all,' Jim said, as if cheated. 'Let's look for more. In November there's a lot of them. They get bronchitis and consumption.'

'It was like a wedding,' Thomas said. Again they stood in a doorway and looked with vacant boredom through the black curtains of rain sweeping the valley.

'My mother had a new baby last night,' Jim suddenly blurted out, frowning. But when Thomas asked what kind it was, Jim said he didn't know yet. But he knew that there were nine of them now, beside his father and mother and two lodgers. He did not complain. But of late he had been expressing an ambition to go to sea when he left school, instead of going to the colliery.

17

Jim, in the evenings, was often pushed out of home by his mother, a bitter, black-browed woman who was never without a noisy baby. Jim's father was Irish; a collier of drunken reputation in the place, and the whole family was common as a clump of dock. Thomas' mother sometimes made one or two surprised remarks at his association with Jim. They shared a double desk in school. Occasionally Thomas expressed disgust at Jim's unwashed condition.

Again they set out down the streets, keeping a sharp lookout for white sheets in the windows. After a while they found a house so arrayed, yellow blobs of candlelight like sunflowers shining through the white of the parlour. Jim knocked and respectfully made his request to a big creaking woman in black. But she said gently: 'Too late you are. The coffin was screwed down after tea today. Funeral is tomorrow. The wreaths you would like to see?'

Jim hesitated, looking back enquiringly over his shoulder at Thomas. Without speaking, both rejected this invitation, and with mumbled thanks they backed away. 'No luck tonight,' Jim muttered.

'There was the small beer,' Thomas reminded him. A wind had jumped down from the mountains and, as they scurried on, it unhooked a faulty door of a street lamp and blew out the wispy light. When they had reached the bottom of the vale the night was black and rough and moaning, the rain stinging hot on cheeks and hands like whips. Here was a jumbled mass of swarthy and bedraggled dwellings, huddled like a stagnant meeting of bats. A spaniel, dragging her swollen belly, whined out to them from under a bony bush. She sounded lost and confused and exhausted with the burden that weighted her to earth. In the dark alleyways they found a white sheet. A winter silence was here, the black houses were glossy in the rain. No one was about.

'Let's go back,' whispered Thomas. 'It's wet and late.'

'There's one here,' Jim protested. 'After coming all this way!' And he tapped at the door, which had no knocker.

The door was opened and in a shaft of lamplight stood a man's shape, behind him a warm fire-coloured interior, for the door opened on to the living room. Jim made his polite request, and the man silently stood aside. They walked into the glow.

But the taste of death was in the house, true and raw. A very bent old woman in a black cardigan, clasped at her stringy throat with a geranium brooch, sat nodding before the fire. Thomas was staring at the man, who had cried out:

'It's Thomas!' He sat down heavily on a chair: 'Oh, Thomas!' he said in a wounded voice. His stricken face was though he were struggling to repudiate a new pain. A tall handsome man, known to Thomas as Elias, his face had the grey, tough pallor of the underground worker.

The boy stood silent in the shock of the recognition and the suspicion prowling about his mind. He could not speak; he dare not ask. Then fearfully the man said:

'You've come to see Gwen, have you! All this way. Only yesterday I was wondering if your mother had heard. You've come to see her!'

'Yes,' Thomas muttered, his head bent. Jim stood waiting, shifting his feet. The old woman kept on nodding her head. Her son said to her loudly, his voice sounding out in suffering, not having conquered this new reminder of the past years. 'Mam, this is Thomas, Mrs Morgan's boy. You remember? That Gwen was fond of.'

The old woman dreadfully began to weep. Her face, crumpled and brown as a dead rose, winced and shook out slow, difficult tears. 'Me it ought to have been,' she said with a thin obsession. 'No sense in it, no sense at all.'

Thomas glanced secretly at Elias, to see if his emotion had abated. Three years ago he used to carry notes from Elias to Gwen, who had been the servant at home. It seemed to him that Elias and Gwen were always quarrelling. Elias used to stand for hours on the street corner until he came past, hurry up to him and say hoarsely: 'Thomas, please will you take this to Gwen.' In the kitchen at home, Gwen would always toss her head on the receipt of a note, and sometimes she indignantly threw them on the fire without reading them... But Gwen used to be nice. She always kept back for him, after her evening out, some of Elias' chocolates. Once or twice she had obtained permission to take him to the music hall and gloriously he had sat between her and Elias, watching the marvellous conjurors and the women in tights who heaved their bejewelled bosoms as they sang funny songs. But Elias, he had felt, had not welcomed those intrusions. After a long time, Gwen had married him. But before she left to do this, she had wept every day for a week, her strong kind face wet and gloomy. His mother had given her a handsome parlour clock and Gwen had tearfully said she would never wind it as it would last longer if unused. Then gradually she had disappeared, gone into her new married life down the other end of the valley.

Elias looked older, older and thinner. Thomas kept his gaze away from him as much as possible. He felt shy at being drawn into the intimacy of all this grief. The old woman kept on quavering. At last Elias said, quietly now: 'You will come upstairs to see her, Thomas. And your friend.' He opened a door at the staircase and, tall and gaunt, waited for them to pass. Thomas walked past him unwillingly, his stomach gone cold. He did not want to go upstairs. But he thought that Elias would take a refusal hardly. Jim, silent and impassive, followed with politely quiet steps.

In a small, small bedroom with a low ceiling, two candles were burning. A bunch of snowy chrysanthemums stood on a table beside a pink covered bed. Elias had preceded them and now he lifted a starched white square of cloth from off the head and shoulders of the dead.

She was lying tucked in the bed as if quietly asleep. The bedroom was so small there was nowhere else to look. Thomas looked, and started with a terrified surprise. The sheets were folded back, low under Gwen's chest, and cradled in her arms was a pale waxen doll swathed in white. A doll! His amazement passed into terror. He could not move, and the scalp of his head contracted as though an icy wind passed over it. Surely that wasn't a baby, that pale stiff thing Gwen was nursing against her quiet breast! Elias was speaking in a hoarse whisper, and while he spoke he stroked a fold of the bedclothes with a grey hand.

'Very hard it was, Thomas, Gwen going like this. The two of them, I was in the pit, and they sent for me. But she had gone before I was here, though old Watkins let me come in his car... I didn't see her, Thomas, and she asked for me—' His voice broke, and Thomas in his anguish of terror, saw him drop beside the bed and bury his face in the bed.

It was too much. Thomas wanted to get away; he wanted to run, away from the close narrow room, from the man shuddering beside the bed, from the figure in the bed that had been the warm Gwen, from the strange creature in her arms that looked as though it had never been warm. The terror became a nightmare menace coming nearer... Unconsciously he jerked his way out to the landing. Jim followed; he looked oppressed.

'Let's clear off,' he whispered nervously.

They went downstairs. The old woman was brewing tea, and in the labour seemed to forget her grief. 'You will have a cup,' she enquired, 'and a piece of nice cake?'

At this Jim was not unwilling to stay, but Thomas agonisedly plucked his sleeve. Elias' heavy step could be heard on the stairs. Then he came in, quiet and remote-looking. He laid his hand on Thomas' shoulder for a second.

'Do you remember when we used to go to the Empire, Thomas? You and Gwen used to like that Chinaman that made a white pigeon come out of an empty box.'

But Thomas saw that he was not the same Elias, who, though he would wait long hours for the indifferent Gwen like a faithful dog, had been a strutting young man with a determined eye. He was changed now, his shoulders were slackened. She had defeated him after all. Thomas sipped half a cup of tea, but did not touch the cake. He scarcely spoke. Elias kept on reminding him of various happy incidents in the past. That picnic in the mountains, when Elias had scaled the face of a quarry to fetch a blue flower Gwen had fancied. 'Didn't she dare me to get it!' he added, with a strange chuckle in his throat. 'And then she gave it to you!' He sat brooding for a while, his face turned away. Then, to Thomas' renewed terror, he began to weep again, quietly.

The mother, hobbling across to her son, whispered to the two boys. Perhaps they would go now. It was only yesterday her daughter-in-law had died, and the blow was still heavy on her son. She had stiffened herself out of her own abandonment to grief. The boys went to the door in silence. Jim looked reserved and uncommenting.

But outside, in the dark alley, he said: 'I wonder how she came to chuck the bucket! The baby was it?' Receiving no reply, he added with something like pride now: 'My mother's always having them, but she's only abed for three days, she don't die or nothing near it.' Thomas still stumbling silently by his side, he went on: 'Perhaps he'll marry again; he's only a young bloke... I never seen a man cry before,' he added in a voice of contempt.

But for Thomas all the night was weeping. The dark alley was an avenue of the dead, the close shuttered houses were tombs. He heard the wind howling, he could feel the cold ghostly prowling of the clouds. Drops of icy rain stung his cheeks. He was shivering. Gwen's face, bound in its white stillness, moved before him like a lost dead moon. It frightened him, he wanted to have no connection with it; he felt his inside sicken. And all the time he wanted to burst into loud howling like the wind, weep like the rain.

'Shall we look for more?' Jim said. A roused, unappeased appetite was in his voice.

Thomas leaned against the wet wall of a house. Something broke in him. He put up his arm, buried his head in it, and cried. He cried in terror, in fear and in grief. There was something horrible in the dark world. A soft howling whine came out of his throat. Jim, ashamed, passed from wonder into contempt.

'What's up with you!' he jeered. 'You seen plenty of 'em before, haven't you?... Shut up,' he hissed angrily. 'There's someone coming.' And he gave Thomas a push.

Thomas hit out. All the world was jangled and threatening and hostile. The back of his hand caught Jim sharply on the cheekbone. Immediately there was a scuffle. But it was short-lived. They had rolled into a pool of liquidly thin mud, and both were surprised and frightened by the mess they were in.

'Jesus,' exclaimed Jim. 'I'll cop it for this.'

Thomas lurched away. He stalked into the rough night. All about him was a new kingdom. Desperately he tried to think of something else. Of holidays by the sea, of Christmas, of the nut trees in a vale over the mountains, where, too, thrushes' nests could be found in the spring, marvellously coloured eggs in them. Jim, who had seen him weep, he thought of with anger and dislike.

At the top of the hill leading to his home he paused in anguish. The bare high place was open to the hostile heavens, a lump of earth open like a helpless face to the blows of the wind and the rain. He heard derision in the howls of the wind, he felt hate and anger in the stings of the rain.

THE DISENCHANTMENT
OF THE WORLD

A Father in Sion

Caradoc Evans

On the banks of Avon Bern there lived a man who was a
Father in Sion. His name was Sadrach, and the name of the
farmhouse in which he dwelt was Danyrefail. He was a man
whose thoughts were continually employed upon sacred
subjects. He began the day and ended the day with the words
of a chapter from the Book and a prayer on his lips. The
Sabbath he observed from first to last; he neither laboured
himself nor allowed any in his household to labour. If in the
Seiet, the solemn, soul-searching assembly that gathers in
Capel Sion on the nights of Wednesdays after Communion
Sundays, he was entreated to deliver a message to the
congregation, he often prefaced his remarks with, 'Dear
people, on my way to Sion I asked God what He meant—'

This episode in the life of Sadrach Danyrefail covers a long
period; it has its beginning on a March night with Sadrach
closing the Bible and giving utterance to these words:

'May the blessing of the Big Man be upon the reading of
His word.' Then, 'Let us pray.'

Sadrach fell on his knees, the open palms of his hands
together, his elbows resting on the table; his eight children –
Sadrach the Small, Esau, Simon, Rachel, Sarah, Daniel,
Samuel, and Miriam – followed his example.

Usually Sadrach prayed fluently, in phrases not unworthy
of the minister, so universal, so intimate his pleading: tonight
he stumbled and halted, and the working of his spiritful

mind lacked the heavenly symmetry of the mind of the godly; usually the note of abundant faith and childlike resignation rang grandly through his supplications: tonight the note was one of despair and gloom. With Job he compared himself, for was not the Lord trying His servant to the uttermost? Would the all-powerful Big Man, the Big Man who delivered the Children of Israel from the hold of the Egyptians, give him a morsel of strength to bear his cross? Sadrach reminded God of his loneliness. Man was born to be mated, even as the animals in the fields. Without a mate, man was like an estate without an overseer, or a field of ripe corn rotting for the reaping hook.

Sadrach rose from his knees. Sadrach the Small lit the lantern which was to light him and Esau to their bed over the stable.

'My children,' said Sadrach, 'do you gather round me now, for have I not something to tell you?'

Rachel, the eldest daughter, a girl of twelve, with reddish cheeks and bright eyes, interposed with:

'Indeed, indeed, now, little father; you are not going to preach to us this time of night!'

Sadrach stretched forth his hand and motioned his children be seated.

'Put out your lantern, Sadrach the Small,' he said. 'No, Rachel, don't you light the candle. Dear ones, it is not the light of this earth we need, but the light that comes from above.'

'Iss, iss,' Sadrach the Small said. 'The true light. The light the Big Man puts in the hearts of those who believe, dear me.'

'Well spoken, Sadrach the Small. Now be you all silent awhile, for I have things of great import to tell you. Heard you all my prayer?'

'Iss, iss,' said Sadrach the Small.

'Sadrach the Small only answers. My children, heard you all my prayer? Don't you be blockheads now – speak out.'

'There's lovely, it was,' said Sadrach the Small.

'My children?' said Sadrach.

'Iss, iss,' they answered.

'Well, well, then. How can I tell you?' Sadrach put his fingers through the thin beard which covered the opening of his waistcoat, closed his eyes, and murmured a prayer. 'Your mother Achsah is not what she should be. Indeed to goodness, now, what disgrace this is! Is it not breaking my heart? You did hear how I said to the nice Big Man that I was like Job? Achsah is mad.'

Rachel sobbed.

'Weep you not, Rachel. It is not for us to question the all-wise ways of the Big Man. Do you dry your eyes on your apron now, my daughter. You, too, have your mother's eyes. Let me weep in my solitude. Oh, what sin have I committed, that God should visit this affliction on me?'

Rachel went to the foot of the stairs.

'Mam!' she called.

'She will not hear you,' Sadrach interrupted. 'Dear me, have I not put her in the harness loft? It is not respectable to let her out. Twm Tybach would have sent his wife to the madhouse of Carmarthen. But that is not Christian. Rachel, Rachel, dry your eyes. It is not your fault that Achsah is mad. Nor do I blame Sadrach the Small, nor Esau, nor Simon, nor Sarah, nor Daniel, nor Samuel, nor Miriam. Goodly names have I given you all. Live you up to them. Still, my sons and daughters, are you not all responsible for Achsah's condition? With the birth of each of you she has got worse and worse. Childbearing has made her foolish. Yet it is un-Christian to blame you.'

Sadrach placed his head in his arms.

Sadrach the Small took the lantern and he and Esau departed for their bed over the stable; one by one the remaining six put off their clogs and crept up the narrow staircase to their beds.

Wherefore to her husband Achsah became as a cross, to

her children as one forgotten, to everyone living in Manteg and in the several houses scattered on the banks of Avon Bern as Achsah the madwoman.

The next day Sadrach removed the harness to the room in the dwelling house in which slept the four youngest children; and he put a straw mattress and a straw pillow on the floor, and on the mattress he spread three sacks: and these were the furnishings of the loft where Achsah spent her time. The frame of the small window in the roof he nailed down, after fixing on the outside of it three solid bars of iron of uniform thickness; the trapdoor he padlocked, and the key of the lock never left his possession. Achsah's food he himself carried to her twice a day, a procedure which until the coming of Martha some time later he did not entrust to other hands.

Once a week when the household was asleep he placed a ladder from the floor to the loft, and cried:

'Achsah, come you down now.'

Meekly the woman obeyed, and as her feet touched the last rung Sadrach threw a cow's halter over her shoulders, and drove her out into the fields for an airing.

Once, when the moon was full, the pair were met by Lloyd the Schoolin', and the sight caused Mishtir Lloyd to run like a frightened dog, telling one of the women in his household that Achsah, the madwoman, had eyes like a cow's.

At the time of her marriage, Achsah was ten years older than her husband. She was rich too: Danyrefail, with its stock of good cattle and a hundred acres of fair land, was her gift to the bridegroom. Six months after the wedding Sadrach the Small was born. Tongues wagged that the boy was a child of sin. Sadrach answered neither yea nor nay. He answered neither yea nor nay until the first Communion Sabbath, when he seized the bread and wine from Old Shemmi and walked to the Big Seat. He stood under the pulpit, the fringe of the minister's Bible-marker curling on the bald patch on his head.

'Dear people,' he proclaimed, the silver-plated wine cup in

one hand, the bread plate in the other, 'it has been said to me that some of you think Sadrach the Small was born out of sin. You do not speak truly. Achsah, dear me, was frightened by the old bull. The bull I bought in the September fair. You, Shemmi, you know the animal. The red and white bull. Well, well, dear people? Achsah was shocked by him. She was running away from him, and as she crossed the threshold of Danyrefail, did she not give birth to Sadrach the Small? Do you believe me now, dear people? As the Lord liveth, this is the truth. Achsah, Achsah, stand you up now, and say you to the congregation if this is not right.'

Achsah, the babe suckling at her breast, rose and murmured:

'Sadrach speaks the truth.'

Sadrach ate of the bread and drank of the wine.

Three months after Achsah had been put in the loft Sadrach set out at daybreak on a journey to Aberystwyth. He returned late at night, and, behold, a strange woman sat beside him in the horse car; and the coming of this strange woman made life different in Danyrefail. Early in the morning she was astir, bustling up the children, bidding them fetch the cows, assist with the milking, feed the pigs, or do whatever work was in season.

Rachel rebuked Sadrach, saying, 'Little Father, why for cannot I manage the house for you? Indeed now, you have given to Martha the position that belongs to me, your eldest daughter.'

'What mean you, my dear child?' returned Sadrach. 'Cast you evil at your father? Turn you against him? Go you and read your Commandments.'

'People are whispering,' said Rachel. 'They do even say that you will not be among the First Men of the Big Seat.'

'Martha is a gift from the Big Man,' answered Sadrach. 'She has been sent to comfort me in my tribulation, and to mother you, my children.'

'Mother!'

'Tut, tut, Rachel,' said Sadrach, 'Martha is only a servant in my house.'

Rachel knew that Martha was more than a servant. Had not her transfer letter been accepted by Capel Sion, and did she not occupy Achsah's seat in the family pew? Did she not, when it was Sadrach's turn to keep the minister's month, herself on each of the four Saturdays take a basket laden with a chicken, two white-hearted cabbages, a peck of potatoes, a loaf of bread, and half a pound of butter to the chapel house of Capel Sion? Did she not drive with Sadrach to market and fair and barter for his butter and cheese and cattle and what not? Did she not tell Ellen the Weaver's Widow what cloth to weave for the garments of the children of Achsah?

These things Martha did; and Danyrefail prospered exceedingly: its possessions spread even to the other side of Avon Bern. Sadrach declared in the Seiet that the Lord was heaping blessings on the head of His servant. Of all who worshipped in Sion none was stronger than the male of Danyrefail; none more respected. The congregation elected him to the Big Seat. Sadrach was a tower of strength unto Sion.

But in the wake of his prosperity lay vexation. Rachel developed fits; while hoeing turnips in the twilight of an afternoon she shivered and fell, her head resting in the water ditch that is alongside the hedge. In the morning Sadrach came that way with a load of manure.

'Rachel, fach,' he said, 'wake up now. What will Martha say if you get ill?'

He passed on.

When he came back Rachel had not moved, and Sadrach drove away, without noticing the small pool of water which had gathered over the girl's head. Within an hour he came again, and said:

'Rachel, Rachel, wake you up. There's lazy you are.'

Rachel was silent. Death had come before the milking of

the cows. Sadrach went to the end of the field and emptied
his cart of manure. Then he turned and cast Rachel's body
into the cart, and covered it with a sack, and drove home,
singing the hymn which begins:

> Safely, safely gather'd in,
> Far from sorrow, far from sin,
> No more childish griefs or fears,
> No more sadness, no more tears;
> For the life so young and fair
> Now hath passed from earthly care;
> God himself the soul will keep,
> Giving His beloved – sleep.

Esau was kicked by a horse, and was hurt to his death; six
weeks later Simon gashed his thumb while slicing mangolds,
and he died. Two years went by, by the end of which period
Old Ianto, the gravedigger of Capel Sion, dug three more
graves for the children of Sadrach and Achsah; and over
these graves Sadrach and Martha lamented.

But Sadrach the Small brought gladness and cheer to
Danyrefail with the announcement of his desire to wed Sara
Ann, the daughter of Old Shemmi. Martha and Sadrach
agreed to the union provided Old Shemmi gave to his
daughter a stack of hay, a cow in calf, a heifer, a quantity of
bedclothes, and four cheeses. Old Shemmi, on his part,
demanded with Sadrach the Small ten sovereigns, a horse
and cart, and a bedstead.

The night before the wedding, Sadrach drove Achsah into
the fields, and he told her how the Big Man had looked with
goodwill upon Sadrach the Small, and was giving him Sara
Ann to wife.

What occurred in the loft over the cowshed before dawn
crept in through the window with the iron bars I cannot tell
you. God can. But the rising sun found Achsah crouching
behind one of the hedges of the lane that brings you from

Danyrefail to the tramping road, and there she stayed, her eyes peering through the foliage, until the procession came by: first Old Shemmi and Sadrach, with Sadrach the Small between them; then the minister of Capel Sion and his wife; then the men and the women of the congregation; and last came Martha and Sara Ann.

The party disappeared round the bend: Achsah remained.

'Goodness me,' she said to herself. 'There's a large mistake now. Indeed, indeed, mad am I.'

She hurried to the gateway, crossed the road and entered another field, through which she ran as hard as she could. She came to a hedge, and waited.

The procession was passing.

Sadrach and Sadrach the Small.

Achsah doubled a finger.

Among those who followed on the heels of the minister was Miriam.

Achsah doubled another finger.

The party moved out of sight: Achsah still waited.

'Sadrach the Small and Miriam!' she said, spreading out her doubled-up fingers. 'Two. Others? Esau. Simon. Rachel. Sarah. Daniel. Samuel. Dear me, where shall I say they are? Six. Six of my children. Mad, mad am I?' She laughed. 'They are grown, and I didn't know them.'

Achsah waited the third time for the wedding procession. This time she scanned each face, but only in the faces of Sadrach the Small and Miriam did she recognise her own children. She threw herself on the grass. Esau and Simon and Rachel, and Sarah and Daniel and Samuel. She remembered the circumstances attending the birth of each... And she had been a good wife. Never once did she deny Sadrach his rights. So long as she lasted she was a woman to him.

'Sadrach the Small and Miriam,' she said.

She rose and went to the graveyard. She came to the earth under which are Essec and Shan, Sadrach's father and mother, and at a distance of the space of one grave from theirs were the graves of six of the children born of Sadrach and Achsah. She parted the hair that had fallen over her face, and traced with her fingers the letters which formed the names of each of her six children.

As Sara Ann crossed the threshold of Danyrefail, and as she set her feet on the flagstone on which Sadrach the Small is said to have been born, the door of the parlour was opened and a lunatic embraced her.

THE BLACK RAT

Frank Richards

We were in the trenches at Hulloch, and a Battalion Headquarters' signaller came in our dugout and handed me Battalion Orders to give to the Company Commander; of course, Dann and I read it before handing it over. It consisted mainly of orders sent by the Lieutenant General commanding the corps we were now in, and ran something like this: 'It has been brought to my notice that a pessimistic feeling prevails amongst the officers, NCOs and men in my corps; such expressions as "We will never shift the enemy out of their entrenched positions" and "The war has now become a stalemate", are frequently made. Officers must eradicate this feeling from their minds and from the minds of the men serving under them, and remember that it is only a question of time before the enemy will be driven headlong out of the lines that they now occupy." There was also too much swearing in the corps for his liking, and the officers were worse than the men: "This practice must also cease." I took the message to the Company Commander, and his language for the rest of the day was delightful to listen to: it would have done that Lieutenant General a heap of good if he could have heard it.

The Corps Commander was right about the pessimistic feeling prevailing: since the Battle of Loos, all along this front from Cambrin to Hulloch and as far as the eye could see, our dead were still lying out in front of us, and looking through the periscopes by day we could see the rats crawling over their bodies. They had a good picking along this front and were as fat as prize porkers. We also knew that from now on any attack that was made by us would involve huge casualties. We old hands were always hoping that the enemy would attack us, so that we could get a bit of our own back for the Loos battle. It was all very well for the Corps General to be so optimistic: he was living in a chateau or mansion many many miles behind the front line from where he issued his orders, which went from him to divisions then to brigades then to battalion commanders, from them to company commanders and platoon officers who with the men had to do the real dirty work. If he had been in a front-line trench on a dark or dirty night, and going around a traverse had been knocked head over heels on his back in the deep mud by someone carrying a roll of barbed wire, or by the burst of a shell, I expect his language would have been a little stronger than what he used back in his abode of luxury. A few weeks previously he had inspected the Battalion in Montmorency Barracks and noticed that the men's brasses were not polished. He gave orders that all men in his corps when out of action must polish their brasses the same as if they were at home. Up to this time it had been a standing order in the Battalion to keep the brasses dull, but after that inspection our brasses were polished good enough to shave in. Many prayers were offered up for his soul, and a few days later when we marched down the main road towards the line with the sun shining brightly and striking on our polished brasses, the enemy in their observation balloons must have thought that hundreds of small heliographs were moving into action. One man called Duffy swore that the Corps Commander was a chief director in one of the large metal-polish companies and another remarked that the old sinner would sooner lose his trenches than his button sticks.

During one spell in the line at Hulloch, Dann and I came out of our little dugout, which was about fifteen yards behind the front-line trench, to clean our rifles and bayonets. We were just about to begin when there appeared, on the back of the trench we were in, the largest rat that I ever saw in my life. It was jet black and was looking intently at Dann, who threw a clod of earth at it but missed, and it didn't even attempt to dodge it. I threw a clod at it then; it sprang out of the way, but not far, and began staring at Dann again. This got on Dann's nerves; he threw another clod but missed again, and it never even flinched. I had my bayonet fixed and made a lunge at it; it sprang out of the way for me all right but had another intent look at Dann before it disappeared over the top. I would have shot it, for I had a round in the breach, but we were not allowed to fire over the top to the rear of us for fear of hitting men in the support trench; one or two men had been hit this way by men shooting at rats, and orders were very strict regarding it.

Dann had gone very pale; I asked him if he were ill. He said that he wasn't but the rat had made him feel queer. I burst out laughing. He said: 'It's all right, you laughing, but I know my number is up. You saw how that rat never even flinched when I threw at it, and I saw something besides that you didn't see or you wouldn't be laughing at me. Mark my words, when I do go west that rat will be close by.' I told him not to talk so wet and that we may be a hundred miles from this part of the front in a week's time. He said: 'That don't matter: if it's two hundred miles off or a thousand, that rat will still be knocking around when I go west.' Dann was a very brave and cheery fellow, but from that day he was a changed man. He still did his work the same as the rest of us, and never shirked a dangerous job, but all his former cheeriness had left him. Old soldiers who knew him well often asked me what was wrong with him. But I never told them; they might have chaffed him about it. Neither I nor Dann ever made any reference about the rat from that day on, and though we two had passed many hours together shooting at rats for sport in those trenches, especially along at Givenchy by the canal bank, he never went shooting them again.

A few months later we arrived on the Somme by a six days' march from the railhead, and early in the morning of the 15th July passed through Fricourt, where our First Battalion had broken through on 1st July, and arrived at the end of Mametz Wood which had been captured some days before by the 38th Welsh Division which included four of our new service battalions. The enemy had been sending over tear gas and the valley was thick with it. It smelt like strong onions which made our eyes and noses run very badly; we were soon coughing, sneezing and cursing. We rested in shell-holes, the ground all around us being thick with dead of the troops who had been attacking Mametz Wood. The fighting was going on about three-quarters of a mile ahead of us.

Dann, a young signaller named Thomas, and I, were posted to A Company. The three of us were dozing when Thomas gave a shout: a spent bullet with sufficient force to penetrate had hit him in the knee – our first casualty on the Somme. Dann said: 'I don't suppose it will be my luck to get hit with a spent bullet; it will be one at short range through the head or a twelve-inch shell all on my own.' I replied, as usual, that he would be damned lucky if he stopped either, and that he wouldn't be able to grouse much afterwards. 'You're right enough about that, Dick,' he said.

A few hours later the battalion moved around the corner of the wood, the company occupying a shallow trench which was only knee-deep. Dann and I were by ourselves in one part of this trench, the Company Commander being about ten yards below us. The majority of the company were soon in the wood on the scrounge; we had been told that we were likely to stay where we were for a day or two. I told Dann that I was going in the wood on the scrounge and that I would try and get a couple of German topcoats and some food if I could find any. The topcoats would be very handy as we were in fighting order, and the nights were cold for July. Just inside the wood, which was a great tangle of broken trees and branches, was a German trench, and all around it our dead and theirs were lying. I was in luck's way – I got two tins of Maconochies and half a loaf of bread, also two topcoats. The bread was very stale and it was a wonder the rats hadn't got at it. Although gas destroyed large numbers of them there were plenty of them left skipping about. I returned to Dann telling him how lucky I had been, and that we would have a feed. 'Righto,' he replied, 'but I think I'll write out a couple of quickfirers first.' (Quickfirers were Field Service Postcards.)

Enemy shells were now coming over and a lot of spent machine-gun bullets were zipping about. He sat on the back of the trench writing his quickfirers, when – zip! – and he rolled over, clutching his neck. Then a terrified look came in his face as he pointed one hand behind me. I turned and just behind me on the back of the trench, saw the huge black rat that we had seen in Hulloch. It was looking straight past me at Dann. I was paralysed myself for a moment and without looking at me it turned and disappeared in a shell-hole behind. I turned around and instantly flattened myself on the bottom of the trench, a fraction of a second before a shell burst behind me. I picked myself up amid a shower of dirt and clods and looked at Dann, but he was dead. The spent bullet had sufficient force to penetrate his neck and touch the spinal column. And there by his side, also dead, was the large rat. The explosion of the shell had blown it up and it had dropped by the side of him. I seized hold of its tail and swung it back in the shell-hole it had blown from. I was getting the creeps. Although Mametz Wood, was, I dare say, over fifty miles as the crow flies from Hulloch, I had no doubt in my mind that it was the same rat that we had seen in the latter place. It was the only weird experience I had during the whole of the war. There was no one near us at the time, and men on the right and left of us did not know Dann was killed until I told them. If I hadn't handled that rat and flung it away I should have thought that I had been seeing things, like many who saw things on the retirement from Mons.

THE GROUSER

Fred Ambrose

'Next, Private Morgan,' shouted the Sergeant-Major. 'Quick march! Left wheel! Halt! Right turn.'

'Sir (to the Colonel), Private Morgan, sir, who is reported by Corporal Thomas for not complying with an order. The offence took place yesterday afternoon at 4.30 p.m. near the man's billet, sir.'

'H'm, yes,' said the Colonel, 'very serious charge indeed – especially on active service. Give me his conduct sheet, Sergeant-Major.'

As the Sergeant Major searched his wallet, the Colonel turned to the Corporal who made the charge. 'Well, Corporal, what was the trouble?'

'It was like this, sir. The Surgunt Major said some officer from Headquarters – sanitary or something – 'ad complain about our billat bein' untidy – tins an' things about the place, sir – an' he was blamin' me because the place was so dirty, so I ordered Shoni Morgan – Private Morgan, I mean, sir – to burn the tins an' then bury them. He refuse to obey the ordar, sir. He said what was the good of burning the tins if they was to be buried after. He said he would burn them tins or bury them, and last of all he did say that he wouldn't bury or burn them, sir. So he did refuse to obey ordars, sir.'

By this time the Sergeant-Major had found the elusive conduct sheet. By no stretch of leniency could Private Morgan's record be regarded as creditable – CB, Stop pay,

Field Punishment, Nos. 1 and 2, figured largely, while the numbers of a few 'Drunk' entries in red ink stared up from the paper.

The Colonel glanced at the sheet, frowned slightly, and looked up. 'Well, Morgan, what have you to say for yourself?'

'They are always on to me, sir, an' it isn't fair to put all the work on to the same chap all the time. There was a lot of chaps sittin' in the billat doin' nothin' and the Copral ought to ask them to 'elp too, an' that is what I told 'im. He always do pitch on to me for the dirty work sir...'

'Yes, Morgan,' said the Colonel, 'but being in the Army...'

'I know, sir, I'm in the Army, but I didn't join...'

'Silence,' thundered the Sergeant-Major; 'Don't interrupt the Colonel when he is speaking.'

But Private Morgan would not be silenced: he commented with extraordinary fluency upon the unfair division of labour in the Battalion in general, in particular upon the unnecessary amount of labour that was the portion of his platoon. He asserted that the Sergeants had their favourites, and the Corporals their pets. Taking a wider survey, he was beginning to develop the thesis that nepotism was widespread in the Army, when the Colonel cut him short with, 'Very well, I sentence you to Field Punishment, No. 1 for fourteen days. In future you will obey orders first, and make your complaints afterwards.'

The Colonel nodded, and the Sergeant-Major addressing the culprit as if he were a regiment of soldiers, shouted, 'Right turn! Quick march! Right wheel!' and Private Morgan disappeared.

This was my first acquaintance with Morgan, who was known to his comrades as 'Shoni'. On the short side, with black hair, and rather squarely built, he was a typical Welsh collier.

I had but recently joined the Battalion from the Depot, and I was beginning to find it no easy matter to aid in administering justice to a Battalion with such a curious psychology. Formed at the beginning of the war, the Battalion had had the usual training, and had now been some time in France. The men were quick and smart, but they had no discipline – I mean they had no 'sense' of discipline. They obeyed orders, but they were outspoken in their criticism of authority in any shape or form. I put it down to the years of tuition they had received in Trades Union and socialistic principles in the South Wales coalfield. And 'Shoni' Morgan was more than representative of the type!

Of Morgan I was destined to see more than was enough. He was a 'grouser' – the super-grouser of the Battalion. It is the privilege of the British soldier to grouse, but grousing was more than a privilege to him: it was an obsession. One day it was the rations – he did not get his fair share. For this he blamed everybody from the Corporal to the CQMS. Another day it was fatigues: they always pitched on him. What were the Pioneers for? They were paid for doing navvy's work. He had joined to fight: he was an Infantry Man, not a navvy.

He was selected for reconnaissance work one night, and orders were given to leave the rifles behind. He remonstrated, as he always did: he did not see why he should not take his rifle. How was he going to defend himself? It was useless to assert that the object of the patrol was to discover without being discovered: he would not be silenced, and even in 'No Man's Land' audibly protested that it was folly to leave his rifle behind.

The Bosches must have heard him, for a machine gun was turned in our direction, and we had to lie flat for half an hour before we could continue our work. 'Shoni', in his perversity, seemed most active when the Very lights went up, and he was cursed silently, but fervently, by every man in the patrol. We got back eventually, apparently without losing a man, the only casualty being my sergeant, who had received a bleeding nose through falling flat with too much celerity when the machine gun forced us to take cover. When I mustered the little party in the trench, 'Shoni' could nowhere be seen, and no one knew anything about him. Blessing him, I was about to return when the crack of a solitary rifle was heard from the direction of a Johnson hole we had crept past a little time before. I remembered remarking in an undertone how it overlooked a German trench and would make a fine sniper's post. Our Very lights showed 'Shoni' lying prone, and putting in some 'rapid fire' – probably hopelessly ineffective – at the Bosches. When he had emptied his pouches, he crept back to our trench. I admonished him for his conduct, but he was, as usual, staunch in his defence. He did not think it fair to go out without his rifle to protect himself. What was his rifle good for? He had gone back 'to get a bit of his own back'.

Another grievance was not long in presenting itself, for one afternoon, marching back from our billets to the trenches, we saw a string of London omnibuses taking down a company of Scotch Bantams from the trenches, where they had been training, and we learnt that they were soon bringing back a fresh company. Whether his equipment galled him more than usual, or whether his feet were more than usually sore I do not know: I know I was surprised by the force of his language. Why should he walk while those bloody Scotchmen were carried? He was as good as any bloody Scotchman any day. Macalister, looking sourly in his direction, brought a torrent of abuse upon himself, and hurriedly disclaimed his obvious Scotch ancestry before 'Shoni' turned his attention from his luckless fellow private to his general grievances. The whole army was in a rotten condition. Favouritism was rampant: it was not fair that one should march while another was carried: all should march, or all should be carried. It was the Sergeant who cut him short with a gruff 'Silence in the ranks'.

I well remember that march. We were returning from billets along the old Rue de Bois. There was a battery of 6" guns roaring away on our left, while behind us, the sun was setting in a blaze of red, against which were silhouetted the quaint red-tiled cottages with their attendant poplar sentinels. The crimson glare shone on the filled ditches and the pools which pitted the roadway. From the fields, weary with their day's toil, came the workers – old and bent peasants, soldiers broken in the war, soldiers on leave, and young girls and lads. We passed their peculiar three-wheeled carts, the driver persisting in his habit of driving in the middle of the road in spite of loud shouts of 'À droit'. The motor transports squelched past us, sending up streams of mud to the accompaniment of curses from the infantry. As it grew darker, the gun limbers hurried past – a long train, stretching out into the gathering night. As we neared the trenches we saw the familiar star shells and Very lights rising and falling, showing up the 'line' as a black ridge. Shrapnel began to find us out, and we separated into small parties. This, apparently, was the opportunity for which Private 'Shoni' Morgan had been looking, for he dropped out. In the dusk and the bustle he was not observed, and he was not missed until we began the inter-battalion relief. Half an hour later he turned up with a platoon of Bantams up for training. He did not see it fair to march while others were being carried, so he had stopped on the road until a bus had picked him up. How to punish him puzzled me. Field Punishment, or loss of pay, seemed not to influence his actions in the least, and yet his offence was flagrant. During that period in the trenches I kept him on fatigue duty all the time, supplying him with sufficient material to grouse about for an average lifetime.

After this he determined to transfer. The formation of a new tunnelling company gave him his opportunity. He, and several of his comrades, applied to the Colonel for the necessary permission, and in his particular case it was readily granted. So 'Shoni' Morgan joined the 'Moles', and the Battalion, officially, knew him no more.

We were, however, not without news of him. The

Sergeant-Major, some time afterwards, told me that he had seen him in a working party coming back from the trenches. He looked well, and was singing. Knowing his officer, a mining engineer, I went across to his billet for a chat. He was most favourably impressed by Morgan. 'He is one of the best miners we have,' he said, 'the most willing, and the most daring.' I was discreetly silent. He stated, further, that he was recommending him for promotion. In the narrow galleries of the mine, it seemed, he had again found his element.

Hearing that he had been seen, with a stripe on his arm, in charge of a small working party, I sent him one of those all-embracing FS postcards, addressed to Second Corporal J. Morgan, RE, scribbling 'Congratulations' where the Regulations state 'Signature only'. I wonder if he ever guessed who sent it.

Weeks passed, and I lost sight of him: his company had, somehow, been attached to another brigade. Cares multiplied, and I forgot his existence, until one day I saw him again – this time at a Battalion Aid Post – coming in on a stretcher. I can see him now, all clay-covered, with his head all battered and bleeding. There he lay, dead, the stretcher dripping with the sticky, brown blood of him.

I turned to one of the stretcher-bearers whom I recognised as having transferred from the Battalion at the same time as Morgan.

'Shoni?' I queried.

He nodded his head, and said, 'Blown up in a mine, sir.' The bearer assisted in carrying the body and returned to me. 'How did it happen?' I asked.

He answered my question with all a Welshman's circumlocutions and irrelevancies, and this was his story:

'Yes, sir, "Shoni" was one of the best minars in the Company – he was a better minar than soldiar, sir, and the Captun said he was one of the best men he 'ad, beggin' your pardon, sir. "Shoni" was a good colliar, an' I remember 'ow 'is stall in the Dyffryn pit was one of the tidiest in the place.

Well, sir, it was like this. We was drivin' a headin' – I mean a gallery, sir – towards a German sap, and we 'ad got well under it, and there was three Engineers workin' in the cross headin' preparin' for the mines and the connections. But the Germans 'ad countermined, an' all at once part of our gallery fell into theirs, shuttin' up the Engineers in the far end. Our top fell in, and there we was in the gallery not knowin' what to do, and every minute we was expectin' the Germans to blow up their mine. To stop in the gallery was dangerous, an' to leave it was to leave them three to be buried alive. The ground was so loose, an' the boys was afraid, and we was beginnin' to make for the shaft when "Shoni" came up. "Where are you goin'," he said, "you aren't goin' to leave them boys there. Come on, Twm," he says to me, "We can get a hole through that fall in ten minutes. I've been lookin' at it." So we went back, an' dug away at that fall like anythin' – all the time expectin' that German mine to go off. I was all nerves, but "Shoni" was as cool as anything – workin' away as if he was in his own pit at 'ome, diggin' an' proppin' with flats an' other things at full speed. At last 'e shouted 'e was through, but we could see that the fall would be settlin' again as the top was working like anything. "Twm," he says to me, "me an' you will get them out – we are used to it. You others get back now." They didn't want to go then, sir, but "Shoni" made them go, sayin' they was only in the way. So we worked our way in, an' we found them: two was very weak an' exhausted, an' the other like dead. We got them out to the top of the slant, and then "Shoni" said, "Twm, it's no use you comin' back again: I'm goin' back for the dead one. We'll try artificial respiration on him." It was no use me arguin' – he would go in himself. So I went back to the neck of the slant, an' 'eard 'im creeping back an' draggin' the body along. He was just pullin' 'im through the hole in the fall, when the mine went off. The wind of the explosion came up the gallery, an' hit me against the trench, an' left me gaspin'. They all rushed up, an' by then I was all right, but a bit shaky. The Germans 'ad fired what is called a "camouflet", which is a small charge which will blow up a gallery, but not make a big crater like a mine would do. They 'ad blown it up just as "Shoni" was clearing the fall, an' 'e didn't have a chance. It had exploded nearly under 'im, an' had blown 'im yards towards the mouth of the gallery before the roof came down an' buried him. We dug like devils an' got 'im out: he was still conscious when we brought 'im out, but 'e was nearly gone. He couldn't speak, an' then 'e went unconscious. He wasn't long, sir, before he died. He was back in the mine again, an' 'e was in awful pain, an' he was moanin'. "Tell the manager," I heard 'im sayin', "I nearly got 'im out. I done my best" – and he was dead.'

And the bearer's voice broke, and the big teardrops coursed down his cheeks.

I went to his burial at the British Cemetery at Windy Corner, where those rows of simple wooden crosses mark the last resting place of many, whose heroic deeds no pen will record. As the Chaplain read those undying words of the Burial Service over the poor, shattered body in the bloodstained blanket, lying in the shallow grave, the snow fell steadily and wrapped it gently in a pure white coverlet: his winding sheet was of the purest white... And there I left him. Far from the Land of his Fathers he sleeps well among the brave.

At the crossroads the German shrapnel was beginning to burst at the usual time; where the road bent sharply to the right passed a working party bound for the trenches; behind us a battery of 18-pounders suddenly opened fire, as if in honourable tribute to the poor clay that was Second Corporal John Morgan, RE, grouser, and man.

Be This Her Memorial

Caradoc Evans

Mice and rats, as it is said, frequent neither churches nor poor men's homes. The story I have to tell you about Nanni – the Nanni who was hustled on her way to prayer meeting by the Bad Man, who saw the phantom mourners bearing away Twm Tybach's coffin, who saw the Spirit Hounds and heard their moanings two days before Isaac Penparc took wing – the story I have to tell you contradicts that theory.

Nanni was religious; and she was old. No one knew how old she was, for she said that she remembered the birth of each person that gathered in Capel Sion; she was so old that her age had ceased to concern.

She lived in the mud-walled, straw-thatched cottage on the steep road which goes up from the Garden of Eden, and ends at the tramping way that takes you into Cardigan town; if you happen to be travelling that way you may still see the roofless walls which were silent witnesses to Nanni's great sacrifice – a sacrifice surely counted unto her for righteousness, though in her search for God she fell down and worshipped at the feet of a god.

Nanni's income was three shillings and ninepence a week. That sum was allowed her by Abel Shones, the officer for Poor Relief, who each payday never forgot to remind the crooked, wrinkled, toothless old woman how much she owed to him and God.

'If it was not for me, little Nanni,' Abel was in the habit of telling her, 'you would be in the House of the Poor long ago.'

At that remark Nanni would shiver and tremble.

'Dear heart,' she would say in the third person, for Abel was a mighty man and the holder of a proud office, 'I pray for him night and day.'

Nanni spoke the truth, for she did remember Abel in her prayers. But the workhouse held for her none of the terrors it holds for her poverty-stricken sisters. Life was life anywhere, in cottage or in poorhouse, though with this difference: her liberty in the poorhouse would be so curtailed that no more would she be able to listen to the spirit-laden eloquence of the Respected Josiah Bryn-Bevan. She helped to bring Josiah into the world; she swaddled him in her own flannel petticoat; she watched him going to and coming from school; she knitted for him four pairs of strong stockings to mark his going out into the world as a farm servant; and when the boy, having obeyed the command of the Big Man was called to minister to the congregation of Capel Sion, even Josiah's mother was not more vain than Old Nanni. Hence Nanni struggled on less than three shillings and ninepence a week, for did she not give a tenth of her income to the treasury of the Capel? Unconsciously she came to regard Josiah as greater than God: God was abstract; Josiah was real.

As Josiah played a part in Nanni's life, so did a Seller of Bibles play a minor part in the last few days of her travail. The man came to Nanni's cottage the evening of the day of the rumour that the Respected Josiah Bryn-Bevan had received a call from a wealthy sister church in Aberystwyth. Broken with grief, Nanni, the first time for many years, bent her stiffened limbs and addressed herself to the living God.

'Dear little Big Man,' she prayed, 'let not your son bach religious depart.'

Then she recalled how good God had been to her, how He had permitted her to listen to His son's voice; and another fear struck her heart.

'Dear little Big Man,' she muttered between her blackened gums, 'do you now let me live to hear the boy's farewell words.'

At that moment the Seller of Bibles raised the latch of the door.

'The Big Man be with this household,' he said, placing his pack on Nanni's bed. 'Sit you down,' said Nanni, 'and rest yourself, for you must be weary.'

'Man,' replied the Seller of Bibles, 'is never weary of well-doing.'

Nanni dusted for him a chair.

'No, no; indeed now,' he said; 'I cannot tarry long, woman. Do you not know that I am the Big Man's messenger? Am I not honoured to take His word into the highways and byways, and has He not sent me here?'

He unstrapped his pack, and showed Nanni a gaudy volume with a clasp of brass, and containing many coloured prints; the pictures he explained at hazard: here was a tall-hatted John baptising, here a Roman-featured Christ praying in the Garden of Gethsemane, here a frock-coated Moses and the Tablets.

'A Book,' said he, 'which ought to be on the table of every Christian home.'

'Truth you speak, little man,' remarked Nanni. 'What shall I say to you you are asking for it?'

'It has a price far above rubies,' answered the Seller of Bibles. He turned over the leaves and read: '"The labourer is worthy of his hire." Thus is it written. I will let you have one copy – one copy only – at cost price.'

'How good you are, dear me!' exclaimed Nanni.

'This I can do,' said the Seller of Bibles, 'because my Master is the Big Man.'

'Speak you now what the cost price is.'

'A little sovereign, that is all.'

'Dear, dear; the Word of the little Big Man for a sovereign!'

'Keep you the Book on your parlour table for a week. Maybe others who are thirsty will see it.'

Then the Seller of Bibles sang a prayer; and he departed.

Before the week was over the Respected Josia Bryn-Bevan

announced from his pulpit that in the call he had discerned the voice of God bidding him go forth into the vineyard.

Nanni went home and prayed to the merciful God:

'Dear little Big Man, spare me to listen to the farewell sermon of your saint.'

Nanni informed the Seller of Bibles that she would buy the Book, and she asked him to take it away with him and have written inside it an inscription to the effect that it was a gift from the least worthy of his flock to the Respected Josiah Bryn-Bevan, DD, and she requested him to bring it back to her on the eve of the minister's farewell sermon.

She then hammered hobnails into the soles of her boots, so as to render them more durable for tramping to such capels as Bryn-Bevan happened to be preaching in. Her absences from home became a byword, occurring as they did in the haymaking season. Her labour was wanted in the fields. It was the property of the community, the community which paid her three shillings and ninepence a week.

One night Sadrach Danyrefail called at her cottage to commandeer her services for the next day. His crop had been on the ground for a fortnight, and now that there was a prospect of fair weather he was anxious to gather it in. Sadrach was going to say hard things to Nanni, but the appearance of the gleaming-eyed creature that drew back the bolts of the door frightened him and tied his tongue. He was glad that the old woman did not invite him inside, for from within there issued an abominable smell such as might have come from the boiler of the witch who one time lived on the moor. In the morning he saw Nanni trudging towards a distant capel where the Respected Josiah Bryn-Bevan was delivering a sermon in the evening. She looked less bent and not so shrivelled up as she did the night before. Clearly, sleep had given her fresh vitality.

Two Sabbaths before the farewell sermon was to be preached Nanni came to Capel Sion with an ugly sore at the side of her mouth; repulsive matter oozed slowly from it, forming into a head, and then coursing thickly down her chin on to the shoulder of her black cape, where it glistened among the beads. On occasions her lips tightened, and she swished a hand angrily across her face.

'Old Nanni,' folk remarked while discussing her over their dinner tables, 'is getting as dirty as an old sow.'

During the week two more sores appeared; the next Sabbath Nanni had a strip of calico drawn over her face.

Early on the eve of the farewell Sabbath the Seller of Bibles arrived with the Book, and Nanni gave him a sovereign in small money. She packed it up reverently, and betook herself to Sadrach Danyrefail to ask him to make the presentation.

At the end of his sermon the Respected Josiah Bryn-Bevan made reference to the giver of the Bible, and grieved that she was not in the Capel. He dwelt on her sacrifice. Here was a Book to be treasured, and he could think of no one who would treasure it better than Sadrach Danyrefail, to whom he would hand it in recognition of his work in the School of the Sabbath.

In the morning the Respected Josiah Bryn-Bevan, making a tour of his congregation, bethought himself of Nanni. The thought came to him on leaving Danyrefail, the distance betwixt which and Nanni's cottage is two fields. He opened the door and called out:

'Nanni.'

None answered.

He entered the room. Nanni was on the floor.

'Nanni, Nanni!' he said. 'Why for you do not reply to me? Am I not your shepherd?'

There was no movement from Nanni. Mishtir Bryn-Bevan went on his knees and peered at her. Her hands were clasped tightly together, as though guarding some great treasure. The minister raised himself and prised them apart with the ferrule of his walking stick. A roasted rat revealed itself. Mishtir Bryn-Bevan stood for several moments spellbound and silent; and in the stillness the rats crept boldly out of their hiding places and resumed their attack on Nanni's face. The minister, startled and horrified, fled from the house of sacrifice.

A Bed of Feathers

Rhys Davies

I

One year Jacob Jenkins, having amassed a little fortune by steady labour in the pit, went for a long holiday amid the rich meadows and stony villages of Cardiganshire. And he brought back to the valley a wife.

To the valley people the union was scandalous and unnatural. For though Jacob was sixty and become arid in a respectable celibacy, the woman he brought triumphantly to the valley was a rose-red blooming young creature of twenty-five, with wanton masses of goldish hair and a suggestion of proud abandonment about her: a farmhand, as everyone knew not long after her arrival. Ach-y-fi. Why couldn't the man marry one of the many local widows near his own age? Jacob Jenkins, a deacon for fifteen years, taking to himself a jaunty-looking slut like that!

But Jacob brought her proudly into the home, presented her to his gaping sister Ann, who for minutes was shocked into silence, and then to his half-brother Emlyn, who accepted her with amused indifference.

'Come to mother us orphans, have you?' Emlyn said with a grin.

'Indeed now, have I been useless, then?' Ann, forty-five and shrewish, demanded at last. She turned to Jacob's wife.

'An awful business you'll find it, looking after colliers,' she said with an unpleasant grimace.

'With two of you not so hard the work will be,' Jacob said.

But Ann announced, drawing off her shawl and folding it calmly: 'Oh, now that you have married like this, so late and cunning, no need is there for me here. Go as a housekeeper I will, somewhere in the country.' Her lips were bloodless, her big body taut with scorn. She loathed the wife at first sight.

Jacob said indifferently, 'Your own way you must go, Ann fach.' He had eyes only for Rebecca now.

'No disturbance do I want to make in this house,' Rebecca said, tapping her foot nervously.

But Ann ignored her and went out. Emlyn, child of their father's second wife, spat into the fire and sat down in satisfied acceptance of the new menage. And he said to Jacob, when the young wife had gone upstairs to take off her new clothes:

'Jacob, Jacob, a sly taste for women you hid in you. And a juicy taste too!'

Jacob lifted his lizard eyelids.

'Easy capture she was,' he said. 'A lot of silly bumpkins were after her, with nothing in their pockets, and a liking for dear things she has. Think you she is worth a brooch that was fifty shillings and a bracelet that cost the wages of ten days' work?' His grey old collier's face shone exultingly.

Emlyn laughed. 'Worth every penny she is, no doubt!'

Jacob looked at him in senile rhapsody.

'Ah, every penny. A fool I was to stay single for so many years. Take advice from me. Don't you be a frog and remain unmarried for so long. A rare bed of feathers is a woman.'

Emlyn stretched his length in yawning indifference. He was not yet thirty, tall and easy with supple strength, and no stranger to the comforting ways of women.

'Don't hurry me now,' he laughed. 'Satisfied I am as things are.' He looked at Jacob. 'But you want me to go? Ann says she is going, and you want to be alone?'

But Jacob shook his head. 'No, stay you as a lodger, Emlyn bach. An expensive woman Rebecca is going to be I am thinking, and not for ever do I want to work in the dirty old pit. Take some of the expense off you will if you will pay us so and so.' Rebecca came back into the room just then, and he said to her: 'Willing you are that Emlyn shall stay as a lodger? Asking he was if we would rather be alone.'

Rebecca's dark watching eyes suddenly became filled with tears. 'Oh,' she said again, faltering a little, her tearful glance upon the young man, 'no disturbance do I want to make here. Emlyn, stay you will, won't you?'

Her thick hand played with the blood-red stone of her bracelet; and her eyes looked a little weary in the shining fruit-like freshness of her face.

II

Rebecca did not become a collier's wife easily. She would *not* boil enough water for the baths, she neglected to dry the sweat-damp garments that Jacob and Emlyn threw into a corner of the kitchen as they undressed to wash in the tub before the fire, she couldn't patch moleskin trousers, she couldn't make broth as a Welsh collier likes it – thick and heavy with carrots, onions and leeks. This last fault was hard to overlook, though both Emlyn and Jacob were strangely forbearing with the young woman.

'Thin is her broth and heavy her jam pudding,' Emlyn muttered. 'No hand has she for tasty cooking.'

'Give the woman time,' Jacob answered with warmth. 'More used to cows' teats her hands have been, remember.'

At first, too, she seemed to dislike being present in the kitchen when the men bathed, to hand them this and that as they stood naked in the tub, and to wash the coal-black off their backs, as the women do in the miners' cottages. But gradually she got accustomed to it, even to washing Emlyn's back, while Jacob, having taken precedence in the tub, read the paper or dozed before the fire, attired only in his flannel shirt. For such is the bucolic simplicity of the miner's cottage life; and Rebecca did not mind, presently.

Though she dreamed of a better life. True, this valley was far nicer than the country of Cardiganshire. Here there were shops filled with blue and red silks and satins, fashionable hats, beads, and thin delicate shoes. Here was a cinema too. The chapel was crowded with observant faces, and she had a position there, as the wife of a deacon. Yet she craved for something else, she knew, gazing at her handsome face in the mirror, that some other wonderful thing was escaping her. And as she realised that, a strained and baffled look would come into her searching eyes and she would cross her pressing arms over her body, a half-strangled moan escaping her distended lips.

There were some evenings when she was left alone, Jacob in the chapel attending to deacons' business; and Emlyn was always out. She had not made friends yet, and in those long weary evenings she would sit and brood over a novelette, her face a little paler after the work of the day. Or she would go into the parlour and lie down on the sofa in the darkness, or stand at the window and watch with gleaming eyes the few people pass. And then perhaps she would go out for a short walk, to the main street, where the men were gathered in little groups about the street corners, peaceful in the night, the hills rising up tall and secretive, each side of the hushed vale. But she would return with a greater loneliness in her heart.

Jacob would come in to his supper and sink with established familiarity into his chair, his face fixed in a contented leer.

'Well, Rebecca,' he would say, watching every movement she made, every expression shifting on her face, 'what have you been doing tonight?'

He never touched or caressed her out of bed. But his pale eyes watched her with a possessive satisfaction that crept about her like the tight embrace of a snake. Sometimes she would notice his large oaken hand tremble as it rested on his knee.

Then she would go into the kitchen and wait until the painful throbbing of her heart was stilled.

And he was aware of that, her sheering off from him like a flame from an icy blast. A strange lipless grin would come to his face then. Still the female was not his. The contented leer passed from his face and in his eyes a fanatical glare shone. As it shone when he prayed aloud in chapel.

III

One Sunday morning she said:

'Staying home from chapel I am this morning.'

Her face was rather yellow, though her cheeks as yet had not quite lost their blooming rose.

'Not well you are?' Jacob enquired gently.

'I will make apple dumplings instead,' she promised, moving away into the kitchen.

'Don't you stay too long over the fire,' he said, looking for his Bible and bag of peppermints. And he went out dressed in his deep Sunday black.

She was alone. Emlyn had gone to the whippet-racing, the Sunday morning amusement of those colliers who have the courage to scorn the chapel respectability; but she wished he was home, so that she would have someone young to talk with. That morning the house had seemed like a dark and silent prison about her soul, and yet she would not have stirred out of it, fearful lest she would cry aloud in the chapel. She worked, going from room to room with a duster, working without method, only conscious that she must move. She prepared the apple dumplings. A little later Emlyn came in. He brought with him a dog, one of the whippets.

'It isn't yours?' she asked, gazing fixedly at the slim animal. It had a beautiful sleek body, long and narrow, its glistening fawn coat like velvet, the most delicate-looking dog she had ever seen. 'Ah,' she cried in sudden excitement, 'lovely he is.'

'Keeping him I am for a while,' Emlyn said, taking the dog's head in his hand with a slow pressure that she watched, bending to stroke the animal. There was a bright glint, almost of passion, in Emlyn's eyes as he held the dog's head tight in his hand.

'Oh, he doesn't like me!' she cried childishly as, her hand touching his sleek coat, the dog winced away. Shaking his head free, the whippet looked at her with a swift regard. Then, sniffing the air delicately, he moved his head towards her, his long narrow head that invited the grasp of a hand. And, fearful but fascinated, her hand moved down over the head until it spanned the jaw in a light and trembling clasp.

'There!' Emlyn said in a satisfied voice, 'he likes you.'

Slowly she released the head. The dog turned to Emlyn with a nervous look, as though he wondered at some atmosphere in the air.

'My little beauty!' Emlyn cried suddenly in delight. 'Just like a funny little child you are.'

Rebecca got up slowly, stood watching them, her eyelids dropped, her face inscrutable. Emlyn was as though unaware of her and was caressing the dog, uttering little noises of satisfaction. He passed his large strong hands over the slender body of the dog, slowly up and down, the thumbs on the back and the fingers over the belly.

'Soft and glossy as the back of a swan,' he whispered ecstatically.

The dog was quivering under his grasp.

'Hurting him you are!' she exclaimed.

'No,' he said, 'he likes it.' And his powerful collier's hands, that spanned the animal's slim body, were certain and intimate in their caressive grasp.

Then when Emlyn released him, the dog immediately lay down on the mat, contentedly burying his head between his paws. Emlyn looked up.

Rebecca was still standing against the table, taut, her eyelids drooped. There seemed a strange tension on her face. Neither spoke for a minute or so and at last her voice, unquiet and unwilling, broke the silence:

'What will Jacob say, bringing one of those dogs in on a Sunday?' Jacob, as was proper in a deacon, sternly condemned whippet racing.

'Ah! what will he say?' Emlyn repeated, a little grin on his mouth.

And then he stared at her, his full moist lips distended in that jeering grin. For a moment she looked back at him. Her eyes seemed to go naked in that moment, their blue nudity, chastened of weariness and pain, gleaming full on him.

She moved away, went into the kitchen and sank upon a chair. The yellow pallor of her face was again evident. She looked as though she wanted to be sick.

Jacob came in, his face still exalted from the chapel prayers. Immediately he saw the sleeping dog.

'Whose is that?' he asked sternly.

'Keeping it for a while I am,' Emlyn said fondly. 'A little angel he is.'

'Bah!' Jacob uttered, violent wrath beginning to burn in his shrunken cheeks. 'Bring you one of those animals in this house? Come I have from the Big Seat of the chapel, the words of our prayers still full of fire in my heart, and this vessel of wickedness my eyes see as I enter my house!'

'Ach, Jacob, if wickedness there is, blame you the men that use the animal.'

'He is a partner in your Sabbath abominations. Take him away from here.' A storm was gathering in Jacob's eyes.

'He likes the warmth of the fire. Look, Jacob, innocent as a little calf's is his face.' The dog had lifted its head and was gazing at Jacob with a pleading expression in his glinting eyes. But his gaze made Jacob more infuriated.

'Out of these rooms where I move,' he began to shout.

'Take him back to his owner or tie him to the tree in the garden. Put evil in the house he does.'

Rebecca had come into the room. She said, her voice scarcely above a mutter: 'Comfort let the little dog bach have, Jacob. Delicate he looks and company for me he'll be.'

Jacob turned to her. 'Ignorant of the wicked sports he is partner to you are, Mrs Jenkins,' he replied angrily. 'No, let him go out of this house.'

Emlyn began to grin. He was really indifferent. The grin on his handsome tolerant face was irritating to Jacob, who began to moan:

'Ach, awful it is for me to have a brother who spends the Sabbath mingling with abandoned and dirty-minded men. Take you warning, young man, the Lord is not mocked and derided long.'

'All sorts come to our races,' Emlyn reflected comfortably, 'and happy and healthy they seem. No sour faces such as gather in the chapels.' He called to the dog and lazily took him to the garden.

IV

That night she dreamed of hands.

They were upon her breasts, outspread and clasping; and there was such a pain beneath them that her lips moved in anguish. She did not know whose hands they were, her mind strove to discover. A horror came upon her, she seemed to struggle. But the hands were immovable and finally she submitted, drifting into the gloom and the horror, moaning until she woke in the darkness, hearing the bell of the alarm clock.

'Jacob,' she called, louder than usual, 'Jacob.'

Jacob grunted. He had been deep in slumber. Rebecca got out of bed and lit the candle. Then Jacob, his face grey and corpse-like in the dim light, moving his limbs with the effort of an old man, followed and put on, with grunts and sighs, his thick striped flannel drawers.

She went downstairs, after calling Emlyn. Her mind was still drugged with slumber and in her too was the shadow of that unbearable pain. With mechanical drugged movements she set about the usual tasks – blew the fire into a glow and set the kettle, prepared the breakfast and the men's food tins for the pit. She was in such abstraction that when she turned and saw Emlyn, who had silently entered in his stockinged feet, she shrank back with a little cry.

'What's the matter with you?' he exclaimed.

For a moment or two she stared at him. His face! Ah, she had never seen it before, not as she saw it now. Her heart seemed to dart in a flame to her throat, her lips could utter no word. And there he stood, strange and watching, looking at her curiously.

Then she woke with a jolt and bent her head, to cut the bread.

'Make a noise coming down you ought to,' she said. 'Not quite awake am I, early in the morning like this.'

Emlyn began to whistle with a shrill male energy that made her shudder, and went into the kitchen for his boots.

Jacob came down, coughing. He seemed to creak as he sat in his chair, his face like a wrinkled stone.

They all sat down to breakfast, Rebecca between them. There was cold ham and thick black tea. Jacob began to grunt:

'Wheezy I am again this morning. Glad I'll be when I'll be able to lie in bed longer.'

Rebecca was looking at her husband. As he uttered the last word he glanced at her and a cunning grin came over his face. She felt her stomach rise, her mind reel.

'Jesus, white you've gone, Rebecca,' Emlyn said quickly.

Jacob looked at her calmly. The cunning grin had become an obscene and triumphant leer.

'Well, well, one must expect such things now,' he said.

'What!' exclaimed Emlyn in a sharpened voice. 'True is it, Rebecca?'

She suddenly swept her hand before her, upsetting her cup of tea.

'No,' she said loudly, 'no.'

'Ach, you don't know,' said Jacob. 'And there's a mess you've made, Mrs Jenkins.'

'No, it's not true,' she repeated loudly. Her eyes glittered.

Jacob sniffed as he rose from the table and loosened his belt.

'See we shall,' he continued hatefully, sniffing laughter over the words. 'Think you are different to other women?'

She sat, her face stretched forward like an animal suddenly aware of some ominous portent. The men gathered their things together.

'Take you heart, Mrs Jenkins,' Jacob said.

She watched them go off – they worked side by side in the pit, on the same seam. Her husband's back suddenly roused a fury of hate in her – she could have clawed in venom the coarse thick neck above the cotton muffler. But Emlyn – going through the door last – turned and smiled at her, a quick brilliant smile that rippled in a delighted shudder over her, until her own moist mouth reflected it.

She removed the breakfast things. How quiet and familiar the house had become! She thought of the day's work in a sudden access of energy; and she began to sing *Merch yr Ydfa*. The rows of polished plates standing on the dresser pleased her – how pretty were the little Chinese bridges and the sleeping trees! She plunged her hands into a bowl of cold water and enjoyed the shudder that ran through her blood.

Then the bark of a dog made her lift her head quickly. She went in haste to the pantry and filled a pan with pieces of bread, pouring milk over. Again came the bark, and she hurried out with the pan to the back garden.

The whippet stood outside its roughly made kennel.

'Well, well now,' she called soothingly, 'is he hungry then?'

She knelt on the earth before it, holding the pan for it to eat; and as the animal ate she admired again the fawn sheen of his coat and the long delicate shape of his body, which quivered in pleasure.

V

Then from that morning Rebecca seemed to awaken as from a long and dull slumber. Her eyes became wider, a blue and virgin fire glowing beneath the thick lids; and as she went about, her body walked with a taut and proud grace, flaunting a fierce health. Her voice became plangent and direct, coming from her heavy lips.

'Ha, agree with you does married life,' Jacob said.

She slowly turned her head to him.

'Ha,' he repeated, 'rich and nice as a little calf you are now.' And he added with lecherous humour, 'Afraid of you I was at first, in Cardigan. More like a Bristol cow you were then.'

She pressed her hands down over her hips, lifting her shoulders and looking at him with drawn brows.

'Not angry with me you are?' he asked with childish complaint. 'A compliment I was paying you.'

She said, a metallic sharpness wavering in her voice: 'Don't you watch me so much. Continually your eyes are watching me.'

Curiously, he dropped his head before her anger. For the first time she realised her power.

'Like a prison keeper you behave,' she added. 'Always you are staring at me as if I wanted to hide something from you. Suspicious of me you are?'

His instinct was aroused by her question.

'Something to hide you have, then?' he asked, jerking his head up.

'What can there be to hide!' she exclaimed with such artless surprise that again his face became expressive of his relentless lust for her.

'Only a thought passing in my head it was,' he muttered.

She roused herself. She seemed to glitter with an ominous vitality, female and righteous.

'A dirty old swine you are,' she said loudly.

He received this with silence. Then his voice became plaintive and ashamed; he said:

'Harsh you are with me, Rebecca. Forgive an old man's errors you must.'

He looked at her with abject pleading in his eyes. She stared back at him. And still she saw behind the flickering childish pleading in his eyes the obsessed leer of the old man, the relentless icy glitter of his lust. She drew back and her voice had something of a threat in it as she said:

'Well, don't you be so suspicious of me at all.'

She went upstairs to their bedroom.

The evening sun invaded the room with a warm and languid light, a shaft falling on the scarlet counterpane of the bed. The soft glow soothed her. She gazed in the mirror and, biting her lower lip, softly murmured his name. 'Emlyn, Emlyn.' Her head dropped, she sank on the bed and covered her face with her hands. But when she lifted her head again her face was smiling. She went to the dressing table and combed her hair. She passed into Emlyn's room and began to look for some odd job to do. She looked over his garments to see if any buttons were missing. All were in their places, and then she opened the drawer in which he kept his ties and collars. As usual, the drawer was untidy. She began to fold the things.

Among other oddments she found a scrap of paper on which was scrawled *May Morgan, 30 Glasfryn Street*, and she stood up to scrutinise it carefully. Then she tossed it back into the drawer with a gesture of disdain.

When she went downstairs Jacob was sleeping in the armchair, his hands clasped over his stomach. His mouth had dropped open and a thin line of saliva was descending from it. She laid the supper quietly, so that he should not waken. Her senses were marvellously tranquil; she moved about with soft, intimate movements, her face relaxed as though she were utterly at peace with the world.

Jacob ate his supper with chastened solemnity. She dreamily watched his wad of bread and cheese decrease. He took her long silence as a sign of grieved anger against him, and he anxiously studied her face, eager to see a sign of compassion.

Emlyn came in and joined them. He was slightly tipsy, and his face, handsome and flushed, seemed to give off a ruddy heat of ardour. He sat at the table and gazed round, a critical smile on his lips.

Jacob sniffed with deliberation.

'God, we had a talk tonight!' Emlyn exclaimed.

'About what?' asked Rebecca.

'Socialism,' he said exultingly.

Jacob sniffed again.

'Wisdom was in your talk, no doubt,' he said suavely. 'Godly seems socialism after five or six pots of beer.'

'Jacob, Jacob, a hard-bottomed old Tory you are getting. No wonder you are such a grizzler.'

'All your evenings you spend like that?' Rebecca asked.

'I like mixing with men,' Emlyn said, 'to save my mind and joints from getting stiff.' He laughed uproariously at this. Rebecca and Jacob remained grave and unsmiling.

'And your pockets from keeping full,' Jacob added unctuously. 'A poor old mongrel you will become, not worth a penny.'

'Ha,' Rebecca cried swiftly, 'a runner after women he is too I should think.'

Emlyn turned his bright, glazed eyes full upon her.

'The wrong way you put it, Rebecca,' he said softly, 'nowadays the women it is who have the pleasantest tongues.'

She drew back her head. Her bosom seemed to rise in a storm.

'Vain as a silly peacock,' she jeered, 'nothing is there in you for a woman to get excited about.'

He laughed again, loudly. There was a coarse maleness in his laughter, a flood of primitive strength.

She sat there, high and proud, the colour deepened and vivid in her face. Jacob seemed to ignore them, sucking up his tea with solemn contempt. He knew that his half-brother was lost to the Baptists forever. His former protests and denunciations had all been in vain, and now Emlyn interested him no more.

Supper finished, Jacob sat by the fire to read a chapter of the Scriptures before bed. Emlyn lit a cigarette and restlessly began to study a racing list which he took from his pocket.

Rebecca cleared the supper things into the kitchen. Her heart beat with a hard painful throb that was unbearable, and as she carried the crockery into the kitchen she seemed to sway with a slight drunken movement, her head drooping.

And as she was washing the dishes Emlyn came noisily into the kitchen and kicked off his boots. Then he turned and looked at her. Through the dim candlelight his eyes shone down on her like a cat's. She crouched over the pan of water in a sudden fright: she thought he was going to advance on her and take her there, suddenly and silently. She began to pant in fear.

They heard Jacob noisily clearing his throat and spit in the fire, and the spell was broken. But Emlyn, with a sleek, drunken smile, came over to her and pressed his hands over her swelling breasts. She moved in anguish and stared at him with remembering eyes. Ah, his grasp was familiar, this agonising rush of her blood suddenly familiar: she remembered her dream. Only the dark horror that had wrapped that dream was not here.

She lifted her face; mutely they stared at each other. Then with a shy and ashamed look she resumed her work.

He went back into the other room, whistling.

VI

Each day passed in an ecstasy of dreaming. When she rose in the early morning she took greater care of her appearance.

But it was a relief to see the two men go off to work – then she was alone to dream as deliriously as she liked. Perhaps she was the only collier's wife in the district who was dressed as though for a jaunt when the men returned from work. She bought a flimsy apron to wear over her frock, and a box of powder to soften the colour of her face: she began to look subtle. Once Jacob exclaimed irritably:

'What's come over you, woman! Extraordinary in your ways you are getting. No respectable woman dresses like that this time in the afternoon. Follow you how the others in the street are – hard-working women they look. A laughing stock you will make yourself.'

Rebecca tossed her head.

'Sluts they look,' she said, 'and sorry I feel for them.'

'Half a dozen children you ought to have, Mrs Jenkins,' Jacob answered warmly, 'and come to your senses you would then.'

Emlyn broke in:

'*Out* of her senses! Like to see women become machines of flesh you do, Jacob. Use them until their wheels are worn out. Yes, use them, that's all you see in women.'

Jacob became angry. 'A worshipper of women I am,' he cried in the manner of a Baptist preacher. 'Did not Jesus Christ come through a woman! And when I see one give herself over to frip-fraps and idle her flesh all day, vexed and disgusted I become.'

'I work all day and change at four o'clock,' Rebecca cried hotly, 'because bright I want to be by the time you come home.'

'Bright with a blouse and petticoat!' Jacob jeered. 'Bright enough it is for me to know that my wife you are. Without meaning are the clothes that cover your body.'

Rebecca shrank back. She went about her work without another word. Not until the time came for washing Emlyn's back did her averted and ashamed face lift itself in ardour again.

She usually washed the thick coal dust off his back with movements that were far too delicate, so that it took a long time before his flesh shone white again. But he did not complain, crouching in the big wooden tub, and did not shiver, like Jacob, for whom she was never quick enough – the nightly bathe was always unpleasant to him.

This evening she felt vengeful. Jacob had had his bath and was sitting in his shirt before the fire in the other room, warming his naked legs. She scooped water over Emlyn's back and passed the soap over the collier's black skin. And with her two hands, softly and ah, with such subtle passion, she began to rub the soap into his flesh, disregarding the rough flannel used for that task. Into the little hollows of his muscular shoulders, down the length of his flawless back, over the fine curves of his sides, she caressingly passed her spread hands. Beneath them his flesh seemed to harden, draw itself together as though to resist her. But – she could feel another answer to her quivering touch. She became exhausted, her breathing difficult. So she rested for a moment or two, and then, as he moved restlessly in his crouching attitude, she took a bowl of clean warm water and poured it over him. The flesh gleamed out, white-gold, a delicate flush beneath, like a heap of wheat burned hot in the sun.

'There,' she breathed, 'you must use the towel yourself. Tired I am.'

He did not answer, neither did he move up from his crouching. She went into the living room. Jacob, his hands clasped over his stomach, was dozing before the big fire. In his multi-coloured flannel shirt he looked gaunt and grotesque. She went up to the bedroom. Her eyes were gleaming with a kind of remorseless brilliance; her mien was profligate and mobile. She squatted on the floor like some brooding aboriginal dark in the consciousness of some terrific deed hovering. She squatted there, dark and brooding, and heard his steps approach, behind her. His hands were upon her shoulders and entering her bosom. A shock, icy and violent, went through her: she dropped her head. Yet she felt as though she lay amid the softest velvet, folds of soothing dark velvet about her. No word was spoken and presently she was alone.

VII

Then came the time of the Cyfarfod, the Big Meetings in Jacob's chapel – a week of important services. A well-known preacher and other ministers came: every night there would be a long service with two sermons. A week of fiery oratory and prayers like flaming gas. Jacob, his deacon's face pompous and weighty, directed Rebecca to see that his Sunday clothes were spotless, that there were seven clean stiff collars ready, and that a new heart-shaped tie was bought.

As these instructions were given Emlyn blew whiffs of cigarette smoke to the ceiling, a secret and ironical smile on his face. Rebecca saw it with a little shudder. Jacob added:

'Enjoy the preaching you will, Mrs Jenkins. The sermons of Mr Prys-Davies can make you cry, enjoy them so much you do. Sometimes, so great is his shouting that crack like a wall does his voice.'

She was silent. Emlyn broke in:

'Darro, Jacob, those meetings are only for brainy men and old women who cannot take pleasure in anything else.'

Rebecca thought this incautious and she said quickly:

'Oh, enjoy them I shall, Jacob. Little outings they'll be for me, instead of staying in this house every evening.'

Emlyn drew in his stretched legs and spat in the fire.

'Gluttons for religion you two are,' he jeered.

The Cyfarfod opened on the Sunday; there was no hot dinner that day, as Rebecca went to the three services. She arrived home at ten o'clock that night, her eyes rather wild and obsessed. Jacob had stayed back with the deacons in the vestry.

Emlyn was reading a periodical, waiting for his supper.

'God!' he exclaimed, 'their beds people ought to take to that chapel.'

'The preaching was good,' she said slowly. Her cheeks seemed to sag, her face was rather pitiful. He watched her.

'Enjoy it you did!' he laughed.

'I *did* cry,' she answered in a subdued voice.

He rose from the chair and clasped her shoulders. But she drew away a little, her head dropped.

'Ah, foolish you are like all of them,' he said, 'all those damned hypocrites.'

She shrank further away. She was in that mystical state that by prolonged hymn-singing and prophetic preaching can so easily be induced in Welsh people.

'No, no,' she muttered, 'peace was there tonight.'

But he followed her, slowly and sinisterly, and as she reached the table pressed her back over it in his destroying embrace. He caught her unwilling mouth and warmed her with his lips. She tasted the sweet, languorous contact of his dripping tongue. She could have screamed in the violence of her soul. Her hands clasping his shoulders, she could have torn him in her agony of hate and lust.

'Tuesday,' he whispered, 'Tuesday you stay home.' Then he let her go and went back to his chair.

Silent and still, she remained for some moments by the table, her arms across her face. Presently she muttered:

'What am I to say?'

'Oh, tell the old fool that your sickness is coming on again. You know, deceive him with soft soap.' His voice was coarse and brutal.

Jacob came in, fiery banners still burning in his soul. His long, arid face was lit with them. He began immediately, sitting down to supper:

'The children of Israel sit down to their meat with thanksgiving to the Lord who gave it them. With singing voices and loud music we have praised his name, and on our bended knees given up our sins. We have listened to the voice of one whose soul is deep with wisdom. Out of his mouth has come big words and exalted phrases.'

Emlyn listened gravely and said: 'Ach, Jacob, strange it is to me that you are not a local preacher yet.'

But Jacob waved this derision aside:

'The wicked shall mock in their ignorance. How can they see the hand of the Lord in their whippet-acing and games of painted cards? But with the people of Sodom and Gomorrah they shall sit in misery.'

He ate his supper with austere dignity, seated patriarchally in his armchair, his jaws working rhythmically. He looked rather fearsome. Rebecca did not say a word, but presently he turned to her:

'Rebecca Jenkins, say you that the meeting moved you?'

'Yes.'

'Did not the wings of angels beat about the singing!'

'Very beautiful was the singing,' she answered.

'Tired you look,' he said sternly.

'Well, after three long services—'

He bent his head to her; there seemed to be iron and fire in his voice as he said:

'Yes, a good wife you have been today. When we were singing did I not think, Blessed is our union today: my wife Rebecca lifts up her voice with mine in Cyfarfod, her voice is as my voice, her body is with my body here.'

She met his burning stare. Every motion seemed to flee from her consciousness and she had the taste of death in her. The fiery purpose of these eyes blasted her.

Emlyn seemed not to hear or see anything; he ate his Sunday night cold beef with head bent at the other end of the table. When he had finished he went back to his periodical, stretched his legs into the hearth, and casually lit a cigarette.

Rebecca's steps dragged with weariness and dread as she cleared away the supper things.

And the following two days she waited in a kind of numbness, her eyes glittering obsessively under her sullen brows. Tuesday, as Jacob hurried over his bath, she told him quietly:

'I am going to stay home tonight and rest.'

'Why, Rebecca fach?' he demanded.

'I— I,' she muttered, her eyes cast down, 'something comes over me lately. I could faint, so crowded does the chapel get.'

His face hung over her; she could hear the roused intake of his breath.

'Better ask Mrs Watkins next door to come in and keep you company,' he said slowly.

'Don't you be silly about me,' she answered hurriedly. 'A little rest is all I want.'

'Broody you will get, alone,' he went on fussily. 'Think you it is— '

'Oh go on, like an old woman you are, making a bother. Wait you for plainer signs.'

'All right. But take you care of yourself.'

Later she went into the parlour and pressed her hands upon her head in an agony of mingled loathing and fear. She felt as though she bore a sword within her, a glittering blade which might at any moment split her being in two. She crouched behind the door, covering her head, her face contorted and ugly; she heard Emlyn go out and she went to her task of clearing the living-room after the men. Then Jacob came downstairs in his chapel clothes and after an admonishment that she was not to do too much, went off in dignified haste to the meeting.

Slowly she went upstairs and entered her bedroom. Slowly and carefully, as though she were following some definite and dictated plan, she removed her clothes. Her face was repulsive, contracted in an orgasm of primitive realisation, her eyes fixed like balls of blue marble, her lips thick and distended. Unclothed, her body looked hewn out of pure hard flesh, barren of light and shade, solid flesh of marble, hard and durable. Her breasts sloped forward like cornices of white stone, her thighs were like smooth new pillars. From her head her loosened hair fell in a shower of silky gold threads, rich and lovely upon the polished stone of her shoulders. For moments she stood still in her gleaming nudity, as though she had indeed turned into a hewn white stone. Only when she moved to the bed there was the sudden grace of life.

She heard the click of the front door latch.

He was mounting the stairs; she called out in a voice strange to her own ears: 'He has gone, Emlyn.'

Emlyn went back to the front door and locked it.

VIII

She came downstairs and into the living-room. Emlyn was sitting in the armchair, smoking easily and contentedly.

'Are you going to stay in then?' she asked.

He smiled at her, a fatuous, contented smile.

'Don't you be nervous,' he said lazily, 'or suspicious Jacob will get at once. I am going to sit in this chair until he comes in.' He lay back deeper, his legs hanging limp. 'A task it would be for me to go out tonight.'

But Rebecca burned with a vivid heat that showed in her mottled face and lithe powerful movements. She looked flushed with strong life. Emlyn watched her move through the living room and said in a sniggering whisper:

'A marvel you are, Rebecca, darling.'

'Ach!' she exclaimed, making a gesture of disgust.

'But considerate of you I've been—' he said calmly.

Her cheeks flushed a deeper red.

'But you wai—' he continued.

His lechery was like the stinging of a whip on her quivering flesh. Again, cleaving up through her desire for him, she felt a sword of destruction within her. She looked at his throat with haunted eyes.

'Now, Rebecca,' he coaxed, 'take things in a natural way. Be ready for Jacob.'

But she dropped on her knees, bowed down on the floor before him, crouching, her arms shuddering over her breasts.

'What shall we do!' she cried, her distorted face thrust to him. 'Living in this house together. What shall we do!'

He leaned to her rather angrily.

'Rebecca, Rebecca, use control on yourself. Shocking this is. What if he came in now?'

'How can we live together here now!' she moaned.

'Ach, certain we can,' he said sharply.

She drew back. 'But how can it go on? Two men, and you his half-brother,' she cried again. There was horror in her face and her eyes seemed utterly lost.

He stooped before her and pressed her between his thighs, lifted her up with his hand, looked at her long and steadily.

'Go on we will all right. You leave it to me. Rebecca, enjoy it you should. A little secret between ourselves.'

She laid her head on his thigh and burst out:

'Oh, I love you, Emlyn. Only with you I want to be. Horrible it will be for me to go to bed with Jacob again. That it is will kill me. Always I am thinking of your arms and your mouth kissing me.'

'Ah! a few good times we will have.'

She wrenched herself free.

'No,' she cried with anger, 'one or the other!'

'Don't you be a fool now! Go you cautious and everything will be all right.' He became impatient with her, and her dramatic and hysterical mien alarmed him. Jacob might come in any moment. 'Can't you take patience with an old man like Jacob? Only a little soft soap he wants.'

'Ha!' she answered venomously, 'a part of his God I have become. When I am with him in the night sometimes he prays as though he was praying through me. Like God he makes me feel.'

Emlyn laughed.

'Don't you laugh!' she shouted.

'Shut up,' he said quickly.

'Well, don't you joke about this.'

He sat back and was silent. Anything to calm her. She went into the kitchen and put the kettle on. And it was just then that Jacob came in.

'No supper laid!' he exclaimed.

'I was just starting—' Rebecca said, coming into the living room.

Jacob gazed at her. 'More colour you have than before I went,' he said. 'In the first prayer tonight I asked God to see to your comfort. For indeed ill you looked.'

She stared at her husband without a word.

'Ignorant that she was unwell I was,' Emlyn said hastily, 'or stayed in I would have, to keep her company.'

Jacob slowly turned his gaze to Emlyn. 'So alone she's been most of the evening!' he said as though pondering over the fact.

In a caught, nervous voice that sent a flame of anger over Emlyn, Rebecca said:

'Go on, don't you worry about me. Accustomed to being alone I am.'

'Not very lonely were you in the evenings in Cardigan,' Jacob said. 'Seemed to me it did that plenty of louts were hanging about.'

'Louts they were,' she answered, regaining something of her natural demeanour. 'And innocent of any behaviour I was.'

Jacob went to hang his coat up in the passageway. And Emlyn shot an angry glance at Rebecca, who tossed her head. There was a strange glint in her eyes now.

During supper she was mostly silent, replying in a short and vague fashion when the men spoke to her. She seemed occupied with some problem, her brow rather sombre. And in that mood Emlyn was afraid of her.

Then from that night something entered the house. It was in the air like the still presence of death, it was in the drawn tension of Rebecca's paling brow, it was in the forced jocular humour of Emlyn. And, too, in the frozen drop of Jacob's eyelids as he sat in his chair, silent for long periods, there seemed a kind of foreboding, a chill.

Rebecca's conduct sometimes infuriated Emlyn. She would look at him with a long and shameless intensity when the three sat at a meal together: the expression of her whole body seemed to cry their secret. Once when they were alone he said to her:

'Behave yourself, you fool. You make your thoughts plain as ABC. Old Jacob might be, but not a blind ape is he.'

She set her jaw sullenly. 'I know,' she said.

'How is it you act so childish then!' he exclaimed savagely.

He was a different Emlyn now. She saw him contemptuously, his fear. Yet she was determined to force the issue. She said coldly: 'A rabbit's mind you've got.'

'Rabbit be damned. Worse it would be for you if Jacob found out.'

She drooped towards him. 'Then always we could be together!' She whispered with a sudden change of mood, her eyes gazing ardently upon him.

He let her caress him: until he fixed his mouth upon hers with a fury that satisfied her. But with that he too had to be content. Rebecca was becoming wily.

'Tomorrow night,' he muttered drunkenly, 'he will be at the deacons' meeting.'

'Suspicious he is getting,' she said derisively. 'Not a blind ape is he.'

'Hell and Satan take him,' he went on, 'my female you will be tomorrow night.'

She laughed.

IX

Tramping together to the pit in the early morning, Jacob said to Emlyn:

'What is coming over the woman? Noticed you have, Emlyn, how changed she is?'

'Yes,' Emlyn answered irritably, 'trying she is. Look you, my vest wasn't dry this morning and my trousers was still damp in the corner where she threw them yesterday. And like a peevish owl she is in the mornings now.'

'Ah,' muttered Jacob, 'more to complain of I have.'

Emlyn glanced aside at his half-brother's face. Its sharp grey profile was outlined in the keen air as though cut out of cardboard, and it had a flat, dead expression. Emlyn felt a moment's pity for Rebecca: what joy could she have from this arid mechanism of dry flesh walking beside him?

'Happy you seem with her,' he said with a note of surprise.

'She keeps herself cold to me,' Jacob said. 'Yet like a playful little mare she was before we were married.'

'Difficult is the first year or so with a woman like Rebecca,' Emlyn observed wisely.

'Mine she is,' said Jacob with sudden intensity. 'Yet I will have her.'

Emlyn said nothing. They tramped along, up the hill towards the pit in the far reach of the quiet vale. Emlyn became aware of something grim and warning in Jacob's demeanour as he strode silently by his side. His face was still grey and inscrutable, but in his movements there was some dark austerity, like a warning. What was brooding in that shut, resentful mind?

They were joined by other colliers, dark-browed under their caps, tramping in a ragged black procession to the pit, under the dawning sky. Across the bridge the sound of their footsteps softened in the thick black coal dust; they trooped into the alleyways between the black-coated sheds and the lines of small coal trucks, up to the lamp-room, where they were given their polished lit lamps.

Jacob and Emlyn kept together: they worked side by side. At the shaft they waited their turn to enter the cage. The two wheels aloft spun against the metal sky and dropped their thick and shining ropes taut into the gaping hole beneath: one cage emerged and clashed loudly into stillness. Jacob and Emlyn, with fourteen others, crowded in, and ahead a bell clamoured. The cage descended like a stone.

Arrived at the bottom, a brick-walled tunnel sloped away in the shrill electric light, slimy and dripping. The colliers tramped on, at the side of the rail track, until the walled tunnel ceased and the workings began, propped up by timber. Now light came only from the tiny flames of their lamps. The narrow rail track twisted its way with them, between the walls of rock and timber, the thin rails like twin nerves going deeper and deeper into the rich silence of the earth.

The two half-brothers trudged on without a word, stooping under the beams that held off the earth above, splashing through the pools of black water, until they were alone in their own working.

It was a small clearing thick with props of timber and heaps of stone: at one side the coalface gleamed and sparkled in the lamplight, jutting generous and lively out of the dead earth.

Jacob was looking at the roof examiningly.

'Lewis put it all right afterwards?' Emlyn inquired.

'He's been here,' Jacob said. He put his hand on a prop and tried to move it: there was a faint creaking sound. 'It's all right,' he added, and passed to examine another part of the clearing. Emlyn threw off his upper garments and began to attack the coalface; soon he was absorbed, sweating, in the task of removing the coal from its bed, oblivious of Jacob, who, half naked also, was working twenty yards away, still fumbling with the timber props and beams.

The hours passed and at ten o'clock the two men paused for a meal. Emlyn's face and body was now black with dust, save where the sweat ran down in streaks; tense from his labour, crouching under the coalface, his eyes shone out blood-red and liquid.

'God above, how difficult the seam is getting, Jacob,' he panted, looking round for his food tin. 'Where's my box?'

'Here,' came Jacob's voice. He was standing, a dark crouching shape beyond the lamplight, ten yards away.

'What you doing there?' Emlyn asked. 'Still messing with the timber?'

He advanced, ducking his head under the low beams.

Then something moved overhead, as he ducked: there was a sharp creak followed by a tearing as of wood slowly snapping. Emlyn turned sharply, and his face showed caught and vulnerable for an instant. Then the space was choked with stone and dust.

Jacob clambered down from his perch in the darkness, ran shouting through the clearing, out into the other workings. His hoarse shout for help leapt with a peculiar deadened sound through the still, hot tunnels.

Men came running up, ducking like strange other-world creatures in the dark alleys, wild-eyed and tense.

'A fall,' Jacob shouted, 'my brother is under.'

There were cries of dismay when they saw the heap of stone.

'Jesus!'

'Quick! Hell, what a job.'

'Ach, not much hope is there.'

They crowded round, worked with feverish haste, shovelling, pulling away with their hands the rock and earth. Jacob clawed like a possessed beast at the rubble, his eyes glaring manically.

'Right on the head, right on the head,' he kept on shouting. 'I saw it falling.'

'Stay you away,' one collier muttered, 'we'll get at him soon enough.'

A large stone had caught him – it lay upon his head and shoulders. There was a heavy smell of blood. They heaved at the rock. Jacob left them alone to their final task. He stood leaning against a prop, his head sunk in his shoulders. He heard a collier's sharp intaken breath as he muttered:

'Christ! a bloody mess.'

And Jacob's nostrils quivered and paled in the stench of blood.

X

They laid him, a shape covered in some dark coarse cloth, on his bed, and, their faces closed and grave, went out softly – the four colliers who had brought him home. They heard the wild, shrill weeping of Jacob's wife in the living room and the comforting voice of her neighbour. Jacob shut the door behind them and upon the little crowd of people gathered on the pavement.

Rebecca's frightened voice was lapsing into sobs now. As Jacob entered the living room she lifted her head from the woman's arms and he stared at her fixedly. Her wild face was drenched with tears, her mouth moving pitiably in its sobs.

'Hush, Rebecca,' he said sternly.

The neighbour protested. 'Let her work it off. Natural is it for her to be frightened. Low enough she has looked lately.'

But his face was stern and sombre, his eyes fixed in a cold, remorseless stare.

'I will wash and change,' he said, 'and go out. Many things are there to arrange. Stay you with her, Mrs Evans, until I come back this evening.'

Rebecca burst into further tears.

'Don't leave me alone in the house,' she wept.

'Why should you fear death?' said Jacob darkly. 'Life it is that we should fear.' And he strode into the kitchen to wash.

Later he went out of the house without another word.

'Strange he is,' commented Mrs Evans. 'Affected by the accident he must be. Daft in the eyes he looked.'

'Yes,' Rebecca whispered, 'it's of him I am frightened.'

'Tut, tut, harmless enough is old Jacob Jenkins,' said the other. 'Shaken him has his brother's death! Fond of each other they were.'

Rebecca shook her head. And she could not keep her

hands from trembling. There was a stern and terrible presence in the house, a horror that was closing round her tenaciously and icily, like a freezing drug gripping into her consciousness. What had she seen in Jacob's face when he looked at her? What dark warning had been there?

Trembling and pale to the lips, she awaited his return. He arrived back about seven o'clock and asked:

'Have you lit the candles for him?'

Mrs Evans said they hadn't, and Jacob took two brass candlesticks from the mantelshelf.

'I will go back now then,' Mrs Evans said. Rebecca made a gesture towards her, then sank into her chair: and the woman went off, after a sharp inquisitive glance at Jacob.

In silence he fixed the candles and lit them. At last Rebecca said tremulously: 'Is it arranging about the funeral you were?'

Without looking at her he answered:

'I have been on the mountain. I fled to the hills for silence and prayer.'

'Awful for you it must have been,' she whispered. 'Killed at once he was?'

Jacob slowly raised his head and looked at his wife.

'No. I had words from him before he died.'

Her eyelids dropped quickly, she moved nervously in her chair. He took the candles and went to the stairs. There he turned and said:

'Come you up when I call, Rebecca Jenkins.'

With a numbed heart she watched him. Ah, what terrible meaning was in his voice and his look! There was something he knew. Her faculties seemed to shrink within her, she felt the horror grip at her will. He knew, he knew. She was seized with panic and yet she could not move. Like a lodestone the will of Jacob held her in its power, she could not move out of the warning of his look. She would have to go to him and tell him all. Emlyn was gone and there was no strength to which she might cling. She would have to tell him all and pray for his forgiveness. She would serve him and give of her body, all she had, to the last shred of her being. She would content herself with buying pretty clothes and going to chapel to display them, she would make a friend of young Mrs Rowlands and they would go out together in the evenings. Tearfully she thought this, her head sunk in her shoulders, her hands still trembling, while the minutes passed. Her face began to look wild and obsessed. Suddenly she dropped her face into her hands and moaned aloud. No, no, she could not bear the thought of living alone with Jacob, it would be horrible, horrible now.

'Rebecca!'

Violently she started in the chair.

'Rebecca.' His voice was stern.

She forced herself to answer. 'What do you want?'

'Here I want you.'

She stood up and her body seemed to droop within itself. She heard him go back into Emlyn's bedroom. What did he want of her up there, what could she do! But she knew that some awful revelation was waiting, that a deathly horror was gathered in that room for her. For a moment she looked round wildly, as though to flee. And yet there was something reassuring in this familiar room, her living room, where she had laboured and lived in so much loneliness the last year. Ach, she would face him. What if he *did* know! She had something to tell him. An old man like him. She would not stand in fear of any man. Yet she felt her heart plunging as she slowly climbed the stairs, into the silent darkness of the upper floor.

The door of Emlyn's bedroom was shut, and for a moment she crouched before it in acute dread. Then again came Jacob's voice, sharp, imperious: 'Rebecca.'

Why should he bully her! The old fool. She opened the door and entered quickly, demanding: 'What do you want?'

The two candles were burning on the little mantelshelf. Jacob was seated beneath them, the Bible open on his knees.

He did not answer her question as she came in – only stared at her with his deadened eyes fixed unswervingly upon her. Then he rose, put the Bible on the seat, and took up a candlestick. Sombre and tall in his black clothes, his sere face began to kindle with a dull wrath. The shape on the bed had been covered with a white sheet.

She crouched against the washstand by the further wall, and again her strength ebbed from her, her face paling to the lips. But she forced herself to speak, her voice coming in a dry gulp:

'Afraid you make me, Jacob! How is it you are so strange?'

He advanced to the bedside, holding the candle aloft.

'There,' he said, extending his finger downwards over the corpse, 'there is your dead.'

She stared at him. He went on: 'Come you and look for the last time.'

Her mouth had gone dry, she could not move her tongue to any word. She lifted her hand to her face, and her eyes were livid with fright.

'Come,' he repeated.

She did not stir. His brows drawn, stern and righteous wrath in his countenance, he went to her and took her arm in his stony grasp. She quivered away from him, a curious sound coming from her lips, but, tightening his grasp, he drew her to the bedside. Her face had become sickly and loose, her breasts panted. Stonily Jacob looked down on her.

'Gather yourself together, woman. Make yourself ready to look for the last time on what you have worshipped.'

For a moment she went stiff and taut in his grasp, then, had he not held her, she would have fallen to the floor like a heap of rags. He put the candlestick down on the little table at the side of the bed, and with one gesture swept the white sheet away from the head and shoulders of the corpse. She saw. Jacob had taken the canvas wrapping from the filthy wax of the head and the horror lay there revealed in its congealed blood. Rebecca's body quaked, her back bent forward, she screamed at last. Then Jacob half-carried, half-dragged her to a chair and sat her on it, as she moaned, her head dropping pitiably on her breast.

He went back to the bed and covered the corpse. Then he took up the Bible again and sat down. And he began to read aloud:

'And early in the morning he came again into the temple, and all the people came unto him; and he sat down, and taught them. And the scribes and Pharisees brought unto him a woman taken in adultery; and when they had set her in the midst,

'They said unto him, Master, this woman was taken in adultery, in the very act.

'Now Moses in the law commanded us, that such should be stoned: but what sayest thou?

'This they said, tempting him, that they might have to accuse him. But Jesus stooped down, and with his finger wrote on the ground, as though he heard them not.

'So when they continued asking him, he lifted up himself and said unto them, He that is without sin among you, let him first cast a stone at her...'

For a moment he was silent, glancing up at Rebecca. Her head still dropped on her breast, she sat immobile as one dead. He went on:

'When Jesus had lifted up himself, and saw none but the woman, he said unto her, Woman, where are those thine accusers? hath no man condemned thee?

'She said, No man, Lord. And Jesus said unto her,

'Neither do I condemn thee: go and sin no more.'

He closed the book, went on his knees, and, leaning his elbows on the chair, prayed:

'Lord, who am I to condemn my wife Rebecca? Thy son forgave the woman taken in adultery and now I ask thee for strength to do likewise with Rebecca. Gone far in sin she has, dear Lord, looking with desire on the flesh of my brother Emlyn. And thou hast punished him with this visitation of death. The voice of the world would say, Stone her, cast her out, let her go from thee into the highways and byways. But have I not read the words of thy son! And what the great Jesus said has opened my heart in pity. Lord, forgive her her great sin against me. Tonight the hills cried out to me to slay her, the rocks mocked at my anguish, her name was written in letters of blood upon the sky. For before he died did not Emlyn confess to their behaviour together? Lord, she has done evil while her husband laboured for thee in thy chapel. Visit her with more punishment if thou wilt. Let her beauty shine no more, let her countenance be marked with grief, let her belly sicken her. But she shall rest quietly in her home with me, for I will not harden my sorrowing heart against her. For little Jesus' sake. Amen.'

He rose. Rebecca had covered her face with her hands. He went to her and touched her hair. She moaned.

'Ah,' he muttered, 'a fool you have been. Think you your sin would not be found out?'

She flung up her head; her face had gone loose and mottled, twitching in tears. 'He told you—' she sobbed.

'But already I knew,' he cried harshly. 'Think you I have no eyes, no sense to see how you flaunted yourself before him, and how his eyes burned with lust for you! Then confessed to me he did before he died that given yourself to him you had.'

Jacob, after one of the Big Meetings, had gone up to his bedroom and found a certain belonging of Emlyn's beside the bed.

She got up, crouched against the wall, swaying and sobbing. She felt all her life falling to pieces, there was no hope or happiness anywhere. Then Jacob's hand was laid upon her arm.

'Come, Rebecca. Young and pretty you are. Like a little wanton mare frisking in a field you have behaved. But look you now, settle down to life you must and there's peaceful we'll be together—'

He drew her to him. He passed his large strong hands over her, his sunken eyes began to kindle. She swayed in his gentle embrace. Then his arms closed like oak about her, and she lifted her face. It was like a shining hot flower. She was his now.

THE CONQUERED

Dorothy Edwards

Last summer, just before my proper holiday, I went to stay with an aunt who lives on the borders of Wales, where there are so many orchards. I must say I went there simply as a duty, because I used to stay a lot with her when I was a boy, and she was, in those days, very good to me. However, I took plenty of books down so that it should not be a waste of time.

Of course, when I got there it was really not so bad. They made a great fuss of me. My aunt was as tolerant as she used to be in the old days, leaving me to do exactly as I liked. My cousin Jessica, who is just my age, had hardly changed at all, though they both looked different with their hair up; but my younger cousin Ruth, who used to be very lively and something of a tomboy, had altered quite a lot. She had become very quiet; at least, on the day I arrived she was lively enough, and talked about the fun we used to have there, but afterwards she became more quiet every day, or perhaps it was that I noticed it more. She remembered far more about what we used to do than I did; but I suppose that is only natural, since she had been there all the time in between, and I do not suppose anything very exciting had happened to her, whereas I have been nearly everywhere.

But what I wanted to say is, that not far from my aunt's house, on the top of a little slope, on which there was an apple orchard, was a house with French windows and a

88

large green lawn in front, and in this lived a very charming Welsh lady whom my cousins knew. Her grandfather had the house built, and it was his own design. It is said that he had been quite a friend of the Prince Consort, who once, I believe, actually stayed there for a night.

I knew the house very well, but I had never met any of the family, because they had not always occupied it, and, in any case, they would have been away at the times that I went to my aunt for holidays. Now only this one granddaughter was left of the family; her father and mother were dead, and she had just come back to live there. I found out all this at breakfast the morning after I came, when Jessica said, 'Ruthie, we must take Frederick to see Gwyneth.'

'Oh yes,' said Ruthie. 'Let's go today.'

'And who is Gwyneth?'

Jessica laughed. 'You will be most impressed. Won't he, mother?'

'Yes,' said my aunt, categorically.

However, we did not call on her that afternoon, because it poured with rain all day, and it did not seem worthwhile, though Ruthie appeared in her macintosh and galoshes ready to go, and Jessica and I had some difficulty in dissuading her.

I did not think it was necessary to do any reading the first day, so I just sat and talked to the girls, and after tea Jessica and I even played duets on the piano, which had not been tuned lately, while Ruthie turned over the pages.

The next morning, though the grass was wet and every movement of the trees sent down a shower of rain, the sun began to shine brightly through the clouds. I should certainly have been taken to see their wonderful friend in the afternoon, only she herself called in the morning. I was sitting at one end of the dining-room, reading Tourguéniev with a dictionary and about three grammars, and I dare say I looked very busy. I do not know where my aunt was when she came, and the girls were upstairs. I heard a most beautiful voice, that was very high-pitched though, not low, say:

'All right, I will wait for them in here,' and she came into the room. Of course I had expected her to be nice, because my cousins liked her so much, but still they do not meet many people down there, and I thought they would be impressed with the sort of person I would be quite used to. But she really was charming.

She was not very young – older, I should say, than Jessica. She was very tall, and she had very fair hair. But the chief thing about her was her finely carved features, which gave to her face the coolness of stone and a certain appearance of immobility, though she laughed very often and talked a lot. When she laughed she raised her chin a little, and looked down her nose in a bantering way. And she had a really perfect nose. If I had been a sculptor I should have put it on every one of my statues. When she saw me she laughed and said, 'Ah! I am disturbing you,' and she sat down, smiling to herself.

I did not have time to say anything to her before my cousins came in. She kissed Jessica and Ruthie, and kept Ruthie by her side.

'This is our cousin Frederick,' said Jessica.

'We have told you about him,' said Ruthie gravely.

Gwyneth laughed. 'Oh, I recognised him, but how could I interrupt so busy a person! Let me tell you what I have come for. Will you come to tea tomorrow and bring Mr Trenier?' She laughed at me again.

We thanked her, and then my aunt came in.

'How do you do, Gwyneth?' she said. 'Will you stay to lunch?'

'No, thank you so much, Mrs Haslett,' she answered. 'I only came to ask Jessica and Ruthie to tea tomorrow, and, of course, to see your wonderful nephew. You will come too, won't you?'

'Yes, thank you,' said my aunt. 'You and Frederick ought to find many things to talk about together.'

Gwyneth looked at me and laughed.

Ruthie went out to make some coffee, and afterwards Gwyneth sat in the window seat drinking it and talking.

'What were you working at so busily when I came in?' she asked me.

'I was only trying to read Tourguéniev in the original,' I said.

'Do you like Tourguéniev very much?' she asked, laughing.

'Yes,' I said. 'Do you?'

'Oh, I have only read one, *Fumée*.'

She stayed for about an hour, laughing and talking all the time. I really found her very charming. She was like a personification, in a restrained manner, of Gaiety. Yes, really, very much like Milton's *L'Allegro*.

The moment she was gone Jessica said excitedly, 'Now, Frederick, weren't you impressed?'

And Ruthie looked at me anxiously until I answered, 'Yes, I really think I was.'

The next day we went there to tea. It was a beautiful warm day, and we took the short cut across the fields and down a road now overgrown with grass to the bottom of the little slope on which her house was built. There is an old Roman road not far from here, and I am not quite sure whether that road is not part of it. We did not go into the house, but were taken at once to the orchard at the back, where she was sitting near a table, and we all sat down with her. The orchard was not very big, and, of course, the trees were no longer in flower, but the fruit on them was just beginning to grow and look like tiny apples and pears. At the other end some white chickens strutted about in the sunlight. We had tea outside.

She talked a lot, but I cannot remember now what she said; when she spoke to me it was nearly always to tell me about her grandfather, and the interesting people who used to come to visit him.

When it began to get cool we went into the house across the flat green lawn and through the French window. We went to a charming room; on the wall above the piano were some Japanese prints on silk, which were really beautiful. Outside it was just beginning to get dark.

She sang to us in a very nice high soprano voice, and she chose always gay, light songs which suited her excellently. She sang that song of Schumann, *Der Nussbaum*; but then it is possible to sing that lightly and happily, though it is more often sung with a trace of sadness in it. Jessica played for her. She is a rather good accompanist. I never could accompany singers. But I played afterwards; I played some Schumann too.

'Has Ruthie told you I am teaching her to sing?' said Gwyneth. 'I don't know much about it, and her voice is not like mine, but I remember more or less what my master taught me.'

'No,' I said, looking at Ruthie. 'Sing for us now and let me hear.'

'No,' said Ruthie, and blushed a little. She never used to be shy.

Gwyneth pulled Ruthie towards her. 'Now do sing. The fact is you are ashamed of your teacher.'

'No,' said Ruthie; 'only you know I can't sing your songs.'

Gwyneth laughed. 'You would hardly believe what a melancholy little creature she is. She won't sing anything that is not tearful.'

'But surely,' I said, 'in the whole of Schubert and Schumann you can find something sad enough for you?'

'No,' said Ruthie, looking at the carpet, 'I don't know any Schumann, and Schubert is never sad even in the sad songs. Really I can't sing what Gwyneth sings.'

'Then you won't?' I said, feeling rather annoyed with her.

'No,' she said, flushing, and she looked out of the window.

Ruthie and Jessica are quite different. Jessica is, of course, like her mother, but Ruthie is like her father, whom I never knew very well.

Next morning, immediately after breakfast, I went for a

walk by myself, and though I went by a very roundabout way, I soon found myself near Gwyneth's house, and perhaps that was not very surprising. I came out by a large bush of traveller's nightshade. I believe that is its name. At least it is called old man's beard too, but that does not describe it when it is in flower at all. You know that it has tiny white waxen flowers, of which the buds look quite different from the open flower, so that it looks as though there are two different kinds of flowers on one stem. But what I wanted to say was, I came out by this bush, and there, below me, was the grass-covered road, with new cartwheel ruts in it, which made two brown lines along the green where the earth showed. Naturally I walked down it, and stood by the fence of the orchard below her house. I looked up between the trees, and there she was coming down towards me.

'Good morning, Mr Trenier,' she said, laughing. 'Why are you deserting Tourguéniev?'

'It is such a lovely morning,' I said, opening the gate for her; 'and if I had known I should meet you, I should have felt even less hesitation.'

She laughed, and we walked slowly across the grass, which was still wet with dew. It was a perfectly lovely day, with a soft pale blue sky and little white clouds in it, and the grass was wet enough to be bright green.

'Oh, look!' she said suddenly, and pointed to two enormous mushrooms, like dinner-plates, growing at our feet.

'Do you want them?' I asked, stooping to pick them.

'Oh yes,' she said; 'when they are as big as that they make excellent sauces. Fancy such monsters growing in a night! They were not here yesterday.'

'And last week I had not met you,' I said, smiling.

She laughed, and took the mushrooms from me.

'Now we must take them to the cook,' she said, 'and then you shall come for a little walk with me.'

As we crossed the lawn to the house she was carrying the pink-lined mushrooms by their little stalks.

'They look like the sunshades of Victorian ladies,' I said.

She laughed, and said, 'Did you know that Jenny Lind came here once?'

Afterwards we walked along the real Roman road, now only a pathway with grass growing up between the stones, and tall trees overshadowing it. On the right is a hill where the ancient Britons made a great stand against the Romans, and were defeated.

'Did you know this was a Roman road?' she asked. 'Just think of the charming Romans who must have walked here! And I expect they developed a taste for apples. Does it shock you to know that I like the Romans better than the Greeks?'

I said 'No,' but now, when I think of it, I believe I *was* a little shocked, although, when I think of the Romans as the Silver Age, I see that silver was more appropriate to her than gold.

She was really very beautiful, and it was a great pleasure to be with her, because she walked in such a lovely way. She moved quickly, but she somehow preserved that same immobility which, though she laughed and smiled so often, made her face cool like stone, and calm.

After this we went for many walks and picnics.

Sometimes the girls came too, but sometimes we went together. We climbed the old battle hill, and she stood at the top looking all around at the orchards on the plain below.

I had meant to stay only a week, but I decided to stay a little longer, or, rather, I stayed on without thinking about it at all. I had not told my aunt and the girls that I was going at the end of the week, so it did not make any difference, and I knew they would expect me to stay longer. The only difference it made was to my holiday, and, after all, I was going for the holiday to enjoy myself, and I could not have been happier than I was there.

I remember how one night I went out by myself down in the direction of her house, where my steps always seemed to take me. When I reached the traveller's nightshade it was growing dark. For a moment I looked towards her house and a flood of joy came into my soul, and I began to think how strange it was that, although I have met so many interesting people, I should come there simply by chance and meet her. I walked towards the entrance of a little wood, and, full of a profound joy and happiness, I walked in between the trees. I stayed there for a long time imagining her coming gaily into the wood where the moonlight shone through the branches. And I remember thinking suddenly how we have grown used to believing night to be a sad and melancholy time, not romantic and exciting as it used to be. I kept longing for some miracle to bring her there to me, but she did not come, and I had to go home.

Then, one evening, we all went to her house for music and conversation. On the way there Ruthie came round to my side and said, 'Frederick, I have brought with me a song that I can sing, and I will sing this time if you want me to.'

'Yes, I certainly want you to,' I said, walking on with her. 'I want to see how she teaches.'

'Yes,' said Ruthie. 'You do see that I could not sing her songs, don't you?'

In the old days Ruthie and I used to get on very well, better than I got on with Jessica, who was inclined to keep us in order then, and I must say it was very difficult for her to do so.

When we got there, right at the beginning of the evening Gwyneth sang a little Welsh song. And I felt suddenly disappointed. I always thought that the Welsh were melancholy in their music, but if she sang it sadly at all, it was with the gossipy sadness of the tea after a funeral. However, afterwards we talked, and I forgot the momentary impression.

During the evening Ruthie sang. She sang Brahms' *An die Nachtigall*, which was really very foolish of her, because I am sure it is not an easy thing to sing, with its melting softness and its sudden cries of ecstasy and despair. Her voice was very unsteady, of a deeper tone than Gwyneth's, and sometimes it became quite hoarse from nervousness.

Gwyneth drew her down to the sofa beside her. She laughed, 'I told you nothing was sad enough for her.'

Ruthie was quite pale from the ordeal of singing before us. 'It is rather difficult, isn't it?' I said.

'Yes,' said Ruthie, flushing.

'Have you ever heard a nightingale?' asked Gwyneth of me.

'No,' I said.

'Why, there is one in the wood across here; I have heard it myself,' said Jessica. 'On just such a night as this,' she added, laughing, and looking out of the window at the darkness coming to lie on the tops of the apple trees beyond the green lawn.

'Ah! You must hear a nightingale as well as read Tourguéniev, you know,' said Gwyneth.

I laughed.

But later on in the evening I was sitting near the piano looking over a pile of music by my side. Suddenly I came across Chopin's *Polnische Lieder*. It is not often that one finds them. I looked up in excitement and said, 'Oh, do you know the *Polens Grabgesang*? I implore you to sing it.'

She laughed a little at my excitement and said, 'Yes, I know it. But I can't sing it. It does not suit me at all. Mrs Haslett, your nephew actually wants me to sing a funeral march!'

'Oh, please do sing it!' I said. 'I have only heard it once before in my life. Nobody ever sings it. I have been longing to hear it again.'

'It does not belong to me, you know,' she said. 'I found it here; it must have belonged to my father.' She smiled at me over the edge of some music she was putting on the piano. 'No, I can't sing it. That is really decisive.'

I was so much excited about the song, because I shall never forget the occasion on which I first heard it. I have a great friend, a very wonderful man, a perfect genius, in fact, and a very strong personality, and we have evenings at his house, and we talk about nearly everything, and have music too, sometimes. Often, when I used to go, there was a woman there, who never spoke much but always sat near my friend. She was not particularly beautiful and had a rather unhappy face, but one evening my friend turned to her suddenly and put his hand on her shoulder and said, 'Sing for us.'

She obeyed without a word. Everybody obeys him at once. And she sang this song. I shall never forget all the sorrow and pity for the sorrows of Poland that she put into it. And the song, too, is wonderful. I do not think I have ever heard in my life anything so terribly moving as the part, 'O Polen, mein Polen,' which is repeated several times. Everyone in the room was stirred, and, after she had sung it, we talked about nothing but politics and the Revolution for the whole of the evening. I do not think she was Polish either. After a few more times she did not come to the evenings any more, and I have never had the opportunity of asking him about her. And although, as I said, she was not beautiful, when I looked at Gwyneth again it seemed to me that some of her beauty had gone, and I thought to myself quite angrily, 'No, of course she could not sing that song. She would have been on the side of the conquerors!'

And I felt like this all the evening until we began to walk home. Before we had gone far Jessica said, 'Wouldn't you like to stay and listen for the nightingale, Frederick? We can find our way home without you.'

'Yes,' I said. 'Where can I hear her?'

'The best place,' said Jessica, 'is to sit on the fallen tree – that is where I heard it. Go into the wood by the wild rose bush with pink roses on it. Do you know it?'

'Yes.'

'Don't be very late,' said my aunt.

'No,' I answered, and left them.

I went into the little wood and sat down on the fallen tree looking up and waiting, but there was no sound. I felt that there was nothing I wanted so much as to hear her sad notes. I remember thinking how Nietzsche said that Brahms' melancholy was the melancholy of impotence, not of power, and I remember feeling that there was much truth in it when I thought of his *Nachtigall* and then of Keats. And I sat and waited for the song that came to:

> ...the sad heart of Ruth, when, sick for home
> She stood in tears amid the alien corn.

Suddenly I heard a sound, and, looking round, I saw Gwyneth coming through the trees. She caught sight of me and laughed.

'You are here too,' she said. 'I came to hear Jessica's nightingale.'

'So did I,' I said; 'but I do not think she will sing tonight.'

'It is a beautiful night,' she said. 'Anybody should want to sing on such a lovely night.'

I took her back to her gate, and I said goodnight and closed the gate behind her. But, all the same, I shall remember always how beautiful she looked standing under the apple trees by the gate in the moonlight, her smile resting like the reflection of light on her carved face. Then, however, I walked home, feeling angry and annoyed with her; but of course that was foolish. Because it seems to me now that the world is made up of gay people and sad people, and however charming and beautiful the gay people are, their souls can never really meet the souls of those who are born for suffering and melancholy, simply because they are made in a different mould. Of course I see that this is a sort of dualism, but still it seems to me to be the truth, and I believe my friend, of whom I spoke, is a dualist, too, in some things.

I did not stay more than a day or two after this, though my aunt and the girls begged me to do so. I did not see Gwyneth again, only something took place which was a little ridiculous in the circumstances.

The evening before I went Ruthie came and said, half in an anxious whisper, 'Frederick, will you do something very important for me?'

'Yes, if I can,' I said. 'What is it?'

'Well, it is Gwyneth's birthday tomorrow, and she is so rich it is hard to think of something to give her.'

'Yes,' I said, without much interest.

'But do you know what I thought of? I have bought an almond tree – the man has just left it out in the shed – and I am going to plant it at the edge of the lawn so that she will see it tomorrow morning. So it will have to be planted in the middle of the night, and I wondered if you would come and help me.'

'But is it the right time of the year to plant an almond tree – in August?'

'I don't know,' said Ruthie; 'but surely the man in the nursery would have said if it were not. You can sleep in the train, you know. You used always to do things with me.'

'All right, I will,' I said, 'only we need not go in the middle of the night – early in the morning will do, before it is quite light.'

'Oh, thank you so much,' said Ruthie, trembling with gratitude and excitement. 'But don't tell anyone, will you – not even Jessica?'

'No,' I said.

Exceedingly early in the morning, long before it was light, Ruthie came into my room in her dressing gown to wake me, looking exactly as she used to do. We went quietly downstairs and through the wet grass to Gwyneth's house, Ruthie carrying the spade and I the tree. It was still rather dark when we reached there, but Ruthie had planned the exact place before.

We hurried with the work. I did the digging, and Ruthie stood with the tree in her hand looking up at the house. We hardly spoke.

Ruthie whispered, 'We must be quiet. That is her window.

She will be able to see it as soon as she looks out. She is asleep now.'

'Look here,' I said, 'don't tell her that I planted it, because it may not grow. I can't see very well.'

'Oh, but she must never know that either of us did it.'

'But are you going to give her a present and never let her know who it is from?'

'Yes,' said Ruthie.

'I think that is rather silly,' I said.

Ruthie turned away.

We put the tree in. I have never heard whether it grew or not. Just as the sun was rising we walked back, and that morning I went away.

THE LAST VOYAGE

James Hanley

The eight-to-twelve watch had just come up. The fo'c'sle was full. The four-to-eight crowd were awake now. Some were already getting out of bed.

'Where is she now?' asked a man named Brady.

'She's home, mate. Look through the bloody porthole. Why she's past the Rock-Light.'

And more of the four-to-eight watch began climbing out of bed. They commenced packing their bags. The air was full of smoke from cigarettes and black shag. A greaser came in.

'Reilly here?' he asked gruffly.

A chorus of voices shouted: 'Reilly! Reilly! Come on, you bloody old sod.'

A figure emerged from a bottom bunk in the darkest corner of the fo'c'sle.

'Who wants me?' he growled.

'Second wants you right away. Put a bloody move on.'

The man put on his dungaree jacket, a sweat rag round his neck, and went out of the fo'c'sle.

'His goose is cooked, anyhow,' said a voice.

'Nearly time too,' said another.

'These old sods think they rule the roost,' said another.

'He's just too old for Rag-Annie,' said yet another.

And suddenly a voice, louder than the others, exclaimed: 'What the hell's wrong with him, anyhow? If some of you bastards knew your work as well as he does, you'd be all right. Who says his goose is cooked?'

'The doctor.'

'The second.'

'Everybody knows it.'

'That fall down the ladder fixed him all right.'

'The old fool'l get jail. D'you know he's sailin' under false colours?'

'False colours?'

'Yes. False colours. The b—'s sixty-six, and he's altered his birthdate. They've got him down on the papers as fifty-six.'

'Has he been found out?'

'I don't know.'

'Some lousy sucker must have cribbed.'

'Give us a rest, for Christ's sake,' shouted a Black Pan man. 'You'd think it was sailin' day to hear you talkin'. Don't you know it's dockin' day? We'll all be home for dinner.'

'And a pint of the best, eh?'

The packing of the bags continued, whilst the flow of conversation seemed unceasing.

'This ship is the hottest and lousiest I ever sailed in,' growled a trimmer. 'A real furnace, by Jesus.'

'Oh, listen to that,' said a voice. 'You want to sail on the *Teutonic* if you like the heat.'

Suddenly the man Reilly appeared in the fo'c'sle. He walked back to his bunk past the crowd of men, who were now so occupied with bag-packing that they hardly noticed his return. Suddenly a voice exclaimed: 'Well, Christ! Here he is back again.'

'Who?'

'Old Reilly.'

All the faces turned then. All the eyes were focused upon the man Reilly.

'Did you get your ticket, mate?' asked one.

'Did he kiss you behind the boiler?' asked another.

'Are you sacked then?' asked another.

Everybody laughed.

'He went down to kiss the second's —,' growled one.

The man Reilly was tall and thin. His eyes, once blue, were black. Heavy rings formed beneath them. His skin was pasty-looking, his hair was grey. He was very thin indeed. When he took off his singlet, they shouted:

'His fifth rib's like a lady's.'

'His arms would make good furnace slices.'

'He's like a bloody rake.'

'The soft old b—. Why doesn't he go in the blasted workhouse.'

Suddenly Reilly said: 'Go to hell.'

Then he commenced to roll up his dirty clothes.

'Here, you! Shut your bloody mouth and leave Reilly alone,' exclaimed a man named John Duffy. 'If half you suckers knew your job as well as he does, you'd get on a lot better.'

'He's an insolent old sod, anyhow,' said a deep voice in the corner.

'I've been twenty years in this ship,' said Reilly.

'Aye. And by Christ, the ship knows it too. I'll bet you must have been growlin' for that twenty years.'

'Who's growlin'?' shouted Reilly. 'You young fellers think you can do as you like,' he went on. 'Half of you don't know your damn job, but you can come up to us old b— and get the information though. Who the hell told you I was sacked? Don't you believe it. You'll have me here next trip whether you like it or not.'

'Oh Christ!'

'By God! *I'll* look for another packet, anyhow.'

'So will I.'

'Why in the name of Jesus don't they let you take the ship home with you? Anyhow we don't all kiss the second's —.'

'That's enough,' shouted Duffy.

A silence fell amongst the group in the fo'c'sle. Reilly, having packed his bag, went out on the deck. He sat down on number 1 hatch. The ship already had the tugs, and was being pulled through the lock. He walked across to the rails and leaned over. He glared into the dark muddy waters of the river. He thought.

'Good God! All my life's been like that. Muddy.'

Duffy came out and joined him. He spoke to him. 'Hello, Johnny,' he said. 'How did you get on with Finch?'

Finch was the second engineer, a huge man with black hair and blue eyes, and a chin with determination written all over it. It was known that he was the only second engineer who had ever tamed a Glasgow gang from the Govan Road.

'This next trip,' said Reilly, 'is my last. It's no use. I tried to kid them all along. But it wouldn't come off. I just come up from the second's room now.'

'What did he say?'

'"Reilly," he said, "I'm afraid you've got to make one more trip, and one only. You'll have to retire."

'"Retire, Mr Finch," I said.

'"Yes. You're too old. I'll admit I like you, for I think you're a good worker, a steady man. You know your job. What I have always liked about you is your honesty and your punctuality. I have never known you fail a job yet. That's why I've hung on to you all this time. You're a man who can always be trusted to be on the job. I'm sorry, but you know, Reilly, I'm not God Almighty. The Superintendent Engineer had you fixed last trip. But I asked him a favour and he did me one."

'"D'you mean that, Mr Finch?" I asked him.

'"Yes, I do. Look here, Reilly. What have you been doing with that book of yours? You're down as being ten years younger than you are."

'"Can't I do my job?" I asked him.

'"Of course you can, Reilly, but that's not the point. You're turned the age now. Once you become sixty-five the company expect you to retire."

'"On ten shillings a week," I said to him.

'"That's not my business, Reilly," he said: "I repeat that I'm sorry, very sorry, but I'm not very much higher than you, and if I disobeyed the Super, I wouldn't be here five minutes."

'"By Christ!" I said.

'"Look here, Reilly," he said, "it's your last trip this time. I can't stand here talking to you all day. I'm sorry, very sorry. It might have been worse. You ran a chance of getting jail, altering the age in your book. Here. Take this."'

'He gave me a pound note,' said Reilly to Duffy.

'He did?' Duffy wiped his mouth with his sweat rag. 'He's not a bad sort himself, isn't the second. Not bad at all.'

'Not much consolation to me though,' said Reilly, 'after thirty-nine years at sea. By Jesus! I tell you straight I don't know how to face home this time. It's awful. I've been expecting it, of course, but not all of a sudden like this. But d'you know what I think caused it?'

'What?' asked Duffy, and he spat a quid of tobacco juice into the river.

'Falling down the engine room ladder three trips ago.'

'But that was an accident,' remarked Duffy.

'Accident. Yes,' said Reilly. 'But don't you see, if I'd been a younger man I'd have been all right in a few days. But I'm not young, though I can do my work with the best of them. I was laid up in the ship's hospital all the run home.'

'Ah, well. Never mind,' said Duffy.

'S'help me,' exclaimed Reilly, 'but those young fellers fairly have an easy time. Nothing to do only part their hair in the middle, and go off to French Annie's or some other place. By God! They should have sailed in the old ships. D'you remember the *Lucania*?'

'Yes.'

'And the *Etruria*?'

'Yes.'

'D'you remember that trip in the big ship when she set out to capture the Liverpool to York speed record?'

'Aye.'

'D'you remember Kenny?'

'I do,' said Duffy. 'The bloody sod! All he thought about was his medal and money gift from the bosses, but us poor b—. Every time we stuck our faces up to the fiddley grating to get a breath of air, there he was standing with a spanner, knocking you down again.'

'"Get down there. Get down there."'

'Half boozed too,' said Reilly. 'I'll swear he was.'

'He was that,' remarked Duffy. 'All in all, nobody gives a damn for us. Work, work, work, and then—'

'You're a sack of rubbish,' said Reilly. 'And by Christ I know it. I know it. All my life. All my life. I've worked, worked, worked, and now—'

'Will you have a pint at Higgenson's when we get ashore?' asked Duffy.

'No. I won't. Thanks all the same,' said Reilly, and he suddenly turned and walked away towards the alloway amidships.

'It's hard lines,' said Duffy to himself, as he returned to the fo'c'sle. All the men were now dressed in their go-ashore clothes. Duffy began to dress.

'Where's the old boy?' they asked in chorus.

'I don't know,' replied Duffy, and he put on his coat and cap. Overhead they could hear the first officer shouting orders through the megaphone; the roar of the winches as they took the ropes; the shouts of the boatswain as he gave orders to the port watch on the fo'c'sle head. The men went out on to the deck.

'She's in at last. Thank God.'

She was made fast now. The shore gang were running the long gangway down the shed. A crowd of people stood in the shed, waiting. Customs officers, relatives of the crew, the dockers waiting to strip the hatches off and get the cargo out. All kinds of people. The gangway was up. The crew began to file down with their bags upon their backs.

'There he is!' shouted a woman. 'Hello Andy!'

'Here's Teddy!' shouted a boy excitedly.

And as each member of the crew stepped on to dry land once more, some relative or other embraced him. The men commenced handing in their bags to a boy who gave each man a receipt for it. He placed each one in his cart. Now all the crew were ashore. The shore gang went on board. An old woman stood at the bottom of the gangway. She questioned an engineer coming down the gangway.

'Has Mr Reilly come off yet, sir?' she asked.

'All the crew are ashore,' he replied gruffly.

But they were not. For Reilly was in the fo'c'sle. He was sitting at the table, his head in his hands. His eyes were full of tears.

'What a time you've been, Johnny,' exclaimed Mrs Reilly, when eventually her husband made his appearance. 'The others came down long ago.'

'I had something to do,' said Reilly, and there was a huskiness in his voice. Near the end of the shed he suddenly stopped and put his bag down. 'Have all those fellers cleared?' he asked. 'I wanted to send this bag home with Daly.'

'I'll carry it, Johnny,' said his wife.

'How the hell can you carry it?' he said angrily. 'I'll carry it myself. Only for this here rheumatism. I've never been the same since that there fall down the stokehole.'

He picked up the bag and put it on his shoulder. They walked on. At the dock gates they had to stop again, whilst the policeman examined his pass.

'I haven't got it,' exclaimed Reilly, all of a flutter now, for he suddenly remembered that he had left it on the table in the fo'c'sle.

'You're a caution,' said his wife. 'Indeed you are.'

'If you haven't a pass, Mister, I'll have to search your bag. Are you off the *Oranian*?'

'Yes. I am. You ought to know me, anyhow. I've been on her for years.'

'I don't know you,' said the policeman gruffly. 'Let's have a look at it.' He picked the bag up and took it into the hut.

'Good heavens,' said Mrs Reilly. 'How long will he be in there? I'm perished with the cold.'

'Serve you right,' said her husband angrily. 'Haven't I told you time after time not to come down here, meetin' me? It's not a place for a woman at all.'

'There were other women here as well as me,' said Mrs Reilly.

'The other women are not you,' said Reilly, more angry than ever. 'Anyhow, here's the bloody bag.'

The policeman said: 'Everything's all right. Goodnight.'

Mrs and Mr Reilly walked away without replying. They passed through the dock gates. The road was deserted. Suddenly the woman exclaimed: 'Did you take those Blaud's pills while you were away, Johnny? I've been wondering. How d'you feel now?'

'Rotten,' he replied.

They walked on in silence.

'Shall I get you a glass of beer for your supper?' asked his wife.

'No.'

Again silence.

'Mary's husband got washed overboard,' said Mrs Reilly quite casually. 'Of course, I wrote to you about it.'

'Jesus Christ! Andy? Andy gone?'

'Yes. Poor feller. He was coming down the rigging after making the ratlines fast.'

'My God!'

They reached the end of the road. Turned up Juniper Street. Reilly spoke. 'How's Harry? Did he get any compensation?'

Mrs Reilly looked at her husband.

'He got twenty pounds. Lovely, isn't it? And him with his jaw gone.'

'Poor Andy, poor Andy,' Reilly kept saying to himself.

'Poor Andy.' And then suddenly he said aloud: 'Holy Christ! What a life! What a lousy bloody life!'

'It's God's Holy Will,' said his wife. 'You shouldn't swear like that, Johnny.'

'I dare say I shouldn't,' he said, and he stopped to spit savagely into the road. They reached the house. The three children, twelve, fifteen, and sixteen, all embraced him.

To the boy, Anthony, who was sixteen, he said : 'Well, are you workin' yet, Anthony?'

'No Dad. Not yet.'

The father sighed. He turned to Clara, twelve years of age, and took her upon his knee. 'How's Clara?' he asked her.

She smiled up at him, and he smothered her with a passionate embrace.

When the children had gone to bed, Mrs Reilly made the supper. They both sat down.

'Eileen has to go into hospital on Wednesday,' said Mrs Reilly.

'What for?'

'Remember her gettin' her arm caught in the tobacco cutting machine?'

'Yes. But I thought it healed up?'

Mrs Reilly leaned across and whispered into his ear. 'The poor darlin' has to have her arm off altogether. Don't say anything, John.'

'I'm sorry I came home. By God, I am. Coming and going. Coming and going. Always the same, trouble, trouble, trouble.'

He put down his knife and fork. He could not eat any more, he said, in reply to his wife's question. He drew a chair to the fire and sat down. Mrs Reilly began clearing the table. She talked as she gathered up the dishes.

'Trouble. God love us, you don't know what trouble is, man. How could you know? Sure you're all right, aren't you. Away from it all. You have your work to do. And when you've done it you can go to bed and sleep comfortable. You have your papers and your pipe. You have your food and your bed. Trouble. God bless me, Johnny, but you don't know what the word means. The rent's gone up, and then Anthony not working, and Eileen's costing me money all the while. And she'll end up by being a drag on me. How can the poor girl work? I get on all right for a while and then something happens. You see nothing. Nothing at all.'

Reilly jumped up and almost flew at his wife. She dropped her hands to her side. She looked full into his face.

'See nothing! Jesus Christ Almighty! You don't know what I see. You don't know what I have to do. What worry I have. You don't know what I think, how I feel. No. No. God's truth, you don't. Me! ME! An old man. And I have to hop, skip, and jump just like the young men, and if I don't, I'm kicked out. And where would you be then? And all the children. In the bloody workhouse. I have to put up with insults, humiliations, everything. I have to kiss the engineer's behind to keep my job. By heavens, you're talking through your hat, woman!'

'Am I? How do you know I'm talking through my hat? Was I talking through my hat that time you fell twenty-five feet down the iron ladder into the engine room? Was I? Was I? Was I talking through my hat when I made you come away from the doctor who examined you? Was I daft? You with a piece of your skull sticking in your brain, and no jaw, and all your teeth knocked out, and three ribs broken. And you actually wanted to take a lousy twenty-three pounds from the shipping company's compensation doctor. The dirty blackguards! You tried to kiss *his* behind. That I do know.'

'Look here, woman. I'll cut your throat if you torment me much longer. You don't know what I have on my mind. God! You don't. Kiss his backside. I had to. Supposing I had done as you say. Asked for a hundred pounds' compensation. I know it would have been all right if we had got it, but we didn't get it, did we? And I knew we couldn't. So I took what they offered – twenty-three pounds, and my job back.'

'Did that pay the doctor's bill and rent and food, for all the eleven weeks you were ill in bed on me? Did it? No. You had a right to ask for the hundred pounds. It's too late now.'

'I had no right.'

'You had. Good God! You know you had.'

'Damn and blast you, I tell you I had no right. I could never have got it. Didn't the union try? Didn't everybody try? It was no use. I got off lucky. I got my job back anyhow, didn't I?'

'Your job,' said Mrs Reilly, sarcastically.

'My job! My job! My job!' he screamed down the woman's ear. 'My job!'

'The people next door are in bed,' she said.

'I don't care a damn where they are.'

'I do,' said his wife.

'Christ, you'd aggravate a saint out of heaven. I feel like chokin' you.'

'Go ahead then. You hard-faced pig. That's what you are.'

'Oh, go to hell,' said Reilly. He walked out of the kitchen. Went upstairs. He undressed and got into bed. He lay for a while. Suddenly he got up again. He went into the children's room. They were sleeping. He went up to each one. He kissed them upon the forehead and upon the lips. He kissed Clara, murmuring: 'Oh, dear little Clara. Dear little Clara. I wonder what you'll do. I wonder how you'll manage.' Then he kissed Eileen.

'Poor Eileen. Poor darlin'. Losing your little arm. Your poor little arm. And nothing – NOTHING can save it.'

He kissed Anthony and murmured: 'Poor lad. God help you. I don't know how you'll face life. No, I do not know. Poor boy.'

Then he tiptoed out of the room and returned to his bed. All was silent in that house now. Below, Mrs Reilly was sitting in the chair just vacated by her husband. She was weeping into her apron. Above, he lay.

He thought. 'First night home. Good Lord. Always trouble. Always something. And me – me defending my job, and I haven't got one after this trip. Finished now. All ended now.'

Mrs Reilly came up to bed. Neither spoke. She got into bed. Lay silent. No stir in that room. All dark outside. Roars of winches and shouting of men they could hear through the window. Mrs Reilly slept. The husband could not sleep. He got out of bed again, and went into the children's room. Anthony was in one bed. Clara and Eileen in the other. He lay down on the edge of the boy's bed.

'Nothing. Nothing now,' he said. 'Things I've done. All these years. Nothing now. How useless I am. Poor children. If only I had been all right. Oh, I wonder where you'll all be this time next year. I wonder.' He closed his eyes but could not sleep. Was nothing now, he felt. Nuisance. And young men coming along all the time. Young men from same street. Street that was narrow, and at the back high walls so that sun could not come in. 'No sun in one's life,' he thought.

Mrs Reilly woke. Felt for her husband. Not there.

'O Lord!' she exclaimed. 'Where is he? Surely he hasn't gone.'

She called. And her voice was thin and cracked and outraged silence of that room. 'Johnny, are you there?' she called.

He heard. He would not reply. Was crying quietly, and one long arm like piece of dried stick was across Anthony's neck. She called again.

'Oh my God! Where are you, Johnny?'

He did not answer. Were now strange feelings in him. Heart was not there. Was an engine in its place. Ship's engine. Huge pistons rose and fell. He was beneath these pistons. His body was being hammered by them. All his inside was gone now and was only wind there. Wind seemed to blow round and round all through his frame. Gusts of wind. Were smothering him. Many figures were tramping in him. Voices. All shouting. All talking together. He could hear them. They were walking through him. Third engineer was one.

'You soft old bastard. Didn't I tell you to watch the gauge?'

Chief engineer was another.

'Watch yourself, Reilly. You're getting old now. Be careful. We'll do what we can for you. We won't forget you.'

Was another. And him a greaser. His name was Farrell

'You sucker. Working longer than anybody else in port. Go and get me some cotton waste. And shift your bloody old legs.'

'I have to keep my job.'

All voices spoke as one now. He could not understand their words. And always this engine was moving, these pistons crushing him. Three o'clock in the morning and no sleep yet.

Mrs Reilly was out of bed. She was downstairs. She looked in the back kitchen, in the yard and closet. Her husband was not there.

'What a worry he is,' she said, and came upstairs again. And there he was in the bed. He looked up at her. She smiled. He did not smile, but closed his eyes. She spoke to him.

'Where were you, Johnny. I thought you had gone down to the yard. Didn't you hear me calling you?'

'No. Was with children,' he said.

'Are you hungry? Would you like that glass of bitter? You had no supper,' she said, and there was a kindness in her voice, and in the tired eyes.

'Not now. Am tired,' he replied.

'Oh, Johnny. If only you'd stuck out for the hundred pounds. It would have been lovely. I was only thinking just now. We could have opened that greengrocer's shop. An' Eileen could have served in it. It would have been grand. We could have got her an artificial arm. They're so wonderful now, these doctors. Artificial arms are just like ordinary ones. You can use a knife and fork with them. If only you'd stuck out, Johnny. And Anthony could have taken out the orders.'

'Shut your mouth, for Christ's sake!' he growled.

Was a silence. Reilly breathed heavily. Light of candle fell upon his face. Was thin and worn. Yellow like colour of flypaper. Hands were hard. White like coral.

'Johnny, what's the matter, darlin'? Aren't you well?'

'I'm all right,' he said. 'It's this rheumatism, and then I'm thinking of Andy. Lord have mercy on him.'

'Poor Andy,' she said, 'was a lovely lad, wasn't he?'

'It's awful about Eileen,' said Reilly. 'Does she get no compo?'

'Not yet. Company said it was her own fault. If comb fell out of her hair and on to machine she had no right to put out her hand for it. Was an accident, they said. Would give her light job just now brushing rooms.'

'And her with her arm off. The soft sons of bitches,' he growled.

'I had an idea,' she said to him, and stroked his forehead.

'Idea,' he said, and sighed.

'Yes. Couldn't you get Anthony away with you as a trimmer?'

'What for?' he asked. And was a strange look in his eyes.

'To help us, of course,' she said; 'we have to get money somehow or other. We have to live.'

'Don't you get mine?'

'Yes. But it's not enough, Johnny,' she pleaded. 'You know Anthony is a strong lad. He would be all right as a trimmer.'

'I don't want any of my children to go to sea,' he said.

''You're very particular in your old age,' she said, with sarcasm.

'In my old age! Particular! Christ! Shut it.'

'Anyhow he wants to go,' she said. 'Is tired being at home. No work for him. Poor lad. Other lads working and money for cigarettes and pictures. None for him.'

'We're a lucky bloody family,' said Reilly angrily.

'Won't you try?' she asked. 'Will help us all this getting him away as trimmer. Will make a man of him. He wants to go.'

'Make a man of him,' said Reilly, and he laughed.

'Yes. Will make a man of him,' she said, and was angry, for colour had come into her cheeks that looked like taut drum skins. 'How bloody funny you are.'

'Me funny. Don't kid yourself, woman. I have to see the doctor in the morning. Nothing funny in that. For the love of Jesus shut up about Anthony and everybody else. Why don't you go to sleep?'

He was angry too, for eyes were burning with strange fire. He turned over on his side. Mrs Reilly mumbled to herself. They both lay on their sides with their backs to each other. He thought.

Bring Anthony with him? No. How funny. What made her suggest that? Especially this next trip. No. He would not.

'Are you awake, Johnny?' she asked him.

'I am,' he replied.

'Are you all right? I'm worried about you. Won't you have that glass of bitter that's downstairs?'

'No.'

Of a sudden were strange sounds in that house. And silence was like a fast-revolving wheel that has just stopped.

'What's that?' asked her husband.

'It's Eileen. Poor child. In the night her arm pains awful.'

'Go to her.'

His wife got up and went in to Eileen. The girl was sitting up in bed. All dark there for though moon shone light could not get in through high wall that faced window. It had a crack in it.

''What's the matter, child?'

'Oh, Mother!' she said. 'Oh, Mother!' Mrs Reilly held her child to her. And in her heart a great fear arose. Could feel now tiny heart of child pulsating against her own, whose tick was slow, like little hammer taps, or like dying tick of clock that is worn out.

'Oh my arm!' sighed Eileen.

'There, there,' said the mother. 'Don't cry, darlin'. God's good.'

Was nothing but heavy breathing of mother and little sobs of Eileen in that darkness.

Mrs Reilly shuddered. Eileen clung to her. In the other bed Anthony snored. His curly hair was a dark mass on the pillow.

Mr Reilly turned and lay on his back. He was muttering to himself.

'Tomorrow. Pay off. Go away. Pay off. Finish.'

Was not much in life, and we are only like dirt, he felt in his heart. He fell asleep. Was morning when he woke. Nine o'clock.

'I've fried you an egg,' said Mrs Reilly.

'Can't eat anything now,' said Mr Reilly. 'Just make a cup of tea. Have to pass doctor and sign on half past ten. Where's Eileen?'

'Gone over to the chemist's.'

'What for?'

'Well, I thought you'd want those pills again. For next trip.'

'Pills. Oh yes,' he said, and his voice seemed to be far away. He sat down and drank the tea hurriedly. Then he went into the back-kitchen. As he was closing the door he said: 'Don't let anybody come in here. I'm washing all over.'

He stripped. Was very thin. And he looked at himself in the glass. Ran hands over his body. He said to himself: 'Forty years at the one job. By God! And now finish. Well, many's the stokehole and engine room as has drawn sweat out of you, and you're alive yet. Many a time was ill with eyes bulgin' out of bloody head, and yet I took my rake and slice like a man and fired up. Many places I've been to. Saw many things. Not much in life.' He began to scrub himself.

'Don't splash all over the place,' shouted Mrs Reilly. 'I only scrubbed that place out last night.'

'All right,' he replied.

Was washed now. He dried himself with tablecloth that

had been on table once and Anthony had spilt tea on it. Was not much of a towel, he said. Again he looked at himself in the glass.

'These varicose veins,' he murmured. 'That's what it is.' And putting on the truss, he added: 'And this. This bloody rupture.'

Remembered fifteen years ago. Was young and strong and worked hard on *Lucania* when her engines broke down in the Western ocean. Heavy shafting to be lifted and he was strong. Was no thought for himself then, only for ship that had to be in New York by Wednesday 10.15p.m. Company were anxious to get passengers for Advertisers' Convention in England, before Red Star liner got them. Remembered that. And Chief Engineer said to second: 'Call the men for'ard, and tell the steward to give each man a tot of rum. Good job that.'

Remembered that. Had the rum. Forgot all about strain on body. Six years later the rupture came. It was bad too. He dressed and went the kitchen.

'You look all right now,' said Mrs Reilly, and helped him to tie his boots, and fasten his collar on. He put his coat and blue serge cap on. Then he crossed to the door.

'Kiss me,' she said.

He kissed her on cheek. The door banged. Mrs Reilly was thinking:

'God help him! He does look bad this trip.'

Reilly walked down the street. There were some people standing on their doorsteps, and children in gutters. Some women were speaking.

'There's owld Reilly home again.'

'He looks bad, doesn't he?'

'Sure that owld devil's as hard as leather.'

Reilly passed a pub where men were standing outside. Were old seamen out of work and they were talking.

'Hello, Johnny! How are you keepin', old timer?'

'Not bad,' Reilly said.

'See you coming back,' he added, and they smiled.

One man was small and had a face like a bird. He smacked his lips for Reilly coming back meant two rounds of drinks at Hangmans.

'He's a tough old devil, all right,' said this man.

Reilly had turned the corner. He had nearly been knocked down by a car. He had jumped smartly out of the way. A man who was young and very tall laughed. He said to the girl who was with him: 'Can't beat that, can you? An old sod like that trying to appear like a schoolboy.'

Reilly walked on. He was near the docks now. He walked down the shed. Were many men in this shed who knew him. They halloed him. Waved hands.

'Hello there?'

'Hello?'

'How goes it, Jack?'

'How do?'

Reilly smiled and shouted: 'Fine.' 'Middlin'.' 'Not so bad.' 'In the pink.' He was walking up the gangway now. A large number of men were standing about in the alloway, waiting to pass the doctor.

'Hello there?'

'How do?'

'Christ, he's back again!'

'Bloody old sucker.'

'How do, Reilly, old lad?'

All the men shouting and joking with him. He stood by the wall. He had his book in his hand.

'Whose — will you kiss this time?'

'How's your arm?'

'Did you have a bite this time home?'

All men taunting him. Were young men. Could not protest. Must hang on to his job.

'Leave the old fellow alone.'

'He's all right.'

'A wet dream is more correct.'

Reilly's heart was almost bursting. Could do nothing. Was tragic for him. 'I feel like a piece of dirt,' he said to himself. He was nearly in tears through anger, humiliation, threats, taunts.

'Doctor.'

All the men commenced to move down the alloway. Reilly was last. He shivered. Was afraid. He drove his nails into the palms of his hands but hands were hard and horny through much gripping of steel slice. He bit his lip until some blood came.

'Jesus, help me!' he said in his heart. 'Don't shiver. Don't be afraid. Be like the others. Remember now. All at home waiting for you. Waiting. Waiting for money. Little children expecting something. Wife expecting to go to the pictures. Keep cool.' The thoughts careered round and round his brain. He felt he was in a kind of whirlpool. 'Keep calm.'

The file moved along and it came Reilly's turn. He was in the doctor's room now. The doctor was young, and whilst Reilly dropped his trousers down, he cast look of appeal at doctor, whose cheeks were rosy, and his teeth beautifully white. Very clean he was. 'Like those men from university with white soft hands,' thought Reilly as he looked him in the face. Terribly clean. And strong too. The doctor spoke to him.

Reilly looked up at him with the eyes of a dying dog. 'Tell the truth now,' he said to himself. 'Anyhow it's your last trip.'

'How old are you?'

'Sixty-four, sir,' replied Reilly. 'I've been in this ship since she was built.'

'That doesn't mean that you can stay in her forever,' said the doctor. Was cruel. Was like a stab in the heart. Was bitter, Reilly thought.

'Step over,' he said to Reilly.

The man stepped across and stood before the doctor. He was a head above Reilly. He examined his chest.

'All right there,' he said quietly.

Then he looked lower down. He stroked his hair with his hand. He placed his hand on Reilly, and he felt how soft it was. Like silk. Beautiful hands. And his own were like steel. 'How long have you had this rupture, Reilly?'

'About six years, sir. I think I got it in the *Lucania*.'

'You didn't happen to get it anywhere else,' said the doctor.

'Again he is sarcastic,' thought Reilly.

'Oh,' exclaimed the doctor. 'Who's been passing you with these varicose veins?'

There was a bitter taste in Reilly's mouth. Like gall.

'On and off, sir,' he said: 'Dr Hunter always passed me. I can do my work well. Second engineer will tell you that, sir.'

The doctor smiled. 'I don't want to know anything about that,' he said. 'I am quite capable of handling you, thank you.'

'Christ!' muttered Reilly: 'How bitter he can be. Bitter as hell.'

'Bend down,' said the doctor.

Reilly bent down. Doctor looked hard at him. Felt him. All over. Legs, thighs, heels.

'All right,' said the doctor. 'But I won't pass you again after this. Next.'

The blood stirred in Reilly's heart. He was angry. He did not, he could not, make any reply to the doctor. He seemed to fly from that room.

'Did you get tickled?'

'Did you cough?'

'Did you do it?'

Again were voices in his ears as he walked down the alloway. Again were many men waiting to pass through to the pay table. Suddenly a voice of a master-at-arms shouted: 'Pass through as your names are called.'

Pay table was in grand saloon where rich carpets are deep and feet sink into them. Was beautiful and rich. Very quiet. Warm. Beautiful pictures on walls. Great marble pillars stretching up to ceiling. Was a place where first-class passengers dined on trips to America, but crew were not allowed to go there, for crew must stay for'ard in fo'c'sle. Crew must eat off wooden table through which iron poles were pushed up to deckhead, to hold table and prevent food from upsetting when weather was rough. Was well for'ard, the men's fo'c'sle. Where, when ship was up against heavy head swell, fo'c'sle seemed to pitch and toss, and often when she pitched badly food would be flung from table into men's bunks. And was dark too, for portholes were down near waterline, and must have deadlights screwed over them, for fear waters poured in, drowning men in their bunks. Men filed past the pay table.

'Reilly.'

His name now. And he stood whilst another man said: 'Five pounds, eighteen and threepence.' Was handed the notes, and they were new and crackled in his horny hand.

'Your book.' And another man handed him his book.

'John Reilly, ship's fireman.' He passed through another room, where he signed on. He handed his book to the officer. He passed out to the other side, and walked along saloon deck, which crew were not allowed to stand on during voyage, descended the companion ladder, walked along well-deck, and then down gangway. Again many men in the dock shed. 'Union,' one said, and that was seventeen shillings.

'Help the blind!' said a voice, and that was one shilling.

'Here y'are,' and it was a bill for carrying the bag to and fro from ship to house for four trips, and that was eleven shillings.

Near gates were Salvation Army women with boxes, and these rattled, for were full of poor men's pennies, that kept hostels open for poor men. Was also a man holding a large box for collection. A card read: 'For widow of Bernard Dollin. Scalded to death on the *Europesa*. No compensation. Please help.' More shillings. Reilly hung desperately on to his money now. He put two shillings in the box for Dollin's widow. On dock road was a woman selling flags that were made of yellow rag. Was for homes for tired horses at Broadgreen.

'Jesus Christ! For tired horses!' exclaimed Reilly, and laughed aloud. He turned up Juniper Street. At Hangmans he stopped and went in with men who had been waiting for him.

'Have a drink on me, mates,' he said.

The bar-lady served seven pints of bitter. 'Good health, Johnny. Best of luck next trip.'

All wished him good health and good luck. He said 'same to you', and drank his pint quickly, like a thirsty horse drinking at a trough.

'Same again,' he said to the bar-lady. 'I must go now, lads,' he said. 'See you again. Good luck.'

'Good luck, Johnny,' all said in chorus, and he went out.

He came up the street and again were women talking on steps as he passed. Also children like pigeons in gutters.

'Good day, Mr Reilly.'

'Good day,' he said.

'Hello, Johnny, how are you?'

'Not so bad,' he said.

People were nice in one's face, and some people had cursed him when he had gone up the street. Was at his home now. Mother had clean tablecloth on the table and children were waiting for him.

'Hello, Dad,' said Clara, and then Anthony said, 'Hello, Dad,' and Eileen too. 'Hello, Dad,' she said. He kissed them all. He sat down in the chair by the fire. Looked in the flames for a long time. Children looked up into eyes of father who had come to them out of great ocean and dark night and was wonder in their eyes. Mother came in from back-kitchen and said: 'Dinner is ready, Johnny.'

He said he was ready too and sat down. Children were seated now. Wild freshness of youth on their faces was a feast for his eyes, and his dinner was going cold through watching them. He looked at them longingly and blood stirred in him when he remembered humiliations of last trip.

'Lovely children. God help them,' he said in his heart.

The children were finished dinner so they got up and went out.

'Here,' he said, and gave each of them sixpence, and they smiled. He kissed them all. 'How happy they are,' he thought. They went out then.

Mrs Reilly said: 'Did you sign, Johnny,' and he said: 'Yes.' He pushed back his plate and put his hand in his pocket. Gave her four pounds.

'Is that all?' she asked, and was a sadness in her voice.

'That's all,' he said. 'Had to give seventeen shillings to union, and coppers here and there. Was going to buy a pair of drawers this trip, but can't afford it.'

'Good God!' she said. 'That's terrible, Johnny.'

'Good Jesus!' he said. 'Can't do any more, can I? You get my allotment money. You can't have it both ways, woman. If you hadn't drawn thirty shillings a week from my wages I could have given you about eight pounds.'

'God! I don't know,' she said, and sighed deeply.

'Can't do any more,' he said. 'Will you go to the pictures tonight?' He stood up and put his hands on her shoulders.

'I don't know,' she said.

'Heavens above,' he said. 'Always something wrong. What would you do if I hadn't signed?' He became suddenly silent. No use to talk like that. Forget all that. Try and be happy.

'Come on, old girl,' he said, 'get cleaned up. We'll go to the theatre or somewhere.'

'All right,' she said. 'You go and have a lie down.'

Reilly went upstairs to bed. He was not long with his head on the pillow before he snored. Below Mrs Reilly cleaned up. When she was finished she washed herself. Changed. Was all ready now and sitting by the fire. Kettle was boiling on the hob. At five Johnny came down. Was feeling a little better after his sleep. He said: 'Good. I see you're ready. Where'll we go, old girl?'

'Anywhere you like,' she replied.

'Righto,' he said, and went to get a wash in the back-kitchen.

When the children came in she said to them: 'Your father and me are going out to the pictures. Now please be good and look after the place.' And to Eileen she said: 'Look after them, Eileen. Tomorrow me and you will go somewhere.'

Were gone now and children all alone in house. Mrs Reilly and her husband got on a tram and it took them to the picture house. Was dark in there but band played nice music and Mrs Reilly said she liked it. He said nothing at all. When picture came it was a story of a man and two women. Mrs Reilly said last time she was at the pictures story was about two men and one woman. Johnny laughed. 'Story was very nice,' he said. Always the people in the pictures were nice-looking, and always plenty of stuff on tables and no trouble for them to get whisky. She said women wore lovely dresses. Interval then and lights went up. Band played music again.

'Come on,' he said, and they got up and went outside. They went to a pub, and he said: 'What'll you have, old woman?'

She said: 'A bottle of stout.'

'All right,' he said.

He drank a lemon dash himself. Was all smoke and spit and sawdust in the pub. Many men and women were drinking there. He said: 'It's cosy here.'

'Have another?' said Reilly, and she said: 'No. Not now.'

'I'm having another dash,' he said. When it came he drank it quickly. Back to pictures. All was dark again. In the next seat to them they could hear the giggling of a girl.

'Gettin' her bloody leg felt,' he said and lighted his pipe.

'Ought to be ashamed of herself,' she said, and was looking at a picture of a comic man throwing pies when she said this. He laughed, and she thought he was laughing at the picture and she said: 'He's a corker, isn't he?'

He said: 'I should think so,' and was thinking of the man

who was with the girl who his wife said should be ashamed of herself.

'I'm tired,' he said. 'Shall we go?'

'Near the end now,' she said. 'Wait, Johnny.'

Comic man had just been chased by a policeman. He knew it was near the end of the picture. Did not want to stand when 'God Save the King' was played by band.

He said: 'Come on,' and pulled her arm. They went out. They hurried home in the tram through dark roads where pale light of gas lamps made all people's faces look yellow as if everybody had yellow jaundice.

'I feel so tired,' he said.

'Will you have a glass of bitter?' she asked him as they were walking up the street.

'No,' he said. 'I'm going to bed now. Too tired for anything.' When they got in he went straight upstairs. As he was closing the kitchen door, he said: 'Don't be long now.'

Mrs Reilly made herself a drink of tea before she went up herself. She ate some bread that the children had left. 'Poor Johnny,' she said. 'Gets tired quickly these days. Is not the man he used to be: God help him.

She put out the light and went upstairs. Undressed and got into bed. Candle was burning on table at his side of the bed and light fell on her husband's face. His eyes were closed.

'He is asleep,' she said. Looked at his face. Was very thin, she thought. 'Good God!' she whispered. 'I hope he doesn't catch consumption.' She kissed him on the forehead where many furrows were. She fell asleep watching him.

Morning for going away had come and he was up early. Mrs Reilly and the children were up. Bag was packed and was standing in the corner by the door. Was beautiful and clean for his wife had scrubbed it well. Was hard work for it was made of canvas. All were at the table having their breakfast. Egg each and some bacon. It was the same each sailing day. An egg each and a slice of bacon for the children. Mr Reilly was shaving in the back. Was sadness in his eyes and he did not like looking at himself in the glass whilst he was shaving. He tried to look downward just where razor was scraping. He finished and washed himself. Came into the kitchen. Were two eggs and a piece of bacon for him. He could not eat all that, he said. Wasn't hungry, he told his wife. But she said, 'Try, because you haven't ate much this trip,' and children were looking from father to mother and to his plate, and each was thinking: 'He will give me the egg that's over.' Mr Reilly started to have his breakfast. His wife said: 'Won't you eat any more?' and he said: 'No.' Children looked only at the mother now, but were disappointed for she said: 'I'll have the odd egg myself.'

Children had gone out into yard. Was quiet now and clock could be heard ticking. Was five past seven by it.

'Must go now,' he said, and voice was soft.

'Now, Johnny,' she said, and got up from the table. Whilst she crossed to the back door to call in the children to say goodbye to their father, she wiped pieces of egg from her mouth, for her husband always kissed her on the lips on sailing day. Children came in. He embraced each one, saying: 'Goodbye. God bless you.' Now his wife. She clung to him.

Nearly in tears he was, for was much in his mind, and 'the heart is a terrible prison,' he said to himself.

'Goodbye, Johnny,' she said. She hung tightly to him. 'God bless you. Take care of yourself now. Don't forget to take the Blaud's pills. Goodbye. God bless you.'

'Goodbye,' he said, and bag was on his back and he was through the door. She closed it and went up to the window, where children were trying to look out in to the dark street and with their noses pressed flat against the windowpane.

'Poor Johnny,' she said in her heart. 'Didn't eat much this trip, was looking very bad, poor fellow. Ah, well!'

'Draw the blind down again,' she said to Eileen, for it was still dark and gas was lighted yet. Dark until eight o'clock. The children came away from the window. Mother's eyes were misty and they were looking at her. Reilly walked down the street in the direction of the dock where his ship lay. Was dark, and all silent. Streets were terribly quiet. Everything seemed gloomy and sad. Raining too. Turned the corner now. Argus Street, Welland Street, Darby Street. Goodbye. Goodbye. Juniper Street, Derby Road. Goodbye. Goodbye. Was near the docks now. Some men were coming out of the gate. They knew him for he was just walking under the lamp when they came out.

'Goodbye Johnny. Good luck,' they said.

'Goodbye. Goodbye,' and his voice was a murmur low in their ears. Ship was there. Like a huge beast, sleeping. Was a light from an electric cluster hanging over number 2 hatch. Was like huge beast's eye. Some steam was coming out of the pipe near the funnel. Was like hot breath coming out of huge beast's nostrils. Was slowly waking. And from funnel itself was much smoke coming. It came out in clouds, then in the air became scarf-shaped. All was very silent except for low moaning. Steady whirr, whirr within ship. It came from for'ard where beef-engine was running. Was never stopped for place where food is kept for passengers must always be cool. The morning was very cold. At the gangway the watchman shivered. As Reilly ascended the gangway, the watchman took his nose between his fingers and blew hard into dock.

'Mornin',' he said dryly as Reilly passed him. Reilly made no reply. Was on his ship now. Going for'ard. In some hours to come he would be right down inside this beast. Down inside huge belly. Sweating. Half past seven. Suddenly many noises filled the air. Ship was full of action. Ship was like great hippopotamus where all ticks were feeding on body. Decks were alive with men. Derricks were moving like long arms, and men seemed like pygmies on the great decks. Crew were now coming on board. All were hurrying towards fo'c'sles and glory holes, for first there was best served. Last trip Reilly had to take bottom bunk in firemen's room where rats as big as bricks stood up defiant against the men when they tried to get them in the corner and kill them with big holystones. Reilly had a top bunk now. Was first man in. Another man came in. His name was Campbell.

'Hello cocky. You took my bloody bunk,' he said.

Reilly did not reply. Thoughts in him were calm. He said in his heart: 'Your last trip. Keep calm. Remain silent. Stand things for sake of wife and children. When you go home you can get the old age pension.'

'Well, Holy Jesus!' said Farrell, coming in. 'The dozy swine's back again.'

Reilly remained silent. Calmly he unpacked his bag. Was something hard in it. Like a little box. 'Good God!' he murmured. 'Fancy that. Poor Eileen. Bought me a box of soap. God bless the darling child.' He fondled the box as if it were made of solid gold. Were many noises now for fo'c'sle was full. Again voices in his ears. He wished they were full of cotton wool.

'Old Reilly's back.'

'Oh Christ! Is he?'

'Can't you see him?'

'Hello there. You old sucker.'

Was a message flashing through Reilly's brain. 'Keep calm.' Nine o'clock now. Second engineer came down the crew's alloway. He crushed past a small trimmer. Said to him: 'Tell Farrell to pick his watch.' Trimmer went into fo'c'sle. Spoke to Farrell. Farrell shouted: 'Outside men.' All the men went out on deck. Some were already wearing their dungarees. Some wore their best clothes. Many were drunk. Farrell looked at the men. His right forefinger was pointing. As if he were pointing a gun at them all. They watched him.

'Ryan. Duffy. Connelly. Hughes. Hurst. Thompson. Reilly. Simpson.'

Eight men stepped forward.

'Eight-to-twelve watch,' he said. 'Stand by till twelve o'clock. Have your dinner. Then turn in.' He walked off amidships.

On the deck also were boatswain and his mate. They picked their port and starboard watches. Lookout men. Day men. Lamp trimmer. Storekeeper. Came a little man, bald, with a sandy moustache. He called eight firemen and they were for Black Pan watch. Then a man named Scully; he picked the 'gentleman's' watch.

Hatches were being put on. The chief engineer was coming along the deck. He was shouting and his face was as red as a turkey cock. 'God damn you. Can't you hear five blasts on the whistle? Get these men up on the boat deck.'

Was a terrible fuss now, for no watches should have been picked before boat muster. Boat drill first because that was most important. Was very important because men must be good sailors in case of ship striking iceberg, and helpless passengers to be saved. Was not right to pick watches before this had been done as it gave men a chance to pick mates and make other arrangements. Confusion. All the men diving into bags for jerseys and sailors caps that made some look like monkeys. Was necessary company said even if they looked like monkeys to have ordered ones.

'Like the bloody navy,' said Duffy, whose hat would not fit him and he had just paid five and sixpence for it at the slop chest. 'Robbers,' he growled. 'Dirty robbers.'

The crew ran along all decks and on flush deck some tripped over hatch combings and falls from the drum-ends. Cargo men cursed them. Crew swore too. Reilly was one. Fell right over hatch cover.

'You dopy old bastard. Where were you last night?' growled a ganger. He did not hear the remainder of the sentence. He did not run up companion ladder to the saloon deck, rather he hopped up like a bird. 'I feel like a poor bloody sparrow,' he said in his mind.

All excitement.

'Lower away.'

'Slack your falls.'

'Hey! What the hell are you doin'?'

'Easy there.'

'Heave away.'

'God blast you! How can you lower away with your rollocks like that?'

'Get clear of chocks.'

The boats were ascending and descending. Then a whistle blew. The men dispersed. Reilly went along the deck with Duffy.

'How are you, old timer?' asked Duffy.

Reilly said: 'Not so bad.' They pressed up the alloway. Reilly undressed and turned in. All the men looked at him.

'Oh hell. He's started again.'

'Who? Oh, him. How are you, my pigeon?'

'Leave the old sucker alone.'

'He's all right.'

'Tickle his ribs.'

'To hell with him!'

Duffy's face went red for was fifty himself and remembered sailing with Reilly years ago when he was young and strong and a good worker. Would not let him be put on, he said.

'You're as bad as him.'

'Who said that?'

'I said it.' Farrell was speaking. Was a glint in his eye.

'Come out on deck,' said Duffy.

Reilly was shivering in his bunk. Was cold. For ship's blankets were thin and iron laths of bed pierced through straw palliasse. Was in singlet but no drawers. 'Good Christ!' he said to himself. 'All this over me. All this fuss. All will hate me now.' Some men playing cards at the table were growling.

'Throw the old bastard over the side. Bunk and all.'

'There's always something wrong when he's here.'

'Awful,' said Reilly in his heart, 'and I wanted to keep calm. Say nothing.'

'Come on. Come on the bloody deck!'

'Put a sock in it.'

'Pipe down.'

Silence then for a moment.

'What time is it?'

'Nearly four o'clock.'

The cook, who was half drunk, came up the alloway from galley and said did any of those b—'s want dinner. Was not going to wait there all day for them. Was going to kip.

Seven bells. Four-to-eight watch were dressing. All had clean sweat rags round their necks. Some smoked cigarettes, others black shag. They passed out of the fo'c'sle in silence. Down alloway and along well deck number 2. Was a great stink now. Very warm. They could hear the thunder of the pistons pounding. Walked slowly. Some dragged their legs after them.

'Bloody steam up all day. Just to keep you workin'. Lousy bastards.' From the alloway could see the entrance to the engine room. The steel ladders glistened. All disappeared through the steel door between two high walls of steel, that were black. One wall was scaly with salt. In the fo'c'sle Reilly fell asleep. He dreamed. Was with the children in a park. Were playing with a rubber ball. All were jolly. Laughing. He bought them ice cream sandwiches. He stroked their heads. They disappeared. He called after them. Could not find them. 'Hey! Hey!' he called aloud. 'Hey! Where are you all?'

'Where the hell are you? Shut your confounded trap. People here have to do their four hours below as well as you.'

Blood rushed to his head. He had been dreaming all right. Raised his head a little. Very quiet in the fo'c'sle now. Eight-to-twelve watch fast asleep. Suddenly he felt cold. Felt in the bed. Was nothing. Felt on top of blanket and his hand was wet. Greasy. Someone had thrown slops on top of him whilst he was sleeping. Was angry.

'Show a leg there! Show a leg there! Seven bells! Seven bells!'

Reilly sat up quickly.

'How soon the time passes,' he said.

Somebody laughed. 'Were you dreaming about her?'

Some were now climbing out of their bunks. Were sullen and silent. They had been drinking heavily and their heads were large and painful. All were ready now.

Five to eight.

'Righto.'

Eight-to-twelve watch left the fo'c'sle and towards amidships. Reilly stopped to tie his boot with a piece of string.

'Come on, dozy,' shouted Farrell, and to himself: 'I'll sweat that sucker this trip.'

Descended ladder now one at a time. Reilly was shaking. Each time he was on a ladder his whole body shook. Remembered that trip falling twenty-five feet on his head. They reached the engine room. Passed through into stokehole. Was all heat and smell of water on ashes for men they were relieving had been emptying their bladders. Was much sweat on these men.

'Number 3, you,' said Farrell, and Reilly went on number 3.

A man said to him: 'What time did she pull out?'

'Half past four.'

'Oh! Must be in the channel now.'

'Yes.'

'Farrell! Are you there?'

Farrell turned round. Reilly was standing there with singlet off and bare to waist. Ribs shone in red glare of furnace.

'What the hell do you want now?' asked Farrell.

Reilly was afraid. Was a sickness at the pit of his stomach. His blood was stirring. It was anxious for rest.

'Number 3. Who is he?' asked Reilly.

'What's that got to do with you?'

'A lot,' said Reilly. 'Isn't he the man I relieve this trip?'

'Well?'

'He wasn't here when I came down.'

'What about it?'

'He should be here. The lousy sod. Look at that.'

'Look at what?' said Farrell, and he smiled.

'You bastard,' said Reilly, but only in his heart.

'The mess he left,' said Reilly. 'The mess he left. What a worker. A pile of bloody ashes here and half the furnace raked out.'

'D'you know who you're relievin'?' asked Farrell.

He bent low towards Reilly, who shivered now.

'Who?'

'My wife's brother,' said Farrell. 'You get on your job, old cock. By Jesus! I'll watch you.'

Was a man stoking up hard at number 4 furnace. Also a little trimmer running to him from between boilers. Had come from bunkers with heavy steel barrow full of coal. Ship lurched and trimmer was pitched forward on to his face.

'You awkward bloody worm,' said Duffy.

'Come on. Christ! Look at him. Standing there,' said Farrell. 'D'you want me to use your slice for you? Hell. Sit down. I'll hold your hand for you.'

'O Jesus!' said the old man to himself. 'Be calm.'

Farrell walked away. Reilly looked towards number 4 furnace. Was a cloud of steam. Duffy had done it on ashes. He could not see him. He looked at his own furnace. Suddenly bent down. Looked right into it. A trimmer had shouted: 'Righto.' Had tipped his barrow for Reilly. Heat was terrible. Reilly took his shovel. Dug into coal and heaved a shovelful into the furnace. Flames roared. Flame licked out at him, scorching his face and thin chest. Reilly said: 'The mean bastard! Knew it would happen. Told trimmer to heave me a load of slack. God strike him dead!'

He shovelled again. Must get her going. Must watch gauge. Gauge going down. Must watch bloody boiler. Might burst. He heaved in again. Flames licked out at him like many little tongues. Suddenly he flung down his shovel. Folded his arms and stared into the roaring furnace. 'How tired I am. How sick and tired of it all. After forty years. O

Jesus! How can I go to them? To see her face when I say: "I'm sacked. Too old." How can I? Poor children. Nothing for them. Nothing for them.' Was silent. Tears were running down his cheeks and drying on his chest. Saw in flames all his past life. Every thought. Every word. Every deed. All endeavours, trials, braveries of the flesh and spirit. Was now – nothing. All ended. Nothing more now. Nothing more now. What is it all for?' he said in his heart. Who cares? Nobody. Who feels? Nobody. Saw all his life illuminated in those flames. Not much for us. Sweat, sweat. Pay off. Sign on. Sweat, sweat. Pay off. Finish. Ah, well! Were voices in those flames now. Were speaking to him. He understood their language which was in sounds of hot air. And suddenly he said, half aloud: 'All to her. All to the sea.' He gripped his shovel. Then suddenly dropped it. He picked up the steel slice. And suddenly dropped that too. All to her. All his life, hopes, energies. Everything. The flames licked out at him.

'ALL,' he shouted, and leaped.

'Hey! Jesus Christ! HELP! HELP! Reilly's jumped in the furnace.'

An Afternoon at Ewa Shad's

Glyn Jones

Em was my friend. He lived with my Ewa Shad and my Bopa
Lloyd in a lonely row of whitewashed cottages on the side
of the hill. It was a lovely sunny afternoon when I went up
there carrying a brown paper parcel, and my mother had
put my blue print trousers on me. These were real trousers
with a button fly and a patch pocket for my handkerchief
on my behind.

Em lived in the end cottage in the row. There was a
pavement in front with gutters crossing it half-filled with
soapy water from the colliers' bathtubs. In front of the
pavement again stretched a flat patch of rusty ground, a sort
of little platform in the side of the hill where the sagging
drying lines stood and a chickens' cwtch built of orange
boxes. At the back of the row, beyond the colliers' gardens,
the steep tips of pit rubbish sloped smoothly up into the sky,
and it was on these tips the men who were out of work used
to scratch for coal. Em's father, my Ewa Shad, had made a
fence round his garden out of old pit-rope and sheets of rusty
corrugated zinc, but the bottom part was formed of the two
end frames of a black iron bedstead, with the bright knobs
and the brasswork still shining in the sun upon them.

I went into the back garden, and there I found Em playing
with his fish. He had a big zinc bath half-filled with water

sunk to the level of the ground to keep it in. He took his finger out of his nose to wave to me. It was a good garden for playing in because only about a quarter of it was set, and the earth of the rest had been trodden hard as the flags of a kitchen. There was a sycamore tree growing in the middle, and a whitewashed lavatory stood like a sentry box in the far corner. Em's father was lying on his back between the lettuce beds, his boots off and his cap over his face. He was dirty and in his working clothes, and every now and then he would take hold of his shirt and start scratching his chest with his fist.

'It's our Mam's birthday today,' said Em, as I went up to him. His jersey was navy blue with a new light blue sleeve to one arm and half a sleeve, from the elbow down, to the other. He was sunburnt, his nose dotted with black freckles like the spots on a bird's egg, and his ginger hair was cut very short and in a notchy way, looking as though something had been nibbling at it. I could see he had a red bloodshot blot in his eye that afternoon, and I thought I would like to have one of those, too. We played with the fish, which was about as big as my middle finger and which had a bright scarlet line all around the gulping edge of its mouth.

Presently Bopa Lloyd came out of the kitchen to throw some potato peelings over the fence. When she saw me she looked glad, and when I gave her the parcel for her birthday she patted my face like a pony. She was a fat woman wearing a black flannel bodice with grey pinstripes and a wet sack apron that hurt you when she wiped your nose with it. On her forehead she had lines across like you use for music, and her grey hair was coming down out of her combs like the feathers of an untidy hen. Her nostrils were black and big enough for her to put her thumbs up them, and there were three or four little round lumps of shiny purplish skin growing on her face, each very smooth and tight-looking and with a high polish on it. And one of these lumps, the glossy plum-coloured one on her chin, had a long brown hair curling out of the top of it. 'Shad,' she shouted, 'come from by there now and wash yourself for dinner.'

Just then a big drop of rain fell into the middle of the pan. The sycamore opened and let out a bird. Loads of dark clouds with torn, wispy edges like black, heavy hay were blown across the sky, soon leaving no blue. It became dark and cold, and big pieces of white water began falling heavily out of the sky and dropping cold as lead right through my thin blouse, wetting my skin. Bopa Lloyd hurried towards the kitchen door with her parcel like a hen off her nest, shouting to us: 'Go and shelter in the dubs while I get your dinner or you'll get wet soaking.' Em and I ran into the WC and Ewa Shad got up too and trotted down the garden, the peak of his cap on his neck and his working boots under his armpits. 'I been with the angels,' he muttered as he passed us, and we sat and watched him till the kitchen door had gulped him through.

Soon it was raining like tap water and we heard the bumming of the thunderclap, but it was a long way off. From where we were we could see a big rain-stream pouring along a gutter the coal pickers had worn down the side of the steep tip outside the garden, and halfway down, where it met a big lump of orange shale, it spouted up into the air, curving high out like a fountain. We sat on the wooden seat of the lavatory watching the inky tips through the open door. Then when Em peeped out he said the pipe from the troughing next door was pouring rain into the garden. I could see it was broken off halfway down, and it swung loose against the wall like the empty coat-sleeve of a man with one arm, making a big rusty tobacco stain on the white-lime of the wall. Em ran out into the rain, picked up the piece of piping that had fallen into the garden, and sloped it from the wall to the edge of his zinc bath sunk into the earth. Then he ran back again, and we waited for the pan to fill with water.

We could see the earth spitting hard with rain, and hear it hissing like poured sugar or a cockle bed. Grey rain-fur grew round the pit ropes of the fence and the iron bedstead and over the sheets of rusty zinc. The surface of the water in the bath swarmed with tall rain, each heavy drop as it fell bouncing up again like the bobbing rod of a sewing machine. Then two of Bopa Lloyd's hens, a white one and a ginger one, struggled through the hedge into the garden, their feathers stuck to them with rain. 'Shoo,' said Em, and the white one fell into the bath. Em laughed, but the chicken made so much noise Bopa Lloyd came out to the door of the kitchen drying her hands on her sack apron. When she saw what had happened she pushed Ewa Shad back, and swinging a towel over her head she ran round the side of the house and got a big shovel out of the coalhouse. It was a collier's shovel, an old one of Ewa Shad's, shaped like a heart-shaped shield. With this she shovelled the chicken up out of the pan while the water ran out of the toolbar hole in the corner. She kicked the piping down from the wall and shouted, 'Come on in now, boys, and have a meal of food.'

It was dark inside Bopa Lloyd's kitchen, but I could smell the fried onions and herrings cooking for dinner in the big fireplace where the row of bright candlesticks was and the brass horses in the hearth. The ceiling was brown wood with beams across, and the stairs curved down into the far corner. Some sheets of newspaper and two pieces of sacking covered the parts of the floor you walked on. When the back door opened it banged against the mangle which had a couch alongside with a bike on it. The wallpaper was brownish with purple birds and upright daisy chains of black roses, but Ewa Shad hadn't put it on well near the curve in the wall made by the stairs, and all along that side the stripes were diagonal. Our Mam said Ewa Shad must have two left hands.

'Emlyn,' said Bopa Lloyd, 'go and fetch your father's slaps.'

Four of us sat down to dinner, Bopa Lloyd, Ewa Shad, Em, and myself. Ewa Shad had washed a bit now, the middle of his face and the palms of his hands. He was a funny-looking man, pale, with a big oval face and round, popping eyes, whitish grey and very shiny and wet-looking. On his head he had a brown covering of my father's armpit hair, and now that he had taken off his red flannel muffler I could see the swelling wen hung in his neck like a little udder, half of it grimy and half of it clean and white. When I went into the kitchen he was rubbing his back up and down against the edge of the open pantry door to scratch himself. He didn't say anything to me, he just rubbed and showed his teeth with the dirty dough on them. Then he sat down and read the tablecloth with his head twisted round on one side.

Bopa Lloyd sat on a chair without a back nearest the fire with her false teeth on the table in front of her. 'There's pretty trousers you've got on,' she said, as she served me half a herring. 'Let me see, a pocket and a coppish and all.'

Ewa Shad ate his potatoes and onions without saying a word, but he looked over all his food before he ate it, and sometimes he gave a loud, wet belch. And every now and then he would start scratching himself, putting his arm inside his shirt and rubbing his chest, working around under his armpit to his back, and at last letting his fingers come back up through his open collar-band on to his wen. I was looking most of the time at the little purple potatoes sprinkled on Bopa Lloyd's face; they were so tight they looked inflamed, like little bladders ready to burst. Then I heard Ewa Shad and Bopa Lloyd talking loudly. Suddenly my Ewa stopped and stared before him with his mouth open. I could see the spittles stretched like thin wires from his top teeth to his bottom ones in an upright row.

'You'll be sorry,' he growled at Bopa Lloyd at last. 'You'll be sorry,' and he left the table and went up the stairs out of sight.

'What's the matter with him now, our Mam,' said Em, as though he was going to cry. 'What's he gone to bed without washing for?'

'Because he's gone dull,' said Bopa Lloyd, running her

finger round her gums, her face very red. 'Since he's lost his job he's not a-willing to eat his fried onions if they're not all in proper rings. He's going daft, that's what's the matter with him.' Then she went quieter. 'Have you had enough of food, bach?' she said to me, putting her teeth back in her mouth. 'Don't take no notice of him. Try a bit of teisen lap, will you?'

When she had sharpened her knife on the doorstep, Em and I sat down there, eating our cake and playing dixstones. We could hear Ewa Shad thudding about in his stocking feet upstairs. The rain was slackening and by the time we had reached fivesy, it had stopped.

'Can we go out now, our Mam?' said Em.

Bopa Lloyd was sitting on the couch by the bike, sewing Ewa Shad's coat up under the armpit, and she said we could. We went into the garden. The heavy rain had made the place look different, there was gravel about and dirty pools with small coal in them like mushroom gravy. And the earth smelt strong as an animal. But the sky was clearing again, although the sunshine seemed weak after the rain. Then after a bit, as Em was pulling up a long worm to give to his fish, we heard someone throwing the upstairs window open, the one with the blue blouse across for a curtain, and Bopa Lloyd, her face very red, leaned her body far out of it with her hands on the sill. 'Stay where you are,' she shouted, waving her arm, and then, clapping her hand to her teeth, she disappeared suddenly like a sloped nail driven out of sight into a piece of wood with one blow. And then we saw a big heap of bedclothes like a large white cauliflower bulging out through the open window, with smoke oozing upwards in thin grey hairs from it as Bopa Lloyd pushed it out; and almost as soon as she had dropped it into the garden she came running out of the kitchen door. She began dragging the smoking bundle of sheets and blankets across the wet garden towards the bath of water. 'The silly flamer,' she kept on saying, 'the silly flamer. Matches with blue heads again. Every time he sees those flaming things he does something dull.' She piled the smoking bedclothes into the bath and at that Em began to cry.

'What are you grizzling at?' she asked, turning her red face towards him as she stooped.

'My fish,' he answered, pulling a little Union Jack out of his pocket. 'You'll kill it, our Mam; it's in the bath.'

'Fish myn ufferni,' she cried. 'Your father sets the feather bed on fire and you grunt about your fish. Get out of the road or I'll brain you.'

She stirred the bedclothes and spat on the garden. Em and I moved away and climbed over the wet bedstead. As we went slowly up the tip, Em wiping his eyes with his flag, we could see her standing in the garden striking a boxful of matches one by one, while Ewa Shad's two big staring eyes watched her without moving over the blue blouse in the bedroom window.

We wandered about on the flat top of the tips for a long time, afraid of Bopa Lloyd. Em showed me the hole where Ewa Shad had been scratching for coal. At last we came in sight of the old air shaft in the distance, and Em said, 'Let's go right up to it.' The shaft was a pale yellow tower shaped like a lighthouse standing far up on the lonely side of the mountain. To get at it we had to go through a lot of brambles and tall bracken with snakes in it, but we didn't get very wet because we kept to the path. There had been a lean rainbow, but as we went towards the tower the sun blazed again, and the tips steamed like a train in a cutting. The shaft was very tall and built out of some cracking yellowish brick like shortbread. Some of the bricks were missing here and there, and right down near the ground we found a good-sized hole in the side. Em put his notchy head in and said, '*Brain*, look down there.' I lay down beside him on the steaming stones and looked into the dim hole. Every small sound resounded there, it was like putting your head into the hollow between the two skins of a drum. The shaft inside was huge, like a vast empty hall, like some shabby ruin with the floor gone through, very cold and bleak, the walls disappearing below us into the blackness, making you feel giddy and sick. And the spiders hung their webs there, round like a gramophone record or strong and dusty as sacking. Then, Em picked up a piece of brick and pitched it into the darkness. It plunged down out of sight like a diving bird and we could hear it striking the sides of the shaft from time to time with a note like the loud pong of a pitchfork and a stone howling over the ice. Then when we had waited and waited, staring down with our heads hanging over the cold blackness, we heard a terrible splash and roar like a train in a tunnel as the stone at last exploded on the water at the bottom of the shaft. The hollow pit broke out at once into an uproar, it was filled with a storm of echoes and the splashing noises of the water, and when at last all the sounds had died away the darkness was as still and silent as before. I felt sick and frightened, and we ran away together, a long loose patch across the behind of Em's trousers flapping like a letterbox in the breeze.

At last we climbed the warm bedstead and Em made straight for the bath to look for his fish. 'Go and ask Mam for a jam jar,' he said to me, 'she'll give it to you.' I went up to the kitchen door and opened it. It was dim inside at first, but I could see Ewa Shad sitting on the bottom step of the stairs that curved down into the kitchen. He had his shirt and trousers on, but although he was wearing his cap he had no boots on his stockinged feet. And his waistcoat was open, the front of it like a looking glass with grease. He was catching hold of the long, curved knife, the carving knife Bopa Lloyd had cut our cake with, and he was sticking the point of it as hard as he could into the side of his neck. He was using both his hands to push the knife in, and it was going through the skin just below his ear. When I saw him cutting himself like that I went cold between my legs. Every time he stabbed he jerked his head sideways to meet the knife blade, keeping his head stiff, so that the baggy wen on the other side gave a little shiver each time the point of the knife went out of sight into the side of his neck. There was blood all round his chin and his throat and down the front of his shirt, red and thick like jam. When I had watched him give two or three slow, hard stabs like this, showing his teeth out of the froth round his lips, he stopped and stared at me with his swollen white eyes. Then he pulled up the leg of his trousers and started to scratch the back of his calf as hard as he could. His scratching seemed to go on a long time and then, just as he was about to start using the knife again, Em screamed behind me and Bopa Lloyd came down the stairs, her nostril holes like thimbles as I looked up into them. When she saw what was happening, she pushed past Ewa Shad, snatched the knife from his hand and threw it on the fire. His eyes were like big, white milk-bubbles staring up at her, and the lining was showing at the back of his cap. Gradually he slipped sideways on his step as though he was going to fall to the ground. Then with a shout Bopa Lloyd pushed Em and me out into the yard, turning the lock behind us. Em stood crying by the kitchen door, rattling the clothes peg latch, and sometimes going to the window to look in over the cardboard mending the bottom panes. In a few minutes Bopa Lloyd unlocked the door and peeped out, and I had a whiff of the handle of the knife smouldering in the grate. Her red face glowed, it was the colour of a low fire, and the grey feathers of her hair were nearly all out of her combs. 'Go home now, there's a good boy,' she said to me, 'and tell your mother, thank you for the parcel and will she come up as soon as she can.'

'What's the matter with our Dad?' asked Em, making a face and crying all over his mouth.

'He's better now,' she answered. 'Go and play with your fish, there's a good boy.'

As I went home down the road I could see the bloodshot mark like a little smudge of red ink on Em's eye, and I thought again how lucky he was to have that. I told my mother how Bopa Lloyd's chicken had fallen into the bath, and how Ewa Shad had stuck a knife in his neck and made it bleed. And every time I went into the pantry in the dark or when I closed my eyes I could see the inside of the air shaft with the big drop below me, and that made me feel sick and giddy. As my mother was dressing to go up to Ewa Shad's, she said, 'The fool couldn't even cut his throat tidy.'

SHACKI THOMAS

Gwyn Jones

Shacki Thomas was fifty-two, shortish, and bandy from working underground. Unemployment was straitening his means but could do nothing with his legs. But play the white man, he would say – though I'm bandy, I'm straight. It was his one witticism, and he was not using it so frequently now that his missis was in hospital.

He was going to see her this afternoon. He gave a two-handed pluck at his white silk muffler, a tug at the broken nose of his tweed cap, and so went out the back way to the street slanting sharply from High Street to the river. The houses were part soft stone, part yellow brick, and grimy; the roadway between them was decorated with dogs and children and three new-painted lamp posts, and each parlour window showed a china flowerpot nesting an aspidistra or rock fern. He passed his own window, and saw that the fern was doing famous, though he'd forgotten to water it since Gwenny – oh, Gwenny, Gwenny, he was saying, if only you was home in our house again!

Twenty yards in front he saw Jinkins the Oil and hurried to catch him up. Owbe, they said.

''Orse gets more human every day,' said Jinkins from the cart, and to forget his troubles Shacki made a long speech, addressing the horse's hindquarters:

'Some horses is marvellous. Pony I used to know underground, see – you never seen nothing like that pony at

145

the end of a shift. Used to rip down the road, mun, if there'd a-been anything in the way he'd a-hit his brains out ten times, over. Intelligent, Mr Jinkins? You never seen nothing like him!'

As they approached the railway bridge, the two-ten to Cwmcawl went whitely over. The horse raised his head.

'Now, now, you old fool,' cried Jinkins. 'It's under you got to go, not over.' He turned to Shacki and apologised for the dumb creature. ''Orse do get more human every day, see.'

But Shacki couldn't laugh. It was Gwenny, Gwenny, if only you was home with me, my gel; and fear was gnawing him, worm-like.

Turning away beyond the bridge into High Street, he found the old sweats around the cenotaph. For a minute or two he would take his place in the congregation. A lady angel spread her wings over them, but her eyes were fixed on the door of the Griffin opposite. GWELL ANGAU NA CHYWILYDD said the inscription. 'Better death than dishonour'; and as Shacki arrived, the conversation was of death. 'I once hear tell,' said Ianto Evans, 'about a farmer in the vale who quarrelled summut shocking with his daughter after his old woman died. Well, p'raps she gave him arsenic – I donno nothing 'bout that – but he went off at last, and they stuck him in the deep hole and went back to hear the will. Lawyer chap, all chops and whiskers like a balled tomcat, he reads it out, and everything in the safe goes to Mary Anne and the other stuff to his sister. So they has a look at the safe, and what's inside it? Sweet Fanny Adams, boys, that's what.' By pointing a finger at him, Ianto brought Shacki into his audience. '"And what'll you do with the safe, my pretty?" asks the sister – like sugar on lemon, so I hear. Mary Anne thinks a bit and then brings it out very slow. "If it wasn't for my poor old mam as is in Heaven," she says, "I'd stick it up over the old tike for a tombstone."' He scratched his big nose. 'What's think of that, uh?'

His brother Ivor picked his teeth. 'Funny things do happen

at funerals. I once heard tell about a chap as travelled from Wrexham to the Rhondda to spit into another chap's grave.'

'Might a-brought the flowers up,' said Ianto.

'No, not this chap's spit wouldn't.'

'I mean, there's spit and spit,' said Tommy Sayce. 'I mean, f'rinstance—.' A moist starfish splashed on the dust, and he changed the subject. 'How's the missis, Shacki?'

Shacki looked from Ivor to the lady angel, but she was intent on the Griffin. 'Thass what I going to see, chaps. Fine I do hope, ay.'

They all hoped so, and confessed as much. But they were all fools, and the worm-like fear was at Shacki's heart like a maggot in a swede. 'I got to go this afternoon, see,' he said; hoping for a chorus of reassurance and brave words, but – 'I remember' – Tommy Sayce took up the tale – 'when little Sammy Jones had his leg took off at the hip. "How do a chap with only one peg on him get about, doctor?" he asks old Dr Combes. "Why, mun," doctor tells him, "we'll get you a nice wooden leg, Sammy." "Ay, but will I be safe with him, doctor?" asks Sammy. "Safe? Good God, mun, you'll be timber right to the face!" Thass what doctor told him.'

'Ah, they'm marvellous places, them hospitals,' Shacki assured them, to assure himself at the same time. 'Look at the good they do do.'

'Ay, and look at the good they don't do! Didn't they let Johnny James' mam out 'cos she had cancer and they was too dull to cure it? And Johnny, thinking she was better – the devils!'

The worm went ahead with his tunnelling. 'I carn stop, anyway,' said Shacki, and low-spiritedly he left them to their talk. Not fifty yards away he cursed them bitterly. Death, death, death, cancer, cancer, cancer – by God, he'd like to see that big-nosed bastard Ianto Evans on his back there, and that brother of his, and Tommy Sayce, and every other knackerpant as hadn't more feeling than a tram of rippings. From the bend of the street he looked back and saw the lady angel's head and benedictory right arm and cursed her too, the scut of hell, the flat-faced sow she was! Nobody have pain, or everybody – that was the thing. He cleared his throat savagely and spat into the gutter as though between the eyes of the world. Self-pity for his loneliness brought too big a lump to his throat before he could curse again, and then once more it was all Gwenny fach, oh, Gwenny fach; he'd like to tear the sky in pieces to get her home again. If only she was better, if only she was home, he'd do the washing, he'd blacklead the grate, he'd scrub through every day, he'd water that fern the minute he got back – he was shaking his head in disgust. Ay, he was a fine one, he was.

Then he went into the greengrocer's, where the air smelled so much a pound.

'Nice bunch of chrysanths,' he was offered, but they were white and he rejected them. 'I ain't enamelled of them white ones. Something with a bit of colour, look.'

He bought a bunch of flowers and three fresh eggs for a shilling and fivepence, and carried them as carefully as one-tenth his dole deserved to the Red Lion bus stop. Soon the bus came, chocolate and white, with chromium fittings. He found the conductor struggling with a small table brought on by a hill farm-woman at the Deri. 'Watch my eggs, butty,' he begged, and stood on the step till at last they fixed it in the gangway, where it lay on its back with its legs up in the air like a live thing gone dead. Through the back window Shacki saw a youngster running after the bus. 'Oi, mate—'

'Behind time,' said the conductor hotly. 'This here blasted table—' He came for his fare and to mutter to Shacki. 'I never had this woman on board yet when she hadn't a table or a hantimacassar or a chest in drawers or a frail of pickled onions or summut. Moving by instalments I reckon she is or doing a moonlight flit. Iss a 'ell of a life this!'

As the bus went on up the valley, Shacki made a gloomy

attempt to put in proper order what he had to tell Gwenny. The house was going on fine, he himself was feeling in the pink, there was a new baby at number five, he'd watered the fern – and he must tell her summut cheerful. Like what Jinkins said to the horse and this here conductor chap – proper devil-may-care this conductor, you could see that with half an eye. Near Pensarn he saw lime on the bulging fields, like salt on a fat woman's lap. The grass under it looked the colour of a sick dog's nose. He saw farming as a thin-lined circle. If you hadn't the grass, you couldn't feed the beasts; if you couldn't feed the beasts, you didn't get manure; if you didn't get manure, you had to buy fertiliser – which brought you back to grass. All flesh is grass, he heard the preacher say, and all the goodliness thereof is as the flower of the field. The grass withereth, the flower fadeth – Duw Duw, what a thought! It made a fellow think, indeed now it did. Yesterday a kid, today a man of fifty, tomorrow they're buying you eight pound ten's worth of elm with brass handles. Oh, death, death, death, and in life pain and trouble – away, away, the wall of his belly trembled with the trembling of the bus, and the worm drove a roadway through his heart.

At Pensarn a girl stood at the bus stop and said: 'Did a young man leave a message for me at the Red Lion?'

'Yes, my dear,' said the conductor. 'He told me special you was to let me give you a nice kiss.'

'Cheeky flamer!' said the hill farm-woman, but the girl looked down in the mouth, and Shacki felt sorry for her. He explained that a young man had run after the bus at the Red Lion. Ay, he did rather fancy he was a fairish sort of chap 'bout as big as the conductor, so— 'It must a-been Harry,' the girl concluded. 'Thank you,' said Shacki, as though she had done him a favour. Indeed, she had, for he could talk about this to Gwenny.

Later a collier got on. 'Where you been then?' the conductor asked. 'Why you so dirty, mun?'

'I been picking you a bag of nuts.' He took the conductor's

measurements, aggressively. 'Monkey nuts,' he added. He did not enter the bus and sit down, but stood on the step for his twopenny ride. 'We got to draw the line somewhere,' the conductor pointed out.

Shacki was cheered by the undoubted circumstance that all the wit of the Goytre Valley was being poured out for his and Gwenny's benefit. What Jinkins said about the horse now. And this about the nuts— And that gel at Pensarn! What funny chaps there was about if you only came to think of it. He began to think hard, hoping for a witticism of his own, a personal offering for Gwenny. She had heard the bandy-straight one before, just once or twice or fifty times or a hundred, or maybe oftener than that. Something new was wanted. A fellow like this conductor, of course, he could turn them off like lightning. Here he was, looking at the flowers. Shacki waited for his sally. They were his flowers, weren't they? Diawl, anything said about um was as good as his, too.

'I likes a nice lily, myself,' said the conductor.

'You look more you'd like a nice pansy,' said the collier. He grinned, the slaver glistening on his red gums, and winked at the hill farm-woman. 'Cheeky flamer!' she called him.

'You askin' for a fight? 'Cos if you are—'

'Sorry, can't stop now.' Still grinning, he narrowed his coaly eyes. 'But any time you want me, butty, I'm Jack Powell, Mutton Tump. That's me – Jack Powell.' He prepared to drop off, and the conductor kept his finger on the bell, hoping to fetch him a cropper. 'Oh no, you don't, butty!' They heard his nailed boots braking on the road and then through the back window saw him fall away behind them, his knees jerking very fast. 'I'll be up here Sunday,' threatened the conductor, but Shacki didn't believe him. He'd lay two-to-one Jack Powell any day, and was glad a collier could lick a bus conductor.

'Don't forget to stop at the hospital,' he said by way of

reminder, and the conductor, as though to recover face, told a tale about the patient who wouldn't take a black draught unless the sister took one too. To please him, Shacki smiled grimly and wagged his head and said what chaps there was about, but he now thought less highly of the humorist, and as they came nearer the stopping place he could feel that same old disturbance, just as though he wanted to go out the back. Bump, bump, bump, the driver must be doing it deliberate, but try to forget, for he might be going to hear good news. She might even be coming home. He grovelled. Home, like Johnny James' mother, hopeless case, cancer of the womb – not that for you, Gwenny fach, he prayed, and Ianto Evans, for speaking of it, he thrust into the devil's baking oven. Bump, bump, bump, if he didn't get off this bus soon he'd be all turned up, only too sure. He felt rotten in the belly, and the worm turned a new heading in his heart.

He alighted.

Inside the hall, he found from the clock that as usual he was five minutes too early for the women's ward. 'Would you like to see anyone in the men's ward?' He thought he would, if only to pass the time. So down the corridor he went, for it was a tiny hospital, run on the pennies of colliers like himself. The men's ward had a wireless set, and the patients were a lively lot. Bill Williams the Cwm borrowed Shacki's flowers. 'Oi, Nurse,' he shouted, ''ow'll I look with a bunch of these on my chest?'

It was the sporty probationer. 'Like a big fat pig with a apple in his mouth,' she suggested.

'There's a fine bloody thing to say, Nurse! Don't I look better'n a pig, boys?'

'Ay,' said Shacki, thinking of the flowers of the field. 'You looks like a lily in the mouth of 'ell.'

Bill started to laugh, and the other men started to laugh, and, seeing this, Shacki became quite convulsed at his second witticism. The blue small coal pitting his face grew less noticeable as his scars grew redder. It was a laugh to do a man's heart good, and it came down on that tunnelling worm like a hob-nailed boot. 'You'll have matron along,' the probationer warned them.

Then Shacki took his flowers from Bill, and grinning all over his face went back through the corridor to the entrance hall. He'd make his lovely gel laugh an' all! He felt fine now, he did, and everything was going to be all right. He knew it. Tell her he'd cleaned the house, and about the baby at number five, and about Jinkins and the collier and the girl and the conductor and Bill Williams the Cwm and him – it'd be better than a circus for Gwenny.

Into the women's ward. Nod here, nod there, straight across to Gwenny with all the news between his teeth and his tongue. Then he swore under his breath. Matron was standing by Gwenny's bed, looking like a change of pillowcases. She was so clean and stiff and starched and grand that he felt small and mean and shabby before her, and frightened, and something of a fool. Respectfully, he greeted her even before he greeted his wife, and when she returned his good day, thanked her.

'We've got good news for you, Mr Thomas. You'll be able to have Mrs Thomas home very soon now.'

'Oh' he said. He was looking down at Gwenny's white smile.

A murderous hate and rage against all living things filled his heart, and he would have had no one free of suffering. ''Cos she's better?'

'Of course. Why else?'

He put the eggs down carefully, and the flowers. Then he fell on his knees at the bedside. 'My gel!' he cried out hoarsely. 'Oh, my lovely gel!' With her right hand she touched his hair. 'There, there little Shacki bach! Don't take on, look!'

'You are upsetting the patient,' the pillowcase said severely, 'and you are disturbing the ward. I shall have to ask you to go outside.'

It was a quarter of a minute before he got to his feet, and then he was ashamed to look anyone in the face. He snuffled a bit and rubbed under his eyes. 'All right, matron,' he managed to say. 'You can send for the pleece, if you like. I'm that happy, mun!'

He saw his old Gwenny looking an absolute picture there in bed, and thought these would be her last tears, and such happy ones. And with the thought he looked proudly around, and could tell that no one in the ward thought him an old softy. He didn't hate anyone any longer. He was all love, and gave old Gwenny a kiss as bold as brass before he walked outside. He knew they'd let him in again soon.

THE LOST LAND

Geraint Goodwin

She stood there, hands on hips, the red-rimmed eyes hard in
malice. Then she stroked a hand backwards across a brow
wet with heat, and shook up her tousled head in defiance.

'You poor...' she began, twisting her mouth.

'Leave be – there's a girl.'

Her husband, frail as a willow, turned up his wide eyes,
edged with sorrow, in a mute appeal for peace. He was a
little man, thin and haggard, dark, uncut hair making a
frame around a face lean and pale, with on it that
incommunicable sense of the mountain-bred – a Welshman
from up the valley who, in the brief flowering of youth, had
ventured out like a chill half-fledged bird. He had got as far
as this little flannel town which lay like a smudge across the
still, narrow Severn Valley, and there he had stayed. He bent
over his littered breakfast as though communing with it,
saying no word.

She stood there, her breasts out, a stub red hand raised to
the door, a woman in her early twenties, overwhelming, by
her very presence, the little man before her. The face was flat
and coarsened, a hard, bitter sheen transfiguring the ribald
lust that rose like a cloud from her.

'Get out!' she screamed.

She reached up for his cap and flung it at him.

'...an' stay out!'

'Have a heart,' he begged.

'Let me ketch sight o' you – that's all!'

She nodded in her viciousness.

'That's all! Dunna you dare set fut in this house afore the *Mail*'s out. An' if you canna set your hand to summat all the day long – Fair Day, an' all – then you'm past all hope an' prayin' for.'

She worked off her fury and bent down over the cluttered table, jerking the things off with a sullen anger.

He stood there forlornly on the step, peering into his home. The sight of him provoked her to a fresh outburst.

'An' our Mam's had about enough,' she nodded in a threat.

He bowed his head, letting it all go over him.

She swept her hand to the few sticks of furniture the bums had left.

'Inna it a nice come down!'

She stood and watched him in a red glare of contempt.

'Inna as good as you? As though I canna do better for myself, *an*' without the askin'.'

'Sally!' he implored, his hands out, his mouth dropped open.

'Sally theeself!' she shouted back at him. 'An' dunna say I anna told you – that's all!'

He wandered out into the foulness of the 'court' with the vague threat tumbling in him. He never dare let it get hold, kept fending it off like some awful dream that lay beyond the mind. And he dared not think. Things were going from bad to worse. They would go on and on until... he did not know – he did not want to know.

He put a hand up to his head wearily. The hard white light hurt his eyes after the squalid half-light of the room. He reached up his head like a setter and took in a long breath, freeing his lungs.

'Damn me! Watch theeself!'

He reached back to the kerb and gave the other man the right of way, a big man with a florid, blue-red face and a nose like a snout.

'Why! Ishmael! Me auld cock robin!'

It was his brother-in-law from up in the country, in for the Fair. He had his bowler hat set at a tilt, and a crop stuck out arrogantly from under his arm. A big Border farmer, he had gone farther west for his wife – Ishmael's youngest sister, with her mild, blue, uncomprehending eyes that looked out on life with a child's stare of innocence. Ishmael, who was nearest her of all, had been hurt at this match: hurt and bewildered as at some sort of outrage, something that had happened that had no right to happen, and he did not want to think about it.

'Goin' to have one?' the big man asked with the grudging, dry familiarity of the family, giving his crop a jerk towards the inn door.

'Just one, like.'

'Aye! Thee and thee one!'

They took their places on the settle, and Ishmael dipped his thin blue nose into the pint mug.

'Nemma God – thee't half clemmed by the look o' thee!'

Ishmael passed a hand over his chin and swept it over his gaunt cheekbones. Then he brought it backwards across his nose with a sniff.

'An' I dunna suppose her'll change her ways for thy askin'.'

Ishmael winced as under a blow.

'Ways...?' he got out.

'Aye – ways I said. An' I seen summat of her, as well as thee. Oh no – young blood dunna lie quiet, never did, never will.'

The big man sat there, hands on knees, nodding dumbly on his chest, his heavy flesh face set in judgment.

'Thee't a lot to learn – so help me God thee hast,' he went on with contempt. Ishmael raised his head and tried to bring his eyes down on the loud cloth before him.

'One of the best,' he got out fiercely.

'Well, aye! O'course! An' who said her inna?'

The big man pulled at the red wen of nose wryly as Ishmael shouted: 'Out with it!'

The little man's head had gone up, a wild frightened glint in his eye. The black hair dropped like a lank wet hand across his moist brow. Then he slid back in a heap, huddled and disconsolate. He put his hands up to his head, clawing at it hopelessly, and then ran them back through his hair.

'Ah – shut thee eye, man! I canna as much as pass the time o' day without thee't halfway down me throat…'

He looked at the little man before him, the thin white hands for ever working, the lean pallor of his face and the tremble of the mouth – looked at him from out of his own world with a dull-edged contempt.

'Thee and thee poetry an' all that fal-da-la. An' a lot o' good it's done thee. There's summat else in life beside poetry, me boy – as thee't find out soon enough.'

He got up to go at last.

'You anna any message for 'em up there?'

He jerked his crop towards the window and the mountains.

Ishmael shook his head wearily. 'No – nothing to say!'

The little man's lips shut in a line, struck mute: he raised his eyes towards the half-open window and shook his head in a hopeless shake.

'Well… s'long.'

The big man reached out his hand with brief familiarity.

'Some day thee't see sense… I shouldna wonder.'

He pulled his nose again, looking down contemptuously at the unkempt, haggard little figure before him. Then he took a final gulp at his glass, as though to destroy any uneasy thought, and heaved his way towards the door.

'I'll tell them I've seen thee.'

'Aye – do.'

The two men looked at one another in farewell, and Ishmael dropped his eyes to the floor again.

'And not to worry,' he called out, as a final word, shuffling his feet over the flags.

He stayed there, toying with his pint, tipping it up meditatively as though plumbing the depths. Once or twice he sighed heavily and then shook himself, as though trying to wake out of a reverie. He was half drunk and he did not know why. He did not know how he had become drunk, and he did not care. And then a sense of terror like a cold douche would go down his back.

He was out in the streets again, moving along with a furtive, aimless shuffle. He went on, letting the Fair crowd buffet him, making his way to the Labour Exchange to draw his money. It was down in the High Street, and he went on in a daze, now on the street, now on the kerb, his head raised to the far-distant fringe of mountains round his home, his mouth working, and a thin dribble trickling down over his blue-chapped chin.

The loafers and mouchers stood around, chewing plug and spitting. At sight of him they put their heads together and fell into a smirk.

'Serve him right!'

'Poor chap.'

'Ach – he canna see for looking.'

At the Smithfield he wandered about from pen to pen. He went peering over at the beasts, the heavy Herefords and Cross Breds with their coats agleam, and then the Kerry Hill sheep, and then, over at the far end, the little nimble mountain sheep from near his home. He stood there, with the reek of the fleeces coming to him, and began to think of his boyhood up in the mountains. It was all gone and he would never go back. He did not know how it was, but he would never go back. Something had gone out of him since, but it still hung about – this sense of his own home and the sour-green, cropped mountain and the stone-clumped farm, and the windblown pines twisted across it, and the whine of the old wind and the dogs barking.

He ought not to have come down into the town but he came and there he met his wife, and since then everything had gone wrong, and would go on going wrong, and he could not help it. And he did not know how it was at all.

'Aye,' he said, giving his head a wag reassuringly. 'One of the best!'

If they could only understand her, make a place for her. Then there would not have been the one way – or the other way. He could have gone back from the town to his home and if he did not go back the home would always be there. He would not have gone down and down like a man in a whirlpool, with the sullen insistent drag on him – unable to lift a hand to save himself.

He could see them all now – that Sunday night when he went home to tell them – sitting round the old hearth, the white, mute lips set hard in a line, and the dropping silence, more awful than speech. And then the old grandmother, stuck upright like a stick, shawl around her, and her dried gums working.

'Ach-y-fi,' she said in disgust, and the old head began to tremble.

But it was too late: it was too late – and there was no way back. The sense of his wife, the slow, heavy animal sense of her, possessed him. He had lost his home and the sight of his home, like a light in the sky that was and is gone in the darkness, groping and bewildered; there was no other sound or sense in all the world but the slow-blooded, lusty strength of her, bound up within her body.

He went into the marquee and dragged a chair across the yellow, trodden grass, and began to drink. The whisky went down into his stomach in a scorch, and then the cloud rose up to his head, taking the edge off him. He could still hear the high tremulous baaing of the sheep: the sound, the smell of them, was the old life made real again. Then he bowed his head on his hands. Once he staggered up and went to the tent flap and looked up the valley to his home and the lighted, flying white-ash face of the sky over the mountains.

He took his place again, only getting up to push his glass over the counter and reach for it with a swing.

He went on drinking, fumbling in his pocket for the Labour Exchange money, his shoulders hunched up about him and his eyes set staring on the ground.

Now he could no longer remember how it had all happened – it was like the sky fading and the old remembered things dropping down into the darkness. But it had to be – he knew that it had to be. And he did not care. He had gone down and down and down, and he did not care. And he would go all the way to hell itself if he was within the reach of her.

'Aye,' he said again in his drunken haze, 'one of the best.'

Their life together passed up before him like a picture blurred and run – the life in the 'court', in the squalid little house, the smell of it, the rising stench, the table in a litter and the faggots and the chips, and the bin forever full with tins, and her curling irons all about, and the blue print dress with the smell of cheap scent on it.

They had gone down and down, and all his little capital – his share of the farm – had dwindled and gone, and the little shop with its window of dead flies and its row of sweet bottles went down with him until it was shuttered up for good and the last bit of stock sold off.

If he had been a man they could have made things go, could have moved off to a better part of the town and she would have been able to go to the Emporium and order what she liked. And she could have taken her place with them all, for she had a way with her.

He saw her first – that Fair Day, how long ago? – going in a clatter through the Market Hall, her shawl about her. There were five or six of them, come with a whiff of grease from the mills, and 'minching' damsons from the old women's baskets and shooting back the stones; then the policeman came and they picked up their skirts and made a run for it, laughing and screaming up the benches.

'A bad 'un,' said the old Sergeant, wagging his head.

And then he saw her again at the Workers' Union dance. It was his first winter in the town and he was learning to dance. And he was learning to drink. The few port and lemons had gone to his head and he stood there on the fringe of the floor, preened up like a young bird, in his navy blue best and wagging his head across his butterfly. Then he saw her, with the same insolent tilt of the head, the ripe full breasts and a solemn swagger in the heavy hips, her snub nose turned up, mocking.

She stared him back straight and insolent and he moved to go across.

'Leave it alone.' His friend had caught him by the sleeve.

But he went across.

That was the beginning of it – he could remember that first night, for it stood out clear with the edge to it – but he could not remember the rest. And he did not want to remember.

Now he had gone past memory. Only in the dark, edgeless nightmare, when past and present ran to meet – this dream without beginning and without end – he knew that somewhere she was, and where she was he had to be.

He got up in a stagger and lurched out of the tent. The pens were emptying and the mouchers had descended, like a flock of drear, half-plucked crows – the ne'er-do-wells who had come to pick up what they could. They went running and jumping over the hurdles, like boys let loose from school. All her family were mouchers, the worst mouchers in the town, but he did not care.

'Ach-y-fi' his old grandmother had said, with her head atremble and her old white hands held hard on the chair rails.

It was dusk and what light there was lay like a wiped smudge at the valley's end. The old mountains up there, lying up against the sky, were always the last to go: the sun went down behind them, leaving that pale gleam of light in darkness around them.

He saw them as they always were, the lost land that was and would for ever be.

On he went into the little town, all tumbled and desolate with its close, smoke-ridden streets, the 'taverns', and the wet, steaming fish shops, and the rancid, grease-laden gusts: the gasworks and the reach of clinkers: the sullen humid life of it. It was his home now, and he did not complain. He had become a part of it and there was no way out – never and never and never.

'Never: no – never!' he said, shaking his fist up to the sky. Then he broke out into blasphemies, his head up in a gibber. As the fit left him he began to sob, his body shaking, and the hot, scalding tears going down in drops to the ground.

'Surrey! What's up?' Somebody caught him by the arm and reached him straight.

'Why! Ishmael!'

Ishmael looked at the man, unseeing, and swept his arms about.

'Ishmael! Nemma God! Thee't squit.'

'One of the best,' said Ishmael, rocking, his teeth come to, his wild eyes wandering in a hopeless search.

'Aye, aye,' said the other reassuringly. 'Hup! Watch theeself!' He straightened him again and saved him from falling. 'An' thee't not half had a skinful.'

He was one of the little toadies of the town, and Fair Day was a day of days. He led him down a back street to a tavern, and they went round through the yard into the parlour.

'Pink gin,' whispered the little man, letting his charge fall into a chair. 'An' dunna put on the light.' He gave Ishmael a nudge. 'Got summat to show?'

Ishmael fumbled in his fob and dropped a handful of coins on to the table.

'Money!' he said, with a toss of his hand, scattering it, and then he raised his eyes, bleary and wandering. 'And I said to my soul – this night eat, drink, and be merry…'

'Shut thee eye!' broke in the other, cutting him short. 'An' a double brandy for me, like.' He gave the barmaid a meaning wink.

'In't he bad?' the girl said, dabbing her big red hands in her apron.

'Go thee on,' he exhorted. 'Thee leave him to me.'

Ishmael took his drink without looking at it. The little man leaned across and loosened his collar for him.

'And I said to my soul…' Ishmael began again, his voice going up in ecstasy.

'Now! Now! No preachin'. Thee't have us out in a minnit.'

Ishmael looked towards him, unseeing.

'I *got* a soul,' he shouted, waving his fist in a wild despair, his dry mouth clamped sourly to.

'Aye, aye. O' course!'

Ishmael's head dropped down on his chest and he began to mutter incoherently.

'What's say? Better get thee home?'

'The *Mail*… gone?'

'*Mail* be damned! Why, it anna left Aber yet.'

Ishmael shook him free and lolloped back into his seat, but the other, hoisting him out of the chair, slipped an arm round him and led him to the door.

'One of the best.'

Ishmael smashed a fist down until the little beer-soaked table before him rocked. 'Shut thee eye! Nemma God – an' we'm be run in in a minnit.'

At the end of the court the little moucher let go of his arm.

'Thee't all right now?'

Ishmael waved him away and lurched up towards his home. He could not open the door and he began to fumble about with the latch.

'You!'

His wife stood on the step. She stood across the doorway barring his way, a red cotton dressing gown pulled across her breasts, her hair down.

'Hey!' she shouted playfully. 'Who you pushin'?'

'Let me in – there's a girl,' he begged.

He put his hands up to his head.

'That bad!'

'Bad! You an' your bad!'

She began to laugh again in a silly high-pitched way, and Ishmael tried to bring his eyes to see her, to search her out in the haze, but he only saw a red, tousled head reach and heave before him.

He lurched into the passage way and fell against the cane stand.

'Hi!' he began to mumble drunkenly. 'What in the name o' God... is this?'

'What?'

Her head jerked round as though on a swivel, her blown, watered eyes harsh and knowing.

'This!'

He clawed up at the little bamboo hat stand and got his fingers on the rim of a bowler hat, and then fell back in a stagger, taking it with him.

'Oh – say so!'

She loosened his fingers off the rim and stuck it jauntily on his head. It came down over his ears and tipped over on his eyes. He shook his head and it rattled down his ears. She began to laugh in the same high-pitched, nervous way.

'There now! An' it dunna fit.'

She stood back and surveyed it dolefully.

Ishmael opened a bleary eye, un-understanding.

'Whose... whose is it?' he got out.

'Whose – well, thine o' course! An' dunna say I never give thee any thin'. I inna in the Rummage but five minnits an'...'

'Well – I never.'

Ishmael's bloodshot eyes drew taut in focus, then his face widened in a beam. He lolloped over and tried to kiss her, his arms clutching involuntarily around her warm, wide waist.

'Saucy thing!' she minced, giving him a playful slap.

And then, getting hold of the banisters, he began to mount the stairs, flushed with a new hope.

'Ladies first,' she giggled, pushing by him in a flurry.

Ishmael put a foot in the air like a horse pawing, and fell down the bottom steps.

'Oh, damn,' he said despairingly, 'too far.'

She began to giggle again, in the same silly, uncertain way, looking at the desolate heap before her. At last she got him into the little front room, his feet working, like a stepping marionette, before him. He dropped down on the little couch, and she slipped a cushion under his head.

'Stay a bit,' he pleaded, his face wide with bliss.

He made to catch at her skirt, unable to let go of her.

'Ssh!'

She put her fingers to her mouth as though chiding a fractious child.

'One of *the* best,' he said, wagging his head drowsily.

Then his mouth fell open in a snore.

It was only then, with one quick glance around her, that she hurried up the stairs.

WAT PANTATHRO

Glyn Jones

I got the crockery and the bloater out of the cupboard for my father before going to bed. He would often cook a fish when he came in at night, using the kitchen poker to balance it on because we didn't have a gridiron. Then I lit my candle in the tin stick, and when I had blown out the oil lamp I went upstairs to bed. My father was a horse trainer, and on the handrail at the top of the stairs he kept three riding saddles, one of them very old, with leather handles in front curved upwards like the horns of a cow. We slept in the same bedroom, which was low and large, containing a big bed made of black iron tubes with brass knobs on the corner posts. Behind our thin plank door we had a cow's-horn coat hook on which hung a trainer's bridle, one with a massive bit and a heavy cluster of metal fingers like a bunch of keys, to daunt the young horses. There were no pictures or ornaments in our bedroom, only a green glass walking stick over the fireplace and my father's gun licence pinned into the bladdery wallpaper. When I had undressed I said my prayers against the patchwork quilt which my mother had finished the winter she died. Then I climbed up into the high bed and blew the candle out.

But I couldn't sleep at first, thinking of my father taking me down to the autumn horse fair the next day. I lay awake in the rough blankets hearing the squeak of a nightbird, and Flower uneasy in her stall, and the hollow dribble of the dry plaster trickling down behind the wallpaper on to the wooden floor of the bedroom. I dozed, and when I awoke in the pitch darkness I could see narrow slits of light like scattered straws shining up through the floorboards from the oil lamp in the kitchen beneath me, and by that I knew my father was home. And soon I was glad to see the light go out and to hear him groping his way up the bare stairs, muttering his prayers to himself and at last lifting the latch of our bedroom door. I didn't want him to think he had wakened me because that would worry him, so I pretended to be asleep. He came in softly, lit the candle at the bedside and then finished the undressing and praying he had started on his way upstairs.

My father was very tall and slender, his hard, bony body was straight and pole-like. At home he always wore a long check riding jacket, fawn breeches and buttoned corduroy gaiters. He had an upright rubber collar which he used to wash with his red pocket handkerchief under the pump, but because he had not been to town there was no necktie round it. His face was long and bony, dull red or rather purplish all over, the same colour as the underside of your tongue, and covered with a mass of tiny little wormy veins. He had thick grey hair and rich brown eyebrows that were curved upwards and as bushy as a pair of silkworms. And when he pushed back his brick-coloured lips, baring his gums to get rid of the bits of food, his long brown teeth with the wide spaces between them showed in his mouth like a row of flat and upright bars.

He stood beside the bed for a moment wiping the greasy marks off his face with his scarlet handkerchief. He did this because when he balanced his fish over the fire it often tumbled off into the flames and became, by the time it was cooked, as black and burnt as a cinder. Then when he had done he blessed me with tobacco-smelling hands and laid down his warm body with care in the bed beside me. I listened, but I knew he had not been drinking because I could not smell him or hear the argument of the beer rolling round in his belly.

The next morning we went down to the fair in the spring body. This was a high black bouncy cart with very tall thin wheels painted a glittering daffodil yellow. It had a seat with a back to it across the middle and a tiger rug for our knees. Flower, my father's beautiful black riding mare, was between the shafts in her new brown harness, her glossy coat shining in the sun with grooming until she looked as though she had been polished all over with hair oil. As I sat high above her in the springy cart, I could see her carrying her small head in its brown bridle a little on one side as she trotted sweetly along. I loved her, she was quiet and pretty, and I could manage her, but I was afraid my father would sell her in the fair and buy a younger horse for training.

The hedges that morning were full of birds and berries. The autumn sun was strong after the rain and the long tree shadows in the fields were so dark that the grass seemed burnt black with fire. The wheels of the light cart gritted loudly on the road and the steel tyre came turning up under my elbow as it rested on the narrow leather mudguard. We sat with the tiger-skin rug over us, my father beside me holding the brown reins loosely and resting the whip across them, his hands yellow with nicotine almost to his wrists. He looked fresh and handsome in the bright morning, wearing his new black riding coat and his best whipcord breeches, and his soft black hat with the little blue jay's feather in it tilted on the side of his head. And round his upright collar he had a thick scarlet scarf-tie smelling of camphor, with small white horseshoes sprinkled all over it.

I said to him, 'We are not going to sell Flower are we, my father?'

'No, little one,' he answered, teasing me, 'not unless we get a bargain, a biter or a kicker, something light in the behind that no one can manage.' And then, with his tusky grin on his face, he asked me to take the reins while he struck a match on the palm of his hand and lit another cigarette.

It was six miles down to town and all the way my father waved his whip to people or drew rein to talk to them. Harri Parcglas, taking his snow-white nanny for a walk on the end of a thirty-foot chain, stopped to ask my father a cure for the warts spreading on the belly of his entire; the vicar under his black sunshade put his hand from which two fingers were missing on Flower's new collar of plaited straw and reminded my father he was due to toll the funeral bell the next day; and Lewsin Penylan the poacher, coming from his shed, brought a ferret whose mouth he had sewn up out of his inside pocket and offered us a rabbit that night if my father would throw him a coin for the shot. It was on the hill outside Lewsin's shed a month or two ago that I had been sheltering from the pelting storm after school when I had seen my father, soaking wet from head to foot, passing on his way home to Pantathro. He was riding a brisk little bay pony up from town, his long legs hanging straight down and nearly touching the road. He had no overcoat on and the heavy summer rain was sheeting over him from the cloudburst and running off his clothes as though from little spouts and gutters on to the streaming road. But although he was drenched to the skin and there wasn't a dry hair on the little brown pony, he was singing a hymn about the blood of Jesus Christ loudly to himself as the rain deluged over him. When he saw me he didn't stop the pony, he only grinned and shouted that it looked devilish like a shower. The boys who were with me laughed and pointed at him and I blushed with shame because they knew he was drunk again.

We came down into the town at a sharp trot and I could see the long narrow street before us crowded with people and animals. There were horses of every size and colour packed there, most of them unharnessed and with tar shining in the sun on their black hoofs, and yellow, red and blue braids plaited into their manes and tails. And there was a lot of noise there too, men shouting and horses neighing and clattering about. The horses were all over the roads of the town and over the pavements as well, standing about in bunches or being led by rope halters up and down the street, or disappearing through the front doors of the public houses behind their masters. I hardly ever came to town and I loved it. From the high position in the cart where we sat, the crowd of bare backs before us seemed packed together as close as cobblestones, so that I thought we should never be able to get through. But my father governed our mare with his clever hands. He kept her going, waving his whip gaily to people he knew, even sometimes urging her into a little trot, easily steering his zigzag way among the mixed crowds of men and horses around us. And as we passed along he had often to shout 'No', with a grin on his face to a dealer who asked him if Flower was for sale or called out naming a price for her. Because our mare was pretty and as black as jet and many people wanted her.

But just when we were taking the sharp turn out of Heol Wen at the White Hart corner, breaking into a trot again, suddenly, without any warning, we came upon Tal y Fedw's big grey mare, a hulking, hairy carthorse standing out at right angles from the pavement, with her thick hind legs well forward into the narrow street. Without hesitating for a moment my father leaned over and took the turn, and the axle-hub struck the big mare a stinger across her massive haunches as we passed, sending her bounding forward and then in a twist up into the air on her hind legs with pain and fright. The Tal y Fedw brothers, two short black little men, ran out at once cursing and swearing into the road to get hold of her head which she had torn loose from them. I was shocked and excited and I clung to the mudguard because the light trap with all the leathers wheezing rocked over on its springs as though it was going to capsize with the suddenness of the blow. And Flower, frightened by the shouting and by the unexpected shudder of the cart behind

170

her, threw back her head and tried to swerve away across the road. I looked up anxiously at my father. He was grinning happily, showing the big boards of his teeth in his reddish face. He didn't stop at all when Tal y Fedw swore and shouted at him, he only whipped the mare up instead.

My father sold Flower after all to a man he met in the bar of the Three Horseshoes, the inn where we put up. Then, after the business was over, we went across to the large flat field which the farmers used for the horse fair. We wandered about for a time talking to many people and listening to the jokes of the auctioneers but I was downhearted because I wouldn't see Flower any more. And in the end my father bought a lovely slender mare with a pale golden coat to her shining the wing-gloss of a bird and a thick flaky cream-coloured tail reaching almost to the grass. She was shod but she seemed wild, only half broken, with wide-open black nostrils, and a thick-haired creamy mane and large dark eyes curving and shining like the balls of black marble on a gravestone. In a nearby field a fun fair was opening and each time the loud roundabout siren hooted the tall filly started as though she had received a slash with a cutting whip, her large black nostrils opened wide with fear at the sound, and she began dancing up her long slender legs off the grass as though a current of terror were shooting through her fetlocks. She edged warily out of my father's reach too as long as she could, keeping at the far end of the halter-rope, and when he put out his hand towards her dark muzzle she shied away in a panic, peeling open the terrified whites of her eyes as they stood out black and solid from her golden head. But he wouldn't have that from any horse and after a time she became quiet and docile, fawning upon him and allowing him to smooth, with hands that were almost the same colour, the glossy amber of her flanks. Then telling me to fetch her over to the 'Shoes, he handed me the halter-rope and walked off laughing with the man who had owned her before.

It was hot and sunny in the open field then, so bright that if a man threw up his hand it glowed crimson like a burning torch in the sunlight. The great golden mare trod heavily behind me, a thick forelock of creamy mane hanging tangled over her eyes, and her frightened ears pricked up sharply on her high head like rigid moonpoints. I didn't want to lead her, perhaps she was an animal nobody could manage, but I was ashamed to show my father I was afraid. I was almost in a panic going in the heat among the tall and awkward horses that crowded in the field, I was afraid of being trampled down, or of having a kick in the face from the hoof of a frightened horse. And most of all I dreaded that the fairground hooter would begin its howling again and scare this wild creature up on to her hind legs once more with terror and surprise. It became more and more frightening leading her across the crowded field with the hot blast of her breath upon my flesh, I was sweating and in agony expecting her to shy at any moment or to rear without warning and begin a sudden stampede among the horses that crowded around us. My panic and helplessness as the tall blonde mare came marching behind me, large and ominous and with heavy breath, were like the remembered terror rippling hotly over my flesh one night as I sat alone in our kitchen through the thunderstorm, waiting for the endless tension of the storm to break.

But all the time my father, using long and eager strides, went ahead with the other man, waving his cigarette about, enjoying himself among the crowds and slapping the horses recklessly across the haunches with his yellow hand if they were in his way. 'Indeed to God, Dafydd,' he shouted, jeering at a sallow man with a fresh black eye, 'you're getting handsomer every day.'

At last the gate came in sight, my hopes began to rise that I should get out of the field before the siren blared into the sky again. To leave the fairground we had to cross a shallow ditch which had a little stream in it because of the rain, and over which someone had dropped a disused oaken house door to act as a footbridge. As soon as the mare heard her front hoofs resounding on the wood panels she recoiled powerfully with fright and flung herself back against the rope, she began plunging and shying away from the ditch with great violence, her nostrils huge in her rigid head with surprise and terror and the fiery metals of her shining hoofs flashing their menace in the sun above my upturned face. I was taken unawares, but I didn't think of letting go. The halter-rope became rigid as a bar of iron in my hands but in spite of the dismay I felt at her maddened plunging and the sight of her lathered mouth I didn't give in to her. I clutched hard with both hands at the rod-like rope, using all my weight against her as she jerked and tugged back wildly from the terror of the ditch, her flashing forefeet pawing the air and her butter-coloured belly swelling huge above me. My father, hearing the noise and seeing the furious startled way she was still bucking and rearing on the halter-rope, ran back shouting across the wooden door, and quickly managed to soothe again. Meanwhile I stood ashamed and frightened on the edge of the ditch. I was trembling and I knew by the chill of my flesh that my face was as white as the sun on a post. But although I was so shaken, almost in tears with shame and humiliation at failing to bring the mare in by myself, my father only laughed, he made nothing of it. He put his hand down in his breeches pocket and promised me sixpence to spend in the shows after dinner. But I didn't want to go to the shows, I wanted to stay with my father all the afternoon.

After the meal I had the money I had been promised and I spent the afternoon by myself wandering about in the fairground eating peppermints and ginger snaps. I was unhappy because my father had been getting noisier during dinner, and when I asked him if I could go with him for the afternoon he said, 'No, don't wait for me, I've got to let my tailboard down first.' I was ashamed, I felt miserable because he never spoke to me that way or told me a falsehood. In the fair-field the farm servants were beginning to come in, trying the hooplas and the shooting standings and squirting water over the maids from their ladies' teasers. I stood about watching them and when it was teatime I went back to the inn to meet my father as we had arranged. My heart sank with foreboding when they told me he wasn't there. At first I waited in the Commercial, hungry and homesick, pretending to read the cattle-cake calendar, and then I went out and searched the darkening streets and the muddy fairground, heavy-hearted and almost in tears, but I couldn't find him anywhere. And after many hours of searching I heard with dismay a tune spreading its notes above the buildings and I saw it was ten by the moon-faced market clock. The public houses were emptying, so that the badly-lighted town was becoming packed with people, the fair-night streets were filled with uproar, and drunken men were lurching past, being sick and quarrelling loudly. I stood aside from them, near the fishes of the monumental lamp, weary with loneliness and hunger, glimpsing through my tears the ugly faces of the men who crowded swearing and singing through the green gaslight, wondering what I should do. And then, suddenly I realised I could hear someone singing a hymn aloud in the distance above the noise of the town. I knew it was my father and all my fears dropped from me like a heavy load as I hurried away because at last I had found him.

I ran along the dark and crowded street until I came to the open square outside the market entrance where the two lamps on the gate pillars had IN painted on them, and there I saw a lot of people gathering into a thick circle. I failed to get through the crowd of men, so I climbed on to the bars of the market wall at the back where the children had chalked words and looked over the bowlers and the cloth of the people. There was my father, his black hat sitting on the back of his head, standing upright beneath the bright gas lamps

in an open space in the middle of the crowd, singing 'Gwaed
dy Groes' loudly and beautifully and conducting himself with
his two outspread arms. But although he was singing so well
all the people were laughing and making fun of him. They
stood around in their best clothes or with axle grease on their
boots, laughing and pointing, and telling one another that
Pantathro had had a bellyful again. By the clear green light
of the pillar globes above the gates I could see that my father
had fallen, because his breeches and his black riding coat
were soiled with street dirt and horse dung, and when he
turned his head round a large raw graze was to be seen
bleeding on his cheekbone. I felt myself hot with love and
thankfulness when I saw him, my throat seemed as though
it were tightly barred up, but I couldn't cry any more. He
soon finished his hymn and the people began cheering and
laughing as he bowed and wiped the sweat off his glistening
head with his red handkerchief. And soon the serving men
were shouting, 'Come on Wat, the "Loss of the Gwladys",
Watcyn,' but I could see now they only wanted to make fun
of him while he was saying that sad poem. I couldn't
understand them because my father was so clever, a better
actor and reciter than any of them. He cleared away one or
two dogs from the open space with his hat and held up his
arms for silence until all the shouting had died down; he
stood dark and upright in the centre of the circle, taller than
anyone around him, his double shadow thrown on the
cobbles by the market lamps pointing out towards the ring
of people like the black hands of a large clock. Then he spat
on the road and started slowly in his rich voice to recite one
of the long poems he used to make up, while I muttered the
verses from the wall to help his memory. As he recited in his
chanting way he acted as well, gliding gracefully to and fro
in the bright light of the ring to describe the pretty schooner
shooting over the water. Or he held his tall, pole-like body
rigid and erect until something came sailing at him over the
mocking crowd, a paper bag or a handful of orange peel, and

at that he cursed the people and threatened not to go on. When I saw them do that I went hot with shame and anger, because my father was doing his best for them. Then suddenly he stood bent in a tense position, shading his eyes, still as a fastened image with a peg under its foot, his eyes glittering under their thick brows and the big bars of his teeth making the gape of his mouth like a cage as he stared through the storm at the rocks ahead. Rousing himself he shouted an order they use at sea, mimicking a captain, and began steering the schooner this way and that among the dangerous crags, pointing his brown finger to the thunderous heavens, burying his face in his hands, embracing himself and wiping away his tears with his coat sleeves. Every time he did something dramatic like this, although he imitated it so well that I could see the mothers kissing the little children for the last time, all the people listening laughed and made fun of him. I didn't know why they couldn't leave him alone, they were not giving him fair play, shouting out and jeering all the time at his good acting. When the ship struck in the imitated howling of the wind he shrieked in a way that made my blood run cold, and began chasing about the open space with his arms outspread and a frightening look of terror and despair on his face. He was acting better than ever he had done for me in our kitchen, the sweat was pouring from him now because he was doing all the parts and yet the people were still mocking at him. Sinking his head resignedly into his hands and dropping on one knee in the middle of the circle he sang a few bars of the pitiful death hymn 'Daeth yr awr im' ddianc adre', in his beautiful bass voice. It was so sweet and sad I was almost breaking my heart to hear him. Some of the farm boys took up the tune, but he stopped them with an angry wave of his hand, which made them laugh again. And then suddenly he gave up singing and as the sinking decks of the ship slid under the water and the mothers and the little children began drowning in the tempest he crouched down low on the cobbles with his hands clenched in agony before him, asking with the sweat boiling out of his face that the great eternal hand should be under him and under us all now and for ever. He forgot he was a drunken actor reciting before a jeering ring of people, he ignored the laughs of the crowd and behaved like a man drowning in the deep waters. He wept and prayed aloud to the King of Heaven for forgiveness, sobbing out his words of love and repentance, and when the ship with her little flags disappeared under the waves he dropped forward and rolled helplessly over with a stunning sound, his face flat downwards on the cobbled road and his limp arms outspread in exhaustion and despair. Just then, as he sprawled still and insensible on the cobbles like a flimsy scarecrow the wind had blown over, one of the spaniels ran up again with his tail wagging and lifted his leg against the black hat which had fallen off and lay on the road beside my father's head. The crowd laughed and cheered more than ever when they saw that and I could feel the scalding tears trickling down my face. I jumped down from the market wall and started to hurry the six miles home with angry sobs burning my throat, because the people had laughed at my father's poem and made him a gazing stock and the fool of the fair.

All the afternoon I had dreaded this, and in the dark street before finding my father I had wept with alarm and foreboding at the thought of it. I knew I should never be able to manage the golden mare alone and bring her in the night all the way up to Pantathro. And now I was doing it, holding the whip across the reins like my father, and the tall indignant creature with her high-arched neck was before me in the shafts, walking along as quietly as our Flower and obeying the rein as though my father himself were driving her. I had prayed for help to God, who always smelt of tobacco when I knelt to him, and I was comforted with strength and happiness and a quiet horse. The men at the

Three Horseshoes who had altered the brown harness for the mare said when I went back that if I was Wat Pantathro's son I ought to be able to drive anything. I had felt happy at that and ever since I had been warm and full of light inside as though someone had hung a lantern in the middle of my belly. At first I wished for the heavy bridle from the horn hanger behind our bedroom door for the mare's head, but now I didn't care, I felt sure I could manage her and bring her home alone. There was no one else on the road, it was too late, and no dogs would bark or guns go off to frighten her. And beside, it was uphill nearly all the way. Only, about a hundred yards from the railway I pulled up to listen if there was a train on the line, because I didn't want to be on the bridge when the engine was going under, but there was not a sound spreading anywhere in the silent night.

And what made me all the happier was that my father was with me, he was lying fast asleep under the tiger rug on the floorboards of the spring body. His pretty horseshoe tie was like a gunrag and the blue jay's feather was hanging torn from his wet hat beside me on the seat, but he was safe and sleeping soundly. When the men at the 'Shoes lifted him still unconscious into the spring body they examined him first, holding his head up near the light of the cart lamp. I saw then the whole side of his face like beef, and when they pushed back his eyelids with their thumbs the whites showed thick and yellow as though they were covered with matter. And on the inside of his best breeches, too, there was a dark stain where he had wet himself, but I didn't care about that, I was driving him home myself with the young mare between the shafts and I was safe on the hill outside Lewsin Penylan's already.

The night was warm, the moon up behind me and the stars burning in front bright and clear like little flames with their wicks newly trimmed. And in the quietness of the country the yellow trap-wheels made a pleasant gritty noise on the lonely road and from time to time the mare struck out bright red sparks with her hoofs. We passed the vicarage where one light was still lit, and came to Parcglas where Harri's snow-white nanny pegged on her chain chuckled at us like a seagull from the bank. I thought the mare would be frightened at this, so I spoke soothingly to her to distract her attention. She just pointed her sharp ears round and then went on smoothly nodding her high-crested head, her golden toffee-coloured haunches working in the light of the candle flame thrown from the two cart lamps stuck in the front of the spring body.

The sloping hedges slipped by me on both sides of the white road. I wanted more than anything else to please my father after what they had done to him, shouting he had dirtied on the swingletree again and was as helpless as a load of peas, I wanted to bring him home safely by myself with the golden mare, and I knew now I should do it. Because at last I saw a star shining over our valley, a keyholeful of light, telling me I was home, and I turned into the drive of Pantathro without touching the gateposts with the hubs on either side.

REVELATION

Rhys Davies

I

The men of the day shift were threading their way out of the colliery. The cage had just clanked up into the daylight, the tightly packed men had poured out and deposited their lamps, the cage swishing down again for the next lot, and, hitching their belts and shaking themselves in the sunlight, these released workers of the underworld began their journey over the hill down to the squat grey town that was in the bed of the valley. As he was passing the powerhouse, just before depositing his lamp, one of these colliers heard his name called from its doorway:

'Gomer Vaughan. A moment, please.'

Gomer went over to the man who called him.

'You live near my house, don't you, Vaughan? I wonder would you mind calling there to tell my wife I won't be home until about eight this evening? I've got a job on here, tell her, and I can't leave it. You see, she's expecting me now... Hope it's no trouble?'

Of course it wasn't. Gomer was glad to take the chief engineer's message. Montague was liked by all the miners: a chief engineer with sympathetic principles, though an Englishman. Gomer nodded and resumed his way, soon regaining the particular companions with whom he always walked home. They were all young men.

'What the blighter want?' asked one.

Gomer told him.

'She's a beauty, she is,' said another, meaning Mrs Montague. 'Proud of herself, too, strutting about and looking as though the world's no more than ninepence to her, whatever.'

'Got something to be proud of she has,' returned a short terrier-looking fellow, perking himself to have his say. 'A sprightlier bird never trod on two legs. Half French they say. Ach, she makes our lot look like a crowd of wet and panicky hens. Got something our skirts don't seem to have.'

'I wouldn't,' said the eldest of them critically, 'swop her for my old 'ooman. Too much opinion of herself she has, by the look on her. A spirited mare she is in the house, I bet.'

Gomer said nothing. He was the latest married of the company. He did not want to say anything on this subject of women. Though he could say a lot, by God he could. He could let flow some language – a lot of language. But he held himself tight, his eye glittering, while the others went on as men will, saying what they'd up and do if any woman had too much lip and bossiness. He had been married a year: and he was all raw and fiery from his encounters with Blodwen. God, he never thought a woman could be so contrary. Soft and simpering as she was before they married... Well, he'd show her yet... And as the colliers swung along together Gomer planked his huge nailed boots down on the pavement with a vicious firmness.

They had descended the hill, and as they reached the long dismal rows of dwellings that constituted the town they separated to climb to their different homes. Gomer lived in the last row reaching up the side of the greyish-green hill. At the end of this row was a detached house, where the engineer and his wife lived. The lonely bare hill swept up above it. Gomer had to pass his own cottage to climb to the villa.

It was a warm sunny summer's afternoon. There was a

clear soft mist in the still air. Gomer wished there was a country lane of shady trees with a clean stream running near, in this part of Wales. He would have liked to stroll there in peace that evening. But no – after his meal and bath there would be nowhere to go but the street corners, the miserable pub, or the bare uninviting hills. Ah, what a life! Gomer sighed. The same thing day after day. Down to the pit, up again, food, bath, quarrel with Blodwen, slam the door and then a miserable couple of hours trying to jaw to the fellows on the street corner, and back home to see Blodwen's face with the jibe on it still.

He cleared his throat and spat before opening the gate of the garden. Ach, he had had enough of her tantrums, and if she wanted a fight he was ready for her. Trying to dictate to him, just as her mother had tried it on him. Save up to buy a piano indeed! And no one in the house who could play it. He'd give her piano...! He knocked the shining brass image on the villa door and glanced about. Natty house. Bright little garden – a rose garden. There were bushes and bushes of them: he'd never seen such big red and white roses. And such a smell! He almost snorted as he breathed in and emitted the perfume.

No one had answered his knock. He turned and knocked again. Where was the servant? Keeping him hanging about like this. He wanted his dinner. He knocked again. Then there came sounds of steps, upstairs it seemed, and as the steps sounded nearer, hurrying downstairs, a shrill voice called:

'Can't you wait a minute, darling!'

It was Mrs Montague, of course, Gomer said to himself. She thought her husband was at the door. And there was laughter and excitement in her voice. Ah, that was the way to greet a tired husband coming home from work. An excited voice calling 'darling'. Made a man think a woman was worthy to be a wife... The door was flung wide open.

Gomer's tongue clave in astonishment to his mouth. The

gaping silence lasted several moments. A naked woman stood before him, and then slowly, slowly retreated, her fist clenched in the cleft between her breasts.

'Mr... Mr... Montague asked me...' stammered Gomer, and could not switch his rigid gaze from the apparition.

How lovely she was!

'...told me...' he went on humbly, '...said...' His voice dropped and he stared at her like one possessed.

She turned at the foot of the stairs... fled up: and it was like the flutter of some great white bird to heaven.

'...told me to tell you he couldn't come home at all until eight o'clock just...' suddenly bawled Gomer into the empty passageway.

He waited a few seconds, wondering if she would answer. He heard her hurry about upstairs. Then she appeared again, wrapped now in a loose blue garment. Her face was flushed as she came down the stairs, but as she advanced to him she laughed. By God, how she laughed! Gomer felt his blood run. She wasn't ashamed, not she. And still her white feet were bare. They were bare and flawless and like lilies pressed on the floor.

'What is that about my husband?' she asked easily.

Gomer told her. Under the pit-dirt his cheeks burned.

She thanked him very prettily; and then she said:

'I thought it was he at the door. I'm sure you'll understand. I was having a bath. You are married, I expect?'

Gomer nodded. She looked up at his gazing eyes again in a queer laughing way and said in dismissal:

'Oh, well. Thank you very much for the message.'

He turned at last, and the door closed. He stepped out of the porch and, his eyes lifted in thoughtful amazement, made his way slowly to the gate. Never before had he seen a naked woman. Not a live one. Only in pictures. Respectable women – it had always been understood – kept themselves a mystery to men. But was that quite right? Ought they to keep themselves such a mystery? When they were so beautiful.

Surely Mrs Montague was respectable enough! Her husband was a fine respected man too. He wouldn't have things done that weren't right… Gomer suddenly made a decision that it was quite natural for a woman to meet her husband naked. It was lovely too.

As he opened the gate he saw a rose bush stretched up the wall. There were several curled pink-flushed roses. One bloom wouldn't be missed. His hand immediately snatched a flower, and, when he got outside the gate, he laid it in his food-tin.

Gomer's shoulders seemed squared and defiant as he went down at a quickened pace to his cottage. He was going to make his peace with Blodwen. But he was not going to be a namby-pamby fool either. After all, she was his wife: and he was not an unreasonable man. He had been quite fond of her too: and there were times when he thought her handsome enough for any man.

II

'You're late,' she said accusingly. And before waiting for him to reply she went on shrilly, 'Don't you blame me if the dinner's spoilt.'

'Which means it is, I suppose!' he said. But he smiled at her, his good white teeth shining out in his blackened face.

'Come in at your proper time then,' she rapped out, prodding the meat viciously.

He leaned forward and playfully slapped her on the back. She uttered a scream and the meat slid off its plate, hesitated on the edge of the table and fell on the floor. His action and the ensuing accident had an exaggerated effect on Blodwen. She arched up her long neck in a tight rigid fashion, her face flamed, and she darted out into the little scullery like an infuriated turkey.

'I've had enough,' she screamed, 'and more than enough.'

And she banged some crockery about.

'Now then,' Gomer called to her soothingly, 'now *then*, my pet. What's the damage! A bit of dust on the old meat! Look, it's all right. Now, Blod, behave yourself. Where's the taters? I'm hungry.'

He knew she'd find his gentle coaxing astonishing. Another time he would have hurled abuse at her. But she remained in the scullery. He sighed and went in there. She turned her back on him and went to the tap. He followed her and whispered in her pink ear.

'Now, now, what's got you, my darling! There's a way to treat a tired man who's been working hard as he can to get you a bit of dough! Turn about, Blod – and show me your chops laughing, the same as you used to! Look, look what I've got you—' He lifted his hidden hand and tickled her ear with the rose, then reached it to her nose. 'Smell! Put it in your blouse.'

She turned and said angrily: 'What do I want with a rose in my working blouse! Where did you get it whatever?' She was relenting.

'Ah, my secret that is.'

'Oh, well,' she said, tossing her head, 'put it in a cup on the table.'

During the meal she reverted again to the piano controversy. 'A catalogue came today from Jones & Evans. Cheaper they seem than anyone else. There's one that works out at seven-and-six a week.'

His brows were drawn in wrathfully for a moment. He did not speak. She went on talking, and at last he dropped in:

'We'll see, we'll see.'

The meal finished, a big wooden tub was dragged in to the place before the fire, the mat rolled up. Blodwen, sturdy enough, lifted the huge pan of boiling water from the fire and poured it in the tub. Gomer stripped. The pit-dirt covered his body. Blodwen added cold water and Gomer stepped into the tub. While he washed she cleared away the dinner things. She was quick and deft enough in her work, and the house was bright and neat.

'I'm ready for my back,' Gomer called.

'Wait a minute,' she said coldly, taking the remainder of the dishes into the scullery.

So he had to wait standing in the tub with the patch of coal dust beneath his shoulders glaring on the whiteness of the rest of his body. He knew she was exercising her own contrary will again. He might have yelled at her, but today he didn't want to. He was holding himself tight in glowing anticipation. When she came at last to rub the hand cloth over his back and swill him down, he said nothing. Only grunted when she had finished:

'Not much respect have you got for a man's naked skin, Blod. You rub me as though I'm a bit of old leather.'

'Bah!' said Blodwen, 'a nice little powder puff I'll get for you.'

He laughed, lingeringly and good-temperedly. He wanted to get her in a good mood. 'Ach,' he said with affection, 'one of these days, Blod fach, perhaps you'll come to know what a nice skin your husband's got on him.'

'Conceit!' she said, and would not look as he vigorously towelled himself.

Early that evening, when he sat comfortable and easy by the fire, he said to her, as she was about to go upstairs and change:

'You're not going out this evening, are you, Blod?'

'Yes. I'm going to the chapel.'

'Don't you go this evening, if you please,' he said.

Amazement was now evident on her face. This politeness and interference with her arrangements was quite unusual. 'Oh, indeed!' she began, ready for a battle.

He cocked his tight-skinned sturdy young head up at her. His eyes gleamed, there was an odd smile on his lips. 'Well, go and change first,' he said.

She shrugged her shoulders and went upstairs.

He sat waiting for her. She appeared in a peach-coloured silky dress. Her face shone clean. She was prepared for the women's meeting in the chapel. He looked at her appraisingly and said softly:

'Come here, Blod.'

'What d'you want now?' she demanded, withheld in spite of her coldness.

She moved near to his chair – but apparently to the mantelshelf looking for something.

'You're looking nice tonight,' he said. And he suddenly leaned out of his chair and caught her. She cried out, disliking this horseplay in her best silk dress. But he held her and she had to keep still. Then he whispered a few words in her ear.

She suddenly wrenched herself free and slapped his face. He sprang up. Her face and slender tightened neck were mottled.

'Indeed,' she breathed, 'indeed! You rude ruffian. What d'you take me for, indeed? Please to remember I'm your wife, will you? I'll teach you to respect me, Gomer Vaughan.' Yet there was an undercurrent of fear in her breathed words of contempt and horror.

But he had caught fire. His head lurched towards her, his eyes like flame-lit glass, he shouted:

'That's just it, my fine lady. Remember you are my wife I'm doing. Look here, you. Enough of your silly airs and graces I've had. A lodger in this house I might be. You do what I tell you to, now.'

'Never!' she screamed. 'Such rudeness I've never heard of.'

'What's in it?' he demanded furiously. 'You see *me*, don't you, when I wash?'

She was retreating from him in obvious fear now.

'Never have I heard of such a thing!' she exclaimed. Her face was contracted, her eyes were strange and hunted. 'Never. A woman is different from a man... And never do I look at you... not in that way.'

He was advancing to her. She saw the clear determination burning in his eye. With a sudden quick movement she darted out of the room and he sprang too late. She was out of the house. He heard the front door slam.

III

He knew where she had fled to. Twice before, after their more furious clashings, she had hurried off to her mother's – Mrs Hopkins, a widow, who kept a sweet shop. Mrs Hopkins had come up 'to see him about it' afterwards. No doubt she would come this evening. He hated her.

She arrived half an hour later. Directly Gomer saw her pale, large aggressive face, he buckled in his belt and thrust out his chin.

'What's this I hear from my Blodwen, Gomer Vaughan?' she began with shocked asperity. She looked startled this time too.

He uttered an exclamation of contemptuous ire.

'That daughter of yours got no right to be a wife at all, Lizzie Hopkins,' he fumed. 'Running to her mother like a little filly! And don't *you* come here poking your nose in this business either. You go back and tell your silly daughter to return at once to the man she's married. See?' And he turned his back on her abruptly.

'Well you might look ashamed' – Mrs Hopkins replied in a rising voice – 'well you might. Scandalous is the thing I have heard from Blodwen now just. Advice she has asked me. Gomer Vaughan, a respectable man I thought you. Please you remember that my daughter is a religious girl, brought up in a good family that's never had a breath of scandal said about them. And now you want her to be a party to these goings-on.' Her voice reached a dangerous pitch. 'Dreadful is this thing I have heard. Surely not fit to be married to a respectable girl you are! Shame on you man, shame on you. What my poor dead Rowland would have said I can imagine. Why, Gomer Vaughan, for forty years I was married to him, and never once was I obliged to show myself in that awful way! Don't you fear the wrath of God, man, don't you think of His eye watching!'

Gomer retained an admirable silence through this tirade. His thumbs stuck in his belt, he spat in the fire and said:

'Pah, you narrow-minded old bigot, you.'

Mrs Hopkins began to breathe heavily.

'Insult and rudeness! Would my poor Rowland was here! And would my dear girl was single again!'

Gomer lost his balance then. He turned and shouted:

'You be quiet, jealous old cat! What do you understand about young married people today? Interfering! Turning Blodwen's ideas the wrong way. A girl she is, isn't she then? Nothing extraordinary was it that I asked her. Only today was it I saw such a thing.'

Mrs Hopkins said quickly: 'Who?'

In his ire Gomer incautiously answered, as though to strengthen his case, 'Mr Montague's wife. I—'

But Mrs Hopkins broke in with a loud exclamation:

'Ha! So that's it then. Ha, now I understand well enough. *She* is the one, is it? Long have I had my feelings about her... Very well, Gomer Vaughan, very well—' And she began to back out of the room, her heavy head nodding with hidden menace, her pale eyes fixed on him triumphantly.

Gomer shouted at her:

'You send Blodwen back here at once.'

Mrs Hopkins whisked her bulky figure out of the doorway in a surprisingly swift way. 'We'll see, young man,' she darted back over her shoulder, 'we'll see.' But Gomer had no doubts that Blodwen would return.

IV

And so she came back – sooner than he expected. Mrs Hopkins scarcely had time to reach home and impart whatever she had to say, and Blodwen was dashing into the room where her husband sat in brooding wrath.

'You,' she panted, 'you been seeing that woman!'

She looked as though she wanted to leap on him. But like an enraged hound on leash she stood prancing and glaring wildly. 'That's where you been, when you came home late! That's your monkey's game, is it—'

'Now, *now*, Blodwen—' he began. Then he was silent, and he did not attempt to deny her accusation. There was a wolfish grin about his mouth. Blodwen continued to heap vituperation upon him. She became wilder and wilder. Her mouth began to froth, her eyes to protrude. And he liked her fierce, savage beauty. She had a splendour thus. His cunning wolfish grin widened. She became desperate.

'Not another night will I spend in this house! Gladly will my mother welcome me back—'

He decided she had reached the pinnacle of fear. He got up and went to her. She shrunk away and he followed. He took her arms firmly and with power.

'Long enough I've listened to your insults, Blod. Where did you get that idea from that I've been running loose? Eh? Has that old bitch been lying to you then?'

'You told her you been seeing Mrs Montague naked—'

'Well, well, and so I have—'

Blodwen struggled to be free. 'Oh, oh!' she cried aloud.

'Some women there are,' he said, 'who are not so mean as you about their prettiness! Mrs Montague's got very good ideas how to make her husband happy. Listen, my silly little pet...' and he told her of the afternoon's event.

She became quiet. Surprise, astonishment, and amazement leaped successively to her wild-coloured face. And, also, there came a slow and wondering dawn in her eyes...

'There now,' Gomer finished. 'See how ready you are to think evil of me. And here I came home wishing to see a better sight than Mrs Montague could give me. And well I could have it too, only you been brought up wrong. That's where the mischief is. Too much shame you have been taught, by half.'

Blodwen's head was a little low. The curve of her healthy red-gold cheek filled him with tenderness. And magnanimity. He said softly:

'I tell you what, Blod. We'll strike a bargain. You want the piano bad, don't you? Well, say, now, we'll give way to one another—'

She hung her head lower. Some threads of her rust-brown hair touched his lips. He quivered. His hand slipped over her shoulder. But she would not speak.

'—And be nice to each other,' he continued, 'not always squabbering as your mother and father used to do! Live in our own way we must, Blod... there now, isn't she a sweet one... there, ah! sweet as a rose, my darling, a better pink and white than any rose's...! there, my pet, my angel!'

THE SHEARING

Geraint Goodwin

All down the two sides of the barn they went, sitting straddle-legged on rough untrimmed benches, their backs against the loose stone walls. Sometimes they would move a sheep across their knees and start the talk going, without raising their heads.

The place stank with the warm-sweat reek of fleeces: they lay there in a growing heap as one man after another, with a final flick of the shears, tossed them on to the stone floor.

They had come in on ponies across the mountains and from the valley farms to lend a hand with the shearing, as they in turn would be so helped themselves.

For the short, harsh spring of the Welsh coast was mellowing into the milder summer and the sheep were going up to the mountain shorn of their wool. And the natural gaiety of the people kept pace with the seasons. In this farm near the village the men were telling the old stories or fashioning new ones with native wit: without in the yard was the commotion of boys mitching from school while from in the old farmhouse itself came the raised laughter of women, making their own fun in the big kitchen, as they busied themselves with the men's food.

Two boys were running endlessly carrying in the sheep. They carried them as they would a child, their bellies up, and laid them down on benches for ever emptying. Only in between times would a man find time for talk, wiping the reek off his hands and leaning his back to the wall as he looked about him.

The old farmer had let go his sheep. It went scuttling through the open door with the lads holding on to the shorn neck as they raced her without, on to the commotion of voices around the boiling cauldron of pitch. The old man wiped his brow with the gesture of a job well done and looked across to his young neighbour. And then, in the casual way of small talk:

'So married life is all right then, Lewis John?'

'Not bad.'

And the lad, whose wild young face set as though there frozen, buried his head still deeper in the fleece before him.

And it was not all casual as it seemed. The old man brought his hand with a comic gesture backwards across his nose and winked around him. He was a great wag and what people call a character, an old man now of seventy but still good for his fifty sheep a day, and all done clean, which was a good deal more than any of the others. There was no harm in John Shadrach Ifons, or John Shad as he was to everyone, with his round, fresh, crab-apple face and the sharp blue eyes that missed nothing, always a twinkle; the white, untidy hair ruffled up heedless on his head; the long, white, arrogant curve of his moustache that gave the face some semblance of age.

At the same time they thought he was skirting near thin ice, and secretly enjoyed the prospect of what was to come. Not one of the others dared have gone so far, but then he had the privilege of age and again of innocence.

'Not bad!' went on the old man, as though taking the words from him and turning them over. 'Well, well, that is one way of putting it, I suppose.' He looked around him again with the same show of dumb innocence. 'When I was a young man I thought it very good.'

And again he rubbed his nose with that sly, backward swipe and reached his tongue out slowly round his cheeks and went on:

'Life is very unfair – to the young people, I mean. Now if I had to choose between coming here and a warm feather bed at the farm of Ty Newydd I *think* perhaps the bed would win. In all this world there is no place like the bed.'

'Myn ufferni – you ought to know: you have been in plenty.'

For the first time the lad raised his head from out the sanctuary of the sheep's belly. There was the quick, bright flash of a smile that seemed to shed light around him. He nodded, knowing that he had scored, and as though to say he was going to play their own game for once and keep his temper on a leash. This was his first initiation into the old hierarchy of married men and he had to submit to the baiting of his elders with as good a grace as he could. And if that was all there was to it, then he was going to let it pass.

'In my time – in my time,' mused the old farmer, not taking it amiss. He clamped his gums together and spoke as to the wall, and his eyes went off into distance. 'And the happiest days of my life, too, and most men know it.'

He was talking to them all now, half banter half serious, with the warm intimacy that their own tongue gave. And for all its frankness it was natural to them as the light they saw or the food they ate, that ancient, undiscoverable life of the mountain farms, which Christianity had touched but not altered. Even in the rapt ecstasy of redemption that followed the first revivals, this old, worn, pagan life endured: the things of the earth, the ways of a man with women, these they knew as the psalmist did, for it was their life.

'Well, well, Nature, after all.'

He was a man named Wili Owain and the thin and rather foolish white face was set gravely, as though to hold in the weight of thought, and a mouth without meaning was clamped down hard in a judicious line. He was no match for these two and the profundity was meant to ease out the distance.

'Nature – ah, Nature!'

The old man calmly pulled out the torn strips of rag from between his teeth and, crossing the ewe's legs, bound them up, and then settled her on his knees. He rubbed a hand softly over the fleece to search for a beginning, prodding carefully with his shears into the thick wool of the neck: a few careful snips and the fleece fell open, and, like a furrow ripped in dirty water, the shears went down the belly to the tail. The fleece fell apart, trailing its ragged edges almost to the floor: what was once a furrow widened, as the uncovered belly showed itself, the short virgin wool beneath as white as drift snow.

He raised his head a moment, and then, looking to the lad Lewis John beside him and as though the young wild head that tossed restless in its life gave him a tag on which to hold his sermon, went on, with a quiet munching of chops:

'She is a funny old girl is Nature – as stubborn as a woman and just as contrary. And you can trust Her just about as much, boys bach! For she is thinking in Her way and we, poor fools, go on thinking in ours. And who is right, think you?'

He tossed this over to them as some stray morsel which in the process of time should be considered, simply for its own sake. And to start them off, and in one of those abrupt changes from the joking to the serious-minded in the way of the Welsh, he leaned forward and raised a free hand over his head, wagging a finger solemnly into space. And then his voice, like a preacher filled with the spirit, went mounting up in invocation:

'And who is right, m'achgen'i? Nature, in all her wonderful glory who sendeth the spring into the valleys and giveth drink to every beast of the fields: yea, yea, who appointed the moon for seasons and who toucheth the hills and they smoke… or Lewis John Williams of the farm of Ty Newydd in the parish of Pantymaen?'

'Me again!'

'I am only *saying*, my boy, for the sake of illustration. It is the same with all of us.' He stroked his chin again in the same sly way. 'Unless perhaps Llew Pryce here who is too timid…'

'Give me a chance, that's all.'

The quiet youth, as though startled into speech, raised his head laughing, in a show of braveness.

'You have had plenty, so they tell me. Only when the girls begin to think things, off he runs to his mam, and that is no good to anybody.'

The sound of low laughter, of men pleased within themselves rose around the high metallic snip of shears. They did not raise their heads, only grunted over their work. There was too much to do. And the old man might catch their eye and out would come a sally at their expense, which they did not want at all.

'Oh, no, that is no good to anybody,' went on old John Shad, heaving the sheep over on his knees. 'Lewis John is better than that, I must say. He knows the way to the ladies' hearts and once you have touched their hearts there is no knowing what… or so they tell me.'

He raised his worn head a moment and cocked a live eye at the young man before him.

'Hush, hush – fair play. He is a married man now,' one of the men broke in.

There was always a time when things began to get out of hand, when a sally with the point of truth in it got home. So the old man, free of the sheep at last, tossed up his hands in a casual way, and in a voice meant to condone all things said simply:

'Wild oats! And better when you are young – a spring sowing, *whatever* the harvest. Ay, Lewis John?'

The lad winced as under a blow and his head jerked up from his work, flung up in anger: the sheep he held reared up her dumb head in a frantic heave.

'Ah – you've touched her, Lewis bach.'

The old man pointed his shears-end to the soak of fresh blood that spread out on the white, shorn belly.

'Hell – can't I see?'

Lewis John threw the shears on the bench before him and, not waiting for the oil bottle but with one brief glare around him, shouted:

'Look here, Mr Ifans – that's enough for one day! Now leave it alone!'

Then he flung himself out through the door.

'Tut, tut – so childish,' went on old John Shad as though nothing had happened. Then he looked round to the others with the same old, all-comprehending look. 'And everyone *knows*, boys bach, which is small wonder as she is a girl of this parish. And whatever his wife might like to think or say that girl was *not* brought to bed by the fairies!'

'She is here today', a man said, in the same way of small talk.

'What! Gwenna?'

The old man's head went up as though startled out of himself: then he cocked it as though trying to distinguish between the shrill laughter of women in the kitchen. Then back to the same easy tone: 'Well – that is awkward, boys bach, to say the least... but they are bound to meet sometime, after all.'

He waved his hands up in the same offhanded way but it was still on his mind: he shook his head several times as though to wipe out the memory of it. These days of shearing, when all came in a spirit of good fellowship, were soon over as it was. It was a pity to see one spoilt. But they were back again to the old talk.

'As though the folk at Ty Newydd will let a small thing like *that* worry them – now that they have got Blodwen off! Myn ufferni, you would think, to hear them talk, that Lewis John had wings, instead of a son by another woman,' broke in Wili Owain in a bitter challenge.

And with the empty seat before them the tongues were loosened and they began to argue among themselves, taking sides as they were bound to do in a thing which touched the village, and its honour, so deeply.

They could not help liking the lad Lewis John still – would have done much to excuse him if only they could. For he was one of those men who do not belong to themselves but to the people: his quick tongue and nimble wit, the flashing, open tilt of mischief in his face, forestalled the angry word. And after some fresh, some daring piece of devilment, there was only a wise nodding of heads and an indulgent holding-up of hands:

'Goodness only knows what we shall make of him.'

And yet no one really wanted him otherwise and so one and all continued to give false evidence to river watchers and angry policemen and he took it all quite cheerfully as his due, promising to behave next time – and with a great show of hurt innocence.

And now the old happy days had gone. He was quick to sense it and it gave a fresh edge to him.

'No,' picked up old John Shad, 'the Ty Newydd folk are not going to let a small thing like that worry *them*.'

Beyond the words the old man sounded his voice so that it had a faintly unfamiliar air of deference that chilled. And it was noticed they were always referred to as the 'Ty Newydd folk', never in the more homely way that warmed.

'Well, he's done well for himself, whatever,' broke in the timid man Llew Pryce, which only provoked Wili Owain to a fresh shout:

'I tell you Gwenna is worth ten of her, any day of the week, *and* she has not two thousand pounds fastened on to her knickers.'

'Now, now. That is unfair – that is unfair,' old John Shad broke in with a gesture of peace. There was bound to be a row – always had been since it happened.

'And two hundred pounds spent on a wedding does not make it any the more *right* – no, nor photos in the *County Times!*' went on Wili Owain in the full flood tide of his indignation. He began beating with the end of his shears on the bench beside him, trying to make himself heard. The three Methodist ministers, the two hundred guests with printed invitation cards, the dinner for the poor in the County Workhouse – he waved his hands dismissing it all, and then leaned over and spat out through the open door. And on a high note of piety:

'Oh, no – a *poor* girl has nothing to offer but herself…'

'Myn ufferni – that's enough, too.'

The sudden burst of laughter that greeted old John Shad's sally eased the feeling between them, and some of the old intimacy came back.

'We are all very foolish indeed, boys bach.' It was old John again. 'The best thing is to marry a girl for love… who has *got* money though not because…'

Again he brought his hand backwards across his nose in the familiar mischief-making swipe. But Wili Owain was now in the full flood-tide of righteousness:

'He did not do the right thing, boys bach, and mark my words, no good will come of this other.'

He brought the shears-end a resounding blow on the bench again and glared round with a light of challenge in his eye. Then leaning towards the door:

'Ty Newydd folk indeed!'

And he spat outside with the passion of the righteous.

It was hard to know why the Ty Newydd folk were not liked. They had made money, which was a good thing, and they had made it out of the English – and that was better still. And what was more they had come back to spend it in the district where they had been born and bred. And yet their own people no longer knew them: they had taken fresh root elsewhere. They knew the old man simply as Tomos Richards, one-time cowman at Ty Newydd, and his wife Sara as the servant girl there. They were simply London Welsh milkmen with 'pots of money', even though they had bought the farm in which they once worked. It did not put them back on the land. And Sara knew this, though it did not daunt her. She was an ambitious woman and in some ways a dangerous one and she straightway set herself the hard task of making herself somebody: her grim, big-boned face with the few sparse hairs of a moustache, her sour, unlighted eyes and the shorn hair which was to keep her for ever young at sixty, was seen everywhere, often enough trailing around her daughter Blodwen.

'Sara had a little lamb' began one of the local penillion and it ended up on a bawdy note, of how Sara had found the little lamb a man. For Blodwen, a spoilt child and oversexed to boot, was not so discriminating as her mother. So ran the local gossip and it was usually right.

Nevertheless Sara was a character, entitling her to her maiden name, and though they laughed at her it was only to hide their fear. And she was a person of some importance, on almost all committees, a magistrate and a deaconess in Shiloh, the Calvinistic Methodist chapel from which she had been married in the long ago. And with her head bobbing in the chapel vestry or over the tea urn in the Sunday School or with two or three people about her in the street, they knew something was going on, though what that something was did not always reveal itself.

It did not seem likely that scandal would ever touch her or hers but she reckoned without Blodwen. Lewis John was going through an awkward time just then: hard things were being said about him. Perhaps it was to spite the parish (which he saw settling on him for ever and ever) or perhaps it was the inducement of the great outside world which he had glimpsed on a short spell of lorry-driving. Or it may have been Blodwen herself, who was attractive enough in a spitefully passionate way. But there is no doubt that she made a fool of herself and Lewis John, who was used to shaking the tree for the fruit to fall, did not mind it coming otherwise. People began to talk. In the end Sara took a hand. She had hoped for a doctor or at least a minister, but the lad, even to her own hostile eye, was presentable enough, like some lanky pup with the promise of turning out well.

There was only one thing in the way – this unhappy affair with Gwenna that still dragged itself on in the life of the village.

'Trust Sara,' they said, with a grim nodding, and they were right. For in ways that no one quite knew, and without ever anything being said in so many words, people were now beginning to believe that perhaps Gwenna was not all that they had thought she was. It came as a shock to people who had known her since childhood but then, it was explained, she was 'at an awkward age'. And as for poor Lewis John – well, 'you know what he is'. And as they most certainly did, they found themselves forgiving him much.

And now for the first time doubts were being thrown on the child's father and it was even said that Lewis John would have a solicitor to defend himself, though everyone knew where the money would come from. And as that young man could believe anything he wanted to believe he was very nearly a party to it. Let it be said to his credit that it did not go any farther. Though stubborn to the end, he suffered an order to be made on him in the court.

'The Ty Newydd folk!' said Wili Owain again, wiping his mouth. 'And as for Blodwen, she is a silly bitch – nothing more nor less.'

'Now, now.'

'...and she can have what is coming to her, for that sort of thing doesn't pay, boys bach.'

He looked around him with the same glare of righteousness and smacked a fist into the palm of his hand.

'Uffern! Here she comes,' someone whispered, and his mouth stayed open in the midst of speech. Into the uneasy quiet that descended on them old John Shad's voice was raised in nonchalant greeting:

'And how does Mrs Blodwen say she is on this fine summer morning? Come in – come in and let us see you.'

He waved her towards them with his shears. The woman in the doorway was getting on for thirty, though the long, sullen face and big eyes, the passionate pout of the thick, childish mouth, made her look younger. She had long, thin, neurotic hands that were never at rest, pulling and unpulling at her gloves, and all the time she was moving from one foot to the other. She was dressed well but without real taste and her pale face was touched with scarlet in a way that one does not expect in the country, giving a ghoulish look to her brittle type of prettiness.

'Oh, I only… is Lewis John about?'

The old man waved his hands to the outside.

'He was,' he ventured.

'Was!'

And then the wide, staring eyes were flecked with panic. She jerked her head around her, unbelieving, and then tugged at her gloves again.

'Where… where has he gone, then?' she got out, trying to keep the voice steady.

'Well, Blodwen fach, where *would* he go, think you?' He held her with his drooping, shadowed eyes as though peering into her very heart. And then, after the cruel pause, with no more than a hint of the coming smile: 'To no harm, surely? A breath of fresh air to cool that hot young head of his would be fairly near the mark.'

The held breath let itself out in the relief.

'Oh, I… I see.'

Yet she was not sure. She looked around them again, looked in the dumb, polite faces for some answer that would never come.

'Any message?' went on the old man, in the same casual way.

'No – I'll call again.'

And then she had picked her way across the muddy yard, holding her tailored coat down over her knees in answer to the rude wind always blowing. A moment later they heard the little car rattle off along the lane.

'Myn ufferni – she is afraid of letting him out of her sight – and you know why!'

Wili Owain, come back to speech, nodded in his disgust.

And then old John Shad took up again:

'Well, she is wiser than you think; she knows what Lewis John has done once he can do again. And though Gwenna has had her lesson you know how they say: it is easy to light a fire in an old hearth. And somehow I don't think those two would be long in striking up the tinder, boys bach: though she is too good for him – made of tougher stuff.'

And he let his mind wander off to the little thing she had been, wild and headstrong with her bit lip and her triumphant, tossing head, the black hair flung loose in defiance.

'Dai Jim, where did you get this little heifer with you?' was his standing joke with her old grandfather, and the old man always had some answer ready. He would give her away for nothing, or for half a crown, depending on how she had behaved herself that day.

As his mind wandered off to her and then to the old grandfather and then to the whole brood of the Vaughans he lifted his weathered face, with the no longer merry eyes, and a sad, hurt smile went over it.

'Silly to themselves,' he said almost aloud and he shook his white, unruly head grimly and his lean mouth puckered up as though under a blow. For his mind had gone off from them to life and all its hard bargaining and he was sorry for them, sorry as for no one else in this world. They were not the people for that: it was as though they were laughing at life, sometimes grimly enough but always laughing, and that nothing would ever bring them face to face with its awful seriousness. Well, they had paid for it and perhaps it was only right that they should. And yet it hurt him that it had to be so: all that big family in a four-roomed cottage and old Dai Jim, with a few years left him, still at work in the quarry: come back, he had, from the pits in South Wales when his only son was killed, so that he could give the children a fresh start.

And then at the same time he felt an old joy warm him and

his hand quivered over the fleece as though stricken, joy to think that in some way they were never down, that nothing in this life could ever make them less than what they were.

'Poor old Dai Jim, it is a hard thing to stomach all the same,' he ventured as he let his thoughts wander on. He could feel for the old man; of all the children left on his hands Gwenna was the one: the old man's spirit and the old man's wit had gone on to her – yes, and the old man's innocence, as though to level things up.

Old Dai Jim was going to give the lad a thrashing – paternity orders he did not understand. He understood asking a man outright what he was going to do, and knocking some sense into him if there was any nonsense. He had a sack over his bent shoulders and he was off down the village when he was first told. The neighbours, however, had warned the minister and he was there to stop him.

'Dai Jim, your old fighting days are over: you have been called to the Lord.'

And the old man surveyed his great gnarled hands that in his days down south had battered their way through three valleys, emblem of the sorrow and pride of the old-time triumphs when he was any man's man for a quart.

'Myn ufferni – pity I left my tools behind!'

And there was the same quick flash of a smile that took off his temper, and a moment later he was talked back into reasonableness, as they knew he would be.

He went on hoping that some sign of manliness in Lewis John would show itself. And he kept on hoping when Gwenna was brought to bed. There was not much Lewis John could do then but show his face: but that was what was expected of him, for it was a near thing. When the district nurse after twelve hours of it sent for the doctor the old women on the doorsteps began to nod their heads gravely.

'It's up to her now,' they said, wondering whether her strength would hold. And old Dai Jim never moved from the range, staring into the red, sullen glow and wiping off the sweat that stood out like dew on his great battered head, his mouth trying to fashion some rough prayer that should not be sounded. When the feeling got too much for him he would let go a breath like a steam escaping and then raise his head quickly as though nothing had happened. It was not his way to show what he felt.

It was the longest day he had ever known. The roads were all snowbound, the topmost bits of hawthorn on the hedges showed up out of the drifts like black rush clumps: over all the mountainside the piled stone walls ran like faint pencil markings in the billowing white. Yet the doctor, who was one of the old school, did get through.

'She is bred the right way, Dai Jim,' was all he said as he came downstairs.

The old man got up and grasped his hand and then flung his head aside.

'There is a cup of tea waiting,' he said with a wave to the table.

Old Dai Jim liked the lad: he made all allowances. One had to come to it of one's own accord and though it was a bad beginning, two young people who were fond of one another would get over that. And they *were* fond of one another. The whole village knew it. It was not somebody he had picked up on a Fair Day night.

And then he heard of this other wedding to be and he seemed to break up overnight. He could not understand it and they had to tell him over and over again; he could not believe that such things were.

And so to that last wretched stage of all – the court. They could do what they liked now, for once it got there it was the end of everything.

But it would place the child's father beyond all doubt, they argued, and now that the Richardses were behind Lewis John it was just as well. It was their doing that the whole thing had got to the court at all.

And it was soon over. The chairman of the Bench made one last plea for them to come together, turning his wide, sorrowful eyes from one to another: the silent lad, stiff with a hurt pride, and the woman to whom he dared not raise his eyes, filling the magistrate's sad heart with the wonder of all unspoilt things.

'It is a great pity to see young people... like this.'

He raised his head once more and turned his eyes to the lad as though to implore him.

'Is there no way at all?'

Lewis John looked up from his feet and shook his head.

'No sir – none at all.'

Gwenna gripped on to the witness box, stiffening as she stood. It was as though a lash had struck her in the face. Was it for this, then, that she had been persuaded to come, so that Lewis John could tell the world that he had finished with her? For a moment the dark, brimming eyes went wider as though unbelieving and then she knew that it was true. It was beyond her understanding but it was true. Things had happened in these few short months that seemed no part of life at all, as though everyone had, in some way, gone out of their minds. So they could talk if they wanted. And a moment later she had flung up her head, with the old spirit shining in the straight, set eyes. They were harder now than they had been, but she was learning a great deal that she had never thought to learn.

That was all, except that her solicitor rose and explained:

'I'm afraid there is an explanation, sir. This young man's affections, for reasons best known to himself, have been transferred elsewhere.'

And the people in the court turned as one, with neck-craning stares, to where Blodwen and her mother sat, staring stolidly into the glum silence.

That was the last time that they were face to face. And who would ever say that they would meet again? Even Blodwen told herself now that it could not, would not, happen. And yet she was not sure. There was the child and there was Gwenna – a shawl around in the old Welsh way of nursing – whenever she went into the village. She had always been a lovely girl but, with that quiet, incommunicable pride of the young mother as though a bud were slowly widening out into life, she was lovelier than ever. It seemed as though this girl was the wife and it seemed sometimes as though the girl knew it. And Blodwen's jealous nature would not let it rest. It began in a small way and seemed to gather to itself fresh torments. She was making herself ill and sometimes she feared for her reason. What was not there she invented: she *knew* now that it was bound to happen for she had told herself so until at last she was sure of it, as of nothing else in this world. And like in some lurid, edgeless dream she tortured herself to be able to see what she dreaded seeing.

'You are not looking too well these days, Blodwen fach.'

The old woman in the village shop, like a great black bird slowly sunning itself, heaved out a sigh and her black stuff blouse rose and fell with it. Dear me – there was plenty of trouble in the world, she seemed to say, without having to listen to the old, old story all over again. And then, more gruffly than she meant:

'Why *are* you so silly?'

But the next moment she was hobbling round the counter for the young wife had fallen into a chair and was near hysterics.

'Oh God – why was I born?' she kept repeating, dabbing her eyes as though to hide out the light of day. She said it in so hopeless a way, so dry and empty a voice, that the old woman, who knew all the wretched story, found her heart touched in spite of herself.

And in the back room, with a cup of tea to revive her, she turned up her hollow eyes in a helpless plea.

'He's not there. I was in the barn just now and he's not *there*!'

She went on wringing the tiny knot of handkerchief until the blood left the helpless hands. She had said too much: she bowed her head in shame. A tiny stretch of colour came into the white face. She had never been as bad as this before: she was getting worse and worse.

'And you know what Lewis John is? With a bit of skirt about.'

The old woman raised her head and pushed the steel spectacles up from the old ringed-around eyes that had now gone hard with a warning glare. She held her white-boned hands up so that there should be no mistake. 'Now that is quite enough of that.'

The wife, sensing the change, got up stiffly from the little wicker chair, preening herself in a new pride.

'She just *happened* to be there, like,' she got in.

'Good gracious, woman!' The old shopkeeper's softly chewing chaps set in anger. And then she stopped herself. 'Indeed, truth, if you go on like this you will throw them into one another's arms and it will be your doing, my girl.'

It was no good talking, as she knew. Instead she drew in a deep breath and sighed once more, as she heard the shop door slam. Where on earth she was off to now no one knew except that she was not going home. To the barn again no doubt.

'Dir annwyl – there will be some doings before the day is out,' she said out loud.

The old woman waved her hands in the same forlorn way: she was too old now, she seemed to say, for this sort of thing.

But in the barn the men were busy. Like grasshoppers in chorus the steel clippers went on, the rumble of voices or a sharp angry rebuke, the sudden commotion of a bolting sheep loosed too soon. The fleeces, folded and packed tight into parcels of wool, stood in an ever-towering heap in the middle, and out in the by-take and beyond that again, in the lower skirt of the mountain, the new-white sheep were straggling up in a thin line.

After a time Lewis John had come back and taken his old

place on the bench. He sat there drumming on his knees waiting for them to bring him a sheep. For some time no one spoke – it was difficult to make a place for him after the outburst. Once the intimate note had gone it was hard to sound again.

But at last old John Shad, with no show of interest:

'Your missis has been here, Lewis John.'

'And what the hell has that got to do with you, then?'

'Tut, tut, tut!' The old man made a noise with his mouth and wagged his hands deploringly. He had meant it as a gesture of friendship, he seemed to say, and look what return he had had.

'I only said she had been here – surely a man can open his mouth?'

'Not your sort of mouth, John Shad.'

The lad nodded towards him in a tight-lipped threat and the old man, finding it hard to stomach the insult:

'If she was to put a bit of rope around you... but leave him alone and he'll come home, wagging his tail behind him.'

The lad jumped up, sending the bench flying to the wall. He held his clenched fists trembling at his sides.

'Iesu mawr,' he got out through his clenched teeth and swung his arms about him in an empty rage. Then, reaching a taut finger at the old man:

'Only for your age, John Shad, I would... oh...'

He ended up on a note of glory and bent his arms up with the still trembling fists.

'Age, indeed! They are always either too young or too old for you, Lewis bach.'

This was a reference to Gwenna: those around looked up with a quick, anxious glance. One or two of them ran between the men, but old John Shad sat there with the dignity age gave.

'I have thrashed better men than Lewis John – when they were men.'

He made a heave towards the old man, struggling to free himself from the men who held him.

At that moment the barn filled with shadow and they all instinctively looked to the door. His wife was there. The men let go their hold, let their hands fall down sheepishly beside them. Old John Shad heaved himself round in his seat and craned his neck to see the cause of the sudden transformation. And then, with an old courtesy that was part of him:

'Come in, Mrs Williams,' and he beckoned her away from the draughty door.

She stood there on one foot and held on to the lintels while her mouth moved as though in a search for words. It was no place for words.

Lewis John had flung himself free. He strode over to her his eyes hard, fists clenched, and stood there before her in a gibber of rage.

'I must see you, Lewis,' she cried out, and made a frantic move towards him.

Then restraint went, like a taut cord bursting. He raised his clenched hands above him and then crashed them down on his head.

'Get out! GET OUT! Oh for Christ's sake...'

He flung his knotted fists towards her, as though to destroy the sight before him, and then ended in a hoarse moan. He stumbled back into the barn and brought a bare forearm across his wet brow, and sank slowly onto a bench.

Outside, they could hear the short, hysterical crying and then that, too, had gone. And within no word: the shears had stopped, a sheep coughed, a bench creaked, a boot scraped over the slate floor. At last the old man's voice, like the gathered voice of all come in judgment:

'Lewis John Williams – you are falling very far short of what you... were.'

The lad lifted his head numbly under the chastisement and then lowered his eyes to the floor. He knew that, too. He wanted to tell himself, more than to tell them, that it was not true, that something had happened to him lately and he did not know what it was.

The old man's voice rose again.

'And we think better of you than *that*, my boy.'

'She has asked for it.'

The lad set his lips in a stolid, incommunicative way and stared before him.

'That is not the way to speak of your wife, either.'

The lad bowed his head under the reproach and the old man went on.

'There are certain things that are not said in public – not said and not done, *whatever* the provocation.'

It was a point, granted the lad who lifted up his face in a dumb show of thanks. 'For your heart is in the right place, Lewis John, I will say that...' The old man paid him this grudging tribute and then went on in a brighter voice, 'And left to yourself there is no great harm in you.'

'No, indeed,' broke in Wili Owain, finding a place for himself. 'But as a man sows, Lewis bach. And Gwenna was the girl for you.'

Wili Owain wagged his head reassuringly in the cocksure way of the knowing.

The lad winced as though cut to the quick. Wili Owain was a foolish man and was privileged to say foolish things so that he could not take him up.

But the others shuffled their feet uneasily and looked hard at the floor – that this of all things should have been said, and now of all times!

'Answer not a fool according to his folly,' broke in the old man in the same tranquil way, 'and there's no fool like the fool who means well. Come on, Lewis bach, we shall be friends yet.'

He got stiffly to his feet and slapped the lad across the shoulders. Lewis John looked up with the same harsh challenge, and then his better nature rose and took hold of him, his face gradually warmed into life again. He could not bear malice for long.

The old man groaned as he took a heavy ewe across his

knee, and rubbed his hand over the timorous muzzle, looked into the sad, disdainful eyes with a comic, meditative squint.

'As a sheep before her shearers is dumb: and a damned good job too, boys bach – one old woman is enough in this life.'

And again the laughter rose, after how long an interval. It was like a thaw in a warm spring sun. The laughter and the native wit, the old stories told again, and a sudden burst of song as someone would take a bar or two out of sheer gladness of heart. And Lewis John threw himself heart and soul into it. It was the old life come back again. He made more droll the droll story and his laughing eye and the wild gleam of mischief in the young face provoked even the glum ones to extravagances. He and old John Shad were the natural leaders through whom all passed: and then they again, with the natural deference paid to each other's greatness, capped the other's sallies.

'Those were the days,' began Wili Owain, as though talking of a time gone. 'Remember, Lewis John, that night on the lake? Keepers all over the place and, myn ufferni, they had enough of it!'

Lewis John raised his head and looked out through the door to the broken, lifting sky over the mountain, and then he made a grimace as though the memory had come back like a known face to torment him. It was all too real. There was a lot about that night that no one would ever know – only he and Gwenna. There was no going back now, and he shook his head bitterly at the remembrance of something gone – the old life which, for all it may have been, was as real as the day itself.

'There's innocent for you!' someone taunted 'Have you ever seen a gaff, Lewis bach?'

'And the dog otter we killed on the way...'

Then old John Shad, raising his mildly browsing head:

'Was that the night that a young man climbed up a ladder to a lady's bedroom? Well, well! The keepers have been after me many a time, but there were never any ladders left lying about – though I was always in *hopes*...'

The laughter rose like a rustle around and he pulled at the white sweep of moustache with a sly, cocked eye.

'...because there are many cosier places than a night in jail. No, boys bach, there were no ladders in my time, but oh dear me, a great deal of red flannel – and rough going it was: the path of true love was not as smooth as it might have been.'

There was no harsh voice now. Lewis John had entered into the life around him, just as though he had opened his hands and gathered it up. The sense of it was as real to him as something he saw and handled. He felt his spirit loosen within him like a hard knot in the belly gradually resolving itself. He gave himself in the same way, felt the touch of the sheep quicken in his hands, until his fingers no longer had a separate sense. The shears went surely, with a new rhythm as they sped over the warm flesh, and his eyes were alight with the felt joy of work.

That night was now so real that the actual physical sights and sounds came to him. He could smell the harsh tarn water in the rushes and raise his head to the taste of salt in the wind from the sea: the sour stink of sea birds that had made sodden the rush-clumps at the far end, and the whiff of peat smoke somewhere far off.

He remembered that night – remembered plucking his cap off and turning his head up into the wind. The fading landscape was going in the way he knew: the deeper blood-red hue of mountains like a slow fuming fire in the thin light, and then a triumphant sky, with no longer a sun, far out over the sea. He remembered throwing his arms up, just in the exultation of being alive, then shaking his fists in defiance at something that he never, even now, understood. The wide, moving splendour overhead, the sense of a world so near that all the live sounds rose up in a last wailing cry in the stillness, and then so remote that the far-off, fading yellow sky over the sea was but a beginning. All this came to him as he stood there. A day like all others, remembered by felt things – by wet earth and the chill of mountain water, and the soft pulp bellies of fish, felt under squeaking rushes: then the blue splendour of mountain and the fired sky far over the sea and a night coming, edged with frost and the blue sparkle of stars.

'Duw – that was a night!' He tossed his head up in the old triumphant way, the level white teeth showing in a grin and the wild gleam in his eyes like a light flashing.

Then, free of the sheep, he reached up to the rafters where some old gaffs lay on pegs, and made play with one. He got the haft bent under his forearm as he reached down to a fish, the body braced into a lean, poised curve and the eyes hard and lightless. And then he struck.

'Got him!' said old John Shad, looking up. 'Oh, he has not forgotten the way, whatever.'

Lewis John flung the gaff back with a gesture of disgust and sat down on the bench again. He pushed his hand up through the wet hair and screwed his eyes shut. Everything about that night had become too real.

The keepers had taken a hiding that time – one that they would long remember. And he, having fallen too far behind, had had to drop the salmon and swim the lake – right across to the Rectory on the far side where Gwenna worked. He had gone into the old church and carried the ladder from the broken bell-cote, through the rhododendron bushes to her window.

It was the end of a daft night. She tried to play off his fooling, as she had done so often before, when he would go off in a sulk, swearing that it was the end of all things. And yet she knew that a time would come when she would not have the strength to do so. She had known that almost as soon as she began to think about Lewis John at all, and she sought desperately to hide it from him in any way she could.

When at last he tried to clamber across the sill she shook her head with a slow, deliberate shake, not daring to trust her voice: but her unquiet, bounding heart and the lit-up eyes spoke for her.

And as he tried gently to unfasten her hands from across the window, she let her head droop downwards on her breast as the last act of surrender. And a look of dismay went, like a shadow, darkening her face, as she asked in an old, grave way:

'*I* know – but do you?'

As he carried her away from the window to the old cast iron bed of the maid's room, festooned with church texts, he tried out the solemn language of love (but with no great sureness), feeling that it was demanded of him.

'Gwenna – I'm... I'm awfully fond of you.'

'So it seems!'

The still grave face broke with the flash of a smile. And the wit was not lost on him. And for all that triumphant note that sounded in him he felt a long way behind, humbled by what she was.

Fused for ever in his own soul was that night. The two were one and indistinguishable: the riding triumph of the sky with its beckon into space, and Gwenna: the first brief bewilderment at life in the slowly widening eyes as passion woke, like a flower warmed out of the still earth. His own live world came back to him at the memory – so real that he felt he could reach out and touch it.

'Duw – what about a song, boys bach?'

He flung his head up in the old wild way. And then without more ado he broke into an old Welsh folk song. Its theme was the burden of young love, so old a song that their fathers had heard their grandfathers sing it at such another shearing, and yet as fresh now as ever. Young love and a sighing lover who in the dawn had followed the foot-tracks of the beloved one in the woodland hollows, so that he might kiss the pressure on the turf. Lewis John sang it very well. He breathed into it that fresh, pliant feeling the Welsh have, making it his own.

'Well done, well done,' chimed in old John Shad, brought up out of himself. They all applauded him. No one really believed it; Lewis John in the dawn, searching for the footprints of the cherished one on the woodland moss: but no one was meant to believe it. And at the same time they were to believe it, what had happened and what had not happened, the real and the unreal becoming one: the foolish, inconsequential lifting of the spirit which worked like leaven in the hard lump of life.

He took his place again and for a long time nothing more was said until, raising his head out of the sheep's belly as he let her go:

'Duw – what is the good of life if... if..."

'If what, m'achgen'i?'

John Shad was not listening: he had a fleece just coming loose at the neck and it needed care. He answered simply to show he had heard, and then bent his head still lower. Lewis John sat there, hands on his knees, head bowed.

'Last one for the morning!'

The old man straightened himself with a sigh. It was nearly time for the midday meal. And then, remembering something that had been said:

'What was that, m'achgen'i?'

'What is the good of...'

And then the words slowly faltered away. Gwenna stood at the door. She had a coarse sack apron round her; arms bare with the morning work were poised on the curving hips.

'Dinner, you men – and not so much singing,' she laughed in her mellow, lilting way.

She looked from one to another as though to ask whose had been the song. They stood back towards the wall in their discomfiture, eyes on the ground, leaving the lad alone before them.

'Oh – I see.'

She bit her lip until it seemed the blood would come and her eyes hardened like the cold gleam of steel. Then the colour surged like a loosened flood into her face, and beyond to her pounding breast.

They stood there for that one brief moment as though unable to free themselves one from the other. Then she turned with a wild toss of the head and ran on towards the house.

One by one the men had gone off in a stagger across the yard, stretching their cramped legs. They stopped at the stone spout and wrung their hands under the cold spring water and then flung them free. And then on towards the house, the high shrill laughter of women, the clatter of plates.

John Shad had stayed behind in the now empty barn. Once more he slipped his arm through the lad's in a final appeal.

'She must get *used* to seeing you, Lewis bach,' he pleaded.

Lewis John raised his head slowly from his knees as though he had heard for the first time.

'Ay – she shall, too!'

He nodded in the same grim, defiant way that she had had for him. Then he drew himself up and cocked his head with his old assurance. It was as if he had said that two could play at that game, and she should see...

But as he went across the yard the anger had already left him – there was only the tumult that welled up, like a hand clutched at the throat.

LET DOGS DELIGHT

George Ewart Evans

The first time anyone heard about him was when young Danny Lewis came home from the mountain and said he'd been bitten by a big brown fox that could run as fast as a train.

The kids had been up on the breast of Gilfach-Y-Rhyd, playing Indians among the rocks. Danny had jumped down from a big boulder nearly on top of this fox. Curled up it was, asleep in the sun. It took one bite at him and was away along the path towards Craig-Yr-Hesg, as quick as a moment.

There was no mistake about the bite – the teeth had gone right into the kid's forearm – but down in Pontygwaith they were not too sure about the fox. They hadn't seen a fox around the Gilfach in years; not since Jenkins the Farm had taken to shooting them.

It was Wil Hughes Flagons who really noticed him first. Just below Craig-Yr-Hesg Farm there's a fairly level shelf of ground bitten into the side of the mountain. Wil Flagons was up there one Sunday morning sitting against a rock. He had his greyhound bitch, the famous Tonypandy Annie, with him, and while he was nearly dozing off after reading the newspaper, the bitch suddenly tugged at the lead and started barking and kicking up no end of a shindy. Flagons looked up and saw what was worrying her.

About two hundred yards away was a big brown

greyhound, poking around among the rocks. When the dog heard Annie barking, he turned round sharply, cocking up his head, like a gossip. And what a head! It was as smooth-lined and well cut as a snake's. The dog held it high, but as soon as he saw Flagons, down it went and he was off towards Craig-Yr-Hesg, up past the quarry on to the moorland.

One glance at the dog in action and Wil Flagons knew he was a right 'un. The dog moved like a champion, taking the rocks and the sheep-wall like a bird; like a fairy; like no milgi that's been in this valley.

A quarter of an hour later the bitch spotted the dog again, right up on top, on the moorland. He was basking quiet in the sun. Flagons stopped, slipped the lead off her collar, and said to her very gentle, like he did before races: After him, gel! When the dog saw the famous Annie blazing towards him, he just cocked up his head and looked interested. But just as he got up to meet her, he saw Flagons standing with the lead in his hand, away in the background. Without as much as a sniff for Annie, the dog turned, and was off in the opposite direction like the wind. And Annie, thinking it was all a bit of sport, went full pelt after him.

Now Wil Flagons has got a few middling words handy when he's surprised. He must have used them all when he saw what happened to his famous Annie when she went after the big greyhound. He couldn't believe his eyes. The dog was leaving her standing, and before they were half-way across the bit of moorland he was as distant from Annie as a rich relation. Tonypandy Annie, mind you, who was meeting all comers and was live fire on the skin of the bookmakers.

Flagons really thought he had the nystagmus when he saw it. He went home after he'd collected the bitch, and he got so worried, trying to think whose dog it was, he couldn't get to sleep. He thought once it may be Twm Aberdare's dog that had got loose; but Twm's dog couldn't raise a gallop, leave alone make Annie look like a lapdog. He had to give it up and he dropped off to sleep dreaming he was riding down to the sea on the back of the big greyhound.

Next day he went round all the pubs in Pontygwaith asking questions; but when he started to talk about the dog on the mountain the blokes didn't take him serious, thinking he was on the cadge for a pint; so he was none the wiser at the end of it.

But after a week or two, one thing was sure: the greyhound was as wild as the bracken. No one came to claim him, though even if they did they couldn't get within a quarter of a mile of him to catch him. As soon as he saw anyone coming he'd look furtive over his shoulder and slink away into the thick ferns, as smooth as a fox.

He must have hated humans like poison. He wouldn't wait for the sight nor the smell of them. The last one he came up against must have treated him like nothing you'd care to tell about. The dog had been beaten till there was no trust left in him. Wil Flagons could see that plain enough, but he couldn't forget how quick the dog was and he would have given one of his eyes to catch him.

Whenever he got a chance he used to be up on the mountain, watching the dog move about. One evening he borrowed a spying glass and went looking for him special. He found him, as usual, up by the Big Rock, and he spent half an hour watching him, sizing him up; his shoulders and the strong curve of his body. Suddenly it struck him that the dog was wearing a collar. Then it came to him in a flash. He shut up his spying glass and off he went for home, with Tonypandy Annie trotting along behind. Catch him? I'll catch him, said Flagons, and then for some fun, Annie gel.

First he looked up Dai Banana, who lived next-but-two, and asked him for a loan of his terrier. Now Dai Banana was proud of the terrier, which was a champion ratter, notwithstanding he had about four breeds of dog in him, and Dai wouldn't hear about lending him to Flagons until he knew what all the fun was going to be about. So he had to let Dai into his secret.

Now it was his idea to train Annie to grab the wild dog by the collar when they were playing together on the mountain. Then Annie would hold him until they came up to get him proper. After a few grunts and grumbles, Dai Banana agreed to lend his terrier for Annie to practise on, on condition, of course, that Flagons would pass on a handful or two of the clover when the wild one would be winning all the races he was talking about.

So the both of them started to train the bitch to do the collaring act. And that was the easiest part of the business; for Annie was as knowing as they make 'em, Flagons had nursed her like a baby and she knew the lift of his little finger. She went at it, natural as walking, and Dai Banana's terrier had a rough time at the rehearsals; though show fight he did at first and raised hell till they calmed him.

Well it all went on fine, and after a week Flagons thought Annie knew enough to have a cut at the wild greyhound. So he and Banana took her up the Gilfach one evening just before dusk and hid with her behind the sheep-wall.

After a bit the greyhound came down and Annie acted her part as cunning as a monkey. The wild one seemed proper tamed at the sight of her. He pranced around, rubbing his flank against her and raising his head, really friendly. Then Annie, quick as lightning, turned and did her act; did it to perfection. She got his collar all right; there was no mistake about that; but then – well, Annie herself didn't know what happened just then. No sooner had the dog felt the pull on his collar after the quick turn of the bitch than he stiffened his neck, and with a sharp twist of his head and his shoulders he sent Annie and the collar flying, ten yards away, into the bracken; and before you could say Jawl the dog was a brown bullet streaking across the moorland. Annie, with tail between her legs, and looking like nobody's bitch at all, brought the broken collar back and dropped it near Flagons' feet. He found the name of a bloke – a bad number from the next valley – written plain upon the brass part of it.

Well, if it had been anyone else bar Wil Flagons he'd have left the dog quiet on the mountain after this bit of business, but being Flagons you couldn't expect him to put all his hopes in his Annie after he'd seen the wild one's paces. One thing the wild life had done to the dog for sure; it had made him yards faster than any Mick of a milgi Flagons had ever seen come after a live hare or a rabbit skin.

Anyhow, the greyhound was on the mountain for another month, with Flagons tickling his brains to think out another scheme to nab him; and when the winter was coming on and there was less chance of him picking anything up about, the women in Top-Row – the houses that have crawled halfway up the side of the mountain – were putting bones and scraps outside their back door in the evening. The greyhound would come down regular after dark to collect them.

Now Flagons' house was in the Top-Row, just handy; so it was natural he got the idea of putting bones and scraps of meat just inside of the gate at the top of the garden, and trying to nab the dog when he came inside to get them.

For a week Flagons was lurking about the top of his garden after dark, with enough bones to start a factory. But he never got his hand near the wild greyhound. He saw him one night, though the dog was away before he could make one step towards him.

But Flagons was a trier, and especially where he could smell out a bit of money; he'd as much patience as a blind spider then. So, although he had failed twice to get the dog, he made up his mind to have another shot at him; three tries for a Taffy, Annie fach, he said one afternoon as he brought the bitch down from a canter on the mountain: we'll catch him this time. He had one more trick left in his bag; Tonypandy Annie herself; an old one, maybe, but the very last.

About this time Annie was not saying no to a bit of

courting, and he was sure that if he tied her up inside the shed, with the door open, she would bring the dog, if he was within five miles of Top-Row and had any blood in him at all.

And, fair play to Annie, fetch him she did. On the second night, Flagons, keeping watch alongside a bottle of something, saw the wild dog slink into the shed. It was him right enough; he saw him plain in the bit of light he'd left shine on purpose through the back-kitchen window. Annie's come-hither had brought him.

Now, although he was aching to run up to the shed, Flagons had enough sense to keep to his hiding place for that night, because he knew he'd have to go slow and be middling cunning to shut the door on the right side of the greyhound. So he waited and saw him slide out silent like a shadow on the mountain.

Next day he made a sort of contraption on the door of the shed, with a cord leading down to his hiding place, so that when he pulled the cord the door would shut with a bang, and stay shut. Proper handy with his wits was Wil Flagons when something pricked him enough to use them.

Waiting that night for the dog to come down, he was as excited as the time his Annie won the hundred pounds and Silver Challenge Bowl. He'd made sure of him this time, and before the dog did actually come through the gate Flagons had spent at least a couple of hundred of the winnings.

The dog came through the gate the same as the night before; very slow and wary; but as soon as he was through he slid into the shed, quick, without a glance to the side of him.

Flagons held his breath and Annie stopped short in her whimpering. The dog was inside. He waited for a few moments to make sure, then he pulled the cord, and the door of the shed shut with a bang. Then there was a snarl and a loud barking.

As he ran up the path, lighting his torch as he went,

Flagons could see his picture in the papers, holding the dog. The Year's Champion: Beat All Comers... He slipped inside the shed. There was Annie in one corner, real frightened, wishing, no doubt, she was somebody else; opposite was the wild greyhound, staring at Flagons enough to burn him. But he made no move to get the dog; he just knelt down and started talking.

Now they say that Wil Flagons had such a way with dogs that he could put his hand out to the fiercest after a bit of talking; and he'd won a few bets over this and never once been bitten. But the more he talked this time the more the wild dog blazed hate and his soft words snarling back at him. And when at last he did stretch his hand out, very gentle, the dog sprang, and with a savage snap at his hand jumped clean over his shoulder. Bang went the dog against the door, and down came the contraption, and he was clear away on to the mountain.

It all came out down in the surgery the next morning, when Wil had three stitches in the back of his hand, and a bit of strong advice from the old doctor.

Well, weighing everything up, it wasn't surprising that Wil went bitter against the wild greyhound; it was only natural. He swore something horrible when anyone mentioned him after that. The dog, he said, was a wrong 'un, with no more worth in him than his looks.

But one morning a few weeks later he rolled into the bar of the Ffynon; proper up in the air with excitement; Annie was going to have pups; he knew it all along; it didn't matter a button that he hadn't caught the wild greyhound; it didn't matter he had gone to all that trouble; had a gammy hand and lost three weeks' work in the bargain; Annie was going to have pups and the wild dog was the father of them; and if the pups didn't turn out to be the fastest things on four legs he'd swear he'd go in for rabbit breeding.

Proper elated was Wil before the bitch had her pups. He had a good few names, like Brown Streak and Treharris

Trailer, stored up ready, and even started to build a place to keep them. But one morning he woke up to find the famous Annie mothering the queerest set of mongrels that had ever been together in a sugar box. There was a bit of Dai Banana's terrier in just every one of them.

Only one man ever mentioned the wild greyhound to Wil Flagons after that; and he was a johnny from away, and since nobody had ever told him, he couldn't know any better.

Twenty Tons of Coal

B. L. Coombes

It happened three days ago. Three days have gone – yet my inside trembles now as it did when this thing occurred. Three days during which I have scarcely touched food and two nights when I have been afraid to close my eyes because of the memory that darkness brings and the fear which forces me to open them swiftly so that I shall be assured I am safe at home. Even in that home I cannot be at ease because I know that they notice the twitching of my features and the trembling of my hands.

That was why I forced myself to go along the street the first day after the accident. I wanted to go on with life as it had been before, and I needed the comfort and sympathy of friends. The first I saw was a shopkeeper whom I had known as an intimate for years. He was dressing the window so I went inside to watch him, as I had done many times.

I expect my replies to his talk about poor sales and fine weather were not satisfactory for he turned suddenly and looked at me before he said:

'Mighty quiet, aren't you? Looking rough, too. What's the matter, eh? Got a touch of flu?'

'No! I wish it was the flu,' I answered, 'I could get over that. I've had my mate smashed – right by my elbow.'

'Good Lord!' He is astounded for an instant, then remembers. 'Oh, yes. I heard something about it, up at that Restcwm colliery, wasn't it? That's the way it is, you know.

Things are getting pretty bad everywhere. The toll of the road f'rinstance – makes you think, don't it?'

'The roads,' I answer slowly, 'yes, we all use the roads. Can't you realise that this is something different? He was under tons of rock, and everything was pitch dark. No chance to get away; no way of seeing what was coming; no – oh, what's the use? If you've never been there you'll never understand.'

'Don't think about it,' he suggests, 'you'll get over it in time. Best to forget about it.'

Forget! The fool – to think that I can ever forget. I know that I never shall and no man who has been through the same experience ever can.

I went back home; soon afterwards one of my friends called. When he saw me he exclaimed:

'Holy Moses! What the dickens has happened to you?'

He had been with me the evening before that accident but that night had written such a story of fright and fear on my face that he could hardly recognise me.

So I stayed indoors, hoping that time would ease my feelings but jumping with alarm at every sudden word or slam of the door, and dreading the coming of each evening when the darkness of night would remind me of that black tomb which had held my mate but allowed me to escape.

Then again, this morning, after I had heard the clock striking all through the night, I must have surrendered to my exhaustion and slept, for I did not remember anything clearly after four o'clock struck. At five o'clock someone hammered on our front door. In an instant I was wide awake; the bed shook with my trembling. That crash on the door was the roar of falling rock; the darkness of the room was the solid blackness of the mine; and the bedclothes were the stones that held me down. When the knocking was repeated I had discovered that I was safe in bed. In bed – and safe; how can I describe what I felt.

Then I pondered what that knocking could mean. It was

obvious that another morning was almost dawning. Griff, that was my mate's name, used to knock me up if he saw no light with us when he was passing to work. Could it be that he was passing: that all else had been a nightmare that this sudden wakening had dispelled? No, I realised it had been no nightmare for I had helped to wash his body – what parts it had been possible to wash without them falling apart.

Then came another thought; could it be that he was still knocking although his body was crushed? I dreaded to look, yet I could not refuse that appeal. I stumbled across the room, lifted the window, then peered down into the darkened street. A workmate was there. He lived some distance away but was on his way to the pit. He had a message for me. He shouted it out so that there should be no doubt of my hearing:

'Clean forgot to tell you last night, so I did. They told me at the office as you was to be sure to be at the Hall before four o'clock today. The inquest, you know. Don't forget, will you?'

Will I – can I – ever forget? Yet so indifferent are we to the sufferings of others that this caller, who is old enough to know better, who is in the same industry and runs the same risks, and who may be in exactly the same position as I am some day, does not realise how he has terrified me by hammering at my door to give that needless message.

Forget it! Is that likely when a policeman called yesterday and, after looking in my face and away again, told me gently that I was asked to be at Restcwm before four o'clock tomorrow – he had to say tomorrow then, of course. Not more than an hour later the sergeant of police clattered up to our door and – very pompously – informed me that I was instructed to present myself at the Workman's Hall, Restcwm, not later than four o'clock on the afternoon of Friday the, etc., etc.

After the caller has gone to his work I get back into bed. I have been careful to put the light on because it will be a while before there is sufficient daylight to defeat my dread of the lonely darkness.

Be there by four – so I must start from here about two o'clock. Restcwm is a considerable distance away and I have other things to attend to before the inquest. I have to draw the wages for last week's work and I shall have to take Griff's to his house as I have been doing for years. Next week I shall be short of the days I have lost since the accident. I wonder if they will pay us for a full shift on the day that he was killed. I have been at collieries where one sixteenth of a shift was cropped from the men who took an injured man home just before the completion of the working day. I think our firm will not be so drastic as that; they are more humane in many ways than most of the coal owners.

I lie abed, and think. The inquest will be this afternoon and I shall be the only witness except the fireman. This is the first time I have been a witness or had any connection with legal things and the police. I dread it all. I shall have to tell what happened in pitch darkness about two miles inside the mountain. They will listen to me in the brightness of the daylight and in the safety of ordinary life; and they will think that they understand. They may put their questions in a way that is strange to all my experience and so may muddle me.

I shall have to swear to tell the truth, and nothing but the truth. Nothing but the truth, it sounds so simple. I will try to recall what happened and whisper it to myself in such a way that I shall be question-proof when the time comes.

Griff was there before me that night, as usual, sitting near the lamp-room. He gave me the usual grin at our meeting, then when he had finished the last of that pipeful and had hidden his pipe very carefully under that old coal tram near the boilers, he took a last look at the moon, then we stepped into the cage and were dropped down.

I remember him saying as he looked upwards before we got under the pit wheels:

'Nice night for a walk ain't it, or a ride through the

country. Nice night for anything, like, except going down into this blasted hole.'

Griff is many years older than I am; I expect he is about fifty. We have worked together for many years. He is well built but quite inoffensive. He has a couple of drinks every Saturday night and chews a lot of tobacco at work because smoking is impossible. He is aware that things are rotten at our job and is convinced that someone could make them a great deal better if they wished to; but who should do it or how it should be done are problems too difficult for Griff to solve. Soon he is going to have one of his rare outings; he is one of a club that has been saving to see Wales play England at rugby football.

We were two of the earliest at the manhole where the fireman tests our lamps and tells us what work we are to do that night, for we are repairers and our place of work is changed frequently. The fireman is impatient and curt, as always.

'Pile of muck down ready for you,' he snaps each word and his teeth clack through the quid of tobacco as he talks, 'there's a fall near the face of the new Deep. Get it clear quick. 'Bout eight trams down now, and you'd best take the hatchet and measuring stick with you because I s'pose as it's squeezing now.'

'Eight trams,' Griff comments as we move away, 'I'll bet it's nearer ten if it's like his usual counting.'

We hurry along the roadway, crouch against the side whilst four horses pass us with their backs scraping against the low roof, then move on after them. As we near the coal workings the sides and roof are not so settled as they were back on the mains. We hear the creak of breaking timber or an occasional snap when the roof above us weakens. The heat increases and our feet disturb the thick flooring of dust.

Where the height is less than six feet timber is placed to hold the roof but where falls have brought greater height steel arches are placed in position. They are like curbed rails, nine feet high to the limit and about the same width. Where they are standing we can walk upright but we must be wary to bend low enough when we reach the roof that is not so high. We have been passing engine houses as we moved inwards. These are set about four hundred yards apart and become smaller in size as we near the workings. Finally we pass the last one where the driver is crouching under the edge of the arching rock.

The new Deep is the last right-hand turn before we reach the Straight Main. Our tools are handy to our work and we are glad to strip off to our singlets for they are sticking to our backs. We see at once that the official was too optimistic for the fall blocks the roadway and it is difficult to climb to the top of the stones.

'Huh,' Griff is disgusted, 'more like twelve it is. Eight trams indeed. I guessed as much.'

It is squeezing, indeed. Stones that have been walled on the sides are crumbling from the pressure and there sounds a continual crack-crack as timber breaks or stones rip apart. As we stand by, a thick post starts to split down the middle and the splitting goes on while we watch, as if an invisible giant was tearing it in half. Alongside us another post that is quite two foot in diameter snaps in the middle and pieces of the bark fly into our faces. The posts seem no better than matchsticks under the pressure and we feel as if we were standing in a forest – so close together are the posts – and that a solid sky was dropping slowly to crush everything under it.

'Let's stick a couple more posts up,' I suggest, 'because most of these are busted up. Perhaps it'll settle a bit by then.'

We drag some posts along the roadway, measure the height, then cut the extra off with a hatchet that must not be lifted very high or it will touch the roof. When we carry the timber forward we listen after every step, with our head on one side and our senses alert for the least increase in that crackling. We have measured the posts so that they should be six inches lower than the roof, then the lid can go easily between, but when we have the timber in position we notice that the top has dropped another inch. When we are tightening the lid we are careful not to hold on top for fear that a sudden increase in the pressure may tighten it suddenly and fasten our hands there. Ten minutes after the posts are in position turpentine is running from them – squeezed out by the weight.

The journey rider – this one is called Nat – comes along and we help him to repair the broken signal wires. He knocks on them with a file; there is a bang and rattle as the rope slackens and a tram is lowered to us. It seems that the roof movement is easing a little so I climb on top of the fall to sound the upper top. I have to stretch to my limit to reach it although I am standing quite nine feet above the roadway. The stones above echo hollowly when I tap them with the steel head of a mandrel so we are convinced that they have weakened and may fall at any minute. The awkward part is that we shall have to jump back up the slope and that the tram will be in the way to prevent us getting away quickly.

One of these trams holds about two tons and we had to break most of the stones, so we were busy to get the first tram filled in the first half-hour. Nat signalled it to a parting higher up where a haulier was waiting with his horse to draw it along the Level Heading where the labourers would unload it into the 'gobs'. Whilst Nat was lowering another empty tram we noticed the small flame of an oil lamp coming down the slope.

'Look out, you guys,' Nat warned us when he stopped, 'here's the bombshell coming and he'll want to know why the heck we ain't turned the place inside out in five minutes, you bet he will.'

It is the fireman and he came with a rush, stumbling over a loose piece of coal and almost falling; whereupon Nat turns away, partly as an excuse for not putting out his arm to steady the official and partly to hide the grin that he has started in anticipation of seeing the fireman go sprawling. The fireman recovers, however, and he glares at Nat as if he had read his thoughts. His hurry has caused him to breathe gaspingly; drops of sweat are falling, from the end of his nose and the chew of tobacco is being severely punished. He glares at the fall, then back at us as if he thinks we must have thrown more on top of it.

'There's one gone,' I tell him, 'and a good nine left still.'

'Huh!' he grunts, 'don't be long chucking this one in agen. There's colliers below and coal waiting.'

He rushed away to hurry the labourers. We were full again when he returned in twenty minutes' time.

'While the rider's taking these trams up,' he ordered us, 'you roll some of these stones and wall 'em on the sides. Put 'em anywhere out of the way of the rails.'

Griff went to have a drink after we had filled the fourth. The water gurgled down his throat as it would have down a drain.

'Blinkin' stuff's got warm already,' he complained, 'and it was like ice when I brought it into this hole.'

His face is streaked with grey lines where the perspiration has coursed through the thickness of dust; when he wrings the front of his singlet the moisture streams from it. The fireman visited us every few minutes and upset us with his impatience. Even when he did not hurry us with words we could sense that he felt we were taking too long. It was nearly three o'clock in the morning when Nat arrived with the tram that would be sufficient to clear the roadway. It seems that the mountain always becomes uneasy about that hour and small stones had been flaking down like heavy raindrops. We peered out from under the edge of the hole and I said that these falling stones must be coming from the upper edge of the right side. I could see some stones there that had half fallen and become checked in their drop. I got the slender measuring stick – it was about nine feet long – and tried to reach those loose stones but when the stick was to its limit

and my arms were outstretched I could not reach the upper
top. I climbed upwards on some of the stones that had been
walled near the side. When I had scrambled up to about eight
feet high it was possible to tap the stones and they fell. It was
warm down below but the heat was intense up in the hollow
of the fall. The increase of temperature almost stopped my
breathing; I noticed the warning smell that is like rotten
apples. My head was so giddy that I could not climb down;
I slid the last part.

'Phew!' I gasped. 'It's chock full up there. My head's
proper spinning.'

'Full? What d'you mean?' the fireman demanded,
although he knew.

'Full up of gas,' I replied, 'and there's enough in that hole
to put us up to the sky.'

'What are you chirping about?' he snapped back at me,
'there's nothing to hurt up there.'

'Try it and see,' I suggested. 'I notice you haven't tested for
any tonight.'

'Get on and clear that fall,' he said, 'there's nothing there.'

'Take your lamp up there,' I insisted, 'it's the only oil lamp
here. I know the smell of gas too well to be sucked in over
it.'

Very reluctantly he began to climb but when he was nearly
up he jerked his hand and the light was extinguished. I had
expected it, for that was better than showing there was gas
present and he was wrong.

'Now just look what you've done,' he complained, 'I'll
have to feel me way back to the re lighter.'

I saved my breath because I knew further comment was
useless. The official stayed sitting on the wall like a human
crow and watched us while we went on with our filling. We
were about half full when I heard a sound like a stifled sob
and the fireman slumped down, then rolled to the bottom
quite near to Nat. The rider jumped back as swiftly as a cat,
then crouched under the shelter of a steel arch.

'Now, where the devil did that 'un drop from,' Nat demanded. Then he turned to look at what had fallen. 'Good Lord!' he added, 'it ain't a stone – it's him. Out to the blinkin' world, he is. So there was some up there, all right.'

Our lights showed us that the fireman was breathing, although faintly.

'Let's carry him back to the airway,' I suggested, 'there's a current of fresh air there and he'll soon come round.'

'Too blasted soon, likely.' Nat was not sympathetic. 'The only time this bloke is sensible is when he's asleep. And why struggle to carry him when I got me rope as I can put round his neck and the engine as can drag him?'

After we had carried him to the airway we went on with our job. We had two pairs of steel arches to place in position and bolt together. We were anxious to erect them so that we could cover them with small timber in case any more stones fell. Nat agreed to sit near the official and shout to us if there was any undue delay in his recovering.

'Fan him with me cap.' Nat was angered when I suggested it. 'Why the hell should I waste me energy on him, hey? Let him snuff it if he wants to, I shan't cry.'

He seemed to be looking forward with delight to the time when the fireman would open his eyes and see the sketches that were chalked on the smooth sides of that airway. We had some skilful artists in that district and no one could mistake who was represented as waving that whip behind those three figures who were carrying shovels.

We had the one arch solid and were well on with the second before the fireman recovered enough to stumble up the road towards us. He did not praise us for our speed in erecting; I do not think he was very appreciative of anything just then. He said nothing as he passed but climbed on to one of the tram couplings. Nat warned him to hold tight in a manner that showed that the fireman could fall off under the trams if he liked, then they moved away up the roadway from us.

As soon as we had covered the steel arches we went to have our meal. We moved to where the roof was stronger, covered our shoulders with our shirts and sat on a large stone close to one another. We leant back against the walled sides, partly to ease the ache in our backs, and partly to lessen the target if more stones should fall.

We were supposed to have twenty minutes for eating food but we had finished before that. Griff looked at his watch; it was ten minutes to four. I remember him stating the time and remarking that we had not been disturbed at our food – for a wonder. Hardly had he said that when we saw a light coming towards us. We could tell by the bobbing of the lamp that the one who was carrying it was running.

Whoever is coming it must be a workman because he is carrying an electric lamp. We can hear him panting as he comes and his boots hit the wooden sleepers with a thud.

'Something have happened.' Griff speaks my own thoughts, 'somebody have been hurt bad or—' He does not finish and we wait, tensed, for the message… The running man reaches us, pauses, then holds his lamp up to our faces. The shadow behind the lamp becomes more solid and I realise that it is Ted Lewis.

'Puff,' Ted blows his cheeks out, 'all out of wind I am. Been hurrying like old boots to get to you chaps.'

Already we are reassured because if someone was under a fall Ted would have shouted his message at once. After taking a deep breath he explains:

'Old bladder-buster sent me to fetch you chaps to clear a fall he did. Said to come at once and bring your shovels and a sledge.'

'Fall!' We are both annoyed. 'Making all this fuss about a blessed fall.'

'Aye, I know,' Ted insists, 'but it's on the main and in the way of a journey of coal. He's in a hell of a sweat about it, not 'arf he ain't. Told me to tell you to hurry up – to run along with your tools, he did.'

'Run! Huh!' Griff is disgusted. 'I s'pose as we'd best go, eh? Allus something, there is.'

With our tools under our right arms and our lamps hanging on our belts we hurry after Ted. We are careful to keep our heads down, to avoid hitting the low places. Near the top of the third Deep we must meet the fireman, who swings around and walks in front of us. Suddenly he shouts back at us:

'There's ten full trams of coal the other side of this blasted fall and they won't be out afore morning if you don't shape yourselves.'

He is wasting his breath, for his threats and hurryings have lost their effect on us. His forcing is as much part of our working lives as the stones that fall or the timber that will break. Our lives are now a succession of delayed coal and falling roof; besides we are hurrying all we can. The sweat is dropping from our eyebrows; I feel it running over the back of my hand where a stone has sliced the skin away; it smarts as if iodine was smeared over it. The official stops suddenly and gasps:

'Just on by there. Not more'n four trams down and all stones, so it won't take you long. Look lively and get it clear.'

I judge the fall and decide that it is nearer six trams than four. My lamp shows me enough light to see to the top of the hole and to detect the stones that hang, half-fallen, around the sides. There is a whitish glint over the shiny smoothness of the upper top. We call that type of roof the Black Pan; it will drop without the least warning.

'What's that smooth up above sounding like?' I ask.

'Not bad,' the fireman answers.

'Have you sounded it?' I ask.

'Course I have,' he answered, and I knew he had not.

'I'm going to do it for myself,' I stated, 'because you can't be too sure.'

I climbed on top of the fall, then tapped the roof with the measuring stick. Boom – boom – it sounded hollow, as would a tautened drum. I scrambled back down.

'That upper piece is just down,' I said, 'it's ready to fall. Best to put some timber under it?'

'It's right enough,' the fireman insisted, 'and by the time we messes about to get timber here the shift'll be gone and it'll be morning afore we gets that coal by.'

'It would make sure that no more fell to delay us,' I argued, 'and it would be safer then.'

'And if you was to slam in it would be clear quicker,' he snapped, 'it seems as you're bent on wasting time.'

'I'm not,' I replied, 'only I wants to be as safe as I can. It's my body, remember, and a man don't want more than one clout from a stone falling from as high as that.'

'Get hold on the sledge, Griff,' he orders, 'and make a start. This chap have got a lot too much to say.'

Griff looks at the official, then at me. He is hesitant.

'Griff can do what he likes,' I said, 'but I'm not working under that top until it's put safer.'

'You'll do as I tells you or you know what you can do,' the fireman snarls, 'and that's pick up your tools and take 'em out.'

'I'll do that too,' I replied and threw my shovel on the side, 'and what about you, Griff? Are you staying?'

'Don't know what to do, mun,' he mumbles. 'P'raps it'll stay all right until we have cleared this fall. We've done it afore, heaps of times. Let's pitch in and clear away as soon as we can.'

I know that Griff has allowed the thoughts of his wife and family to overcome his judgement.

'Aye, that's the idea.' The fireman is suddenly friendly. 'Slam in at it. You won't be long and I'll stand up on the side and keep me eyes on the top. If anything starts to fall I'll shout and you can jump back.'

I know well that before the word of warning could have formed in his throat it would be too late. Griff looks at me in an appealing way. He will not start without me, but I do not want to feel that I am responsible for his losing the job.

I decide to risk it with him but to listen and watch most carefully.

We start to work, breaking the big stones and rolling them back one on top of another until we have formed a rough wall that is about a yard from the rail. The roof is quiet for a while and so we work swiftly. The fireman keeps very quiet because he can see we are working to our limit so that we can escape from under that bad piece, and he knows that the quieter he keeps the better we can hear. He sits on the wall, holding his lamp high and looking continually upward.

We had cleared about half of the fall and I had finished breaking a large stone when Griff asked me for the sledgehammer. Our elbows touched when I handed it to him. As he hit with the sledge I lifted a stone on to my knees but it slid down and dropped a couple of feet from the rail. I moved a short pace after it, bent, then began to lift it again. When I was almost straightened up I felt air rushing past my face; something hit me a terrible blow on the back. I heard a sound that seemed to start as a sob but ended in a groan that was checked abruptly. The blow on the back hit me forward. I felt to be flung along the roadway whilst my face ploughed through the small coal on the floor of the heading. I am sure that fire flashed from my eyes, yet I felt at the same time to be ice cold all over. My legs were dead weights hanging behind me. When I breathed I swallowed the small coal that was inside my mouth. My nose was blocked with dust, so were my eyes. I felt about with my hands before realizing that my face was against the floor and pushing down my arms to lift myself. I whimpered with relief when I found I could use my legs and so my back was not broken.

I could feel something running down my back; obviously it must be blood. Above, below, and around me everything is black with not the slightest sign of light to relieve it. So, whatever has happened the lamps must be smashed and we can have no help from them.

I had just managed to get to my knees and start to collect

my thoughts when I heard a scuffle a few yards away. Suddenly a new sound pierced the darkness. It was a sort of half scream, half squeal. At first I could not realise what this terrible sound meant; I had never before heard a grown man squeal with fear.

'Quick! Quick! Get me out!' It was the fireman screaming, and he sounded to be quite near to me. It seemed that he had been caught but was still alive. I did not hear the least sound from Griff. I collected my strength and shouted, 'Griff-oh! Are you all right?' I am far more concerned about my mate than the official. Griff was near me when I was hit. He was much more in the open than the fireman, who had chosen a part that was sheltered alongside the stronger side. I had no reply from Griff, but the fireman heard my call and I hear him sobbing with relief at knowing that I am alive and near to him.

'Come here, quick,' he appeals. 'I'm held fast over here. Get me out before more comes. Quick!'

I listen for some seconds, trying to puzzle where Griff was standing. I have lost all sense of direction. Am I nearly on top of my mate or will I press a stone still harder upon him if I move in that direction? While I hesitate the fireman restarts his screaming. Small stones drip around me continually, like the early drops of a shower of solid rain. Probably these are the warning that bigger stones are loosening but I cannot see what is above or which way to crawl and escape. I have lifted one eyelid over the other and the water from that eye has cleared away most of the dust. I can now open both eyes, but I can see no more than I could when my eyes were fast closed. I crawl towards the fireman, guided by his screams. Soon I find myself checked by what feels to be a mass of stone. I climb upwards, scramble over the top, then slide down. I call Griff again, softly, caressingly, as if to coax him to answer, whatever has happened, but no reply comes.

I press my shoulder against the solid side of the roadway

so that it shall guide me, then I crawl forward, very slowly. The fireman knows I am nearing him and directs my movements – continually imploring me to hurry. Suddenly I touch something that is softer and warmer than stone. I run my hand along and know it is a human leg. My every nerve seems to grate when I decide it must be Griff's and that he is dead.

'That's the leg.' The fireman's scream relieves me. 'There's a stone on it as is holding me down. Lift it, quick.'

I feel for the stone and set myself to endure the pain of lifting. I might as well have attempted to move the mountain, for three attempts fail to shake the stone. The fireman is speaking near my ear; he is frantic; begs me to hurry; screams at me as would an hysterical woman. I feel about and find a stone that I can move so I push it tightly under the one that holds the leg. This fresh stone will ease some of the weight and will stop any more pressure coming on his foot.

I have realised that I cannot do more until I have help. I must crawl and get others. I tell the fireman so, but he begs me not to go. I know there is no other way, so I turn around and feel my way over the stones. My fingers touch the cold iron of a tram rail, but as there is no sign of a tram on that side I am assured that this is the right way. I crawl alongside that rail, running my fingers on it for a guide.

'Don't you be long,' he screams after me, 'for God's sake don't be long.'

Above, in the darkness, I hear a sound that resembles the ripping of cloth. It is this noise that stones make when they are being crushed and broken by the weight that is moving above them. I must hurry, so that the fireman may be saved and to see if there is any hope for Griff.

I drag myself along a few yards, rest some seconds to ease the pain, then drag along again. I must have crawled more than two hundred yards before I saw a light in the distance. I could not shout, so I had to crawl close to the repairer who was at work there. He was some seconds before he understood the message that I was croaking, then when he did he became so flustered that he wasted some time hurrying back the way I had come before he realised it was useless going by himself. I lay in the darkness while he ran back to call the help that came very quickly. Soon the roadway was brightened by the lamps of scores of men, who hurried along and took me with them, and this time we had plenty of light to see what had happened.

I could see that at least another twenty tons had fallen and the hole under which we had been at work was now higher than ever. The place was all alive again, creaking above and around us. Posts back in the gob were cracking – cracking – as if someone was firing a pistol at irregular intervals.

The fireman was as I had left him. He had his back against the side. His right foot was free but the left one was held tightly under a large stone. We could see no sign of Griff. They lifted a rail from the roadway, then used it as a lever to ease the stone off the fireman so that he could be taken back from the danger. He was only slightly hurt because the weight had only been sufficient to hold him and the main body of the stone was resting on others. He would not sit down but wandered amongst the men continually telling them of his own fright and moaning, 'Who would have expected this?' They lost patience at last and someone told him to sit down and not delay the work.

Above the men who strained to clear the fall, huge stones several tons in weight had started to fall, then had pressed against other stones that were moving and each had checked the downward movement of the other. They had locked each other in that position and now remained balancing – partly fallen – but the slightest jar or movement of the upper top would send them crashing down to finish their drop on the gang of men underneath. There was a continual rolling above us like thunder that is distant. Little stones flaked from the larger ones and dropped on the backs of the men as they worked below. Each time a stone dropped all the men leapt back, for a smaller stone is often the warning from a bigger one that is coming behind.

Several of the men stood erect, with their lamps held high and their eyes scanning the moving stones up above. They kept their mouths open, so that the warning shout should issue with no check. The others, busy amongst the fall, tumbling and lifting whilst they searched under the stones, did not hesitate when a warning came – they sprang backwards at once and made sure that no man stood directly behind the other to impede that swift spring.

Men can lift great weights when fear forces their strength. These stood six in a row, then tumbled big stones away until only the largest one in the centre was left. This one needed leverage, so a man knelt alongside to place the end of two rails in position; they had to be careful not to put the end on a man's body. Several men put their shoulders under the rails then they prised upwards. As the stone was slowly lifted they blocked it up by packing with smaller stones, then started to lift again. When the stone was two feet off the ground they paused; surely it was high enough. There was something to be done now that each man dreaded; then, as if their minds had worked together two men knelt down and reached underneath. Very carefully they drew out what had been Griff.

We retreated with our burden and left the sides to do what crushing, and the roof to do what falling, they wished. The pain of my back had been severe all the while, when the excitement slackened I felt sick and could not stand alone. I leaned against one of my mates for support and he placed his arm around me gently, as if I was a woman.

We all know the verdict well enough, but refuse to admit it. Griff seems to be no more than half his usual size. Someone takes his watch from the waistcoat hanging on the side. They hold the shining back against what they believe is his mouth. Thirty yards away another stone crashes down on top of the others and the broken pieces fly past us whilst dust clouds the air. The seconds tick out loudly through that underground chamber whilst forty men watch another holding a watch; when he turns around someone lifts a lamp near so that they can see. The shining back is not dimmed. We had all known, yet somehow we had dared to hope.

As we are going outwards I notice that the fireman tries to isolate me; he wants to talk. I avoid him and keep in the group. Some distance along. I hear a queer sound and look back to see that he has collapsed. His legs have given under him and he cannot stand. He is paralysed with fright. Two of the men place their hands under him and they carry him along behind the stretcher. They have to lean inwards to avoid the sides and bend their heads down because of the top. The fireman senses the hatred that is in all our minds and he sobs continually but no one asks him if he is in pain.

When we reach the main roadway the journey of empty trams is waiting. We place the loaded stretcher across one tram and four men sit alongside it. The fireman is lifted into another tram and the rest of us scramble on.

Suddenly the fireman tries to reassert himself.

'All of you going out,' he complains, 'didn't ought to go, not all of you. That fall have got to be cleared so's to get the coal back first thing.'

It was as if he had not spoken. The rider knocked on the signal wires. We start to move outwards slowly, for the engineer has been warned that it is not coal he is drawing this time. The fireman starts his mumbling again and we realise that he will tell the manager that the men refused to listen to him. Already he has started to cover his tracks.

Outside, it is dark and raining. The lamps on the pit-mouth are smeared where the water has trickled through the dust on the globes. There is a paste of oily mud and wet small coal that squelches under our feet. The official limps away to the office. We notice, and comment on the fact, that he walks quickly and with hardly any difficulty. He gets inside the office and we hear him fastening the door before he switches the light on. He intends to be alone when making his report. We hand our lamps in, telling the lamp-men to note the damaged ones and we answer their inquiry as to 'Who is it this time?' They return our checks but put Griff's in a small tin box. A smear of light is brightening the sky but it is raining very heavily when we start on that half-hour's journey to his home. We feel our clothes getting wet on our bodies and the blankets on the stretcher are soaking. Water rushes down the house-pipes and it bubbles and glistens in the light of the few street lamps.

All the houses near have their downstairs lights on, for news of disaster spreads quickly; besides, it is time for the next shift to prepare. The handles of the stretcher scrape the wall when we take the sharp turn to get through the kitchen door. This is the only downstairs room they have, so we prepare to wash him there. Neighbours have been busy, as they always are in this sort of happening. A large fire is burning, the tub is in, water is steaming on the hob and his clean pants and shirt are on the guard as if he was coming home from an ordinary shift.

I see no sign of Griff's wife. I remember her as small and quiet; a woman who stayed in her own home and was all her time tending to Griff and their five children. I do hear a sound of sobbing from upstairs and conclude that they have made her stop there, very wisely. Sometimes I hear the voices of the children too, but they are soft and subdued, as if they had only partly wakened and had not yet realised the disaster this dawn had brought to them.

I think that is all. I have relived that night fifty, yes, a hundred times since it happened, and each time I have felt that I hated the fireman more. Had that stone hit my back a little harder I would have been compelled to spend the rest of my days in bed with a broken back – and would have to exist on twenty-six shillings a week as compensation. Had I been a yard farther back I would probably be in similar state to Griff – then I would have been worth eighteen pounds, bare funeral expenses, as I would have been counted as having no dependants.

If I appear stupid at the inquiry, as a workman is expected to be, then I will answer the set questions as I am supposed to answer them and 'the usual verdict will be returned'.

Griff was my mate, and nothing I can do will bring him back to life again, but his wife and family are left. He would have wished that I do the best thing possible for them. If I remain quiet, they may be paid about four hundred pounds as compensation – which is the highest estimate of the value of a husband and father, if he is a miner. They will think that one of the usual accidents robbed them of the father, but if they are told he should not have died, it will surely increase their suffering.

If I speak what is true, the insurance company will claim that they are absolved from liability because we should not have worked there. Had we refused we should probably have lost our jobs. The insurance solicitor will be present – ever watching his chance – and will seize on the least flaw in the evidence.

So this afternoon I shall go to the office and draw two pay envelopes that should contain about two pounds sixteen each. One is mine, the other I will take to his house. There five silent children will be waiting whilst their dazed mother is being prepared to go to the Hall and testify that the crushed thing lying in the kitchen was her husband and that he was in good health when she saw him leave the house.

If the verdict is anything except 'Accidental Death' that pay packet may hold the last money she will have – unless it is the pension and parish relief.

Later, tonight, I shall have to face another fear; I shall have to go again down that hole and restart work, but at four o'clock I will be at the inquest, shall kiss the Bible, and speak 'The whole truth and nothing but the truth' – perhaps. Would you?

GAMBLERS

Leslie Norris

On the hills outside the town, near the river and, further out, on the bleak moor, lie bundles of enormous masonry. The gaunt towers, the unlit, vaulting arches, the great walls of cut stone, are ruined and empty, their heavy margins flawed and irregular where parts have tumbled away. When I was a kid I used often to stand near a single fallen block, looking at it. It was a frowning grey, grass grew about its edges, a golden lichen furred its tiny crevices. Sometimes I'd climb on top of it, lie back, stare to the tops of the dark walls around, ominous, heavy, without purpose. I could not imagine any use for them at all. They were all that remained of the ironworks which had been the reason for the town. I had never seen them working. Perhaps there were old men who had known this, perhaps they had worked there.

I used to wander often about the works, particularly on gloomy days when the sky had the colour and something of the weight of those dull stone ruins and the rain beat without ceasing on those streaming walls. I knew the galleries, their floors covered with a soft dust of powdered limestone mortar, I had examined the cogwheels, taller than I was, rust-covered, much too heavy to think of shifting, that lay abandoned and broken against the walls of mills and cooling towers. It was in the works that I learned to fix a night line. One of the streams coming off the mountain had been channelled underground beneath a maze of ovens and engine rooms. It emerged just below the works, through a low tunnel. You could follow it, walking along a ledge of stone deep into the mountain, your hand on the exquisite, damp curve of the arched roof, until your nerve failed. I never went in far. Some people said there were rats in there. One warm day, sitting on the grass at the tunnel's mouth, I saw three trout swim out of the darkness. Easy and sinuous, they lay facing the current. The water was so clear that I could see their freckled colours, their red and black spots. An uncle of mine showed me how to set a night line. Every evening I'd get a few yards inside the tunnel, my baited hook ready, tie the line to a nail I'd hammered into the wall, lower the line gently into the water. A couple of lead shot about eighteen inches up from the hook kept the worm in an enticingly natural position. I've caught many a breakfast that way. But that was years later. The only other people to use the old works as much as I did were the gamblers.

There is a sense in which life itself was a gamble in our town. Hardly a man had work. In the whole length of our street, only two men could say they were employed, yet there was an air of urgency about the place, and a reckless, bitter gaiety. People kept busy. Many of them were serious gamblers; undeterred by lack of money, they could speak with authority of bloodlines and handicaps, were walking libraries of form, knew the idiosyncrasies of all the race tracks in England, not one of which they had ever seen. They used to lay complex and intricate bets, trebles, accumulators, little side bets on the way, their ramifications causing hours of study and demanding a mastery of reckoning that accountants could envy, and all for an outlay of sixpence. Using matches for stakes, or perhaps cigarettes cut in halves, they would play card games of desperate intensity and skill. They searched for evidence of good fortune wherever they thought it could be found, in racing, in decks of cards, in the spin of a coin. The first gambler I knew was Owen Doherty.

The Dohertys lived near us, and Owen was the oldest of

nine boys. He was shabby and elegant, walking slowly and straight-backed through the world, his thin, Irish face with its high cheekbones expressionless. I never saw Owen Doherty laugh at anything that was funny, although occasionally he'd give a high sharp bark of contempt at any opinion he thought particularly futile. He was much older than I, over twenty years older. I admired him because he was the best pitch-and-toss player in the district.

The young men used to play pitch-and-toss with pennies, or more probably halfpence, in a narrow lane behind the houses. I used to go down and watch them. From time to time, when I was very small, they'd send me away, since the game was illegal, liable to be interrupted by a patrolling policeman, and I at five or six would be a handicap to them and a source of information to the police. But I'd not gone far, continuing to watch from a tactful place higher up the lane.

The game was very simple. The boys used to take their coins between finger and thumb and aim them, with an underhand swing of the arm, at a mark about fifteen feet away. They used a small stone or a peg in the ground at which to aim. The player whose coin landed nearest the mark would collect the coins, place them on the flat of his hand, and toss them, glittering and spinning, into the air. A complicated system of heads and tails, which I never completely understood, decided the winner. Oh, to see Owen Doherty step up to the line, glare about him to demand the silence necessary for his total concentration, take the edge of his jacket in his left hand so that its drape should not impede his throw, lean forward, and sweetly aim! And later, as he placed the coins fastidiously along his palm and thin fingers, examining them so that their positions were absolutely right, holding them, waiting for the wind to die away before he threw them up, then we'd watch, knowing such artistry rare and sacred.

Only once did the police ever raid this game, as far as I

know, and I was older then. I was at the head of the lane, bouncing a tennis ball on my right foot and counting aloud to see how many times I could manage it, when I heard yelps and shouts at the other end and the coin-tossers raced past me, going flat out. I looked down the lane and there was Sergeant Wilson, red-faced, pounding towards me at a frightening speed. I took off at once, despite my innocence, and had overtaken all the fleeing criminals long before they'd had time to scatter. I turned right at the top of the lane, sped along Victoria Street and doubled back through Albert Road. Then I sat on our window sill, looking virtuous and innocent, as I had every right to. I wasn't even breathing hard. I was about fourteen then. This race was the cause of my graduating to the card games, hard, serious, for real money, that were held most nights in the old works.

Every boy in our town would have known the difference between a three of spades and a cup of tea at a very early age. I certainly did, but my knowledge stopped right there. For some reason I could never understand even the simplest card games. I would have been hard put to it to give a blind man reasonable exercise in a game of Snap and the satisfaction of Brag, Pontoon and Bridge have never been known to me. I was teaching Muirhead, our cat, to jump through a hoop. She was refusing consistently, and mewing in a conciliatory manner. Pretty soon, I knew, she would bite and scratch. I was glad when the boys came up. They told me that I was just the fellow they wanted for their card school. Flattered but realistic, I told them that I couldn't play cards and that I had no money.

'No, no,' said Owen. 'We don't want you to play. We want you as lookout. The way you went past us this morning, why there can't be a policeman in the force to live with you. What do you say? A shilling a week, for three evenings' work. Up at the old works.'

We worked out a neat ploy. A disused railway track, its metal and sleepers long ago lifted to leave only the cinder ballast, led through the works, and I was to use it as a running track, supposedly training there while keeping a sharp lookout for policemen. Gareth Stephens had an old pair of shorts he'd grown too big for and he gave them to me. I liked them. They were of white silk, with blue lines round the waist and down the outside of the legs. Wearing these, a white vest and a pair of gym shoes, I began my employment, jogging along, practising my starts, occasionally stopping for deep breathing and bending and stretching. I grew to like it very much. I trained sincerely, revelling in the increasing strength and stamina I began to recognise. I trained every night and on Saturday morning, forgotten were the card players, forgotten the plan by which, if the police ever came, I was to trot gently and inconspicuously towards the gamblers where they sat on stone benches under one of the great arches, warning them by whistling 'The Last Round-up'. Even so, it should have been easy. Down before me, below the slope of the mountain, I could see the roofs of the town small and far away. There was no cover on the mountain, not a tree, not a bush. The scattered remnants of a few low stone walls, which had once contained the fields, the moor had long taken back and could certainly not have hidden a policeman. But nothing had happened for so long; I had been nearly two summers training in front of the works, and I had become unwary. I had become engrossed in my running, the running had taken over. So that one Friday evening, cloudless, in late July, I was suddenly astonished to see five stout blue bodies a couple of hundred yards away.

I turned and trotted back towards the works, prancing, knees high, shaking my arms as they hung limply at my side, as if to loosen the muscles. Behind my neck I thought I could feel the policemen mustering for a brief charge, and I could stand it no longer. I exploded into a frenzied sprint, all thought of 'The Last Round-up' forgotten.

'Police! Police!' I hissed, whipping past the cavern like a short, white Jesse Owens. 'Move, for Christ's sake!'

I kept on running until I was two hundred yards down the track, and then slowed gently to a walk, hands on hips, getting my breath. Then I turned and trotted back, breaking into fast sprints of twenty yards or so, straight out of the trot. I'd read about this in an old book by Jack Donaldson, who had been World Professional Champion in the days when shorts were worn below the knee. That book was a mine of information. It also had details of a high-protein diet which was guaranteed to take a yard off your time, but I knew I'd never have the money for it. I raced past the empty arch. A policeman was bending down, collecting a scatter of cards that had fallen to the ground. The other four were looking up at the hillside. I could see the dark figures of the gamblers bucking like stags up the steep. Decorously, I slowed.

'Do you know them, boy?' said the policeman. 'Do you know any of them?'

'Who do you mean?' I answered.

I shaded my eyes with my hand so that I could look more easily up the hill into the sunset. My friends were satisfactorily away.

The policeman sighed gently.

'Never mind,' he said.

He stood looking at the cards in his hands.

'At least we gave them a fright,' he said.

It was then that Mr Everson appeared, stepping delicately over a bundle of stones at the fallen edge of a wall. Mr Everson was a middle-aged gambler who sometimes sat in with my friends. He held in one hand a small bundle of plants and leaves and under his arm was a thick book with a respectable black cover.

'Good evening, gentlemen,' he said. 'And a very lovely evening too.'

The policemen watched him as he came mildly down the track. They didn't answer;

'Look at these,' said Mr Everson, detaching a few dark

green leaves from his miscellaneous bouquet. 'The leaves of the wild violet, gentlemen, and here, a little late and therefore faded, the flower itself. A marvel, gentlemen, a marvel.'

Mr Everson chuckled with satisfaction over the fistful of flowers.

'It's astonishing', he said. 'Don't you find it astonishing, to think that a mere fifty years ago the glare from these furnaces lit up the sky for miles around and nothing would grow on these hills because of the stench and fume of burning sulphur? And now, see, the violets are growing. Quite astonishing.'

Mr Everson held out his violets. Every time he said 'astonishing', he opened wide his guileless eyes. It was quite a performance. A pair of ravens which lived high in the walls came out and croaked derisively, but the policemen said nothing. Mr Everson walked through their silent suspicion.

'Come along, boy,' he said. 'You've done enough for one night. We don't want you to get stale.'

I picked up my sweater and, side by side, we walked away. All the time I expected the policemen to call us back, but they didn't. Mr Everson was perfectly calm, treating me with courtesy, as an equal. He was not only old, he was lame. He couldn't have run away with the others. When he was young he had injured his right knee playing football and the leg was permanently bent. Yet he walked strongly, taking a very short step off the right foot and gliding down in an immense long stride on his good leg. More excitingly, while he walked he grew tall and short in turn. On his injured leg his face was level with mine, but his left leg turned him into a tall man, a foot above me. So his voice soared and fell, too, as we walked into the town. He spoke to me about the wild flowers mainly. He knew all about them. He could outwit the police. He was a very clever man.

As I grew older my admiration for Laurence Everson grew too. We became friends, in spite of the difference in our ages. He was both intelligent and amusing and in another place and at another time he could have done great things. But in the waste and wilderness of our town he was able to cultivate only his individuality. He was well read, scholarly even, and he belonged to several libraries. His interest in politics was informed and cynical, but he loved all kinds of sport. Whenever I'd call on him, I'd find him reading, his head resting on one hand, bent over his book. He always read at a table, sitting on a hard chair, the book fairly close to his face because he refused to wear glasses. It was a big face, large-featured, and he had flat lemon hair on top of his head, shading to grey around his ears. I didn't know he wore a wig until after his death, when one of his brothers told me.

Laurence was a fine snooker player and twice a week for years we played together. He taught me everything, from the basic grasp of the cue up. He taught me how to let the weight, the lead in the heavy base of the graduated wood, do the work, to bend low over the table so that the forward stroke would brush the knot of my tie, to use side and stop. From him I learned the correct bridge for every shot and to recognise a situation so clearly that I could carry in my mind not only the shot in hand but the next five or six shots. And we bet on every game we played during all that time, sometimes straightforward wagers based on a handicap which decreased as I improved, sometimes on some wild, surrealistic series of events which he improvised as he went along. Laurence Everson would bet on anything.

'Beautiful day,' he'd say. 'Bet you it will rain before two thirty-three.'

And we'd sit there, watching the second hands of our watches. Once we spent a whole afternoon betting in even pennies on his canary, a cinnamon-yellow Border that lived in the kitchen. First we bet on the precise second when it would sing and when that palled, we bet on the pitch of its first note, checking the result on Laurence's piano. This was the time he'd been ill and I'd gone in to see him. Mrs Everson looked pale and anxious, but Laurence looked fine. He sat in an armchair, a rug about his knees, remarkably strong and imposing. He was sixty then.

After he recovered we went to Cardiff to see Glamorgan play Essex in the county Cricket Championship. We went by train and I won a few coppers on the journey, betting on the colour of the shirt worn by the next man to enter our carriage. We were in plenty of time, found good seats and prepared to have a day of it. We couldn't have chosen better weather, hot enough to give the whole game a dreamlike clarity and yet comfortable enough for those of us who sat in our shirtsleeves. In those days Glamorgan had an opening batsman named Smart, and he was very good. He played that day as if inspired and he'd scored fifty before lunch. Laurence and I ate our sandwiches and opened our bottles of beer. A couple of white pigeons fluttered on the grass in front of us, strutting for crumbs. We were perfectly contented. After the interval, Smart continued where he left off, playing shots of perfect timing and invention. Soon he was punching the ball all over the field. The Essex fast bowler, a youngster who never made the grade, suddenly dug one in so fiercely that it bounced head high and viciously, but Smart, leaning elegantly back, hooked it off his eyebrows. It was perfect. The ball came right at us and Laurence, holding up a nonchalant hand, held it easily and tossed it back, laughing. A few people near us called and clapped and he turned around to say something. I could see his face, his amused eyes, and then it seemed to go to pieces, as if every muscle had suddenly snapped. He keeled right over and I held him as he was falling. God, he was a weight. People were helpful and competent. A doctor arrived within minutes and we got Laurence away to the hospital. He was quite unconscious and I stood around helplessly as they worked on him. It was his heart.

After a while he came to. He looked appalling. His skin,

always sallow, was blue, and it seemed he could open only one eye.

'Did Smart get his hundred?' he whispered.

I could scarcely hear him.

'Yes,' I said. I had no idea if it were true.

There was a long pause. I thought he'd lost consciousness again.

'Thank God for that,' he said.

The doctor looked at me. He was a young man, perhaps a year or two older than I was. His white coat seemed a size too large for him and he looked cautious and sad.

'Your father?' he said.

'No,' I said. 'A friend. I've known him a long time, though.'

'He's not good,' said the doctor. 'He's not at all well. I don't think he'll make it.'

We were talking very quietly away from the bed, near the door. Laurence said something and I moved back to him.

'What time is it?' he asked.

I looked at my watch. It was four-thirty.

'Bet you,' he said. 'I'm still going at five o'clock.'

He could barely speak.

'Done,' I said. 'Ten shillings.'

That was an impossibly large bet for us.

'He's game,' said the doctor. 'By God, he's game.'

We sat there for a long time listening to Laurence breathing. It seemed fainter and shallower. At last he spoke. He had no voice at all, but there was expression, somehow, in his terrible halting whisper. You could hear his amusement.

'Pay the wife,' he said, 'if I win.'

He opened his eyes for the last time and I think he would have grinned had it been possible.

'Think of it,' he said. 'At last. At last one of us is on a dead cert.'

I told all the boys that, and they all liked it, all those truthful and gallant gamblers. It was difficult to get Mrs

Everson to take the money, until I explained that it was a debt of honour, Laurence's last wager. She was a small, hard woman, very proud of Laurence.

'Gambling,' she said tremulously. 'It was his life.'

ON THE TIP

Rhys Davies

The 'tip,' as it is called, fringes the colliery like a cliff, falling away precipitately from the plateau on the hillside where the shafts of the pit rise. It is a gigantic cape of black, stony waste stuff, the rubble unearthed with the coal and thrown aside, dumped uglily and sombrely on the landscape, to remain there for ever. Each year it grows larger, encroaches further down the vale, a loose sombre little hill. In prosperous times no one takes any notice of it: a dirty, ugly dump.

Now, however, with more than half the men out of work, those who have the patience and determination to force something out of the idle day, make their way to the tip and spend long, arid hours of searching among the waste. For here and there, shyly hidden among the dull slate and broken black rock, pieces of coal glitter, treasure escaped among the wagonloads of rubbish emptied daily over the tip. The right to search is a concession granted by the pit owners to those men they have thrown out of work.

That cold afternoon only a dozen or so men combed the tip thus, dragging their canvas sacks laboriously up the steep cliff. The sky was shifty with uneasy clouds, there was a shrill bite in the wintry air. Most of the men had been on the tip since the morning: some were luckier than others and had already gleaned a half-sack of small silver-blue pieces. A full sack, weighing about eighty pounds and worth about a shilling, was considered a good day's work: lifted to the shoulders, it was borne off triumphantly to feed a starved hearth.

'How is it going, Walt?' bawled a swart but cheerful-looking young chap, pausing for a minute to munch a wad of bread. 'I just got a lovely piece – look!' Wad of bread held between his teeth, he held up an unusually large segment of blue-shimmering coal in his black hand, exultingly.

'No luck I'm having today,' Walt, also a youngish man, called gloomily. 'You give us a few pieces, Mog,' he appealed, 'you got more than you've a right to. A clout there'll be from my missus if I go home like this tonight.'

Mog grinned and refused to be charitable. Walt was an indolent searcher: he spent a lot of time vacantly squatting on his heels and smoking bits of fags. He was an amateur boxer, but out of the ring he seemed bemused and bedraggled amid his bulgy, overdeveloped muscles. And he was for ever complaining of assaults from his wife, who had married him just before the slump arrived.

Mog popped his lucky find into his already fat bag and contentedly finished the rest of the bread and a thin slice of Caerphilly cheese. He would have a good fire tonight, red and gold, as in the old days when he was working. A leaping big fire on a winter night and a bowl of broth, feet in the fender – it would make life seem as it used to be, a thing to be enjoyed and believed in. He had been out of work for two years.

Higher and higher they climbed, their feet sinking in the loose hill. Hands were bruised, backs were aching. A quarter of a mile away, down the vale, the rows of dwellings began their straggling lengths of grey concrete or black stone: homes! But attenuated homes now, with no hams hanging under the ceiling, no silks for the women, no ale for the men. All down the narrow vale there was an odd quiet and a queer shrunken look, that it had never possessed in the old days, when stomachs were full and people out among shops with pound notes in their pockets. Pound notes!

A wagon appeared at the top of the tip, sliding on a rail from the pithead. The searchers poised below on the cape moved away from the portion where the emptied rubbish would fall: the wagon was tipped, a thick shower of stone running down the slope. When the movements had ceased, the searchers plunged eagerly to where the shower had fallen, dragging their sacks; there was more promise in a fresh load of rubbish.

Gomer Lewis, a silent middle-aged man, searched erratically and wearily that day. He had been constantly turning to stare with a worried scrutiny down the vale, his weak blue eyes short of vision. He was cold and miserable and knew he ought to be at home. But what was to be done about a fire! Not a scrap of coal in the house and the kettle that morning having to be boiled next door. And he hated troubling neighbours and accepting pieces of wood and coal from the lucky ones. In his day he had earned four pounds a week and bought half a pound of best tobacco every Saturday, wearing a gold watch and chain in the evenings: Maggie had her fur and shiny shoes and trips to the seaside. And now this. This, and what was to come?

He began to search feverishly again: he had had a very poor day, the bottom of his sack scarcely covered yet. And there must be a fire in the house the next few days. Dole on Friday, but there were two days to get through yet: Maggie had been craving for grapes and walnuts, yet laughing at herself. Charity: the district nurse: clothes from the depot run by the Quakers – a bundle of small used garments had arrived a week ago.

The sky thickened, dusky clouds scudding at each other as if in icy dispute. The cold became harsher, and snatches of bitter wind swept down from the winter-dead hills and broke across the tip. None of the searchers wore an overcoat and even Mog, the amiable young man with the almost-full sack, ceased whistling to swear at the cold and thrust his black hands under his armpits, though he comforted himself with the thought of the flaring and buxom fire he would sit before that night.

'How goes it, Gomer?' he asked, having scrambled near the short-sighted collier, peering and scraping among the dull rubble.

'Bad,' Gomer muttered briefly. 'I can't see anything at all.'

'You ought to have specs here indeed,' said Mog sympathetically.

'Can't afford them, and I see all right for ordinary purposes,' Gomer added gruffly. 'Sometimes too much I see, nowadays.'

'Aye,' sighed Mog, 'a blessing it would be to have no sight at all sometimes.' Then he grinned. 'Know what four of the women did in our street yesterday?'

'What?' Gomer said, still bent and delving into the tip.

'Clubbed together and bought a scrag of mutton between 'em. A saucepan of broth each had out of it. The scrag dipped in for half an hour in turn, passing from house to house. A bit thin was the broth, but with plenty of leeks and swedes it went over the tongue pretty fair.'

Gomer was startled. Such depths as using a communal piece of mutton Maggie had not reached yet. Yet! But if things went on as they were going... And he who used to carve the juicy sirloin of beef on Sunday, ceremoniously, a good family joint, best home-killed. Now they managed a frozen chop or two, Maggie somehow achieving tastiness out of them.

Mog went on talking. How much longer, O Lord, were the bad times going to last! Had Gomer any news of pits reopening up the valley? Yesterday there was a rumour of one and Mog had tramped eight miles and found it false. Mog alternately grunted and grinned, chatting to the unresponsive Gomer. He blew his nose and examined Gomer for a while. Getting on in years, thin, and a bit grumpy. A lot of chaps seemed to hide themselves in themselves now, get quiet and dark-looking. No use worrying, Mog thought tenaciously. He had been two years out, but wasn't on his knees yet, though married. True, he had no kids, thank the Lord. No kids to stare and ask for toys and cakes for tea.

The afternoon light shifted into a dark stony-grey, the clouds still clashed dangerously and there was a mutter of thunder. Gomer tore into the tip desperately: he must at least find enough for a small fire in the morning. Things would be needed, a piece of steamed fish, perhaps, for Maggie, a custard. He'd have to try and sell the pair of brass candlesticks on the mantelshelf. But would anybody buy, in the starving town, with the pawnshop overloaded and hostile... He felt himself cold and futile and helpless as he chucked the black rock and stone aside.

Mog was saying to him, 'You ought to come and join our choir, Gomer. Rehearsals for The *Messiah* now. Something to do. A grand piece, by Handel.

'I got a solo to sing,' he added with a grin of pride.

'No voice in me now,' Gomer answered, a little impatiently, weary of his continued failure among the rubble. Then, ashamed of his brusqueness to the cheerful and chatty Mog, who used to work near him in the pit, he said reminiscently, 'Aye, Handel's *Messiah*. Grand indeed. Many's the time I've heard it. I heard Madame Lily Jenkins in it, singing "He shall feed His flock" – there's a voice for you, an angel's! Dead now, poor Lily Jenkins. She went into dropsy.'

'We're having Sara Watkins to sing "He shall feed His flock",' said Mog, who was too young to have known the glory of Lily Jenkins. 'Contralto and eisteddfod winner.'

'A wonderful solo it is,' sighed Gomer. And he turned again to the tip, while Mog, also resuming search, began to sing in a hearty voice:

'*He shall feed His flock*
Like a shepherd—'

'Hey, what's that moke neighing for on this tip?' Walt, not far below, demanded.

An exchange of ironical insults began between Walt and

Mog, the latter reminding the amateur boxer of various disgraceful losses he had sustained in the local ring. It was not long before they were throwing pieces of the rubble at each other. Searchers, pausing in their difficult crablike movements over the tip, urged on the combatants. But Gomer, aware of the darkening afternoon, delved deeper into the tip: he found two or three meagre pieces. So absorbed was he that he peered no more down the vale.

A small figure was approaching the tip, climbing the dirty pasturage that lay between it and the first row of houses, a figure Gomer had been half expecting all day. It was that of a young girl of about twelve, wearing a shabby coat tightly belted round her stark, angular body. She walked stiffly over the dust-sodden field and contemptuously ignored a few grumpy geese who lunged out at her with menacing cries. Soon she was climbing the tip, sticking her feet into the loose rubble and balancing herself confidently. She was thin, but hardened; the ice-pallor of her oval face and the purity of grey in her eyes gave her a remote look. She knew that she bore an important announcement, but she carried it as a sealed letter; she did not allow it to be distributed in wonder and contemplation through her own mind. Her father sometimes called her his young snowdrop. And she looked a snowdrop now, an early snowdrop, closed and very pale and pure. There had been no school for her that auspicious day.

Some of the tip-searchers looked at her curiously. Having discovered her father she went on climbing steadily and with assurance towards his bent figure. Gomer still hadn't noticed and it was Mog who called to him.

'This your girl, isn't she, Gomer?'

Gomer started up as quickly as his aching back would allow him. For a minute he couldn't move, the pain in his back gripped him so tight. His daughter and he met near Mog, who waited inquisitively.

'Well now, well now?' Gomer said hurriedly, his breath blown excitedly over the words. 'What is it, Olwen, now?'

For she had not seemed in a hurry to speak. Her grey eyes, wide and remote, had looked at him without expression. Perhaps, deep in her, there was a secret excitement too. Then her lips moved and her voice, fragile and slow with a strange kind of warmth as if early spring sunlight played on it, said:

'A little boy has come.'

Gomer stood still and after a moment wiped his brow with the back of his hand, leaving a big smudge. There was rejoicing and desolation in his heart. He had two daughters, Olwen, who was twelve, and Megan, who was eight. He used to say, when work was regular and pay decent, that he wanted two girls and two boys. Now he had a boy: a boy had come into his world: the day was a festival. But he stood still and was aware of dark lamentations. What had he to give out of his world to this new child? He moved his gaze almost furtively away from the grey eyes of his daughter. A few drops of rain fell on his lifted face: he looked silently into the prowling clouds. Olwen waited, shut and quiet. Mog, having heard the announcement and gaped at it, turned aside and plunged again into the tip. He was shocked. Other searchers were near and looked up, wondering if anything were happening.

Gomer quickly returned to normal behaviour. 'I'll come now, Olwen,' he said.

Olwen's wide gaze moved to the empty-looking sack flung at her father's feet. She had been busy at household tasks that day, while the district nurse bustled about. She felt responsible, and she asked with cool expectancy, since he had been on the tip since the morning:

'A load of coal you're bringing?'

Gomer swung up the sack. It was disgustingly light, enough for an hour's fire perhaps.

'Not a load, Olwen,' he said briefly.

At which Mog lifted himself and said, 'Open that sack now, more luck's than my share I've had. I got just a full bag here.'

'No, no, Mog,' Gomer protested.

But Mog had already snatched the bag out of Gomer's hand, and he began filling it. All the same, he was going to make the others on the tip contribute. He bawled out to them:

'Oi there! Gomer's got to go home. His missus has took to her bed. Come on now and fill his sack.'

Those within hearing scrambled up and down to the little group. Mog repeated his demand, Gomer protesting. They contributed willingly. One or two men made a joke of the news, others shook their heads and deplored. Gomer's bag was soon full. He stood deprecating, but helpless. And relieved; he had to submit to the feeling of relief, miserable as it was to be helped in this way by those who could ill afford to give.

Olwen stood apart, an aloof acceptance of the scene on her face. Coal was wanted; the house was cold. The district nurse had exclaimed loudly. Olwen had scraped and scraped over the floor of the coalhouse for dust and sifted half a shovelful over an old stool she had chopped up and lit in the grate. So a gleam of approval entered her watching eyes as the searchers crammed the precious stuff into her father's sack.

'There now,' said Mog, with a determined gaiety, 'the young chap'll see a real fire on his first winter's night, as is proper.'

Gomer quietly thanked the searchers. They tied the opening of the sack and heaved it up to his shoulders. Carefully and slowly he began to descend the tip, the sedate Olwen preceding him. Joy and foreboding still struggled in his heart. A boy seemed to him now a more serious business than a girl. A girl was usually protected by some man. A man's life depended on the goodwill and prosperity and peaceful disposition of the world. And the world had become like a skeleton. Gomer stumbled from the tip to the frozen field below. Olwen waited for him. As he came to her, she suddenly smiled, with a kind of cool glee.

'I've seen him. He's a pretty little boy, Dad,' she said.

'Is he indeed, Olwen, is he now?' he said, rousing himself.

Then she added, a hint of grave elderly knowledge in her voice:

'Like you he seemed to me.'

'Like me, is he?' said Gomer, laughing at her desire to please him. The rain was swinging down now, but neither of them took any notice of it. Gomer strode along quite easily, with the lumpy bag stretched across his shoulders. And Olwen, alert and stark in her tight-belted coat, looked forward to domestic tasks, aided by a proper fire...

Up on the tip, Mog had followed father and daughter's progress with a troubled mien. His jauntiness had been wiped away for a while; still he was shocked. It seemed to him the most dangerous folly to bring forth young into the world, with times as they were. Yet... yet... He tightened his belt. Why, after all, should the nasty behaviour of the times be allowed to affect a man's true life! Life must proceed. Gomer had a courage which he, Mog, did not possess.

The rain began to slash across the tip, the sodden clouds plunging nearer the dead hills. Mog looked at his diminished sack. He could hear Gwen's exasperated cry when she caught sight of it. But might as well give up now. Cold and wet: the rain spat large icy drops into his face. Mog suddenly lifted his arm and shook his fist menacingly at the heaving sky. He would like to have a fight with someone just then. The world was dirty, untidy, slovenly...

Then he uttered a bark of laughter. What was he doing, shaking his fist at the heavens? Threatening God with a black eye? Snatching up his sack of coal he ran carelessly and easily down the tip, ducking through the whipping rain and flinging a last good-humoured insult to Walt, whose flattened smudge of a nose was pale blue with cold. Three or four searchers, half hidden in the rain, still combed the tip.

EXTRAORDINARY LITTLE COUGH

Dylan Thomas

One afternoon, in a particularly bright and glowing August,
some years before I knew I was happy, George Hooping,
whom we called Little Cough, Sidney Evans, Dan Davies,
and I sat on the roof of a lorry travelling to the end of the
Peninsula. It was a tall, six-wheeled lorry, from which we
could spit on the roofs of the passing cars and throw our
apple stumps at women on the pavement. One stump caught
a man on a bicycle in the middle of the back, he swerved
across the road, for a moment we sat quiet and George
Hooping's face grew pale. And if the lorry runs over him, I
thought calmly as the man on the bicycle swayed towards
the hedge, he'll get killed and I'll be sick on my trousers and
perhaps on Sidney's too, and we'll all be arrested and
hanged, except George Hooping who didn't have an apple.

But the lorry swept past; behind us, the bicycle drove into
the hedge, the man stood up and waved his fist, and I waved
my cap back at him.

'You shouldn't have waved your cap,' said Sidney Evans,
'he'll know what school we're in.' He was clever, dark, and
careful, and had a purse and a wallet.

'We're not in school now.'

'Nobody can expel me,' said Dan Davies. He was leaving
next term to serve in his father's fruit shop for a salary.

We all wore haversacks, except George Hooping whose mother had given him a brown-paper parcel that kept coming undone, and carried a suitcase each. I had placed a coat over my suitcase because the initials on it were 'N.T.' and everybody would know that it belonged to my sister. Inside the lorry were two tents, a box of food, a packing case of kettles and saucepans and knives and forks, an oil lamp, a primus stove, ground sheets and blankets, a gramophone with three records, and a tablecloth from George Hooping's mother.

We were going to camp for a fortnight in Rhossilli, in a field above the sweeping five-mile beach. Sidney and Dan had stayed there last year, coming back brown and swearing, full of stories of campers' dances round the fires at midnight, and elderly girls from the training college who sunbathed naked on ledges of rocks surrounded by laughing boys, and singing in bed that lasted until dawn. But George had never left home for more than a night; and then, he told me one half-holiday when it was raining and there was nothing to do but to stay in the wash house racing his guinea pigs giddily along the benches, it was only to stay in St Thomas, three miles from his house, with an aunt who could see through the walls and who knew what a Mrs Hoskin was doing in the kitchen.

'How much farther?' asked George Hooping, clinging to his split parcel, trying in secret to push back socks and suspenders, enviously watching the solid green fields skim by as though the roof were a raft on an ocean with a motor in it. Anything upset his stomach, even liquorice and sherbet, but I alone knew that he wore long combinations in the summer with his name stitched in red on them.

'Miles and miles,' Dan said.

'Thousands of miles,' I said. 'It's Rhossilli, USA. We're going to camp on a bit of rock that wobbles in the wind.'

'And we have to tie the rock on to a tree.'

'Cough can use his suspenders,' Sidney said.

The lorry roared round a corner – 'Upsy-daisy! Did you feel it then, Cough? It was on one wheel' – and below us, beyond fields and farms, the sea, with a steamer puffing on its far edge, shimmered.

'Do you see the sea down there, it's shimmering, Dan,' I said.

George Hooping pretended to forget the lurch of the slippery roof and, from that height, the frightening smallness of the sea. Gripping the rail of the roof, he said: 'My father saw a killer whale.' The conviction in his voice died quickly as he began. He beat against the wind with his cracked, treble voice, trying to make us believe. I knew he wanted to find a boast so big it would make our hair stand up and stop the wild lorry.

'Your father's a herbalist.' But the smoke on the horizon was the white, curling fountain the whale blew through his nose, and its black nose was the bow of the poking ship.

'Where did he keep it, Cough, in the wash house?'

'He saw it in Madagascar. It had tusks as long as from here to, from here to…'

'From here to Madagascar.'

All at once the threat of a steep hill disturbed him. No longer bothered about the adventures of his father, a small, dusty, skullcapped and alpaca-coated man standing and mumbling all day in a shop full of herbs and curtained holes in the wall, where old men with backache and young girls in trouble waited for consultations in the half-dark, he stared at the hill swooping up and clung to Dan and me.

'She's doing fifty!'

'The brakes have gone, Cough!'

He twisted away from us, caught hard with both hands on the rail, pulled and trembled, pressed on a case behind him with his foot, and steered the lorry to safety round a stone-walled corner and up a gentler hill to the gate of a battered farm-house.

Leading down from the gate, there was a lane to the first beach. It was high tide, and we heard the sea dashing. Four boys on a roof – one tall, dark, regular-featured, precise of speech, in a good suit, a boy of the world; one squat, ungainly, red-haired, his red wrists fighting out of short, frayed sleeves; one heavily spectacled, small-paunched, with indoor shoulders and feet in always unlaced boots wanting to go different ways; one small, thin, indecisively active, quick to get dirty, curly – saw their field in front of them, a fortnight's new home that had thick, pricking hedges for walls, the sea for a front garden, a green gutter for a lavatory, and a wind-struck tree in the very middle.

I helped Dan unload the lorry while Sidney tipped the driver and George struggled with the farmyard gate and looked at the ducks inside. The lorry drove away.

'Let's build our tents by the tree in the middle,' said George.

'Pitch!' Sidney said, unlatching the gate for him.

We pitched our tents in a corner, out of the wind.

'One of us must light the primus,' Sidney said, and, after George had burned his hand, we sat in a circle outside the sleeping tent talking about motor cars, content to be in the country, lazing easy in each other's company, thinking to ourselves as we talked, knowing always that the sea dashed on the rocks not far below us and rolled out into the world, and that tomorrow we would bathe and throw a ball on the sands and stone a bottle on a rock and perhaps meet three girls. The oldest would be for Sidney, the plainest for Dan, and the youngest for me. George broke his spectacles when he spoke to girls; he had to walk off, blind as a bat, and the next morning he would say: 'I'm sorry I had to leave you; but I remembered a message.'

It was past five o'clock. My father and mother would have finished tea; the plates with famous castles on them were cleared from the table; father with a newspaper, mother with socks, were far away in the blue haze to the left, up a hill, in a villa, hearing from the park the faint cries of children drift over the public tennis court, and wondering where I was and what I was doing. I was alone with my friends in a field, with a blade of grass in my mouth saying 'Dempsey would hit him cold', and thinking of the great whale that George's father never saw thrashing on the top of the sea, or plunging underneath, like a mountain.

'Bet you I can beat you to the end of the field.'

Dan and I raced among the cowpads, George thumping at our heels.

'Let's go down to the beach.'

Sidney led the way, running straight as a soldier in his khaki shorts, over a stile, down fields to another, into a wooded valley, up through heather on to a clearing near the edge of the cliff, where two broad boys were wrestling outside a tent. I saw one bite the other in the leg, they both struck expertly and savagely at the face, one struggled clear, and, with a leap, the other had him face to the ground. They were Brazell and Skully.

'Hallo, Brazell and Skully!' said Dan.

Skully had Brazell's arm in a policeman's grip; he gave it two quick twists and stood up, smiling.

'Hallo, boys! Hallo, Little Cough! How's your father?'

'He's very well, thank you.'

Brazell, on the grass, felt for broken bones. 'Hallo, boys! How are your fathers?'

They were the worst and biggest boys in school. Every day for a term they caught me before class began and wedged me in the waste-paper basket and then put the basket on the master's desk. Sometimes I could get out and sometimes not. Brazell was lean; Skully was fat.

'We're camping in Button's field,' said Sidney.

'We're taking a rest cure here,' said Brazell. 'And how is Little Cough these days? Father given him a pill?'

We wanted to run down to the beach, Dan and Sidney and George and I, to be alone together, to walk and shout by the sea in the country, throw stones at the waves, remember adventures and make more to remember.

'We'll come down to the beach with you,' said Skully.

He linked arms with Brazell, and they strolled behind us, imitating George's wayward walk and slashing the grass with switches.

Dan said hopefully: 'Are you camping here for long, Brazell and Skully?'

'For a whole nice fortnight, Davies and Thomas and Evans and Hooping.'

When we reached Mewslade beach and flung ourselves down, as I scooped up sand and it trickled grain by grain through my fingers, as George peered at the sea through his double lenses and Sidney and Dan heaped sand over his legs, Brazell and Skully sat behind us like two warders.

'We thought of going to Nice for a fortnight,' said Brazell – he rhymed it with ice, dug Skully in the ribs – 'but the air's nicer here for the complexion.'

'It's as good as a herb,' said Skully.

They shared an enormous joke, cuffing and biting and wrestling again, scattering sand in the eyes, until they fell back with laughter, and Brazell wiped the blood from his nose with a piece of picnic paper. George lay covered to the waist in sand. I watched the sea slipping out, with birds quarrelling over it, and the sun beginning to go down patiently.

'Look at Little Cough,' said Brazell. 'Isn't he extraordinary? He's growing out of the sand. Little Cough hasn't got any legs.'

'Poor Little Cough,' said Skully, 'he's the most extraordinary boy in the world.'

'Extraordinary Little Cough,' they said together, 'extraordinary, extraordinary, extraordinary.' They made a song out of it, and both conducted with their switches.

'He can't swim.'

'He can't run.'

'He can't learn.'

'He can't bowl.'

'He can't bat.'

'And I bet he can't make water.'

George kicked the sand from his legs. 'Yes, I can!'

'Can you swim?'

'Can you run?'

'Leave him alone,' Dan said.

They shuffled nearer to us. The sea was racing out now. Brazell said in a serious voice, wagging his finger: 'Now, quite truthfully, Cough, aren't you extraordinary? Very extraordinary? Say "Yes" or "No".'

'Categorically, "Yes" or "No",' said Skully.

'No,' George said. 'I can swim and I can run and I can play cricket. I'm not frightened of anybody.'

I said: 'He was second in the form last term.'

'Now isn't that extraordinary? If he can be second he can be first. But no, that's too ordinary. Little Cough must be second.'

'The question is answered,' said Skully. 'Little Cough is extraordinary.' They began to sing again.

'He's a very good runner,' Dan said.

'Well, let him prove it. Skully and I ran the whole length of Rhossilli sands this morning, didn't we, Skull?'

'Every inch.'

'Can Little Cough do it?'

'Yes,' said George.

'Do it, then.'

'I don't want to.'

'Extraordinary Little Cough can't run,' they sang, 'can't run, can't run.'

Three girls, all fair, came down the cliff-side arm in arm, dressed in short, white trousers. Their arms and legs and throats were brown as berries; I could see when they laughed that their teeth were very white; they stepped on to the beach, and Brazell and Skully stopped singing. Sidney smoothed his hair back, rose casually, put his hands in his pockets, and walked towards the girls, who now stood close together, gold and brown, admiring the sunset with little attention, patting their scarves, turning smiles on each other. He stood in front of them, grinned, and saluted: 'Hallo, Gwyneth! Do you remember me?'

'La-di-da!' whispered Dan at my side, and made a mock salute to George still peering at the retreating sea.

'Well, if this isn't a surprise!' said the tallest girl. With little studied movements of her hands, as though she were distributing flowers, she introduced Peggy and Jean.

Fat Peggy, I thought, too jolly for me, with hockey legs and tomboy crop, was the girl for Dan; Sidney's Gwyneth was a distinguished piece and quite sixteen, as immaculate and unapproachable as a girl in Ben Evans' stores; but Jean, shy and curly, with butter-coloured hair, was mine. Dan and I walked slowly to the girls.

I made up two remarks: 'Fair's fair, Sidney, no bigamy abroad,' and 'Sorry we couldn't arrange to have the sea in when you came.'

Jean smiled, wiggling her heel in the sand, and I raised my cap.

'Hallo!'

The cap dropped at her feet.

As I bent down, three lumps of sugar fell from my blazer pocket. 'I've been feeding a horse,' I said, and began to blush guiltily when all the girls laughed.

I could have swept the ground with my cap, kissed my hand gaily, called them señoritas, and made them smile without tolerance. Or I could have stayed at a distance, and this would have been better still, my hair blown in the wind, though there was no wind at all that evening, wrapped in mystery and staring at the sun, too aloof to speak to girls; but I knew that all the time my ears would have been burning, my stomach would have been as hollow and as full of voices as a shell. 'Speak to them quickly, before they go away!' a voice would have said insistently over the dramatic silence, as I stood like Valentino on the edge of the bright, invisible bullring of the sands. 'Isn't it lovely here!' I said.

I spoke to Jean alone; and this is love, I thought, as she nodded her head and swung her curls and said: 'It's nicer than Porthcawl.'

Brazell and Skully were two big bullies in a nightmare; I forgot them when Jean and I walked up the cliff, and, looking back to see if they were baiting George again or wrestling together, I saw that George had disappeared around the corner of the rocks and that they were talking at the foot of the cliff with Sidney and the two girls.

'What's your name?'

I told her.

'That's Welsh,' she said.

'You've got a beautiful name.'

'Oh! It's just ordinary.'

'Shall I see you again?'

'If you want to.'

'I want to all right! We can go and bathe in the morning. And we can try to get an eagle's egg. Did you know that there were eagles here?'

'No,' she said. 'Who was that handsome boy on the beach, the tall one with dirty trousers?'

'He's not handsome, that's Brazell. He never washes or combs his hair or anything. He's a bully and he cheats.'

'I think he's handsome.'

We walked into Button's field, and I showed her inside the tents and gave her one of George's apples. 'I'd like a cigarette,' she said.

It was nearly dark when the others came. Brazell and Skully were with Gwyneth, one on each side of her holding her arms, Sidney was with Peggy, and Dan walked, whistling, behind with his hands in his pockets.

'There's a pair,' said Brazell, 'they've been here all alone and they aren't even holding hands. You want a pill,' he said to me.

'Build Britain's babies,' said Skully.

'Go on!' Gwyneth said. She pushed him away from her,

but she was laughing, and she said nothing when he put his arm around her waist.

'What about a bit of fire?' said Brazell.

Jean clapped her hands like an actress. Although I knew I loved her, I didn't like anything she said or did.

'Who's going to make it?'

'He's the best, I'm sure,' she said, pointing to me.

Dan and I collected sticks, and by the time it was quite dark there was a fire crackling. Inside the sleeping-tent, Brazell and Jean sat close together; her golden head was on his shoulder; Skully, near them, whispered to Gwyneth; Sidney unhappily held Peggy's hand.

'Did you ever see such a sloppy lot?' I said, watching Jean smile in the fiery dark. 'Kiss me, Charley!' said Dan.

We sat by the fire in the corner of the field. The sea, far out, was still making a noise. We heard a few nightbirds. '"Tu-whit! tu-whoo!" Listen! I don't like owls,' Dan said, 'they scratch your eyes out!' – and tried not to listen to the soft voices in the tent. Gwyneth's laughter floated out over the suddenly moonlit field, but Jean, with the beast, was smiling and silent in the covered warmth; I knew her little hand was in Brazell's hand.

'Women!' I said.

Dan spat in the fire.

We were old and alone, sitting beyond desire in the middle of the night, when George appeared, like a ghost, in the firelight and stood there trembling until I said: 'Where've you been? You've been gone hours. Why are you trembling like that?'

Brazell and Skully poked their heads out.

'Hallo, Cough, my boy! How's your father? What have you been up to tonight?'

George Hooping could hardly stand. I put my hand on his shoulder to steady him, but he pushed it away.

'I've been running on Rhossilli sands! I ran every bit of it! You said I couldn't, and I did! I've been running and running!'

Someone inside the tent put a record on the gramophone. It was a selection from *No, No, Nanette*.

'You've been running all the time in the dark, Little Cough?'

'And I bet I ran it quicker than you did, too! ' George said.

'I bet you did,' said Brazell.

'Do you think we'd run five miles?' said Skully.

Now the tune was 'Tea for Two'.

'Did you ever hear anything so extraordinary? I told you Cough was extraordinary. Little Cough's been running all night.'

'Extraordinary, extraordinary, extraordinary Little Cough,' they said.

Laughing from the shelter of the tent into the darkness, they looked like a boy with two heads. And when I stared round at George again he was lying on his back fast asleep in the deep grass and his hair was touching the flames.

And a Spoonful of Grief to Taste

Gwyn Thomas

You know how it is in our part of the valley. They are mad for singing in choirs. If you can sing a bit, you get roped into a choir and if you can keep your voice somewhere near the note and your morals facing due north where the cold is, someone with pull is bound to notice you and before you know it you are doing a nice steady job between the choir pieces. If you sound like a raven and cause the hair of the choir leader to drop out like hail when you go for a hearing, you mope about in the outer darkness acting as foot-warmer for the boys in the Exchange.

I couldn't sing at all. As a kid I was handy enough and did very well as one of a party at school that did a lot of songs about war and storms at sea, with plenty of actions showing how wind and death are when they are on the job. I must have sung and acted myself out with that group. I was good. I sounded like an agent for doom. I put the fear of hell up my father who was a sensitive man, often in touch with terror. He shook like a leaf and supplied most of the draughts he shook in. When I sang that very horrible part-song 'There'll be blood on the capstan tonight', he averaged two faints a verse, and his head went up and down so often with the faints I could almost keep the time by him. That didn't last long. When I was about fourteen I went bathing in that deep, smooth part of the river they call the Neck or the Nack. I dived in. When I came out my voice was broken, broken as if somebody had been after the thing with a hammer. At first I thought my father had dived in after me and arranged some submarine antic that would keep me away from part-songs for a couple of years. Then I was told nature works in this fashion, although some people get more warning. I could hardly talk till I was eighteen, let alone sing. I tried to get into a few of the local choirs as a background noise. I got nowhere near except when the conductor was giving a talk on why his choristers should keep away from rivers when an eisteddfod was coming up. It was only my father who had any use for me. He put me to stand behind the front door to frighten off the bum bailiffs. We had plenty of them coming to our place. It was like a training centre for them. There were new brands of debt that were named after my father. My job was to watch out for them and say in this funny croak I had that there was death in the house, much death, and didn't they know that there was some respect due even to the poor. It always worked. I sounded just like death, gone rusty with the boredom of always pushing people in the same direction and hearing no more of them. Between my long experience with those churchyard chants I had learned in the part-song group and the ten-foot drop my voice had done, I bet those bailiff boys could almost see my scythe as I stood there mooing at them through the door. They would flee, wondering, no doubt, how much my old man still owed on the scythe.

But here I am now, busily engaged in the building trade, driving towards the New Jerusalem at so many bricks a day, putting fresh heart into people in this town of Meadow Prospect who have been living in furnished rooms or sharing a belfry with the bats since the Rebecca Riots. I am the only man in our part of the valley who has found a place in such a tidy and dignified traffic without once having sung the *Messiah* or recited the whole body of Psalms backwards and forwards with an apple in my mouth or done a salaam before the wealthy.

I didn't want to be a builder. At the time I'd have been anything. I'd have gone around the roads collecting fertiliser for the Allotment Union if my father had managed to get me a permanent bucket. But I wanted to get away from behind that door. I was sick of being posted there as a scarecrow for the bum bailiffs. I croaked that statement about death being in the house so often and with such passion it wouldn't have surprised me to see death sitting down with us at meals, chatting cosily and complaining about the quality of the grub, which it would have had every right to do, for the grub we had was rough. When I was about nineteen, my Uncle Cadwallader came to stay with us. He was great on doing jerks to get strong. It was a treat just to sit down and watch Cadwallader on these jerks, wondering what part of him you were likely to see next. He had the biggest chest ever seen in or around Meadow Prospect. At rest, the kitchen walls just about fitted it. But when he had the thing filled to the brim with air, and that was a favourite caper with him, someone or something had to be moved, fast. He was always jerking and practising to get bigger and stronger, and sometimes he looked so much like life's final answer to death I thought he would keep it up until his muscles began to glow like lamp posts with a sense of perfection and eternity, and then Cadwallader would float off the earth and look for larger stamping grounds among the planets. Sometimes, when he came in from a night's drinking at that pub, The Crossed Harps, he'd lift my old man clean off the ground and jerk him up and down. First of all, my father didn't like this, and thought of laying the poker on Cadwallader. But after a while he said that he had grown to like this motion and that it made quite a nice change from just standing still doing nothing much at all except keep from falling. But I think he laid aside the poker idea because at the speed he went up and down in Cadwallader's grasp, Cadwallader made much too blurred a target for any good work with a short weapon. On top of that, Cadwallader was working and paid well for his place. He never lost his job. This was a very rare thing in Meadow Prospect, and he was often regarded as a miracle or a mirage by those freethinking boys who gather in the draughts room at the Library and Institute and talk about life and do a good job between them of burying all hope. Cadwallader was dull as a bat and with his strength he could have picked up a colliery and shaken the thing hard to see if there was any coal left inside. He was a great comfort to all the wealthy and to the coal-owning wealthy in particular. We often had the womenfolk of the mighty come along to see Cadwallader, offer him sugar from their hands or a soft vegetable, coo names at him, stroke him, and generally treat him as a horse. If he could have got into the way of talking in sentences and praising the state of things as they were, he would have been taken up by the Government and made into a prince or a mayor or a rent bloke or something. But all he was was strong and daft, and that, they say, is not enough. He didn't talk much at all, and he had a way of moving the muscles of his chest to show when he wanted something. We had to tell him to open the front of his shirt wider whenever we didn't get the full gist of what he was saying. And Cadwallader got tired of having my father peering in to get the exact intonation.

Anyway, he stopped lodging with us. He went up to the Terraces to live in what they call sin with a very big woman called Agnes who had thick red hair and a fine record in sin. This Agnes had worn out about forty blokes without getting any paler herself and she cottoned on to my Uncle Cadwallader when she saw him throwing a cart at a horse that had nearly run him over. She said here was a man who would see her through to old age without going on the Lloyd George every whip stitch. The old chopping and changing had started to get on her nerves and give her religious thoughts.

This was a big blow to my old man. He had actually begun to pay back some debts that had been going about for a long time past in short shrouds, with the money he got from Cadwallader. His manner with the bum bailiffs had become quite cheerful, opening the door to them four inches instead of three and calling them bastards once and with a smile instead of twice with a meaning frown. The only thing he could think of doing to keep hope alive was to take out a threepenny insurance policy on Cadwallader, with an eye on Agnes' past record, and to keep away from that group in the Library and Institute whose forebodings filled him as full of shadow as a mountain of dirt. I told him openly that from what I had seen of Cadwallader, I would say that if there was to be any passing out, both parties would reach the door together.

After a spell my father got the idea that if I went up to the Terraces where Cadwallader was living and pleaded with him, he might come back to us. I could talk in short simple phrases that Cadwallader could follow without going mad with nervous worry. That is why I was picked to do this pleading. I had also made up a short poem about his tremendous chest expansion that filled him with pleasure. But I could not shift him an inch from the side of Agnes. There was something like the hot middle of the earth in the thick redness of that woman's hair, and I could get the feel of the grip she had on Cadwallader. I made no headway with him and one Tuesday afternoon I made my way up the Terraces for my very last bout of supplication with Cadwallader. By that time I was sick of the sight and sound of my uncle. He was a friendly enough man when he was not twirling you over his head like a club and praising toil, but it wore me down trying to argue him out of his desire for this Agnes, and to move him to pity with stories of my father worrying himself thinner than the poker that he had once thought of crowning Cadwallader with. The only thing that lit a light in his eyes when I talked, was my poem about his chest. He liked that, especially an easy couplet in the middle that got best rhymed off with chest. That notion was near enough to the ground for Cadwallader to see it plain without having to stand on tiptoe. But once off the poem and he dropped into a coma as fast as a stone. He rested in these comas. He got part of his strength from them.

When I reached the Terraces I saw great crowds of people. This was not common. Usually the people in the Terraces were asleep, working, sitting in a stupor on the doorsteps, or stroking their rabbits, pigeons or despair in the backyards. The crowd was thickest in Cadwallader's street, and at first I thought his passion and his strength had carried his lust for exercise to a peak where he had thrust Agnes through the roof without thought for her or the tiles. The people were excited. One voter told me that the colliery company which owned the streets around, and most of the people in them, had put up the rent of twelve of the houses, and the tenants in these houses had refused to pay any more rent until the company saw sense. I found that Agnes' house was one of the twelve. I saw Agnes standing on the pavement talking loudly, swinging her arms and flouncing her hair in great crimson waves upon her neck, and giving an outline of the sort of sense she was waiting for the company to see. I felt sorry for all these tenants who were being put on the wheel, but I could not see the company seeing anything but the company even with someone like Agnes dragging their eyes towards the target. Agnes had persuaded the tenants and their friends to resist. I could see a small group of listless and pallid men standing near her and taking in her commands. The man who was giving me the news of these developments told me that these boys were those lovers of Agnes who had blazed the trail before Cadwallader, the few who could still stand at all. People were building a barricade in the street made out of furniture that nobody wanted any more. Most of the furniture in the Terraces looks as if no one wants it any more, so there was a very poor quality about this barricade altogether. The idea of it was to keep out the band of policemen and bailiffs and so on who were shortly to come in the name of the company and drag out these people who had buried their rent books ahead of themselves, which is not legal. I thought this made my job with Cadwallader all the easier. If he was going to be evicted it would be better all round if he just came down to the bed of the valley with me and took his old lodgings with us straightaway, but I found him in a harsh and brutal frame of mind, his mind all stoked up to a high flame by the speeches and antics of Agnes, his heart full of impatient hatred for the evictors and their assistants. Agnes must have been talking to him in signs to make him understand so much. He seemed really to have grasped the issue neatly, and was now waiting for the action to start which would allow him to lay down the issue and transfer his fingers to some unfriendly neck. I began my pleading, orating hard about the condition of my father, his gloom and hunger, lacing the whole with some selections from that poem. But he would not listen. I got down on my knees, conjuring him to have done with this tomfoolery of conflict and let himself be evicted like a decent citizen. I didn't even give up when Agnes, hearing the drift of my talk, began kicking at me from the rear and Cadwallader, to follow suit and to pander to this Agnes, who was the moontug upon the broad yearning waters of him, started to push my head off my shoulders with his thumb which was about the size of your leg. He kept the effort to this thumb to show me this was only a caution, given without malice even though it might end up with me walking about the Terraces wondering why I stopped so short at my shoulders. Then Agnes said I was probably a spy, sent up there after a lot of coaching by the bailiffs to do this pleading and get just one party to evict himself and set the ball rolling in favour of the law and the coal owners. She quickened her kicks and said she could now see through my game, and if it was that she was kicking I was not surprised. She suggested to Cadwallader that I should be reduced to eight parts and served up raw to the bums when they should start peering over the barricade. She opened her mouth so wide when she said this that she got it full of red hair, and that gave her words an old, flaming, dangerous look. Cadwallader started after me, holding up one finger as if measuring me up roughly for the rending. I gave up and began pelting down the Terrace with him after me. I could hear Agnes tally-hoing after him like a mistress of the wolfhounds. I got to the barricade. I climbed up it like a monkey. As soon as I got to the top a policeman spotted me. He did not look very bright. He had probably come fresh from a long talk by the Chief Constable on the disasters, ranging from a terrible crumbling of the nation's brickwork to the organised ravishing of his womenfolk, if these Terraces were allowed to get away with this defiance. I could see his mouth drooping with concern, ripening into panic as he saw me. He yelled, 'Here they come, boys,' and reached up and gave me a hard clip with his baton that stretched me out cold on some sort of sofa number than the millpuff that came staggering out in armfuls from the torn upholstery. This did not please Cadwallader who remembered, Agnes notwithstanding, that I was his nephew. So he went over the barricade and dealt that policeman a lot harder clip than the one the policeman had given me. The policeman joined me across the sofa and we were both full of nothingness, tickled by millpuff. Then a lot of other people followed Cadwallader on his wild way and the policemen and bailiffs were driven to the bottom of the valley. But not for long.

When I came properly to myself, I found myself being marched by an army of policemen down to the police station. With me were about eighteen other men, Cadwallader among them, looking as dazed as I was but walking significantly in the centre of the group, like a kingpin. At the station we were charged with rioting, and I was still so boss-eyed with the fetcher I had from the baton that I could not even ask them what the hell they were talking about.

Everybody made a great fuss of me as we were waiting for the trial. I came right out from behind the front door when the bailiffs called about my father's debts and there was no need to make a single statement about death or calling next week. They were off. Some of the wisest voters in our part of the valley, boys suckled on grief and unrest, told me that I had struck a fine blow for tenants all over the world. I started to go to those classes at the Library and Institute that my friend, Milton Nicholas, used to run on the 'History of Our Times', giving the light to such subjects as the workers' struggle for lower rents, longer lives, higher ceilings, sweeter kids, and kinder days. Milton, though young and on the frail side, shone like a little sun on the gloom and wilderness of these topics. I started, with a thawed and astonished brain, to understand that it is a very bad thing, a very wrong thing, for colliery companies to go slapping extra rent on voters who don't get enough to eat most of the time, and to send bodies of policemen and bailiffs to evict these voters whenever the landlord is in a mood to disagree. And Milton showed me how I personally fitted into all this. He likened me to that Wat the Tyler who had put a hammer to the head of some tax collector or nark who was eyeing Wat's daughter and taking Wat's mind off the tiles. The boys in Milton Nicholas' class clubbed in and bought me a strong hammer, and Milton, when it was handed over, made a short speech in which he said that sooner or later the world, in its endless devising of discomfort and evil, would yield me some nark or collector who would give just the right kind of lip and have just the right kind of head to send me racing for the hammer. This gave me a proud feeling and I began to hope that when the trial came along the judge would order me to be kept in jail for ever like that poor bloke who was all beard and fish bones in that picture *Monte Cristo*, so that Milton could say something about me from week to week as an example of those who were giving their lives for freedom. My father was very worried when I told him about this hope, especially the part about the beard, because he hates hair on the face in any shape or form and thinks a man should be neat even in the County Jail.

The trial came and I could see that the judge, who was dressed in a way I had never seen before except in carnivals, believed in rent and was stern towards all people who rioted and played hell with bailiffs. Every time he opened his mouth I got to feel more and more like Monte Cristo. But the man who was defending us made out that I should never have been in that street at all, and mentioned that Cadwallader had been clearly seen chasing me, with a promise of murder right across his face, towards the barricade, and that the fetcher I got from the policeman which put me across the sofa as cold as one of the legs, was simply a practice swing let off by the policeman by way of getting his muscles loose and ready to help the landlords lose their chains. It had nothing to do with my head at all. It had come along at the wrong moment. The judge was impressed by this and peered at me and muttered something a few times about me being young, as if I was Cadwallader's father and keeping very fresh for my age. He said, 'Let us separate the chaff from the grain.' The chaff was such personalities as Cadwallader, at whom the judge didn't bother even to peer. 'This boy,' went on the judge, 'has no doubt been seduced by the rash Bolshevik elements who mar this valley. He has been corrupted by idleness. The thing here is to nurse this bent sapling back to mental health. We will have him taught a trade. What trade would you like to be taught, my boy?' At first I was too busy playing up to the judge by looking bent and corrupted and explaining this programme in mutters to my puzzled comrades to make an answer. He asked me again. I remembered that Milton Nicholas had told me that moneylending was a very secure line of business where you didn't have to change and bath every time you came home. It sounded to me just the thing for people who were not in it. I mumbled something about having a strong fancy for moneylending if I could find something to lend. 'Excellent,' said the judge, laughing with pleasure. 'An excellent choice. A bricklayer. A wise choice. I judged rightly. This boy has the right stuff. Let him be taught to lay bricks.' I hadn't said a word about bricks but that is how it happened. They sent me on a six-months' course to a Government Training Centre, and the night I went away Hicks the Bricks, the contractor I've worked with ever since, had a piece in the paper giving his views about the problem of the young, to which Hicks seemed to give even more thought than he gave to bricks, and saying that when I returned he would provide me with a job. Cadwallader and the other boys went to jail for a few weeks, and when he came out he found two other voters going in and out of Agnes' house. He noticed that, put together, these two were just about his weight, and Agnes pleaded that she was only keeping them about the place as mementoes of fuller times and to keep the mats in place until Cadwallader's return. But he had read passages from the large printed Bible he had found in his cell, and he told Agnes she was the sort of woman they had set dogs on in the days when print was larger. And he came back to the house of my father trying his best not to bark, and to pour the rain of his new resolution on the hot ache of his longing body.

That is how I came into the building trade. I was too sorrowful at having fallen so far below the golden hills of a striving martyrdom on which I had been sent briefly to walk by the words of Milton Nicholas to feel gratitude or gladness. The only thing I learned to the depths at that centre was to stay right away from all fish that looked like whale, because I had a poisoned stomach from eating fish that looked like that. Our foreman says I am so bad a hand with bricks I ought to sign articles with the Eskimos and specialise in igloos where the walls are supposed to be curved in just the way I curve them and not meant to outlast a good warm spring. So that is the way to do it. When a man of power, like that judge, asks you to choose your path out of hell, mumble your reply and let him put the pattern out of his own wisdom upon your blur of sound, for in the end it is his choice it will be and the hell of your beginning will face you at the end and the heat of hell grows no less hot; only you and your fibres, with weariness and understanding and the laughter that will ooze from the dampest blankest wall of knowing and feeling, will grow less swift to smart at the pain of its burning. That, and helping a boy like Hicks the Bricks to get his name in the paper. That sets you up and eases the cold, whatever the great distance one's eyes must cross before they light once more upon the golden hills.

JUST LIKE LITTLE DOGS

Dylan Thomas

Standing alone under a railway arch out of the wind, I was looking at the miles of sands, long and dirty in the early dark, with only a few boys on the edge of the sea and one or two hurrying couples with their mackintoshes blown around them like balloons, when two young men joined me, it seemed out of nowhere, and struck matches for their cigarettes and illuminated their faces under bright-checked caps.

One had a pleasant face; his eyebrows slanted comically towards his temples, his eyes were warm, brown, deep, and guileless, and his mouth was full and weak. The other man had a boxer's nose and a weighted chin ginger with bristles.

We watched the boys returning from the oily sea; they shouted under the echoing arch, then their voices faded. Soon there was not a single couple in sight; the lovers had disappeared among the sandhills and were lying down there with broken tins and bottles of the summer passed, old paper blowing by them, and nobody with any sense was about. The strangers, huddled against the wall, their hands deep in their pockets, their cigarettes sparkling, stared, I thought, at the thickening of the darkover the empty sands, but their eyes may have been closed. A train raced over us, and the arch shook. Over the shore, behind the vanishing train, smoke clouds flew together, rags of wings and hollow bodies of great birds black as tunnels, and broke up lazily; cinders fell through a sieve in the air, and the sparks were put out by the wet dark before they reached the sand. The night before, little quick scarecrows had bent and picked at the track-line and a solitary dignified scavenger wandered three miles by the edge with a crumpled coal sack and a park-keeper's steel-tipped stick. Now they were tucked up in sacks, asleep in a siding, their heads in bins, their beards in straw, in coal trucks thinking of fires, or lying beyond pickings on Jack Stiff's slab near the pub in the Fishguard Alley, where the methylated-spirit drinkers danced into the policemen's arms and women like lumps of clothes in a pool waited, in doorways and holes in the soaking wall, for vampires or firemen. Night was properly down on us now. The wind changed. Thin rain began. The sands themselves went out. We stood in the scooped, windy room of the arch, listening to the noises from the muffled town, a goods train shunting, a siren in the docks, the hoarse trams in the streets far behind, one bark of a dog, unplaceable sounds, iron being beaten, the distant creaking of wood, doors slamming where there were no houses, an engine coughing like a sheep on a hill.

The two young men were statues smoking, tough-capped and collarless watchers and witnesses carved out of the stone of the blowing room where they stood at my side with nowhere to go, nothing to do, and all the raining, almost winter, night before them. I cupped a match to let them see my face in a dramatic shadow, my eyes mysteriously sunk, perhaps, in a startling white face, my young looks savage in the sudden flicker of light, to make them wonder who I was as I puffed my last butt and puzzled about them. Why was the soft-faced young man, with his tame devil's eyebrows, standing like a stone figure with a glow-worm in it? He should have a nice girl to bully him gently and take him to cry in the pictures, or kids to bounce in a kitchen in Rodney Street. There was no sense in standing silent for hours under a railway arch on a hell of a night at the end of a bad summer when girls were waiting, ready to be hot and friendly, in chip shops and shop doorways and Rabbiotti's all-night café, when the public bar of the Bay View at the corner had a fire and skittles and a swarthy, sensuous girl with different coloured eyes, when the billiard saloons were open, except the one in High Street you couldn't go into without a collar and tie, when the closed parks had empty, covered bandstands and the railings were easy to climb.

A church clock somewhere struck a lot, faintly from the night on the right, but I didn't count.

The other young man, less than two feet from me, should be shouting with the boys, boasting in lanes, propping counters, prancing and clouting in the Mannesmann Hall, or whispering around a bucket in a ring corner. Why was he humped here with a moody man and myself, listening to our breathing, to the sea, the wind scattering sand through the archway, a chained dog and a foghorn and the rumble of trams a dozen streets away, watching a match strike, a boy's fresh face spying in a shadow, the lighthouse beams, the movement of a hand to a fag, when the sprawling town in a drizzle, the pubs and the clubs and the coffee shops, the prowlers' streets, the arches near the promenade, were full of friends and enemies? He could be playing nap by a candle in a shed in a woodyard.

Families sat down to supper in rows of short houses, the wireless sets were on, the daughters' young men sat in the front rooms. In neighbouring houses they read the news off the tablecloth, and the potatoes from dinner were fried up. Cards were played in the front rooms of houses on the hills. In the houses on tops of the hills families were entertaining friends, and the blinds of the front rooms were not quite drawn. I heard the sea in a cold bit of the cheery night.

One of the strangers said suddenly, in a high, clear voice: 'What are we all doing then?'

'Standing under a bloody arch,' said the other one.

'And it's cold,' I said.

'It isn't very cosy,' said the high voice of the young man

with the pleasant face, now invisible. 'I've been in better hotels than this.'

'What about that night in the Majestic?' said the other voice.

There was a long silence.

'Do you often stand here?' said the pleasant man. His voice might never have broken.

'No, this is the first time here,' I said. 'Sometimes I stand in the Brynmill arch.'

'Ever tried the old pier?'

'It's no good in the rain, is it?'

'Underneath the pier, I mean, in the girders.'

'No, I haven't been there.'

'Tom spends every Sunday under the pier,' the pug-faced young man said bitterly. 'I got to take him his dinner in a piece of paper.'

'There's another train coming,' I said. It tore over us, the arch bellowed, the wheels screamed through our heads, we were deafened and spark-blinded and crushed under the fiery weight and we rose again, like battered black men, in the grave of the arch. No noise at all from the swallowed town. The trams had rattled themselves dumb. A pressure of the hidden sea rubbed away the smudge of the docks. Only three young men were alive.

One said: 'It's a sad life, without a home.'

'Haven't you got a home then?' I said.

'Oh, yes, I've got a home all right.'

'I got one, too.'

'And I live near Cwmdonkin Park,' I said.

'That's another place Tom sits in in the dark. He says he listens to the owls.'

'I knew a chap once who lived in the country, near Bridgend,' said Tom, 'and they had a munition works there in the War and it spoiled all the birds. The chap I know says you can always tell a cuckoo from Bridgend, it goes: "Cuckbloodyoo! cuckbloodyoo!"'

'Cuckbloodyoo!' echoed the arch.

'Why are you standing under the arch, then?' asked Tom. 'It's warm at home. You can draw the curtains and sit by the fire, snug as a bug. Gracie's on the wireless tonight. No shananacking in the old moonlight.'

'I don't want to go home, I don't want to sit by the fire. I've got nothing to do when I'm in and I don't want to go to bed. I like standing about like this with nothing to do, in the dark all by myself,' I said.

And I did, too. I was a lonely nightwalker and a steady stander-at-corners. I liked to walk through the wet town after midnight, when the streets were deserted and the window lights out, alone and alive on the glistening tramlines in dead and empty High Street under the moon, gigantically sad in the damp streets by ghostly Ebenezer Chapel. And I never felt more a part of the remote and overpressing world, or more full of love and arrogance and pity and humility, not for myself alone, but for the living earth I suffered on and for the unfeeling systems in the upper air, Mars and Venus and Brazell and Skully, men in China and St Thomas, scorning girls and ready girls, soldiers and bullies and policemen and sharp, suspicious buyers of second-hand books, bad, ragged women who'd pretend against the museum wall for a cup of tea, and perfect, unapproachable women out of the fashion magazines, seven feet high, sailing slowly in their flat, glazed creations through steel and glass and velvet. I leant against the wall of a derelict house in the residential areas or wandered in the empty rooms, stood terrified on the stairs or gazing through the smashed windows at the sea or at nothing, and the lights going out one by one in the avenues. Or I mooched in a half-built house, with the sky stuck in the roof and cats on the ladders and a wind shaking through the bare bones of the bedrooms.

'And you can talk,' I said. 'Why aren't you at home?'

'I don't want to be home,' said Tom.

'I'm not particular,' said his friend.

When a match flared, their heads rocked and spread on the wall, and shapes of winged bulls and buckets grew bigger and smaller. Tom began to tell a story. I thought of a new stranger walking on the sands past the arch and hearing all of a sudden that high voice out of a hole.

I missed the beginning of the story as I thought of the man on the sands listening in a panic or dodging, like a footballer, in and out among the jumping dark towards the lights behind the railway line, and remembered Tom's voice in the middle of a sentence.

'... went up to them and said it was a lovely night. It wasn't a lovely night at all. The sands were empty. We asked them what their names were and they asked us what ours were. We were walking along by this time. Walter here was telling them about the glee party in the "Melba" and what went on in the ladies' cloakroom. You had to drag the tenors away like ferrets.'

'What were their names?' I asked.

'Doris and Norma,' Walter said.

'So we walked along the sands towards the dunes,' Tom said, 'and Walter was with Doris and I was with Norma. Norma worked in the steam laundry. We hadn't been walking and talking for more than a few minutes when, by God, I knew I was head over heels in love with the girl, and she wasn't the pretty one, either.'

He described her. I saw her clearly. Her plump, kind face, jolly brown eyes, warm wide mouth, thick bobbed hair, rough body, bottle legs, broad bum, grew from a few words right out of Tom's story, and I saw her ambling solidly along the sands in a spotted frock in a showering autumn evening with fancy gloves on her hard hands, a gold bangle, with a voile handkerchief tucked in it, round her wrist, and a navy-blue handbag with letters and outing snaps, a compact, a bus ticket, and a shilling.

'Doris was the pretty one,' said Tom, 'smart and touched up and sharp as a knife. I was twenty-six years old and I'd never been in love, and there I was, gawking at Norma in the middle of Tawe sands, too frightened to put my finger on her gloves. Walter had his arm round Doris then.'

They sheltered behind a dune. The night dropped down on them quickly. Walter was a caution with Doris, hugging and larking, and Tom sat close to Norma, brave enough to hold her hand in its cold glove and tell her all his secrets. He told her his age and his job. He liked staying in in the evenings with a good book. Norma liked dances. He liked dances, too. Norma and Doris were sisters. 'I'd never have thought that,' Tom said, 'you're beautiful, I love you.'

Now the storytelling thing in the arch gave place to the loving night in the dunes. The arch was as high as the sky. The faint town noises died. I lay like a pimp in a bush by Tom's side and squinted through to see him round his hands on Norma's breast. 'Don't you dare!' Walter and Doris lay quietly near them. You could have heard a safety pin fall.

'And the curious thing was,' said Tom, 'that after a time we all sat up on the sand and smiled at each other. And then we all moved softly about on the sand in the dark, without saying a word. And Doris was lying with me, and Norma was with Walter.'

'But why did you change over, if you loved her?' I asked.

'I never understood why,' said Tom. 'I think about it every night.'

'That was in October,' Walter said.

And Tom continued: 'We didn't see much of the girls until July. I couldn't face Norma. Then they brought two paternity orders against us, and Mr Lewis, the magistrate, was eighty years old, and stone-deaf, too. He put a little trumpet by his ear and Norma and Doris gave evidence. Then we gave evidence, and he couldn't decide whose was which. And at the end he shook his head back and fore and pointed his trumpet and said: "Just like little dogs!"'

All at once I remembered how cold it was. I rubbed my numb hands together. Fancy standing all night in the cold.

Fancy listening, I thought, to a long, unsatisfactory story in the frost-bite night in a polar arch. 'What happened then?' I asked.

Walter answered. 'I married Norma,' he said 'and Tom married Doris. We had to do the right thing by them, didn't we? That's why Tom won't go home. He never goes home till the early morning. I've got to keep him company. He's my brother.'

It would take me ten minutes to run home. I put up my coat collar and pulled my cap down.

'And the curious thing is,' said Tom, 'that I love Norma and Walter doesn't love Norma or Doris. We've two nice little boys. I call mine Norman.'

We all shook hands.

'See you again,' said Walter.

'I'm always hanging about,' said Tom.

'Abyssinia!'

I walked out of the arch, crossed Trafalgar Terrace, and pelted up the steep streets.

THY NEED

Gwyn Thomas

Whit Monday was the first day of brilliant sun after a week of mist and rain. Spring was nearly always a wet, diffident affair in the hills around Meadow Prospect and the people were delighted to see the burst of sun, for this Monday was a day of festival and gala. The sixth annual sports organised by the Constitutional Club was being held. The club flag was at the top of its pole, washed and fresh. The junior section of the club had its wooden premises decorated and filled with tables for the tea that was to come off at five that afternoon, and from about noon there had been groups of members' children hanging about the club's front door getting their teeth ready for the start. With these young elements circling for the swoop, Meadow Prospect wore an even hungrier, more watchful look than usual.

Most of the day's sporting events were over when the three friends, Sylvanus, Verdun, and Elwyn sat down on a bench in Meadow Prospect square, near the spot where Lodovico Facelli had his ice cream barrow. It was getting warmer all the time. The boys had their best suits on and were wearing the tight, white, long-peaked collars which were the current fancy among the young of the district. Their faces were red under the strain of strong sun and slow strangulation. Verdun ordered three threepenny wafers from Lodovico. The Italian made them extra thick and, after having handed them over, leaned on the barrow and stared at the boys as if the sight of them gave him genuine pleasure. Lodovico was considered too dreamy and generous to have much of a future in business, but he seemed to manage. Verdun waved his hand genially at Lodovico every now and then to show that the kindness of his expression and the thickness of his wafers were not wasted.

'What you boys been racing in?' asked Lodovico.

'We've been stewards.'

'Stewards? What you do?'

'We were doing little jobs for Mr Marsden, who is the brains of the Con Club. If Mr Marsden sees anything that needs knocking into the ground, like a nail or a stake or some voter who won't listen to the judges, he gives us the mallet and the signal to proceed.'

'So you wait for the tea now?'

'There's one more race, the last of the day. The walking race,' said Sylvanus. 'My uncle Onllwyn is entered and he's going to blind them with science.'

'He good?'

'They used to call him the White Horse, on account of his long snowy drawers and his fine strong stride,' said Verdun. 'He's got a trick in starting, too, a way of twisting his legs and shooting forward like a bullet that is magic. It'll make it useless for the other blokes even to get off the mark. The start is important, because this race is short. Honest, Lodovico, I feel sorry for those other boys when I think of Uncle Onllwyn and the way he shoots off. I've seen him practising in the back lane when things are quiet and I know. I call him the White Flash, because all you see is dust and his butts getting smaller. It'll be a big day for him, too, because things have never gone right for Uncle Onllwyn, and this is the first walking match they've held here, and he's never had the chance to shine before.'

'I hope he win,' said Lodovico. 'I know Onllwyn. He's a kind old voter. He's sympathetic.'

'He'll win all right,' said Verdun. 'Tell Lodovico about the dung, Syl.'

'Oh, no,' said Sylvanus. 'That's supposed to be a secret, and anyway Lodovico wouldn't want to hear about a thing like that, not with him in such a clean line of trade as ice cream.'

'Dung?' said Lodovico, still smiling intensely at the boys, but clearly puzzled. 'Is this why they call your uncle the White Horse?'

'No. I'll tell you. Onllwyn heard about a famous runner called Gito who once lived among these hills. He was fleet as a bird, that Gito. Started after sheep and caught hares, that sort of voter. Uncle Onllwyn, who is a great reader, came across an old book about Gito, and it said Gito kept so supple by sleeping on a bed of old dung. So Onllwyn made a long coffin-shaped box and half filled it with dung, and that's where he's been sleeping for the last week, in this box in the shed behind the house, getting suppler all the time. He was so supple after the second day he was waving about like that flag over the Con Club.'

'Good God,' said Lodovico. 'He must be very poor. Not even in Italy they sleep in dung. But I hope he win.'

'That is certain, Lodovico, because in addition to being supple he also has his grips, home-made contraptions of solid rubber that he fits into his mouth to bite on whenever he feels his wind coming a bit short.'

'Don't tell him about those,' said Sylvanus. 'He's in a fog now after what you told him about Onllwyn sleeping in the box.'

'Those grips are more interesting than the dung, I reckon. He looks full of grip when he's got them fitted in and his teeth seem to come right out at you. Between you and me, I think they called Uncle Onllwyn the White Horse as much for his look as for his stride or his drawers.'

'What Onllwyn going to do with the money he win?' asked Lodovico.

'He's got that all worked out. He's buying gardening tools. He's been very keen to get some of those for a long time. He spends so much time staring into the window of that Phineas Morgan the ironmonger that Morgan has got into the way of giving Onllwyn one flick with the dusting rag for every two he gives the window. Onllwyn wants these tools because he is keen on the earth and wants a smallholding. So long, Lodovico. We're off to The Little Ark, that pub down at the bottom of Gorsedd Row.'

'You drink?'

'No. The race starts from there. It's the landlord of The Little Ark, Hargreaves, who's giving the prize. It'll be the first time Onllwyn ever made anything out of the drink trade.'

The three friends made their way towards The Little Ark. It was one of the older taverns of Meadow Prospect, low-roofed, a rust-red in colour. From a distance they could see Hargreaves the landlord standing in the small cobbled yard which fronted it, giving greeting to the first entrants and their supporters. The boys saw Onllwyn coming towards them down a side street. Verdun and Sylvanus looked at him wonderingly, for the last time they had seen him he had been radiant and lithe, with a hint of mastery in his every word and step. Now he walked slowly and his face was thoughtful and shadowed even beyond the point of darkling pensiveness normal in Meadow Prospect. In his right hand he carried the cheap suitcase which contained his racing equipment. They waited for him to come up with them.

'What's up, Uncle Onllwyn? What are you looking so sad for? You bad?'

'No. I'm all right. I feel quite painless.'

'You look down in the dumps. Come on, Uncle Onllwyn. I've been telling everyone what a champion walker you are. We've been telling everybody that you're going to win.'

'I'm not going to win. There are many things that are certain. One is, I'm not going to win.'

'The bookies have been at him,' said Elwyn, who knew more about these things than his friends.

'You and your bookies,' said Onllwyn, looking at Elwyn

with a calm contempt. 'It'll all be due to Cynlais Moore, if you want to know.'

'Cynlais, the bloke with the limp?'

'He's got a bit of a limp: That's the boy. He came to see me two days ago. Cynlais seemed to be in the deepest sorrow I had ever seen. You know how I get when I see somebody in sorrow.'

'You go daft, Uncle Onllwyn.' Sylvanus' tone was sharply unpleasant. 'You'd be better off deaf when the sorrowful come around. But why ever did you listen to Cynlais Moore? Cynlais is known to be the biggest liar in Meadow Prospect.'

'Cynlais is alive. Men alive change. It is likely that truth may have come to a better understanding with Cynlais.'

'All right then. If you don't want to get on, that's your look-out. There's too much pity in you. You're a clown for stroking the sorrowful, that's your trouble.'

'He came to me and told me about his wife, Elvira Moore, who has been ill for a long time and is taking up a lot of money in tonics. Her bill from the chemist makes the Social Insurance look very trivial, says Cynlais. So he wants to make some money. He also has a young son called Maldwyn Moore. This boy has a fine soprano voice and drives people half mad with religious fervour and the wish to be off on a crusade with his rendering of such songs as "Jerusalem, Jerusalem".'

'I've heard that Maldwyn,' said Verdun. He had never heard Maldwyn sing a note. He wished only to counter Onllwyn's current of thoughtless compassion. 'He's ronk. He sings like a frog. Cynlais was on form with you, Uncle Onllwyn. Mostly he tells the truth about just one item on the list to keep his hand in, but with you he seems to have gone the whole hog.'

'Boys change. He may now be like a lark, this Maldwyn. So an uncle who lives in London tells Cynlais that there are fine openings for young Welsh boy sopranos in those parts. The voters are making big money in that quarter, and they like listening to these boys sing when they are getting tender over their drink. But this Maldwyn is ragged. He likes going down slopes on his backside, and he takes the seat out of a pair of trousers as quickly as you would say hullo. So if Cynlais gets enough money he is going to pack Maldwyn off to London, where he can make a fortune singing, and where it's flat, so that he won't forever have to be putting out money in patches. So Cynlais argued me into letting him win this race.'

'Of all the nerve! Honest, Uncle Onllwyn, you're being silly. Are you forgetting the way you were crying and trembling with excitement when you first read about this Gito the fleet one, and how you said he was the boy who ought to have been the patron saint of the Celts because he was one voter who would have shown nothing but speed and scorn to the Saxons and the coalowners when they came around for their collection of scalps and profits. And are you forgetting the trouble you had waiting for bits to fall off every coalhouse in the street so that you could build the box which would let you try out Gito's recipe of the dung?'

'He's been bewitched by this Moore, if you ask me,' said Verdun. 'They say this Moore is such a liar he hasn't even given the same reason for his limp twice.'

'He knows I'm the best walker about here. He's heard from somebody who used to live down in Carmarthen about how I would go flashing about down there beating all the other boys with my skill and stamina. And he said, "If anybody's got the knowledge and the craftiness to win me the prize, it's Onllwyn Evans."'

'But didn't you tell him you needed gardening tools just as much as Elvira needs tonics or Maldwyn needs trousers to sing to the voters in London?'

'Mine is a selfish wish. I want tools, a smallholding, and the feel of fertile earth for myself. But Cynlais wants the things he wants for others. He made me feel a bit ashamed.'

'So what did you say you'd do for this crook?'

'I told him I would show him all the secrets of victory. I spent two hours the night before last teaching him the special leg-twisting starting method which made such a mock of all those elements in the western counties who were tempted to take the road against me. Cynlais got himself into a five-ply knot to start with, he being such an amateur and having that smack on the leg, besides being very eager for a triumph. But after I had unwound him about six times and given him a lot of encouragement he got into the way of it, and now you can't even stop to talk to the man without having him suddenly bend down and shoot off like a torpedo to show his mastery. For all his limp that Cynlais can move in a handy way.'

'Of course he can. That Cynlais is a bigger crook than any of those boys we see in those serials down at the Dog scheming and burgling weekly and paying no rent. That limp is only something he puts on to fool people and flood tender-hearted elements like you with tears. I bet he hasn't even got a wife called Elvira or a kid called Maldwyn.'

'Oh yes, he has. I've seen them, and they're in the exact condition described by Cynlais: Elvira pale as a ghost and scooping up Oxo direct from the pot every whipstitch, and Maldwyn very vocal in a high-pitched way and as bare-breeched for lack of cloth as a cat.'

'What else did you teach him? Don't tell me you let him into that ancient secret of Gito's, of how to be supple though old and bent nearly double most of the time. You know what a great comfort having that secret has been to you through the years.'

'At first I wasn't going to tell him. But honest, Sylvanus, he looked so pathetic, and his legs and arms creaked so much when he moved I had to shout my directions at him. So I thought that if Gito lived only to silence the joints of this Cynlais he did not live in vain, so last night I granted him the use of the box and he slept in it.'

'Well, I hope that's the last thing you'll do for him. You'll never get on, Uncle Onllwyn. You've got no guile, no hardness at all. You chuck away your trumps, and to the last day of time you'll be nothing but a mat for the voters, being taken in by elements like Cynlais Moore.'

'I'm letting him have the grips as well.'

'Oh no! The mouth grips? Why, they are the best thing you've got.'

'He'll have to have them if he's going to win. If there's one thing that makes a man sure of victory it's those grips. They make a man feel he's got the world itself in the palm of his hand and wondering where to throw it. It would have been heartless showing Cynlais the leg-twist, the secret of the dung, and then keep back the grips which are the very crown of all my paraphernalia.'

They heard Hargreaves shouting on the entrants to come in and get dressed for the start. Hargreaves was the starter and was swinging a pistol in his hand. He looked full of drink and malice, and the friends approached him from behind. There were some very old men among the entrants, for the minimum age was forty. Some of them had already changed, and the ancient, withered look of their limbs and their obvious unfitness to stand up to anything much more than the sound of Hargreaves' gun made Verdun and Sylvanus all the more bitter about the gesture of self-denial that Uncle Onllwyn had been talked into by Cynlais Moore. Several of the men were being served with beer by Mrs Hargreaves in the narrow passageway of The Little Ark.

'Where's Cynlais?' asked Verdun.

'Oh, he'll be here shortly. You'll be able to tell him by the easy springy way of walking he'll have. After a night in the dung-box, Gito's casket, you feel so springy you think all the time you're on the point of floating, and when gladness comes into the heart to supplement the suppleness of your limbs, you have to press hard on your feet to keep on the earth at all. That Gito must have been the son of the wizard Merlin.'

A man in his middle forties with very red thick hair and a

face which in normal mood would have been smooth and cheerful came around the corner. But his face at that moment was neither cheerful nor smooth. There was an expression of settled wretchedness upon it, and he walked slowly, as if every motion of his body was undertaken only after an uneasy chat with pain.

'Either this is Cynlais' dying twin,' said Onllwyn, 'or he didn't follow the directions as set forth by Gito and me.'

'He looks rough,' said Sylvanus delightedly. 'Looks to me as if you're going to have those gardening tools whether you want them or not, Uncle Onllwyn. It doesn't seem that Cynlais could beat a hearse in his present shape. He looks as if he's been sleeping under and not in the box.'

'He'll be a new man when he gets the grips in,' said Onllwyn obstinately.

Cynlais had seated himself on a low stone stile that had been let into the garden wall of The Little Ark. When he saw Onllwyn he raised his right arm stiffly and was obviously on the point of some bad-tempered accusation, but he thought better of it, and did no more than sigh in a loud, hopeless way. Cynlais' face had no cunning and these changes of mental front were conveyed in the shift of his eyes and mouth. 'You know, Onllwyn,' he said quietly, 'that my wife Elvira has many troubles. Among those troubles is nerves.'

'I know that, Cynlais. I've seen Elvira shake when Maldwyn has come singing at her from behind. It was I who got you that extra-large box of the herb skullcap from that nature-healer, Mathew Caney the Cure, to see if it would steady her trembles. But what have Elvira's nerves got to do with the feeble and limping way in which you are walking?'

'It was that box, the casket of Gito, or whatever you call it,' said Cynlais bitterly, again making a clear effort to keep his bad temper in the basement of his mood. 'You told me to lie in it, so that its healing properties could go healing and refreshing into every joint. When you first told me that, I thought that you were out of your head, made jingles by your years in the solitude dreaming of land and sheep of your own. But I took your word for it even though my first inclination was to turn you over to Naboth Jenks the Pinks and those other boys in the Allotment Holders' Union for wasting a boxful of prime stuff. But you have a wise, pitying look and I listened. I didn't like the coffin shape you had managed to work on to that box either, but I carried it home, and until Elvira and the kids had gone to bed I kept it in the shed behind the house. When everything was quiet I carried it down to the kitchen, thinking to myself all the time what a sinister shape this box has, and wondering why you hadn't picked a homelier and less haunting pattern. Between the dung and thoughts of doom I was not happy as I laid that article down in front of the kitchen fire, for it was there I put it, determined to be cosy, if foul. Now, as I said, Elvira has nerves, the longest in all Meadow Prospect. These nerves make her twitch and they also make her dream, and she often thinks her dreams show up the future, and it's no joke when listening to Elvira after a night when her dreams have been full of wise bright eyes to see her next week winking away at last week as they thrust freezing fingers up today. It seems a couple of days ago she had a whole belt of dreams about me being kicked by a horse and killed. She had seen me there in her dreams, dead, and apart from me leaving her unprovided for, having been kicked by a horse even poorer than I was and in no way able to make payment for the use of me, she said I had looked quite nice and she had enjoyed the spectacle of me lying there in dreams, stiff as a board and pale as winter. About an hour after I had settled myself in the box, wriggling about and feeling uncomfortable and cursing you and that silly old fool Gito, I doze off. Then Elvira upstairs notices I am not at her side. This worries her, for with all my other failings I am a whale of a man for sleeping in my own bed, so that the boys from the Government will know exactly where to come when they wish to tell me that my days of doubt and trouble are at an end. So I am never far from Elvira's side at night. She catches a slight smell in the air, which, while a common enough smell, is not often to be smelled in our house. The smell of horse. This makes her twitch, with all her nerves working up to a real loud climax of hallelujahs like the boys in the chapels, because she remembers the dream with me catching it from a hoof and being laid flat. She lights a candle, terrified. She comes cautiously down the stairs. She opens the kitchen door. Now, I ask you, Onllwyn Evans, if you were less keen on getting back to the land and were in the way of seeing the dead lying about in your dreams, what would you do if you saw what Elvira saw then, me stretched out in what looks like a coffin but which is worse than a coffin because I am resting on a layer of pure waste?'

'I'd blow out the candle for a start,' said Uncle Onllwyn, trying to see the problem as best he could from the viewpoint of Cynlais Moore, and sounding very helpful. 'I'd do that so that I would see as little of you as possible.'

'All right for you to be so wise. Elvira nearly went off her head. She goes off into the loudest laughing fit heard in Meadow Prospect, even counting the beaut we had from that burning fanatic Ogley Floyd the Flame when he saw the whole truth about mankind five seconds after having a truncheon broken in three over his pate in the Minimum Wage troubles of 1910. I am standing up in the box now bawling at Elvira that I am simply becoming supple, to read no more into it than that, and telling her to shut up her screeching for God's sake, or she will be bringing down on us a visit from Parry the Pittance, that official who calls on behalf of the County Council to take away the demented. At that moment in rushes Teifion Farr from two doors down, an interfering toad, a busybody, a man who has tufts of coconut matting lodged in his ear from keeping it so often to the ground listening to the approaching hoof-beat of calamity. Teifion sees the scene in the kitchen and he thinks this is what he has been waiting to see all these years. He thinks I am up to some devilry with Elvira, because he doesn't often see voters standing up naked in the kitchen without even a soapsud to take the strain, and Teifion is a Calvinist with a low, malicious view of man. He takes hold of me and beats me around that kitchen in a way I hope I will never know again. If I had been a drum he would certainly have got the message across to Calvin. The sound of me being made into pulp brought Elvira to her senses, and for a whole minute she stood there admiring the quick, nimble shakes of Farr as he half butchered me. Then she remembers about the box as she sees me and Farr running around it for the tenth time. She calls the kids, drags it outside and they burn it, and the back fills up with voters who think from the glow we are celebrating some brand of jubilee or armistice. So that's the end of your box.'

'Poor old Gito!'

'Why sympathise with that old goat? He's dead and as used to slowness as the rest of us. Fix your mind on the problems of the quick and the still-vexed, Onllwyn.'

'It was better for Gito than for me.'

'Why?'

'He didn't have to deal with bunglers and menaces like you.'

'Who are you calling a menace? It was your damned coffin that started it all. And I'm still aching from Teifion Farr's treatment. That's why I feel like one half-raised from the dead. I reckon you ought to feel keener than ever to let me have this prize, although I don't know how I'm going to beat anybody now with this present feeling upon me. How would you like to win and hand me the money, Onllwyn?'

'No, that wouldn't be honest. I like to see the people do the thing for which they get the pay or the reward. I'm not an all-out Marxist, but I'll go as far as that with those boys in the discussion group at the Library and Institute.'

'Don't forget Elvira'll be worse after the shock she got from that box. And when Maldwyn catches the ears of those voters in London he'll pay you the money back five times over.'

'Oh, leave him alone,' said Verdun to Onllwyn. 'This Cynlais is making a fool out of you.'

'Now you file off, Harris,' said Cynlais. 'You've got too much mouth for a small one.'

'You can win, Cynlais,' said Onllwyn. 'Look at all those blokes who've entered. Life has snarled at them all, judging by their look, and they'll have to be carrying each other if they want to advance after the first minute. And you forget that you'll be using my grips. Once you get your teeth in those, boy, you'll forget all about your bruises and failures. They'll give you the fierceness and will to win we elements seem most to lack. They make you feel supple and fleet as if you had made a proper use of Gito's box.'

'I bet he put it on the fire himself to save coal,' said Elwyn, his eyes settled unblinking and hostile on Cynlais.

'Of course he did,' said Verdun. 'And I bet that Teifion Farr was never heard of on this earth until a few minutes ago. Whenever Cynlais Moore talks, truth orders a truss.'

'Now you three wise young rodneys, file off,' said Cynlais. Cynlais and Onllwyn went off into the back room of the Ark, Onllwyn was out again in two minutes wearing his singlet and his curiously long white drawers which caught the eye of his three young friends who had been brought up to think of these articles as either very short or not there at all. He wore a look of solemn responsibility which, taken together with the length of his drawers, made Elwyn laugh out loud. Verdun dug his arm into Elwyn's side.

'Sorry, boy,' said Elwyn. 'You look fine, Uncle Onllwyn; a treat, honest.'

An old competitor, with knicks as long as Onllwyn's, but with limbs much less fitted for racing, came out of the Ark's passageway, led by a friend. They were both staggering a little, but the man in the drawers was crying as well. They sat down on the stone bench near the door. The boys noticed that the weeping man had a long, plain scar running across his brow.

'That's Enoch Vizard,' said Onllwyn. 'The man with the scar is Enoch. And his friend is Luther Mitchell. I didn't know that Enoch was interested in such events as races. Hullo, Luther. What's wrong with Enoch? He seems to be in trouble.'

'He'd be all right if he wasn't so stubborn,' said Luther. 'He makes up his mind to be in this race and there we are. A mule. Just being a mule is bad enough, but a mule within two breaths of the pension is a pitiful sight to see. You know what a fine strong chap Enoch was before he got that smack on his forehead?'

'I remember,' said Onllwyn. 'He was the pride of Meadow Prospect with his great strength. One never knew what he was going to lift next. He was one of the few men who kept things moving during the great slump.'

'We got here soon for the changing, and when Enoch took off his trousers to get into his running drawers he became very sad at the thin look of his legs. He said he had seen them before, of course, going to bed and so on, but he had never noticed before how much they had dwindled. The back room of the Ark is a lighter place than any bedroom in Meadow Prospect and full of truth. So I said what the hell, of course we shrink. I even hummed him that well-known hymn which deals with shrinkage and decline in a very clear way. I added that after that bump he got on the boko when the roof came down he ought to be glad he's not bloody well dead. And I said let's have a drink, boy, and to hell with all such antics as dwindling and age and taking off your trousers when the light is too good. So we started to drink. And there we are. When Hargreaves fires off that great gun we'll have to give Enoch a strong shove in the right direction or he'll be landing up in the wrong town, honest to God.'

The boys closed around watching Enoch Vizard pulling at the legs of his drawers and sobbing hard as he stroked the thin, blotched, emaciated skin of his arms and legs.

Cynlais came out. He was wearing tight white drawers that had an elegant cut alongside such baggy articles as those worn by Vizard and Onllwyn, but his vest was a crimson, shapeless effect that looked as if it had been cut down from a dress with the wearer still wearing it and fighting to keep it intact. He appeared self-conscious and furtive, and gave Onllwyn a sly dig as if to say he was now ready for final instructions. Onllwyn paid no attention to him at all. He was staring at Enoch Vizard.

'It would be a good thing,' said Onllwyn, 'if I could arrange a little victory for Enoch. That poor bloke is half eaten away by despair. I've had a slow and grinding trip through the mill, it's true, but I haven't yet had my head under a ton of rock like this voter, nor does my skin look as if it has just been knitted on by a poor hand with the needles. It would set him up no end if he could turn out to be the best walker in Meadow Prospect.'

'No chance,' said Luther Mitchell. 'No chance. Very nice of you to offer, Onllwyn. But as soon as Enoch walks a bit too fast that crack across his brow gives him a terrible headache and giddiness, and when he is in that state, I've seen falling stars that were nearer to the earth and easier to manage.'

'Very nice of you to offer,' said Cynlais ironically, pushing his head fiercely between Luther and Onllwyn. 'It's a pity everybody couldn't win. Then you'd be very happy, Onllwyn. A proper mixture of Carnegie and Claus, that's what you are out to become, boy. Come on, for God's sake, and show me the magic of those grips.' Cynlais, Onllwyn, and the three boys moved off conspiratorially around the corner of The Little Ark. Onllwyn brought the grips, large rough-hewn objects, out of his case. Cynlais looked at them astonished. 'Where in God's name am I supposed to wear those?'

'Don't be backward, Cyn. In the mouth.'

'What kind of a jack will I need to get my head around those? Is this some kind of sombre buffoonery, Onllwyn?'

'No, no. With these in, you'll be breathing deep and easy when all the rest will be gasping their guts out and dreaming of the iron lung.'

'But just look at the size of them. Just one half of one of those would fill me. Thinking through the years of that Gito has driven you off the hinge, boy. And I didn't tell you this before, but I've got a very small mouth for a grown man. All the Moores have dainty lips.'

'It's the size of the grips that gives them their special quality. That's why I designed them big. You are so busy keeping your mouth around them you pay no heed to the call of fatigue. Once during my fourth year on the Social Insurance, they kept my teeth so occupied I even managed to turn a blind eye to the strong need for death.'

'You wouldn't be able to hear any kind of call with those things blocking you up... wait a minute though...' Cynlais stepped very close to Onllwyn. His eyes narrowed and his nostrils swelled. He was clearly on some crest of cunning insight. Onllwyn blushed and trembled a little in his long drawers. With so little on he did not like anyone to look quite as infrared as Cynlais.

'Now I'm up to you,' said Cynlais in a rising voice. 'I can see through all your tricks now, boy. I didn't think you were so smart, Onllwyn, but lucky for me at the last moment I can see you for the crook you are.'

'You're off your head, Cynlais. Buck up, boy. Your thoughts are farther round the bend than normal.'

'You're as deep as a snake. Now I see the way you planned it. First of all you see I'm the only one who's got a chance of walking you off your feet. You saw my rightful quality as a walker better than I did myself. You decided early on that I must be driven from the race by hook or by crook. With Cynlais Moore a cripple, you said, Onllwyn Evans need have no fears. When I came to you begging your help you must have thanked God for delivering your victim into your hands instead of having to wait and do the job by breaking my toes quietly whenever you stood next to me in the queue at the Exchange.'

Cynlais, his eyes bright, paused here to go back over the details of his first interview with Onllwyn, which were now apparently becoming significant to him for the first time. Onllwyn and the boys, fascinated by the sweep of Cynlais' narrative, sat down to enjoy it the more.

'First,' said Cynlais, 'there was that amazing caper of the starting method. That should have put me on my guard, but I was blind with worry and want. You got me into as many wriggles as a lizard, then you tell me to shoot myself into straightness. What was that but an outright invitation to all the ruptures among these hills to camp out with Cynlais Moore. Abolish rent, ye ruptures. In Cynlais there are many mansions, and if you find them a bit cramped just give Onllwyn the wink; he's the boy to have Moore walking lower than a duck at all points. But that didn't work. So you rig up that coffin and treat me to a lot of chatter about that element Gito, whom you paint as a model Celt because he could run so fast he would have been able to catch even joy and a steady job in Meadow Prospect. I can see now how you meant the box to work. First, the sight of me in it was to craze Elvira, then with her crazed you would nip in and clamp the lid on, leaving me boxed for evermore and Elvira given the blame, you sly, seeing old sausage. Or I was to suffer some mental breakage from finding myself lower, flatter, and on an odder mattress than I have ever known since the Navy took to oil in the boilers and I took to tinned milk on the table. But that failed too. You didn't count on that best of neighbours and ambulance men, Teifon Farr, who is on permanent duty waiting to find the whole of Khartoum Row pinned beneath the very rump of doom and squealing for splints, tourniquets, and testaments. Now, you come to your third attempt, and it's the cool friendly way in which you hand these various courses to me that makes me marvel. Two bits of rubber big enough to choke a grown

bloody elephant, and you ask me to fit them into my mouth.'
Cynlais was now shaking with anger and disappointment.

'Come on,' said Sylvanus to his uncle. 'Give your advice
and grips to Enoch Vizard, who'll know better than to call
you a snake and a crook.'

'Wait a minute,' said Onllwyn. 'Don't be too hard on
Cynlais. He's worried about Elvira and self-conscious about
turning up here with such tight revealing drawers and a
singlet that looks as if it was bitten out of his grandmother's
coms. Now calm down, Cynlais, and tell me, do you or do
you not want to win this race?'

'Course I want to win it. Don't pay any attention to what
I said. I was nervous marching about here half-naked and all
keyed up. I talked to you like an old rodney. You tell me
what to do, Onllwyn.' Around the corner they could hear
Hargreaves marshalling the competitors. Onllwyn showed
Cynlais the grips once more and once more Cynlais fell back,
his face carved into the familiar zones of distrust and horror.

'For God's sake, Onll, isn't there a way of doing without
those?'

'I can't guarantee success without the grips. I've given
speed, endurance, and that fleet, elusive Gito most of my
thought, so don't quibble.'

'All right then, block me up.' Cynlais turned his back to
the boys while Onllwyn helped him to adjust the rubbers.

'This one in the front and the other one a bit more to the
back. You get fanatical once you get your teeth deep into
these.' The boys waited with great interest to see the result
of all the manoeuvres of Onllwyn and the agonised twitching
of Cynlais. Only Verdun among the boys had seen Onllwyn
with the grips in position, and he was better prepared than
Sylvanus and Elwyn to stand the ghastly contortion of
Cynlais' face when he turned round. But even he was
shocked to see anyone look so much like a cross between a
devilfish and a hellhound as Cynlais, his mouth painfully
yawning and his eyes bursting with the strain of his gaping

jaws and ripening indignation. He was letting fly at Onllwyn with a long speech of furious blame, but Cynlais might just as well have been praising Onllwyn up to the skies for all his listeners understood. They led him to the starting point. Hargreaves, still waving his pistol, looked closely at Cynlais.

'Is this man fit to start?' he asked Onllwyn.

'Fitter than you.'

'He's looking as if he's just taken his seat on a spike.'

'As long as the spike's not showing there's nothing in the rules against that.'

Cynlais took his place between Onllwyn and Enoch Vizard. Enoch was recovering slowly from his drink and grief and was wiping his eyes, groaning a little now and then to keep in touch with his receding mood. The first thing he saw when he took his arm down and looked around was the face of Cynlais, spread out in a fashion never before seen in Meadow Prospect, and going dark now with the savage effort of his endurance. Enoch darted from the line and made for the sheltering doorway of the Ark. He was dragged back by Luther Mitchell, who told him that Cynlais was no more than a trick of the shifting light, and also that if Cynlais with his look of being three-quarter strangled was the average sample of athlete entered for this race, then Enoch could afford to dawdle for a round of sobbing at every corner and still win.

Hargreaves was inspecting his pistol. Cynlais was bending down, painfully full of deep, suffering sounds. Onllwyn was busy instructing him in the leg-twists necessary for the bullet-like start. Cynlais was whimpering like a dog now and getting into the most dangerous knot. He was listening too closely to his own welling noises to make any sense of what Onllwyn was telling him to do in the matter of his feet. In his tight drawers his backside was wearing the same expression of staring, mortal, atrabilious strain as his face, and Verdun kept passing from the front to the back of him to get the full flavour of this miracle in two shades.

Hargreaves' pistol went off with a great bang, scaring to death what little was left of Cynlais' overwrought wits. With a tremendous shudder his body flattened out on the floor and he passed gratefully into a dead faint, his very last act before the eclipse being a brief look of loathing thrown at Onllwyn. His outflung arm tripped the feet of another competitor, an earnest man in his middle forties, Samuel Howells, and Howells went crashing to the floor and stayed there, unhurt, but with as little wish to move as Cynlais. A lot of these competitors, said Elwyn to Verdun, as they watched this scene, had been pushed into these events by their families who were greedy for money to make an extra trip to such places as that cinema, the Dog, and the alert, fit look of this Howells as he lay on the floor making no move to be up and doing proved it.

The others set forth. It was clear from the start that there were only two men in it. Onllwyn and Enoch Vizard. There seemed to be the dynamic of some desperate rage in Enoch, as if he knew that if this were to be the last fling then at least he would be really far-flung at the end of it. Onllwyn had all his work cut out to keep an even yard behind him. Their shoulders were working with a broad ugly swing that struck the eyes of Verdun, who was half running along the pavement, as downright sinister and saddening. They all urged Onllwyn to put a spurt on, warning him that Hargreaves seemed to have slipped a drop of elixir into whatever Enoch had been drinking in the Ark. 'I'll let him win,' said Onllwyn. 'I wouldn't have the heart to beat him, honest I wouldn't. This will be some sort of crown for his shrinking head.' And as he said that he shouted to the unheeding Enoch to slow down a bit and take it easy, to watch out for that weakness in his head, that he was among friends, that after this day's racing the White Flash, with an inch or two on his drawers and a bit less gasp in his average breath, would not be Onllwyn but Enoch Vizard.

Eight minutes after the start twilight cracked down on

Enoch. He went deathly pale, raised his hand to his head, and began reeling. Onllwyn and the boys broke into cries of sympathy and encouragement: 'Steady up there, Enoch!' 'No need to strain so much at the leash, Vizard.'

Even people sitting on their doorsteps who had been watching them without interest, thinking that the sight of voters half clad and walking at abnormal rates was only another twitch of the long Crisis, now stood up and started to take an interest in the problem of Vizard's zeal and agony. Enoch was staggering on the largest possible scale. Onllwyn did his best to keep him standing, moving forward, and in the race. It was not easy, for Enoch's movements were as tangential and odd as those of a rugby ball. Onllwyn kept close behind him, supporting him when Enoch showed a tendency to lurch headlong, and dragging him back whenever he went off the official route. Enoch in his bewilderment was going right into houses through doors that were never closed, either because the lines of doors and jamb were no longer parallel, or because the sight of a shut, staring door cooled the sense of community in a place where environment was already causing the blood stream of most voters to slow down and stop taking the thing so seriously. On two occasions Onllwyn had to go to the very foot of a staircase to rescue Enoch, who now seemed intent on going off permanently at a right angle to the course. The second occasion might have turned out awkwardly for them, for Enoch, in his rudderless stupor, went through the open door of Goronwy Blamey, a broad, jealous, fierce man, who lived under the constant delusion of being betrayed on every front by his wife, Gloria Blamey, who had once been an usherette and nimble in the use of her eyes in The Cosy, a cinema of Meadow Prospect where the town seemed to garage the central part of its libido. That afternoon, Goronwy, who had been celebrating the morning of the bank holiday with a few pints in the Con Club, had been letting it in for Gloria on a piled up series of charges and cuffing her in and out of the kitchen, working to a familiar pattern of violence that allowed them both to grab something to eat from the shelves as he backed her into the larder at regular points of climax, Goronwy carrying on just like Othello but smaller, less able at speech, and nowhere near as subtle. But Gloria had given him a fish-and-chip dinner, which always agreed with Goronwy when on the beer, and his mood had softened to a frenzy of wanting, and they had gone upstairs to an eager rhythm. It was when Goronwy was coming out of the kitchen, his mouth smiling and his braces dangling, with a cup of tea to take up to Gloria, who had just made him promise to be less of a silly billy in the future and to put aside his tormenting visions of men coming in and out of the house, love bent, that he saw Enoch and Onllwyn, apparently naked except for a few strips of cotton, come through the front door at a tremendous pace, heading straight for the stairs as if this had long been their rallying point.

'So these are the games that go on behind my back!' shouted Goronwy, 'The rodneys are not even properly dressed.' And he waded into Enoch with all his strength, boxing him hard about the head, sparing one for Onllwyn whenever the latter stuck his head in the way. But he did not single out Onllwyn, for he was reserving him as an item that could be properly dealt with when Vizard was dead. It was Verdun who put an end to this by tugging at Goronwy's sleeve and saying: 'There's a fire upstairs, mate.' A look that had wings of longing and terror came to Goronwy's face and he vanished aloft.

They got Enoch on the road again. But his experience with Blamey had finished off all his sense of balance and he was walking now with a kind of extreme leftward crouch that had the most baffling effect on Onllwyn. They came to a sharp slope on the left. Enoch went down it like a plummet and entered neatly into a bus that chanced to stop at the precise moment of Enoch's arrival at the foot of the slope.

The conductor of the bus tried not to look surprised and rang the bell to proceed. Onllwyn wanted to follow him and get him back, but the boys dissuaded him.

'But what'll he do?' asked Onllwyn. 'He's got no kind of bus fare on him in that costume, and in the state he's in he won't be able to explain even by signs what he's doing dressed in that fashion on a bus to Cwmycysgod or some such place.'

'Don't worry,' said Verdun. 'The conductor of that bus is Morlais Morgan, my cousin, who takes a broad view of the bus company and is full of sympathy for all such elements as Enoch who don't know where they're going or what they are up to. Think of yourself now, Uncle Onllwyn. The race is to the swift. You've been waiting years for the chance to show people what you're made of. This is your day, Uncle Onllwyn. You are crying out to Gito that the years of waiting are at an end. Let liars and madmen like Moore and Vizard find their own way to the culvert. Why should sorrow and pity be pulling you down forever into the marsh? Here we are at the homestretch, the new bypass back to the Ark. Hargreaves is waiting there with the money which will buy you those tools and the smallholding with its promise of new life for you and perhaps for us, too, if you can branch out with the right kind of crops and cattle.'

Onllwyn's face brightened as if a load had been taken off his spirit.

'You're right, boy. I owe it to Gito, to whom I must be a kind of son. I owe it to him and to me to shout up to life to waggle it about a bit and stop letting me have the whole torrent.'

There was only one other competitor in sight as Onllwyn started on his last magnificent spurt along the new road, and as there was no second prize he gave up the ghost as he saw the quality of Onllwyn's final effort. As he breasted the tape there was no cheering from the compact, excited group that had formed around the door of the Ark. Verdun noticed that Cynlais Moore was in the centre of this group, and there was a flushed, depleted look on his face, as if he had just finished a long speech.

'I was first,' said Onllwyn humbly.

'First!' said Hargreaves. 'You, first! And no wonder. I have been a fancier in every kind of sport you can mention, but I've never come up against a dirtier passage of work than we've seen here this afternoon. And never do I wish to set eyes on another such scoundrel as you, Evans.'

Onllwyn did not protest. He simply dropped on to one knee, resting the kneecap on one of the meagre bits of turf still left outside the Ark.

'Go on,' he said, as interested as if Hargreaves were putting on a drama.

'Moore has told us everything. The rupture-stunt with the leg-twists, I saw that myself and it's definitely booked for *The News of the World*. I saw the poor chap curved like an S with you bending over him trying to tie a fourth knot in his legs and cajoling Moore, who was stupefied with pain, to pull it a little tighter. It was cruel. Moore also tells me you had his drawers specially shrunk and if he had raced with those articles pulling at him his manhood would not have survived the first yard. Then there was that caper with the coffin. Who ever heard of anybody but a pagan stretching himself out in dung to get supple? No wonder things have got so slack in Meadow Prospect with boys like you badgering the Christians, Evans. But the final crime was those grips. The last time I saw contraptions of that kind was with a horse dentist, and he was keen on big horses. A deliberate attempt to choke Moore. I've talked it over with the boys here and they agree that short of handing you over to the police the best thing to do is give the prize money to Moore.'

'All right,' said Onllwyn. 'Give it to Cynlais. Cynlais has many needs.'

Cynlais was delighted. He rushed into the Ark. When he came out, dressed, he was holding up the prize money.

'Free beer for you boys tonight,' he said. 'This night will belong to Cynlais Moore.'

'Don't forget Elvira's tonics,' said Onllwyn.

'She's having Teifion Farr in now for massage. He's a marvel.'

'Don't forget Maldwyn's bare behind. He can't sing as he is.'

'To hell with Maldwyn. His butts are better bare and in any case I've trained him to sing with his front to the public.'

'If you'll let me,' said Elwyn quietly to Onllwyn, 'I'll take Cynlais around the back and bring you a part of his head as consolation prize. What bit of Cynlais do you most fancy?'

'Oh never mind, Elwyn. Nice of you to offer but Cynlais is all right. Slow to learn, that's all.'

Onllwyn slipped in for his clothes. The boys remained outside, thinking of Cynlais and of learning and pondering the notion of slowness. As they were about to set out, with Onllwyn between them, Verdun slipped back to the group which was still standing around the front door of the Ark, laughing and congratulating Cynlais.

'I wasn't going to tell you this,' said Verdun. 'But just in case I forget and people start wondering, Uncle Onllwyn also did away with Enoch Vizard half way through the race. He's really ruthless is Onllwyn.'

He turned a satisfied back on the gaping silence that fell upon the group. He ran to join his friends and they made their way to the Library and Institute where, that evening, the librarian, Salathiel Cull, known as Cull the Lull, because he was a political quietist and a preponent of gradualist views, was going to give them a talk on why the world's great herds of driven folk should huddle into a compact and cosy mass and let evil bite them to the heart until its teeth were worn to the unhurting stump.

ACTING CAPTAIN

Alun Lewis

The detachment was a very small one, a single platoon sent from the battalion to guard the dock gates and perimeter, but they had a bugle. Acting Captain Cochrane, the detachment commander, had indented persistently for one, and after two months' nagging on his part, DADOS had grudgingly coughed up a brand new one. It was hanging over old Crocker's bed in the fuggy blacked-out Nissen hut in which the administrative staff were sleeping. There was Crocker, an old soldier who had served in Flanders, Gallipoli, India, and the Far East; he was the cook, Acting Lance Corporal, C3, and used to it. Next to him Taffy Thomas was snoring; the air had grown slowly thicker and more corrupt with fumes from the stove, last night's fish and chips, cigarettes and beer, and all the coming and going since black-out time on the previous evening; so you couldn't breathe it into your lungs without a snore as it squeezed and scraped past your uvula. The fire was still flickering under a weight of grey ash and cinders in the stove.

For no apparent reason Crocker woke up, groaned, yawned, pushed his dirty blankets off, and sat up, vigorously scratching his thin hair. He was wearing his thick winter vest and long pants with brown socks pulled up over the legs so that no part of his flesh was showing except where the heel of his sock was worn through. He listened a moment, to discover whether it was raining; then, finding it wasn't, he unhooked his bugle from the nail above his head, turned the light on to make sure that the office clock, which he always took to bed with him, indicated 6.30 a.m., put out the light again, shuffled to the door, spat, breathed in, closed his lips inside the mouthpiece of the bugle, and blew reveille. He found he was blowing in E instead of G, but, after faltering an instant, laboured through with it in the same key. It was too dark for anyone to notice; not a streak of grey anywhere.

'Gawd curse the dominoes,' he grumbled, shuffling back to his bed. He shook Taffy Thomas hard, relishing the warm sleeping body's resistance.

'Get up, yer Welsh loafer,' he shouted in his ear. 'You'll 'ave the boss on yer tail if you don't get down there wiv 'is shaving water double quick. Get up. You ain't got yer missus besidejer now.'

Taffy didn't get up as philosophically as Crocker. He was still young enough to resent and rebel against things the old cook had long ago ceased thinking about. Most things were a matter of course to Crocker; air raids, sinkings, death were as normal as cutting rashers of bacon in the dark and peeling potatoes in his ramshackle corrugated-iron cooking shed.

However, Taffy got up. He put his hand on his head to feel how hot his hangover was, and then in a fit of irritated energy pulled on his trousers and pullover and searched about for his razor. 'Well, we're a day's march nearer home,' he said, dipping his shaving brush in the jam-tin of cold water he kept under his bed and lathering his face in the dark.

'You pups are always thinking about leave,' Crocker said, fed up. 'D'you know I didn't see my old lady for three and 'alf years in the last bust-up, nor any English girl. Plenty of dusky ones, of course, and Chinese ones that'd scarcely left school—'

'Yeh, I know,' Taffy interrupted. 'You're a real soljer. I know.'

'Well, I didn't want to write 'ome every time I found a flea under my arm,' Crocker scoffed. 'I've sat in the mud scratching my arse from one Christmas to the next wivout arsking to see the OC abaht it.'

'It wasn't your fault we didn't lose the war, then,' Taffy said, wiping his shaved face in his dirty towel. 'And if you're moaning about me asking for leave and asking for a transfer, you'd better shut your trap, old soljer, 'cause I'm not going to sit in this dump doing nothing while my missus freezes in the Anderson and coughs 'er heart up every time Jerry drops a load on Swansea.'

'What you going to do, then?' Crocker taunted. 'Stop the war?'

'No,' Taffy answered hotly. 'Win the bleeding thing.'

'Garn,' Crocker laughed jeeringly. 'Get off and polish the cap'n's Sam Browne. Win the war, be damned. What was you doing at Dunkirk if it isn't rude to ask? We never scuttled out of it, we didn't.'

'Aw, shut up and get a pail of char ready for the lads,' Taffy said. 'I reckon you'd still be in your little dugout if somebody hadn't told you the war was over.'

He slammed the door after him, pulled his cycle from under a ripped tarpaulin, and, tucking his bag of cleaning kit under his arm, pedalled through the muddy pooled ruts, past the sentry shivering in his greatcoat and flapping groundsheet like a spider swollen by the rain, down the lane past the knife rest and Dannert wire obstacle that ran from the sidings to the quay where the Irish packet boat lay moored, and out onto the bleak tarred road that was just beginning to reflect a mildew-grey light along its wet surface. The detachment commander was billeted in an empty house on the hill above the harbour. Taffy's first job was to boil him some water for shaving and tea, make a cup of tea with a spoon infuser, shake him respectfully, salute, collect his Sam Browne and yesterday's boots or shoes, and retire to the scullery to clean them up. Then he swept the downstairs rooms, looked round to see whether there were any chocolate biscuits hidden in the trench coat pocket, threw his sweepings outside for the starlings to swoop and grumble over, and then go back upstairs to fold the blankets and sheets, empty the wash basin and jerry, and let the clean air of the ocean revitalise the room. The whole operation was conducted in silence, broken only by odd grunts and monosyllables from the officer and a sort of absent-minded whistling by the private. Taffy knew his man well enough to leave him alone while he pulled himself together; a glance at his reflection in the shaving mirror was enough to inform him as to the patient's condition. He had a young face, but his narrow grey eyes and almost-pointed teeth, combined with the thin, bony forehead and cheeks, gave him an astringent, intolerant sharpness that only wore off after he had warmed up to the day's task. He was a regular officer who had been commissioned a few months before the war began, and because of his martinet appearance and the facility with which he could fly into an abrupt temper he had spent most of the war drilling recruits on the square at the regimental depot. He had got the square in his blood by the end; muddy boots or tarnished buttons, an indifferent salute, the lazy execution of a drill or an order provoked him immediately to a violent reprimand; all his actions were impatient and smart, his appearance immaculate and important, his opinions unqualified and as definite as they were ill-informed. His nature was bound to insist sooner or later on action; he had got into a bad state at the depot and asked to be posted to a battalion. He considered it a rebuff when he was posted to this small harbour on the featureless north-west coast, and it hadn't improved his frame of mind to consider that a further application for posting would be impolitic while an indefinite stay in his present post could only blur the image of a forceful disciplined soldier which he had so assiduously striven to impress on the depot command. He endured his inactive isolation with some acerbity and sought compensation in other quarters. He was careful of his career, knowing how easy it is to fall down the Army ladder; he paid court to the daughter of the battalion's colonel with the same regard for tact and proper keenness as he employed in his conduct towards his senior officers. But he was not of a firm enough mould to subsist on long-term expectations of advancement. He had to have his fling. And, what with one thing and another, he usually got out of bed on the wrong side and had to work a little blood out of his system before he could sit on his table and argue politics or swop dirty jokes with Sergeant Crumb, his principal stooge, or Private Norris, his clerk general who had a classics degree, an LLB, a mind of his own, and a stoop that barred him from promotion.

'Quiet night last night, sir,' Taffy said amiably when the hair combing stage had been reached and a measure of civility might be expected.

'Was it, hell!' the OC replied, wincing his face. 'Mix me a dose of Andrews Health Salts, Thomas. They're in my valise.'

'Very good, sir.'

'What sort of morning is it?'

'Nothin' partic'lar, sir. What do you want for tonight, sir?'

'My SD suit and my Sam Browne; best shoes and walking out cap. I don't want any Silvo stains on it, either.'

'Very good, sir.

The vexed look left the harsh young face as he tilted the bubbling glass down his throat; beads hooked to the uncombed hairs of his moustache; it was pink at the roots and gold-brown at the tips. 'Gosh!' he said, 'it makes you want to live a clean life always, tasting this stuff. God bless Mr Andrews.'

Having returned and breakfasted with the rest of the lads on old Crocker's lumpy porridge and shrivelled bacon and greased tea, Taffy strolled off to collect his wheelbarrow and begin his second task, cleaning the lines. He had sharpened a beech stick to pick up the chip papers and litter; Curly Norris had suggested the idea, saying it gave the camp a better tone, made it more like a royal park. Curly also wanted to indent for a couple of fallow deer, or if DADOS refused to supply them, purloin them from the grounds of Magdalen College, Oxford. He said Taffy should lead the raiding party, singing the War song of Dinas Fawr.

'You will probably be put on a charge,' he said. 'But what is a charge *sub specie aeternitatis?*'

He was always laughing behind his twinkling spectacles, and even if you didn't know what he was talking about, which was most of the time, his gaiety infected you and you laughed as well or wrestled with him.

When Taffy arrived outside the office Curly Norris was just completing his housework. The office was swirling with smoke from the newly lit fire and dust from the floor. Curly's first task was to sweep all the dust from the floor onto the tables and shelves and files. This ritual was always performed alone, before Sergeant Crumb arrived for the day.

Taffy halted his barrow and respectfully tapped the office door.

'Any old matchsticks today?' he shouted. 'Any old matchsticks?'

'Take your dirty boots off my porch,' Curly shouted. 'A woman's work is never done, don't you men know that yet?'

Taffy jumped in and screwed his arm round Curly's neck. They were wrestling on the table when Sergeant Crumb appeared. At his bull's bellow they stopped.

'What the hell d'you think this is? A tavern?'

'Sorry, Sarge.'

'You'll apologise to the OC if I catch you at it again, either of you.' He smoothed the underside of his waxed moustache with a nicotine-stained forefinger. 'What sort of a mood is he in this morning, Thomas?' Sergeant Crumb always arranged the morning programme on the basis of Taffy's report.

'Got a liver on this morning, Sarge,' Taffy replied. 'Shouldn't be surprised if it turns to diarrhoea.'

'I saw him in the Royal at closing time,' Sergeant Crumb said. 'He was buying drinks all round, so I expected he'd be off his food. Get cracking, Norris. Get the correspondence sorted out, let's see what there is. Then get down to the stores and warn Rosendale to appear before the OC I saw him in town last night when he should have been on duty. Make a charge sheet out before you go. Section 40 – conduct prejudicial to good order. Get weaving.'

Curly thought it a pity there wasn't a mantelpiece for the sergeant's elbows and a waistcoat for his thumbs.

'Very good, Sarge.'

'And you get down to cleaning the lines, Thomas. What are you hanging about here for?'

'Want to see the OC,' Thomas said.

'Too busy,' the sergeant replied, stiffening his weak chin. 'Get out.'

'I can see the OC if I want to,' Thomas replied.

'A-ha!' laughed the sergeant, his shallow blue eyes turning foxy. 'Getting a bit Bolshie, are you? What with you and Rosendale in the detachment we'd better hoist the Red Flag, I'm thinking.' He straightened up, blew out his chest, hardened his characterless eyes. 'Get out!' he shouted.

Curly wasn't laughing now. He looked serious, bothered, and unhappy. The way these foolish and unnecessary rows blew up, these continual petty litigations springing from bad temper and jealousy and animosity; why did they allow their nerves to become public? Why couldn't they hold their water?

Taffy stayed where he was, stubborn and flushing. He had a bony ridge at the base of his neck, a strong chin and a knobbly receding forehead. Huge-shouldered and rather short and bandy in the leg, he gave the appearance of animal strength and latent ferocity.

'That was an order,' the sergeant said.

'OK,' Taffy replied. 'But I'm asking to see the OC. You can't refuse.'

The sergeant began to hesitate, grew a little sick at the mouth, fiddled with the paper cutter.

'What d'you want with him?'

'I want to get into a Commando,' Taffy said.

'You'll get into a glasshouse, maybe,' the sergeant laughed unpleasantly, not at all sure of himself now.

'Yes, for knocking you between your pig's eyes,' Taffy said.

An immediate tension, like the shock of an electric charge, and silence.

'You heard what he said, Norris,' the sergeant snapped. 'I'll want you as witness.'

'Hearsay doesn't count as evidence,' Curly said quietly.

'What did you say?' Sergeant Crumb swung livid on him. 'You bloody little sea lawyer, are you trying to cover him?'

'No. I'm not covering anybody. I simply happen to know that legal procedure excludes my repeating something alleged to have been said by a person not formally warned.'

Sergeant Crumb wrote some words on a sheet of paper.

'We'll see,' he said, uncertainly. 'Now get out.'

Taffy shrugged his shoulders and slouched out. He hadn't meant to say that. Not out loud. All the same, it was OK by him. He pushed his barrow down the muddy path to the stores shed.

Rosendale was shaving in his shirtsleeves. His mirror was a splinter of glass an inch long stuck into a packing case. There was a heap of straw in one corner of the shed; the men were changing the straw of their palliasses; he, as storeman, was in charge; he gave more to some than to others – not to his friends, for he had none, but to the important people, the lancejacks and the lads with a tongue in their heads who determined public opinion in the camp. Rosendale was very sensitive to public opinion, partly because it affected his own advancement, partly because he was politically conscious and wanted to form a cell to fortify his somewhat introvert ideas. He was inept as a soldier, too untidy and slow to get a stripe; consequently he posed as a democrat refusing to be bought over to the ruling classes by a stripe, as one of the unprivileged millions who would be deprived of power and exploited by the boss class for just as long as they were content to endure it. He wasn't making much headway in his campaign. His ideas were too dogmatic to convince men who saw life as a disconnected series of circumstances and poverty as a natural ill and active political opposition as both unpatriotic and unpleasant, something that might get you CB, or your application for a weekend pass rejected. He was popularly known as Haw-Haw.

'Morning, Rosie,' Taffy said, having recovered his equanimity. 'Had a tidy sleep, love?'

'Be damned I didn't,' Rosendale grumbled. 'I slept in that bleeding straw in the corner there and a goddamn mouse crawled under my shirt and bit me under my arm. I squeezed him through my shirt and the little sod squirted all over it.'

'Well, you'd better brass yourself up, Rosie,' Taffy commented, ''cause the snoop has pegged you for being out of camp last night when you were on duty. I'm on the peg, too. So don't start moaning.' At such moments Rosendale lacked the dignity and calm bearing of the representative of the unprivileged millions. He became an anxious, frightened little man seeking an excuse, a lie, an alibi. 'Curly'll come down with the charge in a minute,' Taffy said reassuringly. 'He'll tell us what to say, Curly will.'

Curly brought the mail with him when he came. There was a letter for each of them. Rosendale was too het up to read his letter; he threw it without interest onto the table and bit his nails until the other two had read theirs. Taffy was a slow reader. Rosendale fiddled and shuffled, tears almost touching the surface of his eyes. 'My missus is bad again,' Taffy said, staring at the soiled cheap paper on which a few slanting lines had been pencilled in a childish scrawl. Big crossed kisses had been drawn under the signature. 'She can't touch her food again and her mouth is full of that yellow phlegm I told you about, Curly. And the rain is coming in since the last raid.'

'Why doesn't she go into hospital?' Curly said. 'She's on the panel, isn't she?'

'I don't know proper,' Taffy said, rubbing his face wearily. 'I used to pay insurance when I was in the tinplate works, an' she's been paying twopence a week to the doctor. But *he* don't know what's up with her. I fetched him down last time I was on leave; anybody could see she was had. All yellow and skinny, pitiful thin she was. Not eating a bite, neither, not even milk or stout, but only a drop of pink pop when she was thirsty. I made her bed for her in the kitchen to save her climbing the stairs. I stayed in every night with her. Had to go drinking in the mornings with my brother and my mates. And she was spitting this yellow stuff all the time, see? Very near filled the pisspot with it every day.'

'Well, you've got to get her to hospital,' Curly said. 'What the hell is that doctor doing? It sounds criminal to me.'

'I told her to see another one,' Taffy went on. 'But my mother-in-law it is, she swears by him, see? He's delivered all her kids for her, and he helped my missus through with the twins. So she won't change him. She won't go against her mother, see, Curly?'

'What the hell does a mother-in-law matter?' Curly said sharply. 'Look here, Taff. You've *got* to get home and *carry* her to hospital *yourself* if you don't want her to die. D'you understand? Especially with all these air raids. It's cruel to leave her alone.'

'But what about the kids? She can't take them to hospital with her.'

'Get them evacuated. Or send them to your mother-in-law's.'

'What? That bastard?'

'I'd like to knock your head off, Taffy,' Curly said with cold and exasperated anger.

'I wouldn't care much if you did,' Taffy replied, suddenly plunged in despondency. Like his temper, which had flared against the sergeant, his blues came on him without warning.

'Come on,' Curly insisted crossly. 'Pull yourself together. It doesn't matter about you. It's your wife and kiddies I'm thinking about. Get up to the office and show this letter to the OC. You've *got* to get home.'

'Catch him giving me a forty-eight hours' leave after Crumb has told him what I said,' Taffy said, hang-dog.

'I'll see Crumb at once and ask him to hold the charge back,' Curly said, turning to go.

'What about my charge?' Rosendale asked. He had been hanging round the fringe of Taffy's trouble, like an uncomfortable curate with a dyspepsia of his own. 'Can't you talk it over with me, Curl?'

'Your charge isn't important,' Curly said, hurrying out.

'Bloody intellectuals! They're all the same, the pack of them,' Rosendale muttered.

Sergeant Crumb was already closeted with the OC when Curly got back to the office. The Nissen hut was divided into two rooms by a central plywood partition with a door. Curly stood by the door listening.

They were talking about Sergeant Crumb's wife. It was a matter of long standing, and Curly knew enough about it from the sergeant's occasional confidences to see that he had been ruined by it so gradually and completely that he himself didn't know the extent or nature of the damage. He had joined the Army eight years back to get away from a powerful woman who had him tucked into her bed whenever she wanted him and who was pushing him to divorce his wife. He was afraid of ruining his business, a small garage, by the publicity of a divorce; moreover, he wasn't in love with either of the women though he slept with each in turn. So he joined up to let time and distance settle the mess. Oddly enough it was still unsolved. His wife had gone back to a factory job and taken a small flat. After several years he had called on her on leave, having been discarded by the other woman who preferred a civilian lover. He was very proud of that night. He had wooed his wife back to him; Gable had nothing to show him, he told Curly, recounting in some detail. So things reverted to the old ways for a while, until he received information from a sister of his who lived near his wife that his wife had another man, somebody in the works, a young fellow in a reserved occupation. It wasn't definitely established; Sergeant Crumb wasn't one to beard lions; he hadn't asked his wife point-blank, nor did he intend offering her a divorce. He preferred to use the welfare machinery of the Army. Through the OC he had got in touch with the regimental paymaster and requested him to investigate his wife's conduct through the local police with a view to stopping her allowance, to which he contributed fourteen shillings a week, if her guilt could be established. Meanwhile he continued to prove his manhood and independence by making love promiscuously wherever he was stationed, and displaying a definite penchant for married women. His heart wasn't affected by the affair any more, his affections weren't involved. That was the whole trouble, it seemed to Curly. It was simply a matter of pride, of getting his own back. He took it out of his staff in the same way, blustering at them, telling the OC of their disloyalties and delinquencies, keeping well in with his chiefs, at once toady and bully. At the same time he was efficient and hard-working, smart at drill and a master of office routine and military redtape. His files were neat and complete, correspondence properly indexed, ACIs and Battalion Orders always to hand. Messing indents, pay rolls, men's documents were all open for inspection. The only man who knew that Sergeant Crumb depended entirely upon Private Norris, his clerk general, was Curly Norris himself. And because of his peculiar comic outlook on life he had no desire to split. It amused him to contemplate the sergeant's self-importance and it paid him to be useful in a number of small ways. He could get a weekend pass for the asking. He could use the office at nights to type out his private work – some learned bilge he was preparing for a classical quarterly – and as the war was a stalemate and the Command board had rejected his application for a commission after one look at his stoop, he had grown to consider these small amenities as perhaps more important than the restless discontent that produces poets or heroes or corpses.

Having discussed his marital affairs and got the OC to write another letter to the paymaster, Sergeant Crumb, as was his wont, made deposition against the malcontents, on this occasion Rosendale and Thomas. He suggested that each should be charged under section 40 of the Army Act. Curly, hearing the OC melt under the sergeant's reasoned persuasion, shrugged his shoulders and lit a cigarette. He knew it was poor look out for Mrs Thomas' cancer of the throat. Certainly it was no use making any application at the moment. The OC had given him two weekends' leave in the last six weeks, after air raids, to see that his wife was all right. It was Taffy's own fault, the fool, for not getting her into hospital when he was home last. And now they had no money. Curly had already lent him his last train fare, and had no more cash to spare.

Rosendale came in with a pail of specially-sweet tea at that moment, hoping to mollify the powers. But Sergeant Crumb's voice was unsweetened as he told him to get properly dressed and be ready to answer a charge in five minutes' time.

The upshot of it was that both men got seven days' CB and Curly a severe unofficial reprimand for attempting to shield Thomas. The OC always enjoyed a little adjudication. It gave him strength.

'Sod the Army!' Rosendale moaned, bitter and outraged.

'King's Regulations be damned. Better if they'd spend their

time in strengthening the League-a-Nations or finding a living job for the unemployed or making things better somewhere, not pottering around with King's Regulations.'

'What wouldn't I do to Mr bleeding Crumb if I met him in Civvy Street after the war,' Taffy murmured fondly.

'A lot of use that is to your wife,' Curly snapped.

'Go on. Rub it in,' Taffy flared up, goaded to feel anguish at last. Disconsolate, he wheeled his barrow off to the incinerator, and Curly returned to the office to write letters to his friends.

Acting Captain Cochrane was sitting on the clerk's table, tapping his swagger cane against the brown boots Taffy had brought to a nice shine and chatting to Sergeant Crumb over a cup of lukewarm tea.

'Well, Norris,' he said with a sardonic grin. 'You see what comes of playing the barrister to a pair of fools.'

'They're not particularly fools, sir,' Curly replied with proper deference. They're both men. Thomas has worked in pits and steelworks, he's taken the rap in Belgium, he's trying to maintain a wife and two kiddies – that's more than most of us have done.'

'He's still a fool,' the OC said. 'He's like the rest of the working people. They've been too blind and stupid to help themselves when they had the chance. They could have had socialism any time in the last twenty years. They've got the vote. Why don't they use it to get a Labour government? Because they can't be bothered to lift a finger for their own interests. I'm a socialist at heart, but it's not a bit of good trying to help the people. They don't want to be helped.'

'It isn't entirely their fault, sir,' Curly replied. 'The middle class hasn't helped them very much – the teachers and clergy and newspaper proprietors and business executives. They've all thrown dust in their eyes, confused or denied the real issues and disguised selfish interests and reactionary politics to appear progressive and in the public interest, as they say. They keep the world in a state of perpetual crisis in order to crush internal opposition by the need for national unity, and they buy off their critics by giving them minority posts in the Cabinet. Appeasement at home and abroad; give the beggar a penny and expect him to touch his cap.'

'Hot air,' the OC answered, offering Curly a cigarette. He always came in for a chat after giving anybody a dressing down; Curly surmised that it was a maxim of his that a man who is alternately severe and humane wins the respect as well as the affection of his subordinates. As a matter of fact the men distrusted his geniality and called him two-faced. They never knew how to take him; before asking a favour of him they always consulted Taffy or Curly about his mood. They were nervous of him in a surly way; not from fear, but because they disliked being treated curtly without being able to retort on natural terms. 'Would you like England to become communist?' he continued.

'I should be quite acclimatised to the change after serving in the Army,' Curly replied. 'We live a communal life here; all our clothes and equipment are public property; nobody makes any profits; we serve the state and follow the party line.'

'You think the Army is based on Lenin's ideas, do you?' the OC said. 'That would shake the colonel if he knew it.'

'He needn't worry,' Curly said, laughing. 'The Army hasn't got a revolutionary purpose. It has no ideas worth speaking of except a conservative loyalty to the throne and a professional obligation to obtain a military victory. King Charles I's ideas with Oliver Cromwell's efficiency. That's England all over. They never settle their differences, they always keep both sides going. The Royalists were beaten in the field, yet they dominate the Army. The Germans were licked, yet they've got Europe where they want it. There's plenty of class distinction in the Army, black boots versus brown shoes, but no class conflict. I could go on quite a long time like this, sir. It's more interesting than football.' He laughed to hide his seriousness. He hadn't been speaking in fun, but he preferred to be taken lightly. He knew himself to be a perpetual student, introspective, individualist, an antinomian with a deep respect for the privacy of others. His gentle and slightly neurotic liberalism took the edge off his revolutionary convictions. He lacked the strength to defy what is powerful in men, and he had no heart for extreme action. So he always preferred to be left in peace, to think and observe; his conflicts were within him. He had his own anguish.

'I tell you what's wrong with you, Norris,' the OC said largely. Curly felt something wince in him. To be told again what was wrong with him. People were always presuming to do that, nearly always people who knew too little about him and about themselves. It wasn't so bad if they spoke from kindness and a desire to help; that hurt, but it was understood by him. But when a man, like this young fascist type with his muddled democratic ideas and his desire to exercise his power over men, proffered him advice, he writhed like a split toad.

'You haven't got enough *push*, Norris. That's what's wrong with you. Too soft-hearted, not enough keenness. You don't go for things as if you wanted them.'

Curly laughed.

'My ambitions aren't as tangible as yours, sir,' he replied.

'Well; get some ambitions, then, for God's sake. Your life won't go on forever. Get cracking.'

'Very good, sir. I'll submit my scheme for defeating Germany to Sir John Dill immediately.'

The OC shrugged his shoulders, confessing to himself that here was another man who wasn't worth helping because he refused to be helped. He was browned off with fools.

'If you want to help anybody, you might help Thomas to get his wife into hospital, sir.'

The OC snorted and narrowed his eyes.

'I know the difference between seven days' CB and a weekend leave,' he said curtly. 'Thomas won't pull that old

338

gag over me again.' Curly hadn't enough vigour to insist. He clenched his fists on the table, knowing how important it was that Taffy should get leave, knowing it suddenly with anguish. But, as so often, the conflict smashed itself up inside him like two contrary tides, and he said nothing because the intensity of his feelings made him impotent.

The door opened and Sergeant Crumb came in, followed astonishingly by a very dashing young lady. The sergeant was all smiles and deference, inclining his body courteously to her and pointing with a wave of his hand to the OC.

Curly stood to attention. The OC stood flushed.

'Lady to see you, sir,' Crumb said urbanely.

'Hector,' the lady said, her rouge parting in a slow private smile. She held out her gloved hand, letting her fur coat fall open.

'But – but come in,' the OC stumbled. He pushed open the door of his room and she swept through in a swirl of fur and silk and interesting perfumes. He closed the door after her, humbly.

'Gives you the impression of expensive cutlery,' Curly said softly, 'though I doubt whether she is stainless.'

'It's the colonel's daughter,' Crumb whispered, his head inclined and movements subdued as though he were in the presence of the saints.

Curly hoped she wanted some love, so that he'd have a little peace to write his letters. But he had scarcely started when the door opened and she came out again.

'Don't trouble to see me to the gate,' she said. 'I'm sure you're busy. This private will escort me.'

'Not at all,' said the helpless captain, following her out with her gloves.

'Stand easy, stand easy,' Crumb said as the door closed behind them. 'She must have been jilted or something,' he sneered.

The OC came back in a hell of a tear. 'Where's that bloody fool Thomas? Tell him to go to my billet and polish my shoes and Sam Browne till he can see his face in them. And tell Rosendale I want him to take a message for me. At once.'

'Very good, sir,' Sergeant Crumb leapt to it, realizing the situation was urgent. The room was suddenly in a turmoil, as though the young lady had been a German parachutist.

The OC took a sheet of paper and scribbled a quick note, put it in an envelope, and threw it into the OUT tray.

'Tell Rosendale to deliver that when he comes, Norris.'

He put on his service cap, took his stick and gloves, and went out. He was excited and flustered. Probably going to cool off by catching the sentry sitting down or the cookhouse staff eating the men's cheese rations, or the fatigue party throwing stones into the cesspool they were cleaning.

Rosendale came and collected the letter.

'Forgot to lick the envelope,' he said. 'What is it? Is there a war on?'

'Run away,' said Curly, weary of everything.

Rosendale cycled out of camp and down the road till he was out of observation. Then he opened the letter and read it through.

> Dear Eva, [it said] Sorry I can't meet you tonight as we arranged. I'm on duty again and won't be able to see you this week. I seem to have so little free time these days that I doubt whether it's worth our while carrying on any more. What do you think?
> Affectionately yours, Hector Cochrane, Capt.

'Hector Cochrane, Capt.,' Rosendale repeated, curling his lip. He cycled down coast to the town, knowing where to go; he had been to the little street behind the gasworks on other occasions. Miss Barthgate was the name, and very nice, too. Smart little milliner, deserved better luck than to fall in love with *him*. Rosendale's mind was working by devious ways. He'd seen the flash dame in the fur coat with rich smells about her. Maybe he'd get a bit of his own back for that seven days' CB.

He knocked at the door, propping his cycle against the wall. She worked in the parlour; he could see the sewing machine through the window. But the place sounded quiet today, as though she hadn't started working yet.

There was some delay before she opened the door. She was in a loose-fitting frock let out at the waist. Her face was nervous, her dark eyes looked dilated. Her beauty seemed agitated, on pins. 'Yes?' she said, almost breathing the word, at the same time holding her hand out for the note he held between his fingers. Grinning a little, Rosendale handed it to her, watched her read it, waited a long time while she tried to raise her head...

At last she looked up. She wasn't bothering to hide anything. He could see it clear as daylight.

'There's no answer,' she said.

'No,' he replied. 'No answer.' He shuffled, half turning to go. Then he looked up at her shrewdly.

'He isn't on duty,' he said. 'I thought I'd tell you. I shouldn't mind about him if I were you.'

'No,' she said, looking at him vaguely with her unutterable distress.

He had intended to say more, but her look confused him. He turned, mounted his cycle, and pedalled off. She didn't move all the time.

There was a new sensation buzzing through cookhouse, stores, office, and guardroom when he returned. The sentry told it him as he cycled through the gate; and because of it he decided to withhold his own bits of gossip till the chaps would be readier to appreciate it. He didn't want any competition.

The news was that Taffy Thomas couldn't be found anywhere. His denim overalls were on the floor by his bed, his best battledress and respirator were missing. He hadn't answered Crocker's quavering version of Defaulters bugle, he hadn't come forward to shine the OC's Sam Browne. He'd done a bunk.

Curly was waiting for Rosendale with another message, this time for the Swansea police, asking them to visit Taffy's house at night and instruct him forcibly to return by the next train. The OC had said something about a court martial; it would be the colonel's charge at least. That meant probably twenty-eight days' detention and no pay for himself or his wife. It was a bad business, all things considered; but Curly was glad Taffy had gone. Perhaps he'd save his wife's life; twenty-eight days was cheap at that price.

Acting Captain Cochrane had a considerable liver by the end of the afternoon. The men had been dozy and idle all day. He'd gone round bollocking them right and left. The latrines hadn't been cleaned, the washbasins were still littered with rusty blades and fag ends when he inspected them after lunch. The cesspool stank and the fatigue party complained that there wasn't any hot water for them to clean up afterwards. All the plugs for the washbasins were missing, the kit was untidily laid out on the beds, the rifles hadn't been pulled through since he inspected them last. He was in no mood to be accosted. When he saw Eva waiting for him at the bottom of the lane, he had already had too much.

She was wearing a plain mackintosh, a loose-fitting Burberry, and a little green hat with turned-up brim like a schoolgirl. Her hands were in her pockets, her eyes on the ground. He knew she'd seen him, but she wasn't able to look at him approaching. He walked smartly towards her, very military in his swish greatcoat and service cap flat over his eyes. His face looked narrow and sharp under the severe cap, his fair moustache and rather pointed teeth giving him a stoatlike appearance. When he was within a couple of yards, she looked up and her eyes were wide and lambent, looking at him for some sign.

'Well, Eva,' he said. He coughed and looked at his wristwatch. 'You got my letter, didn't you?'

She stayed looking at him with her pale searching face and her dark transparent eyes. Damn it all, she had a nice face. Was she going to cling? Why did she take things so seriously?

'Well? Say something, Eva.'

His voice was softer, the least bit softer.

'I got your letter,' she said. 'That's why I came to see you.'

'Well, you know I'm on duty, then?' he tried it out, not so sure that he wanted to finish it for good just yet.

'That's what you said,' she replied.

He flushed, but she had turned away from him.

'Well?' he queried, his voice hardening. He wasn't going to be pried into. If his word wasn't enough for her, OK chief!

She looked up again. He noticed she hadn't powdered herself very carefully; her nose had a thick patch on it.

'Hector,' she said, putting her hands on the immaculate breast of his greatcoat, 'Don't you understand, darling?'

He was swept with impatience. His success with women was about equal to his ignorance of them. He wasn't going to have any sob stuff, thank you.

'How the blazes do you expect me to understand?' he said roughly.

'Well,' she said. 'There is something to understand.'

He quailed under her sudden precision of mood; she knew what she was going to do now; she wasn't leaning on him, beseeching him with her eyes. She was very quiet and firm. She looked at him and he got scared.

'There's nothing serious, Eva, is there?' his fear prompted him.

'It is serious,' she said.

'Darling,' he gasped.

He was horrified of the consequences, infuriated with her for getting into this mess, and, for the first time in his life, even if only for a minute, in love.

He spoke slowly, stopping to think.

'Can't you see a doctor, Eva? There are some doctors, you know—'

'I don't want to,' she said, still with this ridiculous composure.

'But – but you ought to,' he said.

'I can do as I choose,' she replied.

He said nothing, sensing a hopeless deadlock.

'Eva,' he said at last.

'Well?'

'We could get married at the Registry Office next weekend if you like,' he said, slowly, never taking his worried eyes off her. She was silent, as if listening to his words again and again in her mind.

He felt a growing exhilaration, a new and wonderful simplicity in him, like sunlight slowly breaking.

'Shall we?' he asked, holding his hand out.

She looked up again. This was always the most active thing she did, disclosing her eyes. Her hands all the time in her Burberry pockets. She was reluctant to answer; there was a sweetness in the possibility, a reflection of his own momentary sincerity. It was what she had come for, to hear him say that; because he had said these words she was happy. She had no sense of tragedy or of shame. She felt indifferent to the future.

'No, we can't get married,' she said slowly at the last.

Something in him was suddenly overpoweringly relieved. He had no sense of a durable daily happiness, of a long companionship in love; but only romantic impulses, like sunlight, and harsher emotions.

'But why not?' he asked, trembling.

'Because – oh well,' she mumbled, seeking blindly to bind up her thoughts into the certainty that was still inchoate in her, 'because you – don't—' she turned away, and in profile he saw her lips finish the sentence, '—love me.'

Her courage shamed him into a greater confusion. He flushed and lost his head and was just about to gallop into the breach with protestations of devotion when a four-seater army car swung round the bend and pulled up with a screech and shudder.

'Christ,' he gasped, this time in a real fluster. 'Look out.'

He sprang to the car and saluted.

The colonel half-opened the door.

'Just coming to see you, Cochrane. Expected to find you in your office, not flirting on the roads.'

'Yes, sir.'

'Hop in. Quickly. I want to get back.'

'Yes, sir.'

The car surged forward.

Eva watched it go. By herself. She pushed her hair back, rubbing her cheeks, rubbing the cold sweat off her forehead. Heavily she turned and walked slowly along the road.

The colonel looked into the first Nissen hut.

'These bricks round the fireplace,' he said. 'I sent an order to all detachments that they be whitewashed. Why haven't you done it?'

'No whitewash, sir.'

'Get some. Christ. What are you here for?'

He picked up a pair of boots from one of the men's beds.

'These boots. Burnt. Look at the soles. Burnt through. Drying them by the fire. Is this man on a charge?'

'Er, no, sir.'

'Why the hell not? Nation can't afford to waste boots every time they get wet. Christ. Send him to me tomorrow under escort.'

'Yes, sir. I don't believe they *are* burnt, sir. The man has been waiting for a boot exchange for five weeks. He's worn them out—'

'I tell you they're burnt. Christ man, you're not a cobbler, are you?'

'No, sir.'

'Then talk about something you know.'

By the time the old man drove off Captain Cochrane was utterly emasculate. He saluted with so pathetic and servile a gesture that the colonel didn't even return the salute. And so his day ended. The duties of the evening confronted him. Dinner in mess, then dance attendance on the old man's daughter. Poleworth was the name. Less respectfully, when the subalterns were hidden away in a pub, the name was sometimes garbled to Polecat. She certainly had a pungent odour. Still, hardy men said she was a good sport. She liked to play, they hinted, twisting the yellow ends of their moustaches. Captain Cochrane emptied his whisky flask before deciding on his tactical plan. Marvellous thing, whisky.

Curly took a walk after drinking his mug of tea and eating a piece of bread and marge and a Lyons' fruit pie. He didn't wash or brass up. He wasn't going to town. He wanted some peace of mind, along the sand dunes running from the harbour to the boarding house promenade where the ferro-concrete seaside resort began. Faintly, as though his tedious preoccupations had taken a musical form, the distant sound of hurdy-gurdy jazz songs blaring in the funfair touched his quietness, accompanying him unobtrusively as he climbed the loose sand. Thinking of the industry of pleasure, he watched the sea, fuming like a thin grey smoke far far out beyond the mudflats, and it seemed as though the purpose of the town had been lost, the balance between sea and land ruined, the fundamental element forgotten. Pleasure had broken away from simplicity, the penny-in-the-slot machine had conquered the sea, people had turned their backs and were screaming with laughter. Watching the sea fuming and grey he found himself suddenly investing the solitary person walking slowly and with downcast head across the wet worm-cast mud with all the attributes which humanity, he decided this evening, had rejected. He wanted to speak to this lonely person; it was a woman; heavy she was; heavy with the rejected attributes of humanity; pregnant she must be, and pale with a serious beauty, bearing so much in her.

Following his fantasy, he walked down from the dunes and across the slimy front towards the girl. He walked quickly, keeping his attenion on her, refusing to allow the usual inhibitions to stop him accosting her.

Eva felt no particular strangeness at his approach. A little soldier with spectacles and curly hair like a wire brush. It was quite natural. She said good evening. She was glad he had come.

'I was standing on the dunes,' he said. 'And there was nobody but you anywhere at all. And so you became important to me, so that I came to ask you something.'

'Don't ask me anything,' she said.

'No, I don't want to,' he said thoughtfully.

'Will you take me back to the land?' she said, looking at him, holding her hand out to him uncertainly.

Her face was as he had imagined it, young and hollow, large hollow-eyed, luminous and vague with distress.

He took her cold hand and led her back to the firm land, the grass and rocks and walls and telegraph poles and houses. In silence.

'Have you ever tried to die?' she asked.

'Yes,' he said.

'What shall I do now, then?' she asked again.

'Walk,' he said. 'Pick a flower. Hurt your shin against a rock. Keep doing things like that for a bit. Do you like coffee?'

'Yes,' she said, thinking back to the taste of such things. 'Yes. I like coffee.'

'Shall we go and have some, and some chocolate biscuits, in the Marina?' he asked.

'Yes,' she said, very seriously. 'That would be nice.'

She looked at the people having coffee and peach melbas and spaghetti on toast at the little green tables, soldiers and girls, commercial men, ponderous wives on holiday with children past their bedtime. The waitresses rustling and slender and deft, rotund and homely – and competent; the warm shaded lights falling on the flowery wallpaper. The strangeness and the fear gradually left her eyes like sugar melting in a lemon glass. She tasted the hot coffee slowly, and its warmth led her to smile.

'Why do you look so serious?' she asked Curly.

He looked at her all the time. She could see the gathering of his thoughts in the dark blue eyes magnified and concentrated by the curved lenses of his spectacles.

'Funny, you having blue eyes,' she said.

Looking at each other over the wispy coffee steam, each wanted to be confessed in the other, each desired to share a new yet ancient community of interest. Neither of them could think now of how different they were, the one from the other, how insulated by separate compulsions and circumstances.

'I live near here. Shall we go and sit by the fire?' she asked.

'I'd like to,' he answered...

'It's only an electric fire,' she said, as he opened the glass door for her.

There were two photographs on the mantelpiece of her little bedsitter. Curly noticed they were both men in uniform. Brothers? Or lovers? Also a sewing machine and dresses half finished. A reading lamp and *Picture Post* and *Lilliput* and a *Sunday Pictorial*.

'I haven't got a shilling for the meter,' she said.

He produced one.

'You're very good,' she said to him, putting the shilling in the slot, bending down as she spoke. 'You stopped me committing suicide and now you've given me food and money and – and what else?'

'What else?' he repeated, his sensitive mind crushed by the sledgehammer blow of her casual confession.

'I don't know,' she said, standing up and smoothing her navy skirt down, picking bits of fluff off her knees. 'I don't know what I'm talking about.'

Her sick soul was in her eyes.

He stayed with her till late in the night, putting another

shilling in the meter, going and queuing outside the chip shop for some fish cakes for their supper while she set the little table and boiled the kettle and cut some bread and butter. The reading lamp on the table, and she telling him about dressmaking, and the poverty she was in now there was no material purchasable, and the requirements of her clients, and their sexy confidences. She was recovering herself and he watched her judgement returning gradually as her comments on people and things reached further and further out from the touchstone of herself, radiating like ripples from a stone dropped into a pond. She had no politics or plans, no criteria; except herself, her intuitions and feelings, aversions. He wanted to restore herself to her, so that she could continue living from day to day, thought to thought, with continuity.

They were talking about the Army; tonight it seemed a remote, unreal topic, a social problem which could be discussed or dropped as they chose. In the same unreal mood she said:

'My husband liked the Army. He's the one on the right there. He had a good time in France, till suddenly it all happened.'

Curly crossed to the mantelpiece and looked at the smiling RAC sergeant in his black beret; a powerful, smiling man, confident and untroubled.

'He never bothered about things,' she said. 'He liked tanks and so he liked the war. I don't think he bothered about dying, or being away from me. He just married me one leave, that's all. He wouldn't have a baby. It never occurred to him. And now he's dead. A whole year now he's been dead. I've forgotten nearly everything about him.'

Curly looked from the second photograph in consternation.

'You know Captain Cochrane?' he asked.

'He's been coming here a lot,' she said. 'He's had enough of me now, though.'

How weary she sounded, telling him all these elemental facts in a flat, indifferent voice.

'I should have thought you'd had enough of him,' he said. 'He's a poor piece of work. You shouldn't have let him take you in. He's nothing at all, just cardboard and paste.'

She smiled, lighting one of his cigarettes.

'Would you have saved me, if you'd known me six weeks ago?' she said. 'I met him in the Plaza at a dance, just six weeks ago. Would you have stopped him touching me?'

'Its your own affair,' he said. 'If I'd known you I would have.'

'Could you have?' she teased him. 'Could you make love as gifted as he did?'

'I don't suppose so,' he said. 'I'm not a cinema fan. Nor am I very enthusiastic about that sort of thing. You know what he used to say? He used to say he had a lot of dirty water on his chest and he knew a woman who would swill it out for him.'

'You're not preaching to me, anyway,' she said. 'You're hitting hard, aren't you?'

'I could hit much harder,' he replied.

'I can't help it now,' she said, dejected. 'He offered to marry me; there's that to be said for him; only he didn't mean it.'

Curly went hot and sticky, as though there were filthy cobwebs all over him. And at once the old despair touched him with its dry unavailing fingers, as when he had tried to get a short leave for Taffy Thomas to see to his wife.

It was difficult for him to go now. Yet she didn't want him to stay. She was normal again, and consequently beginning to understand the task that was on her, the mess she had made, the immense fatigue. She turned on the wireless, late dance music, mawkish and sticky. They both stood up.

'Shall I come and see you again?' he asked.

'Yes,' she said. 'Yes. Unless I go away from here.'

'Where to?'

'I don't know,' she said. 'Where do you go to have a baby? Are workhouses open for that? Or I'll go to my sister-in-law. She evacuated to her father's farm in Borrowdale. I won't go yet. Not for a few months. Perhaps I won't go at all.'

She was only talking round and round.

On his way downstairs he bumped into somebody, stood against the wall to let him pass, recognised Captain Cochrane, smelt his hot whisky-sweet breath, and hurried out into the black streets and the unhurried stars.

Anglo-German hostilities, held in abeyance during the daylight, resumed at a later hour than was customary this particular night. The operational orders of the Luftwaffe gave a certain unity to the experiences of Taffy Thomas, Curly Norris, Captain Cochrane and the women with whom they were connected – a unity which would not have existed otherwise. Taffy reached Swansea on a lorry conveying sheep skins from slaughterhouse to warehouse just as the first Jerries droned eastwards along the Gower coast, droned lazily towards the dark sprawling town, and released beautiful leisurely flares into the blackness below. Taffy was hungry and thirsty and broke, not even a fag end in his field dressing pocket. So he didn't mind a few extra inconveniences such as air raids. Life was like that at present. He wasn't expecting anything much. He hurried past his habitual pubs, past the milk bar where he had eaten steak and kidney pies on his last leave and been unable to get off the high stool on which he sat, drunk at one in the afternoon and his kid brother just as bad at his side, bloody all right, boy; and, as the first bombs screamed and went off with a sickening shuddering zoomph down the docks way, he turned into his own street and kicked the door with his big ammunition boots. It was about the same time as Curly went into Eva's flat, and Captain Cochrane bought the Polecat her first gin and lime. Taffy's missus was in bed on the sofa in the kitchen; she couldn't get up to let him in, she'd gone too weak. He had to climb the drainpipe to the top bedroom and squeeze through the narrow sash. She knew who it was as soon as he kicked the door with his big boots, so she wasn't frightened when he came downstairs; only ashamed, ashamed that she was such a poor wife, so useless a vessel for his nights, skinny thighs and wasted breasts and dead urges.

'Hallo, mun,' he said with his rough vigour, picking up the newspaper and glancing at the headlines. 'Still bad? Where's the kids? Up in your mother's?'

'She fetched them up after tea,' she said. ''gainst there's a raid.'

'By yourself, then?' he said. 'Good job I come. Got anything to drink?'

'No,' she said, ashamed at being such a poor wife. 'I'd 'ave asked Mam to go down the pub for a flagon if I'd thought you was coming.'

'What about yourself?' he asked. 'Still drinking that old pink lemonade? Can't you drink a drop of milk or tea or Oxo or something yet? Still spitting that old yellow phlegm up, too, by the looks of that pisspot. I don't know, bach.' He sat on the edge of the sofa and put his hand idly on her moist tangled hair. 'I don't know what to do. Curly said for to take you to the hospital. I think I'd better, too. Shall I carry you tonight?'

'No,' she said, frightened. 'You can't now. It's blackout and there's bombs again, and I doubt there won't be a bed there. And you got to pay, too.' She pushed her bony hand slowly across the soiled sheet and touched his battledress. 'I don't want to go there,' she said.

She was too weak to wipe the tears out of her eyes.

'Oh Jesu!' he said, getting up in a temper. 'Don't cry, then. I was only suggestin'. Do as you like. Wait till tomorrow if you like. Only I was thinking the redcaps will be coming round to look for me tomorrow.'

'Never mind about tomorrow,' she said.

'The cat's been pissing in the room somewhere,' he said,

sniffing about him. He sat down again and wiped her eyes with the sheet.

'You got to mind about tomorrow,' he said.

'Remember you was jealous of me in a dance at the Mackworth when we was courting?' she said. 'You took me out and slapped me in the face, remember?'

'What about it?' he asked slowly, nonplussed.

'Slap me now again,' she said.

He laughed.

'I'm not jealous of you no more,' he said. 'You get better, and then p'r'aps I'll get jealous again, see?'

She smiled and let her neck relax on the cushion.

'You'll never be jealous of me again,' she said, looking at him with her faraway eyes.

Her soul was in her eyes, and it wasn't sick like her body.

The bombs had been falling heavier and heavier, and neither of them seemed to notice. Till the light went out, and then he cursed filthily. The fire was nearly out; it was cold sitting with her all the time. He tucked her icy hands under the blanket.

'I'm going out for some coal,' he said.

'There's none there,' she said. 'The coalman's killed.'

'Christ, there's plenty more men not killed,' he said. 'I'll get some from next door, then.'

'Don't go,' she whispered.

The house shivered and plaster fell in a stream of dust, as if from an hourglass.

'Can't sit in the cold all night,' he said. 'And the dark. I won't be a minute.'

He slipped the latch and went out into the burning night, straight out into a screaming bomb that tore the sky with its white blade and flung him onto his face in the little backyard and brought the house crashing down with its mighty rushing wind.

The Luftwaffe's secondary objective concerned Captain Cochrane's harbour. The raid began at midnight, by which time Swansea had nothing to do except stop the big fires spreading and wait for the morning to come. Taffy had called at his mother-in-law's, and seen the children; and at the police station, to tell them his wife was buried and ask them to inform his unit; and he was just walking around, trying to keep himself from freezing and crying and lying down in a doorway, when Captain Cochrane, who had also suffered some emotional disturbance, was getting out of Eva's bed and hastily pulling on his shirt and trousers in the dark. When he was half dressed he pulled the blind back to see what was happening. The searchlights were stretching their white dividers over the harbour; and yes, by God, they had a plane in their beam, a little tinsel plane, and the red tracer bullets were floating up at it from the Bofors by the sidings. Christ, it was a marvellous sight. He was thrilled stiff, trembling to sink his teeth into it, to draw blood. Where the hell were his shoes?

'I'll have to run,' he said brusquely, grabbing his cap and greatcoat. Eva, motionless and dark in bed, said nothing at all. Of course he had to go; a soldier like him.

'Goodbye,' he said, stumbling on the stairs.

Eva lay quietly, heavy and as though waterlogged, thinking of the Germans and the English, the soldiers of both sides, her husband and the excitement, the professional coolness with which, firing his two-pounder from the revolving turret of his pet tank, he died. And Hector Cochrane – she always thought of his surname as well as his Christian name – that boy with glasses was right; he wasn't much of a man. When he had come in tonight, drunk and abased, begging her forgiveness – as if *that* was anything to give or to withhold – her infatuation had dissolved like a sudden thaw, leaving everything slushy. And as she stroked his spiky Brylcreemed hair and let him sob into her lap she had felt how small and worthless the two of them were, clumsy bungling people of no moment, passive and degraded by their own actions. She had let him take her to bed. Anything was as good as nothing. He had written her a cheque.

Captain Cochrane had a haggard jauntiness, arriving at the office the next morning. The ethical code of his profession forbade a man to allow a hangover to take the edge off his morning smartness. He behaved in the exemplary manner of a commissioned officer, inspecting the sleeping huts and the cookhouse and the sump, chewing up slovenly old Crocker for overflowing the swill bins, chasing the fatigue party who were rat-hunting round the sump, getting a shake on everywhere. Then to the company office for his morning correspondence. Ration indents, pay requisition, arrangements for boot and clothing exchange, a glance at the medical report to see who was scrounging today. Sergeant Crumb had everything in order, non-committal and deferential, soothing.

'Damn good show last night, sergeant,' he said when he had finished his business. 'Got a cigarette?'

'Certainly, sir.' (Bloody cadger). 'The Bofors crew are going on the beer tonight, sir, to celebrate knocking that Jerry down.'

'Yes. Damn good show it was. All burned to death, weren't they?'

'Yes sir. The plane was too low for them to parachute.'

'Well, that's burned their fingers for them. Something towards winning the war.'

'Yes sir.'

A phone message. Thanks. Captain Cochrane speaking. Good morning, sir.

This is Swansea police. A private Thomas from your company, sir? Yes? Called in at 0025 hours last night, sir. Said his wife had been buried under a bomb, sir. Christ, has she? That's bad luck. Have you confirmed it yet? Not yet, sir. Check up on it, please. He's a bit of a scrounger. If it's OK, put him in touch with the barracks. They'll give him all the dope he needs. Money. Railway warrant. OK? Yes sir. If he's bluffing hand him over to the redcaps. He's absent without leave. Very good, sir. Goodbye. Goodbye, sir.

'Thomas' wife. Killed. They must have had a raid as well.'

'That's bad luck, sir. I'll look up the ACI about coffins. I think the civil authorities supply them, don't they, sir? RASC only issue them to soldiers. She was ailing anyway, sir, I know.'

'Check up on it, sergeant. Also ring through to battalion and inform them. We'll send him a leave pass if necessary. Keep the charge sheet, though. He'll have to go before the colonel for absence without leave just the same.'

'Very good, sir.'

'Anything else, sir?'

'No. I don't think so. Oh yes, there's that return to the adjutant about anti-gas deficiencies. I'll inspect all respirator contents at 1100 hours.'

'Very good, sir.'

'Christ, that reminds me. I've left mine in town. Where's Norris?'

'Up at your billet, sir, I sent him to clean your kit, sir, being that Thomas your batman isn't available.'

'Send a runner up, then. Tell him to go to this address' – he scribbled it down, Sergeant Crumb hiding the faintest wisp of a smile as he did so – 'and ask for my respirator. Miss Eva Barthgate is the name.'

He smiled, too. They were both men.

'Very good, sir.'

Sergeant Crumb saluted smartly and withdrew.

Captain Cochrane yawned and put his feet up for a few minutes, and thought, well, that was that.

Maybe he'd ask the old man to put him in for a transfer to the Indian Army. There were better prospects out there, on the whole.

THE LOST FISHERMAN

Margiad Evans

Emily came flying down the steps, glaring at a piece of paper in her hand.

'May have time to get the tape,' she muttered.

She let the scrap float away, and ran down the street. It was quiet and warm and empty; the only person in it besides herself was a woman in black ringing a door bell. The church clock was striking five behind the roofs which were only a little lower than the tops of the huge chestnut trees: from the churchyard stole the green scent of the sward, the coolness, lightness, peace, of the petal-dripping trees.

But round the market hall trampled these strange crowds that the small townspeople were getting so used to; hot, bewildered people, burdened, with a dazzled look on their faces, looking for hotels, for lodgings, for rest. Some of them were sitting on the stone stairway, with their suitcases; some were eating, and some with their hands loosely clasped were staring downhill into the blue-grey hollow of the town. Many more would be queuing at the bus stop, the cafés would be full; there would be forms being signed in all the sash-windowed offices just as if the whole population were suddenly going to prison or to law or something. For last night London had had another heavy raid, and the three o'clock train had come in at half past four. Emily bought the tape from a country girl who was blind in one eye, and selling buttons instead of looking after her father's poultry. She was sagging on the counter.

'Are you done in? So'm I.'

They had been to school together.

'Lord, you can't believe it,' said the girl, heaving herself up on her elbow: 'poor souls – there's any a host of 'em. God knows where they'll all sleep tonight. It must be *awful* up there! Has your sister come away?'

'Not yet. We wish she would. Keep on writing. Mother's terribly worried.'

'She must be. Yes, it's terrible with children…'

Emily nodded. She wondered if Annie and her family were still alive; if they still existed. Any moment they might not. Any second – the flashes when the truth showed were unrealisable. It was vile and horrible and terrifying, and yet unreal. Thinking was a physical, aching disease trying to conquer another disease – that of not thinking. Allow yourself to be injected – submit to noble advertisements. Save, work, smile. Be poster educated. London was being struck and struck and struck again. Annie and the children lived there. Patrick was a prisoner. England was close, how close, to invasion. Patrick, Patrick.

She came out of the shop and looked at the town hall clock. Slow by the church chimes, she noticed. The white face with its hands like an enormous pair of scissors, what did it mean to her? There would always be only one time now on it. That was because she had been staring at it when she held the telegram. A Prisoner of War. A quarter to three. Queer. How did the telegram come to be in her hand? She would never quite remember. Her mother was away: and she had felt, 'This joy isn't mine. I carry it.'

There was a word *widow* and a word *motherless*, but for the condition of a woman who had lost her son there was no simple expression. Childless was false; a woman whose only son was dead was more his mother than she had ever been: she was as secret, as filled with mystery as when she and her child were one being, only this time she carried his whole life and death – she was the mother of his death.

Emily had gone into the telephone box. Her mother's voice said, 'Yes, dear?'

'Mother, good news. Hold on to something. Patrick is a prisoner.'

Faintly the voice: 'Emily... Emily...'

Now the town hall clock meant that hour. But sometimes these days when she looked at it she thought there was always time for grieving. Yes, always, Emily said to herself, turning round. Not for touching your love, or for seeing or being aware of the landscape you lived in, but always for sorrow.

Down the hill she plunged into the spinning people. The smell of war was the smell of a herd, weary and swollen footed. It wasn't the dead, but the driven, the sweated road, the shambling herd.

To avoid the direct but choked way home, she dashed up a narrow side street, one of the oldest in the town. Years before, a few cottages had been demolished. The walls still stood lodging in their niches the flying weeds of the fields, the winged grass which owned the earth, the nettles of gardenless places. Dandelions were in bloom and seeding, their bare wicks standing stiffly whence the flame had blown. There was the quiet intense odour of wallflowers in sunlight; and out of a doorless doorway two white butterflies lurched as if a breeze had puffed them out of the enclosure.

It was May. Oh, why did that still concern her? What was so urgent that it would not wait until the war was over to be beautiful again? Could you pull mankind like a burr out of your heart? But Emily stopped, swaying, conscious of this other presence in the worn, cracked street – the presence which made itself felt from the trees in the churchyard, and from the sight of the hills from her window.

She happened to stop, and she happened to peer round the doorhole...

The mumbled heaps, the smooth dirt and weeds, had been somebody's garden. It was worn to a gloss with children's games, but in the centre grew a lilac tree, its clusters faded to a bluish-grey, dropping their crumbs in the shade. There, close to the trunk in a rocking chair, a paper tossed over his knees, a man sat sleeping: he was quite unconscious. His powerful, innocent face free from eagerness, away from the frightening smell of people, he slept like a lad in a field, and Emily wished she might wait by him for a little while. She knew him, though not his name. She wondered as she turned away if he lived in that street – she had always wondered, though not in an asking way, where was his home. And what had made her stop? Was it the white butterflies, that had flown as though from his brain almost into her hand?

'Is there any news from Annie?' she asked, as she ran into the kitchen.

Her mother was at the sink, washing lettuce. She said there was no news.

'Mother, I've seen the fisherman!'

'Oh, have you? Do you know where he lives?'

'No, he was asleep!'

'Asleep?' sighed her mother absently.

'Yes, in a rocking chair in one of Saint's Cottages.'

'Well, what a strange place to doze in! I can't bear to walk up that street, it smells so bad.'

'You couldn't smell the gas today. Oh mother – gas. We've had a terrific day. Two gas extractions and both fought like mad. Poor Mr Jones, I bet he's bruised.'

'My dear child! You must be tired. Sit down and eat something. Were you all right?'

Emily had taken a temporary job as a dentist's nurse and receptionist, being quite untrained except in sterilising instruments and comforting people. 'Oh yes, quite,' she said. 'I stood behind them, it was old Jones got the kicks. I say, Mum, I think I'll ring Annie up tonight.'

She was twenty-seven and was to work in the ordnance

factory at Chepsford as soon as the real nurse recovered from an operation. Meanwhile she quite liked her work. She never thought about it after the day was over. It was that kind of job. Teeth, she thought, when handed about, were rather absurd: otherwise she had grown used to the white overall, the sterilisers, the appointment book.

But – seeing the fisherman! As she ate her supper and helped to wash up, everything else that had happened since the morning seemed ugly and monotonous. He belonged to a life that was neither tedious nor terrifying. If her mother had guessed the emotions that filled her, she would have said, Are you in love with him? No, no. It isn't *individual*, like that. He is something – he's part of something that's being lost. And I want it to come back. It's life. At least it is to me. Oh dear. Am I going out of my mind, or is my mind going out of me?

The house that Emily and her mother lived in was at the bottom of the town near the Co-operative Mill. It had stood for centuries and smelled of stone and mice and coal, and the spicy old beams which still had the bark on some of them. It was said to be the oldest house in the town. The street door had a large dented brass knob: when you turned it and stepped into the passage it was as if you came under the shadow of a great cliff, for all the sunlight was at the back where it fell into a tiny paved yard as into a box. A long narrow corridor of a path led past a wall with a fine flat vine, as ancient as the building, to a large plot of garden. Next to that was the Friends' graveyard which had in the middle a cedar tree. This enormous geni, so dark as to be nearly black, seemed dead to all sunshine and looked the same by moonlight as by day. The house was simply Number 17, but to the older spirits of the town it was known by its disused and genial name of The Friends' House.

The room where they were eating their early supper was the kitchen. It was clean and orderly: quiet with polished brown furniture, and lit by the evening sun. The door into the yard, and the well lid in the flagstones were open, for both Emily and her mother liked the delicate, flashing reflection of the water which flickered about the imprisoned space. The ferns and vine leaves were still: flies wove the evening light into their loom, and there was a calling note from a blackbird in the apple tree next door.

Emily looked at the canaries swaying in the window; she gazed meditatively into the corner at the oilstove. When war seemed close, she remembered her mother had said they would have to move the oilstove. How she had laughed! But it had come true, and they had moved it, for the shutters wouldn't close when it was in the window. Not a pinch, not a leaf of light showed after dark now. Emily, glancing at the fuchsias in their pots built up on bricks, recalled how the lit plants were sprinkled on the darkness before the blackout came.

After they had washed up, she went and sat in the front room by the 'town window'. She was as glad of the shade as of a different mood. The mother lay on the sofa, her tired legs lifted high on cushions. She read the paper, her face grim and pale, frowning with anxiety. Emily looked at the chestnut trees behind the warehouse, and the clear sky. She could hear the blackbird singing, 'Bird of Paradise, Bird of Paradise', over and over again, and then most sweetly, gently, 'Come butty, come butty, come butty'.

It was so small a town that ducks swam right through it on the brook. Jays and woodpeckers flew screeching over the roof, regarding it perhaps as no more than a large and stony shadow. The wind sowed hayseeds in the cattle market, and the gardens, even the scratchiest, were scented with their red hawthorns and lilacs. Everywhere one went one breathed them. And there was the river, and the silver-blue hills.

May, all of May, Emily thought, her arm resting on the sill, her body supple and pleasant. The shadow of their gable was falling on the road, and the sun was pouring gold over the pale blue sky. A slow dusty echo tracked each footstep.

But down here in the faded part of the town where there were no hotels but only poor men's lodging houses, they escaped the weary rummaging on the hill.

Slum games were scrawled in chalk on the pavements, women looked at their neighbours' doors, and men in shirt sleeves smoked. The human beings, the trees, bathed in the delight of the evening. Children, grime painting scowls on their faces, sulky mops of hair in their eyes, squealed and squatted akimbo on their games, monkey hands on their knees.

May, May, May! The time of year when all is perfect and *young*. The hills were the same, the trees had the same roots, as when she was a child at Aunt Fran's. How long the grass must be! She could feel her toes combing through it, aching with cold dew, the snapping of a clover head in a sandal buckle. She could see the white billy goat chained to the stone roller. How many horses did Uncle Donovan say it would take to move it? All of them – ten horses. Ten horses in the stable...

Her mother got up and went out. Emily lapsed on. The women came and seized the children; the doors shut, the air grew purer and more and more transparent, as if for silence to shine through it. At last Emily thought of the river, shining smoothly under the mist, on those early morning bathes. Why did it all seem so near, and closer every day, and yet so irrevocably saddened? If one person dies, the past is altered. Uncle Donovan was dead. People she had loved were dead. When you were young everyone was eternal. Her eyes moved, and she wondered at her emotion on seeing the sleeping man. She almost laughed. Yes, people would say she was in love with him. She laughed at the ridiculousness of her being in love with anybody. She couldn't be. And the fisherman – he wasn't like the others. Their talk had been casual, never cautious. They had never seemed to meet for the first time. In fact, although she could remember their first words, they never had 'met' any more than animals or birds meet. He was – what? An atmosphere in her own soul. Something more than a mood which was increasing in her.

'My dear, I wish you'd go and ring up Annie.' Her mother was looking in. A flush was on her cheek and neck, streaking her thinness. Emily knew that this meant great nervous endurance. She jumped up and said she would go at once. Suddenly she shivered. She had to put on her coat.

It was quiet now, growing dusky. She had sat for a long time waiting for her call to come through. The mirror with the lettering on it was sinking into the shadow of the wall, the smoky voices in the bar were thicker. Suddenly someone shouted: 'Do with 'im? Give 'im to the Jewish women, and tell 'em to save something alive for the Poles.' There was a guttural laugh, a hoarse shuffling of tones, and then a blending again. Emily leant on the weak little cane table, the ice-cold edge of a slippery magazine touching her hand. Her heart beat in the long suspense and she sat with her eyes fixed on the telephone hanging in the corner by the door.

Presently the house emptied. There was a shambling noise in the street: the landlord looked in at her, rubbing his bare arms:

'Not through yet?'

'No.'

'Want a light?'

She shook her head.

'It's cold in here,' the landlord said, buttoning his cuffs, and he went out closing the door, leaving the shutters open. The moonlight fell towards the windowsill, creepingly, like a hand edging on to the keyboard. A twist of breeze made the hem of the white curtains writhe.

'There must be a raid on. I'll cancel,' she said to herself. Five more minutes passed. The landlord had gone back into the smoking room. He was crumpling papers, talking in a petulant undertone with louder bursts of sighs and yawns. A woman spoke sharply, '… this time of night?'

'She's trying to get London.'

'Oh! Well, I've locked up—'

The telephone rang.

'Annie?'

'Yes, Emily – you've had my wire?'

'No. Nothing.'

How cold and queer the air felt! And those old magazines with their odour of linoleum—

The receiver spouted words, all unintelligible: it whistled, it gurgled and was hollow with some deep resonance, like a dry pump.

'Tomorrow – tomorrow,' it shouted.

'All right,' she yelled. 'You're coming tomorrow. Is there a raid on?'

'Not 'alf,' said Annie's voice in a little space which it exactly filled. 'It's not too bad yet but I must get ready to take the children down to the shelter. There, did you hear that? Christ, I hope it's not going to be as bloody awful as last night.'

Emily heard her call, 'All right, I'm coming.' It was as if a prompter had spoken for the stage, a half-tone, sibilant, expressionless. Then she seemed to have hung up. She went out into the passage and tapped on the hatch.

'Finished?'

'Yes, thank you.'

The man looked at her as she paid. He stooped, then reached up, and then once more framing himself pushed a little glass towards her. 'Come on, Miss, drink this. I know you won't tell on me.' He winked, but his face was concerned: 'It's bad up there.'

She drank. The blood bristled in her cheeks, she leant against the wall, not because she was overcome, but because for the moment she was concentrating so intensely elsewhere that her own body began to slip sideways. She could see the skies. And those unseen, immeasurable arms which human beings carry folded in their breasts, reached out – out – out to fold back the menace. She stood in this state of extended will, her spirit a vaster version of her physical resistance, for about a minute, and then went out, carefully shutting the street door.

'Emily, how long you have been! Was it all right?'

'Yes, Mother, perfectly. She's coming down tomorrow.'

'Oh, thank God!'

Her mother was in her purple dressing gown, holding it round her throat, her eyes peering over the light of a tiny lamp she held, with a globe like an orange: 'There was nothing happening?'

'No, Mother.'

'But why hasn't she wired?'

'She has. I don't know why we didn't get it. I must just go and finish emptying those drawers.'

'It's a pity you didn't do it this evening. You ought to go to bed. I'm glad we've arranged things.'

For days they had been discussing receiving Annie and the children. There were only two large upstairs rooms, and the mother wouldn't think of using the attics in case of incendiaries. She would share the great brass bed with Annie, and the two little girls would have Emily's room. Emily was to go every night to sleep at Aunt Fran's farm – about a mile away from the town. It was a gentle level walk, by the river: she would love it. It was the possibility of returning to Aunt Fran's roof perhaps which was making such a vividness among her memories of her childhood when she had lived at Ell Hall for a year.

Electricity was expensive. The two women lit a larger lamp and went upstairs. In their dressing gowns and soft shoes they fanned from corner to corner, Emily bending over a trunk, her mother absently touching the walls as if she were planning certain movements.

At last she sat on the end of the sofa to unroll the elastic stocking from her bruised and swollen veins. 'Jamie's cot *there*?' she murmured. She got up and touched the wash-stand.

They moved it: somehow they both wanted to complete everything, to move into their own new positions as far as possible that night.

They continued their soft, hushed midnight work. Sometimes the boards shook under the grey-green carpet, and the young starlings stirred startlingly in the chimney. But at last they were in bed. The blackout curtains of heavy sage-green serge were left across the mother's window in case she might remember anything she might want to collect in the night. But Emily pulled hers back; her sash window looked towards the garden and the faint irridescent colours of a moon cloud. There were the vine leaves and the path leading to the moon and the cedar tree. She lay on her side facing them, her hair all pushed into a heavy sensation at the back of her head. Her hands burned with the restless touching of the day, but at last they were alone.

The night was the ghost of the day, as the moon was the ghost of the sun. And the fragrance which balanced in the window was the ghost within a ghost, neither retreating nor advancing, but fluttering outstretched and withdrawn like a breath.

She didn't sleep. Her eyes refused to close over the dream in her brain. Planes drove over; and it was as if they were seaming together long strips of sky. But when they had gone the wavy stillness of the night still clung about the leaves unchanged.

She began to see Annie in the shelter, the baby on her lap, and the little girls in the top bunk, peeping tearfully over the abyss. Guns, bombs, barrage, and then the screech of a plane being drawn into the vacuum.

She sat up suddenly, and drove her head between her knees, embracing her body with those amazingly powerful thin arms: 'All this! Oh, what a pity I can't go to sleep because then I get there, I get there...'

She rocked, and then driven to stillness crouched in a knot, surprised at her dry voice. Her eyes felt as if they must work, must see everything; not seeing anything, she was reduced to their corner in her flesh.

Unexpectedly she saw. What she saw was the fisherman's peaceful face, asleep. She had started up at the shelter scene, but now she lay down again and turned her face into the shelter of her hands, lined, as it were, with chilly, green grass. She found she could array her thoughts if she couldn't release them.

When you were out of doors your body became the touch, the texture of the world, with all its fluid airs, plants, waters, wind. The wind's flesh crept against yours, and the grass clothed the prone body with its feeling of openness and closeness.

She saw the river meadows, the little red bays in the bank where the turf had slipped into deep pools, and bendings where the river bent, the narrow green path rubbed into the grass. Across it lay a fishing rod. Sitting precariously on one of the jutting turfs which was dead and brown fibre, was a man, feet braced against a lolling alder limb. It was March; he wore a belted raincoat, but he had thrown a scarf into the tree. She was walking towards him: as she came closer he turned his face and looked quietly at her. And then suddenly, but not as if it *were* suddenly, they were speaking to each other. This happened quite often until six weeks ago, but as an image she retained none except the first meeting. She knew that of all the faces she had met, there was none at all like this one. It was secret, if candour can be secrecy; it could have been knowing, but she had never seen it when it was. Very dark shining eyes, oval, olive cheeks and chin, a smooth skin. They couldn't resemble each other physically but she felt as though each of them sent the same lights and shadows up to the surface. She walked on guessing, 'I can look like that.' For a few weeks every time she walked that way she met him, and then one day, not. She didn't see him again until she looked at him in the weedy rooms of the ruins. But she was sure they had understood something instantly, perfectly, and for ever. They were friends. And in their perfect familiarity with each other there was incalculable individual solitude.

She smiled into her hands. And this time it didn't feel as if she were roaring with laughter in the middle of everybody's despair. It felt as if she were talking to the fisherman about the curlews and watching the male bird go round and round the sky, calling and searching. The fisherman always made her think of the bird, the hills and the river, and not of himself: he recalled to her a beam of the true meaning of freedom and fulfilment: with him or thinking of him she became again the real Emily who used to swim across the river in the early mornings, who was free, whose being absorbed and radiated the harmony of the countryside in which she was growing. Perhaps it was talking to him which had made her ponder so much on her childhood this terrible spring.

Sleep was like tears in her open eyes, sharp yet tender. She was getting there. Her mind swayed and she no longer knew herself as separate and conscious. The room was the linen room at Aunt Fran's where she had slept, with the dark brown cupboard at the foot of the stairs and the dull leaded window, like a pattern of muslin in grey and black with another pattern of twigs shadowed through it. She remembered how coarse seemed the texture of the sky seen though the thick glass... She was looking up at the candle Aunt Fran was holding, floating in its haze, blinking... And then the room was gone and she was sitting on the garden seat watching her aunt's fingers as she split filberts open with a silver penknife. They were sitting under the Wellingtonian and the air was full of the scent of resin. Aunt Fran was saying:

'Your uncle and I are very fond of you. You have always been good with us.'

It was evening. Children were shouting; a vast splash of light over the west meadows dazzled through the trees. She put out her hand to lift the basket from the grass when suddenly she was awake and knew there had been an eruption of sound which she hadn't heard. It was like a silent explosion which shattered the perfect sphere of rest in which she was lying, and it was the siren.

The mother woke up convinced that she was young again. Her husband was alive: he was with her in the dream; she was married to him but they were being introduced. She woke, talking; part of her speech still seemed to be joined to her, but part had vanished.

'The wind was so lonely last night with the window bare that I went to bed early. It seemed so long since I had been playing the piano and talking...'

Then she heard herself say: 'Beethoven.'

She lifted her head: 'Where's the cot? Where's Jamie, my little Jamie? Annie! Where are the children?' She struck a match. She was awake now: 'Emily, Emily...'

She could just see the empty corner where the washstand had been.

Emily came in: 'I don't hear anything, do you? It must be Bristol again. Or Gloucester.' She was smoking and seemed tenuous with sleep, her body clinging to the support of the wall.

But as she came wavering round the big double bed, the mother moved to put her feet down, and seeing that unhappy blue and white flesh hovering to reach the floor, a pity and an anger which she could never have mentioned caused her heart to make something like a gesture in her body.

'Don't get up, Mother,' she begged: 'It can't be anything else.'

'I hope they don't bomb the bridge,' began her mother. The bridge was very close, carrying the line across the street where they lived. Like a great many of the older women in this small town, Emily's mother instinctively regarded it as an exceedingly likely target – as indeed it might have been had the raiders ever discovered the whereabouts of the great filling factory at Chepsford. The groan and slow thunder of the ammunition trains was a part of their nights. 'Lethal,' the mother would murmur, and the walls would tremble, like the pillars of the market house when the tanks and dismembered planes came swerving down the narrow streets.

They listened, their chins lifted, their necks stretched. Was that a plane?

'Bombs!'

They looked at each other in incredulous silence. And there fell through the sky two percussions locked in each other's vibrations. Clash, clash – like cymbals, like lightning with music. Emily had never heard two sounds so simultaneous yet so separate. It was most beautiful, distinct, entrancing, the way the skies played for that moment.

No thud came. No blow. The quicksilver fled all over their bodies: in the silence they stared and heard the mice ripping at the lining of the old house, rustling and searching through the crowded pockets of its deep cupboards.

'Put out the light!' said the mother.

About ten minutes passed in darkness. Some soot fell down the chimney and they heard it showering in the fender. A bird squeaked. The hush was the suspense of thousands listening, an underground, underdark thing, conscious and of the earth.

'I'm going to look out of the window,' said Emily. She saw fire on Hangbury Hill, red fire, crawling into the woods. She gazed and remembered how the birds and rabbits and snakes screamed when the heath was burned.

There were three bombs, they heard the next day. The man who is always present, no matter how outlandish the fact or the hour, described how he had seen them burst in the woods. He said the trees had writhed, there had been a kind of ashen light and the furrow in which he was standing had wriggled like a snake. He told the tale in the market square, outside the station, and in seven pubs.

Some of the strangers laughed.

'Well, damn!' they said. 'Fancy bombs here! Well what next, I say?'

But some of the rich ones were packing already, having heard of the neighbouring factories.

To Emily the event of the bombs crowded into an already crowded day. She wouldn't think about them. The weather was clear, but there was something stifling in the air, something sated and flaccid. Through the warm swishing streets the scent of meadows and chestnuts in bloom drifted with the smell of the fire-blighted broom and gorse now scattering in slow smoke. She was busy: a great many patients were admitted, but there was nothing dramatic in this day's work: and as she sat eating her lunch in Mr Jones' conservatory, where somebody had left the hose dribbling among the legs of half a dozen wormy kitchen chairs, her mind returned again and again to that one generous year of childhood with her aunt. There was something then on or behind those smoking hills for her. One by one her passions were being lost, but this – this spirit of place, this identification of self with unregarded loveliness and joy – seemed, after a dormant cycle, to be becoming her life.

She sat breathing the green, double-hot air of the geranium-trellised conservatory, eating sandwiches and seeing Aunt Fran. Sometimes she was in her greenhouse, stretching her nose over the plants, with the perfume of the vine in all her movements, but most vividly she saw her at her bedroom window on a summer evening about seven o'clock. Emily saw her smiling and waving across the buttercup-yellow fields to the distant shallows where the naked town boys were splashing like stars in the burning silver water. 'Look, look – I suppose we can call it summer now,' the aunt would laugh. And it *was*: such summer as it had never been since. There she would sit, and call Emily to her to come and have her hair curled before going to bed. She held the brush on her lap, and the fingers of her right hand she dipped into a mug of tepid water before twisting each strand of hair into the rags. Emily could feel the slight, drowsy tug at her scalp, and the selected lock sliding through Aunt Fran's first and second fingers. The book she was reading aloud lay open on the dressing table among the silver things and the old yellow combs – *The Story of a Red Deer*...

'There! Goodnight. And when you're in bed sing me a song.'

'What shall I sing?'

'Well – 'John Peel' – or – 'The Keel Row'.'

Her voice seemed to stir in her as she remembered, and she heard the air coming from herself as she crouched in the bed.

> *As I came through Sandgate, through Sandgate, through Sandgate,*
> *As I came through Sandgate, I heard a lassie sing...*

The silent voice in her was physical now – she could hear it, feel it rising... she never sang at The Friends' House; she liked to sing out of doors. She saw the leaves in the walnut tree, the wall where Esau, the red cat, sat in the dusk, she heard the owl, and felt the grain of the light fading in the room.

> *I heard a lassie sing.*

Why did it all seem beautiful then? It couldn't have been, not everything. But no Emily nowadays would climb an oak tree to see if sitting in it would make her sing like a blackbird, nor listen to the notes with such an unaffected thrilling expectancy.

When her work was over she went straight home. A little girl in a red check pinafore, whose two hands had swallowed the door knob, was jigging on the doorstep, and peeping through the keyhole. Her laughter and that of another child inside was pealing out into the street. When she saw Emily she peeped up sideways under her arm.

'Hullo, Aunt Em'ly.'

'Hello, Ann.'

'What d'you think I'm doing?'

'I don't know.'

'I'm looking at Diddle. And Diddle's looking at me. I can see her eye. I said I'm going to look *in* at the keyhole. Because I'm not often out in the street. Hullo, Diddle,' she bawled, 'I'm here, are you there?'

'Hullo, Ann, I'm he-ere,' cackled a smaller voice, with bursts of chuckling. Suddenly Ann lost interest. She gave Emily a long stare that was cool, peculiar and consciously measured. And Emily felt shy of the child's sudden gaze and stooped to pick a red hair ribbon off the pavement. Ann triumphed, and yet was reassured. She broke up again into a small skipping, smiling creature.

'*We've* all run away from ole Hitler,' she said cheerfully. 'Mummy's here, and Diddle and Jamie. Did you know?'

She twirled the door knob faster, and the catch inside went clack-clack.

'I knew you were coming,' said Emily.

'Jamie wasn't frightened. Diddle was. Wasn't you, Diddle, eh?'

'Ye-e-s,' chuckled the child inside.

'Diddle cried. Jamie didn't. I'm going to open the door. I want to tell you something.'

They went into the cool stone shadowed passage which was heaped with luggage and a pram. Diddle, a very short fat little thing, was squatting on the mat.

'Don't touch!' cried Ann anxiously: 'This is the-wipe-your-feet mat, Aunt Em'ly. I put something under it. I didn't want to drop it. It's a penny. Here it is. Heads or tails?'

'Tails,' screamed Diddle.

'Not you – Aunt Em'ly,' said Ann with jovial authority.

'Ann!' a voice called.

'She's here, playing pitch and toss,' shouted Emily.

'Toss you for tuppence, Ann, PQ'

'I've won, I've won. I always know. That's what I wanted to tell you. This is tails,' said Ann mysteriously.

'Tails,' said Diddle.

'You look.'

'Ye-e-es.'

'You mustn't look!'

'I muttoned look…'

Annie appeared, slanting out of a doorway, lunging into an apron.

'Ann, for God's sake—' her voice was dry with fatigue. '*Will* you come and drink your milk?' she muttered, seizing each bland child. She was thinner even than Emily, her terse red dress tossed over the wind of her limbs. She held Emily's eyes for a moment, in her own an unconscious hardness and contempt for all things irrelevant to pure animal life – a look which was the mother's at times. Yet far back, there was a friendliness: 'Hullo, sister, when there's a moment I shall see you…'

'See you. See you. See you. No, you won't. I don't live in your eyes,' said Emily to herself. She stepped out into the tiny stone yard; it seemed dull there – something was missing. Oh yes, the lid of the well was down and a great stone on it. The dark, ivy-green water was buried and all its flight of reflections.

'Emily,' said her mother, draining the potatoes over the grating so that the steam climbed the wall like a plant – 'Emily, fetch me that cloth, dear. I'm sorry there aren't any greens. I hadn't time to… thank you. Perhaps before you go you'd get us some nettle tops. Poor Annie has more than she can do.'

'Yes, Mother.'

She could hear the canaries cracking their seeds with a tiny insect-like pop. It was so hot that the stones were tepid in the shade. The pods of broom and gorse burst in the sun with that wee minute crack, with only the linnet to make the stillness alive. Emily remembered, as if she saw the burnt grass and the sky above, the clicking and whirring world of heat. Upstairs the children being put to bed dropped a geranium leaf on her head and laughed in the bow window. She looked at her mother's amethyst beads and thought of the river. Under the drops and the silver, her mother's neck was patched with a scattered flush. Her love for her own children was all anxiety, only what she felt for her grandchildren was physical and enjoyable. She sat at the table straining not to interfere, not to run upstairs with kisses when Jamie cried, not to be upset by Annie's retorting voice. Annie, however, said less and less, and towards the end of the meal abruptly drew her chair back into the window and there sitting bowed with her strangely gnarled nervous hands binding her knees, cried wearily. Suddenly she seemed younger than Emily, younger even than her own children. And her attractive matronly little face which owed some of its beauty to work, but nothing to her everyday mind, became a rarer face – the real face. Seeing her crying, her breath jerking, terrified and childish, they knelt by her and tried to smooth the movements of her frightened body with their touches.

'He'll be killed. Oh Mother, Mother.'

'No, he won't, dear. No, he won't. Please… there,' pleaded the mother.

'Yes…' Annie cried; her tone struck them and they looked at her in silence. In the sunshine her shining tears crusted her: she smeared them from her eyes with her queer powerful fingers whose tips were like drops of coldness: 'Yes. I can't live, I can't live. I don't know anybody here. I want Tom. I want Tom.'

'Annie, darling, you've got the children!'

The temper of hysteria, which is so like mad fury, shook her. She stood up, crying out as she flew through the door: 'To hell with the children! I shall send them all to school and go back to Tom.'

The mother sat down, sighing. A slight breeze came blowing down from the garden and the vine leaves bent as though stroked by the dress of someone coming walking along the path. With that movement came the phase of evening, its entire separation from the day.

'What we shall do with her – what we *shall* we do – if Tom – if anything *should* happen to Tom. She told me before you came in – when she was quite quiet, you know – she told me he says she must be responsible for the children. She said, he said they must have *one...*'

'Yes,' said Emily drearily.

And now the seven o'clock train was in, two hours late, standing in the station releasing puffs of steam, and the light was beginning to bank against the trees and the yellow meadows. With a basket Emily was moving slowly along the coal dust path against a grey hedge of nettles, nipping off their tops with her gloved fingers.

Through the palings she saw the hurrying flickers of people with suitcases, bicycles, push chairs and children – all scuttering, like the pictures on the sticks of a fan which is shaken out and flicked back. The sound of their feet threaded past the new factory site where the hammering had ceased – the sound of their thin words, the tune of a stick being tapped out, towards the town, and three taxis shooting down the road. The greasy dark engine slid away: then came the pure smell of evening, the scent of sky and grazed fields, water and shadows.

She turned and put her basket down. She looked at two chestnut trees in flower, broad green and tapering blossoms balancing, that grew in a piece of willowy waste. The sunlight on them seemed part of themselves, and the flowers looked as if each one had been placed by a hand among the splayed leaves.

The birds sang. Their notes were always like echoes; as though one never heard the voice but only its reflection. The calls were the length of dark woods... as they sang, thought

Emily, in the rain outside the rooms one loved, where the fire was one slow old log charred like an owl's breast.

'I'd love to sit at a window and sew and look out at trees like that. For hours and hours and hours of quiet...'

In that minute she realised that she had achieved the complete vision of her desire and her indifference. Her desire was peace and freedom – the wildness of peace, the speed and voicelessness of it. Her indifference was her duty, which she would do. Try to do. The spirit of life would be laid by for years of spiritual unemployment, that was a part of war. She glanced at the trees, their leaves drooping now in the sinking light. She would take with her their stillness: as she left them she said goodbye.

'If you neglect yourself you must automatically belong to something else. The State. There's nothing else to claim you...'

Some quiet long task at a window looking out on chestnut trees in bloom. Sewing, writing poetry, or just growing older. Aunt Fran shelling peas, gathering raspberries. That kind of order, order not for its own sake, but for the wilder, more ecstatic rhythm which it imitated. Life's natural conformity to life, not to this warped form of death.

War has no seasonableness. No light or darkness, no true time but lies, lies, lies, to make the hands go faster.

She began to hurry, thinking of the clock.

Walking along the river to Aunt Fran's that night Emily met the fisherman. He came up the bank through the willows chewing a grass. She started when she saw him: she had been staring at the sky, all clear light, a sky which she seemed to have seen before but not on earth. As she stood wondering and unconscious, a dream of the night before came back to her with a feeling of distance and quietude. She remembered a kite bursting in space and two giant figures stepping down arm in arm and walking away, never turning round...

The fisherman wished her good evening. For the first time

they shook hands. He asked her where she was going; when she told him, he said that if she liked to walk back with him to the boathouse he would row her up the river.

'It would save you going all round by the bridge,' he said. 'Would you like to? I've got the keys.'

Emily said she would love it, it was years since she had been on the water. So they turned and strolled along the bank. It was quiet and cool: they could smell the meadows up for hay and see the moonlight forming round the moon on the pale horizon.

'The moon looks as if it were made of thistledown,' said Emily.

He looked at her quickly, and away at the water again.

'Are you fond of the country?'

'Sometimes I think I'm fond of nothing else.'

They talked but seemed to give their minds to the river and the twilight. He went before her, holding back the bloom-laden sprays of hawthorn round which little moths were spinning their balls of flight: her legs were damp: in her flesh she felt the familiar chill of the fields at dusk and the clear wakefulness which often precedes sudden and deep sleep.

She was patient now, and at peace... she saw his olive hand with the greenish tan on it, holding back the branches, and she wondered how it came to be that they should know each other so completely and yet so subtly ignore each other.

He walked slowly, his feet making a frail noise in the grass. Over the flowerlit meadows on the other side a shell of mist was closing. There was an exquisite clear coolness and spaciousness. Water under a root fluted like some stationary bird.

'I work at the factory,' he said. 'That's why I haven't seen you for a long time. I'm a chargehand now.'

'I saw you yesterday,' she said, 'in Saint's Cottages. You were asleep, though.'

'Yes.' His voice was expressionless. 'I don't like little rooms in the summer. My shift's changed now. I shall be on days tomorrow.'

She went with him dreamily, her mind full of vague emotion and one sharp thought, that she would never forget this, because somehow she also knew that they would never meet again.

The river was bent like a scythe, and on it a single swan sailed opposite the boathouse. Its whiteness was sharp, distinct, and its being seemed to cease at the water line, it made so little restlessness of swimming.

Inside the boathouse was a huge hollow rolling noise and a wooden banging. That too was familiar: clubmen used it as a skittle alley. While the fisherman went in Emily stood looking down at the deep ditch under the hawthorns where the water was concealed by the white floating petals. The smell of the bloom was like forgetfulness. She held a branch to her face, and when she released it it flew up into the tree with a battering sound like a concealed wood pigeon's wild shudder into flight. She sighed a deep sigh to give her heart room. The fisherman came out with a pair of sculls. They stepped down to the landing. A moorhen whirred the water.

'Get in,' he said.

She walked steadily down the boat. She had a feeling as if her feet were breathing. Weeds wavered under the surface, darkness rose and clung. There was a sense of mist rather than dusk broken around them. The boat rocked and then poised itself into narrow balance. The river under it was taut and vibrant as a gut under a fiddler's finger...

The fisherman pushed out, then all in one movement he sat down and opened the wide embrace of the oars. They glided to the middle and then upstream. They had only a short way to go, the river making less than a quarter of the way that the fields roamed.

Pausing a moment, drawing his fists towards his chest and bunching them there, he looked at her smiling and asked: 'Can you row?'

'No,' she said; 'what does it feel like?'

'Grand.'

He added: 'I like to feel the oars bringing the tremble of the water up to my hands. They almost throb, you know, here and *here*. It's such a strong feeling, though – powerful—'

'Like electricity,' she said.

'Ye-e-es. A sort of connection with something one doesn't know. You think a lot, don't you?' he suddenly asked, fixing his eyes on her.

'No,' she said sadly.

'Well, you look as if you do. But perhaps you call it something else.'

She dipped her hand, sank and floated it, watched its inner fingertips of round green pearls sliding mistily along under the surface. Dandelion seeds were drowning; all the stillness of the grey elf world was flowing and they were silent for a while, the banks piled on either side of this quiet corridor of water darkening its edges.

'I don't know, I don't know,' she sighed in her thoughts.

'I often row up and down here all night,' said the fisherman: 'all night,' he repeated to himself.

'Do you?'

He stooped again as if he were lifting the river on his back, and strokes sent them jetting upward.

'Yes. I love the river. To me there's nothing like it.'

She imagined him at the factory all day and then out here, all night alone, never asleep, never losing sight of himself: 'But don't you ever sleep then? Aren't you tired the next day?'

'No, I don't feel tired. You see I can't live my life among a lot of people all the time, and then just sleep.'

She said nothing for a moment, laying her wet hand on her forehead. Then she asked, puzzled:

'How long are the shifts then?'

'Eleven hours.'

He smiled at her. Emily tried to smile back, but her mouth felt as if it had been trodden on. There was an extraordinary solitude upon his face like that of a man who is standing away, right away beyond the last shelter, watching the lightning.

'My mother was a Frenchwoman,' he told her abruptly: 'but she wasn't a bit the sort of person you'd think. Not thrifty or tidy or anything Frenchwomen are supposed to be. I never knew what it was to have a solid pocket or a weathertight button on me... I used to wander about the fields. I've got the habits of a tramp now... oh, not the visible ones, I hope – no – but I can't stand houses simply because it seems you can never be alone in them. However—'

'I don't expect *a whole house*,' said Emily laughing: 'I like a *room* I can be alone in. And sit near the window.'

'I shouldn't like a country without trees, though,' she went on vaguely; 'you'd feel like a bee in a glass hive. Was your mother scientific?'

'Good God – my mother!'

'Well, I think Frenchwomen are.'

'Well,' he said, 'perhaps you're right. Perhaps she *was* scientific in her way. She liked growing flowers. White flowers – big white daisies – tall ones – I remember them all along our hedge, walking in the wind. Many a time coming home I've taken them for our white cat in the twilight. By jove, yes.' And he pulled an oar out of the water as if it had a root, and looked at the end of it dripping.

'Smell the fields,' he muttered, turning.

'My mother was a musician,' said Emily slowly, 'not one that anyone knew about – she just played beautifully and loved it. She wanted to be a singer, but her father wouldn't let her. Some other girl had failed. Do you know,' she was leaning forward, looking down at her feet and clasping her ankles with her cold wet fingers as she spoke – 'do you know, sometimes I think of Mother all day, and what I'm sure was the happiest part of her life. It was when she was about my age. She had gone from the piano to the organ. Whenever she speaks of Bach she seems to remember herself then, when she was beginning to play his fugues. She used to pay a boy sixpence to blow for her. Just two of them on a weekday in an empty church… her eyes shine when she speaks of it. Oh dear, I think of her then. It's unspeakably sad because one of those days she must have walked out full of ecstasy and never gone back. I seem to imagine her leaving her joy behind forever and then all the troubles and the hard work and the poverty falling on her. And then, I can't help it, I look at her face and feel heartbroken. Isn't it dreadful? I suppose it isn't – not when you think of war.'

'I don't know,' he said. 'She got married?'

'Yes. And had four children. We're a poor substitute for Bach.'

'I don't know,' he said again gravely, thinking: 'Bach himself was probably a substitute for – I mean he took the place of – some woman's single freedom. Don't you think so?'

'Yes. But we are nearly all bad,' she said under her breath.

He was working the oar loosely, turning the nose of the boat towards the old sheep dip where she was to be landed. Glancing back at her, he demanded what she was thinking.

'I?' she said: 'I was thinking we shall never meet again. I don't know how I know it, but I do.'

'It's queer you should feel that, because it's very likely I shall be moved soon. Called up probably. I don't really care much where I go.'

'Don't you feel anything?'

'Yes, I feel something.'

'What?' she cried passionately.

'What?' he laughed, patting the water: 'Why, lost!'

The word seemed to sink down and down into the middle of the river. Her body felt light and chilly: she put her hand on the narrow edge of the boat and looked down at the shadow within the shadow of the reflected sky. A glow of yellowy green, precious light, *the light of darkness* as she saw it, lay on the level behind that they had left. On the top of the bank the enormous hemlocks spread distinctly, neither black nor green but a strange soft brown colour of darkness. This was the place. The current, with its go up or go down, would not let them think.

'Goodnight,' she said, as the grass-swept boat thrilled against the bank.

'Goodnight,' he said at the end of the swaying boat.

'Goodnight and thank you.'

She jumped ashore. She stood on a stone. Hesitatingly he seemed to hover. Then came the clear plunge of the oars. The boat made a bias curve. She stared it away. From the fields the river was all mist, and the slight moonlight was only another kind of invisibility. He had gone. But she heard no stroke. He must be drifting down. He had gone and it was over and they would never meet again.

Emily bent and rubbed her feet which were as wet and cold as if they had been walking in the river. Neither of them had made the least individual acknowledgment of the other. It was from this point of view, the most inscrutable meeting in her life. And yet she understood what it might mean to each of them. Wasn't it the farewell to something each was feeling through the other? Wasn't that why neither he nor she could contradict her instinct that they would never talk together again? Was that too direct, too crude, an explanation? Wasn't it truly what it amounted to tonight?

She stood up, hooking both arms like wings, fists pressed against her, she fled down the tingling, tangled path, the pale yellow moon leaping about in the sky as she ran, the fragrance rising behind her from bruised clover, docks and nettles. In the home meadow each cow was lying still as a rock on the seashore. Her heart seemed to be vaulting in and out of a hole in her breast. A flock of ewes and lambs in the corner by the yard gate trembled on to their feet, shuddering like the echo of thunder in the ground as they shook themselves. The scent of honeysuckle was everywhere in the air as an intenser stillness. And now, the grit of the yard sticking to her wet feet like sand, she bounded up the steps – she was at the house. Weak, dazed, she leant against the porch. There came a pounding vision of machinery, of voices unbroken by silence, into her ears and her closed eyes. The future...

She looked through the window into the room with its parasol of lamplight. Aunt Fran was asleep in her chair over her knitting, a candle in a brass candlestick burning beside her. The dim gold shone through the tangled room and out on to the lawn.

Emily thought, 'With that candle end I shall go to bed.'

THE PITS ARE ON THE TOP

Rhys Davies

Snow whirled prettily about the bus in the bright noon light. Through a hatch in his glass cabin the driver gossiped with a policeman so enormously majestic that the flakes seemed nervous of fluttering on his blue cape; they just melted away in the fiery red of his face. The bus, a single-decker, was slowly filling up; in a few minutes it would begin its steep journey up the vale, right to the top where the pits were.

A girl entered with her young man. They sat near the front. Something of the bright, chill shine of the morning was in her oval face: he was dark, sturdy-looking and brisk, though his face had that azure pallor of the underground worker. As the couple entered and found seats together a little interested silence fell over the other passengers, who, except for the district nurse, were all married-looking women. Everybody, of course, knew that Bryn Jones was courting Dilys Morgan: perhaps they had come down to the shops that morning to buy the engagement ring.

The couple settled, interest was withdrawn from them and conversation resumed to more important matters. There was a youngish, serious-looking woman with a wreath on her knees. It was composed of red tulips, white chrysanthemums and two long-tongued orchids which were the colour of speckled toads. She eyed the wreath with uncertainty and went on with her complaint:

'Fifteen shillings, and in the summer a bigger wreath than

this you can get for seven-and-six. The price of flowers! And soon as I've taken this up I've got to come down again and be fitted for my black. Potching about!' She spoke as if she wanted to administer reproof to someone or something.

'It's bronchitis weather,' sighed a fat woman with a large basket on her knees. Top of the bulgy basket was a loaf of bread, a bag of cakes and a tin of peaches. 'Did he—' she asked the woman with the wreath, hesitant, 'did he *think* he was going?'

'No. A hearty dinner enough he ate and spoke as if it was no different a Sunday to any other. Then he went to lie down on the couch in the front room. Middle of the afternoon my sister heard him coughing but didn't take no notice and went on making the cake for tea. About five o'clock she went to call him – and there he was!' A frown knitted her brow and she touched the closed mouth of a tulip with an uncertain finger. She was wondering if the flowers were quite fresh.

'It's a wonder,' said the fat woman, 'that they didn't open him up.'

'But the plates,' said the district nurse, who had her black maternity bag on her knees. 'He had the X-ray plates took not long ago and they didn't show anything.'

The fat woman did not like to dispute with the district nurse, but, pushing the loaf more firmly into the basket, she said judiciously: 'Oh aye, the plates! Funny though for him to go off so sudden: a young chap too. I wonder,' she turned again to the woman with the wreath, 'your sister didn't *ask* for him to be opened up, like Joe Evans and Dai Richards in my street was, when they went. It's worth it for the compensation. The pits got to pay for silicosis, haven't they!' Indignation had begun to seep into her voice, before it subsided into doubt: 'Of course there *is* a lot of bronchitis about.'

Another woman, who was nursing a baby voluminously wrapped in a thick, stained shawl, said: 'There's two men got it in our street. You can hear them coughing across the road. Jinny James' 'usband one of them, and *she* do say it's the silicosis.'

'What d'you expect,' said another, 'with their lungs getting full of the coal dust and rotting with it.'

'They can always have plates taken,' said the district nurse officially, and looking down her nose. She leaned across to the woman with the baby. 'How's Henry shaping?' she asked, peering at the pink blob of face visible in the shawl's folds. She had brought Henry into the world.

'I just been taking him to the clinic,' said the mother and whispered something in the ear of the nurse, who nodded sagaciously.

A woman, thin and cold as an icicle, climbed hastily into the bus. A crystal drop hung on the end of her nose. She wiped it away with the back of her hand and, having settled into her seat and nodded to the others, she exclaimed rancorously: 'Not a bit of tidy meat in the butcher's! Only them offals, as they call 'em. And my man do like a bit of steak when he comes from the pit. I rushed down to Roberts's soon as I heard he 'ad steak. "Steak", he said to me, "someone's been telling you fairy-tales—"' Something mournful in the air of the bus arrested her, and her roving eye then saw the wreath. Ears pricked, she asked sharply: 'Who's dead?'

''Usband of my sister Gwen Lewis,' said the woman with the wreath.

'Gwen Lewis... let me see...'

'That stoutish piece,' helped the woman with the baby, 'up in Noddfa Street. 'Usband worked in Number One pit. He went sudden Sunday afternoon, lying on the front-room couch. Been coughing and had trouble with his lungs. A young fellow too.'

'Not the silicosis,' exclaimed the thin woman, 'again!'

'Well—' said the woman with the wreath, 'we don't know.'

'He ought to have been opened up,' repeated the fat woman. 'Gwen Lewis could get her compensation from the pits if they found the coal dust had rotted his lungs.'

'He had plates taken,' said the district nurse, 'months ago and there was no sign.'

'He's in his coffin now,' said the woman with the wreath. 'The doctor said it was bronchitis. My sister don't want to go out or anything.' Something of the finality of death seemed to oppress her too, hold her locked. 'I had to buy this wreath for her. Fifteen shillings it cost.' She examined a chrysanthemum; the petal tips were slightly darkening. 'I do hope it's fresh,' she went on worriedly. 'And I've got to come down again this afternoon; my black isn't ready.'

Taking out a red and white spotted handkerchief, the young man with the girl covered his mouth and coughed hard. His girl had sat still as a rabbit; she seemed to look round at the others without looking round. Her ears were flushed.

'It's bronchitis weather,' sighed the woman and pursed her mouth as Bryn Jones coughed again.

The baby suddenly let out a bawl, ferocious and astonishing from such a small leaf of a face.

'He wants his titty,' nodded the thin woman, smiling bleakly.

'Oh, a hungry one he is,' said the mother in a disconsolate way, as if she were complaining.

'What does he weigh now?' benignly asked the district nurse.

Two men jumped on the bus, followed by the conductor, who clipped the bell. The driver put away his pipe. Solid and red-faced among the whirling snowflakes, the policeman stepped back. The thin woman gazed out at him with a kind of disagreeable respect. 'He don't look as if he's got a crave for steaks,' she nodded, speaking to her neighbour as the bus moved safely off.

'And I don't blame him, out in all weathers like they are.'

The bus began its whining climb up the steep slope. The hard, prune-coloured hills each side of the vale were beginning to hold the snow in their wrinkles. Sitting in the recessed back seat, one of the men who had jumped on last thing plucked the conductor's sleeve and said: 'Hey, Emlyn, heard what happened in the cemetery on Saturday night – you know, when them incendiary bombs fell?'

'What?' said Emlyn vaguely, examining his row of tickets.

'Well, you know old Matt Hughes, the cemetery keeper? Well, after them incendiaries fell he went all round the cemetery at midnight to see that everything was OK. And who should be coming down one of the paths in the dark but two funny-looking chaps, and each of 'em carrying a tombstone under his arm. "Hey," said Matt, "what you're doing walking out of 'ere?" The chaps was hurrying, but they stopped and said: "Hell, it's getting too hot for us us 'ere with them incendiaries falling." "Oh aye," said Matt, "they *is* a bit dangerous. But what you're doing carrying them tombstones under your arms?" "Well," said one of the chaps, "there's the Home Guard at the gate, and we heard that people got to have identity cards nowadays, haven't they?"'

The conductor gave a subdued guffaw and called: 'Fares.' Down the bus, where the man's tale had carried, there were smiles. The fat woman tittered. Bryn Jones' neck reddened and swelled with interior mirth, though his young lady did not seem amused... out in the rushing snowflakes a woman had hailed the bus, but it stopped much further up the road and she was obliged to pant through the windy flakes. 'What,' she shrilly scolded, climbing in, 'is the matter with the damn buses? Why can't they stop when they're asst to?' Her snow-wetted eyes glared at Emlyn the conductor; she wore a man's cap skewered to a bun of hair by an ancient hatpin. Sitting down, her gaze pounced on the wreath and she asked, breathless: 'Who's dead?'

'My sister Gwen Lewis' 'usband,' said the woman with the wreath and gazed down heavily at the expensive cluster on her knees. The fat woman added for her:

'Last Sunday. The young fellow went into the front room

after dinner and—' She gave the history. And the woman in the man's cap was sure it was the silicosis: a man in her street had gone off just the same and he wasn't thirty. She agreed he ought to have been opened up, even though the district nurse said the X-ray plates had been negative and the woman with the wreath said the doctor said it was bronchitis.

'It's *proof*,' added the woman in the cap, 'if you open 'em up.'

'*Of course*,' assented the fat woman vigorously, and shoved the slipping tin of peaches further into her basket. 'I wonder she didn't think of the compensation.'

'I've got to go back this afternoon,' lamented the woman with the wreath, but fluffing herself out a little, 'to see about my black. What a potch it is, and snowing like this. My sister, she can't do a thing but sits there by the fire all day, poor 'ooman.'

'The New Inn!' shouted the conductor, roused to his duties by the scolding, though everybody knew every stone and post of the place.

The girl and her young man rose and passed down the silenced bus. He strutted a little, chest before him. She, rather skimped, went looking and not looking, her ears pink. As they stepped out of the door the married women nodded to each other knowingly, with a little grimace of the mouth and lowering of the eyelids. The bus swung on.

Bryn spat as soon as he was out of the bus, then coughed again, in the bright, sharp air. Dilys opened her small fancy umbrella and held it against the snowing wind. She shivered. She was slight, unlike the dumpy older women in the bus. But there was a tenacity in her body and in the way she put her face into the wintry air. 'Goodness me,' she said with a worried kind of irritation, 'I wish you'd do something about that cough.'

'Hell, it's nothing,' he barked. He wore no hat. His shoulders were broad, his limbs and hand thick and hard. The snowflakes turned into a grey liquor in the warm grease on his brisk black hair. The faint bluish pallor of his face was a little more evident. This week he was working on the night shift.

They went down a side turning. They lived in the same street. But before they reached it he put his hand in hers and stopped her against an old building where there was shelter from the whirling flakes and wind. It was a bakehouse, and the oven was inside the wall: they could feel the heat coming out. He would not be seeing her again until Sunday. 'What's the matter?' he said.

'It's those women in the bus!' she exclaimed in a little burst of half-curbed hysteria.

'What's the matter with 'em?' he asked, mystified.

She frowned, trying to concentrate. She did not quite know. But she struggled to know. He tried to help. 'Talking about opening that bloke up?' he suggested.

'No,' she almost wailed. 'It's... it's their *way*. Sitting there and... and talking, and—' No, she couldn't express it. But she went on: 'And looking at me when we came out, looking at me like as if I'd soon be one of them... even,' she added, the hysteria getting a hold, 'carrying a wreath in my lap!'

He was a bit shocked. 'Dilys,' he said, 'they're not bad; they're not bad women.'

As suddenly the hysteria coiled down. But she spoke with bitterness: 'No, that's the worst of it.' She knew she had failed to express the fear knotted deep in her.

With a thick finger, grained with coal dust, he brushed a stray snowflake off the tip of her nose.

'Ooh,' she said. 'It felt like a biff.'

'Just a bundle of nerves you are!' he said in a loving, gratified way. Then he coughed.

'That cough!' she cried, the irritation returning. 'Why don't you wear a hat and a muffler?'

'Oh, shut up,' he growled, squirming in her irritation. 'Didn't you hear it's bronchitis weather?'

After they parted in their street she felt – for she was not one to stay ill-tempered and sulky for long – that she was lucky really. He was in a reserved occupation, and he was a good miner, with a place of his own down under. They were going to be married in three months' time. He would be by her side for her to look after him.

THEY CAME

Alun Lewis

The evening was slowly curdling the sky as the soldier
trudged the last mile along the lane leading from the station
to the Hampshire village where he was billeted. The
hedgerows drew together in the dusk and the distance,
bending their waving heads to each other as the fawn bird
and the blackbird sang among the green hollies. The village
lay merged in the soft seaward slope of the South Downs;
the soldier shifted his rifle from left to right shoulder and
rubbed his matted eyelashes with his knuckles. He was a
young chap but, hampered by his heavy greatcoat and
equipment, he dragged his legs like an old clerk going home
late. He cleared his throat of all that the train journey,
cigarettes and chocolate and tea and waiting had secreted in
his mouth. He spat the thick saliva out. It hung on a twig.

Someone was following him. When he heard the footsteps
first he had hurried, annoyed by the interfering sound. But
his kit was too clumsy to hurry in and he was too tired. So
he dawdled, giving his pursuer a chance to pass him. But the
footsteps stayed behind, keeping a mocking interval. He
couldn't stop himself listening to them, but he refused to look
back. He became slowly angry with himself for letting them
occupy his mind and possess his attention. After a while they
seemed to come trotting out of the past in him, out of the
Welsh mining village, the colliers gambling in the quarry, the
county school where he learned of sex and of knowledge, and

college where he had swotted and slacked in poverty, and boozed, and quarrelled in love. They were the footsteps of the heavy-jawed deacon of Zion, with his white grocer's apron, and his hairy nostrils sniffing out corruption.

But that was silly, he knew. Too tired to control his mind, that's what it was. These footsteps were natural and English, the postman's perhaps... but still they followed him, and the dark gods wrestling in him in the mining valley pricked their goaty ears at the sound of the pimping feet.

He turned the corner into the village and went down the narrow street past the post office and the smithy, turned the corner under the AA sign and crossed the cobbled yard of the hotel where the officers' and business men's cars were parked. A shaggy old dog came frisking out of its straw-filled barrel in the corner, jumping and barking. He spoke to it and at once it grovelled on its belly. He always played with the dog in the mornings, between parades. The unit did its squad drill in the hotel yard, kitchen maids watching flirtatiously through the windows, giggling, and the lavatory smelling either of disinfectant or urine.

He pushed open the little door in the big sliding doors of the garage which had been converted into a barrack room for the duration. The electric bulbs high in the cold roof dangled a weak light from the end of the twisted, wavering flex. Grey blankets folded over biscuits or straw palliasses down both sides of the room. Equipment hanging from nails on the whitewashed wall – in one corner a crucifix, over the thin, chaste, taciturn Irish boy's bed. He was the only one in the room, sitting on his bed in the cold dark corner writing in his diary. He looked up and smiled politely, self-effacingly, said 'Hallo. Had a good leave?' and bent his narrow head again to read what he had written.

'Yes, thanks,' said the soldier, 'except for raids. The first night I was home he raided us for three hours, the sod,' he said, unbuckling his bayonet belt and slipping his whole kit off his shoulders.

Last time he returned from leave, four months back, he had sat down on his bed and written to his wife. They had married on the first day of that leave and slept together for six nights. This time he didn't ferret in his kitbag for notepaper and pencil. He went straight out.

The hotel managament had set a room aside for the soldiers to booze in. It was a good-class hotel, richly and vulgarly furnished with plush mirrors and dwarf palms in green boxes. The auctioneers and lawyers and city men, the fishermen and golfers and bank managers, most of whom had weekend cottages or villas of retirement in commanding positions at the local beauty spots, spent the evening in the saloon bar and lounge, soaking and joking. So the soldiers were given a bare little bar parlour at the back, with a fire and a dartboard and two sawdust spittoons. The soldiers were glad of it. It was their own. They invited some of their pals from the village to play darts with them – the cobbler, the old dad who lived by himself in the church cottage and never shaved or washed, the poacher who brought them a plucked pheasant under his old coat sometimes – all the ones the soldiers liked popped in for an evening. A few girls too, before the dance in the church hall, on Tuesdays.

Fred Garstang from Portsmouth and Ben Bryant, from Coventry, the two oldest soldiers in the unit – regulars who had never earned a stripe – were playing darts, two empty pint glasses on the mantelpiece by the chalk and duster.

'Owdee, Taffy?' they said in unison. ''Ave a good leave, lad?'

'Yes, thanks,' he said automatically, 'except for raids. The sod raided us for three hours the first night I was home.'

'Damn. Just the wrong side of it,' said Fred examining the quivering dart. 'I deserve to lose this bloody game, Ben. I 'xpect you're same as me, Taff; glad to get back to a bit of peace and quiet and a good sleep. My seven days in Pompey's the worst I've ever spent in India, China, the Rhineland, Gallygurchy, or anywhere. But we're nice and cosy here, thank God. They can keep their leave. *I* don't want seven nights in an Anderson. I'd rather stay here, I would.'

Old Fred never stopped talking once he started. The soldier tapped the counter with a shilling and leaned over to see whether the barmaid was on the other side of the partition. He saw her silky legs and the flutter of her skirt. He hit the counter harder, then, while he waited, wondered at his impatience. His body wasn't thirsty; it was too damned tired to bother, too worn out. It was something else in him that wanted to get drunk, dead, dead drunk.

The barmaid came along, smiling. She was natural with the soldiers. She smiled when she saw who it was and held her pretty clenched fist to him across the counter. He should have taken it and forced it gently open, of course. Instead, he just put his flat palm underneath it. She looked at him with a hurt-fawn reproach in her sailing eyes, and opening her hand let a toffee fall into his.

'One from the wood, Madge,' he said.

'I'll have to charge you for *that*,' she said.

'That's all right,' he replied. 'You always pay in this life.'

'Why don't you take the girl, Taffy?' said old Fred as he came and sat by them, their darts over. 'If I was your age...'

He had been in the army since he was fifteen. Now he was past soldiering, wandering in the head sometimes, doing odd jobs; in peace-time he kept the lawns trimmed at the depot, now he was tin-man in the cooking shed, cleaning with Vim the pots and pans Ben Bryant used for cooking. 'Vermicelli tastes all right,' he said. 'Better than anything you can pick up in the streets. Yellow or black or white, German or Irish. I've never had a Russian though, never. It's not bad when you're young, like a new crane when the jib runs out nice and smooth; it's better than sitting in the trenches like an old monkey, scratching yourself and not knowing whose leg it is or whose arm it is, looking in his pockets to see if there's anything worth taking, and not knowing who'll win the race, the bullet with your number on it or the leaky rod you're nursing. But I like it here. It's nice and peaceful up here, in the cookhouse all day. We ought to try some vermicelli, Ben, one day.'

'Don't you get impatient now, Freddy,' Ben said with the calmness of a father of many children. 'We'll stuff your pillow full of it next Christmas and put a sprig of it on your chest. Don't you worry, boy.'

But old Fred went on talking like an old prophet in a volcanic world, about and about. 'There's no knowing when you've got to fight for your king and country,' he said. 'No matter who you are, Russian, or Frenchy, or Jerry – and the Yankee, too. He'll be in it, boy. I've seen him die. It's only natural, to my way of thinking. I wore a pair of gloves the Queen knitted herself, she did, last time. The Unknown Soldier I was, last time.'

None of us are ourselves now, the Welsh boy sat thinking: neither what we were, nor what we will be. He drained his pint glass and crossed to the counter to Madge smiling there.

'You never looked round all the way up from the station,' she said, pulling her shoulder straps up under her grey jumper and exposing the white, rich flesh above her breasts.

'So it was you followed me, eh?' he said, sardonic.

'Why didn't you turn round?' she asked. 'Did you know it was me? You knew someone was behind you, I could tell.'

'I didn't turn round beccause I didn't want to look *back*,' he said.

'And you mean to say you don't know how the Hebrew puts out the eyes of a goldfinch?' Freddy's aggrieved voice swirled up.

'Afraid of being homesick for your wife, eh?' she jeered.

He covered his eyes with his hand, tired out, and looked up at the vague, sensual woman playing upon his instincts there like a gipsy on a zither.

'Not homesick,' he said dryly. 'Death-sick.'

'What d'you mean?' she said.

'Well, she was killed in a raid,' he shouted.

He went up to the orderly room then, having forgotten to hand in his leave pass to the orderly corporal. The room was in the corner of an old warehouse. The building also housed the kitchen and the quartermaster's stores. About the high bare rooms with their rotten dry floors and musty walls, rats galloped in the darkness; in the morning their dirt lay fresh on the mildewed sacks and the unit's cat stretched her white paws and got a weak and lazy thrill from sniffing it.

The orderly corporal was dozing over a Western novelette from Woolworths, hunched up in a pool of lamp and fire light.

'Hallo, Taffy,' he said. 'Had a good leave?'

'Yes, thanks,' he replied. 'Except for raids. Am I on duty tomorrow?'

'You're on duty tonight, I'm afraid,' the orderly corporal replied with the unctuous mock regret of one who enjoys detailing tired or refractory men for unexpected jobs. 'Dave Finley had a cold on his chest this morning and didn't get out of bed. So they fetched him out on a stretcher and the MO gave him pneumonia pills before Dave could stop him; so he's got pneumonia now. You'll go on guard at midnight and at six hours.'

'OK.'

He turned to go.

'Better get some sleep,' said the orderly corporal, yawning noisily. 'Hell! I'm browned off with this war.'

The soldier yawned too, and laughed, and returned to the barrack room to lie down for a couple of hours. He rolled his blankets down on the floor and stretched out.

Old Ben and Fred were back also, Ben fixing bachelor buttons into his best trousers and singing 'Nelly Dean' comfortably to himself, Fred muttering by the stove. 'There's some mean and hungry lads in this room,' he said; 'very hungry and mean. It's an awful nature, that. They'll borrow off you all right, but they won't lend you the dirt off their soles. And always swanking in the mirror, and talking all the time, saying, Yes, they can do the job easy. The fools! Whip 'em! Whip 'em !'

Ben was toasting bread on the point of his bayonet and boiling water in his billy. A tin of pilchards left over from tea was for them all.

'Come on, Taffy. Have a bellyful while you can,' he said.

'No, thanks,' said the soldier, restless on his blankets, 'I don't feel like food tonight, Ben, thanks.'

'Ain't you never bin hungry?' Fred shouted, angrily. 'You don't know what food is, you youngsters don't.'

'I've been without food,' the soldier said, thinking of the '26 strike; and going without peas in the chip shop by the town clock in college, when a new book must be bought. But not now, when everything is free but freedom, and the doctor and dentist and cobbler send you no bills. What survives I don't know, the soldier thought, rubbing his hot eyelids and shifting his legs on the spread-out blankets. What is it that survives?

He got up and buckled his battle order together, adjusting his straps, slipping the pull-through through his Enfield, polishing boots and buttons, tightening his helmet strap under his chin.

'There was a religious woman used to come to our house,' Ben was saying, 'and one day she said to me, sociable like, "You're a Guinness drinker, aren't you, Mr Bryant?" and I says, "I am, mum." And she says, "Well, can you tell me what's wrong with the ostrich on them advertisements?"'

The soldier went out to relieve the guard.

They were only twenty soldiers altogether sent up here to guard a transmitting station hidden in the slopes of the Downs. A cushy job, safe as houses. There was a little stone shed, once used for sheep that were sick after lambing, in a chalky hollow on the forehead of the hill, which the guard used for sleeping in when they were off duty. Two hours on, four hours off, rain and sun and snow and stars. As the soldier toiled up the lane and across the high meadow to the shed, the milky moon came out from grey clouds and touched with lucid fingers the chopped branches piled in precise lengths at the foot of the wood. The pine trees moved softly as the moon touched their grey-green leaves, giving them a veil that looked like rainy snow, grey-white.

The lane running up through the wood shortened alarmingly in perspective. A star fell. So surprising, so swift and delicate, the sudden short curved fall and extinction of the tiny lit world. But over it the Plough still stayed, like something imperishable in man. He leant against the gate, dizzy and light-headed, waves of soft heat running into his head. He swallowed something warm and thick; spitting it out, he saw it was blood. He stayed there a little, resting, and then went on.

He went along the sandy lane, noticing as he always did the antique sculptures of sea and ice and rain, the smooth twisted flints, yellow and blue and mottled, lying in the white sand down which the water of winter scooped its way.

At the top of the lane was the lambing shed – guard room. He slipped quickly through the door to prevent any light escaping. There was gunfire and the sound of bombs along the coast.

The sergeant of the guard was lying on a palliasse in front of the stove. He got up slowly, groaning lazily.

'So you're back again, Taffy, are you?' he said, a grudge in his too hearty welcome. 'Relieving Dave Finley, eh? He's swinging the lead, Dave is. I've a good mind to report him to the OC It's tough on you, going on night guard after a day's journey. Have a good leave, Taff?'

'Not bad,' the soldier replied, 'except for the raids. Raided us the first night I was home.'

'Everybody's getting it,' the sergeant replied, yawning. 'They dropped two dozen incendiaries in our fields in Lincs last week.'

He was drinking a billy can of cocoa which he had boiled on the fire, but he didn't offer any. He had weak blue eyes, a receding chin, fresh features of characterless good looks, wavy hair combed and brilliantined. He was always on edge against Taffy, distrusting him, perhaps envying him. He lived in terror of losing a stripe and in constant hunger to gain another promotion. He sucked and scraped the officers for this, zealously carrying out their orders with the finnicky short temper of a weak, house-proud woman. He polished the barrack-room floor and black-leaded the stove himself because the boys refused to do more than give the place a regulation lick. And he leaped at the chance of putting a man on the peg, he was always waiting to catch somebody cutting a church parade or nipping out of camp to meet a girl when he should be on duty. Yet he was mortally afraid of a quarrel, of unpopularity, and he was always jovial, glassily jovial, even to the Welsh boy whom he knew he couldn't deceive.

'Who am I to relieve on guard?' the soldier asked.

'Nobby Sherraton. He's patrolling the ridge.'

'OK.' He slipped his rifle sling over his shoulder and put his helmet on. 'You marching me out? Or shall I just go and send Nobby in?'

For once laziness overcame discretion.

'There's nobody about. Just go yourself,' the sergeant said, smiling, posing now as the informal honest soldier. 'I'll be seeing yer.'

'Some day.'

He left the hut and crossed the dry dead-white grass to the ridge where Nobby was on guard.

Nobby was his mate.

He had only been in the unit about a month. Before that he had been stationed just outside London and had done a lot of demolition and rescue work. He was from Mile End, and had roughed it. His hands and face showed that, his rough, blackened hands, cigarette-stained, his red blotchy face with the bulbous nose, and the good blue eyes under tiny lids, and short scraggy lashes and brows. His hair was mousy and thin. He had been on the dole most of the time. He had been an unsuccessful boxer; he cleared out of that game when his brother, also a boxer, became punch-drunk and blind. He had plenty of tales of the Mosley faction. He was sometimes paid five bob to break up their meetings. He always took his five bob, but he let the others do the breaking up. Who wants a black eye and a cut face for five bob? 'Tain't worth it. He rarely said anything about women. He didn't think much of lots of them; though like all Cockney youths he loved the 'old lady', his mother. He wasn't married. No, sir.

He was a conscript. Naturally. He didn't believe in volunteering. And he didn't like the Army, its drills and orders, and its insistence on a smart appearance. Smartness he disliked. Appearances he distrusted. Orders he resented. He was 'wise' to things. No sucker.

Taffy felt a warm little feeling under his skin, relief more than anything else, to see Nobby again. He hadn't to pretend with Nobby. Fundamentally they shared the same humanity, the unspoken humanity of comradeship, of living together, sharing what they had, not afraid to borrow or talk or shut up. Or to leave each other and stroll off to satisfy the need for loneliness.

Nobby was surprised so much that he flung out his delight in a shout and a laugh and a wave of his arms. 'Taffy, lad!' he said. 'Back already, eh? Boy!' Then he became normal.

'Can't keep away from this bloody sannytorium for long, can we?' he grumbled.

Taffy stood looking at him, then at the ground, then he turned away and looked nowhere.

'What's wrong, kid?' Nobby asked, his voice urgent and frightened, guessing. 'Anything bad? Caught a packet, did you?' He said the last two phrases slowly, his voice afraid to ask.

'*I* didn't,' Taffy said, his voice thin and unsteady. '*I* didn't. *I'm* all right. *I'm* healthy.'

Nobby put his hand on his shoulder and turned him round. He looked at the white sucked-in face and the eyes looking nowhere.

'Did *she* get it?' and he too turned his head a little and swallowed. 'She did,' he said, neither asking a question nor making a statement. Something absolute, the two words he said.

Taffy sat down, stretched out. The grass was dead; white, wispy long grass; Nobby sat down, too.

'They came over about eight o'clock the first night,' Taffy said. 'The town hadn't had a real one before. I've told you we've only got apartments, the top rooms in an old couple's house. The old ones got hysterics, see, Nobby. And then they wouldn't do what I told them, get down the road to a shelter. They wouldn't go out into the street and they wouldn't stay where they were. "My chickens," the old man was blubbering all the time. He's got an allotment up on the voel, see? Gwyneth made them some tea. She was fine, she calmed them down. That was at the beginning, before the heavy stuff began. I went out the back to tackle the incendiaries. The boy next door was out there, too. He had a shovel and I fetched a saucepan. But it was freezing, and we couldn't dig the earth up quick enough. There were too many incendiaries. One fell on the roof and stuck in the troughing. The kid shinned up the pipe. It exploded in his face and he fell down. Twenty-odd feet. I picked him up and both his eyes were out, see?'

He had gone back to the sing-song rhythm and the broad accent of his home, the back lanes and the back gardens. He was shuddering a little, and sick-white, sallow.

Nobby waited.

'I took him into his own house,' he said, controlling his voice now, almost reflective. 'I left him to his sister, poor kid. Then I went in to see if Gwyneth was all right. She was going to take the old couple down the road to the shelter. She had a mack on over her dressing gown. We'd intended going to bed early, see? So I said she was to stay in the shelter. But she wanted to come back. We could lie under the bed together.

'I wanted her back too, somehow. Then some more

incendiaries fell, so I said "Do as you like" and went at them with a saucepan. I thought sure one would blow my eyes out. Well, she took them down. Carried their cat for them. Soon as she'd gone the heavy stuff came. Oh Christ!'

Nobby let him go on; better let him go on.

'It knocked me flat, dazed me for a bit. Then I got up and another one flattened me. It was trying to stop me, see, Nobby. I crawled out of the garden, but it was dark as hell and buildings all down, dust and piles of masonry. Then he dropped some more incendiaries and the fires started. I knew she must be somewhere, see? I knew she must be somewhere. I began pulling the masonry away with my hands, climbed on to the pile of it in the fire. I couldn't see with the smoke and I knew it wasn't any use, only I had to do it, see?'

'Then suddenly the masonry fell downwards. The road was clear on the other side. I thought it was all right after all, then. I thought she'd have reached the shelter… but she hadn't.

'I found her about twenty yards down the road.

'She wasn't dead. Her clothes were gone. And her hands. She put them over her face, I reckon.

'She couldn't speak, but I knew she knew it was me. I carried her back in my arms. Over the fallen house. The fire wasn't bad by then. Took her home, see, Nobby. Only the home was on fire. I wanted her to die all the time. I carried her over a mile through the streets. Fires and hoses and water. And she wouldn't die. When I got her to the clearing station I began to think she'd live.

'But they were only playing a game with me, see?'

He stood up, and made himself calm.

'Well, there it is.' He rubbed his face with the palm of his hand, wiping the cold sweat off.

'I knew she was going to die. When they told me she was – I didn't feel anything, Nobby…

'But she died while they were messing her body about with their hands, see?… And she never said anything. Never said anything to me. Not that it makes any difference, I suppose.

We never did speak about those things much. Only, you know how it is, you want a word somehow. You want it to keep.'

'Sure, I know,' Nobby said.

'What's it all for, Nobby?' he said in a while. He looked so tired and beat. 'I used to know what it was all about, but I can't understand it now.'

'Aw, forget all about that,' Nobby said. 'You're here, aincher, now?'

He put his hands on his mate's shoulders and let him lean against him for a bit. 'I reckon you belong to each other for keeps, now,' Nobby said.

'You believe that, Nobby?' he asked, slow and puzzled, but with a gathering force as his uncertainty came together.

'Yes. For you and 'er, I do. It wouldn't be true for me, or the sergeant in there, but for you two it is.'

Taffy was still against his shoulder. Then slowly he straightened himself, moved back on to himself, and lifting his face he looked at the milky-white fields and the sentinel pines and the stars.

'I knew it was so, really,' he said. 'Only I was afraid I was fooling myself.'

He smiled, and moved his feet, pressing on them with his whole weight as if testing them after an illness.

'I'm all right, now, Nobby. Thank you, boy.'

'I'll go, then,' Nobby said. He slipped his rifle over his shoulder and as he moved off he hesitated, turned back, and touched his mate's arm lightly.

'Two's company, three's none,' he said, and stumped off slowly to the lambing shed through the dead straw-grass.

And the soldier was left alone on the flat upland ridge.

Below him the valleys widened into rich, arable lakes on which the moonlight and the mist lay like the skeins which spiders spin round their eggs. Beyond the pools another chain of downland lay across the valleys, and beyond those hills the coast. Over him, over the valleys, over the pinewoods, blue fingers came out of the earth and moved slanting across their quarters as the bombers droned in the stars over his head and swung round to attack the coastal city from inland. The sky over the coast was inflamed and violent, a soft blood-red.

The soldier was thinking of the day he received his calling up papers, just a year ago. Sitting on the drystone wall of his father's back garden with Gwyneth by him; his ragged little brother kneeling by the chicken run, stuffing cabbage stumps through the netting for the hens to peck, and laughing and pulling the stumps out as the old hen made an angry jab; his father riddling the ashes and the ramshackle garden falling to bits, broken trellis and tottering fence; his mother washing her husband's flannel vest and drovers in the tub, white and vexed. He had taken Gwyneth's hand, and her hand had said, 'In coming and in going you are mine; now, and for a little while longer; and then for ever.'

But it was not her footsteps that followed him down the lane from the station.

Now over his head the darkness was in full leaf, drifted with the purity of pines, the calm and infinite darkness of an English night, with the stars moving in slow declension down the sky. And the warm scent of resin about him and of birds and of all small creatures moving in the loose mould in the ferns like fingers in velvet.

And the soldier stood under the pines, watching the night move down the valleys and lift itself seawards, hearing the sheep cough and farm dogs restlessly barking in the farms. And farther still the violence growing in the sky till the coast was a turbulent thunder of fire and sickening explosions, and there was no darkness there at all, no sleep.

'My life belongs to the world,' he said. 'I will do what I can.'

He moved along the spur and looked down at the snow-grey evergreen woods and the glinting roofs scattered over the rich land.

And down in the valleys the church bells began pealing, pealing, and he laughed like a lover, seeing his beloved.

Boys of Gold

George Brinley Evans

The steamer was a small, thirty year old, coal-burning cargo/passenger boat, that until Pearl Harbour had plied her trade quietly between the ports on the shores of the Bay of Bengal. Now with a number in place of a name, painted fleet grey, she was steaming as part of a battle group.

He had been brought back from Akyab with the rest; a week in Calcutta and Captain Belton had asked for volunteers. Two trucks took them to a hot empty plain, miles from anywhere, just seven tents set alongside a sparkling river. Most of the next day was spent swimming, until the medics arrived, along with the ammunition. It was jabs all round.

The evening was spent charging Bren magazines with ball, tracer and incendiary bullets. The following morning they were aboard ship, on their way. Two days out, under the bluest of blue skies, they were ordered to check their kit. They had handed their pay books to the QM before embarking. He had handed them proxy forms, for the coming parliamentary elections, back home. Not one of them had been old enough to sign. Belton's kindergarten, someone mocked. He felt for his dog tags; they were there, one red, one black, strung on his army issue cord necklace. Thomas Samuel. 11741178. C of E. The armourer at Brecon had punched on the information. He had stopped thinking of himself as a Samuel. Now, when people called his name, he automatically answered to Taff. He sat down on the deck next to Bagley, closed his eyes and listened to the rhythmic slap-slap of the bow wave; not long now.

The Afon Pyrddin gleamed and shimmered as it slid over the smooth stones, swirled, spun, and turned, then bent itself over the Sgwd Fach, the first of its three waterfalls. On and over, headlong down the one hundred foot drop of the Horseshoe Falls, into a dark, dank gorge, filled with the sound of angry, hissing water, breaking and splitting itself into a grey boiling mist; only to fall back into the iron grip of the millstone grit. Raging in its narrow channel, it rushed for the freedom of the smooth, wide shelf above the Lady Falls, to billow out like clouds of white silk, into the sun-filled pool below.

What a wonderful place for a body to live, he thought. He looked over Mrs Strong's garden to Ianto the Farm's big field. It shone a warm buttercup yellow in the morning sun. Almost in the centre stood a nursery, a stand of some thirty to forty full-grown Scots firs. A hideaway place that could turn into a steaming jungle, if you wanted it to. Where every shadow was an envelope for some new terror and so frightening, warned Billy Whitticker, 'It would give you lockjaw right enough! Right!'

Or if you held your head on one side and looked through the cobweb of your eyelashes, it would become a desert fort. Standing in the long shadow of an Arabian sunset, with white capped legionnaires standing sentinel. Once it was the Metz Wood they had read about in *The Wizard*. They had become the heroic, defiant men of the Welch Regiment. Up from their young souls had surged the craving of an ancient inherited valour; through their milk white teeth they had cried the cry, 'Stick it the Welsh!' and they had meant it.

'Sammy! Sammy! Sa...mmy!' His mother's voice sang out. He hated people calling him Sammy, except his mother, and that best of all when they two were alone together. He liked everyone else to call him just plain Sam.

'Come on then, if you're going with Owen to pick whinberries. Sit in your place.' He looked at his brother, two years older than himself, who said without malice, 'Won't wait for you mind, if you can't keep up.'

'Mammy! Owen's going to leave Sammy on the mountain,' his sister piped up. She was sat in their father's chair, still in her nightdress; her hair tied up in rag curlers. She was the youngest and only girl, so could do and say what she liked.

'If they only dare!' his mother had said. The clean scent of her skin close to him, a wisp of her hair brushed his cheek and a small voice inside him whispered, 'I love you, and I'll bring you back more whinberries than anybody's ever seen.'

She gave him one of his father's old tommy boxes, burnished to a bright pewter by the emery rough hands of a collier. To Owen she gave the Christmas biscuit tin and the bottle with the home-made pop. They bought the ginger pop off a girl called Dolly, who brought it around, on a Friday, in a handcart, that ran on an old set of pram wheels and bore on its sides the words 'Polar Ajax Explosive', from the days when it was a box that carried gelignite to the colliery.

Alan was ready and came around.

'You mind Sammy, now!' their mother called after them.

The sound of her voice made Mr Gay, the Frenchman who lived opposite, lift his head from the storm of colour that was his flower garden. The tough old peasant from the Ardennes raised his hand in greeting to the boys.

'Good morning, Mr Gay!' they shouted back respectfully. He was the only foreigner they knew and hadn't he shown them the merry-go-round he had made for his grandson, with its painted, prancing horse?

'Takes a Frenchman to make something like that,' Alan had said.

'And where are you away to, Sam?'

'Hello, Mrs Strong,' he smiled at the kind eyes that looked

down on him. 'Going to pick whinberries, I am,' he announced his impending venture to the tall figure leaning against the gate. 'I'll bring you some if you like,' realising that perhaps he had found a way of repaying the soft-spoken lady for all the sprigs of mint she'd passed over the fence to little Mrs Thomas, as she called his mother, every time they had lamb for dinner. And every St David's Day since he had started school she'd brought him the best leek in her garden, the one with the greenest leaves and the whitest root, to pin on his coat; and one for Owen.

Mrs Strong laughed. Her life had begun in a small village outside Whitehaven that stood right in the way of the North Atlantic wind as it came in like ice off the Solway Firth and took its spite out on the half a dozen cottages that some insolent Cumberland miners had built right in its path. She accepted and forgave his extravagances with the natural compassion bred into those born in such places.

When they reached the bridge by the Pant, Rafferty was waiting for them.

'Got money for your permits? MacDermitt the shepherd is up by the Bwthin,' warned Rafferty.

He felt in his pocket for the silver thrupence his mother had given him. MacDermitt lived alone in a small valley hidden high on Mynydd Cefn Hir, tending a flock of sheep and guarding that part of the estate that belonged to the Williams family of Aberpergwm. He had only ever seen MacDermitt once, when the man had been making his monthly trip down to the village to shop. The memory of him came flooding back, as he lengthened his stride to keep up with the others. How could such a small pony carry such a big man? He was as wide as a piano.

They went down over the quoit pitch and behind Hopkins' shop. He looked across the colliery horse's field to Banwen colliery, the world's biggest anthracite mine. Owned by David Martin Evans Bevan, one thousand, two hundred men worked there. His father was one and he would be another.

'Do you know how MacDermitt do disbaddy young rams?' Rafferty was asking 'Just tips them up and bites their balls off!' Liar, he thought. But winced all the same.

The Bwthin was nothing more than a ruin. When David Thomas, a fireman at Banwen colliery, lived there with his family, it was called Ty-yr-heol (The Road House), for this was no ordinary road. The road they walked on was Sarn Helen, built on the orders of the Emperor Maximus and the road, it was said, along which St Patrick was led to slavery by Irish raiders, from his home at Banwen.

This time the raider was a massive Scot, sat on a pile of stones. And although the sun had already made the stones warm to the touch, MacDermitt was wearing a heavy tweed shepherd's coat, a tweed hat, leggings and half-sprung boots. The hair that showed from under his hat was snow white, as were his bushy eyebrows and the stubble of his moustache and beard. His eyes were light blue and clear like a boy's and shone out over the weather-raw skin that covered his cheekbones.

'Can my brother and me pick on the same permit, Mister?' asked Owen.

'No. One picker, one permit, laddie.'

He gave his brother his thrupence. Owen handed over the sixpence. 'Thrupence each,' Owen said.

'What do you call the wee boy?'

He stepped out from behind Owen to show himself. MacDermitt smiled at him. At the sight of those long tobacco-stained teeth, he stepped back, and was sorry he had thought Rafferty a liar.

The second part of the climb up Cefn Hir was steep and could only be made on hands and knees. Owen kept looking back at him; he was sorry he was making Owen feel guilty. But the windburnt grass was making the bottoms of his boots shine and chafing the skin between his fingers.

'Not much further now, Sam,' Owen encouraged from a

little higher up. The tone of his voice regretting the earlier hard looks.

Alan got to the wall first, and was standing on top of it. They had reached the top of the mountain. Owen held out his hand.

'Come on, Sam. The Roman Wall!' He scorned the helping hand and ran on to the wall. The wall stretched for as far as the eye could see, along the topmost ridge of the mountain, held together by nothing more than the builder's ability to balance one stone on top of another.

'Get up on it, Sam!' his brother urged. 'Take a look.'

It was like looking over the edge of the world. Below him lay MacDermitt's domain. The beautiful landlocked valley of Blaen Pergwm. Its shape reminded him of the fans the girls had carried in the school play, *Princess Chrysanthemum*. Tucked down, hundreds of feet below, MacDermitt's cottage was the thumb that drew the centre folds together. The lovely golden fabric of the fan rippled like a summer sea, as the tall mountain grass bent its head to the soft breeze. Dotted out like painted flowers were the pickers, their heads bowed and deft fingers urgently plucking the ripe fruit from its stalk.

'Come on, mark your name on the wall,' shouted Rafferty. Alan had already finished scraping his name through the powder-dry moss. It was as well; two summers away lurked the consumption.

'You have a rest, Sam. I'll do your name for you,' offered Owen. 'Samuel Thomas 1932', Owen finished off his name and the date neatly. He was glad Owen was his brother.

'No good picking on top by here, better go down a bit,' organised Rafferty.

When they reached the first group of pickers, Owen warned, 'Mind where you're putting your feet now, in case you step into one of their baskets.'

Mrs Morgan and her children made up the first group, all picking into helpers, old teacups, that when full were tipped into two fourteen-pound wicker baskets. The whinberries, still in their powdered bloom, lay like a purple cushion against the shining brown wicker walls. If there was such a thing as professional whinberry pickers in Banwen, then this family was it. When a basket would become full, one of the children would take it down the mountain and give it to Shurry, the bus conductor. At Neath he would give the basket to the man who kept the centre stall at the market.

Four or five pence a pound, Mrs Morgan got for her whinberries. A full day's work brought them in seven or eight shillings, if they were lucky. They found a place to pick, but only after religiously observing the laws of 'Bara-y-cwtch'. This was a custom that designated territorial rights to the picker already on the spot. The size of the allotment was nowhere stated but usually the bigger and more ferocious the picker on the spot was, the larger the area of his preserve became.

There were whinberries everywhere; how he wished he had brought two of his father's old tommy boxes, or a bigger tin. The first whinberry he picked burst between his fingers. Never mind, he thought, there's plenty more. The next one dropped into a tangle of stalks and leaves. Then the insects, that until then had been busy feeding on the long grass, found him. They buzzed their inquiries around his head, in his hair, into his ears and nostrils, along his bare legs and down his shirtfront. The others picked diligently, insects or no insects.

'All right, Sam?' Owen called.

'Yes, all right.' He looked down at the few badly mauled whinberries that rattled around the bottom of the tin. And about two hours later, he could have done without Rafferty announcing to the world, 'Hey! Look lads, poor old Sammy hasn't covered the bottom of his tin yet.'

They stopped to eat. Owen gave him the sandwiches from the bottom of the pack, because they had stayed the freshest. But not even the banana sandwiches and the ginger pop improved his efficiency. Then it was time to go home. The bottom of his tommy box was covered by about two inches of whinberries, no more; and that included squashed whinberries, red whinberries, not to mention the bits of grass and pieces of stalk.

The pledges he had so readily made weighed on him. His feet dragged themselves through the bracken, not wanting to carry him to where he would have to confess that those pledges would not be kept. In the evening light, he was frightened by the massiveness of the mountain's dark curves. He would never come after whinberries again, never. Nor would he, he was going to think, ever come on this ugly mountain again, but stopped himself, thinking that perhaps he'd better wait until he got home first.

At the side of the house, Owen took the lid of his tin: 'Tip yours in here, Sam.'

He opened his tin and looked at the jammy mess.

'Go on. Never mind, tip 'em in, Sam.'

Their father was in the back yard, legging a mandrill. He looked up and smiled, 'How's it going, Owen-Sam?'

He grinned back at the smiling man and the fear of the mountain flew from him.

The table was laid for supper, and the kitchen full of the smell of newly-pressed linen their mother was folding on to the airer.

'Well then?' She stood there, with a snow-white pillow slip over her hands, like a muff.

Owen lifted the lid of his tin; the Christmas biscuit tin was full to within an inch from the top.

'Sam and me managed this much between us, Mam.' He looked at Owen; Owen was looking at their mother, looking at her eyes. Looking for what only a son can see in the eyes of his mother. And no man ever born has seen it in any other place. In that instant of light, you bask, you bathe; you become the boy of pure gold.

* * *

'Come on, Taff, move!'

The bump against the jetty brought him to his feet. He waited to follow Bagley up the rope ladder. The loop he had made in the cotton bandolier slipped. He fastened it to the 'D' buckle of his pack and shinned up the ladder after Bagley. Bagley bent to help him over the edge of the jetty. He saw it coming through the air towards him. For a moment, he thought it was a bundle of rags. Until it thumped down heavily on the deck in front of him. The mouth wide open, showing strong white teeth bloodstained from having almost bitten the tongue in half. He rose to his feet and his eyes met the eyes of the Indian sepoy, who had booted the head at them. The sepoy stopped grinning.

'Taffy!' Bagley's voice was a mixture of impatience and concern, something the young Englishman often felt at his comrade's seemingly unending ability to wander into trouble. They ran across the jetty, over the road and jumped through the window of a bank. They landed up to the tops of their boots in money. They picked it up by the armful, useless paper money. They kicked it around.

'Bagley! Thomas!' They ran out into the street to where the captain's shout had come from and formed into Indian file with the rest. Now they had to make their way through the city to the main railway station. He looked down and let the worthless paper money, still in his hand, slip through his fingers. And thought of the death head, the matted blood-soaked hair a mother had once washed and gently brushed into curls. The eyes, so full of the terror of death, a father had looked into to see the reflection of his own dream. Of the torn and bruised lips, pressing and receiving loving kisses.

The sun blazed down, turning the green of their shirts to black with rivers of sweat and scattering the stench of death to every corner of this once shining city.

'Right! Everybody got one up the spout! And check your safety catches!' Sergeant Hopper's voice banged around the empty street.

The soft, gentle breath of a mountain breeze passed across his face, his feet were on mountain bracken and his mouth filled with the clean, clean scent of his mother. He stepped off along the road behind Bagley.

Thirty yards away, crouched behind a pile of rubble that not long ago had been a shop of sorts, a twenty year old Japanese infantryman felt a pulse racing in his finger as he bent it around the trigger. Knowing the moment he pressed that trigger, his life would end in minutes. His strong, young body smashed to pulp in a hail of tracer, ball and incendiary bullets.

Carefully, he framed the face of the British soldier in the aperture of his rifle sight, felt the soft warmth of the palms of his mother's hands against his temples, sucked in a deep sigh and pressed the trigger.

WARD 'O' 3 (B)

Alun Lewis

I

Ward 'O' 3 (b) was, and doubtless still is, a small room at the end of the Officers' Convalescent Ward which occupies one wing of the rectangle of one-storeyed sheds that enclose the 'lily-pond garden' of No. X British General Hospital, Southern Army, India. The other three wings contain the administrative offices, the Officers' Surgical Ward and the Officers' Medical Ward. An outer ring of buildings consists of the various ancillary institutions, the kitchens, the laboratory of tropical diseases, the mortuary, the operating theatres and the X-ray theatre. They are all connected by roofed passageways; the inner rectangle of wards has a roofed verandah opening on the garden whose flagstones have a claustral and enduring aura. The garden is kept in perpetual flower by six black, almost naked Mahratti gardeners who drench it with water during the dry season and prune and weed it incessantly during the rains. It has tall flowering jacarandas, beds of hollyhock and carnation and stock, rose trellises and sticks swarming with sweet peas; and in the arid months of burning heat the geraniums bud with fire in red earthenware pots. It is, by 1943 standards, a good place to be in.

At the time of which I am writing, autumn 1942, Ward 'O' 3 (b), which has four beds, was occupied by Captain A. G.

419

Brownlow-Grace, Lieut. Quartermaster Withers, Lieut. Giles Moncrieff and Lieut. Anthony Weston. The last-named was an RAC man who had arrived in India from home four months previously and had been seriously injured by an anti-tank mine during training. The other three were infantrymen. Brownlow-Grace had lost an arm in Burma six months earlier, Moncrieff had multiple leg injuries there and infantile paralysis as well. 'Dad' Withers was the only man over twenty-five. He was forty-four, a regular soldier with twenty-five years in the ranks and three in commission; during this period he had the distinction of never having been in action. He had spent all but two years abroad; he had been home five times and had five children. He was suffering from chronic malaria, sciatica and rheumatism. They were all awaiting a medical board, at which it is decided whether a man should be regraded to a lower medical category, whether he is fit for active or other service, whether he be sent home, or on leave, or discharged the service with a pension. They were the special charge of Sister Normanby, a regular QAIMNS nurse with a professional impersonality that controlled completely the undoubted flair and 'it' which distinguished her during an evening off at the Turf Club dances. She was the operating theatre sister; the surgeons considered her a perfect assistant. On duty or off everybody was pleased about her and aware of her; even the old matron whose puritan and sexless maturity abhorred prettiness and romantics had actually asked Sister Normanby to go on leave with her, Sister deftly refusing.

II

The floor is red parquet, burnished as a windless lake, the coverlets of the four beds are plum red, the blankets cherry red. Moncrieff hates red, Brownlow-Grace has no emotions about colours, any more than about music or aesthetics; but he hates Moncrieff. This is not unnatural. Moncrieff is a

university student, Oxford or some bloody place, as far as
Brownlow-Grace knows. He whistles classical music, wears
his hair long, which is impermissible in a civilian officer and
tolerated only in a cavalry officer with at least five years'
service in India behind him. Brownlow-Grace has done eight.
Moncrieff says a thing is too wearing, dreadfully tedious,
simply marvellous, wizard. He indulges in moods and casts
himself on his bed in ecstasies of despair. He sleeps in a gauzy
veil, parades the ward in the morning in chaplies and veil,
swinging his wasted hips and boil-scarred shoulders from
wash-place to bed; and he is vain. He has thirty photographs
of himself, mounted enlargements, in SD and service cap,
which he is sending off gradually to a network of young
ladies in Greater London, Cape Town where he stayed on
the way out, and the chain of hospitals he passed through
on his return from Burma. His sickness has deformed him;
that also Brownlow-Grace finds himself unable to stomach.

Moncrieff made several attempts to affiliate himself to
Brownlow-Grace; came and looked over his shoulder at his
album of photographs the second day they were together,
asked him questions about hunting, fishing and shooting on
the third day, talked to him about Burma on the third day
and asked him if he'd been afraid to die. What a shocker,
Brownlow-Grace thought. Now when he saw the man
looking at his mounted self-portraits for the umpteenth time
he closed his eyes and tried to sleep himself out of it. But his
sleep was liverish and full of curses. He wanted to look at
his watch but refused to open his eyes because the day was
so long and it must be still short of nine. In his enormous
tedium he prays Sister Normanby to come at eleven with a
glass of iced nimbo pani for him. He doesn't know how he
stands with her; he used to find women easy before Burma,
he knew his slim and elegant figure could wear his numerous
and expensive uniforms perfectly and he never had to exert
himself in a dance or reception from the Savoy in the Strand
through Shepheard's in Cairo to the Taj in Bombay or the

Turf Club in Poona. But now he wasn't sure; he wasn't sure whether his face had sagged and aged, his hair thinned, his decapitated arm in bad taste. He had sent an airgraph to his parents and his fiancée in Shropshire telling them he'd had his arm off. Peggy sounded as if she were thrilled by it in her reply. Maybe she was being kind. He didn't care so much nowadays what she happened to be feeling. Sister Normanby, however, could excite him obviously. He wanted to ask her to go to a dinner dance with him at the Club as soon as he felt strong enough. But he was feeling lonely; nobody came to see him; how could they, anyway? He was the only officer to come out alive. He felt ashamed of that sometimes. He hadn't thought about getting away until the butchery was over and the Japs were mopping up with the bayonet. He'd tried like the devil then, though; didn't realise he had so much cunning and desperation in him. And that little shocker asking him if he'd been afraid to die. He hadn't given death two thoughts.

There was Mostyn Turner. He used to think about Death a lot. Poor old Mostyn. Maybe it was just fancy, but looking at some of Mostyn's photographs in the album, when the pair of them were on shikari tiger hunting in Belgaum or that fortnight they had together in Kashmir, you could see by his face that he would die. He always attracted the serious type of girl; and like as not he'd take it too far. On the troopship to Rangoon he'd wanted Mostyn to play poker after the bar closed; looked for him everywhere, couldn't find him below decks, nor in the men's mess deck where he sometimes spent an hour or two yarning; their cabin was empty. He found him on the boat deck eventually, hunched up by a lifeboat under the stars. Something stopped him calling him, or even approaching him; he'd turned away and waited by the rails at the companionway head till Mostyn had finished. Yes, finished crying. Incredible, really. He knew what was coming to him, God knows how; and it wasn't a dry hunch, it was something very moving, meant a lot to him somehow. And by

God he'd gone looking for it, Mostyn had. He had his own ideas about fighting. Didn't believe in right and left boundaries, fronts, flanks, rears. He had the guerrilla platoon under his command and they went off into the blue the night before the pukka battle with a roving commission to make a diversion in the Jap rear. That was all. He'd gone off at dusk as casually as if they were on training. No funny business about Death then. He knew it had come, so he wasn't worrying. Life must have been more interesting to Mostyn than it was to himself, being made that way, having those thoughts and things. What he'd seen of Death that day, it was just a bloody beastly filthy horrible business, so forget it.

His hands were long and thin and elegant as his body and his elongated narrow head with the Roman nose and the eyes whose colour nobody could have stated because nobody could stare back at him. His hands crumpled the sheet he was clutching. He was in a way a very fastidious man. He would have had exquisite taste if he hadn't lacked the faculty of taste.

'Messing up your new sheets again,' Sister Normanby said happily, coming into the room like a drop of Scotch. 'You ought to be playing the piano with those hands of yours, you know.'

He didn't remind her that he only had one had left. He was pleased to think she didn't notice it.

'Hallo, Sister,' he said, bucking up at once. 'You're looking very young and fresh considering it was your night out last night.'

'I took it very quietly,' she said. 'Didn't dance much. Sat in the back of a car all the time.'

'For shame, my dear Celia,' Moncrieff butted in. 'Men are deceivers ever was said before the invention of the internal combustion engine and they're worse in every way since that happened.'

'What is my little monkey jabbering about now,' she replied, offended at his freedom with her Christian name.

'Have you heard of Gipsy Rose Lee?' Moncrieff replied inconsequentially. 'She has a song which says "I can't strip to Brahms! Can you?"'

''Course she can,' said Dad Withers, unobtrusive at the door, a wry old buck, 'so long as she's got a mosquito net, isn't it, Sister?'

'Why do you boys always make me feel I haven't got a skirt on when I come in here?' she said.

'Because you can't marry all of us,' said Dad.

'Deep, isn't he?' she said.

She had a bunch of newly cut antirrhinums and dahlias, the petals beaded with water, which she put into a bowl, arranging them quietly as she twitted the men. Moncrieff looked at her quizzically as though she had roused conjecture in the psychoanalytical department of his brain.

'Get on with your letter writing, Moncrieff,' she said without having looked up. He flushed.

'There's such a thing as knowing too much,' Dad said to her paternally. 'I knew a girl in Singapore once, moved there from Shanghai wiv the regiment, she did. She liked us all, the same as nurses say they do. And when she found she liked one more than all the others put together, it come as a terrible shock to her and she had to start again. Took some doing, it did.'

'Dad, you're crazy,' she said, laughing hard. 'A man with all your complaints ought to be too busy counting them to tell all these stories.' And then, as she was about to go, she turned and dropped the momentous news she'd been holding out to them.

'You're all four having your medical board next Thursday,' she said. 'So you'd better make yourselves ill again if you want to go back home.'

'I don't want to go back "home",' Brownlow-Grace said, laying sardonic stress on the last word.

'I don't know,' Dad said. 'They tell me it's a good country to get into, this 'ere England. Why, I was only reading in the

Bombay Times this morning there's a man, Beaverage or something, made a report, they even give you money to bury yourself with there now. Suits me.'

'You won't die, Dad,' Brownlow-Grace said kindly. 'You'll simply fade away.'

'Well,' said Sister Normanby. 'There are your fresh flowers, must go and help to remove a clot from a man's brain now. Goodbye.'

'Goodbye,' they all said, following her calves and swift heels as she went.

'I didn't know a dog had sweat glands in his paws before,' Brownlow-Grace said, looking at his copy of *The Field*.

The others didn't answer. They were thinking of their medical board. It was more interesting really than Sister Normanby.

III

Weston preferred to spend the earlier hours in a deck chair in the garden, by the upraised circular stone pool, among the ferns; here he would watch the lizards run like quicksilver and as quickly freeze into an immobility so lifeless as to be macabre, and the striped rats playing among the jacaranda branches; and he would look in vain for the mocking bird whose monotony gave a timeless quality to the place and the mood. He was slow in recovering his strength; his three operations and the sulphanilamide tablets he was taking had exhausted the blood in his veins; most of it was somebody else's blood, anyway, an insipid blood that for two days had dripped from a bottle suspended over his bed, while they waited for him to die. His jaw and shoulder-bone had been shattered, a great clod of flesh torn out of his neck and thigh, baring his windpipe and epiglottis and exposing his lung and femoral artery; and although he had recovered very rapidly, his living self seemed overshadowed by the death trauma through which he had passed. There had been an

425

annihilation, a complete obscuring; into which light had gradually dawned. And this light grew unbearably white, the glare of the sun on a vast expanse of snow, and in its unbounded voids he had moved without identity, a pillar of salt in a white desert as pocked and cratered as the dead face of the moon. And then some mutation had taken place and he became aware of pain. A pain that was not pure like the primal purity, but polluted, infected, with racking thirsts and suffocations and writhings, and black eruptions disturbed the whiteness, and coloured dots sifted the intense sun glare, areas of intolerable activities appeared in those passive and limitless oceans. And gradually these manifestations became the simple suppurations of his destroyed inarticulate flesh, and the bandaging and swabbing and probing of his wounds and the grunts of his throat. From it he desired wildly to return to the timeless void where the act of being was no more than a fall of snow or the throw of a rainbow; and these regions became a nostalgia to his pain and soothed his hurt and parched spirit. The two succeeding operations had been conscious experiences, and he had been frightened of them. The preliminaries got on his nerves, the starving, the aperients, the trolley, the prick of morphia, and its false peace. The spotless theatre with its walls of glass and massive lamps of burnished chrome, the anaesthetist who stuttered like a worn gramophone record, Sister Normanby clattering the knives in trays of Lysol, the soft irresistible waves of wool that surged up darkly through the interstices of life like water through a boat; and the choking final surrender to the void his heart feared.

And now, two and a half months later, with his wounds mere puckers dribbling the last dregs of pus, his jaw no longer wired up and splinted, his arm no longer inflamed with the jab of the needle, he sat in the garden with his hands idle in a pool of sunlight, fretting and fretting at himself. He was costive, his stockings had holes in the heel that got wider every day and he hadn't the initiative to ask Sister for a needle and wool; his pen had no ink, his razor blade was blunt, he had shaved badly, he hadn't replied to the airmail letter that lay crumpled in his hand. He had carried that letter about with him for four days, everywhere he went, ever since he'd received it.

'You look thrillingly pale and Byronic this morning, Weston,' Moncrieff said, sitting in the deck chair opposite him with his writing pad and a sheaf of received letters tied in silk tape. 'D'you mind me sharing your gloom?'

Weston snorted.

'You can do what you bloody well like,' he said, with suppressed irritation.

'Oh dear, have I gone and hurt you again? I'm always hurting people I like,' Moncrieff said. 'But I can't help it. Honestly I can't. You believe me, Weston, don't you?'

Disturbed by the sudden nakedness of his voice Weston looked up at the waspish, intense face, the dark eyebrows and malignant eyes.

'Of course I believe you, monkey,' he said. 'If you say so.'

'It's important that you should believe me,' Moncrieff said moodily. 'I must find somebody who believes me wherever I happen to be. I'm afraid otherwise. It's too lonely. Of course I hurt some people purposely. That dolt Brownlow-Grace for example. I enjoy making him wince. He's been brought up to think life should be considerate to him. His mother, his bank manager, his batman, his bearer – always somebody to mollycoddle him and see to his wants. Christ, the fellow's incapable of wanting anything really. You know he even resents Sister Normanby having to look after other people beside himself. He only considered the war as an opportunity for promotion; I bet he was delighted when Hitler attacked Poland. And there are other people in this world going about with their brains hanging out, their minds half lynched – a fat lot he understands.' He paused, and seeming to catch himself in the middle of his tirade, he laughed softly, 'I was going to write a lettercard to my wife,' he said. 'Still, I haven't got any news. No new love. Next Thursday we'll have some news for them, won't we? I get terribly worked up about this medical board, I can't sleep. You don't think they'll keep me out in India, Weston, do you? It's so lonely out here. I couldn't stay here any longer. I just couldn't. '

'You are in a state, monkey,' Weston said, perturbed and yet laughing, as one cheers a child badly injured. 'Sit quiet a bit, you're speaking loudly. Brownlow'll hear you if you don't take care.'

'Did he?' Moncrieff said, suddenly apprehensive. 'He didn't hear me, did he? I don't want to sound as crude as that, even to him.'

'Oh, I don't know. He's not a bad stick,' Weston said. 'He's very sincere and he takes things in good part, even losing his arm, and his career.'

'Oh, I know you can preach a sermon on him easily. I don't think in terms of sermons, that's all,' Moncrieff said. 'But I've been through Burma the same as he has. Why does he sneer at me?' He was silent. Then he said again, 'It's lonely out here.' He sighed. 'I wish I hadn't come out of Burma. I needn't have, I could have let myself go. One night when my leg was gangrenous, the orderly gave me a shot of morphia and I felt myself nodding and smiling. And there was no more jungle, no Japs, no screams, no difficulties at home, no nothing. The orderly would have given me a second shot if I'd asked him. I don't know why I didn't. It would have finished me off nicely. Say, Weston, have you ever been afraid of death?'

'I don't think it's as simple as that,' Weston said. 'When I was as good as dead, the first three days here, and for a fortnight afterwards too, I was almost enamoured of death. I'd lost my fear of it. But then I'd lost my will, and my emotions were all dead. I hadn't got any relationships left. It isn't really fair then, is it?'

'I think it is better to fear death,' Moncrieff said slowly. 'Otherwise you grow spiritually proud. With most people it's not so much the fear of death as love of life that keeps them sensible. I don't love life, personally. Only I'm a bit of a coward and I don't want to die again. I loathe Burma, I can't tell you how terribly. I hope they send me home. If you go home, you ought to tell them you got wounded in Burma, you know.'

'Good God, no,' Weston said, outraged. 'Why should I lie?'

'That's all they deserve,' Moncrieff said. 'I wonder what they're doing there now? Talking about reconstruction, I suppose. Even the cinemas will have reconstruction films. Well, maybe I'll get a job in some racket or other. Cramming Sandhurst cadets or something. What will you do when you get home?'

'Moncrieff, my good friend,' Weston said. 'We're soldiers, you know. And it isn't etiquette to talk about going home like that. I'm going in where you left off. I want to have a look at Burma. *And I don't want to see England.*'

'Don't you?' Moncrieff said, ignoring the slow emphasis of Weston's last words and twirling the tassel of his writing-pad slowly. 'Neither do I, very much,' he said with an indifference that ended the conversation.

IV

The sick have their own slightly different world, their jokes are as necessary and peculiar to them as their medicines; they can't afford to be morbid like the healthy, nor to be indifferent to their environment like the Arab. The outside world has been washed out; between them and the encircling mysteries there is only the spotlight of their obsessions holding the small backcloth of ward and garden before them. Anyone appearing before this backcloth has the heightened emphasis and significance of a character upon the stage. The Sikh fortune tellers who offered them promotion and a fortune and England as sibilantly as panders, the mongoose-fight-snake wallahs with their wailing sweet pipes and devitalised cobras, the little native cobblers and peddlers who had customary right to enter the precincts entered as travellers from an unknown land. So did the visitors from the Anglo-India community and brother officers on leave. And each visitor was greedily absorbed and examined by every patient, with the intenser acumen of disease.

Brownlow-Grace had a visitor. This increased his prestige like having a lot of mail. It appeared she had only just discovered he was here, for during the last four days before his medical board she came every day after lunch and stayed sitting on his bed until dusk and conferred upon them an intimacy that evoked in the others a green nostalgia.

She was by any standards a beautiful woman. One afternoon a young unsophisticated English Miss in a fresh little frock and long hair; the next day French and exotic with the pallor of an undertaker's lily and hair like statuary; the third day exquisitely Japanese, carmined and beringed with huge green amber stones, her hair in a high bun that only a great lover would dare unloose. When she left each evening Sister Normanby came in with a great bustle of fresh air and practicality to tidy his bed and put up his mosquito net. And he seemed equally capable of entertaining and being entertained by both ladies.

On the morning of the medical board Brownlow-Grace came and sat by Anthony among the ferns beside the lily pool; and this being a gesture of unusual amiability in one whom training had made rigid, Weston was unreasonably pleased.

'Well, Weston,' he said. 'Sweating on the top line over this medical board?'

'What d'you mean?' Weston asked.

'Well, do you think everything's a wangle to get you home or keep you here like that little squirt Moncrieff?'

'I don't think along those lines, personally,' Weston said. He looked at the long languid officer sprawled in the deck chair. 'The only thing I'm frightened of is that they'll keep

me here, or give me some horrible office job where I'll never
see a Valentine lift her belly over a bund and go grunting like
a wild boar at – well, whoever happens to be there. I got used
to the idea of the Germans. I suppose the Japs will do.'

'You're like me; no enemy,' Brownlow-Grace said. 'I didn't
think twice about it – till it happened. You're lucky, though.
You're the only one of us four who'll ever see action. I could
kill some more. What do I want to go home for? They
hacked my arm off, those bastards; I blew the fellow's guts
out that did it, had the muzzle of my Colt rammed into his
belly, I could feel his breath, he was like a frog, the swine.
You, I suppose you want to go home, haven't been away
long, have you?'

'Six months.'

'Six months without a woman, eh?' Brownlow-Grace
laughed, yet kindly.

'Yes.'

'I'm the sort who'll take somebody else's,' Brownlow-
Grace said. 'I don't harm them.'

Weston didn't reply.

'You've got a hell of a lot on your mind, haven't you,
Weston? Any fool can see something's eating you up.' Still
no reply. 'Look here, I may be a fool, but come out with me
tonight, let's have a party together. Eh?'

Surprisingly, Weston wasn't embarrassed at this extreme
gesture of kindness. It was so ingenuously made. Instead he
felt an enormous relief, and for the first time the capacity to
speak. Not, he told himself, to ask for advice. Brownlow-
Grace wasn't a clergyman with a healing gift; but it was
possible to tell him the thing simply, to shift the weight of it
a bit. 'I'm all tied up,' he said. 'A party wouldn't be any use,
nor a woman.'

'Wouldn't it?' Brownlow-Grace said drily, standing up.
Weston had a feeling he was about to go. It would have
excruciated him. Instead he half turned, as if to disembarrass
him, and said, 'The flowers want watering.'

431

'You know, if you're soldiering, there are some things you've got to put out of bounds to your thoughts,' Weston said. 'Some things you don't let yourself doubt.'

'Your wife, you mean?' Brownlow-Grace said, holding a breath of his cigarette in his lungs and studying the ants on the wall.

'Not only her,' Weston said. 'Look. I didn't start with the same things as you. You had a pram and a private school and saw the sea, maybe. My father was a collier and he worked in a pit. He got rheumatism and nystagmus and then the dole and the parish relief. I'm not telling you a sob story. It's just I was used to different sounds. I used to watch the wheel of the pit spin round year after year, after school and Saturdays and Sundays; and then from 1926 on I watched it not turning round at all, and I can't ever get that wheel out of my mind. It still spins and idles, and there's money and nystagmus coming into the house or no work and worse than nystagmus. I just missed the wheel sucking me down the shaft. I got a scholarship to the county school. I don't know when I started rebelling. Against that wheel in my head. I didn't get along very well. Worked in a grocer's and a printer's, and no job was good enough for me; I had a bug. Plenty of friends too, plenty of chaps thinking the same as me. Used to read books in those days, get passionate about politics, Russia was like a woman to me. Then I did get a job I wanted, in a bookshop in Holborn. A French woman came in one day. I usually talked to customers, mostly politics; but not to her. She came in several times, once with a trade union man I knew. She was short, she had freckles, a straight nose, chestnut hair, she looked about eighteen; she bought books about Beethoven, Schopenhauer, the Renaissance, biology – I read every book she bought, after she'd gone back to France. I asked this chap about her. He said she was a big name, you know the way revolutionary movements toss up a woman sometimes. She was a communist, big speaker in the industrial towns in north France, she'd been to Russia too. And, well, I just wanted her, more and more and more as the months passed. Not her politics, but her fire. If I could hear her addressing a crowd, never mind about wanting her in those dreams you get.

'And then the war came and most of my friends said it was a phoney war, but I was afraid from the beginning that something would happen to France and I wanted to hear her speaking first. I joined up in November and I made myself such a bloody pest that they posted me to France to reinforcements. I got my war all right. And I met her, too. The trade unionist I told you about gave me a letter to introduce myself. She lived in Lille. She knew me as soon the door opened. And I was just frightened. But after two nights there was no need to be frightened. You get to think for years that life is just a fight, with a flirt thrown in sometimes, a flirt with death or sex or whatever happens to be passing, but mostly a fight all the way along. And then you soften up, you're no use, you haven't got any wheel whirring in your head any more. Only flowers on the table and a piano she plays sometimes, when she wants to, when she wants to love.'

'I've never been to France,' Brownlow-Grace said. 'Hated it at school, French I mean. Communists, of course – I thought they were all Bolshies, you know, won't obey an order. What happened after Dunkirk?'

'It was such burning sunny weather,' Weston said. 'It was funny, having fine weather. I couldn't get her out of my mind. The sun seemed to expand inside the lining of my brain and the whole fortnight after we made that last stand with Martel at Cambrai I didn't know whether I was looking for her or Dunkirk. When I was most exhausted it was worse; she came to me once by the side of the road; there were several dead Belgian women lying there, and she said "Look, Anthony, I have been raped. They raped me, the Bosche." And the world was crashing and whirring, or it was doped, wouldn't lift a finger to stop it, and the Germans crossing the Seine. A year before I'd have said to the world, "Serve you right". But not now, with Cecile somewhere inside the armies. She'd tried.'

'And that was the end?' Brownlow-Grace said.

'Yes,' said Weston. 'Just about. Only it wasn't a beautiful end, the way it turned out. I had eight months in England, and I never found out a thing. The Free French didn't know. One of them knew her well, knew her as a lover, he told me; boasted about it; I didn't tell him; I wanted to find her, I didn't care about anything else. And then something started in me. I used to mooch about London. A French girl touched me on the street one night. I went with her. I went with a lot of women. Then we embarked for overseas. I had a girl at Durban, and in Bombay: sometimes they were French, if possible they were French. God, it was foul.'

He got up and sat on the edge of the pool; under the green strata of mosses the scaled goldfish moved slowly in their palaces of burning gold. He wiped his face which was sweating.

'Five days ago I got this letter from America,' he said. 'From her.'

Brownlow-Grace said, 'That was a bit of luck.' Weston laughed.

'Yes,' he said. 'Yes. It was nice of her to write. She put it very nicely, too. Would you like to read it?'

'No,' said Brownlow-Grace. 'I don't want to read it.'

'She said it often entered her mind to write to me, because I had been so sweet to her, in Lille, that time. She hoped I was well. To enter America there had been certain formalities, she said; she'd married an American, a country which has all types, she said. There is a life, she said, but not mine, and a war also, but not mine. Now it is the Japanese. That's all she said.'

'She remembered you,' Brownlow-Grace said.

'Some things stick in a woman's mind,' Weston said. 'She darned my socks for me in bed. Why didn't she say she remembered darning my socks?'

Brownlow-Grace pressed his hand, fingers extended, upon the surface of the water, not breaking its resistance, quite.

'I don't use the word,' he said. 'But I guess it's because she loved you.'

Weston looked up, searching and somehow naïve.

'I don't mind about the Japanese,' he said, 'if that were so.'

V

Dad Withers had his medical board first; he wasn't in the board room long; in fact he was back on the verandah outside 'O' 3 (b) when Weston returned from sending a cable at the camp post office.

'Did it go all right, Dad?' Weston asked.

'Sure, sure,' Dad said, purring as if at his own cleverness. 'Three colonels and two majors there, and the full colonel he said to me, "Well, Withers, what's your trouble? Lieutenant Quartermaster weren't you?" And I said, "Correct, sir, and now I'm putting my own body in for exchange, sir. It don't keep the rain out no more, sir." So he said, "You're not much use to us, Withers, by the look of you." And I said, "Not a bit of use, sir, sorry to report." And the end of it was they give me a free berth on the next ship home wiv full military honours and a disability pension and all. Good going, isn't it now?'

'Very good, Dad. I'm very pleased.'

'Thank you,' Dad said, his face wrinkled and benign as a tortoise. 'Now go and get your own ticket and don't keep the gentlemen waiting...'

Dad lay half asleep in the deck chair, thinking that it was all buttoned up now, all laid on, all made good. It had been a long time, a lifetime, more than twenty hot seasons, more than twenty rains. Not many could say that. Not many had stuck it like him. Five years in Jhansi with his body red as lobster from head to toe with prickly heat, squirting a water pistol down his back for enjoyment and scratching his

435

shoulders with a long fork from the bazaar. Two big wars there'd been, and most of the boys had been glad to go into them, excited to be posted to France, or embark for Egypt. But he'd stuck it out. Still here, still good for a game of nap, and them all dead, the boys that wanted to get away. And now it was finished with him, too.

He didn't know. Maybe he wasn't going home the way he'd figured it out after all. Maybe there was something else, something he hadn't counted in. This tiredness, this emptiness, this grey blank wall of mist, this not caring. What would it be like in the small council house with five youngsters and his missus? She'd changed a lot, the last photo she sent she was like his mother, spectacles and fat legs, full of plainness. Maybe the kids would play with him, though, the two young ones?

He pulled himself slowly out of his seat, took out his wallet, counted his money; ninety chips he had. Enough to see India just once again. Poor old India. He dressed hurriedly, combed his thin hair, wiped his spectacles, dusted his shoes and left before the others came back. He picked up a tonga at the stand outside the main gates of the hospital cantonment, just past the MD lines, and named a certain hotel down town. And off he cantered, the skinny old horse clattering and letting off great puffs of bad air under the tonga wallah's whip, and Dad shouting, 'Jillo, jillo,' impatient to be drunk.

Brownlow-Grace came in and went straight to the little bed table where he kept his papers in an untidy heap. He went there in a leisurely way, avoiding the inquiring silences of Weston and Moncrieff and Sister Normanby, who were all apparently doing something. He fished out an airgraph form and his fountain pen and sat quietly on the edge of his bed.

'Oh damn and blast it,' he said angrily. 'My pen's dry.'

Weston gave him an inkbottle.

He sat down again.

'What's the date?' he said after a minute.

'12th,' Moncrieff said.

'What month?' he asked.

'December.'

'Thanks.'

He wrote slowly, laboriously, long pauses between sentences. When he finished he put his pen away and looked for a stamp.

'What stamp d'you put on an airgraph?' he said.

'Three annas,' Moncrieff said patiently.

Sister Normanby decided to abolish the embarrassing reticence with which this odd man was concealing his board result. She had no room for broody hens.

'Well,' she said, gently enough. 'What happened at the board?'

He looked up at her and neither smiled nor showed any sign of recognition. Then he stood up, took his cane and peaked service cap, and brushed a speck of down off his long and well-fitting trousers.

'They discharged me,' he said. 'Will you post this airgraph for me, please?'

'Yes,' she said, and for some odd reason she found herself unable to deal with the situation and took it from him and went on with her work.

'I'm going out,' he said.

Weston followed him into the garden and caught him up by the lily pool.

'Is that invitation still open?' he asked.

'What invitation?' Brownlow-Grace said.

'To go on the spree with you tonight?' Weston said.

Brownlow-Grace looked at him thoughtfully.

'I've changed my mind, Anthony,' he said – Weston was pleasurably aware of this first use of his Christian name – 'I don't think I'd be any use to you tonight. Matter of fact, I phoned Rita just now, you know the woman who comes to see me, and she's calling for me in five minutes.'

'I see,' Weston said. 'OK by me.'

'You don't mind, do you?' he said. 'I don't think you need Rita's company, do you? Besides, she usually prefers one man at a time. She's the widow of a friend of mine, Mostyn Turner; he was killed in Burma, too.'

Weston came back into the ward to meet Sister Normanby's white face. 'Where's he gone?' she said.

Weston looked at her, surprised at the emotion and stress this normally imperturbable woman was showing.

He didn't answer her.

'He's gone to that woman,' she said, white and virulent.

'Hasn't he?'

'Yes, he has,' he said quietly.

'She always has them when they're convalescent,' she said, flashing with venom. She picked up her medicine book and the jar with her thermometer in it. 'I have them when they're sick.'

She left the ward, biting her white lips.

'I didn't know she felt that way about him,' Weston said.

'Neither did she,' said Moncrieff. 'She never knows till it's too late. That's the beauty about her. She's virginal.'

'You're very cruel, Moncrieff.'

Moncrieff turned on him like an animal.

'Cruel?' he said. 'Cruel? Well, I don't lick Lazarus' sores, Weston. I take the world the way it is. Nobody cares about you out here. Nobody. What have I done to anybody? Why should they keep me here? What's the use of keeping a man with infantile paralysis and six inches of bone missing from his leg? Why didn't the board let me go home?'

'You'll go home, monkey, you'll go home,' Weston said gently. 'You know the Army. You can help them out here. You're bound to go home, when the war ends.'

'Do you think so?' Moncrieff said. 'Do you?' He thought of this for a minute at least. Then he said, 'No, I shall never go home, I know it.'

'Don't be silly, monkey. You're a bit run down, that's all.'

Weston soothed him. 'Let's go and sit by the pool for a while.'

'I like the pool,' Moncrieff said. They strolled out together and sat on the circular ledge. The curving bright branches held their leaves peacefully above the water.

Under the mosses they could see the old toad of the pond sleeping, his back rusty with jewels. Weston put his hand in the water; minnows rose in small flocks and nibbled at his fingers. Circles of water lapped softly outwards, outwards, till they touched the edge of the pool, and cast a gentle wetness on the stone, and lapped again inwards, inwards. And as they lapped inwards he felt the ripples surging against the most withdrawn and inmost ledges of his being, like a series of temptations in the wilderness. And he felt glad tonight, feeling some small salient gained when for many reasons the men whom he was with were losing ground among the whole front to the darkness that there is.

'No,' said Moncrieff at last. 'Talking is no good. But perhaps you will write to me sometimes, will you, just to let me know.'

'Yes, I'll write to you, monkey,' Weston said, looking up.

And then he looked away again, not willing to consider those empty, inarticulate eyes.

'The mosquitoes are starting to bite,' he said. 'We'd better go now.'

MRS ARMITAGE

Emyr Humphreys

I

'This unfortunate woman' was the phrase that tapped away in the Rector's brain as he listened to Mrs Armitage's high-pitched yet well-controlled voice speaking fluent and idiomatic English with an accent that remained obstinately German. She sometimes spoke of her *schloss* in Kärnten, but the only dwelling he had known her to have was the two rooms of the Charitable Institution, bluntly in Welsh Yr Elusendy (the almshouse) but in English *The Endowment for Decayed Gentlewomen* of which he, all honour and worry to him, was Secretary. It added one hundred pounds a year to his stipend and involved little administrative work. The main task was to listen sympathetically to the endless complaints of six or seven difficult and discontented old women.

'It is not that I am afraid of dying, Mr Mayrick. It's just that I dislike the idea of my body lying in one of those two rooms for days on end without anyone knowing.' Her voice, like her large eyes, still had vitality and power, but the rest of her seemed the work of a tipsy taxidermist: her long legs bent in an untidy bow, her back hunched, and her large well-powdered face suspended above her trunk, sometimes trembled slightly as if about to fall off. It was a remnant of personal dignity, not bodily strength, that still gave her power over her movements. 'Will you please take this duplicate key of my door? I've attached a label with my name and number, in case the key gets mixed up with others.'

Nodding wisely, but with a spasm of inward discomfort, the Rector accepted the key and dropped it into one of the drawers of his large untidy desk. No doubt his wife had told the old girl more than once that he was untidy. It was rather unfair of Meg really. This old Austrian was a difficult case. She attended service regularly, English or Welsh (unlike Miss Hoxham who never saw the need for a Welsh service since she didn't know the language herself). In fact, she did not complain half as much as the other inmates. But when she did complain she did so with such precision, usually suggesting a reasonable seeming remedy, which was uncomfortable, because whatever you did in that place, it always led to more trouble.

There could be no doubt about it that she was most unpopular among her neighbours at the institution. Some of them hated her with astonishing violence. Miss Hoxham, for example, saying, all out of her picture-book-little-old-lady-lace-bonnet appearance: 'I tell you, Mr Mayrick, it would be no crime to stick a knife into that black foreign heart.' That had really shaken him. In fact, he had never got over it and it had made him think seriously of seeking a new living. The Bishop had no idea of what he had to put up with. A living in a Depressed Area in the South would in many ways be preferable.

Most of the old women were jealous because 'the Austrian witch' was so friendly with his wife. That was the source of more than half the trouble. Meg had spent three months in the Tyrol in her undergraduate days and knew, or fancied she knew, German. She could never hear enough of the old girl's stories of foreign royalty, especially the Hapsburgs, which was odd really, because, before the war, with his wholehearted approval, of course, Meg had belonged to the Left Book Club in the most enthusiastic way. The old Bishop had been rather annoyed about Meg's politics in those days. But there we are, imaginative people are not expected to be consistent.

'I know I am asking too much of you, Mr Mayrick.' He wondered anxiously what was coming next. (She always gave you time to wonder but never time to escape.) 'But you and your dear wife had shown me so much Christian kindness, I dare to ask for a little more.'

'We have done nothing at all, Mrs Armitage, I assure you...' His pipe went out and he stopped talking, trying to light it again and glad not to have to finish the sentence.

'It is time I made my will, Mr Mayrick. May I ask you to draw it up for me?'

'I could try, Mrs Armitage,' he smiled nervously.

'Your wife told me how you help poor people sometimes in this way.' (Confound Meg's easy tongue.) 'My will is really very small. I have nothing except my bits of furniture and a few things of sentimental value. Hardly any money at all. Nothing more. But what I have I should like to bequeath to your wife.'

The third match burnt his finger before he shook it out. She was quite the most difficult of his parishioners. It was so embarrassing, what on earth could he say?

'Well, Mrs Armitage, I really don't know what to say... that is... well... it is difficult, you know... to advise you for the best. It's extremely kind of you, of course... very kind indeed... but I don't really think, well to be perfectly frank with you it would be, well... rather improper of me to draw up such a will, much as I want to help you, all I can, of course, all I can...'

After all, after leaving her things to his wife, wouldn't she have some kind of a claim on them? That was a difficult point really. The Rector came of a family of Cardiganshire hill farmers who took property seriously. Property was like life itself, infinitely desirable and yet involving endless obligations. She might even try to move into the Rectory, so many empty rooms. That was really intolerable! Meg had enough work to do. And how could he get on with his work if his peace of mind was disturbed? Was that perhaps what she was after? She was always longing to get away from the institution.

'There is no one else. I have no one. She has been kind to me. She is interested in Austria. It would please her to have them. I don't want those vandals and harpies at the institution to get at my things. I know how they would enjoy stepping over my dead body and smashing up my room.'

'Really, Mrs Armitage!'

'I am sorry, Mr Mayrick. But you see, I am a realist. I know how terrible old women can be. After all, I am one myself.'

There was such sudden charm in her smile, such gracious calm, how could he but smile back, even though he had not the slightest desire to do so.

'And my wife, Mrs Armitage...?'

'She knows nothing about my little scheme. She is so charming, Mr Mayrick, so innocent if that is the right word. Innocent in a special way, a Welsh way. And yet a way all her own too. Her face can light up with pleasure like a child's. You are a very fortunate man.'

At this point, after a light knock on the door, Mrs Mayrick came in, a shopping basket on her arm, breathless and smiling. Usually her girlishness (after all she was thirty-eight) tended to irritate Mr Mayrick; but at this moment her presence warmed and excited him, and almost against his will, under the spell of the old woman's words, he saw her as Primavera in a raincoat, a visitation on the threshold of his so familiar room.

'How nice to see you, Mrs Armitage! Now you must stay to tea. I won't be a minute. Pop on the electric kettle. You won't mind having it with us in the kitchen? It's Elsie's day off, you know. Cosy cup of tea and a chat. I'll knock the wall when it's ready, Hywel.'

Out she went, leaving him alone with Mrs Armitage again, and even more uncertain what to say next. As he lit his pipe he allowed himself to wonder for a second time, what exactly Mrs A. (as he and Meg usually called her) *had* got to leave. This annoyed him by making him feel guilt for something he hadn't even contemplated doing. He was also feeling cross with her for disturbing tea-in-the-kitchen a meal he always enjoyed having alone with Meg.

Mrs Armitage's silence, too, was becoming extremely annoying; sitting on the edge of one of his armchairs like a living reproach. That so talkative a person should find it easier to remain silent now than he did, seemed to reflect against his character. All his life he had prided himself on his ability to keep his mouth shut, among people given to speaking first and thinking afterwards. Would it be too rude for him to get up and ask her to excuse him? There were some raspberries he knew of unpicked in a corner of the garden. And he could think much more clearly when left alone.

'Do you think' – she had struggled out of the chair and was hobbling towards the door – 'I could help your dear wife?' The door open, she called down the corridor: 'Mrs Mayrick, may I come along and help? I do so enjoy cutting bread and butter.'

The muffled answer was some kind of acceptance. The Rector was left alone with his thought and his pipe. He heaved an agreeable sigh, picked up the *Manchester Guardian* and tried to forget her.

After all, the unfortunate woman was not nearly so interesting and exceptional as Meg chose to believe. All over Europe there were thousands of broken-down aristocrats, flotsam left behind by the ebb-tide of an epoch. (Put that somewhere in sermon. Need for sympathy, toleration, broadview, etc.) It was also part of the rough justice of history. (Not so easy to fit into an acceptable sermon.) She was just much luckier than the rest, married to an

Englishman. An improvident and reckless type no doubt, the late Mr Armitage, something of an adventurer; but nevertheless an Englishman, partaker of rights and privileges; *civis Romanus sum*, bestowed by marriage also on this alien woman.

She was also fortunate to have found refuge in the institution. It was neat and clean there. She had a wireless. There was a view of the mountains and of the sea. Her two rooms were self-contained. There was an extensive garden and orchard for the use of all the inmates equally. Well away from the road, very, very quiet. Wonderful spot really. It really was time he stopped calling her an unfortunate woman.

A knock on the wall summoned him to his tea. As he feared they were already lost in some cloud cuckoo land of the kind that most annoyed him. A dream of the Continent that implied that Cardiganshire and the place of his birth were both dreary and barbarous, outside the pale. The Rector was deeply attached to his birthplace and therefore this kind of talk was not merely uncongenial, but wounding.

'Well, that summer, I was only sixteen at the time – the Emperor spent a week at the *schloss*. He asked especially for Lisa. You wouldn't believe it but I was considered good looking and good company in those days. I had to accompany him on the most unexpected excursions. Fishing, walking, boating on the Ossiachersee, visiting one of the elementary schools and opening a new road...'

Living in the past. Fifty years ago, nearer sixty. It annoyed him. Spoiling his tea with the Emperor story again. Vienna Woods next. Old Splendour. If he'd heard that tale once... and Meg had heard it even oftener... and there she was listening, enchanted. Puerile romanticism, that's what it was. This unfortunate woman was forever hymning the glories of her foreign past, or bemoaning the discomforts and miseries of her present. Everything was wonderful fifty years ago, everything was better, especially in Austria. Should he bother to argue? Ask her about the peasants, how they fared, and the non-German nationalities? And the hill farmers, leading their hard and virtuous lives? She was impossible to argue with. She would just wear you down. No possibility of changing her mind. She'd been brought up a Roman Catholic of course; no idea that there were two sides to every question. Best to keep quiet and think of something else.

'But here I am, living on charity in dear little Wales and boring your poor husband to tears. You really shouldn't encourage me, Mrs Mayrick.'

'Oh, but not at all.' The Rector smiled stiffly.

'You mustn't notice Hywel, Mrs Armitage. The poor dear always looks bored, even when he's reading the *Manchester Guardian* cricket reports. And that's about the most exciting thing, apart from rugby football, isn't it, dear?'

Meg was inclined to go too far in front of strangers.

'Do you know, dear Mrs Mayrick, I sometimes have the most weird feeling as if I were making it all up, as if people don't really believe that it all happened, that such a world ever existed, that I ever belonged to it. I feel now as if all my life, all my years, and I've got so many of them, had been spent in the institution. And yet I've known how wonderful it can be just to be alive – skiing when the air is so cold and still the movement of your body seems to cleave the air. But who would believe an old wreck like me had even seen skis, let alone been on them.'

'You ought to write,' Mrs Mayrick said impulsively, as if hit by a great idea for the first time. The Rector had heard her say it at least twice before. 'Write your memoirs, Mrs Armitage.'

It was an astonishing fact to realise, that for the moment neither of them was conscious of having been through the whole conversation on several previous occasions – and in his presence. Even that bit about the air being so still. Really the capabilities of the female mind for self-delusion! Now she was saying she would have to write in German and that her German was by now rusty and bad, almost as bad as her French. No doubt it was true that when talking about their favourite subjects people never noticed how often they repeated themselves. While he was wondering whether he could decently get away, to his great relief, the old woman began to say it was time for her to go.

'Not that I have any pressing engagements.' Her head trembled humorously. 'But it is time I relieved you of my presence. You have been too kind as it is.'

He was, he felt, as he genially followed them to the front door, being let off unusually lightly. He hadn't had to listen to her usual tale of woe about the institution. But wait a moment, what were they whispering about so animatedly outside the front door?

'Hywel!' Now what was it?

'Has that cottage at the end of the lower village been let, do you know?'

Confound Megan, encouraging the woman! 'Not yet, but it soon will be.'

'Do you think Mrs Armitage could apply? How could you help her, Hywel?'

They misunderstood his silence, assuming he was thinking of ways and means. Actually he was attempting to suppress his rage.

'It would be so wonderful,' there was a false-blissful continental note in her voice that deeply invoked him: her eyes turned shakily heavenwards; at her age, he thought, it was clearly immoral, 'to be left in peace. Those terrible caretaker's children and Miss Hoxham and Miss Whitely have been really terrible this week.' Then she put a crooked finger to her mouth, and smiled, a grotesque caricature of a girlish smile. 'But I swore to myself I wouldn't complain this time, and I'm not going to.'

'My dear Mrs Armitage,' the Rector burst out so loudly that both women were quite startled, 'it would be very wrong of me to raise your hopes. There is absolutely no prospect of your getting that cottage. There are at least six *families* competing for it. I sympathise greatly with your position, I really do, but the housing position in general being what it is, you cannot hope to obtain a cottage or a small house for rent. It's very hard I know, but—'

'Hywel, dear! Hywel! Please don't get so excited. We were only wondering and hoping. Mrs Armitage, that knee of yours looks stiff again. Hywel, why don't you bring out the car and run Mrs Armitage down to the institution?'

'Of course, of course.'

'No! Please. I won't hear of it. It's very kind of you both, but I insist on walking. It will do me good. A beautiful evening. I am too much indoors. Sometimes I get afraid to venture in and out, I'm so silly. Goodbye, both of you. Goodbye.'

She was hobbling awkwardly down the drive, turning occasionally to wave.

'Shall I go after her?' Hywel asked doubtfully.

'She wants to walk, poor dear. And you want to get back to your paper. Mustn't leave the *Manchester Guardian* unfinished, darling.'

He wanted to say she was trying to make him feel small. And yet she was smiling sweetly enough. So instead, he drew on the store of his wisdom and resorted to his deepest Cardiganshire silence.

II

Mrs Armitage made her way up the narrow lane, leaning heavily upon her ebony stick, and breathing hard. It had been unwise of her to stay so long at the shoemaker's on her way home from the Rectory. She hated the institution so much, she had wanted to delay her return to the last moment, until after dark if possible so as not to see the great square prison of a building stuck down among weedy fields and straggling anaemic trees on the edge of the top village.

But the shoemaker was an amusing man and his eldest daughter was learning German at school and they always made her welcome. It was about the only place in the village, where she had something to give and could really be sure she wasn't a nuisance or a burden. At the shoemaker's they treated her – not like visiting royalty of course; no, better than that, like a fellow human being worthy of real respect. That was it.

But now struggling up the ominously silent lane, too weak to hurry, fear took a stronger grip on her than ever in her life before. There had been a time once on Triglav, seeking edelweiss, when feeling an effort to ascend the crevasse was beyond her strength and that death was waiting – forty years ago, why should she think of it now? – she had shivered with uncontrollable fright, but this was really far worse. This was an humiliating, cruel, beetle-crushing fear, that jeered at her and told her she was worth nothing, a parasite, a wasp, a filthy worthless fly, fit only to be exterminated. She felt too weak to disagree with the verdict; therefore at any moment the fatal blow would fall.

She heard a distinct titter. A moon-faced child with red eyes showed its unpleasant face over the top of the bank.

'Fancy face! Fancy face! Fancy face!' Oh God, they had started. Why couldn't she walk faster? Now they were in the gloomy lane behind her, jumping and jeering. 'Foreign spy, yah, wicked witch! Burn the witch! Yah! Yah! Burn the witch!'

Grasping the wooden handrail, panting, she felt she would never gather enough strength to drag herself up the stone stairs to the first floor where she lived. She didn't want to collapse on the stairs. God knows what they would do to her, what insults. She just had to get up and that was what she had to do, and she would do it and do it quickly and not kill herself, and put herself decently the other side of the locked door of her room.

How delectable the inside of that little room looked now,

her refuge. Yes, it was after all quite cosy. It was there. She could get to it. Not like the *schloss* which had gone forever out of her reach, dissolved into a dream. So far, far away. Somebody else's life. This was her life, this terrible struggle.

And at the top of the stairs, Miss Hoxham and Miss Whitely would be lurking, their little front doors ajar, ready to hear the clump of the struggling footsteps on the wooden stairs, cats waiting to pounce, to fix their claws in her. Couldn't she fight back? No. Her breeding was against her, kept her silent, infuriating them more, leaving her open, helpless, defenceless victim, inviting attack.

On the last step, the old woman dropped her stick and it went clattering down, to be retrieved by the enemy below with subdued yells of triumph. Here they dared not shout so loudly but their whispers came shooting up the stairs: 'Ah ha, old witch, we've got your stick! Ah ha, old witch, we've got your stick! We'll break your back with it! Come on, Fancy face, come down and get it.' Their worthless, whining parents knew very well they were at it. No doubt they were listening now or trying to make out the fun from behind the dirty lace curtains of their back window. Would she ever get that stick back, the Archduke's stick? Not now. Mr Mayrick perhaps could get it for her, if he wouldn't be too cross.

'What's all the noise?' Miss Whitely's voice grated like nutmeg on a scraper. 'Oh! It's you. Making trouble again, eh? It's time you cleared out of here. I'll report you. You're not entitled to be here anyway.'

Miss Hoxham's door opened. The pretty little old lady's voice hissed like a snake. 'I should say so too. No right at all. She should be behind bars, that's where she should be, put away. She's a spy. A German spy!'

'Report to the Chairman, right over Mr Mayrick's head, that's what I'll do.' Miss Whitely's harsh bass mingled freely with Miss Hoxham's bittersweet hiss. 'Thinks because she's friendly with the Rector's wife. Who's she anyway? There are those above him.'

'Quite a simple matter. All traitors should swing. She'd look good hanging up by the neck. She would... straighten her crooked back I don't doubt. No right here at all...'

Mrs Armitage stumbled blindly along to her own door.

'I've told the police about her. It's a public disgrace that we have to have her here.'

'She ought to swing and that's a fact.'

'The trouble she causes. This is a rest home for English gentlewomen of good birth, so what right I ask...'

Mrs Armitage fumbled desperately with the lock.

'Bolting like a rabbit into her hole without a word.'

'Thinks she's too good to speak to the likes of us.'

'They hang traitors, why shouldn't she swing...'

At last the door was closed. The relentless voices cut off. Some kind of peace attained. But her heart was hurting. Her whole body was in pain. She was worried about the precious walking stick the Archduke had given her. If she could light the paraffin stove, prepare herself a cup of coffee. Find a book to console her for the loss of the stick. Somehow get into bed. Read about the old times and forget all this. She would like to read poetry. Something to remind her of better days, old days, golden days. Something romantic to take away the bad taste. What were those charming poems that came out just before the first war, about the Slovene legend of the Chamois with the golden horns and about the snow roses – the red snow roses? The Archduke had given them to her for her birthday. Such a beautiful edition and such a special day, a special dedication: *To my dearest Liza, with a prayer for her happiness.*

It was on top of the glass cupboard wrapped in brown paper, a private treasure. On top of a chair she could reach it. Stretch a bit. Oh, where was her strength? She must have it, it would soothe her so. Those horrible people had reduced her so, beaten down her spirit. She was so weak. She must not forget what she had once been, once known. Must not forget. Stretch! The book was between her fingers. A dizziness swept over her suddenly; she lost control; she came toppling down.

All that night the room was dark and completely silent, like a tomb.

III

'I should have been informed sooner. She may be lying there.'

'Don't, Hywel.' Mrs Mayrick sat beside her husband in their pre-war Wolseley. 'Do you think the car will go up the lane?'

The caretaker's children scrambled up a bank to get out of the way of the advancing car that filled up the entire width of the lane.

'Wouldn't be a bad idea to accelerate and go over them.'

'Meg! Really!'

'Little pests. It's time you looked around for new caretakers. They've made her life hell. These really aren't fit...'

Together they hurried up the stone stairs. Miss Whitely, masticating the last remnants of her late lunch, peeped excitedly through an inch of open door. The Mayricks hurried on to No. 3. He glanced at the key in his hand, with the label written in long Central European handwriting.

'Wait outside, Meg,' he said firmly.

'She may only have fainted, Hywel.'

'We'll soon see.'

Shaking with apprehension, she remained outside, closing her eyes, but counting instead of praying.

'Meg!' His stout form seemed extraordinarily bulky on the small threshold. She looked at him anxiously. He nodded slowly. She thrust her gloved fists into her face and began sobbing.

'You'd better go to the car, my dear...'

'No, Hywel. I want to see her. And see her poor little room for the last time.'

With gentle, friendly curiosity at last she knelt beside the twisted black form. The head was thrown backwards, the face frozen in animal surprise.

'She must have been trying to reach down this parcel from the top of the cupboard. She still had her hat on. It's a book.' Hurriedly, as if she feared her husband might stop her, Meg tore off the tattered brown paper. 'A German book. Poetry. Hywel, may I keep it?'

He spoke slowly, heavily. 'Oddly enough everything in this room should now be yours.'

'Mine?'

'She wanted me to draw up a will, leaving her belongings to you, dear.'

'Oh the poor darling, the poor old thing. She had nobody, nobody but me.'

Mrs Mayrick wept bitterly. 'Oh, if only I'd have done more for her,' she kept saying. She would not leave with her husband when he went to fetch the doctor and the police. She was going to stand guard, she said. She told him firmly but calmly to shut the door. 'In case those vandals come peeping,' she said. 'It's the least I can do.'

The Rector hastened about his business, worried about his wife.

The doctor, who knew him well, was surprised about what appeared to be the Rector's unconcern. When he broke the news he seemed to be preoccupied with other things as if her death was a matter of small importance. This was unlike Mayrick because normally he took every aspect of his duties very seriously, and to the doctor's way of thinking, too ponderously.

They found Mrs Mayrick sitting at the old lady's small bureau. Anxiously her husband hurried to her. She was smiling and seemed quite unaware now that she was in the same room as a corpse. The Rector put his arm protectively about her shoulders. Had he known Meg really wanted it, he would have drawn up the will on the spot. She was a wonderful wife and he did not appreciate her enough. Also some of these things, part of the property, could be of some value. Prices of antiques were sometimes high. There was a price to historical value too.

'Hywel!' she said. The three men looked at her, struck by the elated note in her voice. 'She was the daughter of an archduke – a natural daughter. She was the niece of the last Emperor. A Hapsburg. Can you believe that?'

The doctor and the policeman shook their heads simultaneously and turned to look at the body.

ONE LIFE

Alun Richards

On the day of her husband's funeral, Lydia Skuse was more composed than anyone had expected. Leonard had always said he would go in February and although the funeral took place on the first of March, his death had about it the predictable order of things which she had come to expect of life. He had died as he said he would, in the first months of his retirement, and when she returned from the grave and the few mourners had gone, she declined her sister-in-law's offer of tea and retired alone to the front room of the terraced house in Dan y Graig Street.

She wanted to sit by herself and put her thoughts in order. She had decisions to make. Soon her sister-in-law, Ada, would ask what she intended to do with the house and whether or not she would leave it and come and live with their family; and since that implied leaving her home town and all that she had known, Lydia wanted to go over it in her mind carefully before she gave her answer. She was a careful, neat little woman, not given to chatter, methodical and reasoned in all she did and, although at sixty-five she was not as agile as she had been once, age was a great blessing because it relieved her of the pressure of feelings and anxieties which had once tortured her beyond belief.

'I am,' she had always seemed to be saying, 'and that is enough.' But now she could say with some satisfaction, 'I am, and I look as I am.'

Now more than ever, she appeared truly as she really felt and this simple register of the emotions on her face was itself a miraculous thing, because she was born a foundling, a workhouse child, and all her life, her expressions, her voice itself, revealed the flat, calm, passively accepting demeanour of the permanently institutionalised. She never looked as she felt and her very presence in a room was always something of an anticlimax. And yet, within her small wizened frame, her tight-skinned, immobile face whose sharp, darting eyes betrayed or missed nothing, she had felt all of the passions it was possible for her to feel, and if ever she was patronised as she had been by the boyish clergyman in the afternoon, she had learned to smile secretly to herself.

She, Lydia Skuse, knew a thing or two. What could she not say of all the swirl of experience that had carried her to this point in time! The clergyman saw the childless widow of a small-town baker, unusually composed, but diminutive and insignificant before the fact of death itself. But she had stood before bigger chasms and felt the future yawning before her with an awful incomprehension inside her, and she had mastered that too. There was nothing she had not learned to live with, and as she sat alone, she prepared herself for the immediate decision by allowing her attention to slip a little, going over the comparative tranquillity of the last years of Leonard's life to an earlier time when their son Bobby was alive. That was *the* time to think about, and it was natural that she should do so now in peace.

But in the next room her brother-in-law, Walter, bestirred himself uneasily and voiced the fear which had haunted him since well before the funeral. He gave his wife a sour look.

'Ada, it's no good avoiding it, Lydia won't fit in with us. She won't feel at home there, and that's it in a nutshell,' he said aggressively. He spoke of the bungalow on the South Coast which he had recently bought and retired to himself.

His wife agreed but she did not like him raising his voice so soon after the funeral. As it happened, she felt even more apprehensive than he did. She had always had unrealised social pretensions and remembered the shock of her brother Leonard bringing home a girl who was in service all those years ago.

'*In service*, Leonard?' She knew then that he could have done so much better.

'She's had a hard life, but now it's going to stop,' Leonard had said.

'But marrying the Workhouse Master's Maid?'

'Lydia Skuse is her name, and from now on, you're to call her by it.'

Ada remembered Lydia then. Nothing to commend her in looks, manners, money. A docile little thing without a spark of humour. Said very little, only looked at you disapprovingly. Not even winsome, more like hard-faced. And if Leonard was going into business on his own, someone with an engaging manner by his side would be a godsend. There were two girls he could have married whose fathers would have helped him financially, and that was important because it was the year of the General Strike, the miners were locked out for nine months, and all the local tradesmen were in dire straits.

Oh, that he could be so foolish! A girl with nothing to say, a surly domestic marrying literally out of the workhouse. What a comedown for a favourite brother! More than that, she felt it reflected on the family who were grocers in a small way, and she had since harboured the feeling of having been let down by Leonard all her life.

Aware of her thoughts, Walter tried to sound cheerful.

'Lydia's taken it all very well. She may not want to come to us. She's always been a tough nut.'

Ada sniffed and raised her eyebrows. 'She wouldn't even let me make a cup of tea – and we've come all this way! She doesn't want sympathy, I know that, but we have come,' she said complainingly.

Walter agreed. They'd come for Leonard's sake, but the

funeral was very disappointing. 'It's a good job we did come. Not many there. You'd have thought some of his old customers would have turned up. I can't remember a Welsh funeral with under a dozen present before. And the singing was terrible!' said Walter peevishly. Although he had disguised both his origins and his accent for business reasons on the South Coast, he had the old Welsh appreciation of a good funeral and he felt let down.

'The valleys have changed,' Ada said, and she pursed her lips as if to say, '*Since we left!*'

But there was no avoiding the topic. Lydia and Leonard had spent summer holidays with them on the South Coast where Walter had also been in business since the war. Lydia had liked the change and it was suggested that they might retire there themselves. Walter and Ada had two grown-up children and several grandchildren with whom Lydia got on famously, and besides the change of scenery, they knew that Lydia was very attached to their own children who worshipped her. This was another thing.

Lydia had an uncanny knack with children, was always willing to babysit and generally help out, and this forthcoming expertise was in a way a criticism of them for they were somewhat uneasy parents, immensely house-proud since the purchase of the bungalow, and, to tell the truth, they felt they had given enough to their children. It was all very well for Lydia to queen it for a fortnight a year. There were, and always had been, the remaining fifty weeks. But the matter was further complicated because they were jealous of Lydia's success with their children and although they couldn't find a single reason to justify any criticism of themselves, there remained this remarkable quality of Lydia's which they just couldn't see.

It was as if she radiated a special kind of light which others saw and they couldn't, and it annoyed them intensely. They felt she did it on purpose, and the joke was, she was so ordinary, a cut below them in every way. They saw nothing special about her at all. You'd pass her in a crowd and not notice her. In an empty room she was part of the furniture. And yet, Leonard had never hesitated, and thirty years later, their own grandchildren began to smile as soon as they came into Lydia's presence. They just couldn't put their finger on it, but whatever it was she had, it maddened them. All very well for her, but they'd had to raise the family. They'd had their troubles too and they hadn't saved and succeeded just to spend their last years watching Lydia reap the benefit of their children and grandchildren. They had, after all, themselves and their own old age to think of, and they felt Lydia's personality to be both a remonstrance to the past and a threat to the future.

'No,' Ada said firmly. 'We must ask her because of Leonard, but there's no doubt about whether she'll fit in or not. We know very well, she won't!'

'I quite agree,' Walter said, nodding. He had never had a moment's regret about the woman he married. He was that shrewd.

But both of them knew that they must make the offer to Lydia. They owed it to Leonard and to what remained of decency from the past.

In the next room, Lydia heard their muffled voices and smiled. With all they had, they were such unhappy people and she paid them scant attention. Instead, enjoying the moment of quiet, she stretched herself out. She would have a morning in bed the next day, a luxury she had not experienced more than half a dozen times in her life. Even when Leonard had retired, years of habit still made him keep baker's hours. He simply could not lie in bed for long and always awoke with the dawn when he would get up and prowl about the kitchen, doing odd jobs like black-leading the fire grate, or fetching coal and sticks which had previously been her lot. Baker's hours had always meant that she had to be far more self-sufficient than most wives and now that he was gone, she would have to be more self-sufficient still.

But she smiled confidently. She knew she had the training for it. One of the reasons why she could savour the sweet luxury of lying in bed was that she had for so many years to clean rows and rows of boots in the early morning, and she could still picture them laid out in the institution. She began always, as was fitting, with the workhouse master's, and then worked down through the hierarchy, missing most of the children, except for the toddlers in the annexe who were too small to clean their own. She could remember the hard, stiff leather of those boots and their bony toecaps. As hard as frost, she used to say, but she was not so foolish as to attribute a wonderous glow to the past. She had had to prove herself all the way up as a scullion from slop-pails to boots, from boots to vegetables, vegetables to brass, and after brass, the golden jump to waiting at the master's table and the cushioned intimacy of the master's separate quarters. Finally, she had been given her own room, free of the smell of disinfectant with curtains and an actual bedspread.

Remembering, she gave a little laugh. How she had valued that room! She had told Leonard about it. But he was very sentimental. A thing like that, the mental picture of rows and rows of toddlers' boots laid out in regimental order was enough to bring tears to his eyes.

'You shall have a house with six rooms,' he promised wildly.

They had to wait seven years, but she didn't mind. Leonard couldn't understand that every privation was like a coiled spring loaded against her withdrawn emotions. She could wait seven years or more, but the moment she actually walked into her own rooms, the release of pleasure inside her was like a gun going off! If her face betrayed very little – she could do no more than smile her pinched, small-mouthed smile – her heart beat faster and her excitement was voluptuous. So it had been all her life. It was not that waiting for things made them better, that was too simple. Rather, it was that for so many years she expected nothing that she could not actually touch at the moment of wishing, and it was a fact of life that you could not touch much in the workhouse.

She laughed again. What a thought these days! What would she have been like if she had seen a car like Walter's with a cigar lighter and a toy tiger slung in the back as a mascot? Or Ada's electric toothbrush and Scandinavian cutlery? It was very curious that her in-laws owned nothing that needed cleaning, except the car and they still continued to change that every year on their accountant's advice. How strange anyway, not to have to clean anything! Her own kitchen was festooned with brass, two German shell cases that Leonard had saved from the first war, candlesticks galore, the handles of the dresser and a large Victorian hob that the Master's wife had given her as a wedding present.

The whole room was alight with polished brass and the coals from the fire reflected in all of it so that the impression of warmth was heightened by all the added focal points of light. It glistened because she cleaned it every day and she would not know what to do without it. She had even prevented Leonard from usurping that function when he retired. She loved brass and the abundance of it made her feel rich while it depressed her in-laws. They couldn't say it was old-fashioned for it was now fetching a price, but in some way it must seem to hem them in. Perhaps it was also uncomfortable evidence of labour which she loved for its own sake.

Leonard always used to remonstrate with her.

'It'll kill you. You'll die with a Brasso tin in your hand.'

She always had a tart reply.

'Hard work never hurt a fly.'

But she was wrong, of course. It had killed him. For the last fifteen years, he had no help in the bakehouse and they had made very little profit. He could have made more money working for somebody else. The baker's round had diminished when a new council estate brought a supermarket and cheaper bread. Leonard's demise lay in his stubborn nature. He would make no capital outlay and would not replace the dated machinery. It was obvious that the day of the batch and the freshly scrubbed basket of loaves and the baker's cheery call was over, but Leonard would not admit it.

His old customers stuck to him, mostly the colliers, but one by one, the pits shut, the men were transferred to work elsewhere and the young wives were working and simply weren't in when he called. They all preferred to shop on the way home and made bulk purchases of all their goods in the same store. You couldn't blame them, but Leonard refused to change. While they were shopping at night, he was baking. He was like a man shoring up an ancient sea wall while the inland river flooded at his back. He couldn't or wouldn't change. He wouldn't work for anybody else, and finally, he watched the round diminish until he was working for nothing and then suddenly sold the ovens for scrap with a last defiant gesture and retired.

Fortunately, they'd put money by and were comfortably off by their standards, without debt or hire purchase, but Leonard couldn't live without the baker's round and he had died, she thought, because he could not adjust himself to idleness. He fretted about the past and dwelt on it, his mind pacing out each trivial incident of the years until he was exhausted. It was a frightening thought, but she did not avoid it. She had learned to face everything, and now deciding for herself about the future, Lydia knew that it would be wrong for her to avoid anything.

Anything at all! She had to tell the truth to herself about Leonard too. The decline of the round was part of his death, but not the whole of it. There was one day there in the past that had haunted him, sticking like gall in his mouth and clamping its awful shadow on everything he did afterwards. They had never spoken of it fully. She was ready always to comfort him, but he was beyond that, a maimed man, put beyond his conscience.

Poor Leonard... if she could have cried, it would have been now. It was terrible for him and he could not live with the memory of that awful day. His funeral was a joyous time beside it, but she had to face it, and all the phrases which echoed in her ears all the way to his grave. You had to face everything. It was what she had always lived by.

'Hard work never hurt a fly.'

They had both been brought up on this principle. They had always needed to work, but they believed in the virtue of it, for its own sake. Perhaps it was a drug, she had come to think, but at the time, there was no room for doubt. Work was a bread and butter matter.

She could hear Leonard's voice and see Bobby's face, pimply with the acne of adolescence. Ah, she had had her son, there were seventeen years of caring for him that no one could take away. They were arguing about Bobby's attitude to the bakery. The war was on. Labour was short. Leonard needed help and did not see why Bobby, still in grammar school, could not do his homework and help out on the van.

'When I was your age, I was up at three in the morning. I had to scrub and bake. I had a basket and a brown sack, and I scrubbed that basket white!'

'Oh, give it a rest,' Bobby said sullenly. 'Take it easy will you?'

'I can't,' Leonard said. 'I can't take it easy! I never have been able to take it easy. It's not in my nature.'

'Oh, give him a medal, Mum!'

She could still smile. The adolescent-parental battle never changed. The surly tones, the smart remarks, the limp sarcasm, they were perennial. Even the clothes were as offensive then as they were with Ada's grandchildren now. She remembered Leonard going on about Bobby's sloppy lumberjacket.

'When I was your age, I wore a blue suit, a stiff collar and a dark tie on a Sunday. But you look like a woman in that thing. Doesn't it affect you?'

'Yeah,' Bobby's lip curved unattractively into a sneer. 'I feel the draught above my knees.'

Leonard gave a gasp of exasperation. 'You'll start work three evenings a week, and that's that.'

'Oh, no.'

'You wouldn't want to see your mother do it? Or would you?' Bobby shrugged his shoulders insolently and she intervened.

'Leonard, you're upsetting him.'

'Upsetting him? What about me? Haven't I got to work?'

Leonard had craggy, black eyebrows and a small impatient mouth. He was too quick-tempered for an argument and his face was a mask of pique. 'Well, haven't I?'

'Perhaps that's all you're good for,' Bobby said sulkily. 'Work…'

That was going too far. Leonard's hand was raised to strike in the instant, while Bobby, awkward and gangly and already flushed with embarrassment moved quickly to the door.

'You raise your hand to me and you'll be sorry!'

'You'll feel it in a minute.'

'I won't! I'll go to sea,' Bobby screamed in his cracked, scarcely broken voice. 'I'll go with Hector Trencherman, he's going back Friday.'

'Go then,' Leonard shouted. 'Go and good riddance!'

Of course, he did not mean it, Lydia knew. But the words were said. Such a mundane and ordinary little scene, a tiff between father and son, such as must have happened in every family. It was so commonplace that under any other circumstances it would be difficult to remember it.

But there was only one Bobby.

'You shouldn't have threatened to hit him,' she said afterwards. 'You shouldn't hit children.' She had been hit herself.

'I wouldn't have,' Leonard replied, but they both knew it wasn't true. Leonard had a simple fear that the boy might turn out a waster. 'Ah, he'd never go to sea. He couldn't stick it.'

Neither of them took Bobby's threat seriously. They both knew Hector Trencherman and the Trencherman family, and while they were not exactly ne'er-do-wells, all the Trencherman family had at various times been at loggerheads with authority. Ben Trencherman, the father, was blacklisted in the colliery for activities as an agitator and had cracked open a militiaman's face during the industrial riots, and there was an aura of lawlessness and violence about the whole family. Hector, Bobby's acquaintance, was nineteen, well cast in the family stamp, with strong, muscular shoulders, black curly hair, and the same way of standing, hands casually lolling about his belt, as if forever tempting others to attack. He had been at sea since the war began and was by way of being a local hero since he had survived bombardment and torpedoing on several occasions. Lydia remembered him displaying a hand of frostbitten fingers with modest bravado to the girls in a local café. Bobby had witnessed this display and, while there was no doubt that the Trencherman family came into their own in a war of attrition, neither their spirit nor the times seemed to have anything to do with her Bobby. He was slight and delicate, an overgrown child still subject to bronchitis in the winter months. If she feared anything, it was that he was tubercular.

But a week later, without note or word, they learned that Bobby had gone to sea, signed on before the mast as deck boy. One of the Trencherman girls called when the bakery had closed and dropped the news almost casually after they had spent a night thinking he had gone to Cardiff and missed the last train to the valleys.

'Gone?' Leonard said. 'It's impossible.'

'They're sailing for Liverpool.'

'Bobby wouldn't do that,' she said.

'Of course not. It's not true. There are papers and things to sign. He's only just seventeen,' Leonard said. 'I've signed nothing.'

'Oh, Len, what if he has?' Lydia caught her throat.

The girl was taken aback at their distress. In the Trencherman household, men went out into the night to jail or across the world without fuss. They had the industrial peasant's acceptance of leave-takings without ceremony. The Skuses were of Welsh stock and although the language had gone, they remembered ancestors who had worked the land and did not have the anarchic indifference to catastrophe which the coal mines bred.

The girl wanted to get out of the room as quickly as possible.

'Oh, well,' she said. 'I'm sure he'll be all right. Hector'll look after him. He's been all over.'

'All over?' Lydia said.

'The world.'

Their throats were dry with apprehension. As soon as the girl left, Leonard began to rush around seeing people. He got a cousin to come in and look after the bakery and left for Liverpool the next morning. They had no information, nothing to go on, not even a postcard. The local grammar school headmaster rang the shipping offices, finally contacted the Seamen's Pool and found that Leonard's signature had been forged on the consent forms. Later, they found that some unknown person had impersonated Leonard in the shipping office and that if Leonard had not missed a train at Crewe, they might even have stopped the ship. But it was all too late. The ship had sailed in convoy and Bobby was at sea.

Leonard told her he'd wandered around the hinterland of the docks like a lost sheep. It was a prohibited area and they shunted him from office to office, and to make matters worse, there was an air raid in the middle of the afternoon and he had no chance. Lydia pictured him shouting at the officials, his rage giving way to guilt and finally despair. She remembered his homecoming, the peak of his trilby almost worn through with the marks of his fingernails and fidgeting. She could see his face all through the journey. He was red-eyed and exhausted when he returned and stepped into the tiny kitchen.

'It's no good. He's gone, sailed.'

'Oh, Len...'

'They couldn't tell me where, but I've got a forwarding address.'

And that was all. But then came the weeks of waiting until a pathetic allotment note arrived and then more silent, dogged weeks. Nothing more until the telegram came, and that was like some savage blow sent up with a snarl of fate into the middle of the anguish they were already suffering. She could not speak the words aloud, but the précis of them stayed as if carved in her skull for years. MISSING, PRESUMED...

'Oh, Bobby... Bobby...'

It was too much for the human soul to bear. Not a postcard, a letter, a kind word, an expression of regret, or hope, or remorse, or forgiveness. Nothing. A dead void whose circumference was infinity lay before them and an abyss arose between them, an aching and immediate gulf of sorrow that welled in her body like some unnatural destructive sea of feeling itself. Not another word.

They sat in the kitchen helplessly. A cross word, a tiff, and death. Leonard moaned.

'Oh, no... no... no.'

It was Lydia who felt that there was no hope immediately. With the telegram in her hands, she knew it was final.

But Leonard was already building up his hopes.

'It depends,' he said, 'where the convoy was going. If it was the Mediterranean, there's a chance.'

'Why?' she asked flatly.

'There are more ships to pick them up. The water's not so cold.'

But the convoy, it turned out, was going to Russia.

Two days later there was a letter from the shipping company with details, but no hope. Yet Leonard stuck out his jaw and willed hope.

'Hector was a good swimmer. He'd look after Bobby. Say what you like about him, he's from the same street. They're local boys together. I mean, they're both Welsh.'

But she looked away from him. She had already accepted it. It had happened and it was past. She was too old to have more children. She was a woman who had had a son. She stated it simply. After all, she had previously said, 'I am an unwanted child who was deserted before I was five.' All these things were facts. She went about her daily tasks automatically and dared not share her feelings because Leonard could not have stood them. But she knew, and for the following weeks, she was like a wounded animal limping about her lair in silence. There was nothing she could say that made any difference. Bobby was gone. She was already preparing for the future without him.

But there was a night that week in which she seemed to feel her heart stop, experiencing a physical pain that made her gasp.

Without bothering to knock, flushed with drink and hoarse with shouted jubilation, Ben Trencherman came booted and black with pit-dirt into the kitchen, bearing a second telegram. His eyes were bloodshot and jaundiced and they could smell his sweat and the clammy dankness of the pit.

'The Ruskies have got him. Archangel. The bloody water couldn't stop him.'

'Who?' Lydia gasped.

'Hector,' he said blandly, flourishing the second telegram. 'Haven't you got yours?'

No, they had not. There was not one for them.

Lydia saw Ben Trencherman's white teeth glisten behind the coal dust as his jaw fell open. The immensity of his blunder dawned upon him.

'Oh, Christ, sorry,' he said. 'Oh, Jesus Christ.'

He backed out helplessly, leaving a stain against the wall where he had stood.

A month later, Hector came home, frostbitten again, his features indelibly coarsened and his clothes hanging on him. Lydia saw his back in the street first, but eventually he came to see them, bolstered with rum. He could not keep his eyes on her and Leonard went sobbing with rage and anguish out of the room.

'He passed on very comfortable,' Hector said laconically. 'In his sleep, in the night, like. He was very brave. They was all very fond of him. Game, he was. I give him my blanket, tack an' all, but it was hopeless in that weather.'

'Yes,' she said. Although it was obvious that Hector had passed a point of no return in his own life, she did not believe a word he had said. But what was the point of accusing him now? 'Thank you for coming,' she said. And that was all.

Leonard did not speak that night, but months later he wanted all the details. Hector had one story for them and another for the girls on the street corner. Bobby had died screaming in his arms while the lifeboat was being dashed against the ship's side and they'd had to cut away the fall. He was dying when Hector got him into the boat, both his hands mangled to pulp. And when she heard this, she believed. It would be like Hector to carry a dying Bobby into the boat, anxious to do the right thing at last, as if by some dumb gesture, he could bring the body home to her to atone in some way. No matter how much Hector had suffered, the war was to him a schoolboy escapade. It sounded like the truth and she believed it and then put it out of her mind.

But not Leonard. The night of torment became the central point of his life. What she had come to think of as the death word, was on his lips.

'If... if... if...'

She knew there could be no *if*. There never were any second chances.

'It's happened,' she said simply. She never wasted words. 'But we've still got each other.'

'Yes,' he said, but she could see then that he did not really believe it, or that if he did, she was not enough. That was really the great tragedy of their life, not that Bobby had been taken from them, but that without him, there was nothing else they could create together. Leonard could never communicate any sense of the present afterwards. When the brief period of praying passed, he retracted from life altogether and aged prematurely because from then on, he functioned like an automaton, all his responses conditioned. She could not waken anything in him. She tried, in the initial stages, to join him in prayer. But it was an idle practice. She had faith in herself but not in God. She had not the experience of life to prepare her for that luxury and following her own intuitive stands, she felt there was something not quite right about the Church. There was so much faith consciously aired that it smacked of disbelief. She was too much a realist to depend that much on others or on a supreme being. Not her, she said to herself. They allowed you freedom of action but not of thought, and all her life, while her actions were curtailed, her mind remained her own and the use of it was the only blessing she had left.

But Leonard tried everything else, religion, bowls, a working men's organisation dedicated to good works, only to find that there always came a point when he suddenly saw Bobby's face and there were always lonely hours when his mind returned to that night. He thought about the killing so intensely that it was as if he drowned himself a thousand times, and try as he might, his ear seemed never to be far from the sounds of the sea. She heard him mutter in his sleep as if he had heard Bobby cry out and one night when she woke him, he protested about the curses of the sailors – a child in the midst of all that.

She watched him pass through that stage until he hardened his heart to life, and slowly, all the arteries of feeling in him contracted in the face of the pressures of an existence that could allow such barbarous strokes of fate. It was not right. Life was not right. It was more than the human heart could bear and the imagined scenes too awful for the eyes to comprehend. He was their only son, could nobody understand that? From then on, any life outside the ordered treads of the familiar baker's round seemed to be leading him into that unknown where such things happened. Any life outside the known was a blasphemy and he feared it as a prim man might fear an obscenity. Hear it, and it contaminated you; touch it and examine the fingertips afterwards with terror. So Leonard turned his back upon the living.

He had died, she thought now, sitting peacefully in the armchair, with the blinds of the little room still drawn to his memory, twenty years ago. She had been a widow all that time. But how fruitless to think your life ended in a lifeboat even if it bore the dead body of your son. Poor Leonard, he could never realise it. But she had done her duty by him and now she was free. Freedom was the courage of facing things as they are.

Presently Ada entered with tea.

'I made another pot. I know you didn't want it, but I'm sure it'll do you good. I've put a few aspirins in the saucer.'

'Oh, thank you,' Lydia smiled.

'Of course,' Ada said, 'you'll want a few days to think things out, but you know you're always welcome to come to us.'

'Welcome?'

'To come and live with us,' Ada said, raising her voice as if she was speaking to one afflicted. 'Leonard would have wanted it.'

'Yes, he would,' Lydia took the tea and stirred it. It was true. He didn't like people to be alone, perhaps because his own aloneness was so complete.

'Of course, it would be a big step to give up everything here. You know how you like to be independent. I mean, we're all getting on and we're not the company we used to be. We're all getting tetchy. And our place does get a bit crowded. But you *are* welcome. Leonard would have wanted us to ask.'

'Yes,' Lydia said. But she could have hooted with laughter. Other people's lies only confirmed her own strength. One cryptic sentence and she could have sent Ada packing, exposed as a person to whom nothing had happened, one of those unfortunates hardly touched by living.

'Well,' Ada hesitated. 'I expect you'd like a few days to think about it?'

'No, I've made up my mind now.'

'Oh,' Ada flushed nervously. She would ever after be ashamed of her next thought. It would be typical of the workhouse brat to say she'd come. But thank God she never uttered it. What would she have to answer for in the hereafter!

'I won't move,' Lydia said. 'But I'd like to stay a little longer with you in the summer when the children are on holidays.'

'Oh, of course,' Ada said hastily.

'In furnished rooms,' Lydia said.

'There's no need for that.'

Lydia smiled. 'I'd prefer it if it's to be more than a fortnight. But I shall always be very grateful to you for asking me. Leonard would be too. He always said how kind you were really.'

Ada flushed. She felt herself humiliated and could not understand why or how it had happened. After all, she thought, how many people in their sixties would welcome an in-law like Lydia? And she *had* offered. Moreover, she'd brought up children and lived her own life free from the tarnish of the major sins, and she still looked more worn than Lydia. To cap it all, the March wind had given Lydia a high colour, whereas Ada was sure she herself looked positively sallow from contact with the open air. And she felt chesty, fit to crumple. But Lydia sat there stiff-backed, her chin tilted, her small pointed features and smooth grey hair, a picture of health, and still – she had to say it – definitely a charity figure. Completely without style. Perhaps it was the unmarked, tight skin? She did not know. *What was she thinking?*

Lydia smiled. 'Poor Ada,' she said quietly. 'D'you think I can't manage?'

'Oh, no,' Ada said hastily. 'No, of course not.' She could find nothing more to say, nodded solicitously at the aspirins in the saucer, and left the room uncomfortably.

Watching the door close behind her, Lydia summed it all up. As the workhouse master had told her all those years ago, life was very unkind to those who did not help themselves. A human being had an allotted span. You did what you could, that was all. What was the point of complaining? Why sulk? What was the value of pretence? You could grieve a life away by wishing. And of course, he was right. Everything that had happened to her was beyond her wildest expectations. If she had learnt anything, it was to take people as they are. And hadn't her skill in this direction won her a husband, a son, a house with six rooms, the luxury of in-laws even!

She smiled as she thought of them, lifting her ear to the wall. She knew there'd be silence in the next room and she had the teeniest pleasure in knowing it would be an uncomfortable silence. Whoever would have thought that a little mouse like her could have reduced such a notability as Ada to silence? No; more than that, she'd positively dismissed her!

Gulping, Lydia reached again for the cup of tea and dutifully took the two aspirins from the saucer. Of all the ideas which had been impressed upon her, the most important was that she should never get above her station.

'I really am grateful to you for offering,' she said later. 'And *Leonard* would have liked it.'

And then she smiled one of her secret smiles and went quietly upstairs to bed, Lydia Skuse, widow, Dan y Graig Street. From now on, this was how she would be described. It was yet another experience.

AFTER FOREVER

THE RETURN

Brenda Chamberlain

It isn't as if the Captain took reasonable care of himself, said the postmaster.

No, she answered. She was on guard against anything he might say.

A man needs to be careful with a lung like that, said the postmaster.

Yes, she said. She waited for sentences to be laid like baited traps. They watched one another for the next move. The man lifted a two-ounce weight from the counter and dropped it with fastidious fingers into the brass scale. As the tray fell, the woman sighed. A chink in her armour. He breathed importantly and spread his hands on the counter. From pressure on the palms, dark veins stood up under the skin on the backs of his hands. He leaned his face to the level of her eyes. Watching him, her mouth fell slightly open.

The Captain's lady is very nice indeed; Mrs Morrison is a charming lady. Have you met his wife, Mrs Ritsin?

No, she answered; she has not been to the Island since I came. She could not prevent a smile flashing across her eyes at her own stupidity. Why must she have said just that, a ready-made sentence that could be handed on without distortion. She has not been to the Island since I came. Should she add: no doubt she will be over soon; then I shall have the pleasure of meeting her? The words would not come. The postmaster lodged the sentence carefully in his brain ready to be retailed to the village.

They watched one another. She, packed with secrets behind that innocent face, damn her, why couldn't he worm down the secret passages of her mind? Why had she come here in the first place, this Mrs Ritsin? Like a doll, so small and delicate, she made you want to hit or pet her, according to your nature. She walked with small strides, as if she owned the place, as if she was on equal terms with man and the sea. Her eyes disturbed something in his nature that could not bear the light. They were large, they looked further than any other eyes he had seen. They shone with a happiness that he thought indecent in the circumstances.

Everyone knew, the whole village gloated and hummed over the fact that Ceridwen had refused to live on the Island and that she herself was a close friend of Alec Morrison. But why, she asked herself, why did she let herself fall into their cheap traps? The sentence would be repeated almost without a word being altered but the emphasis, O my God, the stressing of the *I*, to imply a malicious woman's triumph. But all this doesn't really matter, she told herself, at least it won't once I am back there. The Island. She saw it float in front of the postmaster's face. The rocks were clear and the hovering, wind-swung birds; she saw them clearly in front of the wrinkles and clefts on his brow and chin. He coughed discreetly and shrugged with small deprecatory movements of the shoulders. He wished she would not stare at him as if he was a wall or invisible. If she was trying to get at his secrets she could till crack of doom. All the same. As a precautionary measure he slid aside and faced the window.

Seems as though it will be too risky for you to go back this evening, he said; there's a bit of a fog about. You'll be stopping the night in Porthbychan? – and he wouldn't let her go on holiday in the winter: said, if she did, he'd get a concubine to keep him warm, and he meant—

A woman was talking to her friend outside the door.

478

You cannot possibly cross the Race alone in this weather, Mrs Ritsin, persisted the postmaster.

I must get back tonight, Mr Davies.

He sketched the bay with a twitching arm, as if to say: I have bound the restless wave. He became confidential, turning to stretch across the counter.

My dear Mrs Ritsin, no woman has ever before navigated these waters. Why, even on a calm day the Porthbychan fishers will not enter the Race. Be warned, dear lady. Imagine my feelings if you were to be washed up on the beach here.

Bridget Ritsin said, I am afraid it is most important that I should get back tonight, Mr Davies.

Ann Pritchard from the corner house slid from the glittering evening into the shadows of the post office. She spoke out of the dusk behind the door. It isn't right for a woman to ape a man, doing a man's work.

Captain Morrison is ill. He couldn't possibly come across today. That is why I'm in charge of the boat, Bridget answered.

Two other women had slipped in against the wall of the shop. Now, four pairs of eyes bored into her face. With sly insolence the women threw ambiguous sentences to the postmaster, who smiled as he studied the grain in the wood of his counter. Bridget picked up a bundle of letters and turned to go. The tide will be about right now, she said. Good evening, Mr Davies. Be very, very careful, Mrs Ritsin, and remember me to the Captain.

Laughter followed her into the street. It was like dying in agony, while crowds danced and mocked. O, my darling, my darling over the cold waves. She knew that while she was away he would try to do too much about the house. He would go to the well for water, looking over the fields he lacked strength to drain. He would be in the yard, chopping sticks. He would cough and spit blood. It isn't as if the Captain took reasonable care of himself. When he ran too hard, when he moved anything heavy and lost his breath, he only struck his chest and cursed: blast my lung. Alec dear, you should not run so fast up the mountain. He never heeded her. He had begun to spit blood.

By the bridge over the river, her friend Griff Owen was leaning against the side of a motor car, talking to a man and woman in the front seats. He said to them, ask her, as she came past.

Excuse me, Miss, could you take us over to see the Island?

I'm sorry, she said, there's a storm coming up. It wouldn't be possible to make the double journey.

They eyed her, curious about her way of life.

Griff Owen, and the grocer's boy carrying two boxes of provisions, came down to the beach with her.

I wouldn't be you; going to be a dirty night, said the man.

The waves were chopped and the headland was vague with hanging cloud. The two small islets in the bay were behind curtains of vapour. The sea was blurred and welcomeless. To the Island, to the Island. Here in the village, you opened a door: laughter and filthy jokes buzzed in your face. They stung and blinded. O my love, be patient, I am coming back to you, quickly, quickly, over the waves.

The grocer's boy put down the provisions on the sand near the tide edge. Immediately a shallow pool formed round the bottoms of the boxes.

Wind seems to be dropping, said Griff.

Yes, but I think there will be fog later on, she answered, sea fog. She turned to him. Oh, Griff, you are always so kind to me. What would we do without you?

He laid a hand on her shoulder. Tell me, how is the Captain feeling in himself? I don't like the thought of him being so far from the doctor.

The doctor can't do very much for him. Living in the clean air from the sea is good. These days he isn't well, soon he may be better. Don't worry, he is hanging on to life and the Island. They began to push the boat down over rollers towards the water. Last week Alec had said quite abruptly as he was stirring the boiled potatoes for the ducks: at least, you will have this land if I die.

At least, I have the Island.

Well, well, said the man, making an effort to joke; tell the Captain from me that I'll come over to see him if he comes for me himself. Tell him I wouldn't trust my life to a lady, even though the boat has got a good engine and knows her own way home.

He shook her arm: you are a stout girl.

Mr Davies coming down, said the boy, looking over his shoulder as he heaved on the side of the boat. The postmaster came on to the beach through the narrow passage between the hotel and the churchyard. His overcoat flapped round him in the wind. He had something white in his hand. The boat floated; Bridget waded out and stowed away her provisions and parcels. By the time she had made a second journey Mr Davies was at the water's edge.

Another letter for you, Mrs Ritsin, he said. Very sorry, it had got behind the old-age pension books. He peered at her, longing to know what was in the letter, dying to find out what her feelings would be when she saw the handwriting. He had already devoured the envelope with his eyes, back and front, reading the postmark and the two sentences written in pencil at the back. He knew it was a letter from Ceridwen to her husband.

A letter for the Captain, said the postmaster, and watched her closely.

Thank you. She took it, resisting the temptation to read the words that caught her eye on the back of the envelope. She put it away in the large pocket of her oilskin along with the rest.

The postmaster sucked in his cheeks and mumbled something. So Mrs Morrison would be back here soon, he suddenly shot at her. Only the grocer's boy, whistling as he kicked the shingle, did not respond to what he said. Griff looked from her to the postmaster; she studied the postmaster's hypocritical smile. Her head went up, she was able to smile: oh, yes, of course, Mrs Morrison is sure to come over when the weather is better. What did he know, why should he want to know?

It was like a death; every hour that she had to spend on the mainland gave her fresh wounds.

Thank you, Mr Davies. Goodbye Griff, see you next week if the weather isn't too bad. She climbed into the motor boat and weighed anchor. She bent over the engine and it began to live. The grocer's boy was drifting away, still kicking the beach as if he bore it a grudge. Mr Davies called in a thin voice... great care... wish you would... the Race and...

Griff waved, and roared like a horn: tell him I'll take the next calf if it is a good one.

It was his way of wishing her Godspeed. Linking the moment's hazard to the safety of future days.

She waved her hand. The men grew small, they and the gravestones of blue and green slate clustered round the medieval church at the top of the sand. The village drew into itself, fell into perspective against the distant mountains.

It was lonely in the bay. She took comfort from the steady throbbing of the engine. She drew Ceridwen's letter from her pocket. She read: if it is *very* fine, Auntie Grace and I will come over next weekend. Arriving Saturday teatime Porthbychan; please meet.

Now she understood what Mr Davies had been getting at. Ceridwen and the aunt. She shivered suddenly and felt the flesh creeping on her face and arms. The sea was bleak and washed of colour under the shadow of a long roll of mist that stretched from the level of the water almost to the sun. It was nine o'clock in the evening. She could not reach the anchorage before ten and though it was summertime, darkness would have fallen before she reached home. She hoped Alec's dog would be looking out for her on the headland.

The wind blew fresh, but the wall of mist did not seem to

move at all. She wondered if Penmaen du and the mountain would be visible when she rounded the cliffs into the Race. Soon now she should be able to see the Island mountain. She knew every Islandman would sooner face a storm than fog.

So Ceridwen wanted to come over, did she? For the weekend, and with the aunt's support. Perhaps she had heard at last that another woman was looking after her sick husband that she did not want but over whom she was jealous as a tigress. The weekend was going to be merry hell. Bridget realised that she was very tired.

The mainland, the islets, the clifftop farms of the peninsula fell away. Porpoise rolling offshore towards the Race made her heart lift for their companionship.

She took a compass bearing before she entered the white silence of the barren wall of fog. Immediately she was both trapped and free. Trapped because it was still daylight and yet she was denied sight, as if blindness had fallen, not blindness where everything is dark, but blindness where eyes are filled with vague light and they strain helplessly. Is it that I cannot see, is this blindness? The horror was comparable to waking on a black winter night and being unable to distinguish anything, until in panic she thought, has my sight gone? And free because the mind could build images on walls of mist, her spirit could lose itself in tunnels of vapour.

The sound of the motor boat's engine was monstrously exaggerated by the fog. Like a giant heart it pulsed: thump, thump. There was a faint echo, as if another boat, a ghost ship, moved near by. Her mind had too much freedom in these gulfs.

The motor boat began to pitch like a bucking horse. She felt depth upon depth of water underneath the boards on which her feet were braced. It was the Race. The tide poured across her course. The brightness of cloud reared upward from the water's face. Not that it was anywhere uniform in density; high up there would suddenly be a thinning, a tearing apart of vapour with a wan high blue showing through, and once the jaundiced, weeping sun was partly visible, low in the sky, which told her that she was still on the right bearing. There were grey-blue caverns of shadow that seemed like patches of land, but they were effaced in new swirls of cloud, or came about her in imprisoning walls, tunnels along which the boat moved only to find nothingness at the end. Unconsciously, she had gritted her teeth when she ran into the fog bank. Her tension remained. Two ghosts were beside her in the boat, Ceridwen, in a white fur coat, was sitting amidships and facing her, huddled together, cold and unhappy in the middle of the boat, her knees pressed against the casing of the engine. Alec's ghost sat in the bows. As a figurehead he leaned away from her, his face half lost in opaque cloud.

I will get back safely, I will get home, she said aloud, looking ahead to make the image of Ceridwen fade. But the phantom persisted; it answered her spoken thought.

No, you'll drown, you won't ever reach the anchorage. The dogfish will have you.

I tell you I can do it. He's waiting for me, he needs me.

Alec turned round, his face serious. When you get across the Race, if you can hear the fog-horn, he said quietly, you are on the wrong tack. If you can't hear it, you're all right; it means you are cruising safely along the foot of the cliffs...

When you get home, will you come to me, be my little wife?

Oh, my dear, she answered, I could weep or laugh that you ask me now, here. Yes, if I get home.

Soon you'll be on the cold floor of the sea, said Ceridwen.

Spouts of angry water threatened the boat that tossed sideways. Salt sprays flew over her.

Careful, careful, warned Alec. We are nearly on Pen Cader, the rocks are near now, we are almost out of the Race.

A seabird flapped close to her face, then with a cry swerved away, its claws pressed backward.

Above the noise of the engine there was now a different

sound, that of water striking land. For an instant she saw the foot of a black cliff. Wet fangs snapped at her. Vicious fangs, how near they were. Shaken by the sight, by the rock death that waited, she turned the boat away from the Island. She gasped as she saw white spouting foam against the black and slimy cliff. She was once more alone. Alec and Ceridwen, leaving her to the sea, had been sucked into the awful cloud, this vapour without substance or end. She listened for the foghorn. No sound from the lighthouse. A break in the cloud above her head drew her eyes. A few yards of the mountaintop of the Island was visible, seeming impossibly high, impossibly green and homely. Before the eddying mists rejoined she saw a thin shape trotting across the steep grass slope, far, far up near the crest of the hill. Leaning forward, she said aloud: O look, the dog. It was Alec's dog keeping watch for her. The hole in the mist closed up, the shroud fell thicker than ever. It was terrible, this loneliness, this groping that seemed as if it might go on forever.

Then she heard the low-throated horn blaring into the fog. It came from somewhere on her right hand. So in avoiding the rocks she had put out too far to sea and had overshot the anchorage. She must be somewhere off the southern headland near the pirate's rock. She passed a line of lobster floats.

She decided to stop the engine and anchor where she was hoping that the fog would clear at nightfall. Then she would be able to return on to her proper course. There was an unnatural silence after she had cut off the engine. Water knocked against the boat.

Cold seeped into her bones from the planks. With stiff wet hands she opened the bag of provisions, taking off the crust of a loaf and spreading butter on it with her gutting knife. As she ate, she found that for the first time in weeks she had leisure in which to review her life. For when she was on the farm it was eat, work, sleep, in rotation.

I have sinned or happiness is not for me, she thought. It

was her heart's great weakness that she could not rid herself of superstitious beliefs.

Head in hands, she asked: But how have I sinned? I didn't steal another woman's husband. They had already fallen apart when I first met Alec. Is too great a happiness itself a sin? Surely it's only because I am frightened of the fog that I ask, have I sinned, is this my punishment? When the sun shines I take happiness with both hands. Perhaps it's wrong to be happy when half the people of the world are chain-bound and hungry, cut off from the sun. If you scratch below the surface of most men's minds you find that they are bleeding inwardly. Men want to destroy themselves. It is their only hope. Each one secretly nurses the death wish, to be god and mortal in one; not to die at nature's order, but to cease on his own chosen day. Man has destroyed so much that only the destruction of all life will satisfy him.

How can it be important whether I am happy or unhappy? And yet it's difficult for me to say, I am only one, what does my fate matter? For I want to be fulfilled like other women. What have I done to be lost in winding sheets of fog?

And he will be standing in the door wondering that I do not come.

For how long had she sat in the gently-rocking boat? It was almost dark and her eyes smarted from constant gazing. Mist weighed against her eyeballs. She closed her eyes for relief.

Something was staring at her. Through drawn lids she felt the steady glance of a sea creature. She looked at the darkening waves. Over an area of a few yards she could see; beyond, the wave was cloud, the cloud was water. A dark, wet-gleaming thing on the right. It disappeared before she could make out what it was. And then, those brown beseeching eyes of the seal cow. She had risen near by, her mottled head scarcely causing a ripple. Lying on her back in the grey-green gloom of the sea she waved her flippers now outwards to the woman, now inwards to her white breast, saying, come to me, come to me, to the caverns where shark bones lie like tree stumps, bleached, growth-ringed like trees.

Mother seal, seal cow. The woman stretched out her arms. The attraction of those eyes was almost strong enough to draw her to salt death. The head disappeared. The dappled back turned over in the opaque water, and dived. Bridget gripped the side of the boat, praying that this gentle visitant should not desert her.

Hola, hola, hola, seal mother from the eastern cave.

Come to me, come to me, come to me. The stone-grey head reappeared on the other side, on her left. Water ran off the whiskered face, she showed her profile; straight nose, and above, heavy lids drooping over melancholy eyes. When she plunged showing off her prowess, a sheen of pearly colours ran over the sleek body.

They watched one another until the light failed to penetrate the fog. After the uneasy summer twilight had fallen, the woman was still aware of the presence of the seal.

She dozed off into a shivering sleep through which she heard faintly the snorting of the sea creature. A cold, desolate sound. Behind that again was the bull-throated horn bellowing into the night.

She dreamt: Alec was taking her up the mountain at night under a sky dripping with blood. Heaven was on fire. Alec was gasping for breath. The other islanders came behind, their long shadows stretching down the slope. The mountaintop remained far off. She never reached it.

Out of dream, she swam to consciousness, painfully leaving the dark figures of fantasy. A sensation of swimming upward through fathoms of water. The sea of her dreams was dark and at certain levels between sleeping and waking a band of light ran across the waves. Exhaustion made her long to fall back to the sea floor of oblivion, but the pricking brain floated her at last on to the surface of morning.

She awoke with a great wrenching gasp that flung her against the gunwale. Wind walked the sea. The fog had gone, leaving the world raw and disenchanted in the false dawn. Already, gulls were crying for a new day. Wet and numb with cold, the woman looked about her. At first it was impossible to tell off what shore the boat was lying. For a few minutes it was enough to know that she was after all at anchor so close to land.

Passing down the whole eastern coastline, she had rounded the south end and was a little way past Mallt's bay on the west. The farmhouse, home, seemed near across the foreshortened fields. Faint light showed in the kitchen window, a warm glow in the grey landscape. It was too early for the other places, Goppa, Pen Isaf, to show signs of life. Field, farm, mountain, sea, and sky. What a simple world. And below, the undercurrents.

Mechanically she started the engine and raced round to the anchorage through mounting sea spray and needles of rain.

She made the boat secure against rising wind, then trudged through seaweed and shingle, carrying the supplies up into the boathouse. She loitered inside after putting down the bags of food. Being at last out of the wind, no longer pitched and tumbled on the sea, made her feel that she was in a vacuum. Wind howled and thumped at the walls. Tears of salt water raced down the body of a horse scratched long ago on the window by Alec. Sails stacked under the roof shivered in the draught forced under the slates. She felt that she was spinning wildly in some mad dance. The floor rose and fell as the waves had done. The earth seemed to slide away and come up again under her feet. She leant on the windowsill, her forehead pressed to the pane. Through a crack in the glass wind poured in a cold stream across her cheek. Nausea rose in her against returning to the shore for the last packages. After that there would be almost the length of the Island to walk. At the thought she straightened herself, rubbing the patch of skin on her forehead where pressure on the window had numbed it. She fought her way down to the anchorage. Spume blew across the rocks, covering her sea boots. A piece of wrack was blown into the wet tangle of her hair. Picking up the bag of provisions, she began the return journey. Presently she stopped, put down the bag, and went again to the waves. She had been so long with them that now the thought of going inland was unnerving. Wading out until water swirled round her knees she stood relaxed, bending like a young tree under the wind's weight. Salt was crusted on her lips and hair. Her feet were sucked by outdrawn shingle. She no longer wished to struggle but to let a wave carry her beyond the world.

I want sleep, she said to the sea. O God, I am so tired, so tired. The sea sobbed sleep, the wind mourned, sleep.

Oystercatchers flying in formation, a pattern of black and white and scarlet, screamed; we are St Bride's birds, we saved Christ, we rescued the Saviour.

A fox-coloured animal was coming over the weedy rocks of the point. It was the dog, shivering and mist-soaked as if he had been out all night. He must have been lying in a cranny and so missed greeting her when she had landed. He fawned about her feet, barking unhappily.

They went home together, passing Pen Isaf that slept: Goppa too. It was about four o'clock of a summer daybreak. She picked two mushrooms glowing in their own radiance. Memories came of her first morning's walk on the Island. There had been a green and lashing sea and gullies of damp rock, and parsley fern among loose stones. Innocent beginning, uncomplicated, shadowless. As if looking on the dead from the pinnacle of experience, she saw herself as she had been.

She opened the house door: a chair scraped inside. Alec stood in the kitchen white with strain and illness.

So you did come, he said dully.

Yes, she said with equal flatness, putting down the bags.

How sick, how deathly he looked.

Really, you shouldn't have sat up all night for me. He stirred the pale ashes; a fine white dust rose.

Look, there's still fire, and the kettle's hot. He coughed. They drank the tea in silence, standing far apart. Her eyes never left his face. And the sea lurched giddily under her braced feet. Alec went and sat before the hearth. Bridget came up behind his chair and pressed her cheek to his head. She let her arms fall slackly round his neck. Her hands hung above his chest. Tears grew in her eyes, brimming the lower lids so that she could not see. They splashed onto his clenched fists. He shuddered a little. Without turning his head, he said: your hair's wet. You must be so tired.

Yes, she said, so tired. Almost worn out.

Come, let us go to bed for an hour or two.

You go up, she answered, moving away into the back-kitchen; I must take off my wet clothes first.

Don't be long. Promise me you won't be long. He got up out of the wicker chair, feeling stiff and old, to be near her where she leant against the slate table. One of her hands was on the slate, the other was peeling off her oilskin trousers.

He said: don't cry. I can't bear it if you cry.

I'm not, I'm not. Go to bed please.

I thought you would never get back.

She took the bundle of letters out of the inner pocket of her coat and put them on the table. She said: there's one for you from Ceridwen.

Never mind about the letters. Come quickly to me. She stood naked in the light that spread unwillingly from sea and sky. Little channels of moisture ran down her flanks, water dripped from her hair over the points of her breasts. As she reached for a towel he watched the skin stretch over the fragile ribs. He touched her thigh with his fingers, almost a despairing gesture. She looked at him shyly, and swiftly bending, began to dry her feet. Shaking as if from ague, she thought her heart's beating would be audible to him.

He walked abruptly away from her, went upstairs. The boards creaked in his bedroom.

Standing in the middle of the floor surrounded by wet

clothes, she saw through the window how colour was slowly draining back into the world. It came from the sea, into the wild irises near the well, into the withy beds in the corner of the field. Turning, she went upstairs in the brightness of her body.

He must have fallen asleep as soon as he lay down. His face was bleached, the bones too clearly visible under the flesh. Dark folds of skin lay loosely under his eyes. Now that the eyes were hidden, his face was like a death mask. She crept quietly into bed beside him.

Through the open window came the lowing of cattle. The cows belonging to Goppa were being driven up for milking. Turning towards the sleeping man, she put her left hand on his hip. He did not stir.

She cried then as if she would never be able to stop, the tears gushing down from her eyes until the pillow was wet and stained from her weeping.

What will become of us, what will become of us?

HOMECOMING

Nigel Heseltine

Coming back after a long time overseas, everything is very small and falling to bits. Especially the front gates of big houses with the manorial balls leaning off the posts towards the ditch. My car, by contrast, was very large and well held together, being well-made in the US and about thirty feet long.

Down in the village nothing stirred because it was ten o'clock in the morning, but the big house was not in earshot of the village and never had been. Nor had there been anything to hear about the big house since Mr Robert was sold up and that was the last of all of them. That is to say, there was an auction at Llwyn-y-brain for the carved-ivory-inlaid-chippendale occasionals and the dirty, dark Dutch pictures: and I believe all Mr Robert rescued was a print of a laughing girl, and the *Death of Admiral Lord Nelson*, on glass, in red and yellow.

The rooks stayed. They cawed round the house, built their nests, did a shillingsworth of damage and eighteenpennorth of good, as ever. And in the church they bought the parish magazine under Mr Robert's uncle's cross from Flanders, decorated with a button or two from his coat: and above this was Mr Robert's great grand-uncle's marble slab: the Admiral RN. 1809.

These are the humped green hills of Wales of which the exiles in Ohio, and beyond, think. Sound your hooter man and try the gate, I said to myself. But there is no one to open it, and that sort of gate has a joke that if you blow on it it falls on you. The house, too, though I hope not.

The grand thing, I remembered, about Mr Robert's disgrace, is that no one knows what it was. Maybe I could ask in the village. But how do I ask in the village? Try asking.

'D'you... of course you'd remember Mr Robert, I mean young Mr Robert?'

O yes, they remember both Mr Robert, and Mrs Robert. And I remember Mrs Robert, too. Or do I? Or is she the old woman with the swollen leg and the bandage dropping down: and half a petticoat hanging down, and the heels of her shoes worn down, and a torn old fur coat worn down to the skin, and a feathered hat? Yes, she is.

When I was a little boy I dreamed of lawns and balustrades, lead statues and peacocks like Lord Mum has. Had. Mum's dead? Dead. My old father used to say he threw coal out of the window to stop the peacocks screeching at four o'clock in the morning. I well remember the coal in the scuttles year after year, for no one ever had a fire in their bedroom so no one used the coal but the cat.

I have an idea old Mr Robert shot.

'Old Mr Robert now, a good man with the gun now?'

'O ah,' they'll say, 'With the gun,' and we know who was good with the gun.

Did young Mr Robert take after old Mr Robert?

No, he sold up and went.

Where?

Ah.

Coming home after a long time abroad I didn't expect to find the same old faces, though there was Morgan Watkin went into the Bear after eighteen years in Thibet and elsewhere and they said 'Haven't seen you lately.' If young Mr Robert went to Thibet, he went some time ago, because it was about the time I went that it happened.

Mum's a great loss, they said: the loss of the head of the

tail. And Lord Jones, too, another loss for Wales: another madman the less for poor old Wales. All will long remember the schemes of Lord Jones and the fortunes of time and energy poured out on them; all will recollect the fantastic fetes of Lord Jones and the crop of arterioscelerosis which followed them among the weak. Few will find monuments of lasting worth left after him, for it was for the mountains of paper and cubic yards of wind that Lord Jones was loved. I well remember him in my poor old father's time, sprawling his stomach across our dinner table at Sunday supper, and my poor father struggling with his breeding and his collar whenever Lloyd George's name came up, and Lord Jones looking up to heaven whenever he spoke of God's annointed of the Welsh Nonconformists.

Mum was a different sort of Lord from Jones, since he looked like one. His heir killed himself out of a red racing car, the chorus-girl was, as usual, unhurt, and the title is extinct.

It was Mum up there in the Castle entertaining the Prime Minister, and our (Wales' too) ambassador to Tokyo, that helped us all to look down on the doctors in Trallwm, even when they bought our farms off us out of death and illness: and down too, on the bank managers and their red-haired daughters, and down on the poor, lean-chapped solicitors and their lean wives. And owing to Mum, we never saw the secondary school teachers, nor did a dissenting minister ever fumble at our tables.

Old Mrs Robert's dead, too, and after all the lingering on and patching the roof and patching their legs when they fell to bits through the bandages. This gate doesn't need paint, it needs a new gate. My father said a house is all right till the roof goes, and he should have known.

There was a time we came to dinner here, through this gate, before Mrs Robert's leg fell to pieces. My poor father and I came over in the old black car, and my poor mother stayed at home with a cold. And there we sat like gentlemen before a plate of tough mutton, like gentlemen, without our bellies and elbows sprawling on the table before us.

'Idris is he?' said old Mr Robert, meaning my name, and young Mr Robert would have sniggered at me if he had been at home, which he wasn't.

Then there was some joke about Taffy was a thief because Idris was a Welshman, and very loud laughter from my father and old Mr Robert.

Then I half stood up, half screeched that our name being Brain we should live at Llwyn-y-brain, not somebody called Mr Robert.

And all the laughter stopped.

On the way home, my poor old father told me how Mr Robert was the grandson of the heiress of a black-toothed little lawyer who won Llwyn-y-brain at cards from somebody called Devereux Brain in 1790.

'Then whose is the carved stone coat of arms over the door?' I asked.

'Ours,' said my poor old father.

I dare say the people at the Mill might remember about young Mr Robert. I came across the sale bill when I was home from school, and the Mill stuck in my mind since it was held in fief. I had some ideas then about leet courts, and hommagers, and manorial dovecots.

Seated in the sunlight under the pine trees by this decayed gate, into my mind floated a picture of me standing by my nurse's side in the dark by some gate, while she warded off a man with her right hand.

At another time she joked with me that I would one day come and see her in a Rolls-Royce and she would give me tea.

'That is another person I must see if she is alive. Old Hannah.'

I had several times meant to come home in a large car, and here I was at the gate in a large car. But not my gate.

My home was down in a hole, faced north. And is it now further down in the hole and used as a cow-house?

I do not know.

Nor have I yet asked anyone. There was no one on the road coming up, but an old man I did not know.

Driving up from the boat, the country looked small enough all set about with hedges; but there people on the roads and pigs and sheep and hens. But here all objects were half-size, and there was no one at all but this old man, and he had gone round the corner.

There are two ways of visiting my old home: one way is to stumble about the mud which was my poor mother's garden and about the forage where was our drawing room floor. The other way is not to visit it.

When I was a boy they told me the Kingdom of Heaven was at hand, and I left home. There followed a time of being in the world and round the world and through the mill and up the tree. Now follows the car thirty feet long and the trip to the home county.

Cariad.

I am not young Morris Williams went to America and patented his screw cutter and lives in luxury among the film girls. Nor am I Dicky Pugh became Professor at McGill. Nor poor Gwalchmai the Tailor's son who made God knows what wheels go round in Sidney.

No.

When I was a lad, and leaning on my red leather I looked at the fields and the pleasant shimmer that hung on them this morning, and I thought a farmer was the best sort of man and I wanted to be a farmer. Did they give me a farm? No. They laughed. And they put the money into Buenos Aires Pacific and Malayan Jungles, Ltd. And the roof fell in. But not till I'd gone and so I never had to listen to Mother thanking God my poor old father hadn't lived to see it.

I saw my poor old father into his yellow box and under the ground, and I didn't cry for him until I got drunk and fell down the cellar in Salt Lake City, where poor old Father bought a watch when he went round the world in two years. And I remembered his silver watch and I sat down in that cellar and wept.

Now if I had the house I could farm all the thirty acres on the finest principles of science. One old horse in a field by himself was the farming I remembered old Mr Robert doing. I might take them for a drink tonight and find out about young Mr Robert. But no one knows anything, and into the pub I see myself going and good fellowship going up the chimney. Did you ever walk into the pub at home when you were a boy and order drinks?

No.

Hannah.

I'm by her and holding her skirt, and all down the dark lane she beats a man with her hand and giggles: beats him off and I crouch down against her leg and clutch.

Hannah.

I don't expect to see much except an old face without any teeth, and grey hairs streaming about on top.

Where are the Hannah and I who picked oak apples in the August sun?

I cried because when I was five last summer had gone.

Mother clutched the radiator in church and looked out of the window in the hymn, and only brightened for the General Confession. We had 'done those things we ought not to have done.' We never went inside a chapel, but Hell burned with its flames a few feet below the grass of the fields. And I was afraid to dig a hole in case I should fall down into Hell.

Who told us?

It was in the air and the ground, coming from many pulpits out of earshot. Our mild Mr Bach preached of his duty to our neighbour, and the messages of Christmas and New Year.

I read of the old fellows like the Lloyds who had a tame

parson in the house: a humble sort in a spotted coat down the back of it. And a pied harper with a white face and black eyes. My poor old father used to tell me about the Tenants Dinner at the Canal House every year when they brought the rents, and how they toasted his old father and sang songs.

'Ah,' said my father, 'The Banks give them no dinners, now they've changed their landlords for the Banks.'

And every evening when Old Batty Trow brought up the *London Times* from the station, my poor father read it all through.

The old boy was sorry we never sent a Conservative to Parliament but a Liberal. I remember the time some of them sounded me, Idris Brain, about that same Parliament. Mr Robert was the sort, the young one, they'd have liked, but he was sold up first.

If I came back, what sort of men would I get about the place? It takes twenty-five years to make an 'old retainer'. And if I settle here in the sun, how about the young heiress in the bedroom, and the grooms to muck the stables out, and a man in a yellow waistcoat to look at people through the door? What about the girls in the village? Or is the whole country empty? Away on the deserted fields what stirs but the little haze?

We had a theory that the land was finished, and I could always get my poor old father talking about all the families that had sold up in his lifetime, and their heirs drunk their peaceful way about the Empire in its service. Also he knew who was the grandson of a Liverpool merchant and a Manchester merchant, and who was in the merchant's house before him. We were all descended from Brochwell Ysgythrog, with the exception of the Lloyds, who sprang from Cunedda Wledig.

Mother used to say young Mr Robert had every natural advantage, and on top of it he was in the Guards for a time. It was never clear why he left. Then, it seemed that the Roberts would be in Llwyn-y-brain for ever: though it will be I suppose, the wheel of fortune if I am, and old Devereux Brain will be said to rejoice in his grave, though he's very dead and very gone.

My poor old father used to cut the laurels and tidy up the trees in the autumn, and he had one or two days a week in the season shooting with Lord Mum. Old Mr Robert had a few decent coverts where nothing lived but fat pheasants, till he turned it over to a syndicate. Then there was the County Council and every other sort of Council, and the Vestry Meeting and the Cricket Club.

Mother found plenty to do, she was so interested in other people. A man, I often thought, might build himself a replica of Blenheim Palace in the prairies.

No one seems to live here at all. And the gentle haze hovered. No one in the fields moved about the fields. No dogs barked, nor hens crowed nor crows cawed. 'Hoot your horn man and open the gate and have a look where the Roberts lived and look at Devereux Brain's coat of arms if that's all that's left of him.'

With very modern methods I could farm these bits of pasture, but I'd be cramped. On Committees I could not sit for ever. Nor on the Benches, sending the poor away to prison and discriminating according to the unreformed Law. Nor indeed, remembering the stations of everyman according to his neighbours' opinion, or who is better than who.

My mother used to cry 'too too' like an owl after the dogs, and shouted after them in a very threatening way, and sat up with them all night when they were sick giving them teaspoonfuls of white of egg and brandy.

My eye travelled over the little rounded hills and the small sunny valley where the river flashed sudden silver patches, but my thoughts were on the evening of childhood with my face leaning out of the friendly window of home just before my supper, when the sky was an aquarium green and the rooks flew cawing home in the green sky, and the blackbirds called and chaffered in the darkness of the laurels, and the sky melted into the hills of the night. I sniffed away the tears that collected in my nose, and on my heart lay the ache of dear childhood lost, and on my heart also the images of girls smiling who'd have shared my life as they say, but dear, dead images of faces lost in the stream of past years.

Hannah.

I looked down through the haze, and in tangled recollection looked for traces of her cottage. There was a turnpike cottage with the falling chimney: that was in the middle of my eye when as a child I gazed up the valley towards the glorious future of my advancing life.

When I looked over the hills the whole gleaming, glittering world was beyond the hills for me to tread.

Hannah.

My mother said when she left us and married, she'd be broken up by the life, rearing chickens, running a smallholding, as poor Evan's wife. I saw her greying hair, my beautiful Hannah whom I kissed and hugged when she kissed me lovingly goodnight; I saw her gapped teeth and the tired skin falling about her bones.

What is she now?

Can I bear to see Hannah broken, and an old woman, like my mother said?

I have no one to bring back with me, as I'd pictured. That I'd re-enter my country with a glorious partner by my side. The years slip by very quickly, and people slip out of them, and you have no one. I come back to my country as I left it, alone, barring this long, rich car. How could I give away my heart to a woman, and throw it down before her, when it was buried here among the woods and damp pastures and the little rounded hills?

Or if I close my eyes and up the road she comes swinging and walking like she did, and holding her arms out to me.

But whose face?

Hannah's?

Mother's?

I opened my eyes and they opened on the same view of the same valley.

'Practically speaking,' I began thinking, but no practical speaking was possible sitting here at this old gate. I ought to be looking instead at the old cow-house which they made our home into. I remember the stream that Mother swore ran under the house summer and winter.

I ought to be visiting Hannah, however old she is, and I ought to help her, not sit here with tears in my nose. Its a fact that I can get this place very cheaply from what I've been told, and what have I then? A house called Llwyn-y-brain and my name contained in it. And a bigger house than I lived in as a child. And no child of mine to bring up in it.

As I walked the distant cities I thought of other resting places. Rest, I wanted: to rest like I rested in loving arms where I could cry out my heart and bury my face in their loving arms.

Hannah.

My poor old father knew. 'You'll never live here,' he used to say sadly to me when I was a boy, 'Everything's going.' And I was very sad. But he was right; the roof fell in and I went away, and what little I left behind has vanished like grass. You carry a huge heritage about with you, as you think, and rich memories and visions, and smiling faces, and many people. And now when my eyes are shut I see it all, and when I open them I see only the empty beautiful valley, empty for me, beautiful for every one, through my wretched tears.

Young Mr Robert had enough sense never to come back. Or if he did, no one ever knew. I doubt if he ever came and sat at his own drive gate to sniff tears.

It isn't my drive gate.

Our gate fell off its hinges and rotted and an old bedstead probably blocks up the hole. In one of her last letters I remember my mother writing to me half across the world, and she said, Why don't you write? I am so very lonely. I never see anyone. The gate fell off its hinges and there's no one I'm afraid to put it up.'

I pressed the starter to start up the engine, thinking: If I go away what have I but the two pictures? The old ones I had with me all these years, and the new one of the beautiful empty valley, smiling no more for me than for any spectator.

'And I'm no spectator,' I said, 'if I inherited a country, and this valley with it. And my inheritance fastened to me like a chain, pulling me back across the world.'

I looked down at the empty road, as the engine purred, and nobody walked on it.

'What is the future?' I thought, and thought how the future rushed on you like a river and left you suddenly old and lonely like an old stone standing unwanted in the land of your fathers.

A WHITE BIRTHDAY

Gwyn Jones

With their next stride towards the cliff edge they would lose sight of the hills behind. These, under snow, rose in long soft surges, blued with shadow, their loaded crests seeming at that last moment of balance when they must slide into the troughs of the valleys. Westward the sea was stiffened to a board, and lay brown and flat to the indrawn horizon. Everywhere a leaden sky weighed upon land and water.

They were an oldish man and a young, squat under dark cloth caps, with sacks worn shawl-like over their shoulders, and other sacks roped about their legs. They carried long poles, and the neck of a medicine bottle with a teat-end stood up from the younger man's pocket. Floundering down between humps and pillows of the buried gorse bushes, they were now in a wide bay of snow, with white headlands enclosing their vision to left and right. A gull went wailing over their heads, its black feet retracted under the shining tail feathers. A raven croaked from the cliff face.

'That'll be her,' said the younger man excitedly. 'If that raven—'

'Damn all sheep!' said the other morosely, thinking of the maddeningly stupid creatures they had dug out that day, thinking too of the cracking muscles of his thighs and calves, thinking not less of the folly of looking for lambs on the cliff face.

'I got to,' said the younger, his jaw tensing. 'I got reasons.'

'To look after yourself,' grumbled the other. He had pushed his way to the front, probing cautiously with his pole, and grunting as much with satisfaction as annoyance as its end struck hard ground. The cliffs were beginning to come into view, and they were surprised, almost shocked, to find them black and brown as ever, with long sashes of snow along the ledges. They had not believed that anything save the sea could be other than white in so white a world. A path down the cliff was discernible by its deeper line of snow, but after a few yards it bent to the left, to where they felt sure the ewe was. The raven croaked again. 'She's in trouble,' said the younger man. 'P'raps she's cast or lambing.'

'P'raps she's dead and they are picking her,' said the older. His tone suggested that would be no bad solution of their problem. He pulled at the peak of his cap, bit up with blue and hollow scags of teeth into the straggle of his moustache. 'If I thought it was worth it, I'd go down myself.'

'You're too old, anyway.' A grimace robbed the words of their brutality. 'And it's my ewe.'

'And it's your kid's being born up at the house, p'raps this minute.'

'I'll bring it him back for a present. Give me the sack.'

The older man loosed a knot unwillingly. 'It's too much to risk.' He groped for words to express what was for him a thought unknown. 'I reckon we ought to leave her.'

Tying the sack over his shoulders the other shook his head. 'You leave a lambing ewe? When was that? Besides, she's mine, isn't she?'

Thereafter they said nothing. The oldish man stayed on the cliff top, his weight against his pole, and up to his boot tops in snow. The younger went slowly down, prodding ahead at the path. It was not as though there were any choice for him. For one thing, it was his sheep, this was his first winter on his own holding, and it was no time to be losing lambs when you were starting a family. He had learned thrift the hard way. For another, his fathers had tended sheep for

504

hundreds, perhaps thousands of years; the sheep was not only his, it was part of him. All day long he had been fighting the unmalignant but unslacking hostility of nature, and was in no mood to be beaten. And last, the lying-in of his wife with her first child was part of the compulsion that sent him down the cliff. The least part, as he recognised; he would be doing this in any case, as the old man above had always done it. He went very carefully, jabbing at the rock, testing each foothold before giving it his full weight. Only a fool, he told himself, had the right never to be afraid.

Where the path bent left the snow was little more than ankle deep. It was there he heard the ewe bleat. He went slowly forward to the next narrow turn and found the snow wool-smooth and waist high. 'I don't like it,' he whispered, and sat down and slit the one sack in two and tied the halves firmly over his boots. The ewe bleated again, suddenly frantic, and the raven croaked a little nearer him. 'Ga-art there!' he called, but quietly. He had the feeling he would be himself the one most frightened by an uproar on the cliff face.

Slowly he drove and tested with the pole. When he had made each short stride he crunched down firmly to a balance before thrusting again. His left side was tight on the striated black rock, there was an overhang of soft snow just above his head, it seemed to him that his right shoulder was in line with the eighty-foot drop to the scum of foam at the water's edge. 'You dull daft fool,' he muttered forward at the platform where he would find the ewe. 'In the whole world you had to come here!' The words dismayed him with awareness of the space and silence around him. If I fall, he thought, if I fall now… He shut his eyes, gripped at the rock.

Then he was on the platform. Thirty feet ahead the ewe was lying on her back in snow scarlet and yellow from blood and her waters. She jerked her head and was making frightened kicks with her four legs. A couple of yards away two ravens had torn out the eyes and paunch of her new-dropped lamb. They looked at the man with a horrid waggishness, dribbling their beaks through the purple guts. When the ewe grew too weak to shake her head they would start on her too, ripping at the eyes and mouth, the defenceless soft belly. 'You sods,' he snarled, 'you filthy sods!' fumbling on the ground for a missile, but before he could throw anything they flapped lazily and insolently away. He kicked what was left of the lamb from the platform and turned to the ewe, to feel her over. 'Just to make it easy!' he said angrily. There was a second lamb to be born.

'Get over,' he mumbled, 'damn you, get over!' and pulled her gently on to her side. She at once restarted labour, and he sat back out of her sight, hoping she would deliver quickly despite her fright and exhaustion. After a while she came to her feet, trembling, but seemed rather to fall down again than resettle to work. Her eyes were set in a yellow glare, she cried out piteously, and he went back to feel along the belly, pressing for the lamb's head. 'I don't know,' he complained, 'I'm damned if I know where it is with you. Come on, you dull soft stupid sow of a thing – what are you keeping it for?' He could see the shudders begin in her throat and throb back the whole length of her, her agony flowed into his leg in ripples. All her muscles were tightening and then slipping loose, but the lamb refused to present. He saw half a dozen black-backed gulls swing down to the twin's corpse beneath him. 'Look,' he said to the ewe, 'd'you want them to get you too? Then for Christ's sake, get on with it!' At once her straining began anew; he saw her flex and buckle with pain; then she went slack, there was a dreadful sigh from her, her head rested, and for a moment he thought she had died.

He straightened his back, frowning, and felt snowflakes on his face. He was certain the ewe had ceased to work and, unless he interfered, would die with the lamb inside her. Well, he would try for it. If only the old man were here – he would know what to do. If I kill her, he thought – and then: what odds? She'll die anyway. He rolled back his sleeves, felt for a small black bottle in his waistcoat pocket, and the air reeked as he rubbed Lysol into his hand. But he was still dissatisfied, and after a guilty glance upwards reached for his Vaseline tin and worked gouts of the grease between his fingers and backwards to his wrist. Then with his right knee hard to the crunching snow he groped gently but purposefully into her after the lamb. The primal heat and wet startled him after the cold of the air, he felt her walls expand and contract with tides of life and pain; for a moment his hand slithered helplessly, then his middle fingers were over the breech and his thumb seemed sucked in against the legs. Slowly he started to push the breech back and coax the hind legs down. He felt suddenly sick with worry whether he should not rather have tried to turn the lamb's head and front legs towards the passage. The ewe groaned and strained as she felt the movement inside her, power came back into her muscles, and she began to work with him. The hind legs began to present, and swiftly but cautiously he pulled against the ewe's heaving. Now, he thought, now! His hand moved in an arc, and the tiny body moved with it, so that the lamb's backbone was rolling underneath and the belly came uppermost. For a moment only he had need to fear it was pressing on its own life cord, and then it was clear of the mother and lying, red and sticky on the snow. He picked it up, marvelling as never before at the beauty of the tight-rolled gummy curls of fine wool patterning its sides and back. It appeared not to be breathing, so he scooped the mucus out of its mouth and nostrils, rubbed it with a piece of sacking, smacked it sharply on the buttocks, blew into the throat to start respiration, and with that the nostrils fluttered and the lungs dilated. 'Go on,' he said triumphantly to the prostrate ewe, 'see to him yourself. I'm no damned nursemaid for you, am I?' He licked the cold flecks of snow from around his mouth as the ewe began to lick her lamb, cleaned his hand and wrist, spat and spat again to rid himself of the hot foetal smell in nose and throat.

Bending down to tidy her up, he marvelled at the strength

and resilience of the ewe. 'Good girl,' he said approvingly, 'good girl then.' He would have spent more time over her but for the thickening snow. Soon he took the lamb from her and wrapped it in the sack which had been over his shoulders. She bleated anxiously when he offered her the sack to smell and started off along the ledge. He could hear her scraping along behind him and had time at the first bad corner to wonder what would happen if she nosed him in the back of the knees. Then he was at the second corner and could see the old man resting on his pole above him. He had been joined by an unshaven young labourer in a khaki overcoat. This was his brother-in-law. 'I near killed the ewe,' he told them, apologetic under the old man's inquiring eye. 'You better have a look at her.'

'It's a son,' said the brother-in-law. 'Just as I come home from work. I hurried over. And Jinny's fine.'

'A son. And Jinny!' His face contorted, and he turned hurriedly away from them. 'Hell,' he groaned, reliving the birth of the lamb; 'hell, oh hell!' The other two, embarrassed, knelt over the sheep, the old man feeling and muttering. 'Give me the titty-bottle,' he grunted presently. 'We'll catch you up.' The husband handed it over without speaking, and began to scuffle up the slope. Near the skyline they saw him turn and wave shamefacedly.

'He was crying,' said the brother-in-law.

'Better cry when they are born than when they are hung,' said the old man grumpily. The faintest whiff of sugared whisky came from the medicine bottle. 'Not if it was to wet your wicked lips in hell!' he snapped upwards. He knew sheep: there was little he would need telling about what had happened on the rock platform. 'This pair'll do fine. But you'll have to carry the ewe when we come to the drifts.' He scowled into the descending snow, and eased the lamb into the crook of his arm, sack and all. 'You here for the night?'

Their tracks were well marked by this time. The man in khaki went ahead, flattening them further. The old man followed, wiry and deft. Two out of three, he was thinking; it might have been worse. His lips moved good-humouredly as he heard the black-backed gulls launch outwards from the scavenged cliff with angry, greedy cries. Unexpectedly, he chuckled.

Behind him the ewe, sniffing and baaing, her nose pointed at the sack, climbed wearily but determinedly up to the crest.

The Medal

George Ewart Evans

Peregrine stood on the kerb watching him and at the same time watching himself, and asking: 'Why should I be here, out of my orbit and out of all reason, waiting for an old man who knows less of me than I of him?' But he stayed, in spite of his impulse to turn and walk away down the grey street whose flagstoned pavements glistened with a mercy of light after the quick shower of rain. He could not be wrong because of the old man's colour; but he would have recognised him apart from this. Although the fifteen years had whitened the old man's hair and bent his knees, the features and the straight back with the head well set on the shoulders were still the same. He wore a white coat; and this with his fringe of white hair and straggle of beard made his colour shout out. But the children he was shepherding over the road clasped his dark hands without hesitation; and kept hurrying across with his great-footed shuffle as they collected in groups on the opposite kerb.

He watched the old man's face, and the half-smiling absorption he saw there made him decide to stay. But how could he get into conversation with him; and – more difficult still – how could he bring the talk round to his own purpose? The old man glanced his way suddenly and nodded – but not with recognition, but as he would have to any stranger who was interested in his task.

And it was unlikely that he would have recognised him:

Peregrine was only a boy then, barely sixteen, when it happened; and it was unlikely that there was on the old man's side any impress of the event to make him remember. It had probably melted back into his sixty-odd years as easily as a flake of snow disappearing into the tightened surface of a pond. As he recalled the afternoon it happened he glanced up towards the hill. The field hung over the narrow valley a couple of hundred feet above them, a narrow strip of fairly level turf, lit up now to a light yellowish-green by the fitful sunlight. Powderhouse Field they called it; and it was here that sports had been held and football matches played for as far back as he could remember.

But that afternoon had passed in another world. The sun had been a raging furnace, blistering across the sky, driving all the damp and mist out of the valley, making the length of field a bright, torrid strip of scant shade, with the air rising to the bare hilltops in quick, agitated ripples. The feel of that day was still in his limbs: he remembered the vague glow of promise, the sense of being released as he sped over the turf of the roughly prepared track – effortless, as though his body had lightened, brought to a pitch of harmony by the simple miracle of the up-drawing sun. His limbs still held that feeling of power, and he relived the experience so vividly that he paced restlessly about the pavement; until the old man glanced his way and looked at him curiously.

He did not know in what part of him the other feeling lay – the quirk, the twist in the fibre that the afternoon had also left. But this, too, had persisted with the years and had brought him here; powerfully causing him, in spite of himself, to wait on an old man who was now leading little children across a busy road.

They came now in a continuous stream that showed no sign of stopping; and he could do nothing while the old man was so occupied. He would have to wait until the whole school of children had crossed before approaching him.

The long-past afternoon held his mind again, shutting out

the grey morning and the watery, ineffectual sun. He was in the first heat, and was pacing about waiting for the starter to order the runners to their marks when he saw a woman at the side of the track nudge her neighbour and heard her loud whisper:

'Look, there's Mr Brown the Black. He's going to run in the race!'

The coloured man was standing near the start, his jacket under one arm, and his boots, stuffed with tattered socks, held in his other hand. He was trying to catch the starter's attention. Tommy John, handicapper as well as starter, shouted across to him: 'All right, Lewis; we'll have you in the last heat.'

He must have been well over sixty years old then; and the crowd laughed with good humour at the thought of Mr Brown the Black running with all those young men: *Of course he was a champion runner in his own day; but now! What can you expect at his age?*

Peregrine had a very good mark and won his heat easily. Tommy John had whispered to him just before: 'You got the best lane on the track, young 'un. Keep going!' He rose like a bird from the tremendous crash of the starting gun, became conscious of his light limbs, and felt the dark forms and the white faces of the crowd slip harmoniously past him. Then he felt the tight, momentary pull of the tape across his down-thrusting chest. As he paced luxuriously back to the start to get his sweater Tommy John gave him a nod and a smile he could not read.

Afterwards he stayed on the side of the track to watch the other runners. When it came to Brown's heat a man who stood on the track shouted down:

'Where shall I put the black fellow, Tommy?' The starter waved his programme casually.

'Take him for a walk up the course will you, Seth?' Brown grinned as he was led to a mark ten yards in front of the others. He tucked up his sleeves, and then his trousers carefully above his knees, showing his lean, sinewy legs and big feet shining with sweat. The women screamed with laughter. *Look! Mr Brown the Black. He's black all over. Deer-foot they used to call him when he was a runner. But look at his feet now!*

Lewis Brown the Black paid little regard to this: he stood solidly on his mark in the standing start of the old timer. When the gun went off he sprang forward, running with long, ungainly strides which nevertheless ate up the ground in front of him. He finished yards ahead of the nearest runner. As he came back the crowd shouted with delight; but he paid little attention to them as he paced down the track with a slow dignity.

There were no cross-ties and the final came an hour later – an hour that was filled with the tinny uproar of the jazz bands. Peregrine was strung up and anxious to get it over; and he was one of the first of the finalists to take up his mark. Brown the Black was the next to come out on to the course: he halted yards in front of Peregrine and stayed there immovable while the other runners paced around him like a bunch of restless colts prancing about an old warhorse. *Come on, Deer-foot! Show 'em your heels!* came a quick challenge from the crowd, and Brown grinned in answer. But the starter was nodding towards him; and the starter's man came purposefully up the track and gently caught Brown by the arm:

'Back you come, Lewis. By here your mark is,' and nodded towards a spot two or three yards to the rear.

'No, no!' Brown protested, 'here my mark is, for sure. Here I was standing in the heat.'

'But here you got to stand now, boyo.' The starter's man was firm. 'There was some mistake, no doubt, the first time.' And Brown shrugged his shoulders and took up his old, dated stance on the fresh mark. It all happened so quickly that few of the crowd noticed it.

But Peregrine, standing a few yards behind Brown, took

in every move of the incident; and the look of resignation on the coloured man's face hit him. It was wrong to pull him back! That was his mark in the heat: he was entitled to hold the same mark in the final. Peregrine was about to speak to the starter's man; but the man spoke to him first, whispering urgently without turning his head as he passed: 'Keep going, young 'un. You can win it.' Then came the compelling shout of the starter, 'Get on your MARKS!' driving out all thought except the many-times rehearsed response to the signal and the low obeisance towards the tape stretched out across the field a hundred yards or so in front of them.

After the gun's report Peregrine gained immediately on Brown's slower impetus; but it was a struggle, even so, to pass him. Then in the whole-bodied thrust forward he saw no other runner, but hearing behind him a desperate *tck, tck, tck*, a disembodied sound chasing him – the urgent and chilling challenge of another runner's feet gaining rapidly upon him. But he breasted the tape before the sound caught up with him; and then he became aware for the first time of the crowd and their loud shouting. Brown the Black – he learned afterwards – was third.

Back again out of the clear, blueprinted past to the urgent and disturbing present where right action is hidden in a mist of numberless possibilities: his hand closed round the medal they had given him on that day. He had often recalled how he had gone up for it before a crowd quiet in a precarious hush, and had heard a voice say in pure denunciation: 'Brown the Black should have won that. It's his by right. If he had his proper mark you never would have caught him!' And that voice had long echoes because it was his own voice, reminding him that he was not whole, that a part of him had been left on the field that afternoon, not to be recovered until he had tried to put things right with this old coloured man.

Then on his return after many years he had found the medal thrust away in the drawer, hidden from the light as he had often willed his memory of it to be; and hearing that

Brown was still alive and living in the village the urge to seek him out had brought him to the edge of the kerb where he was now standing like a diver estimating the steel-smooth water which he sensed rather than saw beneath him. Brown the Black! Well, he had better tackle him and get it over: pluck out the small snag that had been irritating his self-respect for so many years. Besides, it would be rather pleasant to put this matter right; to give the coloured man his proper due, although the day was rather late for doing so. He watched the old man escort two more children across to the kerb. Would he remember? Or would he have to lead him laboriously back to the event on Powderhouse Field?

At that moment the stream of children suddenly ceased. He walked across to the old man and got into conversation with him. Yes, he remembered the afternoon well; even remembered his name and that he had won the sprint. And when Peregrine told him that he was not very happy about winning it, Brown shrugged his shoulders with the same gesture and said in the same high-pitched voice he so well recalled:

'You had to win it, mun. It was rigged.'

'Rigged?'

'Ay, didn't you know? But perhaps you were too young: you were carrying a pile of money, most of it Tommy John's, the starter's. You had to win! All that money was betted on you.'

Peregrine felt a jolt: he had gone to pick up an empty vessel and it had turned out to be full. He was going to put things right, and now it seemed the old coloured man was putting things right for him. But rigged! That explained a number of things. Peregrine shifted his stance: the old man was not as he had pictured him. He had been too eager for good works and had made a blunder. Yet as he watched the old man's lined face and friendly eyes he knew that was not his thought:

'It was a very hot afternoon,' Brown said with a smile.

'I remember it well.' Then nodding towards the cemetery on the other side of the valley: 'Tommy John won't handicap no more: he's up there now, back right behind scratch himself.' But he spoke without bitterness.

Peregrine's hand closed again on the medal in his pocket; and with a stubborn resolve to see his purpose through he took it out and showed it to the old man. He looked at it with interest:

'I knew there was a medal, but I never saw it.'

'It's yours by right,' Peregrine said with relief, and with the satisfaction of saying a long-rehearsed line. 'Wouldn't you like to take it?'

The old man glanced up quickly and Peregrine immediately saw the look as a refusal. Another false move. He saw his impulse to return the medal for what it was: his wish to right a wrong had been mixed with something less pleasant, and the old man had instantly spotted it; and he was now brushing aside the brash gesture with all the grace of a natural good breeding. He wanted to snatch the medal from the old man's hand and return it to his pocket where it should have stayed. For a moment they both stood awkwardly on the pavement. Then a sudden clear note interrupted them: the sound of a boy's voice from the opposite kerb calling insistently:

'Mr Brown. Mr Brown the Black.'

The old man looked up and held up his hand to signal the small boy to stay where he was. Then after looking up and down the road he shuffled across, taking the boy's hand and bringing him over the road. They were both smiling as they reached the pavement where Peregrine stood: the old man out of a natural pleasure, the boy with the satisfaction of a lesson rightly carried out.

When they stood near Peregrine, Brown – who was still holding the medal – asked the boy:

'So you are the last today?'

The boy nodded, his hand still in the old man's.

'Well, the last shall be first, so they say. And the first ought to have a prize, for sure.'

And bending over, the old man pinned the medal on the boy's coat. The boy flushed as he realised that he was meant to keep it, and without another word he ran up the pavement as hard as he could go – eager to bring his good fortune home to his family.

For a moment Peregrine stood amazed at the old man's action. But as he saw the small boy scuttling exultantly up the street a deep laughter took hold of him; and it was not long before the old man was laughing with him. Then the hard light of the too enduring past broke up instantly into a spatter of bright and quickly vanishing colours. And their laughter continued, long after the sound of the boy's footsteps had gone right out of the narrow, echoing street.

A STORY

Dylan Thomas

If you can call it a story. There's no real beginning or end
and there's very little in the middle. It is all about a day's
outing, by charabanc, to Porthcawl, which, of course, the
charabanc never reached, and it happened when I was so
high and much nicer.

I was staying at the time with my uncle and his wife.
Although she was my aunt, I never thought of her as
anything but the wife of my uncle, partly because he was so
big and trumpeting and red-hairy and used to fill every inch
of the hot little house like an old buffalo squeezed into an
airing cupboard, and partly because she was so small and
silk and quick and made no noise at all as she whisked about
on padded paws, dusting the china dogs, feeding the buffalo,
setting the mousetraps that never caught her; and once she
sleaked out of the room, to squeak in a nook or nibble in
the hayloft, you forgot she had ever been there.

But there he was, always, a steaming hulk of an uncle, his
braces straining like hawsers, crammed behind the counter of
the tiny shop at the front of the house, and breathing like a
brass band; or guzzling and blustery in the kitchen over his
gutsy supper, too big for everything except the great black
boats of his boots. As he ate, the house grew smaller; he
billowed out over the furniture, the loud check meadow of
his waistcoat littered, as though after a picnic, with cigarette
ends, peelings, cabbage stalks, birds' bones, gravy; and the

forest fire of his hair crackled among the hooked hams from the ceiling. She was so small she could hit him only if she stood on a chair, and every Saturday night at half past ten he would lift her up, under his arm, on to a chair in the kitchen so that she could hit him on the head with whatever was handy, which was always a china dog. On Sundays, and when pickled, he sang high tenor, and had won many cups.

The first I heard of the annual outing was when I was sitting one evening on a bag of rice behind the counter, under one of my uncle's stomachs, reading an advertisement for sheep dip, which was all there was to read. The shop was full of my uncle, and when Mr Benjamin Franklyn, Mr Weazley, Noah Bowen, and Will Sentry came in, I thought it would burst. It was like all being together in a drawer that smelt of cheese and turps, and twist tobacco and sweet biscuits and snuff and waistcoat. Mr Benjamin Franklyn said that he had collected enough money for the charabanc and twenty cases of pale ale and a pound apiece over that he would distribute among the members of the outing when they first stopped for refreshment, and he was about sick and tired, he said, of being followed by Will Sentry.

'All day long, wherever I go,' he said, 'he's after me like a collie with one eye. I got a shadow of my own *and* a dog. I don't need no Tom, Dick, or Harry pursuing me with his dirty muffler on.'

Will Sentry blushed, and said: 'It's only oily. I got a bicycle.'

'A man has no privacy at all,' Mr Franklyn went on. 'I tell you he sticks so close I'm afraid to go out the back in case I sit in his lap. It's a wonder to me,' he said, 'he don't follow me into bed at night.'

'Wife won't let,' Will Sentry said.

And that started Mr Franklyn off again, and they tried to soothe him down by saying: 'Don't you mind Will Sentry'… 'No harm in old Will'… 'He's only keeping an eye on the money, Benjie.'

'Aren't I honest?' asked Mr Franklyn in surprise. There was no answer for some time, then Noah Bowen said: 'You know what the committee is. Ever since Bob the Fiddle they don't feel safe with a new treasurer.'

'Do you think *I'm* going to drink the outing funds, like Bob the Fiddle did?' said Mr Franklyn.

'You *might*,' said my uncle slowly.

'I resign,' said Mr Franklyn.

'Not with our money you won't,' Will Sentry said.

'Who put dynamite in the salmon pool?' said Mr Weazley, but nobody took any notice of him. And, after a time, they all began to play cards in the thickening dusk of the hot, cheesy shop, and my uncle blew and bugled whenever he won, and Mr Weazley grumbled like a dredger, and I fell to sleep on the gravy-scented mountain meadow of Uncle's waistcoat.

On Sunday evening, after Bethesda, Mr Franklyn walked into the kitchen where my uncle and I were eating sardines with spoons from the tin because it was Sunday and his wife would not let us play draughts. She was somewhere in the kitchen, too. Perhaps she was inside the grandmother clock, hanging from the weights and breathing. Then, a second later, the door opened again and Will Sentry edged into the room, twiddling his hard, round hat. He and Mr Franklyn sat down on the settee, stiff and mothballed and black in their chapel and funeral suits.

'I brought the list,' said Mr Franklyn. 'Every member fully paid. You ask Will Sentry.'

My uncle put on his spectacles, wiped his whiskery mouth with a handkerchief big as a Union Jack, laid down his spoon of sardines, took Mr Franklyn's list of names, removed the spectacles so that he could read, and then ticked the names off one by one.

'Enoch Davies. Aye. He's good with his fists. You never know. Little Gerwain. Very melodious bass. Mr Cadwalladwr. That's right. He can tell opening time better than my watch.

Mr Weazley. Of course. He's been to Paris. Pity he suffers so much in the charabanc. Stopped us nine times last year between The Beehive and The Red Dragon. Noah Bowen, ah, very peaceable. He's got a tongue like a turtle-dove. Never a argument with Noah Bowen. Jenkins Loughor. Keep him off economics. It cost us a plate glass window. And ten pints for the Sergeant. Mr Jervis. Very tidy.'

'He tried to put a pig in the charra,' Will Sentry said.

'Live and let live,' said my uncle.

Will Sentry blushed.

'Sinbad the Sailor's Arms. Got to keep in with him. Old O. Jones.'

'Why old O. Jones?' said Will Sentry.

'Old O. Jones always goes,' said my uncle.

I looked down at the kitchen table. The tin of sardines was gone. By Gee, I said to myself, Uncle's wife is quick as a flash.

'Cuthbert Johnny Fortnight. Now there's a card,' said my uncle.

'He whistles after women,' Will Sentry said.

'So do you,' said Mr Benjamin Franklyn, 'in your mind.'

My uncle at last approved the whole list, pausing only to say, when he came across one name: 'If we weren't a Christian community, we'd chuck that Bob the Fiddle in the sea.'

'We can do that in Porthcawl,' said Mr Franklyn, and soon after that he went, Will Sentry no more than an inch behind him, their Sunday-bright boots squeaking on the kitchen cobbles.

And then, suddenly, there was my uncle's wife standing in front of the dresser, with a china dog in one hand. By Gee, I said to myself again, did you ever see such a woman, if that's what she is. The lamps were not lit yet in the kitchen and she stood in a wood of shadows, with the plates on the dresser behind her shining – like pink-and-white eyes.

'If you go on that outing on Saturday, Mr Thomas,' she said to my uncle in her small, silk voice, 'I'm going home to my mother's.'

Holy Mo, I thought, she's got a mother. Now that's one old bald mouse of a hundred and five I won't be wanting to meet in a dark lane.

'It's me or the outing, Mr Thomas.'

I would have made my choice at once, but it was almost half a minute before my uncle said: 'Well, then, Sarah, it's the outing, my love.' He lifted her up, under his arm, on to a chair in the kitchen, and she hit him on the head with the china dog. Then he lifted her down again, and then I said goodnight.

For the rest of the week my uncle's wife whisked quiet and quick round the house with her darting duster, my uncle blew and bugled and swole, and I kept myself busy all the time being up to no good. And then at breakfast time on Saturday morning, the morning of the outing, I found a note on the kitchen table. It said: 'There's some eggs in the pantry. Take your boots off before you go to bed.' My uncle's wife had gone, as quick as a flash.

When my uncle saw the note, he tugged out the flag of his handkerchief and blew such a hubbub of trumpets that the plates on the dresser shook. 'It's the same every year,' he said. And then he looked at me. 'But this year it's different. *You*'ll have to come on the outing, too, and what the members will say I dare not think.'

The charabanc drew up outside, and when the members of the outing saw my uncle and me squeeze out of the shop together, both of us catlicked and brushed in our Sunday best, they snarled like a zoo.

'Are you bringing a *boy*?' asked Mr Benjamin Franklyn as we climbed into the charabanc. He looked at me with horror.

'Boys is nasty,' said Mr Weazley.

'He hasn't paid his contributions,' Will Sentry said.

'No room for boys. Boys get sick in charabancs.'

'So do you, Enoch Davies,' said my uncle.

'Might as well bring *women*.'

The way they said it, women were worse than boys.

'Better than bringing grandfathers.'

'Grandfathers is nasty too,' said Mr Weazley.

'What can we do with him when we stop for refreshments?'

'I'm a grandfather,' said Mr Weazley.

'Twenty-six minutes to opening time,' shouted an old man in a panama hat, not looking at a watch. They forgot me at once.

'Good old Mr Cadwalladwr,' they cried, and the charabanc started off down the village street.

A few cold women stood at their doorways, grimly watching us go. A very small boy waved goodbye, and his mother boxed his ears. It was a beautiful August morning.

We were out of the village, and over the bridge, and up the hill towards Steeplehat Wood when Mr Franklyn, with his list of names in his hand, called out loud: 'Where's old O. Jones?'

'Where's old O?'

'We've left old O behind.'

'Can't go without old O.'

And though Mr Weazley hissed all the way, we turned and drove back to the village, where, outside The Prince of Wales, old O. Jones was waiting patiently and alone with a canvas bag.

'I didn't want to come at all,' old O. Jones said as they hoisted him into the charabanc and clapped him on the back and pushed him on a seat and stuck a bottle in his hand, 'but I always go.' And over the bridge and up the hill and under the deep green wood and along the dusty road we wove, slow cows and ducks flying by, until 'Stop the bus!' Mr Weazley cried. 'I left my teeth on the mantelpiece.'

'Never you mind,' they said, 'you're not going to bite nobody,' and they gave him a bottle with a straw.

'I might want to smile,' he said.

'Not you,' they said.

'What's the time, Mr Cadwalladwr?'

'Twelve minutes to go,' shouted back the old man in the panama, and they all began to curse him.

The charabanc pulled up outside The Mountain Sheep, a small, unhappy public house with a thatched roof like a wig with ringworm. From a flagpole by the Gents fluttered the flag of Siam. I knew it was the flag of Siam because of cigarette cards. The landlord stood at the door to welcome us, simpering like a wolf. He was a long, lean, black-fanged man with a greased love curl and pouncing eyes. 'What a beautiful August day!' he said, and touched his love curl with a claw. That was the way he must have welcomed The Mountain Sheep before he ate it, I said to myself. The members rushed out, bleating, and into the bar.

You keep an eye on the charra,' my uncle said; 'see nobody steals it now.'

'There's nobody to steal it,' I said, 'except some cows,' but my uncle was gustily blowing his bugle in the bar. I looked at the cows opposite, and they looked at me. There was nothing else for us to do. Forty-five minutes passed, like a very slow cloud. The sun shone down on the lonely road, the lost, unwanted boy, and the lake-eyed cows. In the dark bar they were so happy they were breaking glasses. A Shoni-Onion Breton man, with a beret and a necklace of onions, bicycled down the road and stopped at the door.

'Quelle un grand matin, monsieur,' I said.

'There's French, boy bach!' he said.

I followed him down the passage, and peered into the bar. I could hardly recognise the members of the outing. They had all changed colour. Beetroot, rhubarb, and puce, they hollered and rollicked in that dark, damp hole like enormous ancient bad boys, and my uncle surged in the middle, all red whiskers and bellies. On the floor was broken glass and Mr Weazley.

'Drinks all round,' cried Bob the Fiddle, a small, absconding man with bright blue eyes and a plump smile.

'Who's been robbing the orphans?'

'Who sold his little babby to the gyppoes?'

'Trust old Bob, he'll let you down.'

'You will have your little joke,' said Bob the Fiddle, smiling like a razor, 'but I forgive you, boys.'

Out of the fug and babel I heard: 'Come out and fight.'

'No, not now, later.'

'No, now when I'm in a temper.'

'Look at Will Sentry, he's proper snobbled.'

'Look at his wilful feet.'

'Look at Mr Weazley lording it on the floor.'

Mr Weazley got up, hissing like a gander. 'That boy pushed me down deliberate,' he said, pointing to me at the door, and I slunk away down the passage and out to the mild, good cows. Time clouded over, the cows wondered, I threw a stone at them and they wandered, wondering, away. Then out blew my uncle, ballooning, and one by one the members lumbered after him in a grizzle. They had drunk The Mountain Sheep dry. Mr Weazley had won a string of onions that the Shoni-Onion man raffled in the bar. 'What's the good of onions if you left your teeth on the mantelpiece?' he said. And when I looked through the back window of the thundering charabanc, I saw the pub grow smaller in the distance. And the flag of Siam, from the flagpole by the Gents, fluttered now at half mast.

The Blue Bull, The Dragon, The Star of Wales, The Twll in the Wall, The Sour Grapes, The Shepherd's Arms, The Bells of Aberdovey: I had nothing to do in the whole, wild August world but remember the names where the outing stopped and keep an eye on the charabanc. And whenever it passed a public house, Mr Weazley would cough like a billygoat and cry: 'Stop the bus, I'm dying of breath!' And back we would all have to go.

Closing time meant nothing to the members of that outing. Behind locked doors, they hymned and rumpused all the beautiful afternoon. And, when a policeman entered The Druid's Tap by the back door, and found them all choral with beer, 'Sssh!' said Noah Bowen, 'the pub is shut.'

'Where do you come from?' he said in his buttoned, blue voice.

They told him.

'I got a auntie there,' the policeman said. And very soon he was singing 'Asleep in the Deep'.

Off we drove again at last, the charabanc bouncing with tenors and flagons, and came to a river that rushed along among willows.

'Water!' they shouted.

'Porthcawl!' sang my uncle.

'Where's the donkeys?' said Mr Weazley.

And out they lurched, to paddle and whoop in the cool, white, winding water. Mr Franklyn, trying to polka on the slippery stones, fell in twice. 'Nothing is simple,' he said with dignity as he oozed up the bank.

'It's cold!' they cried.

'It's lovely!'

'It's smooth as a moth's nose!'

'It's *better* than Porthcawl!'

And dusk came down warm and gentle on thirty wild, wet, pickled, splashing men without a care in the world at the end of the world in the west of Wales. And, 'Who goes there?' called Will Sentry to a wild duck flying.

They stopped at The Hermit's Nest for a rum to keep out the cold. 'I played for Aberavon in 1898,' said a stranger to Enoch Davies.

'Liar,' said Enoch Davies.

'I can show you photos,' said the stranger.

'Forged,' said Enoch Davies.

'And I'll show you my cap at home.'

'Stolen.'

'I got friends to prove it,' the stranger said in a fury.

'Bribed,' said Enoch Davies.

On the way home, through the simmering moon-splashed dark, old O. Jones began to cook his supper on a primus stove in the middle of the charabanc. Mr Weazley coughed himself blue in the smoke. 'Stop the bus,' he cried, 'I'm dying of breath!' We all climbed down into the moonlight. There was not a public house in sight. So they carried out the remaining cases, and the primus stove, and old O. Jones himself, and took them into a field, and sat down in a circle in the field and drank and sang while old O. Jones cooked sausage and mash and the moon flew above us. And there I drifted to sleep against my uncle's mountainous waistcoat, and, as I slept, 'Who goes there?' called out Will Sentry to the flying moon.

MATCH

Roland Mathias

The night had been uncertain of rain or moon and the grass in the longer patches on the slope towards the pill showed silver and green impartially, as though it had been dewed and combed then, roughly and to and fro. It would be a wet ball for a while, no doubt of that. On the lower touch three boys in wellingtons who had completed their office with the flags were beginning to chase each other, ducking under the grabs that went for tackles. Up the hill there was whistling and a workman or two behind the rising walls of the craft block, Saturday-happy and lost. Apart from these, Wynford Hughes was the first on hand. From where he stood the farther posts, barely safe from a sudden fall-away of ground to the thorn bushes at the pill bottom, masted into the full grey waters of the reach. Tide was up, and the calm envelope of morning seemed at pressure.

A hubbub at the field gate told of the arrival of the bus, and as the players, hooped with black and yellow and blue and gold, spread like a hot breath outward on the slope, Wynford knew that he needed to come to a sort of understanding, and that with himself. He had made the effort, he had come out early deliberately in the hope of being cheered up. It would be nonsense now to be girding round and round upon his bitterness when for an hour at least he could be caught up in a fight not his own. No, not his own narrowly. But he had always accustomed himself to loyalty, to being inside the skin of the bodies he belonged to, to enthusing when his enthusiasm was asked for and expected. Some members of the staffroom, he knew very well, regarded this weakness of his with silent pity. Others were not so silent. 'Adolescent,' Garro Davies would no doubt remark if he had the chance. His intentionally audible asides from Intellectual Corner had been a trial for years. Adolescent. Well, what of it? He was a member of the School. Why not shout for it? It was just this self-regarding falsity, this lofty absence of loyalty, that so infuriated him in every walk. Was it only boys, working in a house system without houses, playing for a team ideal that was talked up too much, who would undertake to suffer inconvenience, exhaustion and injury? Who cared if the ideals didn't go much beyond the physical? It was something to have an ideal, wasn't it, and to work towards it? Damn Garro and all his spawning superiors! His very being at Bush this morning was his answer. To hell with them! He couldn't help it and why should he? He was born to enthusiasm as the heart pumps faster. To hell with Garro!

But this was the very thing he had come out not to do, to get bitter again. Look at the game, Wynford boy. Whistle blowing now. Its shrill peep ran round the edge of the plantations, sounded warningly against the quarry, and came back in a huff from the reach, where the morning still waited for a wind. The mudflats were well covered. It was surely high tide.

When Wynford switched back from long sight he was still in time to see Gethin standing, hands on hips before the referee, watching the quick ceremony of the toss. Gethin, small, black, barely five foot two and smiling the more because of it. Gethin Du he would have been in the Welsh parts. But here just Gethin. Or Geth. Or even Wait, or Weight (no one would care to produce a definitive spelling), presumably from some half-forgotten middle school joke about Geth your Weight. Possibly too a tribute to the bulging muscles of Gethin's thighs and the thickening pillar of his neck. None of his friends and equals called him Weight. Only perpetual up-and-comers like Ceffyl Collett, who was just the sort of feeble middle-school crackpot to have stuck together such a joke in the first place. Ceffyl Collett. A silly name Ceffyl. But he had been one of those who for rugby's sake had wanted to learn Welsh, and the sound of it had been for him the noise of his zeal. 'Ceffyl, ceffyl, ceffyl a horse,' he went when older boys were about. And Ceffyl he had become and went on becoming, the great sandy mane and twitching ears growing a hand or two higher every time one looked. Running the line today was Ceffyl, an expert whose own play, some rearing and bucking in the tight excepted, rarely went beyond whinnying the side from a yard or two back. No peace on the field if Ceffyl had the flag and wind left.

Well, there it was, Wynford reflected. Ceffyl on the lower touch meant peace, comparatively, till half-time. Ah, there was Sam Toogood of the Staff in sight now, pegging along at speed, afraid of missing a minute. He would be no trouble. The world was well lost to Sam once the game started. A column of mist, barely distinguished at its base from the plinth of wood and misted hill beyond the quarry, stood up like the morning-sign of prophecy over Monkton Cave. In that half-world of heights and shapes it seemed no great step from the hyena bones under the rock and the middens of the gnawed-at ages. Perhaps only additional physique and a stripier jersey.

But to attend. Gethin had kicked off, downhill towards the reach. The fresh hide of the ball as it flew was lost for a moment in the stealing water greys behind. A clean catch from one of the Gwendraeth lumps in the second row, and a boot to touch. Regulation so far. A deal of rucking and mauling followed, all on the lower side over against Ceffyl, whose voice made raucous encouragement. But it soon appeared that of the two packs, that of Gwendraeth was much the heavier and harder. Ben Thomas, their captain, muscles squared-off and head shaven, was worth two men at close quarters, and his up-shouldered, angular form came through again and again like an auger through lath. Once he ran clear and was pulled down more by luck than judgement. Then a stoppage. And out. Out it came, the ball thudding from hand to hand. Roberts, the tall red-headed centre, went streaming out into the open spaces beyond the hands of Ogley and Russ in the middle of the home line. The long stride lengthened, short-cut red-gold hair seeming to balance and helmet the figure as it ran. Roberts was away. But no. No. Gethin Du was coming. Across, across short thick black legs cutting into the arc of danger. The full back challenged. Roberts thought to dummy and did not, feeling Gethin's breath. Out went the ball to the wingman, left, up the hill. Out, up the hill came the short legs, quick steps calculated, converging on the wingman running blind, head back, for the line. A sudden bulge of spectators shut Wynford out of view. There was a thud and a cheer. 'Good boy, Weight,' came clear across the field from Ceffyl. The ball was now passing high over Wynford's head at an angle into touch. Gethin was up already, had played the ball and cleared. As the spectators stood back, the wing was slowly getting up.

Exaltation shuddered up Wynford's spine. He was involved and fully, as he had not been for more than odd minutes in the past year. 'School!' His voice tingled out from the top of the spine with a primitive volition of its own. He *was* the black and yellow, jersey and man and heart.

And yet the moment ebbed. Mauling had begun again on the far touchline. The tickling seconds when he had *been* Gethin Du, calculating and heroic, had slipped away. Back and fore slopped his spirit now, in the sump of the game, and over the slug and beat and repeat he could see again the look that he had come here to forget – the look of Kathy's head against the reddened edges of his anger. It was not, by this time, a tearful visitation. Neither was it a vision changeable or topic for argument. Kathy's head, how well he knew it! – black and fit and curled as for a medallion, tidy and composed and short of conversation, yet tearing grouts in his composure day in, day out. Heaven knew he had tried to be dispassionate. Iorwerth was not a bad fellow, he supposed. There were points about him, that cool ability to dissect and analyse, for instance, which impelled both respect and dislike, that more charming Garro-ishness which left one tamping and without a cause. Not difficult to understand that Kathy's ordered mind should prefer Iorwerth to his own moody evasions and wayward enthusiasms. Mind, ordered mind? What had that to do with it? He could have borne Iorwerth's mental superiority and agreed that Kathy should admire it. But who knew that it stopped there? Mind, bah! There was no mind about it. Just a damned dirty intrigue, growing and growing ever since Iorwerth came to lodge with them. What a fool he had been to believe that such an arrangement *could* work! All in the cause of kindness. All towards the end of a world.

Where were they now, while he worked out his stupid enthusiasms? God, wouldn't it be something to die in a moment of complete, honest, spiny engagement, not knowing or caring for anything but the reach of arm and heart and the blessed cry of battle about the head? Wouldn't it? Ceffyl was shouting. That was it. That was the nearness he had in the ears. Ceffyl was shouting, at full stretch, hoarse. Ceffyl was shouting. God, the noise! What about, for heaven's sake? He looked. There was a heap near the lower touch. Something had just happened. Scurlock, perhaps, in a scrap again. Still shouting. No. Out came the ball. Gwendraeth, Gwendraeth. On to Evans, on to Roberts. And Roberts was away again, pushing off from Ogley's chin and cutting left. Roberts with his red-gold Mercury-head and his long stride was beautiful, beautiful. And he kicked. This time he kicked. Short and neat over the full-back's head. He's in, he must be. No, no. What's that? What is it? What's happening? Gethin again! Doubling back on the far side and under the ball first after all. Down on one knee and Roberts flat out over the top! Up and away now, Gethin, running forward again and pointing the ball high and long towards the lower touch.

No matter. It could not last. Wynford's identification with the School had ebbed entirely. Something about Roberts obsessed him. The red-gold helmet of his head. The purity in the lines of his body. The determination, the severity, the will to conquer. The will to pierce clean through and wound, wound, wound. To strike here, there, anywhere. To ward off with arms like flails that little black figure, that composed little black figure, to upset his calculations and trample him and leap over him and go on, on. So far, oh yes, so far, those little tricks had held out. That composed manner, the black hair still in place. But it would not be so much longer. No, he would go through, and through, and through. Hit 'em again, boy. And again. Let there never be any answer, any comeback. Ever again.

Roberts drew Wynford's eyes magnetically all over the field. Monkton Cave and its flanking woods had thrown off their hieratic mist and the slate-smooth of the sea-reach was no more than a mirror for the nearer action. No outside portent now would sway the issue. The battle was here. The sun threatened presently from behind an aqueous pall, but for the moment withheld.

Half-time came and went, with no more effect on Wynford's trance of vengeance than the barest registration of a temporary stillness. It was a time for girding on, for red-gold preparation, for sharpening the shaft of righteousness. It was a time too that brought Ceffyl up from the lower touch. Ceffyl, a little hoarse and glassy with exhaustion. But Wynford cared nothing for him now. He might screech as he wished, sweat as he wished for school, for the dark ranks of obstinacy, for man and his puny endeavours, for the trickiness of sin. Bellow, boy, bellow! Much good may it do. Shout! The grace is departed and the glory with it. To your tents, O Israel. God shall smite you with his red-gold shaft and thereafter there shall be no truth that you can bear that cannot I. No meddling truth that can touch me. Not of Kathy or Iorwerth or Garro or any damned infidel among you. Go back, back. Because you must. Must.

'Hir,' said Ben Thomas suddenly from near at hand. Gwendraeth were throwing in from touch. 'Watch the long, boys,' yelled Ceffyl in a translator's ecstasy. 'Watch the long! – O Connie, get your man, for God's sake get your man.' But Gwendraeth were boring through, punching holes with every moment of possession. Ben Thomas, angular and shaven, was talking away, first on one side, then on the other, working every trick he knew. Ogley went down to a rush and sagged over the shoulders of those who helped him up, his head fixed in one direction and eyes staring, unlidded, like those of a lizard caught in the open. Gethin picked up off Ben Thomas' toes and aimed a neat punt at Ceffyl. But it was no good. The forces of Wynford's vengeance were pressing on. Back, back went the School, back against the sea, and no wind stirred to their aid. Up in the air, down on the ground, Gwendraeth were the masters. Of all save Gethin. Gethin, unsmiling now and breaking his usual rule. 'Cover, boys, cover,' he shouted in the distance, crossing and crossing again like the pattern of darkness. Cover? Cover what? And with what? Wynford's thoughts moved in eagerly. There is no cover for you, my boys. You'll be pierced through and through and behind that line you'll know what I've put up with and lived. No time so long as the time behind the line. You'll know.

Here it comes. Roberts, away again. Away on the left. Red-gold head moving against the grey of the sea, not quite distinct in the lower field corner, but moving in, practised as an arrow. Out to Devonald on the wing. Full back takes him. In to Roberts again. Oh this is it! He must be in, must be! Wynford screwed up his eyes in a haze of conviction. His red-gold, righteous victory...

Suddenly Ceffyl, fifteen yards off, whinnied himself several hands higher than usual. 'Weight, O Weight, well done boyo! Ruddy marvellous!' From the lower touch there was a deeper roar. Through a momentary lane left by the fast-gathering forwards Wynford, not believing, saw Roberts, arms outstretched for the line, lying flat on his face, and nearer, lower, a black form leeching his ankles. It could not be. It could not. There was nothing they could say against his cause, was there?

But it went on. Minute after minute and still no score. Gethin, the outhalf of darkness, was under every ball that Gwendraeth kicked and thudding into every man who came through. Back and across and back and kick and across. How dare he pit his rotten cause against the stride of vengeance? How dare he? Back and across and back and into touch. And Russ. Russ was backing him now. And Scurlock, there, catching Roberts in the open for the first time. Black hearts, how can you? Know you not justice and the meaning of wounds? Ben Thomas talking now, cursing under breath, trying every trick that forward dominance could manage. Evans and Roberts switching and scissoring. Devonald cutting inside. On, on. Time yet. On. No. Russ challenging. Taking Devonald high and hard. Ball loose. On, on. Roberts following. No, Gethin coming in with a swoop and picking off his feet and twisting, down – caught! Caught at last by Ben Thomas and two others. Caught in possession. Down on the ground. Now, now for it. On the line itself. No – no, godfathers no, Gethin up and playing the ball and twisting again. Back and fore, weaving, held by his jersey. Touch, screw kick to touch. And the whistle! The whistle!

Wynford could not believe it. The rest of the morning passed bitterly through his mind. A drawn match. So much right and so much power on one side... All of the game, the very rules themselves, on one side. And a drawn match. Intricate the manner of darkness, and the effrontery, the effrontery of those that should be cast away... He stopped suddenly and looked.

Gethin was passing, overhung with Ceffyl and the gamut of words. 'Boy O boy, didn't the School play well?' Ceffyl was stuttering. 'Didn't they just?'

Gethin said nothing. His face, grimed with sweat, was composed. He looked at Wynford as though about to say something, and then neither smiled nor spoke. Presently he had passed on up to the gate.

The world was turning, turned. The sun, where was it? Right overhead, and it was noon. High noon unrealised. Shafts everywhere. Among the trees, the grasses. Neither for nor against. Light upon the unshadowed, emptying field and the sky windless. Was it always a draw if one had enough courage?

Looking up to the gate, Wynford could just see Ceffyl's mane hanging over the last incomers to the bus, jogging and demonstrating still. Against all his feelings of an hour he stared, and heard the blood run back to his heart. Ceffyl, voluble, idiotic enthusiast, beyond reason and beyond bitterness! The School play well, did he claim? Man alive, there had been no team but Gethin! And no fight but in that composed black courage. But *the School* played well. So said Ceffyl in his folly. Could it be that so many collective feeblenesses, so many miseries, so many downright sins of commission could be retrieved in part by playing on to the end with nothing but courage? And did not that courage speak to him now against the heat of blood, against conviction of right, against the very wounds dealt and not paid for? To play on to the end hiding regret and only learning the rules too late to win. But never too late to draw.

With a shift of shoulder he settled his heart in place. So his medallion head might fight a draw against all odds and remain silent, the same but unrecognised. The sea's reach was shorter now and the tide less full. Copper of beech and yellow of lesser trees ringed the field's southern edge where the quarry lay. The hyena bones were at one remove in their cave. 'Kathy!' he cried for only himself to hear, and turned to face the hill.

HESTER AND LOUISE

Siân James

When I was a girl, women looked their age, particularly if they were widows. My grandmother could only have been in her early sixties when I remember her, but she had settled comfortably into old age; wiry grey hair scraped back into a tight bun, round cheeks reddened by sun and broken veins, dark shapeless clothes, grey woollen stockings baggy round the ankles.

She'd once been a district nurse. On the mantelpiece in the parlour, there was a photograph of her standing importantly at someone's front door, large bag in hand, round hat pulled down to the eyebrows, but I found it difficult to believe in this starched image, could only see the untidy old woman she'd become; shooing the hens away from the back door with a dirty tea cloth, bending to cut a lettuce in the garden, her large bottom in the air, or her most typical pose, standing at the gate, squinting into the sun, her big heavy breasts supported on her folded arms.

I stayed with her for five or six weeks every summer, not for her benefit or for mine, but because it eased the pressure on my parents who kept a dairy in St John's Wood.

I liked London far better than the Welsh countryside. I missed the Friday evening dancing class, the Saturday morning cinema, the big public library which was only two streets away and my friends, Jennifer and Mandy.

There was no dancing class, cinema or library in Brynawel

and the village children scorned me. The much praised fresh air always seemed to have an overlay of cows' shit; I much preferred stale air with petrol fumes.

I didn't like Gran's meals either; runny boiled eggs with orange yolks for breakfast, dirty looking potatoes, greens and grey meat for dinner, rough brown bread with cheese and salad for supper, with the occasional addition of caterpillar or little black flies.

I didn't like my bedroom although it had once been my father's; the bed was hard, the pillows lumpy and the sheets coarse. But worst of all, my grandmother had no bathroom and expected me to strip-wash in the back-kitchen with carbolic soap and the same wet towel she'd used. The summer when I was twelve, she promised to keep out when I was washing, but twice she forgot and came barging in and once the coalman came to the door and saw me in vest and knickers. 'Oh, the man will never be the same again,' was all she said when I complained.

When I was thirteen, I begged my parents to let me stay home; pleaded and cried, promising to serve in the shop, wash dishes, even peel potatoes. 'I'll do anything, anything, but please don't send me away to Gran's.'

My father thought I was mad. He and his brother Bob had had an idyllic childhood, he said; all the freedom of the fields and woods, fishing, ratting, scrumping apples, helping the farmers with the harvest, earning sixpence a day. 'This one's a girl though, Isaac,' my mother said. 'She likes different sorts of things, girls' things, going round Woolworths and Boots and the market, buying shampoo, trying on lipsticks, things like that. Try to understand.'

'It's not just those things,' I said, since he was looking at me as though he'd never seen me before. 'It's just that Gran doesn't have a bathroom, so I don't have any privacy. And I'm not a child any more. I have my periods now and I have to wear a bra. And I'm not going to bath in a back-kitchen and you shouldn't expect me to.'

That shut him up. He could never tolerate any talk of bodily functions. And my mother promised to write a polite letter to Gran, explaining how I felt.

We had a letter back by return of post.

She quite understood the position. I was going through a little phase, that was all, and they were not to worry. She'd spoken to Hester and Louise, the Arwel sisters, though, and I was most welcome to use their bathroom any time I wanted to, twice a day if I'd a mind. And they, as I probably remembered, had an all-pink bathroom the size of a small ballroom with bottles of this and that and loofahs and sponges and a special brush for scrubbing your back, pale grey carpet on the floor and a little fluffy cover on the WC

'The Arwel sisters,' my father said, casting his eyes to the ceiling.

'I'll go,' I said. 'I love Miss Hester and Miss Louise. The Sundays they invite me to their house after church are the only days I enjoy.'

'She's a girl, Isaac,' my mother said again. 'Try to understand.'

Miss Hester and Miss Louise didn't seem to belong in Brynawel, but to a world I knew only from the cinema. I'd often try to describe them to my friends, Jennifer and Mandy. 'No, they're not really young, perhaps thirty-five or so, even forty, and they're like ladies in old-fashioned films with tiny waists and delicate faces like flowers. Well, I think they may have had sweethearts once, but perhaps they were killed in the war. No, they're definitely not spinsters, spinsters are altogether different. No, they don't have jobs, they just have money, plenty of money, so they can do whatever they want to. Sometimes they hire a car to take them out shopping or to the seaside or to church on Sunday. Otherwise they stay at home doing tapestry, reading magazines and changing their clothes. Oh, they're very gentle and kind. Just think of me going there each day! And I know they'll give me home-made lemonade and iced biscuits every time. I'm really looking forward to staying with Gran this year.'

The sisters called on the very afternoon I arrived, to remind me of their promise. 'Isn't she pretty,' one said, smoothing down my rough curly hair. 'Isn't she pretty,' the other replied. They always repeated each other's pronouncements. 'Hasn't she grown tall and slender.'

'Hasn't she grown tall and slender.'

'Don't turn her head,' Gran said. 'She's foolish enough already.'

'We've heard different. We've heard that she had an excellent end of term report and that she's a marvellous little pianist.'

'A marvellous little pianist, as well.'

'We want her to play for us. We've had our piano tuned.'

'We've had our old piano tuned specially.'

I'd forgotten the way they so often stood with their arms clasped tightly round each other's waists, as though they wanted to be one person instead of two.

They were dressed that day in cream high-necked blouses, full, dark-green skirts, black belts pulled tight and cream high-heeled shoes. They always dressed identically, though they weren't twins. Hester was a year and a half older and she was also a little taller and perhaps a little more elegant. Louise's eyes were a brighter blue, though, and her lips were fuller. I could never decide which was the more beautiful.

'Well, I must ask you to go now,' Gran said, 'because I always listen to my serial at four o'clock. I'll send the girl round after supper.'

I could never understand how Gran had the nerve to treat them so casually, even rudely, when she was ugly and poor and they were so beautiful and so rich.

'Who told them about my report?' I asked her when they'd left.

'I did, of course. I told them you were going to college to

be a teacher. In case they have any ideas of turning you into a lady's maid.'

'Are they so rich?'

'Oh yes. Their father had the best farm in the county, but when he knew he was dying and with no son and heir, he had to sell it all, land and livestock, to buy an annuity for those two. Their mother had died, you see, when they were toddlers; soon after Louise was born, and he spoiled them, of course, and everybody spoiled them. Even when they were schoolgirls, they never had to do a hand's turn for themselves, let alone anything in the house or the farm. It was hard on him in the end. But what could he expect? He'd brought them up to be butterflies.'

'Why didn't they get married?'

'No one from round here was stupid enough to ask them, I suppose. To tell you the truth, your Uncle Bob seemed to be thick with them at one time, but he never seemed to know which one of them he liked best and then he was called up and met your Auntie Dilys, so he lost them both.

'He was a born farmer, Bob was, ready to do a day and a half's work every day. Their father would have been proud to have him as a son-in-law, and he would have been the making of those girls, but which one of them?'

'But which one of them?'

'God help us, if you're going to start being an echo like those two.'

'God help us,' I began. But she cuffed me on the head and turned the wireless on.

To think that one of them could have been my auntie. My Auntie Dilys was nice enough, but she wasn't special in any way.

If I hurried over my supper and the washing up, I had two whole hours to spend at the Arwels and I savoured every moment.

I'd be shown first into the drawing room where we'd have

coffee, real coffee, served in a silver coffee pot, where I sat in a fat velvet chair and was passed a cup and saucer of green and gold eggshell china, pink crystals of sugar and exotic dark chocolates. After this delightful ritual, I might look at their photograph albums; two plump little girls sitting together on a garden seat, chubby legs and solemn round faces, two young girls in frilly party dresses with ribbons in their hair, two young ladies in their first ball gowns.

'This one is you, isn't it Hester?' I'd ask.

'Wait a minute, now. I really can't tell. No one seemed sure, even at the time. They always called us the girls or the sisters, you know, never our names. We hardly knew ourselves which of us was which, did we Louise?'

'We hardly knew ourselves, did we, Hester?'

The house was so beautiful, so wickedly luxurious; thick carpets everywhere and floor-length velvet curtains, heavy as the falling darkness outside. They lent me a dressing gown of plum-coloured chenille and after I'd bathed and washed my hair, they'd take me to their bedroom and take it in turn to brush my hair, brushing gently, gently, almost as though they were in a trance. They each had an ivory hairbrush, I remember, one with a silver H on its back, the other an L. I wished my hair was long and straight and raven-black instead of short and reddish-brown. Gran had forbidden me to use make-up, but they insisted that complexion milk didn't count, so they smoothed it into my face and my neck and my shoulders. It felt soft and silky and smelt of little white roses and purple violets, so different from Gran's carbolic soap. 'She's got such delicate skin, hasn't she Hester?'

'Her skin is as soft as a baby's, isn't it, Louise?' Afterwards I was encouraged to try on their perfumes – luckily Gran had lost her sense of smell – and I loved repeating their grand French names; *Je Reviens, Bal de Nuit, Ma Griffe, L'Air du Temps, Mon Désir, Arpège.*

Their house had several bedrooms, six or seven I should think, but they slept together in the largest and grandest one in the front. (The long small room at the back of the house was where their maid, housekeeper, cook slept, a bustling little woman called Gwladys who had been with them since their birth. They always got her to walk home with me, but she never came very far because she was frightened of the dark and I wasn't.)

They slept in a high, old-fashioned bed with a brass bedstead. The quilt was a bright turquoise silk, the colour matching the tiny rosebuds on the cream wallpaper, and the carpets, the heavy curtains and the satin lampshades were a deep, voluptuous pink. There was a highly polished bedside table on either side of the wide bed with a framed photograph on each.

One evening Hester picked up the photograph from her side, gazing at it as though willing me to notice it. I didn't need much prompting. 'What a handsome man,' I said. He was handsome; dark curly hair, slanting eyes, straight nose and full, curved lips. And as I might have guessed, Louise then brought me the photograph from her bedside, and at first I thought it was the same man in a different pose.

'Brothers,' I said then. 'Twin brothers.'

They smiled at each other, but didn't volunteer any information and I was too shy to ask.

One evening towards the end of my holiday, though, when it was mothy and dark as Gwladys walked me back to Gran's, I ventured to ask her about the handsome young men.

She seemed flustered. 'What young men?'

'The brothers in the photographs on the bedside tables.'

'Yes. Very nice young gentlemen,' she said then. 'Sons of a very good family. Not from round here at all.'

'What happened to them?'

'Killed in the war.'

'Both of them?'

'Both of them. Nice young men. Real gentlemen. Not from these parts, of course.'

'Poor Miss Hester and Miss Louise.'

'Yes indeed. 1944. Ten years ago now, very near. And never anyone else after.'

'Gran told me that my Uncle Bob was friendly with them once.'

She was furious. 'Nonsense. Your Uncle Bob was a labourer. He worked on the farm but he never came to the house. He knew his place, Bob did. Your Gran likes to boast, that's all. I'm turning back now. You can run from here, can't you.'

'Gwladys *was* in a stew when I told her about Uncle Bob courting the sisters,' I told Gran.

'She knows nothing about it. She was in Swansea nursing her mother during the war. It was I who had to look after the sisters then.'

'Do you mean when their young men were killed?'

'Their young men? What young men are talking about now?'

'Real gentlemen, Gwladys said they were. Sons of a very good family.'

'Gwladys is getting soft in the head.'

Now that I had my interesting association with the Arwel sisters to sustain me, Gran didn't seem so much of a trial; indeed she often seemed nothing but a fairly harmless relic from an unhygienic past. Sometimes in the evening, I sat at her side on the old rexine sofa, leaning my head on her shoulder, almost able to ignore the dirty dishcloth smell coming from her.

'Tell me a secret, Gran.'

'What about?'

'You know. About the sisters. About their past. Tell me why they're different from other people.'

'I'll tell you when you're older.'

'Gran, you'll be dead when I'm older.'

She chuckled at that. She liked straight talk. She leaned forward, looked me straight in the eye and cleared her throat. 'They never had any men friends, real gentlemen or

otherwise. They only had one man between them and he...
he was an Italian prisoner of war.'

'Is that all?'

'Isn't that enough?'

'He was a handsome man, anyway. I saw his photo, two
of his photos.'

'Married, of course.'

'So they were in disgrace, is that it?'

'You could say that, yes.'

I could see her hesitating about going on, but I squeezed
her arm and gave her an imploring look.

'Their father found him in bed with them, you see. In
between them, he said. That seemed to be the last straw. I
don't think he'd have minded quite so much if he'd been
either firmly on one side or the other, but there he was
cuddled up between them. All three of them naked as babies,
he said.'

'Naked?' I swallowed hard. Of course I knew about sexual
intercourse, but I found certain of the details very unsavoury.

'Naked as new born babies.'

'And after the war, I suppose he went back to Italy?' I tried
to keep the quiver out of my voice.

Gran paused again. 'No. No, sometime later he was found
shot in Henblas woods.'

'Murdered? Do you mean murdered?'

'That's right. Murdered. The Italians weren't exactly loved
at that time, especially the very handsome ones. No one
found out who'd shot him. There were no clues. It could
have been anybody, I suppose.'

'I think it was their father don't you, Gran, who murdered
him.'

'It could have been their father. He had a massive heart
attack six months later. It could have been guilt, I suppose.'

'Poor things. Poor Hester. Poor Louise.'

'Don't cry. You wanted the truth and now you must accept
it.'

'And you had to look after them. Were they very unhappy?'

'They were, of course. Very unhappy.'

She glanced at me again, as though wondering how much more I could take. 'Go on,' I said.

'And pregnant as well. Very pregnant. Five or six months pregnant.'

'Both of them?'

'Both of them. Well, that's what happens when you lie naked in bed with a handsome young man, especially an Italian.'

'Both of them pregnant?'

'Yes.'

'Oh Gran, whatever happened to their little babies?'

'I looked after their babies, one boy, one girl, until they were old enough to be adopted. And it was straight after that their father died.'

'Gran, it's a terrible story, a cruel story.'

'That's why I didn't want you to hear it.'

We were both silent for a while. I felt there was a hand twisting my stomach. I wanted to be sick, wanted to vomit up everything I'd heard.

'But they've still got each other, haven't they,' I said at last.

'Yes, they've still got each other, God help them, foolish as they are.'

I thought of them, their arms tightly clasped round each other's waists, repeating each other's sentences, spending hours laying out their dresses on the wide bed, deciding which to wear, trying on their lovely jewellery.

'Shall I spend the whole day with them tomorrow, Gran? Because it's my last day? They said I could.'

'Then I suppose you can. Silly girl. Go to bed now. You can come again next year... unless I'm dead before that, of course.'

I bent to kiss her good night. 'Silly girl,' she said again.

A VIEW ACROSS
THE VALLEY

Dilys Rowe

What was left was a presence in a room where all the wood
was scrubbed white. The presence, already disembodied,
had assumed a power it never had before. It was hard for
those present to know what they felt in the presence of an
event so difficult to understand, so impossible to reconstruct.
Feelings ran like mercury between compassion and awe.
Fortunately routine provides a set of phrases and even a tone
of voice which concealed this confusion. Time that morning
was short. The man considering the case said he must ask
himself what else it could be but misadventure; he found no
answer, he said. No one unfortunately would have been
likely to pass by that place, not at that time of day and on a
Sunday. He paused again and found the next part of the
formula. All too often, he went on, in that place the deaths
of children came before him, but it would have been unfair
in this case to expect the parents to start a search
immediately because a girl whose habits must have been a
little out of the ordinary did not return in time for her lunch.
He sighed and made a gesture with his open hand. He was
disgruntled like a good workman who had not been given
the right tools for the job. He was returning this verdict, he
said, because they did not know what went on up there.

The child had been alone on the slope of the hill. She drew

547

all her hair down before her face, pressed her chin to her neck, and knelt there for something to do in the brazen afternoon. Through the back of her neck the sun drove a boomerang of light grown solid, a creature consumed by light, as light had consumed the pieces of white hot metal pulled out of the furnace to amuse her as she stood at the foundry door. They would pick them out for her on the long tongs, shapes like toys distorted and fantastic, shapes pure with light and possessed by it; they held them out to her so that the heat flew at her face like an angry swan restrained. She felt the white-hot boomerang now probing through her neck to meet her chin at the other side. She pressed her chin still closer. She created dusk with the heavy curtain of hair, and at the day's height she put out the sun. It was a new state of being, and labouring with her breath she enjoyed to the full its exquisite pain. She opened her eyes to the thick falling hair, blew on it and felt the moisture returning from it to her face. She shook it three times. It swung in its own weight like a pendulum, and then hung still. Sweat started on her forehead and spread. When it became unbearable she raised her head and through the hair falling back around her face she saw the scar cut by the valley white after her own dusk, until in a moment the sun drenched it again.

She hitched up at her waist the green pleated skirt which the last wind before the heat of the day blew against her legs. Haze was beginning to rise on the summer Sunday. Occasionally gorse cracked in the heat. It must have been between one and two o'clock because below nobody was moving in the toy streets. She saw the tower of feathers where a train crawled on its stomach amongst the black hulks of the steel works and the bright red boxes of the new factories. A car visible only in the sun's searchlight moved where a road must be. From the cemetery something too small to see, a glass shade it may be with two dirty joined hands inside it, flashed her the living sun from amongst its deaths. No one moved in the streets. They were all in their houses stifling in the fumes from roast beef, lamb and mint, hot jam and rhubarb. The valley had life as a wound has microbes, but not on a Sunday between one and two o'clock. Stripped of its power, it lay harmless and neutral in the sun.

She was high above it where woods had been, where there was nothing to wreck. Somewhere behind her foxes and badgers played, and beyond that further than she could walk there was a lake. But only men with their heads in the clouds and gentle happy madmen would use this right of way with wind strumming in their ears when there were other ways in and out of the valley. And so it was no part of the landscape where the girl was now. Where she was four white clovers might spring up in all her footsteps, or she might be a girl conjured for convenience out of flowers. But she was not. She was a girl who was out at a forbidden time on the muted Welsh Sunday.

From her pockets she took the six bracelets. She put three on each arm and shook them towards the sun. She held her thin arms out and admired them hanging at her wrists, then pushed them hard up her arm as far as each would go. The sharp edges cut into the white freckled flesh. She had chosen them carefully for their graded sizes, two from jam jars, two from jars of chutney and two from jars of fish paste. She pulled them down again to the wrists and ran her fingers through the grooves of the red weals, three on identical places on each arm. She sat on, above the valley, shackled in the six bracelets.

From here the river was only a river, winding its way on a map through the lie of the land. Its banks were not doomed by memories of old deaths; it was not a place where pitiful drowned dogs covered with the grey plush that is left of them show the holes of their eyes. Down the valley the viaduct leapt in three great bounds across it, and she could see now that when trains stopped on it, sprawled in their monstrous immobility, people would be up there with their heads well out of the smoke, parcelled eight at a time in little boxes. In a musty book which might have been the only one an illiterate old man long dead had in his house for sentimental reasons, she had once seen a drawing on a page hanging off the thin cords of the binding. 'A landscape in Tuscany', it said, showing a long arched bridge in the fields with hills behind it. This might have been a landscape in Tuscany under the sun.

Time in this new dimension of sun and space was long and vacant, solid so that she felt she could have cut it into little blocks. She was appalled by the length the afternoon would be. She cupped her hand and called, not seriously thinking that at this time it would bring the others up to her from the valley. Calling still she beat her hand against the sound. She was the child the children follow in the streets; when they form their little groups conferring against walls, it is she who bends the lowest in the centre and walks first away, upright carrying the threat and the secret of the destruction they have planned. If she says there are to be no spitting games today nobody spits for the furthest, the longest, the slowest, although the game has been devised by her. To this call they did not come.

But it was then for the first time that the hare showed itself, its haste less like fear than the movement of a dance. Seeing her he ran back to the slope below all in the flick of his tail. She went to the place where she had left her shoes and made on them the two crosses for seeing a hare. She took them off again, and threw herself down with her face into the sun. Turning she watched the leather of her shoe lapping up the crosses for as long as, in a more familiar dimension, a kitten would take to drink its saucer of milk. Then time came over her again, and pressing her fingers to her eye balls she walked about in the yellow halls behind her eyes in the greatest nothing she had never seen.

Into the depths of this endless time she threw at random one thought after another and watched them ripple slowly outwards and outwards in the lazy afternoon. It was between one and two o'clock on a Sunday in the whole long history of the world, and the moment that had just passed and this minute had gone for ever into the whole world's past. There would never be another time when one girl and one only, 13 years and 6½ days old, would be lying alone on the hill hungry and damp from the sun between one and two o'clock. She thought of valleys which are green and fruitful and yellow with corn; a slow river would be winding through green banks. Cowslips would be lying like newly-washed children around it and poplars and larches would be beyond the water meadows. This valley was not green, but sometimes a piece of slag would have the print of a fern stamped deep into it. Sometimes a stream would turn red with copper like the biblical sea or yellow like the Tiber with filth. When the snow came the birds left their confident footprints on the slag heaps mistaking them for hills. When it was two o'clock the hooter sounding between hills sent packs of soiled and sweating men moving through the valley. And when it was dark the furnace opened its inflamed mouth and caught stars for flies.

The vaporous halls behind her eyes turned solid, and through the skin of her lids she saw the cloud that was passing for a moment over the sun trailing with it a wind that was no more than a message. She sat up. Purple lights blocked her newly opened eyes. When they cleared the hare came again running in the arc of a circle from below. She called to him, and crossed her shoes and ran to where it had disappeared. Licks of flame were playing in the bracken and in the grass at its edge. Over its blazing purity the river was full of the thick and various filth it collected, there were leprous deaths on the grave stones and the black hulks of the steel works were crusted with barnacles of soot and grime. On the canal she could pick out the galleon, the treasure boat, with the gold breast plates and the rings with stones like blood on the sandals and the bracelets. It was rotting and sodden, the coal barge that had not been used for thirty years. Every year of her life its swollen timbers had become a little more decayed until now their ends were fraying. Sitting in the sun with the fire beginning she remembered one of many deaths. Men stood with ropes and poles for the whole of a day; children looking for sensations as hens peck for anything that comes out of the ground were shooed away only to gather again and again. The boy lay only where he had fallen in the discoloured yellow water. He did not get himself destroyed in a lonely place. He fell quietly, almost under their eyes, with a low wall between him and the road, and the path was there for anybody to be walking on at a lucky time.

But where he fell the barge imprisoned him, weeds parcelled his nine-year-old body with the awful precision of accident, and the men dragged in shallow water through a whole day, and when they were meant to find him they did find him tangled in weeds. The canal is not like the sea, the powerful destroyer, returning its dead when the deed has been accomplished. The canal only gives them reluctantly after a struggle covered with the long green slime with which it brands the bodies of dead dogs. The girl was dappled in sunshine and hatred for his wilful destruction. And the hare came again.

He was running now in no hurry, as children run to music when they expect it suddenly to stop. The afternoon had reached its turning. The sun was a blatant disc of light, from which the wind had snatched the warmth to give it to the fire. The fire burnt now on three sides of the hare. The child thought she would look at the sun through a flame. She ran into the middle of the hare's circle to catch a sight of this miracle of miracles. She lay outstretched in the middle of light and the soft unburdened flame leaping and the tireless hare running in his sacrificial pleasure as far away from her as he could go. They all lay about her like gifts she did not deserve. She felt the angry swan straining again for her flesh. She saw the hare moving in now closer to her than he had dared. He was beyond caring now for her presence or she for his. Pleasure moved inside her mounting from the pit of her stomach to her throat in waves of exquisite agony. The wind changed on the turning of the afternoon tide. The fire was already a great bracelet all around her just open for the arm. She lay enchanted, and the circle closed.

TIME SPENT

Ron Berry

Doctor Gammon dogs-eared the buff envelope. 'This report confirms the X-rays. Set your mind on it, Lewis, you are finished in the pit. You're one hundred per cent. Neglect, man, sheer neglect. I've sent scores of colliers to the NCB medical board.'

Lewis Rimmer crossed his legs. He had wide, upward-tilting eyes, dark, vulpine above the bony ridge of his white-glazed nose, tight-skinned like his forehead. Forehead and anchor-boned jowl trapped him: a man estranged by passions. 'I'm fifty-seven,' he said. 'They can't expect a bloke to change his job at fifty-seven. All I've ever done is work on the coal, driving headings in Fawr pit, been driving headings for nigh on thirty years.'

The Doctor tutted impatience. 'Let's be frank. If you don't leave the coalface you won't reach sixty.'

'By the Jesus...' .

'Here's my advice. Live outdoors as much as possible, cultivate an allotment, grow vegetables, flowers, then you'll increase your chances of lasting to a good age.'

Lewis jigged his foot. 'My pigeons keep me occupied. Where'll I find a job though, ah?'

'Forget about employment. See your lodge secretary, see him today. He'll put you in touch with the compo sec. You are entitled to full compensation.'

From the doorway, Lewis said, 'Crime in my opinion, shoving a man on the street. Goes against the grain with me.'

Doctor Gammon aimed his forefinger. 'Lewis, you are finished in the pits by *law*! The Coal Board dare not employ you after serving fourteen days' notice.'

'By the Jesus... so long, Doctor,' he said.

Head sunk, hands fisted in his jacket pockets, Lewis walked the wet pavements. Pen Arglwydd mountain towered behind shifting drizzle. He crossed the road to the chemist shop. Alert behind the counter, her lips stretched, the girl said, 'Good morning,' – glancing at his prescription – 'Mr Rimmer.'

'Bit of chest trouble,' he said, staring at her, thinking, nice piece, aye, guaranteed banker for the old through-and-through stakes. She makes my Bessie look like a bag of slurry tied 'round the middle. 'What's the damage, gel?'

A shivering spasm wriggled her shoulders. The rawness of his ugly face, his huge, black-nailed, gripping fingers. Ugh, stupid old miner. 'Seventy pence, Mr Rimmer.'

'Reckon Nye Bevan's turning in his grave', he said, grinning, slapping his sides.

'Mmm, I don't know what you mean.' She heard the soft rustle of maple peas in his jacket pocket. 'Please take a chair. I shan't be a few minutes.'

A talkative group of matronly women filed in, ranged themselves along the counter. Lewis fell away into himself, his foot jigging, sight and hearing emptying away. The girl reappeared, still smiling, lost for Lewis, vanquished. He left the shop without thanking her for his tablets.

Drizzle thinned to creeping mist across the massive frontal nub of Pen Arglwydd. As he came out of the corn chandler's store Lewis saw his bus leaving the curb. He decided to walk home. Take it steady. Nothing spoiling in the house. His pigeons were fed and watered. Bessie's morning job. Least she could do, by the Christ, after living off his back since she clicked for William. Just gave birth once. Barren ever since. Therefore waste. Swill chucked down the drain.

Single paced, unamazed, Lewis paused at a street corner,

shuffled a narrow half-circle, muttering, 'Well-aye, shortcut.'
He climbed the up-and-over footbridge, sulphur-tasting
smoke flooding above the full trucks. Lewis crouched, held
onto the handrail, coughed, coughed, his heart hammering.
Down on the pavement again, he cursed his weakness. Then
he cursed having to walk home. He came to a road bridge,
Melyn brook flowing below, black as enamel. Leaning on
the parapet, Lewis cleared his chest, 'Chhhhachhh,' and he
spat into the brook. He examined the tablets, swallowed one,
and dropped the plastic bottle into the water.

Resting for a while, he wondered if he should bring his
tools out from Fawr pit. If a man can't use his tools best
forget about them. Never do a bad turn when you can offer
some bugger a good turn. Let one of the night-shift repairers
have them, buckshee, some poor sod on bare wages.

Lewis coughed again, down to hissy grunts. Hundred per
cent, he thought. By Jesus. Men are pegging out with fifty per
cent. I'm miles from that state. Rough chest first thing in the
morning, short of breath until the circulation starts moving.
Good Christ almighty, fifty-seven, packing it in at my age.
Doesn't make sense. Bloody hell. There're colliers in Fawr
close on pension time, old plodders clearing their yardage
every shift. Me, bloody scrapheap. Doctor Gammon, his
mouth about gardening, he's never done a day's graft in all his
natural. Him sat there on his arse, telling me what to do.

Before leaving the bridge, Lewis spat a gobbet of coal
streaked phlegm into Melyn brook. Fretting about his age
and the pneumoconiosis, he raised his head, breathed deeply,
held himself firm, striding, but ache fired his shoulder blades,
his ribs, so he relaxed, hands in pockets, chin out-thrust,
sight fixed on the coming and going of his toecaps. A six-
foot man in his prime, the curvature of his spine lowered him
six inches, the curve prominent, hard packed under the shiny
serge of his long, double-breasted jacket. His shoulders and
sleeves were stained with wiped-off pigeon droppings.

There were three glossy caravans propped in a line behind

the roofless smithy of derelict Number 2 pit. Outsiders, he thought. Bloody NCB, they bring in these outsiders to dismantle while our own men are signing the dole. On impulse he walked past stacks of pit props, thrown higgledy-piggledy, rotting reminders of pit closure. 'Shwmae,' he said formally, repeating, 'Shwmae,' the three young wives nodding, smiled posed together, smoothing frocks and pinafores. He strode clump-footed through the colliery office, a square, echoing building. Looters had stripped doors and windows. Long slits of daylight glimmered beneath the eaves. Everywhere the smell of urine and sheep droppings. From the office he walked to the top pit stables. Mildewed horse collars hung on spikes driven into the walls. Ruination, he thought, nothing but ruination. He followed railway tracks to the end of the colliery siding. Red-rusted truck buffers were bolted to mossy baulks of timber. Turning left, he picked his route between ancient greening slag heaps back to the main road.

Bessie Rimmer had her hands in chicken meal, a heavyweight woman, grossly slack-bodied like a primordial Venus.

'What'd he say, Lew?'

'I got it al'right. The full dose, hundred per cent.'

She said, 'Lord above.' Her fingers ploughed through the meal. 'Want me to write to our William, tell him about you?'

Lewis sat near the fire. He rested his heels on the hob, his long, dark specked hands dangling from the arms of the chair. 'Leave it be. The boy's minding his own affairs.'

'Duw, hopeless you are, Lew Rimmer. Should have gone for a board ages ago. No, stubborn, think you know everything better than anybody else, go your own way regardless. Now see what it's come to! D'you ask Doctor Gammon about a fortnight in that convalescent place on Gower? Don't suppose you did. Couple of weeks rest is what you need, for def'nite!'

He said, 'Your fowls are waiting for that mash. Come straight back and lay some grub on the table.'

Bessie went out and through the kitchen door. She met her neighbour in the dirt lane, Esther Rees, spinster, the school cleaner.

'Hundred per cent he is,' Bessie said.

'Oh, shame,' sympathised Esther.

'Should have known it himself, yes he should have.' Bessie hugged the pan of steaming chicken meal. Her mouth pouted resentment. 'My Lewis won't be told. Always out to prove himself diff'rent, nothing at all like anybody else God ever put breath into. From now on he'll have to knuckle down, stands to reason with hundred per cent dust.'

Esther sloped her head, sighing resignation. She was forty-nine, tall, lean as a distance runner. Bessie marched down the lane, pale grey whiffs of steam rising from the chicken meal. Esther rotated from the waist, her head perched, watchful, blue eyes watery, lips puckering, ageing within the defensive wedge of her cheekbones and chin. She lifted her empty ash bucket off the backyard wall, 'Tch-tch-tch,' and hurried indoors to inform her son – Lewis Rimmer's son, Bernard. Of course Bessie knew about Bernard Rees, but all that happened a long time ago. Not worth bothering about any more. Bernard was thirty-two, a bachelor, two years younger than Bessie's son, William.

Lewis rested, unaware of resting himself. He sat without thinking. The sideboard clock chirruped, stroked twelve pinging chimes. Roused, Lewis jabbed the firegrate with the sole of his shoe, sparks and dead ash spluttering into the hearth. He huffed while climbing upstairs. From the landing window he looked to see if Bessie was in the lane, before entering the small bedroom, William's bedroom until he left home to join the Army. Lewis used his fingernails to lift out a length of floor board. His secret place. Counting the money, mumbling, each note was passed from hand to hand. Seven hundred and eighty-four pounds. My sweat, he thought, carelessly piling the notes on the plaster lathes between two joists. He felt no excitement.

The back door rattled. Lewis clumsily tiptoed out of the bedroom to the lavatory, pulled the chain and fiercely slammed the door.

'Use some bloody elbow grease on the bowl of the lav,' he said.

'Fancy anything special to eat?' asked Bessie.

Lewis grunted, slumped in his fireside chair. 'I'm off my food, gel.'

'Obvious an' all, after what Doctor Gammon said to you this morning. I'll be down his surg'ry later on, find out regarding that place on Gower coast. Years an' years you've paid the NUM without so much as a pint of beer off of 'em. There's facilities for compo cases, Lew, laid on for the likes of you'self.'

'Aye,' he said, 'and leave you to look after my pigeons.'

'Pigeons! Health comes before pigeons!'

'You mind your own business, Bessie.'

'Suit you'self, if that's how you want it.'

'Right, that's al'right,' he said calmly.

Bessie persisted. 'You drove our William away as if he was a total stranger. My own son! Seems to me you haven't got any feelings left at all, only for them blasted pigeons. Fat lot of good they'll be after…'

'Shurrup!'

'You can't frighten me no more.'

'Shut it. Just lay some food on the table, and shut it.'

Bessie waddled to and from the pantry with cheese, pickles, cold ham, tomato sauce, bread and butter. Elbows on the table, Lewis began eating while she brewed the tea. By the time she sat down, Bessie felt uncomfortably flustered. And her toes were itching. Slipping off her shoes, she rubbed her toes with her heels, hard, rubbing and rubbing. The torment and ecstasy of her itching feet.

'You wash your hands after mixing the mash?' he demanded quietly.

'Course not, 'tisn't as if I've been messing with filth.'

'Sit still then, you're fidgeting like a woman with the piles.'

'My toes are burning hot!'

'Guh, you're the bloody limit.'

'As if you cared about anybody 'cept you'self,' she grumbled.

Lewis chewed methodically, false dignified as an old captive lion.

'How much is full compo these days?' she inquired, friendly now, leaning towards him.

'No idea, gel.'

'Be enough for us two I expect, Lew. We'll manage.'

'I daresay.'

'There's our William, he'll send us a few pounds if ever we run short.'

'I shan't take a penny off the boy. He's got a houseful of kids.'

'William's earning big money,' protested Bessie. 'Any case, he's our son. It's his duty.'

Lewis levered himself away from the table. 'Duty, no such thing,' he said indifferently. He opened the back door, pleased to see bright sunshine drying out the damp morning. 'I'm off up to the loft. Lissen, gel, fetch me a couple of cartridges from the drawer.'

His shotgun hung in the cupboard beneath the stairs. He greased the action with smears of lard, cleaned both barrels and slotted in the cartridges.

'Lew, how long will you be?'

He hefted the gun at point of balance. 'Be back at three o'clock.'

'Can't I write a letter to our William?'

'No.' He shook his head. 'Scrub the lav, Bessie, don't forget.'

His pigeon loft stood on a green mound sheltered by willows. The school playground fence ran below, some fifteen yards of clay-blotched turf between school and fence. There was a turnstile gate, hub of half a dozen footpaths winding the lower hillside. Lewis climbed the shallowest gradient. He released his pigeons, forty birds, reds, blues, dark and light chequers, mealies, grizzles, a bunched swarm, primaries whirring. They swept out free, wider, higher, turned, plumed and twisted headlong over the village, climbed, hurtled towards the mountain, their colours winking like shell fragments against the green background. Lewis watched them, his private delight, his own expert joy. They were a part of himself. Closer to his heart than Bessie or Esther. His birds, and driving headings in Fawr pit.

He scraped the loft, sprinkled nest boxes and perches with anti-lice powder, then he carried fresh water from a cask at the back of the lean-to roof. The pigeons were roving in unison under ragged white clouds. Lewis sat beneath a pollarded willow with the shotgun across his knees. He gazed along the distant horizon of the hills. 'Stay away from my birds, Johnny-hawk,' he said, lowering his bent shoulders against the tree. He watched his flock performing. The shotgun symbolised his youth, when falcons stooped from the sun, downing his beloved homers. Years gone by. Now peregrines very seldom wheeled above the valley.

The flock drifted overhead, swung upwind, disappeared over the mountain. Lewis closed his eyes. Thoughtlessly he went, 'Ssss-huhssss-ssss-ssss,' through his teeth, a cold sound, tuneless, like wind pressing itself through a cracked windowpane. He was resting himself.

The pigeons returned, swishing a tight trajectory around the willows, V-winged, legless, knobbled beaks and glinty, popping eyes. They plunged upward, flight line broadening, heading for the shadowed face of the old quarry. They flew yet higher, seeming mechanically driven, speeding like flecks of hail over the mountain top. Lewis laid aside the shotgun. He coughed, cleared his chest, ending on throaty sibilance until he spat phlegm.

Esther called, 'Lew!'

He moved gawkily stiff-legged to the edge of the mound. She beckoned from the turnstile gate. 'Come on up,' he said.

'Can't, not now. Busy in the school. Lew, your Bessie told me about the report from Doctor Gammon. Won't they give you a light job?'

'Not down the pit.'

'Well, what have you got in mind, Lew?'

'Don't know yet.'

'I've told my Bernard. That's only fair, isn't it?'

'Why not... aye.'

They were linked by silence, her thin elbows held horizontal, clutched by her fingertips, forearms pressing her skimpy bosom. 'Pity too,' she said. 'Bye-bye for now, Lew.' She gave him a subdued little wave and hastened into the school building.

Lewis propped his shotgun in the loft. There were slatted flight runs each side of the aisle, the aisle itself littered with scrapers, a hammer, skewed handsaw, tins of nails, stunted cane brush without a handle, and a small sack of maple peas. Above the shotgun were two shelves of medicine, powders, artificial eggs, earthenware nesting bowls, broken rings and a Flit gun.

He returned to the pollarded willow. Old longings stirred, disturbing his dryness like the peckings of feeble squabs. Lewis sat up, wrists on his knees, hands dangling. He remembered Esther, the cool girl of seventeen. Cool, helpless, useless – his desperate, wild rage. She'd sickened his guts. Was it worse, any worse than this, the X-rays, the medical board, the final evidence: hundred per cent dust? She stayed cool, always. Bloodless Esther. Daft, her and Bessie, both daft. Young Bernard, he followed his mother. Tall rope of a bloke, no strength in him anywhere to do anything. Lewis flapped his hands. 'All of it's bloody senseless, the whole lot.'

He cursed quietly to himself, stream upon stream of cursing. Incoherence waned to misery. He drooped back against the tree. She meant nothing. Bessie, nothing. William, nothing. Bernard, nothing. It's me, Lewis Rimmer, fifty-seven, that's all, fifty-bloody-seven. Man for man I've filled more coal than any collier in Fawr pit. Now this. Here I am. What's my next move? How carry on? What's next? Jesus Christ.

He glanced around for his pigeons. Bare sky, two carrion crows winging down, down below the high level rim of Pen Arglwydd. His dark eyes blinked, kindling memories, falcons shot on the mountain, hours spent waiting for Johnny-hawk to cop in to roost. Warm, dusky summer evenings hiding in a den of fallen boulders, puffing Gold Flake fags inside his folded cap, blowing the smoke down between his knees. Long, long time ago. It's well over twenty years since I climbed Pen Arglwydd. Can't manage it now. Finished. Christ, aye, I'm finished. What shall I do? Gardening. Huh, mess about like some old betsy. Not likely. I'd sooner jack it in altogether.

He heard his pigeons, the frantic clap of pinions as a bird tumbled against telephone wires strung from the school down to the road, wires dotted with split corks. Lewis cursed. Plodding slantwise down the mound, he cursed the wires. Aware of his violence as he banged into the kitchen, Bessie left him alone.

At four o'clock he whistled the birds in, fed them, and carried his shotgun back to the house. Bessie replaced the cartridges in a drawer of the sideboard.

On Monday morning the manager visited Lewis' heading. Behind him came the overman, safety stick tucked under his arm. 'Lew,' said the manager, 'I've got some bad news.'

Lewis sent his young butty up into the low face – a narrow layer of rider coal and shale. They were driving through to a virgin seam. 'Pack the right-hand side, boy. Make sure you wall it up properly.'

The men hunkered beside a half-full tram of rubble. 'I know all about this bad news,' said Lewis.

Elderly, with blue scars freckling his left temple, the manager unclipped his cap lamp. 'I'm down for ten per cent myself. Early stages.'

The overman said, 'Take it from me, Lew, these quacks don't know everything.'

The manager scowled. 'Wait now, wait. Regarding Lewis, there's no question of error, and there's damn all I can do about it. Not a damn thing. Understand, Lew, my hands are tied. Truth is, Lew, your fourteen days' notice is in my office.'

The overman squirted tobacco juice. 'First hundred per cent case since we worked the old Four Foot seam through to the boundary. Real hard coal up there, hard as the hobs of hell.'

Lewis spoke to the manager. 'Job on the screens would suit me.'

'Impossible, only wish to God I could put you somewhere on top pit. If I can do anything for you, Lew, let me know. Anything at all outside the colliery. And listen, try not to worry. The man isn't born who can cure worry.'

Lewis watched their cap lamps retreating from the heading. He shouted to his butty. The youth jumped down into the roadway. Lewis continued prising rock from the blasted roof. Behind him, his butty filled rubble into the tram. Bent over his shovel, the boy said, 'So you're going on compo, Lew.'

'You're all ears,' said Lewis.

'Last night, mun, I heard it in the club last night.'

'Never mind what you bloody heard.'

'You're hundred per cent, right? That's what they reckon.'

'Let's see that dram filled,' Lewis said. He knew the arguments in the club. Lew Rimmer's finished. All the slashers travel the same road to Coed-coch cemetery. Pig-headed Lew, never wears a mask when he's boring holes. Tight-fisted money grabber, won't wait for the dust to clear after shot firing. Big Lew, he's packing muck in the gob walls when you can't see your hand in front of your eyes. Typical slasher. They all go the same way. Silicosis or pneumo. Loaf around on street corners until they're only skin and bones. Nothing but skeletons by the time the undertaker comes to measure them.

Conscious of damaged pride, of his reputation in Fawr pit, Lewis elbowed out his gaunt arms, hung his whole weight on the crowbar, pressing evenly. The long slab of rock cracked on, then he shuffled backwards, prised again, arms outstretched until the rock crashed down. Lewis broke it with a sledgehammer. His butty lifted the stones into the tram. Lewis moved forward, he swung a heavy pick, ripping back the sides of the road. Soon he had a pile of rubble in front of his working boots. Stepping up on the loose stones, he struck ahead with his pick. Pride again, remorse, smothered grunts, his spoiled self-esteem turned vicious, aiming the pick, his body angled away by instinct, teetering, the soft-jointed stone sliding soundlessly out from the side where he'd been ripping, falling edgewise on his outflung forearm, breaking the bone.

The youth dragged Lewis around the tram. Frightened, running out, around to the next heading for help, he kept hearing the muffled crack of bone breaking, and Lewis blaspheming like a lunatic.

For two days Bessie endured a brooding husband. Lewis slept and ate in the armchair near the fire. Unshaven, sullen, he remained there with his feet set straight on the coconut fibre hearth mat. She fed and watered his pigeons. Early on the third morning she heard him cursing in the hallway. Bessie pulled the soiled double-breasted jacket across his shoulders.

'Be careful, please, Lew,' she said.

Humbled, the plaster-cased left arm swung up to his chest, he walked the dirt lane, moving stiffly, jerking along, Esther Rees watching him from her kitchen doorway. He climbed the mound in sharp zig-zags, the humped shape of him alternately profiled. Poor Lew, she thought, letting himself go to rack and ruin. Distaste wrinkled her nose. She closed the door and returned to ironing Bernard's white shirts.

Lewis freed his pigeons, he cleaned out the loft, scraping laboriously, wheezing breath through irregular, dry clickings of his false teeth. He felt tired, inwardly softened, sluggish in his blood. Something had drained out of his system, seepage finding outlet while he waited behind the tram with his numb arm held to his stomach. He sat on the wooden steps outside the loft. Down-valley, he could see the smoke stack above Number 2 pit, the railway footbridge and far off, hazed by morning sunshine, the dwarfed spread of terraced houses, shops, stone-built chapels and pubs mapped each side of Melyn brook. His tiredness succumbed to alien contentment.

Images of Bessie flowed, from her gamin childhood to nubile adolescence to the hulking slovenliness of her middle age. Soft sniggers warmed Lewis's throat. After a while he filled the food hoppers, brought fresh water into the loft and he shut the wire screen entrance door.

He walked down in a state of infantile euphoria. Bessie cooked breakfast. He mocked her chickens. Bantams laid bigger eggs.

'My life,' she vowed, humouring him, 'I haven't seen you like this since I went pregnant on William. Anyway, my fowls show more profit than them bloody racing pigeons. Now look, I'm doing my shopping this morning. Mind how you go with that arm of yours.'

'Old gel,' he said, 'never panic over Lew Rimmer. There's no need.'

Alone in the house, he sat on the lavatory for an hour, broken circulation deadening his shanks. Lewis giggled, stamped his feet on the landing. Giggling induced coughing, a harsh, prolonged bout toppling him to his knees. Time went by. He crossed to the small bedroom, raised the floor board and stuffed seven hundred and eighty-four pounds into his pockets. Downstairs again, Lewis emptied the tea caddy, a sweeping fling showering tea grains around the kitchen. He crammed the notes into the caddy.

Very slowly in warm midday, he climbed the green mound to his loft, shotgun held balanced, carried at arm's length.

His birds were down. Lewis carefully stepped among them, he named his favourites, praised their courage and suddenly, gently, he shooed them all way.

Stooped in the aisle, cursing, pressing off the safety catch, blindly cursing, his broken arm hanging, clenching the mouth of the double barrel between his teeth, Lewis gagged curses as the trigger slicked back under his thumb.

Time went by. The pigeons came floating down. A few copped on the roof of the loft. Crop puffed out, a dark chequer cock made deep, rich cooings, strutting around a grizzly hen. She responded, nibbling his shoulder feathers, her wings partly opening on the instant as she rolled slightly sideways beneath his tread. They frisked apart, the dark chequer volplaning into the loft, where he gobbled two maple peas spilt from Lewis' pocket.

Boy with a Trumpet

Rhys Davies

All he wanted was a bed, a shelf for his trumpet and permission to play it. He did not care how squalid the room, though he was so clean and shining himself; he could afford only the lowest rent. Not having any possessions except what he stood up in, the trumpet in an elegant case and a paper parcel of shirts and socks, landladies were suspicious of him. But he so gleamed with light young vigour, like a feather in the wind, that he kindled even in those wary hearts less harsh refusals.

Finally, on the outer rim of the West End, he found a bleak room for eight shillings a week in the house of a faded actress purply with drink and the dramas of a succession of lovers.

'I don't mind a trumpet,' she said, mollified by his air of a waif strayed out of a lonely vacancy. 'Are you in the orchestra, dear? No? You're not in a jazz band, are you? I can't have nightclub people in my house, coming in at all hours. No?… You look so young,' she said wonderingly. 'Well, there's no attendance, my charwoman is on war work; the bathroom is strictly engaged every morning from ten to half past, and I do not allow tenants to receive visitors of the opposite sex in their rooms.' Behind the blowsiness were the remnants of one who had often played the role of a lady.

'I've just committed suicide,' he said naively. She saw then the bright but withdrawn fixity of his eyes, single-purposed.

'What!' she said, flurried in her kimono, and instinctively placed a stagey hand on her bosom.

'They got me back,' he said. 'I was sick. I didn't swallow enough of the stuff. Afterwards they sent me to a – well, a hospital. Then they discharged me. From the Army.'

'Oh dear!' she fussed. And, amply and yearning: 'Did your nerve go, then…? Haven't you any people?' There had been a suicide – a successful one – in her house before, and she had not been averse to the tragedy.

'I have God,' he said gravely. 'I was brought up in an orphanage. But I have an aunt in Chester. She and I do not love each other. I don't like violence. The telephone is ringing,' he said, with his alert but withdrawn awareness.

She scolded someone, at length and with high-toned emphasis, and returning muttering; she started to find him still under the huge frilled lampshade by the petunia divan. 'Rent is in advance,' she said mechanically. 'Number eight on the second floor.'

He went up the stairs. The webby carpet, worn by years of lodgers, smelt of old dust. A gush of water sounded above; a door slammed; a cat slept on a windowsill under sprays of dusty lacquered leaves. Later, as he was going out to the teashop, two young girls, silent and proud, sedately descended the stairs together in the dying sunshine. They, too, had that air of clear-cut absorption in themselves, unacknowledging the dangerous world. But they were together in that house of the unanchored.

And he was alone, not long back from the edge of the dead land, the intersecting country where the disconnected sit with their spectral smiles.

That evening, in the tiny room, he played his trumpet. His lips, as the bandmaster of his regiment had told him, were not suitable for a trumpet; they had not the necessary full, fleshy contours, and also there were interstices in his front teeth; his face became horribly contorted in his effort to blast 'Cherry Ripe' out of the silver instrument. Nevertheless, when the benevolent spinster in the cathedral town where he had been stationed and sung Elizabethan madrigals asked what she could buy him after he had left the asylum, he said: 'A trumpet.' And, alone, he had come to the great city with his neurosis and a gleaming second-hand trumpet costing sixteen guineas. On arrival he spent half his money on four expensive poplin shirts and in the evening went to a lecture on world reform; the night he had spent in Regent's Park, his trumpet case and parcel on his lap.

The landlady rapped and came in. Violet circles were painted round her eyes and her hair was greenish. Within a wrap large, loose breasts swam untrammelled as dolphins. She looked at him with a speculative doubt.

'It's very noisy. Are you practising? There are neighbours.'

'You said I could play my trumpet,' he pointed out gravely.

She said: 'I am artistic myself, and I have had actors, writers, and musicians in my house. But there's a limit. You must have a certain hour for practice. But not in the evenings; the mornings are more suitable for a trumpet.'

'I cannot get up in the mornings,' he said. The trim, fixed decision of the young soldier stiffened his voice. 'I need a great deal of sleep.'

'Are you still ill?' She stepped forward, her ringed hands outstretched. He sat on the bed's edge in his clean new shirt, the trumpet across his knees. From him came a desolate waif need. But his round, fresh-air face had a blank imperviousness, and down his indrawn small eyes flickered a secret repudiation. 'Are you lonely?' she went on. 'I play the piano.'

'I don't like trembling young girls,' he said. But as if to himself: 'They make me unhappy. I usually burst into crying when I'm with them. But I like babies; I want to be a father. I used to go into the married quarters in barracks and look after the babies... Sometimes,' he said, with his grave simplicity, 'I used to wash their napkins.'

In her slovenly fashion she was arrantly good-natured and friendly. 'Did you have a bad time in the orphanage, dear?'

'No, not *bad*. But I cannot stand the smell of carbolic soap now; it makes me want to vomit... I would like,' he added, 'to have known my mother. Or my father.'

'Hasn't anyone ever cared for you?' she asked, heaving.

'Yes. Both girls and men. But only for short periods.' Detached, he spoke as if he would never question the reason for this. The antiseptic austerity of his early years enclosed him like a cell of white marble; later there had been the forced, too-early physical maturity of the Army, which the orphanage governor had induced him to join as a bandboy, just before the war. He had no instinctive love to give out in return for attempts of affection: it had never been born in him. 'People get tired of me,' he added, quite acceptingly.

After that, in her erratic fashion, he obsessed her. She occasionally fed him; in his room she put cushions and a large oleograph of Dante and Beatrice on a Florence bridge; she even allowed him to play the trumpet when he liked, despite complaints from the other lodgers. She badgered her lover of the moment, an irate designer of textiles, to find him a job in the studio of the huge West End store. But the boy categorically refused all jobs that required him before noon. His head like an apple on the pillow, he lay in bed all the morning sunk in profound slumber.

In the afternoons he would sit at his window drinking her tea or earnestly reading a modern treatise on religious problems. He insisted to her that a fresh upsurge of religious awareness was about to arrive in the world. He had already passed through the hands of a hearty, up-to-date Christian group, and he corresponded regularly with a canon whose sole panacea, however, was an exhortation to pray.

'But I can't pray,' he grieved to her. There was a deadlock of all his faculties.

Only when playing his trumpet he seemed a little released. Harshly and without melodic calm, he blew it over a world in chaos. For all the contortions of his round face he bloomed into a kind of satisfaction as he created a hideous pattern of noise. Cast out of the Army as totally unfit for service, it was only in these blasts of noise that he really enjoyed his liberty – the first that had ever come to him.

'Your rent is a fortnight overdue,' she reminded him, with prudent urgency. 'You really must find work, dear. Think of your future; now is your opportunity, with so many jobs about.'

'What future?' he asked curiously. 'Why do you believe so confidently in the future?'

He could always deflate her with this grave flatness. But her habit of working up emotional scenes was not easily balked. She would call him into her sitting room and, stroking his hand, among the billowy cushions, heave and throb about the rudeness of her lover, who was younger than herself. 'We are two waifs,' she said, while the telephone concealed under the crinoline of a doll rang yet again.

But he did not want the sultry maternalness of this faded artificial woman; unerringly he sensed the shallow, predatory egotism of her need. Yet neither did he want to know the two beautiful and serious girls, flaxen-haired and virginal, who lived on the same floor; he always ducked his head away from them. He wanted to pick up a prostitute and spend a furtive quarter of an hour with her in the blackout. But he could not afford this. He was destitute now.

'You are horrible,' she exclaimed angrily when, in a long talk, he told her of this. 'You, a boy of nineteen, wanting to go with prostitutes!'

'You see,' he insisted, 'I would feel myself master with them, and I can hate them too. But with nice, proud girls I cannot stop myself breaking down, and then I want to rush away and throw myself under a Tube train... And that's bad for me,' he added, with that earnest naiveté of his.

'But *is* it bad for you to break down?' she asked with some energy.

'Yes; I can't stand it.' Beyond the fixed calm of his small crystal eyes something flickered. 'When I was discharged from the Army the MO advised me to attend a clinic. I've been to one. It made me feel worse. I don't want to feel I'm a case.'

'The clinic,' she said sagely, 'couldn't be expected to provide you with a mother. You've got nineteen years of starvation to forget.'

She had got into the habit of giving him a glass of milk and rum at nights. Nevertheless, she had her real angers with him, for she was of tempestuous disposition. She knew that he would not – it did not occur to her that he could not – unfold to her other than in these talks. He did not weep on her waiting bosom; he did not like his bright glossy hair to be stroked. And sometimes when he played the trumpet in his room she was roused to a transport of queer, intent fury and she would prowl about the staircase in helpless rage.

He had been in the house a month when one afternoon, after he had been playing for an hour, she walked into his room. Her green hair was frizzed out, the heavily painted eyes sidled angrily, the violet lips twisted like a cord. There was something both pathetic and ridiculous in the frenzy of this worn and used woman gallantly trying to keep up an air of bygone theatrical grandeur and, indeed, of ladylike breeding. But she was so brittle. Carefully looking at her, he laid the trumpet on his knees.

'Why must you *keep on*!' she fumed. 'That everlasting tune, it's maddening. The neighbours will ring up the police and I shall have them calling. You are not in a slum.'

'You said I could play my trumpet.'

And still there was about him that curious and impervious tranquillity, not to be disturbed, and, to her, relentless. It drove her to a vindictive outburst, her gaze fixed in hatred on the trumpet.

'Why don't you go out and look for *work*? Your rent – you are taking advantage of my kindness; you are lazy and without principle. Aren't you ashamed to sit there doing nothing but blowing noises on that damned thing?' She heaved over him in the narrow room, a dramatic Maenad gone to copious seed and smelling of bath salts.

He got up from the bed's edge, carefully disconnected the trumpet's pieces and put them in the elegant case and his shirts and socks into a brown paper carrier. She watched him, spellbound; his crisp, deliberate decision was curbing. At the door he raised his hat politely. All recognition of her was abolished from the small, unswerving eyes.

'Good afternoon,' he said in a precise way. 'I will send you the rent when I earn some money. I am sure to find a position suited to me before long.'

He stored the trumpet in a railway station. On no account would he pawn it, though there was only a shilling or two left of the pound the canon had last sent him, together with a copy of *St Augustine's Confessions*. He knew it was useless to look for a job even as second trumpet in the cabarets; not even his fresh, shiny, boy appearance, that would look well in a Palm Beach jacket, could help him.

That night he hung about the dark, chattering Circus, not unhappy, feeling vaguely liberated among this anonymous crowd milling about in an atmosphere of drink, flesh, and boredom. He listened carefully to the soldiers' smudged catcalls, the female retaliations, the whispers, the ironical endearments, the dismissals. But as the night wore on and the crowd thinned, his senses became sharpened, alert, and at the same time desperate. Like a young hungry wolf sniffing the edge of the dark, he howled desolately inside himself. In the blackout the perfumed women, dots of fire between their fingertips, passed and repassed, as if weaving a dance figure in some hieratic ceremony; his mind became aware of a pattern, a design, a theme in which a restated lewd note grew ever more and more dominant. He wanted to play his trumpet. Startle the night with a barbaric blast.

He began to accost the women. He had heard that some would give shelter to the temporarily destitute, exercising a

legendary comradeship of the streets. But none had use for
him. After a brief assessment of his conversation they passed
on rapidly. Only one was disposed to chatter. She told him
he could find a job, if his discharge papers were in order, as
a stagehand in a certain theatre; she gave him a name to ask
for.

'Nothing doing, darling,' she replied promptly to his
subsequent suggestion. 'No fresh pineapple for me tonight.'

Waiting for morning, he sat on a bench in the ghostly
Square garden and returned to an earlier meditation on the
nature of God. In this mental fantasy he continually saw the
embryo of a tadpole which split into two entities. The force
that divided the embryo was God, a tremendous deciding
power that lay beyond biology. It was eternal and creative,
yet could one pray to it, worship it? Would it be conscious
of a worshipping acknowledgement, and, if so, could it
reward with peace, harmony, and contentment? He ached to
submerge himself in belief and to enter into a mystic
identification with a creative force; he wanted to cast himself
at the knees of a gigantic parent of the universe. But on every
side were frustrations, and the chaotic world, armed for
destruction, was closing in on him triumphantly. Yet he knew
it was that creative force that had driven him to attempt
suicide as a solution and a release; he had believed that the
power within him would not die but return to the central
force and be discharged again. But he shivered at the memory
of the hours before that act of suicide, those furtive, secret
hours that had ruptured his mind. Outside himself he had
never been able to kill even a spider.

'You must think of your future!' he suddenly whinnied aloud,
causing a bemused sailor on an adjacent bench to lift his round
cap off his face. He tried to envisage a concrete picture of that
future, but saw only a ravaged place of waste with a few tufts
of blackened vegetation against a burnt-out sky.

He began working among acres of painted canvases
depicting idealised scenes in a world devoted to song, hilarity,

and dance. Rainbow processions of girls passed in and out, pearly smiles stitched into glossy faces, the accurate legs swinging like multi-coloured sausages. Watching these friezes in tranced gravity, he sometimes missed a cue, rousing the stage manager to threats of instant dismissal, despite the labour shortage. The hardworking young girl dancers, lustrously trim and absorbed in professional perfection, took no notice of the new stagehand fascinated in attempts to adapt their integrated patterns to his consciousness. But though hypnotised by this new revelation of idealised flesh and movements, he still could not identify himself with them. He was still cut off, he had not yet come through to acceptance that the world breathed, and that these pink and silver girls actually could be touched.

He started and listened carefully when a distinguished young man, a hero of the sky, sent a message backstage that he 'would like to collaborate' with a certain starry beauty of the chorus. 'She'll collaborate all right,' remarked another of the girls in the wings; 'I never heard it called that before.' That night he went home straight from the theatre and filled the house with the blasts of his trumpet.

He had rented a small partitioned space in the basement, its window overlooking the back garden. It contained a camp bed and one or two bugs which he accepted as outcomes of the God-force. The street was not of good repute, but it was beyond the West End, and an amount of lace-curtained and fumed-oak respectability was maintained.

'You can blow your trumpet as much as you like,' Irish Lil said. 'Blow it in the middle of the night if you like – it might drive some of the bastards out. Can you lend me five bob till tomorrow morning?'

There had been a quarrel among the five prostitutes upstairs: four accused the fifth of bringing in clients during the daytime – they declared the house would get a bad name. They were entirely daughters of the night; in daylight there was a moon glisten on their waxen faces, their hair looked

unreal, and their voices were huskily fretful. They called him
the Boy with a Trumpet, and he was already something of a
pet among them. He shared the roomy basement with four
refugees off the Continent who came and went on obscure
errands and everlastingly cooked cabbage soup.

Irish Lil was the disgrace of the house. Though she always
had real flowers stuck in the two milk bottles on her
sideboard, she was a slut. Her slovenly make-up, her regular
OMS lover in the Guards who got roaring drunk, and her
inability to discriminate and to insist on prepayment angered
the four younger women. Blonde Joyce carried on a year-old
vendetta with her. Over a stolen egg. Irish Lil was creeping
downstairs one evening with the egg, which she had taken
from Joyce's room, when a bomb fell in the Avenue. Kathleen
rushed out of her room with a Free French client and found
Lil struck daft on the stairs with the crushed egg dribbling
through her fingers.

'Don't trust your trumpet to her,' Joyce said. 'She'll pawn
it.' For, as his room had no lock, he asked where in the house
he could hide his trumpet while he was at the theatre.

'She weeps,' he said gravely. 'I've heard her weeping.'

'If,' Joyce said, hard, 'she was on fire, I wouldn't pee on
her to put her out.'

But they all, in their idle afternoons, liked him about their
rooms. He fetched them newspapers and cigarettes; he was
a nice boy and, yawning in their dressing gowns and
irremediably nocturnal, they discarded their professionalism
with him. Their calm acceptance of the world as a
disintegration eased him; his instinct had been right in
seeking a brothel to live in.

Yet he saw the house, for all its matter-of-fact squalor, as
existing in a world still spectral to him. Still he lived behind
thick glass, unreleased and peering out in dumb waiting.
Only his old Army nightmare was gone – the recurrent
dream in which he lay sealed tight into a leaden pipe under
a pavement where he could hear, ever passing and returning,

the heeltaps of compassionate but unreachable women. But the tank-like underwater quiet of the observation ward in the asylum was still with him, always. And he could not break through, smash the glass. Not yet.

It was Kathleen who took quite a fancy to him. They had disconnected conversations in her room; she accepted him amicably as a virginal presence that did not want to touch her. She was plump as a rose, and a sprinkle of natural colour was still strewn over her, the youngest girl in the house. She promised to try to find him a job as trumpeter in one of the clubs; he could earn a pound a night at this if he became proficient.

'But I don't want to earn a lot of money,' he said earnestly. 'It's time we learned how to do without money. We must learn to live and create like God.'

'I've met all types of men,' she said vaguely, tucking her weary legs under her on the bed. 'And I hate them all. I tell you I've got to have six double gins before I can bring one home. That costs them a quid or two extra; I make the sods spend.'

He said dreamily: 'When I took poison I felt I was making a creative act, if it was only that I was going out to search.' He could still rest in the shade of that release; the mysteriousness of that blue underworld fume was still there, giving him a promise of fulfilment. 'I saw huge shapes... they were like huge flowers, dark and heavy blood-coloured flowers. They looked at me, they moved, they listened, their roots began to twine into me, I could feel them in my bowels... But I couldn't rise, I was lying in the mud. I couldn't breathe in the new way. I tried to struggle up... through. But I fell back, and everything disappeared—'

'Don't you go trying to commit suicide in this house,' she said. 'Mrs Walton would never forgive you. That Irish tyke's doing enough to advertise us already... You're not queer, are you?' she asked, desultory. 'I like queer men, they don't turn me sick... Always at one,' she ruminated of the others.

She attracted him more than the other four, but, to content his instinct completely, he wished her more sordid, lewd, and foul-tongued, more disintegrated. The ghostly lineaments of a trembling young girl remained in her. They conversed to each other across a distance. But she was the only one of the women who still appeared to observe things beyond this private world of the brothel. He sometimes tried to talk to her about God.

The taxicabs began to purr up to the front door any time after midnight. Sometimes he got out of his bed in the basement, mounted the staircase in trousers and socks, and stood poised in the dark as if waiting for a shattering revelation from behind the closed doors. There was the useless bomber pilot who broke down and shouted weepingly to Joyce that his nerve was gone – 'Well,' Joyce had said in her ruthless way, 'you can stay if you like, but I'm keeping my present all the same, mind!' That pleased him, as he carefully listened; it belonged to the chaos, the burnt-out world reduced to charcoal. He laughed softly to himself. What if he blew his trumpet on this phantasmagoric staircase? Blew it over the fallen night, waken these dead, surprise them with a new anarchial fanfare?

One week when the elder tree and the peonies were in blossom in the once-cultivated back garden, Irish Lil declared she had a birthday. She opened her room on the Monday night – always an off night – to whoever wished to come in. Ranks of beer flagons stood on the sideboard, and Harry, her Guards sergeant regular, roared and strutted before them in his battledress like David before the Ark. Three refugees from the basement ventured in; Joyce forgot her vendetta, but refused to dress or make up; Pamela sat repairing a stocking. When he arrived from the theatre the beer was freely flowing. Irish Lil, in a magenta sateen gown, was wearing long, ornate earrings in a vain attempt to look seductive. Kathleen, on this off-night occasion, gazed at him with a kind of sisterly pensiveness.

'Heard that one about Turnham Green—?' bawled Harry, and took off his khaki blouse before telling it, owing to the heat.

He was a great tree of flesh. His roots were tenacious in the earth. The juice in his full lips was the blood of a king bull; the seeds of war flourished in the field of his muscular belly. For him a battle was a dinner, a bomb a dog bark, a bayonet a cat-scratch, and in the palm of his great blue paw statesmen curled secure. He was the salt of the earth. The limericks flying off his lips became more obscene.

But they fell flat. The prostitutes were bored with obscenity, the refugees did not understand English humour. Joyce yawned markedly.

'Hell, what's this?' Harry panted a bit – 'The funeral of the duchess...? Reminds me. Heard that one about Her Grace and the fishmonger?'

'Fetch your trumpet, will you?' asked Irish Lil, feeling a little music was necessary.

'What!' shouted Harry, delighted. 'He's got a trumpet? I been in the band in my time. A kick or two from a trumpet's jest what's needed.'

He snatched the beautifully shining instrument and set it to his great curled lips. The bull neck swelled, the huge face glowed red. And without mistake, unfalteringly, from harmonious lungs, he played the 'Londonderry Air'. A man blowing a trumpet successfully is a rousing spectacle. The blast is an announcement of the lifted sun. Harry stood on a mountain peak, monarch of all he surveyed.

Kathleen came in, hesitating, and sat beside him on the campbed. 'What's the matter?' she asked. He had flung away with the trumpet as soon as Harry had laid it down. He sat concentratedly polishing it with a bit of chiffon scarf she had once given him, especially the mouthpiece. 'Has he spoilt it, then?' she murmured.

He did not answer. But his fingers were trembling. She said wearily: 'He's started reciting "Eskimo Nell" now.'

'I wish I could play like him,' he whispered.

'You do make an awful noise,' she said in a compassionate way. 'You haven't got the knack yet, with all your practising … I wonder,' she brooded after a while, 'if it's worth going down West. But they're so choosy on a Monday night.'

'Don't go.' He laid down the trumpet as if abandoning it for ever. 'Don't go.'

She seemed not to be listening, her preoccupied eyes gazing out of the window. The oblong of garden was filled with the smoky red after fume of sunset. Their low voices drifted into silences. Two pigeons gurgled in the elder tree; a cat rubbed against the windowpane and became intent on the pigeons. Kathleen's mouth was pursed up thoughtfully. He was conscious of the secret carnation glow of her thighs. Her thick hair smelled of obliterating night.

'I won't ever play my trumpet.' His voice stumbled. 'I have no faith, no belief, and I can't accept the world… I can't *feel* it.'

'Christ, there's enough to feel,' she protested. 'This bloody war, and the bombs—'

'In the Army they taught us to get used to the smell of blood. It smells of hate… And to turn the bayonet deep in the guts… There were nice chaps in our battalion who had letters and parcels from home… from loving mothers and girls… and they didn't mind the blood and the bayonets; they had had their fill of love and faith, I suppose. But I was hungry all the time, I wanted to be fed, and I wanted to create, and I wanted children… I am incomplete,' he whispered – 'I didn't have the right to kill.'

'But you tried to kill yourself,' she pointed out, though vaguely, as if her attention was elsewhere.

'My body,' he said – 'that *they* owned.'

'Well, what can you *do*?' she asked, after another silence. 'You ought to take up some study, a boy with your brains…

It's a shame,' she cried, with a sudden burst of the scandalised shrillness of her kind: 'the Army takes 'em, breaks 'em, and chucks 'em out when they've got no further use for 'em. What *can* you do?'

'There's crime,' he said.

'It don't pay,' she said at once.

'I believe,' he said, 'there'll be big waves of crime after the war. You can't have so much killing, so much teaching to destroy, and then stop it suddenly... The old kinds of crime, and new crimes against the holiness in the heart. There'll be fear, and shame, and guilt, guilt. People will be mad. There's no such thing as victory in war. There's only misery, chaos and suffering for everybody, and then the payment.... There's only one victory – over the evil in the heart. And that's a rare miracle.'

His voice faltered in defeat. 'I've been trying to make the attempt. But the air I breathe is full of poison.'

She let him talk, pretending to listen. Clients sometimes talked to her oddly and, if there was time, it was professional tact to allow them their airings.

'Harry, up there,' he went on dejectedly, 'carries the world on his shoulders. But he'll rob his mother and starve his wife and pick his neighbour's pocket.' He took up the trumpet off the bed, turned it over regretfully, and let it drop back. 'I can't even play my trumpet like him,' he reiterated obsessively. 'Would I make a better criminal?'

'Now, look here,' she said, her attention arrested, 'don't you go starting down *that* street! Boys like you alone in London can soon go to the bad. I've seen some of it. It won't pay, I'm telling you.'

'But crime as a protest,' he said earnestly. 'As a relief. And don't you see there's nothing but crime now, at the heart of things?'

Professionally comforting, she laid her hand on his, which began to tremble again. Yet his small crystal eyes remained impervious, with their single-purposed rigidity. She stroked his hand. 'Don't tremble, don't tremble… Do you ever cry?' she asked, gazing into his face in the last light.

He shook his head. 'I can't.' But something was flickering into his eyes. He had leaned towards her slowly.

'If you could,' she said, but still with a half-vague inattentiveness – 'I'm sure you ought to break down. You're too shut in on yourself.'

He breathed her odour of flesh. It seemed to him like the scent of milky flowers, living and benign, scattered in a pure air. As if it would escape him, he began to breathe it hungrily. His hands had stopped trembling. But the rigid calm of his appearance, had she noticed it in the dusky light, was more disquieting.

'There!' she said, still a little crouched away from him; 'you see, a little personal talk is good for you. You're too lonely, that's what it is.'

'Will you let me—'

'What?' she asked, more alert. The light was finishing; her face was dim.

'Put my mouth to your breast?'

'No,' she said at once. She shook her head. 'It wouldn't be any use, anyhow.'

But, now that the words were out, he fell on her in anguish. 'Stay with me! Don't go away. Sleep with me tonight.' He pressed his face into her, shuddering, and weeping at last. 'Stay!'

She heaved herself free, jumping off the bed with a squirm, like anger. 'Didn't I tell you that I hated men!' She raised her voice, very offended. 'I could spit on them all – and you, too, now.' She opened the door. 'But I will say this' – her voice relented a degree – 'I wouldn't sleep with you if you offered me ten pounds! I know what I am, and I don't want any of your fancy stuff.' She flounced out with scandalised decision.

He rolled over and over on the bed. Shuddering, he pressed his face into the pillow. When the paroxysm had passed he half rose and sat looking out of the window. In his movement the trumpet crashed to the floor, but he did not pick it up. He sat gazing out into the still world as if he would never penetrate it again. He saw grey dead light falling over smashed cities, over broken precipices and jagged torn chasms of the world. Acrid smoke from abandoned ruins mingled with the smell of blood. He saw himself the inhabitant of a wilderness where withered hands could lift in guidance no more. There were no more voices and all the paps of earth were dry.

AUTHOR BIOGRAPHIES

Arthur Machen

Arthur Machen was born in 1863 in Caerleon, Gwent. Unable to complete his education due to his family's poor finances, he moved to London with hopes of a literary career in 1881. After a number of writing commissions, which included translating *The Memoirs of Jacques Casanova*, he published his first book, *The Anatomy of Tobacco*, in 1884. However, it was in the 1890s that Machen achieved literary success and a reputation as a leading author of gothic texts with the publication of works such as *The Great God Pan* (1890), 'The Shining Pyramid' (1895) and *The Three Impostors* (1895), many of which bear the imprint of the Welsh border country of his upbringing. He died in 1947.

Caradoc Evans

David Caradoc Evans was born in 1878 in Llandysul, Cardiganshire and brought up in the nearby village of Rhydlewis. While he did write solely in English, his vocabulary and syntax was heavily influenced by the Welsh fluency of the community in which he lived. He released eleven books throughout his lifetime, but it is his first, the short-story collection *My People* (1915), which is most remembered. A highly controversial release at the time due to its invective directed towards, among others, the Welsh religious system, the book has since been re-evaluated, and is now considered one of the most significant examples of the new Anglo-Welsh literature. He died in 1945.

Rhys Davies

Rhys Davies was born in 1901 in Blaenclydach in the Rhondda Valley. Leaving school at the age of 14, he managed to live by his pen for fifty years. He was among the most dedicated, prolific and accomplished of Welsh prose authors, writing over a hundred short stories, eighteen novels, including *The Withered Root* (1927) and *The Black Venus* (1944), the autobiography *Print of a Hare's Foot* (1969), and the play *No Escape* (1954). He died in 1978. Following his death, the Rhys Davies Trust was established in 1990 with the intention of promoting Welsh authors writing in English.

Frank Richards

Frank Richards was born in 1883 in Monmouthshire. Orphaned at nine years old, he was brought up by his aunt and uncle in the industrial Blaina area, and went on to work as a coal miner throughout the 1890s before joining the Royal Welch Fusiliers in 1901. A veteran soldier who served in British India and many areas of the Western Front, he wrote his seminal account of the Great War from the standpoint of the common soldier, *Old Soldiers Never Die*, in 1933. This was followed by *Old Soldier Sahib*, a memoir of his time serving in British India, in 1936. He died in 1961.

Fred Ambrose

Fred Ambrose contributed 'The Grouser', which was taken from his 1917 collection *With the Welsh* as it appeared in *The Western Mail*, to this volume. Unfortunately, details about him remain elusive, other than he was a Welsh soldier in the new conscript Army, and that 'Fred Ambrose' was a pseudonym.

Dorothy Edwards

Dorothy Edwards was born in 1903 in Ogmore Vale, a small mining community in Mid Glamorgan. She took a degree at Cardiff University in Greek and philosophy, but literature was her passion and soon after graduating her short stories began to appear in magazines and journals. These were collected in *Rhapsody* (1927), along with several previously unpublished stories written during the nine months Edwards spent in Vienna and Florence. Her novel *Winter Sonata* (1928) followed shortly afterwards. She spent the following years trying to supplement her mother's meagre pension by writing stories and articles for magazines and newspapers, and doing some extra-mural teaching at Cardiff University, but she never undertook full-time employment. She died in 1934.

James Hanley

James Hanley was born in Dublin in 1897 and grew up in Liverpool. He saw active service in the Navy during the First World War and was briefly in the Canadian Army. His literary career began with the publication of *Drift* in 1930, which was also the year he moved to Wales, and was followed by *Boy* in 1931 and later a sequence of five novels set in working-class Liverpool. He lived first in Merionethshire and later at Llanfechain in Montgomeryshire, where he developed a friendship with the poet R. S. Thomas, who dedicated a book to him. He wrote prolifically throughout a long career and his output includes novels, short stories and plays. He moved to London in 1964 but continued to regard Wales as his home. He died in 1985.

Glyn Jones

Glyn Jones was born in 1905 in Merthyr Tydfil and worked for many years as a schoolteacher in South Wales. He began publishing poetry and short stories in the Thirties, and his first novel *The Valley, the City, the Village* followed two decades later in 1956. Two other novels were published in the following ten years, *The Learning Lark* (1960) and *The Island of Apples* (1965), as well as poetry, short-story collections, translations and works of criticism. In 1972, he received the Welsh Arts Council's premier award for his services to literature in Wales. He was elected the first Chairman, and later President of the English section of Yr Academi Gymreig. He died in 1995.

Gwyn Jones

Gwyn Jones was born in 1907 in Blackwood, Gwent. As a writer, scholar and translator, he made huge contributions to Welsh, Anglo-Welsh and Nordic literature. He translated a number of Icelandic works, the first scholarly English translation of *The Mabinogion* (1948), and also wrote two Nordic histories which brought him widespread acclaim. As a fiction author, he wrote a number of novels and short-story collections, including *Richard Savage* (1935), *The Flowers beneath the Scythe* (1952) and *The Walk Home* (1962). He also founded *The Welsh Review* in 1939, which he edited until 1948, chaired both the Welsh Committee of the Arts Council of Great Britain and the first editorial board of *The Oxford Companion to the Literature of Wales*, and published three sets of lectures on Anglo-Welsh literature. He died in 1999.

Geraint Goodwin

Geraint Goodwin was born in 1903 in Newtown. He started writing at an early age, and as a young man he made his living as a journalist with the *Montgomeryshire Express* before moving to London, where he wrote his first book, *Conversations with George Moore* (1929). He was diagnosed with a tubercular condition in 1929 and, after treatment at a sanatorium, travelled abroad to convalesce. He used his travel experiences in his next book, *Call Back Yesterday* (1935). It was followed by his first work of fiction, *The Heyday in the Blood* (1936), which enjoyed immediate critical acclaim. Three more books, *The White Farm* (1937), *Watch for the Morning* (1938) and *Come Michaelmas* (1939) followed, the last of which was written during an increasing struggle with ill health. He died in 1942.

George Ewart Evans

George Ewart Evans was born in 1909 in Abercynon. He was one of a family of eleven children whose parents ran a grocer's shop, the setting of his semi-autobiographical novel *The Voices of the Children* (1947). After education at Mountain Ash County School and University College Cardiff, where he read classics and trained as a teacher, he had ambitions of being a writer. He published verse and short stories, many with a Welsh background, in various literary journals. He taught from 1934 until 1948, when he gave up teaching and turned from writing fiction to oral history, and his series of works beginning with *Ask the Fellows Who Cut the Hay* (1956) established his reputation as a pioneer in this field. He died in 1988.

B. L. Coombes

Bert Lewis Coombes was born in 1893 in Wolverhampton and raised in Herefordshire, but moved to Resolven to work in the Neath Valley before the outbreak of World War I. He turned to writing when he was in his forties, and became a protégé of English writer John Lehmann. A miner for many years, he used his writing to dissect the industry and its corrupt underbelly, and his autobiography, *These Poor Hands* (1939), is considered one of the most authentic accounts of mining life ever published. He also published two other works – *Those Clouded Hills* (1944) and *Miners Day* (1945). He died in 1974.

Leslie Norris

Leslie Norris was born in 1921 in Merthyr Tydfil. In 1948, he enrolled in teacher training, and by 1958 had risen to the position of college lecturer. From 1974 onwards, he earned his living by combining full-time writing with residencies at academic institutions on both sides of the Atlantic. Aside from a dozen books of poems, his prose works include two volumes of short stories, *Sliding* (1978), which won the David Higham Award, and *The Girl from Cardigan* (1988), as well as a compilation, *Collected Stories*, released in 1996. He died in 2006.

Dylan Thomas

Dylan Thomas was born in 1914 in Swansea. Arguably the most famous Welsh writer of all time, he achieved lasting recognition predominantly for his poetry, although he published works across a number of forms. Indeed, aside from a number of poetry collections, he wrote radio and film scripts and took part in radio programmes broadcast by the BBC, published a book of autobiographical short stories, *Portrait of the Artist as a Young Dog*, in 1940, and managed to complete a 'play for voices', *Under Milk Wood*. Infamous throughout his career for his predilection for drink and the riotous lifestyle, he struggled with poor finances and ill health. He died in1953.

Gwyn Thomas

Gwyn Thomas was born in 1913 in the Rhondda Valley. He studied Spanish at Oxford and spent time in Spain during the early 1930s. He obtained part-time lecturing jobs across England before deciding to become a schoolteacher in Wales. He retired from that profession in 1962 to work full-time as a writer and broadcaster. He wrote extensively across several genres including essays, short stories, novels and plays, and was widely translated. His fictional works include *The Dark Philosophers* (1946) and *All Things Betray Thee* (1949), the drama *The Keep* (1962) and an autobiography, *A Few Selected Exits* (1968). Gwyn Thomas was given the Honour for Lifetime Achievement by Arts Council Wales in 1976. He died in 1981.

Alun Lewis

Alun Lewis was born in 1915 in Cwmaman in Cynon Valley. He read history at the University of Aberystwyth, where he began to write poetry. A failed period as a journalist gave way to a career in supply teaching, before he joined the British Army in 1940. A pacifist at heart, his experiences during World War II depressed him, and he died in 1944 by his own hand when on active service in Burma. During his lifetime, he published only two collections: one of poetry – *Raiders' Dawn* (1942) – and one of short stories – *The Last Inspection* (1942). However, these were followed posthumously by several further compilations of poetry, prose and letters.

Margiad Evans

Margiad Evans – the pseudonym of Peggy Whistler – was born in 1909 in London. Her family moved to Ross-on-Wye, Herefordshire, in 1920 and it was with the Border counties that she chose to identify as a writer. She is best known and widely admired as a prose writer. Her novels are *Country Dance* (1932), *The Wooden Doctor* (1933), *Turf or Stone* (1934) and *Creed* (1936), while *The Old and the Young* (1948) is a volume of short stories; her journal and a selection of her essays are to be found in *Autobiography* (1943) and *A Ray of Darkness* (1952). Her two books of verse are *Poems from Obscurity* (1947) and *A Candle Ahead* (1956). Having suffered from epilepsy from about 1950, she died of a brain tumour in hospital in 1958.

George Brinley Evans

George Brinley Evans was born in 1925 in Dyffryn Cellwen. He began work in Banwen Colliery, aged 14, in 1939. He joined the army at 18 and served in Burma with the 856 Motor Boats, first with the 15th India Corps then the 12th Army. He returned to Banwen Colliery after the war, married and raised a family before losing an eye in an accident in the

Cornish Drift. He began to produce work as a sculptor in addition to his painting after his accident and also wrote scripts for independent television and the BBC. He returned to industry and finally to opencast mining in 1977. His fiction, painting and sculptures have been widely published and exhibited. His short-story collection *Boys of Gold* was published to critical acclaim in 2000. He still lives and works in Banwen.

Emyr Humphreys

Emyr Humphreys was born in 1919 in Prestatyn. A former theatre and television director, drama producer and lecturer, in a long and illustrious career he has written and released twenty novels, several short-story and poetry compilations, and a history volume, as well as produced a number of screenplays. He has won several literary prizes during his career – the 1958 Somerset Maugham Prize for *Hear and Forgive* (1952), the 1958 Hawthornden Prize for *A Toy Epic* (1958), and the Welsh Book of the Year Award twice, for *Bonds of Attachment* (1992) and *The Gift of a Daughter* (1999). He lives in Llanfairpwll on Anglesey.

Alun Richards

Alun Richards was born in 1929 in Pontypridd. After spells as a schoolteacher, probation officer and as an instructor in the Royal Navy, from the 1960s he was, and successfully so, a full-time writer. He lived near the Mumbles, close to the sea which, coupled with the hills of the South Wales Valleys, was the landscape of his fiction. Alongside plays for stage and radio, screenplays and adaptations for television, a biography and a memoir, he wrote six novels and two collections of short stories, *Dai Country* (1973) and *The Former Miss Merthyr Tydfil* (1976). As editor, he produced bestselling editions of Welsh short stories and tales of the sea for Penguin. He died in 2004.

Brenda Chamberlain

Brenda Chamberlain was born in Bangor in 1912. In 1931 she went to train as a painter at the Royal Academy Schools in London and five years later settled in Caenarfonshire. During World War II, she temporarily gave up painting in favour of poetry and worked, with her husband, on the production of the Caseg Broadsheets, a series of six which included poems by Dylan Thomas, among others. In 1947, she went to live on the Welsh island of Bardsey, where she remained until 1961. After six years on the Greek island of Ydra, she returned to Bangor. Despite her predilection for poetry and painting, Chamberlain also produced prose works, including a novel, *The Water-castle* (1964), and *A Rope of Vines* (1965), a memoir of life on Ydra. She died in 1971.

Nigel Heseltine

Nigel Heseltine was born in 1916 in London: the true identity of his mother remains unknown, but his father was believed to be the famed composer Peter Warlock. As an adult he travelled around Europe and Africa, was married at least five times, including to an aristocrat in Budapest, and worked as a playwright for the Olympia Theatre company in Dublin. He published a number of books in his lifetime spanning several literary forms and genres, including travel writing in *Scarred Background (a Journey Through Albania)* (1938), poetry in *The Four-Walled Dream* (1941), fictional prose in *The Mysterious Pregnancy* (1953), and memoir in *Capriol for Mother* (1992). He died in 1995.

Roland Mathias

Roland Mathias was born in 1915 in Talybont-on-Usk, Breconshire, and read modern history at Jesus College, Oxford. He taught in schools until 1969, when he resigned from his job as a headmaster and settled in Brecon in order to write full-time. His contribution to the study of Welsh writing in English, as editor, critic, anthologist, historian, poet and short-story writer, is substantial. He helped to found *Dock Leaves*, later the *Anglo-Welsh Review*, which he edited from 1961 to 1976. He published one collection of short stories and nine volumes of poetry. The majority of his writing has to do with the history, people and topography of Wales, especially the Border areas. He died in 2007.

Siân James

Sîan James was born in 1932 in Llandysul, Carmarthenshire. After attending the University of Wales, Aberystwyth, she has gone on to on to write and publish a number of acclaimed novels and short-story collections, several of which have won awards, including the Wales Book of the Year Award in 1997 for *Not Singing Exactly* and the Yorkshire Post Fiction Prize twice. Her third novel, *A Small Country* (1979) was adapted for film as *Calon Gaeth* (2006) by Stan Barstow and Diana Griffiths, winning a BAFTA Cymru award in the process.

Dilys Rowe

Dilys Rowe was born in Swansea in 1927. She started writing at an early age, and had a story published before she began studying for an English literature degree at the University of Wales, Swansea. Upon graduating she worked as a freelance journalist in order to fund her writing, and moved to London. There, she worked for the *Guardian* and the *Times*, and during the late 1950s and early 1960s edited the *Observer*'s women's page. She married American writer David Dorrance, and went to live in the south of France.

Ron Berry

Ron Berry was born in 1920 in Blaenycwm in the Rhondda Valley. The son of a coal miner, he worked in mining until the outbreak of war saw him serving in both the British Army and the Merchant Navy. He studied at the adult education college Coleg Harlech in the 1950s but had further spells in mining and as a carpenter as his writing was never entirely successful enough to sustain him. His fictional output, which included works such as the novels *Flame and Slag* (1968) and *So Long, Hector Bebb* (1970), depicted a hard but positive view of the industrial Welsh valleys, entirely bereft of sentimentality and the hype which he scornfully left to others. He died in 1997.

EDITOR BIOGRAPHY

Dai Smith was born in 1945 in the Rhondda. He was educated in South Wales before reading modern history at Balliol College, Oxford and comparative literature at Columbia University, New York. He has been a lecturer at the Universities of Lancaster, Swansea and Cardiff, where he was awarded a Personal Chair in 1986, and was subsequently a Pro-Vice Chancellor at the University of Glamorgan. In addition to his academic career, he has also been a constant broadcaster on radio and television since the 1970s, and he became Head of Programmes (English language) in the 1990s at BBC Wales where he commissioned, presented and scripted a number of award-winning documentary programmes and other series. His many publications, which span books, articles and journalism, have centred on the dynamics – culture and society, politics and literature – of his native South Wales, and most recently have expanded into the form of biography (*Raymond Williams: A Warrior's Tale*, 2008), memoir (*In The Frame: Memory in Society*, 2010) and the novel (*Dream On*, 2013).

Dai Smith was the founding Editor of the Library of Wales Series. He has led Arts Council Wales as its Chair since 2006. He holds a part-time Research Chair in the Cultural History of Wales at Swansea University. He is now writing more fiction.

Published list

- 'The Gift of Tongues' – published in T.P.'s and Cassell's Weekly, issue dated Dec 3, 1927
- 'The Coffin' – published in *The Illustrated Review*, issue dated Jul, 1923
- 'The Dark World' – published in *A Finger in Every Pie* (Heinemann, 1942)
- 'A Father in Sion' – published in *My People* (Andrew Melrose, 1915)
- 'The Black Rat' – published in *Old Soldiers Never Die* (Naval & Military Press, 1933)
- 'The Grouser' – published in *With the Welsh* (Western Mail, 1917)
- 'Be This Her Memorial' – published in *My People* (Andrew Melrose, 1915)
- 'A Bed of Feathers' – published in *A Bed of Feathers* (The Mandrake Press, 1929)
- 'The Conquered' – published in *Rhapsody* (Wishart, 1927)
- 'The Last Voyage' – published in *The Last Voyage* (William Jackson, 1931)
- 'An Afternoon at Ewa Shad's' – published in *The Water-Music and Other Stories* (George Routledge & Sons, 1944)
- 'Shacki Thomas' – published in *The Buttercup Field, and Other Stories* (Penmark Press, 1946)
- 'The Lost Land' – published in *The Welsh Review*, Vol. 1, No. 3, Apr, 1939
- 'Wat Pantathro' – published in *The Water-Music and Other Stories* (George Routledge & Sons, 1944)

- 'Revelation' – published in *A Pig in a Poke* (Joiner & Steele, 1931)
- 'The Shearing' – published in *The Welsh Review*, Vol. 3, No. 2, Jun, 1944
- 'Let Dogs Delight' – published in *Welsh Short Stories*, ed. by Gwyn Jones (Penguin, 1941)
- 'Twenty Tons of Coal' – published in *New Writing* (new series), No. 3, Christmas 1939
- 'Gamblers' – published in *The Girl from Cardigan: Sixteen Stories* (Seren, 1988)
- 'On the Tip' – published in *The Things Men Do* (Heinemann, 1936)
- 'Extraordinary Little Cough' – published in *Portrait of the Artist as a Young Dog* (J. M. Dent, 1940)
- 'And a Spoonful of Grief to Taste' – published in *Where Did I Put My Pity? Folk Tales from the Modern Welsh* (Progress Publishing Co., 1946)
- 'Just Like Little Dogs' – published in *Portrait of the Artist as a Young Dog* (J. M. Dent, 1940)
- 'Thy Need' – published in *The Welsh Review*, Vol. 7, No. 2, Summer 1948
- 'Acting Captain' – published in *The Last Inspection and Other Stories* (George Allen & Unwin, 1942)
- 'The Lost Fisherman' – published in *The Welsh Review*, Vol. 5, No. 1, Mar, 1946
- 'The Pits are on the Top' – published in *A Finger in Every Pie* (William Heinemann, 1942)
- 'They Came' – published in *The Last Inspection and Other Stories* (George Allen & Unwin, 1942)
- 'Boys of Gold' – published in *Boys of Gold* (Parthian, 2000)
- 'Ward 'O' 3 (b)' – published in *In the Green Tree* (Allen & Unwin, 1948)
- 'Mrs Armitage' – published in *Welsh Short Stories*, ed. by George Ewart Evans (Faber and Faber, 1959)

- 'One Life' – published in *Dai Country* (Michael Joseph, 1973)
- 'The Return' – published in *Life and Letters*, Vol. 54, No. 121, Sept, 1947
- 'Homecoming' – published in *Celtic Story*, No. 1, ed. by Aled Vaughan (Pendulum Publications, 1946)
- 'A White Birthday' – published in *The Still Waters and Other Stories* (Peter Davies, 1948)
- 'The Medal' – published in *Welsh Short Stories*, ed. by George Ewart Evans (Faber and Faber, 1959)
- 'A Story' – published in *A Prospect of the Sea and Other Stories and Prose Writings* (J. M. Dent, 1955)
- 'Match' – published in *The Eleven Men of Eppynt and Other Stories* (Dock Leaves Press, 1956)
- 'Hester and Louise' – published in *Outside Paradise* (Parthian, 2003)
- 'A View Across the Valley' – published in *Pick of Today's Short Stories*, No. 6 (Putnam, 1955)
- 'Time Spent' – published in *Pieces of Eight*, ed. by Robert Nisbet (Gomer, 1982)
- 'Boy with a Trumpet' – published in *Boy with a Trumpet* (Heinemann, 1949)

ACKNOWLEDGEMENTS

PUBLISHER'S ACKNOWLEDGEMENTS

Parthian would like to thank all the writers, estate holders and publishers for their cooperation in the preparation of this volume. We would also like to thank the editor, Dai Smith, for his energy and engagement with the world of the Welsh short story.

Although every effort has been to secure permissions prior to publication this has not always been possible. The publisher apologises for any errors or omissions and will if contacted rectify these at the earliest opportunity.

FURTHER ACKNOWLEDGEMENTS

The publishers would like to thank Mick Felton of Seren Books for assistance in the preparation of this volume. We would also like to thank the estate of Dylan Thomas, David Higham Associates and Liam Hanley for permission to publish the stories of Dylan Thomas and James Hanley. Ravinda Jasser for the estate of Brenda Chamberlain. Meic Stephens for copyright assistance with the estates of Rhys Davies and Leslie Norris. Merryn Hemp for the estate of Raymond Williams. Dr Lesley Coburn for the estate of Ron Berry. Geoffrey Robinson for the estate of Gwyn Thomas. Helen Richards for the estate of Alun Richards. Myfanwy Lumsden for the estate of Geraint Goodwin. Matthew Evans for the estate of George Ewart Evans. Glyn Mathias for the estate of Roland Mathias. Viv Davies for the estate of B.L. Coombes.

Editor's Acknowledgements

First and foremost, as now over a lifetime, to Norette for allowing me (again) to sequester myself away for months on end with other people's lives. And their stories. To particular friends and advisers, especially Meic Stephens; and to Sam Adams, Peter Finch, Tony Brown and Daniel Williams. To the various editors and selectors who stepped out onto these highways and byways before me, and, of course, to the odd (sometimes very odd!) tipster who nudged me into unexpected diversions. All at Parthian have proved as exemplary in the arduous production of these two volumes as they have been since the inception of the Library of Wales Series in 2006. But, here, I need to single out the principal editorial assistance of the indefatigable Robert Harries who, like me, has now read all the words all of the time, and more than once.

LIBRARY OF WALES

The Library of Wales is a Welsh Government project designed to ensure that all of the rich and extensive literature of Wales which has been written in English will now be made available to readers in and beyond Wales. Sustaining this wider literary heritage is understood by the Welsh Government to be a key component in creating and disseminating an ongoing sense of modern Welsh culture and history for the future Wales which is now emerging from contemporary society. Through these texts, until now unavailable or out-of-print or merely forgotten, the Library of Wales will bring back into play the voices and actions of the human experience that has made us, in all our complexity, a Welsh people.

The Library of Wales will include prose as well as poetry, essays as well as fiction, anthologies as well as memoirs, drama as well as journalism. It will complement the names and texts that are already in the public domain and seek to include the best of Welsh writing in English, as well as to showcase what has been unjustly neglected. No boundaries will limit the ambition of the Library of Wales to open up the borders that have denied some of our best writers a presence in a future Wales. The Library of Wales has been created with that Wales in mind: a young country not afraid to remember what it might yet become.

Dai Smith

LIBRARY of WALES
FUNDED BY

Noddir gan
Lywodraeth Cymru
Sponsored by
Welsh Government

CYNGOR LLYFRAU CYMRU
WELSH BOOKS COUNCIL

LIBRARY OF WALES

SERIES EDITOR: DAI SMITH